COMMANDING BLOOD AND BONDS

GRAYSHELL RISING

S.J. BARNETT

Commanding Blood and Bonds

AUTHOR'S NOTE

Well, hello my darling! Long time no see. I've been working on this book since circa 2023 and to have it finally committed to paper is WILD.

Let me start by saying thank you for sticking with me and coming back to continue the adventure. I fell absolutely head over boots in love with Freya along the way. She is the savage bundle of chaos this series needed.

Like both prior installments, the ending came to me first (rude), and the big moments came after, leaving me to weave together the details. This book threw me happily back into the fantasy adventure genre, and thanks to my beta team, I have some nostalgic films to watch now (namely, *Tomb Raider* and *Indiana Jones*. Don't judge me).

As promised, Ally and August are back to continue their tale, and I absolutely loved reuniting with the Porters.

As always, your mental health matters. As a reminder, this series deals with dark topics that may be disturbing to some readers. *In addition to* the triggers listed in books one and two, this book includes but isn't limited to: mention of sexual assault (**no** on-page rape), physical + verbal bullying of a minor, violence, gore, war, loss of loved one(s), depictions of anxiety/panic attacks, explicit language, explicit sexual content, diverse religious themes, anti-religious rhetoric, and criticism of societal constructs and governments. This series is intended for mature audiences 18+.

So I'll leave you with this; welcome back, and buckle up.

Until we meet again,

Xoxo-SJB

GLOSSARY + ALEC CARTER'S RAPID RECAP

Because we can't always re-read or retain an entire 600+ page book, here's a refresher! I'm a firm believer that fantasy novels (especially those of the 700+ page variety) should feature a 'previously on' section. You know how those dramatic television shows always do them at the beginning of every episode (as if we didn't just binge the entire series in rapid succession)? And who better to bring us back up to speed than our fan favorite character? Hope this helps!

Ascension: *The process of a soul 'ascending' into their new, immortal gifts and abilities when they hit their physical prime in a new body, and/or when a near-death experience forces them to adapt quickly (like Freya in CFAS).*

Braid/Familiar: *Fragment of an angel soul, or spirits, 'braided' into a mortal or animal soul for a certain mission. Grayshell guards braids in human form to ensure they complete their work. Animal braids are called familiars. Paladins predominantly bond with ravens.*

Calling: *When a soul is ascending, an older and more powerful soul is 'called' to them to protect their transition into their power.*

Coven: *Smaller groups, or cadres of souls within a hierarchy. Most often, covens are comprised of soul groups that are energetically entangled. As they tend to reincarnate together through life after life, these groups are intensely* *intimate. No souls are as trusted as deeply as a covenmate. Covens operate within the laws and structure of their hierarchy.*

Hierarchy: *A tribe/kingdom/clan of souls. Hierarchies are sovereign and operate under their own belief systems, structures and rules.*

The Middle/Middle Realm: *The dimension that recharges souls. This is their true home. Benefits of inhabiting their Middle Realm homes include speed healing, and a celestial power up. Some clans chose to live there (Grayshell, Westerlund, etc.) while others use it for ceremonial purposes, safe harbor, and emergency healing (Hazelharbor, Paladin, Bellaton, etc.). A Commander/King/Queen connected to The Middle allows the entire hierarchy to communicate mind-to-mind. Being detached from The Middle significantly limits the connection.*

Soul: *Nephilim souls reincarnating into new bodies on an unending cycle. Hazelharborians consider themselves witches (not nephilim), but still use the term to refer to those with 'magic'.*

PREVIOUSLY IN *GRAYSHELL RISING*...

So...about that shit show of an ending...

Please remember that you loved me once and everybody makes mistakes, and I honest to God didn't know that Mags darling didn't know, mmmkay?

Oh. By the way. **Don't read this recap if you haven't <u>finished</u> Commanding Earth and Shadow** because the spoilers be spoiling (duh).

I mean it. If you didn't finish the last story, **turn back now**.

Okay, I warned you.

Now, for the good girls and boys that have reading comprehension and are here because you belong here, if you read the first half of this story forever and a half ago, this might be a good refresher.

Oh! This is Alec, by the way. I guess I should lead with that. I'm not feeling quite so spunky this go-round, what with my foot jammed down my throat. Alas. Here we are. And yes, this part of the story happens at the same time as the last one, but I promise, we'll get to the point at the ending, and the next one will answer a boatload of questions, but for now, here's what you need to remember:

Ally and August headed out to unite our people and our allies in preparation for Adrastos' war.

Fae and I went east to learn from the Westerlunds and brush up on illusion magic. It just seems...necessary.

Lana and Ansel came with us for a beat to help the Old General heal from that scrape with death.

And Aren...

Well. Aren headed West...*You know what Aren did.* Our beloved Commander followed Ally's vague-ass vision on a mission to protect the Hazelharborian witches from a relentless assault on their hierarchy. Which was beyond needed, because they were dropping like flies. Even with Aren's help—and the skilled blades of men we thought were Magnolia's friends, but turned out to be enemies—they lost a few remarkable healers to the plight of the demons.

Aren, Lana, and Ansel hunted for a door back home to Grayshell after Adrastos locked us out, and he was quested with finding this pretty ancient circlet looking thing that turned out to be the cursed diadem of Rhiannon Hadrianna—the last rightful Bellpost Queen.

Bellpost. *That Bellpost.* Home to Magnolia's now infamous *not*-nomads. But I don't need to remind you how that shit show went down. How the fuck would anybody forget Magnolia squaring off with a shadow dragon that beat the absolute daylights out of her? Or her trying to save her dying Guardian?

Or...or that motherfucker bleeding out outside Aren's house. *Fucking cocksucker.*

Anyways. That's neither here nor there. While Aren was hunkered down chasing leads and protecting the world's best healers, Ally and August embarked on a mission to find our allies for the war, and meet with another Soul Bound couple to understand their Bond. And Freya—the half-baked, adorable shit head—was sent deep south, USA, to the Paladin-Bellaton divide to secure the alliance of Aren's old flame.

That's where we come in. As a matter of fact, you should recognize *exactly* where our stories parted ways, and I know damn well you'll recognize where they collide again.

I gotta warn you, Buttercup. The road to come is not for the faint of heart. But I know you're no pussy (by the way, did you know that's actually short for pusillanimous? Crazy, right? Look it up).

If you still love us after all of *that*, you're in it for the long haul.

Just like all of us.

So with that, all I can say, is godspeed, little soul.

Welcome back to Grayshell.

TANDEM GUIDE

Commanding Earth and Shadow and *Commanding Blood and Bonds* occur on a tandem timeline.

Some chapters and events overlap.

They can be read independently or simultaneously, However, the tandem read is recommended **for re-reads**.

It is <u>not</u> designed for readers who have not finished *CEAS*, as it will impact the reader experience.

For those of you who want to weave the pieces together, here's the tandem outline:

Commanding Earth and Shadow (Ch. 1- 9)

Commanding Blood and Bonds (Ch. 1- 6)

Commanding Earth and Shadow (Ch. 10-12)

Commanding Blood and Bonds (Ch. 7)

Commanding Earth and Shadow (Ch. 13-17)

Commanding Blood and Bonds (Ch. 8-10)

Commanding Earth and Shadow (Ch. 18)

Commanding Blood and Bonds (Ch. 11-16)

Commanding Earth and Shadow (Ch. 19-21)

Commanding Blood and Bonds (Ch. 17-18)

Commanding Earth and Shadow (Ch. 22-27)

Commanding Blood and Bonds (Ch. 19-20)

Commanding Earth and Shadow (Ch. 28-29)

Commanding Blood and Bonds (Ch. 21-29)

Commanding Earth and Shadow (Ch. 30-32)

PRONUNCIATION GUIDE

The bulk of CBAB takes place in the deep south, USA. There are a handful of colloquialisms and commonly truncated words we might not generally see in print. For example, 'gonna' for 'going to', 'wanna' for 'want to', 'haveta' for 'have to' etc. These are not typos, but regional dialect patterns.

Beyond those, here are some new-to-Grayshell words and names that might be new-to-you:

Cairis: KAIR-iss

Cher: Sha (french Louisiana)

Chérie: sha-REE (french Louisiana)

Lainalei: Lane-uh-lee

La Lune Noire: lah loon nwahr (french Louisiana)

Lonan: Low-nun

Marais: mah-REH (French/Louisiana)

Ma moitié: ma mwah-TEE

Morrieth: MOH-ree-ehth (MOH like 'morrow' - ree - ehth, **Scottish** inspiration)

Nais pas: nay-pah (regional slang for 'don't know', from French, *Je ne sais pas* = "I don't know.")

Rougarou: Roo-GAH-roo (french Louisiana)

Solskari: SOHL-skah-ree (Swedish inspired)

Solskivall: sOOL-chi-val (Swedish inspired)

Umbrabàs: UHM-bruh-bahs (latin Umbra = shadow, bàs= **Gaelic**, death)

Umbrithan UHM-brih-thun – "umbra" (shadow)

PART 1
THE BISHOP'S PATH

ONE

PANDORA'S BOX

FREYA

Eight weeks before the portals opened...

That bitch slit my throat.

That thought alone kept me compliant with Ally's grand plan—one that would rip me from my family just as we'd finally found our way back to each other after centuries apart. Lana. Ansel. Even Aunt Fae. A soul-uncle I'd never known in any role beyond one of Aren's callings. And, for some Godforsaken reason, Ally believed I'd be beneficial to the cause. But I wasn't any happier about being stationed thousands of miles away than my soul mother was. She'd made her displeasure about being sent to "babysit the hippies" more than obvious.

Still, guilt twisted in my stomach as Aren lowered his voice, his gaze following suit. "Freya."

The man was anything but subtle as he cleared his throat, his protective glower somehow muting the crash of waves beyond the Florida estate. Even Brody and his brothers' chatter faded beneath the glare of the sun.

I resisted the urge to roll my eyes and instead batted my lashes, pasting on a doe-eyed smile.

"What?" I said innocently, swaying on my feet with false bravado.

Unless last week's battle had given him a severe concussion, Aren knew me too well to fall for that bullshit. Knew that this was personal. Every millisecond I'd spent clawing my way back here had been fucking *personal*.

"Leave it be."

My lips curled into a mischievous grin. I winked up at him. "I don't know what you're talking about."

Right. Reagan had been my friend—or at least had fooled me into thinking she was—right up until the moment the skill set she'd most admired in me revealed a truth she wasn't willing to be held accountable for. And like hell was I going to let her slink away, believing her sins were forgotten.

Sure, telling Aren and Ansel I couldn't remember who had sent my body careening into that swampy-ass river had been a questionable decision. But not nearly as contentious as what I had planned for the next few weeks. Nothing tasted as exquisite as retribution, and I was already salivating at the thought of her face when I ripped her hierarchy from her blood-soaked talons.

Aren's eyes narrowed. "Don't go digging up old history. You deserve answers—hell, we *all* do—but now's not the time to open Pandora's box. Stay focused on the mission. We survive this war, and *then* you get your chance to unleash hell. Understand?"

Understand? No. I didn't understand. When was the last time *he* had gone to question a friend only to end up with a blade through his jugular before being kicked off a muddy riverbank, *King Leonidas* style? I still wasn't sure if I had drowned in my own blood or the murky water first.

I fought the urge to touch my throat, where that slender silver birthmark had always piqued my curiosity growing up with the Porters.

My official mission had nothing to do with my personal side quest, and I'd make damn sure one didn't impact the other—beyond what was absolutely inevitable, anyway. The Paladins were everywhere in the South. Conflict was unavoidable. But come hell and high water, I would return with Reyna as our ally and Reagan face-down in a goddamn swamp, and a big-ass army for this man to wield.

One trip. Three problems solved.

I flashed Aren a bright smile, swaying side to side as though mulling it over. "I'll do my best."

"*Freya.*"

Smirking, I reached up and patted his muscular arm. Had his biceps gotten bigger since last time? *Jesus.*

"Easy, old man, you'll burst a blood vessel."

He barked a laugh, then spun me around and kicked me in the ass. When I parried, he grinned back at me with the same level of defiance I felt. *There.* That was close enough to permission, right?

"I mean it, Porter. Stick to the plan. I'll personally help you get closure when this is over."

"Fine," I huffed, rolling my eyes like a petulant teenager before flashing him a wink and striding across the perfect lawn to my new babysitters.

He *would* help me get closure. Already had by sending me back to where this all started.

When I glanced over my shoulder, Aren's expression told me he didn't believe me as far as he could throw me. Considering his particular skill set, that might have been generous. With a nod, I averted my eyes. No need to disrespect him by lying more than I already had.

He knew. He had to know. You didn't run a hierarchy for this many centuries without knowing when someone was full of shit.

With one barked order, Aren could have brought me right to heel if he chose.

No order?

Free reign, in my opinion.

As our little envoy bowed our heads to pray, I relished the caress of sunlight on my skin, the coastal breeze threading through my hair. We were going to need every bit of divine intervention we could get.

Reyna would side with us—we already knew that, thanks to Ally and the Bellatons track record of protecting the innocent—but we needed her allegiance in following Aren and August into this war.

As for her sister?

That was just a debt long owed.

With one last fortifying breath of Florida humidity, I nodded farewell to The Commander.

A beat later, Brody jumped us out.

Lichen and mildew tangled in what should have been air but felt like fog. I wrinkled my nose, scowling. Seventy-percent humidity—even in the dry season —was not for me. Looking up and around, I took in the draping sage-green moss that hung from great oaks like fabric, their prickly-looking limbs reaching skyward on either side of the clearing and path ahead. Endless flora sprouted in every direction, some bushes even bearing colorful flowers. Jesus, it was so *green* here. The air scraped into my lungs, and I turned on my companions. Brody, blond hair in a bun, grinned and quirked his head as he moved past me.

"Welcome back to the Bellaton-Paladin divide, little Wraith."

"Joy," I mumbled, hiking my duffle bag higher on my shoulder as I glared at the familiar landscape. Ajax chuckled darkly, adjusting his own pack to make space for the dagger slung at his hip.

"Come on, little lady, we've got an ally to win over," Alastair said, the smile in his voice sharper than the one threatening to activate his dimples.

Kicking out a foot, I smirked and bit out, *"Little lady?"* I laughed aloud as he stumbled past me.

"Prove me wrong, *pipsqueak*, and you can pick your moniker."

I followed in his wake as my eyes adjusted to the darkness. "Get me to Grayshell so I can properly grow, you *giant*."

"Working on it."

"You know, maybe some of us reach our optimal height and stop. I'm The Wraith. A thief. Hard to sneak when you're colossal. Does it sound like thunder when you tiptoe?"

"This vessel has served me just fine."

"Do a lot of *sneaking*, do you?"

"I prefer a more direct approach."

"No wonder Aren loves you."

Alastair choked on a laugh, then jerked his chin up ahead. I'd always liked the trio. Brody—or Ambroise, if Grayshell bothered to use proper names—had broody big-brother vibes but cracked to accommodate thunderous laughter when it was earned. He was next in line for Grayshell Commander after Saraya—not that anyone could stomach the idea of a Grayshell without Aren. I was queasy just thinking about it. Then there were the twins, Ajax and Alastair. Ajax took absolutely everything seriously, while Alastair, the black sheep of the family—literally, with his brunette waves in contrast to his brothers' blond—took absolutely *nothing* seriously.

Go figure my now-brother affectionately nicknamed them *The Greeks*. Perhaps the fact that we'd gotten on well in past lives was why they'd been saddled with this acquisition mission alongside me. Still shaking his head, Ajax led the way through moss curtains that parted to reveal a sprawling, manicured emerald lawn, and I sucked in a breath.

Well, this should be fun, I muttered internally, mind just as sarcastic as my foul mouth.

Every clan has their strengths and weaknesses, Ajax offered as we closed the gap.

And Reyna? Pompous, pretentious, bigoted ass—if my memory served me correctly.

Possesses the second strongest legion of warriors in North America.

I thought the Westerlunds were second.

He shrugged, but it was Brody who answered. *The Westerlunds are an extension of us at this point. Family.*

Still confident Grayshell bears the crown? I arched a brow, not that he turned to see it.

The location of our pillows doesn't dictate the might of our forces, Brody thought mind-to-mind. *The devil himself can't rob us of that. Mano a mano, we'd steal the clothes off their backs.*

But they're still linked to The Middle, I pointed out.

Ajax bobbed his head as we caught up to Brody, just as he crested the divide between looming shadows and striking sunlight.

And it was Marcus and his brothers who came to our aid in that duel, I added. *Not Reyna.*

Marcus would sooner chew his own arm off than allow the hand at the end to betray a brother. This time, it was Alastair's voice that rang in my head.

And Reyna?

Has too much damn pride to admit she played a part.

And I'm supposed to fix this? I skeptically protested before barking a harsh laugh.

If Alvara says you're meant to be here, you're meant to be here, Brody encouraged.

Nodding, I blinked into the blinding yellow, squinting as the white glare gave way to a sprawling, palatial estate—a colonial, white plantation erected over rolling green grass. But my eyes fell to the men standing on the front porch steps. Three of them, feet shoulder-width apart, hands braced behind their backs. Two visible firearms each, and a knife sheathed in leather hanging off each belt. Inevitably, more lay concealed beneath their crisp slacks and button-ups. Two guards roamed the back corner of the perimeter, and one sentinel stood at the back porch, barely visible before we closed too much distance to see him. Not outrageous numbers, but a decent line of defense for a supposedly peaceful estate.

Anyone who knew about the Bellaton-Paladin divide knew better than to believe the pretty little lie of this idyllic painting she'd crafted. Still, I softened my expression, going for that dumb, young, doe-eyed look that disarmed most men.

The loose-limbed brunette's muscles were taut, shadowed eyes locking on us as we approached. The center one was the tallest, though not the broadest. His blond hair was brushed back into a meticulous, gelled wave, and even from the closing distance, I could tell his bright eyes stared back at me. The broad one to his left absently moved his hand to the blade at his side, and I battled the obtuse desire to do the same. *Friends.* We were here to make friends.

With that in mind, I tossed my hair and plastered the softest, most innocent smile onto my face before dropping my eyes when the center one returned it. Let them see me as the innocent little doe, and perhaps I'd get to Reyna that much sooner. Last go-around, she had been hard to gain a private audience with—though hopefully, the urgency of the timeline would change that.

The Greeks moved to flank me, allowing my spine to straighten as I took the lead at the center. I lifted my eyes to the blond, who descended the stairs in swaggering steps, gaze flicking between me and my escorts. His tan face was still a bit boyish, and he cracked a smile meant to be disarming.

"Welcome to Bellaton, Miss Porter." His baritone voice was smooth, each word draped in that southern lilt as he stretched out his hand. I accepted in a rush. "The name's Blaz. I'll be making sure you and your companions are comfortable." He gave my fingers a little squeeze before releasing them and motioning to the lanky one beside him. "This is Montague—Mont, G, it's up to you. He answers to either."

Montague grinned and nodded, adding, "For you, darlin', I'll answer to just about anything."

I kinda liked the look of 'G' and took a moment to admire the high set of his cheekbones, dark eyes, and panty-melting smile set against rich mahogany skin. I giggled, flashing a grin that sent his full bottom lip rolling between his teeth before those deep eyes dropped to his feet.

Blaz was quick to rescue his easily flustered companion, gesturing to the brunette beside him. "This is Darius. He's the head of security for the estate."

"At your service, ma'am. I'm afraid I only answer to that, no matter how sweet the bestower of names is."

I turned that practiced smile on the broad-shouldered one, softening my expression and biting my lip as if nervous—a feeling I hadn't sincerely experienced in lifetimes. Darius had that polished air my brain immediately categorized as a Bellaton: coiffed dark brown hair, hazel eyes framed in thick lashes, sun-kissed skin that crinkled around his smile. Interesting. Likely the oldest of them. But not the alpha.

"Nice to meet you, gentlemen."

"Pleasure is all ours, I assure you, Miss Porter," Blaz said, bowing his head before motioning toward the double doors beyond the front porch. Damn, you could cut glass with that boy's cheekbones, and there was something undeniably charming about the way his caramel eyes flashed when he smiled. Maybe this brief field trip would hold some fun after all.

Mirroring his expression, I skipped up the steps, regretting not listening to Aunt Fae and slipping into a dress just to let it sway as I ascended. The faster I had these men wrapped around my finger, the faster I could win over their Commander—*Queen*, whatever damn title she took—and be back beside my family.

Spinning on my heel, I traced the immense details of the looming columns and swaying porch swing, hoping to look fascinated by the history or architecture or whatever conceited feature I could plant in their pretty little heads. Meanwhile, I cataloged every visible escape route and vulnerability. The Queen of the South had four damn cameras on the front of the house alone.

Blaz reached a tan hand for Brody, his smile shifting to one of camaraderie as they exchanged that weird bro-mance handshake-embrace thing guys always did with old friends.

"Nice to see you, Brody."

"You look good, kid. Nineteen suits you well."

"Feels alright. Just waitin' for those celestial genes to turn on."

"In time," Alastair said with a low chuckle, reaching forward to clasp forearms. Ajax stepped in next.

"How you been, Blazzy?" Ajax's chest shook with amusement as Blaz rolled his eyes before glaring at him.

I swallowed my laugh, batting my lashes when his gaze flicked my way.

"For Pete's sake, I thought that died a decade ago."

Mocking innocence, Ajax raised his hands. "Old habits, *big man*."

"Sure," Blaz drawled, and I caught the start of an eye roll as I turned back around, reminding myself to move light and airy like Fae.

Four windows, two on either side of the entry. Two benches, one beside each door, with work and riding boots propped below them. A swing at both ends of the porch. A wire-pronged hedgehog beside the benches. I quirked my head, narrowing my eyes as I made mental bullet points. Honestly, the place had an inordinate amount of glass to be called a safe house. No wonder it was crawling with celestial security.

Eyeing the hedgehog, I internally noted: *peculiar decor style.*

Boot scraper, Brody supplied.

G and Darius lunged ahead to open both looming white doors. My gaze scraped up to the grand vaulted ceiling and dramatic crystal chandelier. Twin staircases greeted us just beyond the entryway, their graceful curves caging in a hallway illuminated by lantern-style lights, flickering flames dancing within the glass. A marble round table and ornate centerpiece with draping greenery sat between them.

I snapped my mouth shut, realizing it had fallen open for real, and glanced to Blaz, whose lips twisted with something like satisfaction.

"This place is..." I swallowed thickly. *Intimidating. Creepy. Rigid.* "Magnificent," I finally supplied breathily.

"Thank you, ma'am. Quarters get a little tight, but it'll do."

My brows could have kissed with the depth of my confusion, but then the hair on my arms prickled. I turned to the young man now beside me, smirking down as realization dawned.

"Ohh, you're funny," I teased, laughing lightly.

"And you're wearing shoes past the foyer."

My eyes flicked up to the saccharine ghost of a voice abruptly cutting our conversation short just as Blaz looked to his own feet. Standing at the railing overlooking the entrance was a woman too perfect to be real. Worse than I remembered. The southern belle incarnate—skin glowing, bright blonde hair swept back into a chic style at her nape, with strands framing her heart-shaped face—Reyna wore an overtly feminine chiffon dress. Bright buttercream yellow. It should have clashed with her hair, but somehow, she owned every inch of the graceful, flowing fabric. Lightly hooded eyes, sharp as the wings that lined them, stared down at me before she offered what was supposed to be a smile but felt closer to a grimace.

"You must be Reyna." I smiled, knowing full well she was the mirror image of the bitch I was actually here for.

Reyna mimicked the expression, the movement sickly sweet as she curved around the railing. Long fingers, crowned with perfect French tips, trailed the wooden banister as she descended with theatrical grace.

"And you must not be from around here."

"We were just catching up," Blaz offered, his hand settling at the curve of my back. Familiar enough to let it linger—but if he dropped lower, he might lose it.

"Very well," Reyna's voice hovered over the space. Gritting my teeth, I followed Blaz's lead to the bench beside the opposing staircase, setting down my duffle to remove my boots.

"Reyna!" Brody boomed, a smile curving the sharp lines of his cheeks.

"Ambroise," her voice softened as her eyes did, reaching out a hand as her pedicured feet touched marble. Blush polish. Shocker.

As Brody kissed her fingers, I turned to Ajax, who smirked.

Rusty mask, madam Wraith.

Bite me. It's been a minute.

His cough failed to cover his snort, drawing Reyna's gaze. After pleasantries, she turned to me.

"Freya Porter, correct?"

"Yes, ma'am."

"Welcome to Bellaton."

Despite her sweeping gesture toward the hallway beyond, I couldn't shake the feeling that I was anything *but* welcome. But I needed Reyna to justify my presence here for these final weeks before the war, so I nodded and followed her lead deeper into the estate.

She ushered us into a sunlit room, its warmth wrapping around us like a well-worn cloak. Brody and his brothers leaned against the wall perpendicular to an ornate wooden desk, while Reyna took her place behind it, framed by towering bookshelves. Wasting no time on small talk, she launched straight into the string of flawlessly executed burglaries they'd suffered. As I settled into the plush cornflower blue chair across from her, she detailed the strange assortment of targets—each theft somehow connected, though they couldn't decipher the pattern. A greenhouse. A manufacturing plant that reported nothing missing. Her antique storage.

And these petty, mismatched thefts were why I was here under the pretense of negotiating an alliance. Naturally.

"I was goin' to let the rats scuttle home," she snapped, voice dripping with disdain, "until they targeted my lab and roughed up my doctors. Now, enough is enough."

With the flourish of a ship captain, she unrolled a map—acrylic nails clacking against the polished wood. I tilted my head, scanning the red markings denoting each heist. If I connected them with strings, they formed a crooked star.

Well. Hello, old friends.

"It appears they're centrally based in the River District."

TWO

HAUNTINGS

CYRUS

God fucking dammit.

Sighing, I ceased the steady stroke up and down Carissa's back, snaking my arm out from under Melody before palming my face and extricating myself entirely. I tapped the icon on my phone, silencing the shrill alarm screeching into the dead of night. Fucking Bellatons. Retaliation was inevitable, but to be sloppy enough to trip an alarm at three in the damn morning?

That was either aggravatingly lazy or simply incompetent.

Yanking my jeans into place, the quiet purr of the zipper was cut off by a breathy, "Cy?"

"Go back to sleep," I ordered softly, jerking my chin at the bed as Melody sat up, her full breasts popping free from the sheet I'd tucked around the girls. I pulled on my black long-sleeved shirt before running a palm over my hair. "All good. Just some pest control."

Nodding, Melody snuggled in toward Carissa, her blonde hair nearly iridescent in the moonlight streaming through the window. This wasn't new to either of them. Hierarchy business was family business. *My* business. And over my dead body would anybody trip Uptown and not expect a response. Much like our lovely government, the Paladins didn't negotiate with terrorists, thieves, rival clans, or psychotic twin sisters hellbent on interfering with our every damn move. Uptown was home. Our watchtower. Our space to play as much as work. Anybody within a three-thousand-mile radius with at least two brain cells to rub together knew better than to touch Uptown.

Furthermore, Uptown was *mine*.

According to the soft blue glow of my security monitor beside the front door, my sister, Calypso, and our cousin, Carr, were already dressed and yanking on their boots as they stumbled into the hallway. The clip of my pistol clicking into its holster cut off my thoughts as my agile fingers marked weapons and mags, all fitted precisely into place.

Straightening, I snagged my black peacoat off the rack and exited the room, clicking the door closed behind me. I motioned for them to join as soon as I caught eyes with my heiress and our third, whose wreathing shadows mirrored my own displeasure, and as one, we shifted into mist and shadow.

The realm between realms whisked us away into the darkness, re-materializing in my Uptown office where alarms blared. The ancient warehouse was lit with the harsh light of rotating strobes, the echo of rushed footsteps reverberating off steel walls as I slowly braced myself over the desk to study the screens. My team prepared for orders, shadows whispering intel between us.

Chaos.

The screens were chaos. Oh, fuck me—Mercury really was in retrograde, wasn't it?

Cameras were cracked, others blacked out, and those with clear views surveyed absolute destruction. This wasn't the Bellatons. Too damned sloppy. This was the livid tantrum of a rival or the lashing out of a disgruntled employee. *Personal.* A growl lodged in my throat as I snatched the steel baseball bat from behind my desk—extracting answers was often accompanied by the pleasure of cracking kneecaps, and whatever rat was in my home would owe us an explanation. Quirking my head as I studied the new squares on the screen, my eyes caught on the center.

"Cali." She was beside me before the breath could return to my lungs. My sister was the one soul on the planet I trusted without question, the future Queen of our Hierarchy, and it was her analysis I needed now. I nodded at the screen, and she tucked a silky strand of black hair behind an ear, brows furrowing as she studied it.

"Is that a motherfucking...*star?*" she deadpanned.

"Sure as fuck ain't a circle."

"What the fuck?"

Jerking my head toward the bustling hallway, I said, "Let's go find out."

Together, we misted through the warehouse, solidifying outside the pillaged file room. Shouts reverberated, competing with the thud of combat boots against the harsh floor and the jostle of equipment as our response crew searched the building. Forehead pinched, heart rate accelerating, I surveyed the mess within. Black metal cabinets had been knocked sidelong, a broken fluorescent light flickering feebly where it hung from the ceiling, a pathetic attempt to keep the wrecked space lit. Our computer monitors had been absolutely obliterated, and judging by the shatter marks, it had been done with my own steel bat. Papers *everywhere*. The ceiling fan was broken, creaking in a frantic spin as the blades raced in useless grinding rotations.

My jaw protested how tightly I clenched it.

What. The fuck.

"Looks like a smash room," Calypso muttered under her breath. Nodding, I scanned the space. No footprints. No items that didn't belong. But the floor was covered in litter, every damn surface layered in *something*. I knelt down to flip open one of the manila envelopes that our raider had used to outline a *star* on the floor, with one standing black cabinet that—judging by the gouges in the linoleum—had been *dragged* to the center. Scowling, equally intrigued and infuriated, I opened a drawer, finding it entirely vacant.

"Cy!" Carr's voice cut through the tension as he swung his head around the door frame. My cousin was tall, like me and Dad, though his seven-foot frame was packed with more muscle than either of us. He shared my blond hair and tan skin, but while my eyes were a light hazel, his were a rich sapphire blue. A deep furrow between them, those razor blues were trained on me now.

"You're gonna wanna see this."

"What?" I barked, irritation oozing from the word.

"Come on, man. The whole place is torn to pieces."

Which meant...they hadn't *tripped* an alarm in the *process*. They got what they came for and wanted us to fucking know. *That,* or they made one shitty move at the end of a long series of life-ending stupidity. As I followed Carr around the corner, the hair on my neck rose to attention, halting my feet as I glanced over my shoulder. Were we being *watched*? My shadows certainly seemed to think so.

"Your mom just got here and—"

"Where is she?" I cut in impatiently. Now wasn't the time for yammering; I needed to run dispatch for our crews and do so quickly. A strike like this could never be tolerated, and with the world on the brink of chaos, now was not the time to hesitate.

"In the mess."

"Why?" I demanded, glaring down at him as we rounded the corner towards the mess hall.

"You'll fuckin' see. This is some sick joke, Cy. Whoever did this is out for blood. Literally."

"Find them."

"Reyna?"

"No, you dumb shit. This is too bold for Bellaton. Find our thief." Dark smoke began to creep from the nearest door frames, stretching toward the center of the room, climbing up the walls toward the ceiling as I burst through the swinging double doors. "And get that damned fire out."

"On it," Carr barked, turning calmly on his heel—as if we weren't under siege—as he drew water between his palms before kicking open the nearest door.

My boots screeched against linoleum as I took in the mess hall. Mom was staring up at the wall I learned to play dodgeball on. *Blood* dripped down the aged white paint. I stepped up beside her, mouth popping open as I took in the words.

Did you think I would forget?

"Ma'?"

Eyes glazed with something perilously close to fear—an emotion I'd never seen on her before—my mother, Queen of the Southern Paladins, turned to look at me. Her lips parted, disbelief etched into every line of her face.

The shadows whispered, *She's still here.*

"She?" I demanded aloud. The single word widened my mother's bright blue eyes as she dragged a shaky hand over her mouth. What the hell was *wrong* with her?

"She's back," she managed, voice scraped raw.

"What?" I blinked.

She's escaping, the shadows hissed.

"Get her out of here," I barked at Cali, who nodded sharply and moved past me. I turned back the way we came, leaving my incoherent mother to her stupor, irritation burning in my veins. Whatever had rattled her could wait—I had bigger problems.

Gun drawn, I followed the shadows deeper into the warehouse, rounding two corners before a thin curl of smoke snagged my senses like a hooked lure, reeling me forward.

Motherfucker—who the hell was stupid enough to set fire to Paladin territory? Our *home*, at that.

Dread coiled in my gut. The sinking sensation had me breaking into a full sprint toward my mother's office at the end of the hall just as the fire alarm shrieked, splitting the night in two.

Carr, get the fucking fire out, I snapped mind-to-mind, yanking the lower half of my mask into place—partially for the smoke, but mostly because instinct warned I didn't want this intruder seeing my face.

Trying, he gritted back.

Sprinklers burst to life, water striking my skin a beat before I crashed into Ma's office—or what was left of it. The room was a goddamned inferno, flames hissing against the weak spray overhead.

Perched casually in the window was a figure dressed head to toe in black—an ancient Paladin uniform to rival my own. A mask covered both the upper and lower half of a pale face, hidden further by a dark hood.

Female, judging by the frame.

Bright green eyes locked onto mine as I raised my gun. A smirk flickered in them a heartbeat before she fucking *winked,* waggling a folder in her grip before she vaulted through the second-story window like a bird, cloak fanning out behind her.

I didn't shoot.

I *could* have.

Had the opportunity, and fucking froze.

Too stunned to move.

Shield flaring over my skin, I lunged through the fire, nearly throwing myself out the window to chase her into the shadows—only for blinding light to swallow the alleyway.

My escape route vanished as a helicopter swiveled into position, its spotlight trained on my window in eerie, predatory grace.

Holy shit.

I recoiled just as the thudding roar of the rotor blades filled the air.

Burnt.

The whole warehouse was about to go up, and the best move I had left was making sure the flames erased every last trace before the humans in that chopper—law enforcement, no doubt—found anything they shouldn't.

We might not need much from the mortal world, but replacing aliases for thousands of souls? I wasn't equipped for that level of bullshit tonight.

I pulled the air with me, stoking the blaze as I bolted down the hall.

Dad? Mortal police—helicopter out front, which means SWAT is right behind them. What's the order?

I already knew the answer before it came, my chest tightening with grim certainty as my father's voice echoed back.

Burn everything.

"Two dead. Countless documents lost."

"Two burn victims with the healers." My parents rattled off statistics as I paced behind the billiards table. Calypso had her face buried in her hands, elbows braced against the old wooden bar top. Named after Louisiana's favorite childhood nightmare, *The Rougarou* had started as a laundering front but had grown into our hierarchy's favorite haunt. Dimly lit, an abundance of booze, souls behind the bar with watchful eyes, billiards, darts, disruptively loud live music—it all amassed into the best kind of chaos. The perfect place to go unnoticed when needed.

Now, it was empty, save for our coven. Dad's jaw was clenched so tightly he might crack a molar. He was the genetic bestower of my bizarrely long frame, like a mirroring carnival freak. But where my hair echoed Ma's bright blonde, Dad and Calypso had raven black. An entangled twin dance of yin and yang.

The master of immortal stillness, Dad perched in an armchair and, tone steady, demanded, "Can *anyone* offer me an explanation?"

I sucked in a long breath, bracing for the recoil. "No."

"You are the head of our entire fleet of security personnel, Cyrus," he gritted out, "and you're telling me we have *nothing*? No explanation for why two souls are now recirculating? Why a ninety-year-old building is now a skeleton with ash for innards?"

"No, sir," I said, eyes flicking to my mother, who stared daggers through the countertop. The very same countertop my father nearly eviscerated as he abruptly rose, slamming his broad hands down atop it. Unflinching, I supplied, "But we will. Carr is working on the video feed."

"And you honestly expect me to believe one soul demolished a *guarded* safe house *on her own*, and nobody heard a *damn thing*?"

Gritting my teeth, I replayed that moment—that hair's breadth of hesitation as she flashed that cocky wink and sailed out the two-story window. Like she knew I wasn't gonna shoot her.

I knew better than to hesitate. Knew the price that so often accompanied it was steeper than my skin cared to pay. But as I barreled into that room, the last thing I expected to see was a mortal-sized female wearing a Paladin uniform—the same as the ones my parents wore in old photos. Unable to articulate any of that in a way that wouldn't send the King's temper flying, I flatly admitted, "Nais pas. I can only verify that I saw one soul flee out the east window with one folder in hand." I glared at my mother, who still said nothing. Who was blatantly not discussing whatever was terrifying her into silence. She knew *something*.

When her bright blues landed on me, I asked, "Anything you feel like sharing with the coven?"

My dad's dark eyes flicked to her, a scowl in place as she tongued at a molar. "Not at the moment," she drawled, back in possession of her usual level of disdain. Nearly growling, Dad began to pace, hands braced behind his back. This was personal. Because Ciaran Stuart was The Seer of The

South. His place at the head of this hierarchy was largely based on oversight. Despite his gifts, not even Dad saw this coming.

"How the hell did we miss this?" Mom piped up, scowling as her eyes tracked Dad's pissed-off circuit through the space between us. The 'we' was kind, considering we all knew it was a 'you' in her question.

"Didn't see shit. Nothing. Not a devil-damned warning. The threads have been manic since the battle up north. Changing much too quickly to keep up with. There was a flicker of chaos the night before last, but nothing solidified. Even then, it was wisps of darkness, like some kind of phantom."

Slowly, nearly motionless, I raised only my eyes as realization dawned in my chest. Not a *phantom*. A decade before my lifeline, Mom had a friend. A friend the legends painted with a proclivity for theatrics, combined with brutal efficiency. At least, when she *wanted* her target to know what she was up to. If subtlety was the name of the game, there wasn't a legend more adept at entering and exiting undetected, without shadows.

...A friend her estranged sister's men dredged out of the East River, throat slit ear to ear. Mom's glare could have incinerated me where I stood, leaving me to wonder what the fuck she had gotten us into.

Eyes flicking to my pacing father, I supplied simply, "The Wraith."

THREE

THE GUARD

CYRUS

My mother's snarled protests echoed in my mind as I watched the war room fill, one seat at a time.

"Don't be preposterous," she'd barked. "The Wraith was slain three decades ago."

"Which gives her just enough time to recirculate and ascend," I countered, my tone bored.

"Your mother and Miss Lamb were friends," Dad argued, a pinch of concern settling between his dark brows. While my mother had reduced herself to feral pacing, our king had returned to lethal stillness as they took turns belittling my theory.

"Right—until she turned up dead in the water, and you dismissed it as coincidence—"

My rebuttal was cut short by a barked, "*Enough!*" My mother's power snaked its way to the surface, her words edged in command. Not enough to bring me to a knee, but enough to remind me she was a breath away from forcing me to heel. She had never been shy about wielding her gift, and neither Calypso nor I were exempt from her wrathful enchantments. I wasn't naïve enough to think we didn't get away with more than her subjects, but that didn't ease the anger simmering in my veins at being silenced. For a woman devoted to balance, she had a hell of a knack for silencing information she didn't want to hear—unless, of course, it came from Calypso, her precious heiress.

I should have known better than to present my idea myself, but time was of the essence.

I glanced at my sister, who merely shrugged, resigned.

On my own. Got it.

Clenching my jaw, I gave a quick nod, eyes cast to the floor as I followed them to the gatehouse. Conversation over. Time to present a unified front as the ruling family.

Every hierarchy leader had a back way through their gate, and the gothic mansion on the edge of town and marsh was ours. Much too formal for daily use, the monstrosity loomed with spires and stretched cathedral windows, eerie in its silence. Locals believed it was haunted, and we did nothing to dissuade the rumors. If anything, as children, we used them to our advantage—terrorizing our peers, feeding the myths.

We might've been assholes, but we weren't entirely wrong—a fact I was reminded of as the haunting melody of a cello and harmonized vocals rang out from the attic.

Goosebumps rippled across my skin as the familiar chill of something *other* dropped the room's temperature by at least ten degrees. Restless spirits rarely left without guidance, and since the only clan capable of escorting them to the next life wouldn't do house calls without a hefty price, we were left with their company.

Bracing one arm beneath my elbow, I ran my opposite hand over my mouth, then along my jaw, grounding myself in the sensation, even as irritation churned beneath my skin.

I hated this place.

More than the house, I hated these meetings. Hated watching my mother's Guardians rush to her side, no longer convinced my father's presence alone was enough to ensure her safety. How my father allowed any of them to draw breath was beyond me.

I loathed the arrogance of our swaggering Wings—Paladin's most elite warriors, their familiars' blessings imbued into their flesh like ink—as they exchanged greetings and somber handshakes.

Only the worst kind of trouble brought the Wings back to Luminark Manor, and whoever—or whatever—had burned Uptown had just declared war.

My shadows hissed as they slithered up my arm to my shoulder, pressing against my neck in warning.

Captain Nix has arrived, my prince.

Great.

Carr might've been my ride-or-die, but as kids, his brother had been synonymous with getting my ass beat with a rod. Nix was built like a truck, while Carr and I had been lean, and though his intentions were noble enough to earn those damned Wings inked into his forearms, his grasp of *balance* was murky at best.

Moral or immoral was subjective in his eyes. As long as our queen didn't deem his actions *out of balance*, he didn't much care for rules. Or civility.

Nor had he ever cared for our objections—he'd just pummel us into compliance with his meaty fists.

It was Nix's preference for chaos that landed us all in trouble more often than not growing up, and when he was finally deployed elsewhere, Carr, Calypso, and I all breathed a sigh of relief.

His return did not bode well.

Look who it is, Calypso snarled in my mind, leaning back to drape one leg over the other, arms crossed in irritation. The tall slit in her black dress revealed bare legs none of the men in proximity missed. Of all life's cruelties, a sister so beautiful she turned heads was the worst of them.

I all but snarled as a group of Wings strode by, flashing her smiles.

In their fucking dreams.

Oh, good. The devil himself, Carr added dryly, shaking his head as he followed her gaze.

While the claim was an exaggeration, the two of them couldn't have been more different in nature, despite the undeniable similarity in their features.

Nix shook out his blond hair, droplets of water hitting the floor as the storm tapped against the glass above us.

A shit-eating grin stretched over his face as he spotted a few of the Wings summoned for the war room, embracing them like this was some happy reunion rather than a strategy meeting called on the heels of the fall of our stronghold.

Discomfort settled in my stomach. Reaching into my jacket, I found the pocket lining and pulled out a sucker, popping the sour candy into my mouth. The stick rolled between my fingers as I studied the inpouring reinforcements.

Ma abhorred smoking, but she didn't wield her authority to forbid it anywhere but Luminark Manor.

Something about working my mouth helped dispel the anxiety.

Our war room was modeled after the Six's gathering hall—the Paladin crest carved into the enormous stone wall. Six flags hung from the black ceiling beams, designating our covens' roles within the hierarchy. Simple navy velvet-backed chairs surrounded the Goliath of a table, all except for the two winged armchairs sitting at opposite sides—one for my mother, the other for her mate.

While I didn't agree with everything my parents did, I had to commend them for the respect they commanded, because the moment they entered the room, a hush settled over the gathering.

Dad led Ma to her chair, pulling it out before scooting her in close. He poured her tea, then set the kettle one space to the right, making the trek around the table to take his seat at the opposite end.

Jaw set, I watched as three Guardians took their places beside my mother, a fourth looming behind. Orion, Lynx, and Mars—heads of the third coven and Winged generals in our legion—stood at her side, willing sacrifices should her safety require it.

Perhaps that alone was why they were still breathing.

Carr and Nix's father—my uncle Juno—claimed his place to Ma's right, beside Orion. Next came Vesper, then Sidra, and Portia, the final coven leaders. Calypso, Carr, and I were last to take our seats, all gazes turning to us as we settled and met Mom's blue eyes.

"A stello venomous, et ad aethera redibunt omnes." *From stardust we came, and to the ether, all shall return.*

We bowed our heads in confirmation. The remaining souls found their places along the stone walls—there to observe, never to speak.

Nix, the arrogant bastard, sprawled into his seat against the far wall behind his father, somehow making sitting look like a challenge to authority. Irritation had me grinding the candy into crystals between my teeth as I refocused on our queen, who had just begun the meeting.

"Sound off," she ordered by way of greeting, scooping up her teacup as Orion poured his own.

"Orion, first ascension, third coven, accounted for."

"Juno, first ascension, second coven, accounted for…" And so it continued, each council member stating their name as they passed the kettle, filling their cups. The steam thickened in the room, infused with a spice that made my mouth water, promising relief. If *The Rougarou* was for letting loose, the war room's herbs were for steady hearts and clear minds.

When the tea finally made it from my hands to Carr's, Ma cleared her throat.

"Very well." With an impartial flick of her gaze, she added, "Lynx, Vesper—you both have my condolences for your coven's losses this evening."

"From stardust we came, and to the ether, all shall return," the gathering chorused, heads bowing before our queen continued.

"Nix will be the voice of our Wings this evening."

Oh. Great. So the motherfucker could speak freely after all.

Irritated, I fiddled with my signet ring, focusing on my breathing. The difference between us and the bane of my existence? The matriarchal line of power welded Calypso and me into a throne of authority, while Nix's father was merely her advisor—a role I would take when my sister replaced Ma', per tradition. That was, of course, assuming a more powerful female didn't ascend before the magic marked her on the equinox.

It was that magicline that earned us both a ring bearing Ma's family crest—a raven clutching a dagger in his talons, our initials where his heart should be. That heirloom granted us the authority to govern the hierarchy in her absence, to vote at this very table, to hold council, and, should the Six summon the royals, to speak in her stead at conclaves. It also gave us one vote should some crazy bastard ever attempt to conquer the Crucible and become a Paladin—to approve or disapprove of the Wing they challenged in their final task.

Somehow, over the years, the ring had become my anchor in moments of frustration. Like now, as my bastard cousin was handed a platform from which to speak.

Nix bowed his head in acceptance before lifting his chin, his expression insufferably cocky as usual, eyes locking on Ma'. "Our trackers have been deployed, ma'am."

Ma nodded.

I scoffed.

Nix's gaze snapped to mine from where he sat behind Juno and Vesper, one sapphire eye and one gold alight with challenge. "Something funny, Stuart?"

"Your trackers won't find anything," I stated matter-of-factly.

"And why the hell not?"

"This wasn't some petty thief."

"I'd certainly hope not, considering that would call into question the efficacy of our head of security, wouldn't it?"

Refusing to take the bait, I kept my tone bored. "This was a professional. I've never seen anyone move like that without shadows to soften their landing. Our thief moved like a damned bird. She was—"

"She?" he scoffed. "You're telling me you lost our base to a single female?" His golden brows arched skeptically. A murmur of agreement rippled around the table—everyone, it seemed, except Calypso and Carr, whose anxious eyes flicked to mine.

"I stand by my assessment."

Cyrus, Ma warned mind-to-mind.

Deciding to take my lashes later, I lifted my chin. "A solo assailant ransacked a building before alarms tripped or security detected a thing. It's a rather auspicious match for a figure prominent in Bellpost lore, don'tcha think?"

"Can't say I'm familiar—you were always yammering on about the Obsidian Crown," Nix countered, a cocky smirk tugging at his lips. If making people look bad was a sport, Nix was its reigning champion. He knew damn well my obsession with that particular legend had led to the worst tragedy of my life, yet his grin didn't falter when I didn't snap.

The council watched us volley like spectators at a game, their flickering gazes itching my skin like a physical touch.

"You never were one for book smarts."

Carr poorly concealed a snicker behind a cough as Nix's expression soured.

"So let me fill you in on the tale of our ancestors."

"No need to condescend," my father reprimanded. The weight of the council's stares shifted toward him.

"No need to veil reality either," I countered, eyes locked on that mismatched pair across the room. "Nix was never one for studies. *I* was. And I'm telling you all—the style of this attack is not coincidental. We are the descendants of Bellpost proper. And for centuries, our people have encountered an enemy that manifests when we're in the throes of an acquisition. Historically speaking, we're right on schedule." I folded my hands, resting my elbows on the table, rolling the sucker across my tongue before tucking it into my cheek with a clink. My gaze flicked to my sister, willing her to hear reason.

"We're weeks away from finalizing a counterattack to the weapons we acquired during the conflict with the Renown. A sudden manifestation of a rather elusive thief? That is, historically, par for the course."

"The Wraith?" Orion barked in disbelief before his chest shook with husky laughter.

My eyes met seething blues across the table before Ma spoke. "We have no evidence to support this suspicion."

"Except for the elaborate style of the attack," Calypso pointed out. My head whipped toward her, finding her staring Ma down.

I fucking *loved* my sister.

"Cyrus doesn't act unless he's certain, and I, for one, believe him."

"Heiress," Lynx admonished, "with all due respect, neither you nor your second were alive when we last encountered the Wraith. Those of us who met her would know if she were back."

"So explain the warning on the wall," Carr demanded.

"This is undoubtedly a personal assault," Father assured. "But jumping to conclusions serves no one. We will ensure a proper investigation—"

"In which we will find *nothing*," I promised, irritation brewing in my blood. If I was right—and my gut was certain I was—the Wraith wouldn't have left breadcrumbs beyond what she wanted us to know. Which meant she had once again reincarnated under well-enforced wards.

"You can send Nix and his Wings after whatever glimmers remain behind the human police, but unless she wants us to know something, it will be wasted effort."

"Why so certain?" Portia inquired, her jaw set but eyes more curious than suspicious.

I stared at my hands for a long minute before lifting my face to meet her gaze.

"Call it intuition."

"CYRUS!"

My sister's voice rang off the walls, halting my steps with a rubber screech over the marble. The meeting had gone as well as I'd expected— which is to say, *terribly*. Until Calypso sat at the head of that table, my knack for history and analysis would serve precisely no one. I pulled a cigarette from its case as I turned to face her.

"Don't start, Cal."

She would, in fact, start. Evidently with my smokes, as she plucked mine from my fingers. Pursing my lips in irritation, I fished another from the pack.

"You know better than to come at her head-on like that."

"By now, she should know better than to discount *research*."

"Tempers are high," she said, canting her head when I ran my tongue over a molar before popping the roll between my lips. I slid my hand into the silky interior of my jacket pocket to grab a lighter.

"And tolerance was already running low," she added, in the most unnecessary understatement of the century.

Of three things, I was certain:

One—January was always a terrible time for confrontation with our mother. The echo of our brother's loss hung heaviest in the weeks leading up to the anniversary of Charles' death. Unfortunately, that also explained my lack of propriety. Everyone—the queen included—could get fucked.

Two—We stood on an unforeseen precipice, both historically and personally. Calypso was weeks away from reverse-engineering a weapon wielded against the Wings last month that could change the face of not only the coming conflict but the future power dynamics of every hierarchy on the planet. It was not the time for added drama.

Three—Tensions on my aunt's border were at an all-time high. No doubt due to the acquisitions our team had recently prioritized to facilitate said weapon. Petty bitch though she may be, Reyna Gwyne commanded some of the best healers east of the Rockies. Their medicinal gardens were second to none. That didn't mean any of them took kindly to us utilizing them without permission. A Paladin caught in Bellaton territory would face no mercy. Which made investigating an enemy on their side of the river annoyingly daunting.

Of course, tolerance was low. Begrudgingly lighting my cigarette with a click, I mumbled, "You think?" before taking a long drag. With a glare, my sister took three long strides to throw open the front door, motioning for me to lead the way. Only once we were in the crisp air on the front step did she hold out a hand for the lighter.

"I believe you, Cy, but the council will require more than a penchant for folklore and a gut instinct."

"Clearly," I grunted, blowing out a long stream of smoke.

"What would you have me do?"

"You're the heiress, not me."

My sister held my stare for a long moment, both of us taking another drag as she chewed over that rebuttal before calmly responding.

"Humor me. When I am queen, you will still be my advisor. You're already my second. So *advise me*, Cyrus. From a tactical standpoint, as our head of security, what would you have me do?"

Huffing my irritation that our own mother couldn't trust me to do my damn job, I made my way down the stairs, heading for the edge of the wards, even as she groaned her frustration behind me.

"Send shadows across the river," I said matter-of-factly. Calypso's rushed steps before grabbing my elbow told me she didn't approve of that answer—or my walking away—very much.

"Fuck, Cyrus. The last thing we need is Bellaton breathing down our necks again."

"Hence, *shadows*."

"Like the wicked witch doesn't have an abundance of walkers on her side of the divide."

"Ours are better."

"I also don't think she's dumb enough to start something right now."

"I never said she was."

"So what *are* you saying?" Calypso snapped, glowering as she sucked down a deep drag, the cherry glowing red.

"That our only lead is a star on the damn floor and the precision of Uptown's swift dismantling. Reyna might not be preparing to revive the feud, but after the battle out west and the timing of your research, she might be harboring a new recruit or an ally's assets. *That's* what I'm saying."

She hesitated to respond, taking another pull before holding it for a long beat. Slowly, she released a cloud of smoke, the motion rounding her words as she asked, "Who?"

"Would I send?" I filled in the end of her question, rocking on my heels and rolling the cigarette between my fingers. I took a long breath of fresh air, allowing my head to settle as I thought it over. "Vesper and Portia."

Vesper was the most skilled at vanishing within our realm between realms, and Portia had held my eyes in that meeting like she was chewing over what I'd said. Their rank would be of concern, but when it came down to who would get the damn job done without raising too much suspicion around their absence, those were my picks.

"What about Nix?"

I shook my head. "Talented? Yes. But his tactics are too volatile. Keep your friends close—"

"And enemies closer," she finished. I nodded, and she did the same.

"I'll see what I can do through unofficial channels."

Without another word, we split ways into mist and shadow.

FOUR
PETULANT, PATRONIZING
LITTLE SHIT

FREYA

Five Years Ago…

"Freya, come on!" Shay called over her shoulder, impatience thick in her voice. Her silky blonde hair was swept into a high ponytail, tan legs—two miles long—tucked into black-and-pink Vans. We weren't besties by any means, but she was the cool girl who tolerated me every summer at camp. "We're going to be late."

"Chill, Shay. It's the last night—what are they going to do? Send us home?"

"I want to see the show."

Show. Shay had never been to a "show" in her life.

I lived for music—not in the way August did, with his piano, guitar, and whatever other instrument he deigned to pick up—but in the way a designer loves paint chips. I wanted to sample and review, feel the bass in my chest, hear the shift of rubber soles on a sticky floor my parents would say I was too young to be dancing on.

By show, Shay meant the end-of-summer talent show, a long processional of nearly-always-talentless misfits in color-coded camp T-shirts, doing their best to belt out lyrics to trending songs and tap-dance their way across the stage like gangly leprechauns. I rolled my eyes, dropping the charcoal into my tin with a little clink before dusting my hands on my denim shorts.

"Very nice," Shay scolded, glaring at the black streaks.

I snorted, grabbing my worn, button-adorned jean jacket off the hook and making for the door. As we crossed the lawn from our cabin to the lodge, a *posse of babbling girls joined us, always tight on our heels when we could be bothered to attend the festivities. Their high-pitched, anticipatory voices merged into one collective buzz in my ears as my mind wandered back to the shading on my latest sketch.*

Freaking talent show.

We clomped up the front steps and tossed open the doors, not bothering to be quiet as we entered the now-silent hall. Cali, a girl a few years older—and fully filled in with curves I couldn't wait to get—was standing at the mic, swaying her hips as she sang.

As far as voices behind the mic went, theirs were actually worth pausing for. I shook my head, knowing the show was over before it even began.

Ding, ding, ding—your winners, folks.

It didn't help that Cali was unfairly beautiful, her voice curved with that southern-belle twang that made boys stupid. Curtains of sleek black hair framed her face, and generous cleavage peeked through her camp tank. Naturally, every camper with a dick was mesmerized.

Tit-matized, if you will.

The girls too, I noted as I looked around, though most of them glared at the stage with the kind of loathing reserved for the popular girls.

I headed for the back of the room, sighing as the entire posse followed—now silent, eyes glued to the performance. But my gaze scanned the shadowed faces in the crowd until I found him.

Balanced on the back two legs of his chair, Crew had his combat boots propped on the seat in front of him, a lanky arm stretched over the backs of the chairs to either side. A girl was tucked into each—one blonde, one brunette—both watching his face more than the actual performance. Idiots.

But it was the guys in the rows around him I anticipated, and a sneaky smile curved my lips as they teased him. The guys loved driving Crew crazy —using Cali and her appeal to make his temper boil on the regular.

His face, though, was schooled into neutrality, oozing boredom as he flipped his straight, sun-bleached blond hair out of bright hazel eyes.

Eyes that landed on me.

My throat tightened as his gaze slid down, all the way to my Converse— the pair I had signed in silver Sharpie by all of my favorite lead singers and guitarists that year. His lips curled into an aggravating smirk, like he knew a secret he wasn't supposed to.

I held his gaze when it returned, lifting my chin as I marched for the back row.

Crew turned, kissed the blonde's forehead, but his eyes stayed glued to me until he'd have to crane his neck.

Relief washed over me when he finally turned back to his sister instead.

Crew's scrutiny carried a searing weight, branding my skin.

Older boys were trouble.

And Crew was the worst of them.

He'd always held attention—a silent dominance radiating from every inch of him—but this summer, he wasn't just a boy anymore.

It wasn't his now-towering height, or even that low voice that caught my attention when he arrived. It was the way his arms had corded with muscle, veins pronounced. And then the asshole had to play every sport with his shirt off, casually tucked in his waistband instead of actually covering the lean muscles of his body.

I had been spellbound.

An uncomfortable, fluttering heat filled my belly.

And he freaking knew it.

All of the girls were entranced by him and his pack of mischief-wreaking wolves.

The crowd's applause jerked my gaze from the back of his head to Cali as she beamed, tossing her dark hair over her shoulder.

Her brother didn't bother clapping as she scampered down the stage, but his eyes were trained daggers on her boyfriend as he settled beside her in the row in front of him.

I snorted.

But when Crew turned toward the sound, I locked my gaze on Shay and Katie, pretending to be held rapt by their conversation.

I couldn't have cared less about the be-there-or-commit-social-suicide event of the school year, or the outfits they were strategizing, but I nodded and smiled anyway.

Even as he branded the side of my face.

"THIS IS A TERRIBLE IDEA," *I hissed for the umpteenth time as Katie and Shay swiped on sticky-looking lip gloss later that night. Our cabin mates slept soundly, oblivious to the ruckus of the three of us wriggling into too-tight skinny jeans.*

"Loosen up, Grandma," Katie shot back. She and Shay wore their matching blonde locks in double French braids, and despite all my better judgment, I was finishing the last twist of my own. Shaking my head, I glared at Shay, silently pleading with her to back out.

"These are literally the boys your mom warns you to avoid like the bubonic plague." I fastened the hair tie and tucked my Buck knife into my back pocket. Technically, it was my brother James's, but the idiot had left it behind when he was home for break, so it was mine now.

"If you're gonna be a freaking drag, just stay here, Freya." Katie glowered, tucking her lip gloss into her front pocket.

"Seriously," Shay mumbled. Even as she crossed her arms, I caught the flicker of fear beneath her dark brown irises.

I sighed. "Jesus Christ. Fine. Let's go."

Katie chuckled in victory, and two heartbeats later, we were out the door and down the steps. Blinking into the darkness, I spotted the gaggle of girls waiting in a circle of pine trees. They were all freshmen—a year ahead of us— and a few had made it onto JV and varsity cheer at their schools, which explained Shay and Katie's obsession.

Personally, I'd rather fling myself off a cliff in my birthday suit than trust another girl to hold me six feet in the air in front of the entire student body for sport. Back home—miles away from this Appalachian music camp—I'd grown up in gymnastics. That was how I met Shay, but unlike my friend, I had no interest in the spotlight.

"You came!" one of the girls squealed, throwing her arms around Katie's neck. I sighed, earning a concerned glower from the freshman—Ashley, I was almost certain. Some generic '90s name I was tired of trying to remember. Raising my brows pointedly, I all but dared her to challenge our presence.

She didn't. Instead, she motioned for us to be quiet and follow. Silence fell as we trudged deeper into the woods. The camp's perimeter faded behind us, swallowed by trees so thick they blotted out the moonlight.

I snatched Shay's wrist, yanking her back just as probably-Ashley—who was supposed to be a camp counselor—raised her voice.

"We're going snipe hunting tonight, ladies."

A chorus of oooohs rippled through the group. She lowered her voice, flipping her flashlight upward to cast eerie shadows across her face, the kind of scary-story-around-the-fire effect that kids always ate up.

I huffed in exasperation as she continued.

"But be warned," she said. "They say these woods are haunted. That deep within them lurks a pack of great beasts, stealing away campers every summer when the full moon glows—just like tonight. Some say it's a pack of werewolves. Others claim Bigfoot roams these mountains. The truth..." Her voice dropped to a whisper. "...is one you never want to know."

As another high school girl moved through the group, handing out blindfolds with an absurd level of theatrical foreboding, Ashley droned on.

"But also within these woods is a little gold bird worth nearly a million dollars. Does anyone know why the snipe is so valuable?"

The campers shifted—some rapt, others skeptical, and then there was me, already annoyed.

Ashley took their silence as an invitation to continue.

"The snipe has the power to grant one wish to its bearer, making it the

most valuable animal in the world. Tonight, we're going snipe hunting. Now, snipes are drawn to glitter, which is why we'll all put these—" she flashed her light onto a sheet of glittering star stickers "—on our cheeks. But beware—the beasts must look into your eyes to steal you under their spell. That's why we've given each of you a blindfold." She gestured ahead. "We've marked the path and will lead you through until we find our snipes."

I tugged on Shay's wrist, staring at her pointedly. "This is the part in the movie where the audience is insulting our intelligence."

"Oh, come on, Freya, lighten up a little. It's all good fun." Shay shook her head, more frustrated with me than with the ridiculous game.

"They hang out with Crew and his thugs."

"Yeah," she said, nodding enthusiastically. "That's the whole point."

Shay turned away, tying her blindfold into place as she stepped into line.

My gut twisted—one of those moments where you just knew things would end badly. But I wasn't about to let Shay wander into the woods with these idiots alone.

So, with a resigned sigh, I stepped into line.

Ashley stopped beside me, eyes flicking to the blindfold in my hands before a smirk curled across her lips.

"Oh, here, let me help you!" she said with forced cheerfulness.

"I'm good," I shot back.

"You can't go if you don't wear your blindfold—don't want the beasts coming for you."

"I said I'm good."

Her smile sharpened. "Then I'll have Tara and Jess walk you back to your cabin if you're scared, little girl."

I rolled my eyes, more irritated that she was pretending not to know me than the fact that I gave enough of a crap to follow Shay into this mess.

With another sigh, I yanked the blindfold over my eyes.

"That's what I thought," the big idiot chirped before stepping away. I listened to the gravel shift under her feet as I stood there, blinking into nothing.

Shuffling forward, I stretched my arms until I collided into Shay, who giggled like the rest of them.

August would give me absolute hell if he ever found out about this. So, I resolved right then and there not to let him.

Hand gripping Shay's shoulder, I followed her deeper and deeper into the mountains. Time dragged. My eyes ached beneath the blindfold's forced darkness. Then—suddenly—the line came to an abrupt halt.

I slammed into Shay's back.

Someone gasped.

Gravel skidded.

Screams tore through the night.
And my friend's body was yanked away.

Seven weeks before the portals opened...

BLAZ YANKED his shoulder away from my grip, and I snarled in response. I'd been a decent fighter in all my lives, but it had never been something I craved like a Goddess of retribution. Not like Alvara, who lived and breathed bloodshed, or my soul-parents, who could slit a throat and wipe the blade clean in the next breath with all the finesse of opening a package. You didn't have to be a stabby menace to society to get the job done. I'd always preferred my enemies to know exactly who had thwarted them and what I had stolen from them—over leaving them a husk on the earth. Besides, if killing was necessary, there were cleaner ways to do it.

I ducked, dodging his next swing, and threw a jab, which he promptly outmaneuvered. Five straight days of this incessant twelve-hour routine had passed, all thanks to Reyna's relentless insistence. She was worse than Aren, forcing me to train until my body failed, loading my plate with enough protein to make any carnivore go vegan, and acting like my skill set was useless unless I polished the rust off my past-life hand-to-hand.

"You know." I panted, dancing around my opponent. "If you let them get their hands on you, *you already failed.*"

"That why you've recirculated so many times?" he sniped back, earning a snort of laughter from Brody, who was sprawled across two chairs, feigning sleep beneath the cowboy hat on his face. "Maybe you'd die less often if you learned to fight."

Landing my right hook, I grunted as he grabbed my retracting arm and yanked me forward. "Death is the *lone inevitable* in a life of variables. It's unwise to fear that which cannot be avoided."

"Poetic," he growled, attempting to throw me to the ground, surprise flashing across his face when I stayed on my feet.

"*Factual,*" I countered. "Besides—" My uppercut had him reeling back as I panted, "—we come back stronger every damn time. What are you so afraid of, Blazzy?" My sneer curled into a smirk as he glared, circling like a predator. The kid hated that nickname, much to my amusement.

"Wasting my first cycle," he breathed just before dropping his shoulder and tackling me like a damn football player. Ribs screaming, every scrap of air was knocked from my lungs as we hit the mat, my pride reeling as he straddled me. If this damn vessel couldn't remember how to jump soon, that might be the end of my usefulness. "Not bein' there when my people need me." A rattling gasp wheezed out of me as he mimed a blade to my throat, sly smile on his face as he barked, "There are fates worse than death, Miss Porter. You'd do kindly to remember that Bellatons fight not just to preserve life, but dignity."

"Nice form, Blaz." Reyna's cold tone caressed my senses, my eyes sliding closed in frustration.

Seven rounds, and naturally, *this* was the moment she'd waltz in. With a growl, I bucked my hips and flipped him off me.

"You're needed in the war room," she said simply before unceremoniously turning and sashaying away with that irritating bell-like sway of blush-draped hips.

No one wearing tulle and kitten heels should be permitted to bear the title of *Commander*.

Scrambling, I lunged forward to knock Blaz aside before straightening and rushing to follow. His barked laughter bounced off the training room walls.

Still fighting to catch my breath, I stepped up to keep pace beside the Queen of Bellaton, who held her neck long and shoulders back like some prim Southern belle when a warrior should have stood in her place. Lurking under all those pastels, she had to be fierce, or there was no way she would have lasted this long. No way Aren would believe we needed her.

Aren.

Yikes. The idea of the longest-lived Commander *ever* giving this rigid little blonde his time made me vaguely nauseous. Shaking off the unease, I asked, "Why are we convening in the war room?"

"*We?*" she drawled, those blonde Hollywood curls bobbing as she sneered at me. "You're mistaken, Miss Porter. You are an unfortunate thorn in my side—a payment to an ally to whom I owe a life debt—nothing more. I will train you while Aren doddles off to fraternize with those heathens out west, but that is the end of this dynamic. There is no *we*."

Gritting my teeth, I hurried to keep up as footsteps followed behind us. "I'm training, as you ordered."

"One business week does not justify risking an ally's prized *asset*."

"I'm not some newblood infant," I countered. Or at least, I wouldn't be the moment I could force this vessel to complete its ascension. "I've served Aren for centuries."

"And in this incarnation, you can't even jump," she pointed out with mock sympathy. Would've been a hell of a lot more convincing if she wasn't smirking.

"Perhaps if you'd lend me access to Bellaton's *Middle*, I could complete the transformation and remedy that."

"I like you, Miss Porter."

I highly doubted *that*.

"But that doesn't mean you get access to our sacred ground."

"So...what? You expect me to sit down here on my hands while you and your council deliberate on whether or not you'll ally with the only resisting forces against Adrastos—"

"Grayshell is not the center of this continent or any other," she pointed out with a huff. "Don't delude yourself into believin' Aren's name alone is enough to win the forces you were sent to retrieve."

"Aren is the greatest Commander in Nephilim history," I stated, fighting to keep my tone even and my face blank.

"That may very well be," she bit out, whirling on me like a pissed-off viper coiling to strike, "but he's not *my* Commander. And he is not the *only* Commander keepin' an eye on the escalating situation with your mysterious adversary. Keep that in mind."

"*Mother*," Blaz's controlled tone had us both turning to where he was scolding her with his eyes. Blaz, at least, had warmed to our little cadre from the moment we arrived. Brody hovered just behind him, my lone remaining chaperone, as his brothers were out on a mission. With a huff, Reyna straightened, softening her expression as she looked me over.

"You are welcome to retire to your rooms, Miss Porter. We have business to attend to."

Like that would ever happen. Ally and Aren sent me here to win an alliance. I wasn't about to sit in my buttercream yellow, floral-bedecked guest suite reading Proust while the Bellatons ran off to do God knows what.

Plus, their ongoing intel from spies within Paladin walls had already proven immensely valuable. Much to my satisfaction. Dismantling what Reagan built wouldn't be enough. I needed to bring her entire hierarchy to heel. I needed to conquer the trials, expose the truth of what happened on the east side of the river, and in turn, take the throne. If I managed to pull all of it off, I'd return to Aren with not one, but two armies at our disposal.

But that required me to fully embody my power and amass all the information I could glean from the resources at my disposal.

I wouldn't be missing any of *that*, either.

Staying in step with the three of them, we marched through the palatial estate and into her war room, where the heads of *six* additional Bellaton covens had convened.

I nearly made it. *Nearly.*

But Reyna spun around, looking smug as hell, and held up a manicured hand inches from my face to halt my momentum. My jaw nearly cracked with the force of my clench.

"Bless your heart. But you're a newborn." *In this life, you petulant, patronizing little shit.* "This is the end of your walk for the day."

Motioning Brody in, she glared at me as I stood there, seething like the toddler she was accusing me of being.

"You go get your rest, and I'll see you for trainin' in the mornin'. You understand?" she drawled, adding an obnoxiously girlish little finger wave.

How that damn Southern accent could be so endearing in Blaz and Darius but make me want to smash her face in, I wasn't sure.

"Yes, ma'am," I ground out, resisting the deep-rooted urge to punch a hole through her wallpapered drywall as she slammed the door in my face.

I anchored myself in centuries of training, willing it to counteract the reckless youth of this damn vessel and the adrenaline of a lingering forced ascension. Inhaling deeply, I honed in on Brody's thoughts. Once I knew he'd leave that connection open, I turned and stalked back to my damn rooms.

Watching the meeting through Brody's eyes, I muttered curses, begrudgingly stripping down to wash the sweat of the morning off my skin. The updates consisted of two planned strikes on *human* targets, along with a status report on the Paladins as they worked to recover from those *unfortunate fires.*

Pity.

Reyna was taking full advantage of their distraction, reclaiming a warehouse they'd seized, as well as the disputed territory border still at odds between the twin twats.

Not a damn word was said about Adrastos. Or about the fact that all major hierarchies were seeing unprecedented attacks on healers. Or about the war bearing down on us.

Ask her about her response to the threats on humanity, I told Brody.

But something tugged at my attention, like two magnets pulling too close in proximity.

I was still surveying my room, warily eyeing the windows, when Brody said, *Easy, kid.*

I have more than a millennium of experience in this dimension, you douche nozzle. Ask the damn question.

His snort of amusement caught Reyna's attention.

Using our connection this way was odd—the updates came more as thoughts than images. It wasn't like Alvara's ability to *see* what we saw. Blurry outlines at best. Just words or intentions at worst.

The idiot feigned a cough to cover his slip-up, then cleared his throat and asked my question.

It seemed Bellaton was considering alliances with a handful of sovereign hierarchies, including a few nomadic clans. Grayshell wasn't the only one that had stayed away from The Six when their council formed. And with good reason.

My focus on the meeting below cut off as that magnetic pull had me whirling toward the balcony—just in time to see black leather gloves clasp onto the rail.

Smirking, I sauntered over as Ansel and Lana Callahan scaled the terrace, their boots landing so softly they were barely audible.

For a man who had stood behind the world's deadliest Commander, he sure had soft eyes for his shithead soul daughter.

Grinning, I stepped into his immediately open arms.

"Hey, babygirl," he murmured, resting his face against my hair as he crushed me in his embrace.

Hah. That was oddly endearing modern vernacular for The Old General. Not that I was complaining.

"Didn't expect to see you so soon," I mumbled into his strong chest. His strong, *miraculous* chest.

How cruel to nearly lose him the day I finally ascended as his calling.

"Us either," he breathed as Lana set a gentle hand on my hair.

Stupid, to have tears prick in my eyes after centuries cleaved apart, but I couldn't help it.

Perhaps it was the freshly eighteen-year-old body.

Perhaps it was the agony of never knowing if we'd find each other again.

Or maybe it was just the connection between soul daughter and mother.

Whatever the reason, I had to steel myself to keep from weeping like some hormonal mortal.

"But Marcus has always been efficient," Ansel finished.

"We can't stay long," Lana amended. "Ally needs us heading west."

"Just had to see you before things escalate," Ansel explained, as though he needed a reason to drop by unannounced.

I pulled back, holding him at arm's length to study him.

"You all good now, old man?"

Smirking dryly, he nodded. "The Westerlund Middle finished what our healers couldn't."

"Good," I breathed, lifting my chin when concern flickered in those chrome eyes. "Aren needs you," I supplied, forcing my stubborn throat to swallow. It hid all the unsaid things. *I need you.*

Lana, and Ally, and August need you.

He seemed to understand, nodding sagely.

"We're just doing a flyby, but I wanted to make sure you have this."

As the dagger emerged from the bag over her shoulder, Alana Callahan —Aren's notorious assassin—looked close to tears.

Certainly as close as I'd ever seen her in this life. Or our first.

Lana didn't cry. Didn't show much range of emotion beyond anger, humor—usually at someone else's expense—and a fierce loyalty that drove her to violence more often than not.

Gingerly, she held out a dagger with a sheath.

"That was—" My breath hitched in recognition, the sound muffling Ansel's explanation. I slid the metal from its case with a little screech. "Mine," I whispered, studying the enchanted blade. They had preserved it for me all these years, complete with nicks, dents, and scratches.

Just like Ally's pocket watch.

Like my mother's tin, the one Ansel had held so dearly through their years apart.

When all they could manage was a nod, I realized how desperately we had all needed just *five minutes*—the three of us, away from the hierarchy's hive of eyes.

Clearing my throat, I slid the blade back into place before meeting their gazes.

If my official mission was going to be an absolute pain in my ass, I could at least make sure my own kicked off with a bang.

"Do you have time to fill me in on what you know of Paladin movements since I left?"

A bit perplexed, the Grayshell assassins exchanged a look before Ansel said, "For you? Alvara can wait."

FIVE

WAKE UP

ALVARA

"Wake up, El."

Damp heat slicked my fingers as our eyes met, terror and recognition warring in my enemy's dark brown irises.

"Elizabeth," he rasped.

My eyes flew wide. I dropped my gaze to the blade trembling in my grasp as he stumbled back, sliding off it. Horror curdled in my stomach. The vision had altered the blade's angle but hadn't stopped it in time.

I'd stabbed him.

I'd stabbed Adrastos.

Impossible. This was impossible. This was—

"No," I breathed as Adrastos crumpled to the ground, the ruby-hilted blade clattering beside him. A shard of earth and stone speared toward me.

"Elizabeth." His agonized warning tore through me, ribs constricting as my eyes burned.

A lie. A trick of the mind.

I whirled, throwing myself into the throng of combatants, all caked in carnage. Then I froze.

Ice-blue eyes, ringed with exhaustion. A face marred with scars and bruises.

Aren bellowed, the sound guttural, desperate—and then he moved. But this wasn't sparring. This wasn't training. I dodged and deflected, but his strikes came with lethal intent.

"Traitor," he growled.

"Aren!" My voice cracked, fatigue shaking my limbs. "Aren, it's me!" He lunged, disarming me in a swift motion.

"Aren!" I cried again. "Ar, stop!" His elbow cracked against my face, sending blood spurting as I hit the ground, head spinning. Splintering agony registered somewhere in my mind, my vision blurring red. Then Aren's massive frame crashed onto me, fists relentless. I barely guarded my face, screaming his name over and over.

"Please," my voice cracked. "You have to believe me!"

His hands locked around my throat, his weight pinning me. Inhuman rage warped his features.

"I trusted you," he snarled.

"Ar," I croaked, his fingers squeezing, cutting off my air. Panic sent my hands clawing at his grip, my body writhing in vain. Darkness scraped at the edges of my vision.

Then he seized.

Blue sparks danced up his arms. His hands ripped from my throat, his body convulsing as electricity arced through him. I wanted to yell for him, to reach for him, but my throat burned raw. I rolled away, gasping, and when my hands met the ground, it was no longer bloody mud—

But cold, hard marble. White. Luminescent.

Grayshell. Home.

The slap of my palms echoed off the cavernous walls. I sucked in a rattling breath, turning for Aren—only to scramble away, putting distance between us.

Red seeped from his lips, a crimson gash seeping across his neck. His eyes remained closed. Lifeless.

Around him lay countless corpses.

Humans. Souls.

My gaze flicked frantically from one familiar face to another. Ansel. Brody. Lana. A desperate cry cracked my ribs. Trembling hands moved toward Aren but stopped as I caught sight of my palms.

Crimson.

Crimson with souls.

My breath hitched. I lunged forward, dragging bodies from the pile. A stiff wind whipped through my hair, singing a haunting melody through the void of Grayshell.

"August?!" I sobbed, pushing through the carnage, mind racing to sort them by family, by hierarchy. Then, my heart cracked.

The Hazelharbor crest. Two red-haired females. Nathara's kin.

Frantic, I moved to the next pile.

"August!" I screamed for my mate.

"They took him, Ally."

Knees aching, I whirled. Fae stood at the hall's end, blonde curls cascading to her waist. She trailed her fingers along the grand table's surface.

"Who?" I demanded.

"Adrastos." Her brow furrowed. "We lost, Ally." She blinked. "Don't you remember?"

I shook my head, throat thick. I stumbled over a body.

Saraya.

Dead at my feet.

Fae stepped toward me, eyes glistening. "Ally, sweetie, you failed."

"No," I breathed. "The threads—we can fix this." My heel caught another body, and I fell, colliding with the corpses below.

"A bit late for that," a melancholy drawl cut through my panic.

Alec knelt beside me, agony shadowing his gaze. "It's over, Al. We all failed."

"No," I rasped, shaking my head. "We had a chance—"

"We trusted the wrong souls, Ally." He steadied me, then turned to Fae. "We have to go."

"Go?!" I barked. "Go where?"

"Away." His voice was empty. "I can't look at you anymore."

But his steps faltered. His body swayed.

"Alec," I hedged. "Where's August?"

His head dropped. Fae sobbed.

When he turned, blood poured from three brutal claw marks across his torso.

"I'm sorry," he gasped. "They're coming." Agony cracked his face, amber eyes pleading. "Save Fae and the baby, Ally."

"Elizabeth."

That haunting, honeyed British bass echoed in my mind, tugging me from Alec's scream.

"Wake up, El. They're coming."

Adrastos' voice drifted like a memory, distant but insistent. *Move, damn you.*

My eyes snapped open to the softly illuminated cob ceiling of our Arizona safe house. My lungs sucked down air in a panicked gasp. Hands flying to my face, I rubbed at my aching eyes as August's familiar warmth wrapped around me.

Memories flickered. Laughter. Lovemaking. Brutal demise.

His lips found my neck.

God, I'd forgotten what it was to be touched in such a way, touched by a man that cherished me above all else.

Mate. Husband.

"Hey," he breathed. "We're okay, baby. We're okay."

"Yeah," I murmured. "We have time." A fleeting truth.

"One more stop before we head north, correct?"

"Zeke and Livvy," I confirmed, nodding. We'd hit the ground running, rounding up allies with the precise speed of funneling sheep into their pen. Most interactions had been effortless, as few were naïve enough not to know what my presence promised.

Bloodshed.

Brutal and imminent.

You didn't get a summons from Grayshell's third coven unless we were well and truly fucked or you were in desperate need of assistance. Today marked the end of our first leg of campaigning before we'd head up to Terramyst territory in the north.

Zeke and Livvy were the heads of a peaceful nomadic clan, mixed between braids and Nephilim, that spent their winters in the red desert of Arizona. Comprised of warriors, healers, and plant whisperers, I didn't anticipate any trouble getting them on board.

With a sigh, I continued, "And then we track down the Thornquists."

"Get answers for this Bond," he supplied simply. Not buying my suspiciously mellow responses, August shifted his weight over me, a speculative brow raised. "*Together*. Right, Mrs. Porter?"

I raised a hand to capture his fingers where he grazed my face, turning to kiss into his palm. The uncertainty in his voice killed me. Mostly because I put it there. "From here to the encore, baby."

A distant howl keened through the desert, and August's emerald eyes closed in resignation. "Is that—"

"Blood wolves," I confirmed, already moving. "We gotta go."

Wake up, El. They're coming...

"YOU KNOW, Alvara, I have a doorbell. You might try using it sometime."

August, casually sprawled across the black leather recliner, chuckled as his eyes flicked open and settled on me—now safely tucked inside Zeke's wards. Steam curled over my forearm as I poured cups of tea, sliding them across the wooden island.

"I did," I lied, smiling.

"Silence is generally the equivalent of saying '*go away*,'" Zeke quipped as he stepped cautiously into his own home. "You know that, right?"

"You're out of cream," I replied matter-of-factly, turning back to stir the water.

"And fucks to give, if I'm honest. I don't suppose this is a wellness check?"

"Would it help if I said I was in the neighborhood?"

He huffed, mumbling, "Think I'd prefer the wellness check." Smart man. If we were outside our territory, Grayshellians were simply following where trouble led us.

Zeke dropped his bag by the door, smirking as he crossed the room. "Livvy swore the wards were solid. Promised up, down, and sideways. But if any old riffraff can just wander right the hell in..." He shook his head, amusement settling across his deep terra-cotta complexion, before throwing his arms around my neck and tousling my hair.

A laugh bubbled up, and I set down the wooden spoon on a colorfully hand-painted ceramic dish, turning into the embrace just before he pressed a kiss to my cheek. When he pulled back, Zeke tilted my face one way, then the other, his eyes narrowing.

"You look...different."

"Do I?"

His lids narrowed further, hazel irises barely visible. "Like...really different."

"Bad different?"

"You look like *a girl*."

I rolled my eyes and smacked him in the chest before turning back to the stove, stirring the veggies nonchalantly as he sniffed and smiled. Then his attention shifted to August, who looked as if he'd been carved specifically for that chair—hair carelessly tousled, combat boots unlaced around his ankles, exuding the quiet detachment of a soldier who had lived too many lives before.

"I suppose you're to blame for Ally going all soft on us?"

"God, I hope so."

"Ezekiel Flores. Friends call me Zeke."

Zeke had allied with Aren nearly a century before I'd found my way back to him, which made the sight of him—and his irreverent welcome—nearly as comforting as the Westerlund brothers.

"August Porter. Friends call me August," he quipped, his smile beautifully disarming. He was made for this. Uniting the hierarchies with me and Aren. Unlike us, nothing about my mate spelled trouble.

"*No way*. Marcus told us about you, but somehow I imagined you'd be..." Zeke glanced between August and me before repeating, "different."

"Hope I don't disappoint." August stood, cracking his neck as the two sized each other up.

Zeke considered him before nodding. "You know, from what I've heard, I don't think you do." He turned for the fridge, grabbed an armful of beer bottles, then tossed one to August and set another beside the dish on the counter. "Well, I suppose you intend to wait for Liv to get back before dropping whatever bomb you arrived with."

"She's about to turn onto your street," I said mildly.

Zeke exhaled sharply. We'd worked together long enough that he shouldn't startle easily, but he still wasn't used to having his future plainly laid out for him.

"*Of course,* she is. What's Alec up to these days?"

"Getting himself into trouble." I scraped the wooden spoon over the bottom of the pan before flipping off the burner. Right on time.

"So, the usual?"

Zeke had one of those crooked, flashy smiles that demanded imitation. My own cheeks ached as I mirrored his knowing grin.

August snorted, plopping down into a wooden kitchen chair, twisting the cap off his beer before raising it in offering. "Pretty much," he supplied.

Zeke clinked his bottle against August's in easy acceptance.

"August and Alec have cycled before," I explained, pulling four dishes from the cabinet as the boys propped their feet up.

"That tracks." Zeke canted his head. "Which draft of our boy did you first encounter?"

"Robert."

The sound of Zeke choking on his drink made me turn. His feet smacked against the wooden floor as his cheeks puffed, fighting to contain the liquid before he finally managed to swallow. He was about to bark an expletive when the vision shimmered through my mind.

The dogs outside went mad.

"Liv's home."

On the end of one last cough, Zeke jerked his head toward the door, and August followed him onto the porch. I finished dishing up the shepherd's pie and sautéed vegetables before stepping out into the crisp night air.

Liv, like her mate, rarely utilized her ability to jump—she'd only just mastered it. Her expertise lay in all things earth, a trait Fae and Alec had always loved immensely. She hopped out of her black SUV, her expression cautious as she took us all in, tucking her slick black hair behind an ear.

We hugged, and after a brief introduction with August, she turned to look up at me, her dark eyes narrowing with what could only be fear.

"I've seen the signs. Disease in the roots. Birds, dead in the woods."

Her mate's face fell as she continued, dropping onto the dark porch.

"You're here to ask us to fight with you."

"I'm here because Aren needs you." While the truth was that my mate and I needed them, it was Aren's network we were calling in. His centuries of camaraderie would determine the outcome of this war.

"The time's really come, then?" Zeke breathed, his swallow audible. "Amadeus wouldn't call if it hadn't."

I sucked in a breath, glancing at August. His fingers found mine, and as he jerked his chin toward our companions, I nodded, lips pressed together.

"We'll discuss it over dinner. But yes. The first horseman was promised before spring. The others won't be far behind. Our enemy will ally with them. And we need our people."

"REMEMBER, ELIZABETH. REMEMBER."

Glimpses of a young boy with raven-black hair, dressed in the rich navy of royals, running through stone hallways ahead of me, laughter spilling over his shoulder.

The image of a foreign hierarchy kneeling before me.

An angry mob. My mother's hand in mine, her gifts sputtering out.

Fragments of light, laughter, and terror...

"Wake up, El. They're coming for you."

I rocketed upright, my heart lodged in my throat as Adrastos' low, unmistakable voice echoed through my mind. Cold sweat slicked my palms, my bare legs tangled in damp sheets. Twisting, my gaze raked over the converted van—tiny countertop and kettle, quaint curtains Rosaleigh had scavenged. We'd stolen the damn thing after the third Thornquist safe house turned up empty. If Kingsley was going to be a pain in my ass, I could at least return the favor.

A warm, broad palm settled against my back. August. His voice was mellow when he finally spoke.

"Ally." A slow stroke up and down my spine. "You're safe. *We're* safe. We're camped in Idaho."

Idaho. We'd made it to Idaho.

"Holy shit." I buried my face in my damp palms, cursing as I kneaded the tension from my forehead and temples, wishing for something stronger than the teas we had stashed by the kettle. Swallowing hard, I scoured the darkness, but before I could ask the time, August's answer slid through my mind.

"Four thirty-five," he said.

I balked. "Are you kidding me?" Irritation coiled in my chest. Even earthbound, this body refused to rest.

"At least you made it most of the night this time," he pointed out.

Every. Night. Every damn night, I woke from these nightmares. Every night since the battle. Since the vision that changed everything—and nothing—all at once.

Saliva burned like acid as I forced myself to swallow. My breath still came in ragged gasps.

"Did he talk to you again?" August tried to mask the concern in his voice, but I heard it in the slight tension, the way it always tightened when we spoke of Adrastos. Keeping the truth from the coven was eating us both alive, but he didn't press. Didn't try to dissuade me from the razor-thin thread I'd decided to tiptoe down—the one that started by uniting our allies.

As expected, Liv and Zeke hadn't even needed dinner before agreeing to return from their hiatus, pledging to serve Aren—and by extension, August—however they could. Their sizable nomadic hierarchy stood behind them. They might not have our numbers, but they were neck and neck with Hazelharbor.

Every stop we'd made had been the same. The clans were small but mighty. And with many leaders, we could shift the tide of the visions, rewrite the fate of humanity.

Liv's worried lip, white-knuckled grip on her tea, and wide, fearful eyes burned into my vision. My stomach ached with the ancient memory of perpetual hunger—not for food, but for peace.

She was lovely, gentle, nurturing. But she was neither healer nor warrior, and I saw the war between her fear and her determination unfold in real time. Ultimately, even if it meant building bunkers, cooking rations, or brewing tinctures, she'd find her place. I told her as much. We all had a divine calling, something we'd been born and bred to do.

Until now, I had believed—with absolute certainty—that I knew mine.

But ever since the battle, ever since that damn vision, it was my enemy's voice warning me of danger.

August and I weren't the only ones hunting.

Finally remembering his question, I nodded. "Told me to wake up. That they were coming."

August tongued at a molar, then sighed irritably.

"We should get moving."

SIX

HIDE AND SEEK

AUGUST

I lifted my bloodied hands, cupping both sides of her captivating face. Loose strands of hair clung to her damp cheeks, and when I pushed them away, a sob broke past her lips, scorching me from the inside.

"Frida. With me and my father gone, the city will not hold. You must run. Promise me. Promise me you'll run."

"Stop!" she begged. The wound in my abdomen, the spinning of my mind —none of it compared to the sound of her breaking.

But I couldn't stop.

Didn't have a choice.

My heart thundered in my ribs as screams shattered the air. I turned, my back pressed against the cold stone wall, bile burning my throat as I fought to keep standing. "Run, my love."

Too late.

The enemy descended on our hidden refuge. A guttural cry tore from my chest as she was yanked from my grasp by her hair.

The spray of her blood across my face had me welcoming the blade that came for me next...

Without a reprieve, the next reading crashed over me in a relentless tide, memories slamming through me one after another.

...Layla riding me, head thrown back in ecstasy, bare breasts peaked...

...Niamh, bleary-eyed and bloodied, pulling herself over my balcony with trembling limbs. Her black braid had been severed, the cut too clean—too sharp—to be anything but a sword.

I rushed for her as she fought her way over the railing.

Somewhere distant, I heard my voice say her name, but it was the hopelessness in her gaze, the way she panted in a futile attempt to catch her breath, that had the world growing fuzzy.

Saoirse. They'd killed my wife. It was a knowing before Niamh even said a word.

"No," I breathed.

She nodded, a lone tear escaping down her tawny cheek.

"Betrayed," she whispered, her shaking fingers coming away from her abdomen, slick with crimson. "We've been betrayed..."

...James, slipping beneath the ice. Sam and my mad dash across the frozen lake, blades scraping, ice flying.

I dove onto my belly, crawling toward the black void he had vanished into...

...A flash of emerald eyes and midnight hair. A face I could never be permitted to love, breaking into a radiant smile as she turned to her raven-haired brothers. Their faces were obscured by the fire's flickering shadows.

Their laughter should have been a comfort.

Instead, it was a barrier keeping her at an unbearable distance...

...Freya, stepping into my Jeep after summer camp, a fresh gash slashed over her cheekbone. Another fight. Another mess I had to clean up...

...Her brother, draped in a navy jacket, dark hair pulled back at the nape of his neck, handing the woman I should have never desired to a man actually fitting of her station.

I stepped back into the shadows, swallowing the lump in my throat as her wide eyes found mine across the shifting bodies.

The world stilled for one long, agonizing beat.

In her gaze, I saw every touch, every stolen moment, every breathless, whispered fear we had shared.

Then the moment snapped shut.

A shoulder bumped mine.

And he turned her away from me...

...My fingers fumbled over abandoned fabric, finding only cold sheets where her body should be.

Groggily, I called, "Ceana?"

Silence.

I cleared my throat. "Ceana?"

Dread pooled in my stomach like tar.

No creak of wood. No hum of her voice as she drew.

Only emptiness.

Throwing the threadbare blankets from my sweat-slicked skin, I padded across the floor. My voice cracked with panic. "Ceana?!"

A blur of color. A doorway. And then—

The slick warmth beneath my foot.

I looked down. A trail of blood snaked down the hallway. Ice clamped around my spine. My breath turned ragged.

Snatching a blade, I crept forward, my heart a relentless drum in my ears.

Thump-thump. *Step.* Thump-thump.

A pained whimper from the hearth room turned my vision red.

I pressed against the wall, edging around the corner—

And froze.

Thump-thump.

Ceana.

My Ceana.

Pinned to the table. Bound and gagged.

Six men, their hulking forms outlined by the fire's roaring glow.

Her eyes fluttered open. Landed on me.

She shook her head. Imperceptibly.

No time.

No time to fetch reinforcements.

Her blood was pooling.

The tallest man turned, a leather mask concealing his face, a red-hot iron glowing in his grasp.

Ceana began thrashing.

I launched forward.

I was sliding my blade across the first man's throat when her muffled scream split the world in two.

"I didn't do anything, I—" Her words reached a crescendo before her scream shattered what little remained of me.

Another fell. The third whirled, barking a warning as he lunged.

"Keep the witch still," one snarled.

The scent of their blood was thick in the air as the fourth abandoned his post to counter the threat at their back. Singed flesh filled my nostrils. The one with the iron turned his sadistic gaze on me, brandishing the glowing metal as Ceana sobbed uncontrollably.

The fourth hit the floor a beat before the fifth charged.

I wasn't fast enough.

Not fast enough to meet his blows and defend against the sixth. Not fast enough to stop what was coming. Powered only by bloodlust and the inhuman monster clawing at my skin—fueled by the sound of her cries—I fought.

Fought even as my flesh burned. As a blade buried itself between my ribs.

Mortal agony was nothing compared to the eternal ache of her scream embedding itself in my skin.

When the last assailant crumpled, I staggered toward her. She was standing—barely—legs trembling beneath her shift. Livid red crisscrossed her chest.

The devil's mark.

They'd branded my wife.

Ceana collapsed.

I went with her.

A grunt tore from my throat as we hit the ground together. She trembled violently in my arms, wracked with silent sobs, and I pulled her closer, trying —futilely—to shield her from what had already been done.

Her hands rose, her eyes going wide with terror.

"You're bleeding," she whispered.

I shook my head. "It's nothing," I assured her, though my vision was tunneling. Panting, I shook my head again. "'M alright. You're safe."

I pressed a desperate kiss to her shaking lips, running my hands over her back, grounding myself in the reality of her presence.

She was here. She was real.

I'd endure anything to keep her safe.

I'd kill as many monsters as came calling.

The last thing I saw was her wide, frantic eyes searching mine, her hands reaching to slow my collapse.

Her mouth opened in a cry I couldn't hear.

I couldn't summon the words I owed her.

But I prayed she knew them as the darkness claimed me.

Thump-thump...

Alvara. Mouth open, eyes closed in ecstasy as I drove into her. The sound of her pleasure filling my mind...

...Empty emeralds in a face so bruised and swollen I could barely recognize her.

An animal sound ripped from my throat.

I pulled her limp body into my lap, cradling her against my chest on the icy cobblestones.

Horrified brown eyes met mine...

"Jesus fucking Christ, I can't fucking do this."

I snapped upright, yanking my hands away from her as I stood.

I broke.

Just as I had in every goddamn life before this one.

Her pain—*our* pain—fucking broke me.

I meant it, just as I had when that hellish battle first set this into motion.

I'd do anything for this woman. This soul. And watching her suffer, time and again...

"*August.*" Her voice was firm, scolding.

I opened my burning eyes and found glassy emeralds staring back at me, tracking my every movement as I turned away, pacing from camp.

Was she fighting back bile like I was? Losing the battle against the spasms wracking my back?

Locking her shields so tightly into place they might never fully retract?

So many lives. So many memories in so many languages. And every one of them ended in agony. In grief so raw I could feel it in my chest, even now. For all our love, for all her light, in every life, we ended in pain so exquisite there weren't words to articulate it. And it was fucking killing me.

Killing me now, as unprecedented odds stared us down. As we raced against an enemy that had outpaced us at every single goddamn turn.

Heart pounding, I counted my shaking breaths, trying to return to this body.

"Your skin has already tanned since we've been here," she noted, voice flat, far from pleased. As if I hadn't pieced it together, she added, "We're not healing as quickly. And it's only been a few weeks since that motherfucker locked us out. Something has to give, baby." The reproach lingered in her tone, barely restrained. "We need to know what's under the worst of the reading. Knowing who you are...There are answers in that soul of yours. But the only way out is through."

"I—I'm sorry," I breathed, the weight of these damn readings pressing against my chest.

This was why she'd waited. Why she'd told me it would be better if we sat—potentially for an entire *week*. She understood—saw it settle over me.

I wasn't just sorry for breaking the reading. I was sorry for everything this one revealed. For everything she had to see. For ever touching another woman in any life. For every failure. Every stolen moment of peace.

I thought back to the terror that consumed me that first night she and Ansel guarded Lana alone in the park. To the ridiculous challenge I'd thrown at our Commander. To the relief when he allowed it.

A flicker of the rage I'd felt then surfaced now. Her death was a fear rooted deep in my marrow. Not just because she was my mate, but because we had already lived that brutal severing too many times before. Like my beating heart carved from my chest, she was ripped from me again...

And again.

And *again*.

"I'm sorry." My ribs ached with the weight of it.

To my relief, her face crumpled. The mask of our second fell away, leaving only the raw, shared agony of my mate. She swallowed back a sob as she rose from the cot, making a beeline for me. Not being alone in this hell —this unrelenting grief—was its own fragile reassurance.

Because the pain couldn't be imagined if we both felt it.

Only when she collided with my chest and my arms wrapped around her did I finally breathe. Burying my face in her hair, I inhaled her telltale honey, sage, and cinnamon, memorizing the faint echo of summer in her scent.

I grasped for anything to give her. Any promise of a different ending. But I had seen those in her mind, too. And most were just as gruesome as the ones we'd already endured.

On a shaky exhale, I whispered the only words left to me. "I'm sorry."

I was.

For the brutal cycle of endings. For never being enough to save her. For breaking a reading that had already been shattered beyond recognition. For the battle that had stolen what she'd so carefully tried to make sacred. For the truth buried beneath centuries of pain. For not being strong enough to push through it.

"You have nothing to be sorry for," she murmured. "It's not your fault."

"Kinda is," I muttered dryly.

"It's not easy, reliving those things. August...Alec and Fae nearly broke under the reading. Why do you think Ansel and Lana have avoided it for so long? And the horrors in Aren's mind...Those nearly broke *me*."

"What if it's not worth it?" I finally voiced the fear lodged in my ribs.

"We don't need to see how many lives we *nearly* ascended in. We need to know *why*. Who is interfering? Why, when capturing me would have been infinitely more valuable."

"It is worth it," she swore.

"How do you know?"

"I just do," she whispered. But the torment in her eyes told me she was just as haunted as I was.

And somehow, that only made it worse.

Needing to feel her, I traced my hands over every curve, memorizing the hard lines, the warmth of her beneath my palms.

Cradling her face, I pressed my lips to hers.

"I love you," I breathed.

"I love you, too." Her voice wavered, emeralds shining as she met my gaze.

"Take me to dinner?"

"Fuck." I exhaled in relief. Dinner at some shitty little inn in this nothing mountain town? That sounded like heaven.

"*Yes*, please."

ALVARA LOUNGED in the passenger seat of the van after dinner, feet propped on the dash, fingers interlaced behind her head. After a much-needed break and a full meal, I felt marginally better as we set off to check another one of Kingsley's safe houses.

I wasn't entirely sure of the lyrics to the song playing from her playlist, so instead, I reveled in watching her. *Listening*. My gaze danced between her and the winding road ahead as it hugged the mountains.

"So we'll be at Kingsley's tonight?" I finally asked, needing something tangible to focus on before my mind wandered back to darker places.

"Fifty-fifty chance he lets us find him today." She reached out absent-mindedly, long fingers trailing over my arm.

"Eccentric, this Commander?" I pushed, fishing for *something*.

"More than you know. He knows someone's coming—has his own gifts —but he hasn't decided whether he'll hang around to see us."

"What kind of gifts?"

"He...senses more than sees what's coming for him. And he's a shifter, like Marcus."

"Is his form top secret too?"

"He has two."

"Oh." I hiked a brow, curiosity piqued. "You said our northern cousins were wolves?"

"Yes. His *pack*."

"And the second?"

"He's a stag."

If I was going to magically transform into a creature, a deer would likely be my last pick. "Interesting choice."

"I don't know how much of a choice it is. I think it's more of...a reflection of who he is at his core, if that makes sense. The qualities he possesses."

"Virility?" I chuckled, reaching over to cup the back of her neck. She smirked at me.

"I meant like—the forest, the woods. They're a Celtic symbol of nature and power. Kingsley has always been...close to the earth."

"So we're driving across the north, in the dead of winter, for a tree hugger?" From the moment we'd abandoned our coven, I'd been acutely aware of my inability to keep her safe. The readings were just an excruciating reminder of that fact. If this Commander wasn't worth the risk, what were we doing here?

"Be nice." She grinned, and I gave her neck a reassuring squeeze. "Kingsley is a warrior too. He's just stayed closer to our roots."

"Anything specific to expect?"

"They're a very—*um*—*structured* hierarchy. They operate much more like a royal court than Aren does with Grayshell. Kingsley *is* their king."

"Do you think he'll help us?"

"With Adrastos, or getting to Grayshell?"

As though his name had been a summoning, Ally winced, and I yanked my shield up like a Roman shade.

Black leather gloves wrapped around a man's jugular, slamming him against a wall. A snarled demand for a confession he couldn't breathe deep enough to give. The echo of boots on concrete. An explosion of livid shadow fire, igniting fleeing men.

"Forgive them, Prince. They do not know our history."

Blood splattered across leather boots.

Silence settled over the cab as we both stared at the winding road. Since the battle, her visions had been spotty, but when they came through clearly, they nearly always involved our enemy. But this wasn't like normal visions. It was as if she was watching through his eyes rather than as the omniscient marvel she was.

"It's getting worse," I finally pointed out.

"I know," she groused, massaging her temples. The glimpses into Adrastos' world brought her intense, stabbing headaches. For me, they brought an indescribable sense of panic.

What if he could see through her eyes, too?

Was he using the connection to manipulate the war in his favor?

Why the fuck was he warning us when the tormentors were close?

What was the point in warning her to run if he was the one chasing us?

"How do we keep him out?" I pressed, panic spiraling in my chest.

"I don't—" She clamped her jaw shut, sucking in a slow breath. "I don't know," she admitted, shaking her head. Staring out the passenger window, her eyes went distant, reaching past the mountains and into the *other*. "I've never exactly had an adversary on this plane." Eyes refocusing, she studied me, then circled back to our conversation before our unwelcome preview of our enemy's mind. "I think Kingsley will always ally with what is good—right. He's like Aren in that way."

The abrupt shift in topic had me scowling at the jagged peaks. Swallowing my protests, I cleared my throat. "But he's playing hide-and-seek?"

"He doesn't know it's us, per se—but he will have sensed our power in his territory. He's very in tune with his surroundings."

"So where is he?" This was the first 'ally' making it this hard to find them. While our clash with the Renown wasn't old news, it was certainly rippling through the hierarchies.

"Kingsley will leave when he feels our strength. He tells Rosaleigh he doesn't know anyone that powerful. He doesn't realize we're a couple." She laughed, shaking her head. "If we stay in the safe house, he'll come to investigate—"

Her breath stopped mid-sentence.

No warning. Just silence.

My heart kicked into a gallop. I turned to face her, finding her gaze glazed over in vision. Then, with a violent *whoosh*, her breath returned. She slammed her bare feet onto the dirty floor mat, eyes clearing as she focused on me.

"*No.*" Blinking, that little stress-v imprinted between her brows. I might have still been the coven's rookie, but I knew better than to interrupt. So I waited, watching her as much as the road.

"Turn onto the bridge, flip a u-ie on the other side, and park on it toward the mouth."

I flicked my gaze up the road, spotting a narrow iron-and-wood bridge arching over the river.

This couldn't be good.

Leaning into the accelerator, I locked onto my target. The urgency in her voice left no room for doubt. Her eyes returned to that other place as we sped toward the metal monstrosity. I followed her instructions exactly, the van clunking over wooden slats. When we parked at the mouth, Alvara seemed to come back to herself. She blinked at me, then gave a little shrug that seemed to say, *Here we go.* My pulse ticked faster, anticipation warming my veins.

Still silent, my wife rubbed her palms together as though warming them. Then, rotating her hands, she pressed her long fingers down the opposite forearm. She inhaled deeply through her nose, eyes closing, and the van rattled as she summoned her power.

Her hands splayed, fingers dragging down her arms.

Then, she moved—fluid, precise. Her left arm rotated up, palms aligning. I sat, spellbound. I'd never seen any of them conjure power quite so demonstratively.

The van shook. The trees trembled. The wind roared.

Her wind.

Holy shit.

Alvara's eyes snapped open just as a black truck sped around the bend.

"Now," she commanded, voice quiet but absolute.

I hit the accelerator, whipping our van out onto the road behind the lifted black pickup.

"There are children in there," she said, her voice laced with anger.

Then, the truck hit black ice.

I slammed on the brakes. The world stretched into slow motion and high speed all at once. The truck fishtailed, spinning out of control, teetering on the edge of the ravine.

Too late, I threw out my hands, desperate to stop the momentum—

But before it could tip over the embankment, the wind *slammed* into it, and Alvara spoke a quiet prayer as she yanked her cupped hand back.

The truck crashed back onto all four tires.

Windows shattered. Screams filled the air before abruptly cutting off as the world went eerily silent.

And before the tires had fully halted, Alvara was already running. Barefoot. Straight toward the vehicle, suspended in...suspended *in time*.

"Holy shit," I said again as Ally threw open the back door. A young girl —maybe three years old—sat in her car seat, eyes squeezed shut as shattered glass rained down, her little mouth open in alarm. A thin red line had begun to form across her arm.

"Get the boy," she ordered over her shoulder, knocking glass onto the floor mats. She plucked a shard from her skin and tossed it onto the seat between the children.

I rounded the truck bed and yanked open the other door, my mind still caught in the bizarre, impossible amazement of what was happening. The boy—one, maybe two years old—was still rear-facing. His tiny reflexes had only managed to scrunch his eyes into a squint. I cleared the air around him, brushing glass off his seat and onto the floor. A few pieces landed on his lap.

Alvara hissed, and I looked up to see her shaking her head.

"The pieces will carry the momentum of the crash when we leave," she warned. "They might cut through the blanket."

Fuck. I hadn't thought of that. Then again, I'd never fucked with time before.

Holy shit. She had frozen time.

I shoved the burning curiosity away for later.

When Alvara straightened, satisfied with our work, our motions synced, and the doors clunked shut. She strode to the driver's side, a deep scowl carved into her face.

This time, she reached through the shattered window and pressed her fingers to the man's temple. He was young—late twenties, maybe. His face was twisted in terror, but buried in his wide eyes was something unexpected. *Guilt.* Guilt settled in the shadows of his expression.

And that's when I realized what Ally hadn't said.

He knew. He'd known he was reckless, knew he was rushing on those winter roads. Known and done it anyway, impatience nipping at his heels.

She connected with his mind, embedding her commands into his consciousness. I used the moment to brush glass from the woman's exposed skin. Alvara's glare flicked toward the young man one last time before she jerked her head toward our van. I followed without question.

The instant our doors slammed shut, time snapped back into place.

The truck lurched forward. Their screams filled the air.

I turned to Ally. Her expression was carefully schooled into shock and awe—an eerie mirror of my own. Wordlessly, we stepped out of the van for the second time.

LATER THAT NIGHT, Ally pushed open the door to Kingsley's silent safe house. The overhead light flicked on with a click, illuminating the sleek A-frame structure. The exterior was a modern gunmetal gray, with an onyx-black metal roof and copper-trimmed windows.

Inside, it was just as polished—an industrial escape in the woods. Kingsley might have been the most connected to the earth and his elements, but his taste was top-tier.

"You can still smell him," I noted. "They literally *just* left?"

"Probably around the time we set our intention to come here." She waved a hand, and the logs in the wood-burning stove ignited.

"But you think they'll come back."

"When he realizes we made it through his wards and are using the safe house, he'll come back."

I knew better than to challenge Ally. She didn't even have to clear the house like we were trained to. She had already watched the visions. Already knew the outcome. Fucking remarkable.

"So," I said, leaning against the doorway, "when exactly were you going to tell me you can...*stop time?*"

A startled laugh escaped her before she clapped a hand over her mouth, her dark lashes lifting as she met my gaze.

"I didn't know," she admitted. "Not until..."

"The visions showed you."

She nodded. "And then I just...did it."

"That's a nice trick."

"I don't think it was all of time, though, if that makes sense. Because you came with me. I've heard of souls with super speed. We thought Alec was the fastest, but I guess..."

"You've got a new trick to show him when he catches up."

She exhaled sharply. "Yeah. If I can do it again." She hesitated, her voice quieter. "All I could think about was getting to those babies. And then, when I was able to freeze their momentum, I just tried to leave it as explainable as possible."

"Makes sense."

I smirked, but the *absurdity* of it all finally hit me. *Time freezing. Visions. Elemental magic.* After everything I had seen—living in a different dimension, wielding power, fighting demons—you'd think nothing could shock me anymore.

And yet, here we were.

Laughter bubbled up, unstoppably. Slowly, Ally's nervous chuckles turned real, and before long, we were sprawled out on the hardwood floor before the hearth, hands intertwined at our sides, free palms clutching our aching stomachs.

Eventually, I turned onto my side, propping myself on my forearm to look down at her. Tears of laughter streaked her cheeks. Strands of hair had long since come loose from the wind. Black mascara had smudged beneath her eyes.

And yet—watching her beam up at me—I was certain God had never made anything more beautiful.

SEVEN

PERHAPS SWAMP BARBIE HAS BRAINS

FREYA

Hollywood would have you believe there was no career more exhilarating than that of a spy. Perhaps only thieves were depicted as living more thrilling lives. But the reality? Surveillance, of any kind, involved an obscene amount of waiting for a whole lot of nothing. It was grueling work, because the instant you let your guard down, something always happened—and you'd miss your one window of opportunity.

Had my earlier incarnations mastered the art of scaling buildings and slipping through rooftops unseen? Yep. Were there few things more satisfying than scaring the absolute bejeezus out of an unsuspecting mark by appearing out of nowhere? Also yep. But what had truly made me good at this was my ability to sit, still as a statue, for as long as it took.

One of Reyna's accounts had been emptied Monday morning, which had resulted in me being stationed here—watching the new bank where she'd tucked away a conspicuously placed safety deposit box after the thief drained her capital. The challenge, of course, was that I was new to town and wouldn't have known innocent Aunt Patricia from our perp. Which is why Darius, Bellaton's head of security and my second tentative friendship within the hierarchy, handed me an iced donut hole without taking his eyes off the rooftop across from us. We were perched atop the building opposite the bank for the third day in a row, casing the area.

We made a decent team, if I was honest. He wasn't a man of many words—a lot like Ansel in that way—but he kept an astute watch on the roof's vulnerabilities while I surveyed the street, and then we'd swap roles every thirty minutes to keep our eyes fresh. Just as we had for the last half a dozen hours.

"Do you think Reyna just needed us out of the house?" I said, making small talk, earning an uninterested grunt in response. "I mean it—this is a bit below your pay grade, don't you think?"

"It would appear my queen believes this is precisely my pay grade," he said flatly, keeping his gaze where it belonged.

Three air conditioners and one rooftop access point that could only lead to a stairwell. One fire escape zig-zagging across windows to the flat top. That was his assignment.

Mine was a bit more colorful—the street buzzing with well-dressed townsfolk dripping wealth in diamond rings and heavy gold chains. The whole place was a bit too picturesque for my liking. Like I'd stepped into some *Stepford Wives* fever dream.

"Right, but couldn't she just be sending us out to get us out of her hair?"

"I don't follow," he groused, tone bored as he handed me another donut hole.

"She could be getting laid," I suggested, fully expecting a glare from my companion, but only earning the slight twitch of his lips.

"She hasn't had a caller in quite some time."

"A *caller*," I mocked, pursing my lips as I surveyed the mortals going about their day. Thirteen shops, fifteen doors, twenty-seven windows, all within my scope of vision.

"You take offense to the idea of courting?"

"Such formality for the twenty-first century."

"The Commander prefers formality to the alternative."

"I hadn't noticed," I deadpanned. Everything about Reyna Gwyne was formal—her clothes, her stance, her immovable posture, the composed way she delivered every lilted word. A thought occurred to me—not for the first time—and I tilted my head as I asked, "Who was Blaz's father?"

"Pardon?" The feel of those evaluative eyes on the side of my face reminded me of Ansel, his scrutiny unsettlingly familiar.

"Miss Prim and Proper doesn't seem like she'd take lovers casually."

His focus returned to the building across from us. "She does not."

"Did she have a mate?"

"Not that I'm aware of."

"So she's just as susceptible to the desires of the flesh as the rest of us."

"She is part-human," he pointed out flatly.

"And a tremendous fan of passing judgment."

"I think if you slowed your own judgments to understand her story, you'd be surprised at the results you'd find."

"You admire her?"

"I've sworn my loyalty to the leader of my hierarchy."

Snorting, I pointed out, "That wasn't exactly an answer."

"Yes."

"Yes, that wasn't an answer, or yes, you admire her?"

"The latter."

"Come on, Darius, give me something."

"Stop distractin' yourself with gossip. Shift change is in an hour."

With a sigh, I lamented, "Don't hold out on me now. I've got to keep myself awake somehow."

Grumbling, he said, "Reyna took a husband."

"Took a husband," I repeated, rolling my eyes at the continued formality. "Where is he now?"

"Dead."

My head snapped up. I turned to look at him, voice suddenly mouse-ish as regret thickened my throat. "What?"

Darius exhaled the weight of history in that single breath. "Blaz's father was killed by the Renown when Reyna was six months pregnant."

"Jesus."

"She stood down from a mission, and he went to the divide without her. Her guards delivered his body hours later. The Reyna I swore allegiance to —the Reyna your Commander adored—died that day with him. The woman you see now is a result of that loss."

Silence, befitting the cruelty of the truth, settled between us. My grudge against her cracked, just slightly. It was a long stretch later when Darius finally broke it.

"Few know how to build walls as efficiently as my queen, but you'll meet fewer still who can dismantle evil as efficiently as she does. Give her a chance, Freya, and her tactics might make sense someday."

Before I could respond, something—instinct—pressed against my center, like a string pulling taut. My head whipped down to the bank's front door as a tall male figure held it open for a curvy woman with long black hair. The collar of his peacoat was popped up, a buffer between him and the world, a rimmed fedora blocking my view of his face.

Power. That was power I was sensing.

Canting my head, I watched as he slung an arm around her shoulders in undeniable familiarity before guiding her inside the bank.

"That's interesting," I murmured.

"Her story would be."

"Not that," I said, words clipped as I stood from my perch, brushing icing and pastry crumbs from my jeans. I adjusted my Guns N' Roses cropped tee and straightened my jacket before heading for the fire escape. "Watch the door."

"Where do you think you're goin'?"

"Following a hunch."

"I'll accompany you," he said, shifting to stand. My outstretched hand stopped him.

"Watch the door, and my back, big guy. I'm gonna get closer."

"I'm not supposed to leave you unsupervised."

"And you won't," I insisted, quirking my head. "As long as you watch. The. Door."

"No confrontation, Porter. Do ya' hear me?"

"Yes, D, I hear you."

"Don't call me that," he groused for the dozenth time.

I smirked, tossing him a lazy salute before swinging over the railing. Darius shook his head but didn't argue further.

It was only when I blew him a kiss that he groaned, "Lord, spare me."

"FUCK," I mumbled, passing the bottle back to Blaz, my legs swinging idly as I gazed out over the plantation. Below us, the landscape slowed to a peaceful crawl, buttery warmth melting across the grass, illuminating the bearded oaks and winding trunks as the sun crept down behind the manor. It was a day for rooftop perches, apparently.

"We were close—so close this time."

We had been. I knew it to the depths of my core. The duo I'd watched vanish into the bank had reappeared a short while later, their lowered faces obscured—his by a hat, hers by a hood. Intentionally so, if I hadn't lost my touch. I'd dropped a line to Damien Westerlund, who pulled security footage from the interior cameras, only to find they'd evaded those as well. Perfectly.

It was only once I'd followed them into a narrow alley between brick buildings that the hair on my neck stood up. *I was onto something.* Every goosebump confirmed as much. Right up until *fucking Brody* barked a demand for me to get my ass back to the truck, and when I rounded the corner—nothing. Just a swirl of shadows where the two should've been.

Bitterness still thick on my tongue, I muttered, "Hence. The *fuck*."

Blaz snorted, taking a long pull of whiskey before holding the bottle up in offering. I wrinkled my nose. I welcomed the heat of the drink but didn't want to muddle my thoughts before I could properly dissect them. He shrugged, smirking as he took another swig.

"I don't think Mother Dearest would approve of you drinking on the roof with the Grayshell brat." Darius might have instilled an ounce of sympathy for the Bellaton queen, but her tirade against my incompetence when we returned had promptly squashed it.

"What Mama doesn't know won't hurt her." Blaz shook his blond curls out, playfully elbowing me as the liquid sloshed in response.

"Some guard dog you are."

"I'm only here as long as I have to be."

"Well, we have that in common." I snatched the bottle, pressing the neck to my lips for a tiny swig before setting it down on the opposite side. Getting him rip-roaring drunk might have been a good idea initially, but that was kid shit. I needed him sober—or close enough to it that he'd feel coherent, and I wouldn't feel like I was taking advantage of a friend. Because that's what he'd become in our weeks together. I wasn't planning adjoined tombs or anything, but he was good company.

"Listen, Blaz. I need a favor."

"This can't be good." His tone was flat, but his expression flashed pearly white teeth, all smiles.

"I'm going crazy here. My guard dogs are a handicap I can't afford if I'm to win over Reyna."

"Says the girl on her *roof*, drinking whiskey with her son."

"Yes, well, what Mama doesn't know." I rolled my eyes. "Focus, Blaz. The point is, the three bodyguards my coven sent with me? I need to lose them."

"Come again?"

"If I'm going to get close enough to the rat pack to learn anything, I can't exactly have the *Three Stooges* looming behind me, barking orders, can I?"

Blaz narrowed his eyes. "You want me to help you *ditch your escort?*"

"That sums it up, yes." Because lacing their nightcap would only work once without raising suspicion, and I hadn't seen Ajax take a sip of liquor since I'd ransacked the Paladin's warehouse. My escape routes needed to get more creative.

"They're here for a reason, Freya. As am I."

"I don't need protectors."

"This is a new body. Don't get cocky."

"A new body that got you in a chokehold twice in the last twenty-four hours. At this rate, I'll be bailing you out, rather than the other way around."

He snorted before huffing, "In your dreams, little Wraith."

"For fuck's sake, are you my friend or not, Blaz?"

"Friends don't let friends ditch security."

"Friends absolutely *help* friends ditch security."

"And invite Aren of Grayshell and the Great Commander to personally take turns beating me to death? I don't think so."

"Drama queen."

"Says the teenager trying to ditch her team." He leveled me with a sardonic glare.

"They're enormous, loud, and impossible to hide long enough to get close."

"They're here to keep you safe and help with your training."

"And they're wonderful. The greatest chaps you've ever met, and yet..."

"You honestly think you'd get better answers without them?"

I raised my brows pointedly. "I've always worked better alone."

"For someone claiming to have a *doesn't-play-well-with-others* warnin' label, you sure have this hellhole wrapped around your finger."

"*Doesn't* play well with others and *can't* are two very different things."

"So, *play.*"

"I am." I huffed, the sound a bark of exhaustion. Blaz laughed. "One solo reconnaissance mission. That's all I'm asking. If I don't get answers, I'll drop the subject. But I'm going crazy here. If I wait on Reyna's intel, we'll always be one step behind. I need to get ahead."

Blaz shook his head, tousling his tight blond curls. Disappointment coiled in my chest, but then he mussed my hair, earning a snarl. He laughed before clarifying, "One. You want one *recon* mission, solo?"

I perked up, nodding enthusiastically. He rasped out a long sigh before shrugging, evidently resigned. "*Intel* has it, they're gonna be out on the town tonight. Perhaps it's a good night for an evening stroll."

I lunged forward, pressing a kiss to his cheek before rising to my feet and making for the window we'd climbed out of thirty minutes earlier. I needed food. And a plan. Hopefully, in that order. But I didn't miss the way Blaz's fingers absently traced where my lips had grazed his skin before he took another draw from the bottle. Nor could I help the way that made me smile.

MY HEART SHOULDN'T HAVE BEEN POUNDING. I'd completed more missions than any reasonable person would bother counting in my lifetimes, yet my pulse fluttered like butterfly wings against my throat.

Rusty. That was all.

This body wasn't used to the thrill of the job. At least, that's what I told myself as Ajax slid into one of the pristine white porch swings, kicking his dirty boots up onto Reyna's meticulously painted rails. Could he not hear my heart? Did he not feel the nerves settling in my stomach like a trapped hummingbird? Or was he playing ignorant, waiting for the moment my focus drifted from the Paladins to ruin my fun?

I'd told them I needed a walk—to clear my head, to get some alone time—because I felt like I was about to start my cycle and was ready to knock someone's teeth out. A lie, of course. My monthly bleed had predictably stopped when I ascended, and while I knew it would return every blue moon, I had no clue when. But it was enough for the trio to scowl from their scattered perches, granting me the space I needed to *get a grip on my emotions.*

Men. Good lord.

Fog curled lazily around the massive oaks that loomed over the sprawling acreage, their moss-laden branches twisting together in a canopy above me. The setting sun filtered through the leaves, its golden light scattering across the ground in flickering patterns.

Five minutes. Five minutes for the sun to dip below that sprawling green and coat me in shadows.

Five minutes for Blaz to send the Greeks scrambling.

Five minutes, forty-five seconds until I had to disappear.

I smiled, glancing down at my watch, barely registering the time as I casually swung my arms. Rounding the path around one of those looming trunks, I trailed parallel to the fence line, making sure Brody still had eyes on me. I tilted my face toward the fading sunlight, well aware that if the Greeks were pissed enough about my disappearing act, this little stunt might be the last time I found solitude.

The hair on my arms stood on end. A chill prickled across my skin—the unmistakable sensation of being watched. My heart faltered as I scanned my surroundings, muscles tensing the moment Reyna stepped from behind a curtain of moss.

"Evening, Commander," I said, my voice blessedly casual despite the adrenaline impaling my heart and lungs. My plan had just gone to shit. I had to abort. Had to reach Blaz. Couldn't waste my one shot—

"About damn time," Reyna said, lips curving in a subtle, spider's smile.

"Pardon?" My pulse stuttered.

"You're different this time. Commander Amadeus warned me you'd likely go rogue." First of all, *rude*. "You showed up determined to play pacifist, and I worried Aren's little ghost wouldn't return to him in time to be useful. But then my sister's base went up in flames, and my shadows didn't see a thing." A knowing glint entered her sharp blue eyes as she clasped her hands behind her back, hips swaying ever so slightly.

I shrugged. "I don't know what happened there. Tragedy, really."

"Mm-hmm," she purred, clearly unimpressed with my bullshit.

"Aren underestimates my capacity for diplomacy."

"Perhaps." Reyna took a few graceful steps away, then turned in a tight circle, her ballet flats gleaming in the twilight. "And perhaps he underestimates your capacity for pettiness."

"Of that, he is well aware, I assure you."

She halted, amusement glimmering in her gaze. "You notified the mortal feds of illegal activity?"

"As I said, I've no idea who set the trap for your rivals."

Reyna resumed pacing, her tone measured, calculating. If my deflections irritated her, she didn't show it. If anything, admiration flickered in her gaze. Unease settled in my stomach as she matched my stride along the perimeter. "Although," I added, "it does sound like something Aren would do for a good laugh."

"Indeed." She studied me sideways before throwing down a challenge. "I loved him once, you know?"

Her words stopped me cold. My wrist hovered over my watch, half-raised to text Blaz. I quirked my head, eyes narrowing as Reyna tucked honey-colored hair behind her ear.

"Him?" I clarified, though my gut already knew the answer. Reyna's resentment for my leader was born of something deeper than politics.

Her bright blue eyes glinted knowingly. "You're goin' to make me say it out loud?" Humor laced her voice, though her face remained calm, detached. "Aren wasn't always the king of chastity, you know? He had a hell of a reputation when he was younger—straight off the arena floor and back onto the battlefield, rising from there. He could have had whomever he wanted. For a brief window of alliance, I thought he wanted me. When he sided with us over Reagan, I..." She trailed off, jerking her eyes past me toward the estate as silence stretched between us.

After a beat, Reyna sighed. The setting sun bathed her in gold, highlighting the faint tension in her jaw.

"Why are you telling me this?" I hedged.

"You've proven he hasn't changed. And I say that as someone who knows him better than most."

My brow furrowed. Compliment or insult? I risked a glance towards the sunset, watching the base of the orb dip below the harsh horizon line as my nerves tangled into a congealed knot. Could I sneak off a text without her catching me? Would Blaz know I'd been cornered? Was he watching?

This fucking timing.

"He was always the best," Reyna continued. "What he did with you in a few short weeks would have taken other trainers months. The memories he pulled from you so quickly…" She shook her head. "I can't deny it. Even now, locked from the Middle, Grayshell's strength is undeniable. His faith in your loyalty on the dawn of your ascension tells me enough."

I hesitated. "Are you saying—?"

"I'm considering it, *Wraith*. So are my allies. Your skill set hasn't changed, and you can follow orders."

Guilt twisted like a serpent in my gut. She was only half of my plan. If Aren knew my full intent—to dismantle an entire hierarchy and usurp the Paladin throne—he'd have locked me down. Reyna, for all her cunning, would never tolerate evil unopposed. Which meant her alliance was inevitable.

Blaz, where are you?

"I wish he'd come himself," Reyna mused. "Perhaps my ego was… injured that he sent a child for such a big ask. But Blaz and Darius have a kinship with your companions. And with you. I trust them."

"They're good people."

Her smile turned lethal. "Is that why you're about to ditch them?"

I swallowed. Ninety seconds left. Reyna was a legend in her own right, as much as Aren in his. A warrior whose blades were sharp and disciplined, her elegance deceptive. A woman who had ruled unchallenged for decades.

Perhaps in that, we had something in common.

I smiled, lifting my brows. "Blaz."

"He wouldn't have had to say anything." Reyna's eyes gleamed. "I've been waiting for you to pull a stunt like this. Watching as you tried to force yourself into compliance when every bone in your body is bred for rebellion."

I didn't bother hiding my laugh. She smiled in turn. Stunning, in a way that was terrifying.

"I found a peculiar dossier in your room today."

"You *searched my rooms*?" I bit out.

"It's not in my nature to trust without verification—not even for one of Aren's people."

"So, that's a yes?" I snapped.

Reyna took a long step to the side, prowling like a cat around its prey. "Color me curious, Miss Porter, that your notes on the Paladins predate your arrival here."

"I'm thorough when researching allies, and even more so with enemies."

"I noticed my surviving niece and nephew were absent from your file. Perhaps you're not as thorough as you think."

"Children don't belong in blackmail," I stated flatly. Lana had disagreed with me on that. Any ammunition was worth leveraging in a worthwhile acquisition. But using innocents had never been my style. Even if it were, Reagan and Ciaran Stuart's offspring were ghosts.

Cyrus and Calypso Stuart had no social media accounts, no professional pages, not even birth certificates. The only documentation of their existence came from Grayshell's spies. The only reason I *believed* in them at all was because the Oracle owed me a favor and had answered my questions this week. While Cyrus had won the power ranking, Calypso was the expected heir to the throne through matriarchal enchantment. Much like their sisters to the west, Paladin power flowed from the strongest female to the next. The magic itself would choose the heiress, *marking* its chosen soul every thirty years.

Their Queens were magically bound to their partners through a Guardianship Bond, ensuring no man could seduce his way into power. Any such attempt would cost him his freedom—the Guardians compelled to place their Bonder above all else.

Unlike the witches of Hazelharbor, the Paladins had no shortage of males, and royal marriages had been arranged for centuries to preserve their bloodlines. By ensuring only the strongest magic lines mixed, they had all but forced the enchantment to secure their reign. If an outsider emerged with a power ranking that threatened that sacred line, they were bound in contracts—heirs spoken for before they were even conceived. An agreement I knew all too intimately in my last life.

To refuse the pairing was tantamount to challenging the matriarch to a duel—a moment of idiocy none had survived.

Yet.

"They're scarcely children," Reyna contradicted with a smirk, unraveling the knot that train of thought had tied in my belly. I wasn't sure if she was baiting or sincere, as my soul mother had been. "The Paladin Heiress is five years your senior, and her second only two years younger. Both fully ascended. Both active in the family business."

Well, that was intriguing. "That's very young to have both ascended."

"Renown," she said curtly, her jaw working before she wet her lips, her next words rushed. "Forced rapid ascension, same as you."

I arched a brow. More often than not, souls that young failed to ascend. "That can't be coincidence."

"There are no coincidences, Miss Porter. God doesn't make mistakes.

Not in your ascension, not in your skillset, not in who honed it, or in who you'll meet while you're here. Not in who you'll kill or who you'll ally with. You are here when you are because you are meant to be. And your Commander and his second know it."

"You sound like Alec."

"Mr. Carter and I always made for amusing company," she said, tone unreadable, though I was almost positive her lips quirked again. Had she waited until we were alone for this conversation? If so, was it fear of what confessions might spill from my lips, or knowledge that my defiance could undermine her before her men? "But none of this explains why you were gathering intel before I even assigned you the task."

For a long moment, I stared her down, but Reyna was as unflinching as an asp, her gaze unwavering. Ally would be eternally disappointed to know I blinked first. When it was clear she would outlast me, I admitted, "Past life debts are long overdue. I intend to collect."

"I remember," she said. "I remember dredging that body from the water and Aren's ensuing devastation. You're one of his favorites."

"And he's one of mine."

"But it's not Aren confronting old demons tonight, is it? This would be a very different conversation if that were the case." She arched a lone, expectant brow, walking the perimeter as she surveyed the estate, delicate hands clasped before her chest. "You know who claimed your life last time, don't you?"

"You're smarter than you look, Commander."

"And your mother is just as adept at backhanded compliments. She'd be proud, you know?" Pausing, she took a breath. "Dress like a doll—check the boxes of a prim princess, and it's amazing how candid men become when they think you're a doe. *My*, are they surprised when a wolf emerges from the skin they so love to objectify."

"You're like a poisonous plant," I teased, taking far too much pleasure in the lethality in her eyes.

"Aphaea Carter taught me that. Well...she wasn't called that then, but that's how you know her." She glanced at her watch, then at the sinking sun. "Find me the thieves ransacking my city and burning my buildings, and you have my allegiance."

"They've burned *your* buildings?"

"The barn, the storage lot, the bank you investigated—all mine. Yes. This is personal. I can't cross the border without them knowing...*you*, however."

"You baited my temper, sending me out with a full escort."

"You've historically worked well alone."

"Why not start that way?"

"Why not tell me your plans from the beginning?" she countered.

I grinned. "Better to beg forgiveness than permission."

"Arrogant."

"Perhaps," I conceded, smile still in place.

"Blaz is ready. Best you be."

The commotion erupted suddenly. I grinned before schooling my expression.

"Stick to the shadows."

I sprinted for the property's edge just as the sun vanished over the horizon.

EIGHT
UNWELCOME GUEST

CYRUS

The disconcerting monotony of daily tasks hollowed me out as I watched reports roll in from my shadows.

Nobody had shit. Not on our target. Not on The Wraith. Not on gathering another suspect for last week's attack.

My hunch was unsubstantiated, especially with my mother silencing any further attempts at conversation on the subject. There was no arguing with the Queen of the Paladins. But it was the only lead I had.

The only progress for the day came when my cousin slapped a folder onto my desk—details on the warehouse we were acquiring to rebuild Uptown.

A spark of something hopeful lit up Carr's dark blue eyes as they met mine when I turned my chair to face him. On the tail end of a yawn, I asked, "What do ya got?"

"Seventeen thousand square feet, finished interior, six bay doors. It's a start."

"It's a start," I agreed. But it wouldn't replace it. Nothing could. The history our thief had unknowingly—*or knowingly*—robbed from us wasn't something that could be duplicated. I rubbed my palms over my aching cheeks, willing away the exhaustion settling into my bones. Sleep wasn't a luxury granted to a second-in-line whose security lapse had resulted in such a catastrophic loss. Had anybody else been responsible for the failure, their reception likely wouldn't have entailed family fucking dinner on Friday night.

Carr cleared his throat. "You alright, Cy?"

"Yeah," I said, tone clipped.

"Very convincing."

"Tired. That's all."

"Sure," he said, rotating to lean against my desk as I stretched out in my office chair. "Nothing?"

"She's a fucking ghost."

Carr consolidated the scattered papers on my desk into a neat pile, straightening them against his lap as he said, "It's in the name, man. Nobody's gonna find shit. Not until they make another move."

"Still not convinced she's female?"

"Fuck no. Did you see how decimated that place was? You're telling me a solo woman tore up Uptown like a damn tornado?"

"Just because we only saw one person doesn't mean that's the truth of it."

His shrug convinced no one. "Trackers still out there?"

"Yep."

"Welp," he declared, tapping the stack once on my desk before setting it down. "Not jack shit you can do here tonight. Come grab a drink."

"I'm alright."

"Come on, get your mind off this shit. Grab a drink, get some pussy. Do *something*. You're too pretty to rot in this office all weekend."

"One," I decided, rising and ignoring the pained protest of joints I'd kept too still for too many hours. I snatched my jacket off the chair and followed him out of my office, through the marble-drenched lobby of my family's hotel, *La Lune Noire,* and into the bustling Friday night. Jamming my arms into the sleeves, I exhaled a harsh breath before pulling a pack of cigarettes from my pocket and selecting my lone smoke of the day.

Fuck addiction.

One a day was a ritual, not a lapse in control.

The bite of late winter still clung to the air, the damp cold stinging my skin. A lifetime in the South, and I still hated how the evening chill settled in on the rare occasion it rolled through. Not freezing, but not comfortable —the air more fog than breathable substance. Cold and humidity didn't play well together.

Carr snapped his fingers to light his cigarette before extending the flame to me. Inconsequential magic, but convenient enough, especially for a couple of first-lives. "Any progress on Weston?"

Karl Weston. Sick motherfucker. My current mark took the form of an insurance titan whose existence I was days away from dismantling. We didn't make a habit of interfering in human business, but when that business crossed the lines of morality, tipping society into imbalance, we made moves. And we did so quickly.

Balance was sacred.

A concept so few mortals ever bothered to consider as they filled their minds with garbage news and biased media, spinning a flat paper into a threat. The great age of technology—where every motherfucker screamed their vitriol into the void with megaphones nobody should've signed up to hear. If they'd all shut the fuck up for two damn minutes, they'd hear that the melody of their differences was a symphony called balance.

Too far to either side—control versus anarchy—and society collapsed into a dystopia colored in various shades of 'fucked up,' the hue determined by which side had overextended their power before the fall.

At the root of it all, human greed was the bleeding heart of this world's eternal imbalance.

And I fucking loathed it.

Born and bred within Paladin walls, I was nothing but an instrument to *maintain* the world's equilibrium. Some days, that meant walking a granny across the street. Others, it meant putting some sick fuck in the ground or dismantling the corrupt empire of a narcissist parading as a champion of the little guy.

A narcissist like Weston, whose life was about to turn on its head when we drained his accounts and put that money back where it belonged—with the people he'd burned alive to get it.

With the children whose dead parents weren't covered by their 'accidental death' policies because their car rolled once instead of twice.

With the elderly spouses whose 'whole life policy' conveniently devoured itself before they could touch a cent.

With the countless families swallowed by hurricane season, who wouldn't see a penny because that blowhard was a crook spinning sales to those naïve enough to trust the system.

Yeah. I'd enjoy this takedown as much as any other. The bankers, the brokers, the swindlers—those motherfuckers were the lifeblood of my coven. And we drank their pain like fine wine after every sting.

Karma was a bitch.

And I had the pleasure of being her executioner.

"You look like you need to fight or fuck."

"Hmm?" I grunted when Carr's voice dragged me back to the sidewalk, bumping into my shoulder when I clearly wasn't listening.

"So, which is it? We ducking back in the ring, or am I playing wingman?"

His prior words registered, and I pinned him with a glare. "I don't need a wingman."

"So, we're sporting black eyes at the team meeting tomorrow?"

"No, asshole. Shut up and get inside," I said, opening the door to our favorite watering hole—a place that embodied disorder personified. The floor alone could guarantee an STD or some kind of rash if we spent too much time out of The Middle. Not a single lightbulb knew how to illuminate the space without flickering. Fights broke out at least twice a night, usually around the pool table. Cliché metal hair bands blared from blown-out speakers, and you couldn't step through the door without catching a contact high.

And yet, it was home.

Which was why the bartender—a blonde shifter named Elise—brought out our drinks without asking. She knew. Always did. With a nod, I took my scotch and settled into the high-top in the corner, the best vantage point to watch the debauchery unfold.

Contrary to my cousin's assumption, getting laid was the last thing on my mind. My thoughts were trapped in that burning room, replaying a thief's wink before she leaped out the damn window, like it was all some cosmic joke.

Wink-flight. Wink-flight.

That's why my teeth were grinding when my mother's Guardians marched through the front door, temper in their strides.

That didn't look good.

Tossing back my drink, I stood from the stool and cut them off, our paths converging at my parents' crowded table in the back. Dad's dark eyes flicked between Lynx and Orion as the other Guardians straightened. Worse yet, Nix was on their heels, looking murderous.

"What?" Dad bit out, bracing for the inevitable impact. I ran my thumb over the rim of my signet ring—an infuriating nervous tic, as if I subconsciously expected it to vanish.

Orion glanced at his companion, his dark hair pulled into a tie at the nape of his neck. "The labs were just ransacked."

"I WANT her head on a fucking pike," Calypso snarled, black hair fanning around her shoulders as she paced like a feral cat through the wreckage of her safe haven, wiping the back of her shaking hand over her mouth.

"I know," I said, careful to keep my tone level as I rocked on my feet.

Two. *Two* Paladin strongholds dismantled in as many weeks, like she was checking boxes off a grocery list. The most feared hierarchy south of the Rockies, and this bitch was picking off our treasures. *Alone.* Which was fucking impossible, yet there was no evidence of anyone else. The only confirmation that these attacks belonged to The Wraith was the damn calling card she left behind.

One star.

Always a star.

At least she left everyone alive this time—used some kind of gas to knock them out. True to her name, she was in and out before we could respond. No theatrics, no human police.

Forcing my jaw to unclench, I insisted, "I swear to you, you'll get your retribution. I'll see to it."

Uptown had been mine. But the lab? That was my sister's. Years of data earned over sleepless nights, and literal blood, sweat, and tears. I would know—I'd witnessed more than one of them as she poured herself into unraveling the mysteries of our bloodlines. What made us different from mortals? What, if anything, could kill a soul on a biological level? What triggered ascension, and why did some souls die before it kicked in, while others rose into power regardless of age?

The two of us should never have ascended as young as we did. Unfortunate necessity yanked us from adolescence and thrust us into eternal life.

Our younger brother, Charles, hadn't been so lucky.

This was personal.

"Big talk, and for what?!" she threw her hands up. "The attacks don't even seem connected."

"They are."

"You can't know that. The first one—sure, it was out of character for the Bellaton brats, but this one?! In and out, no fatalities? No smoke show? What grounds do you have to assume it was this *phantom* you've been so enamored with?!"

"Wraith," I gently corrected. The Wraith was a legend, and my penchant for history—particularly our hierarchy's—had engraved her conquests in my mind years ago. I certainly never thought I'd actually be hunting a campfire story.

"More than likely, it's one of Reyna's new recruits earning their fucking stripes, and we're not even retaliating," she protested, throwing her hands into the air, demanding an answer. Chest heaving, eyes hard—my usually reserved sister was miles beyond hysteria. I wasn't sure I could bring her back until she could blow off some steam.

"I said I'll take care of it."

"Over a week ago, Cy! What are we waiting on, an engraved invitation? You said you'd handle our pest problem a *week* ago, and in that time—"

"I know!" I snapped, cutting her off as heat throbbed in my forehead. Stepping into Calypso's space was always a gamble. She was just as likely to raise hell as hug me, and there was no telling which I'd get until she did it.

Lip curled, I braced for the former. "I fuckin' know, Cal. Mom's gone off the deep end. The Guard is hitting the streets with the trackers, and Dad's gone with them. Our Wings are waiting for our command. Carr's on point on the cybersecurity front, trying to figure out where the hell she's coming from."

My sister huffed a breath, but I held her glare, waiting for a fist to fly. Instead, her eyes went glossy, and she shook her head as she jerked away. Tears were reserved for death and heartbreak in Calypso's world. The fact that she was teetering on them revealed how deeply this bitch had struck.

A relieved inhale steadied my hammering heart, but my mind was still spinning. When my sister looked back, she was uncharacteristically melancholic.

"My *data*, Cy." My name came out like a broken sob. Lower lip wobbling, she pulled herself together and said, "I was so close to working out the kinks in that compound."

The Wraith had ripped every external hard drive from their ports, and we hadn't even seen her do it. Security cameras captured nothing but a black hoodie on a slight frame and a gas mask over her face. She destroyed the refrigerators, flipped over the lab tables—their contents now puddles of color and glass. Whatever she sought was on those drives, unless they were a misdirect for something not yet accounted for.

"Yeah," I breathed, opening my arms as she closed the gap, burying her face against my chest. Sighing, I wrapped her up. Brilliant beyond her years, my sister was working on something crucial. Even more so given the tenuous blade our continent's hierarchies balanced on. The compounds she'd been developing could make or break the coming war. With that in mind, I muttered, "We'll get it back."

She nodded against me, then stepped out of my grip with a monotone, "Okay." When she stared up at me, big hazel doe-eyes blinking, I sighed.

"Now?!"

"Now," she ordered firmly.

"*Night, Cal.*"

She said nothing, already using her magic to begin a melancholy cleanup. It was only as I reached the door that she muttered, "Skewer this bitch, Cy."

"With pleasure," I promised, before turning and marching from my sister's desecrated temple.

The shadows whispered of my guest the moment my boots hit the hardwood floor of the estate. Our family didn't sleep here—too Gothically regal for my taste—but we preserved it for sentiment, knowledge, and ceremony.

Whoever was waiting for me here was no Paladin. But their shadows greeted mine the instant I arrived, the swell of power in our walls sending goosebumps down my skin. To breach the magic around this estate, this shadowwalker was either invited at some point or immeasurably powerful. Perhaps both.

Palming a blade, I followed that pull without hesitation, sending a mental calling card to my cousin.

Carr, we have company.

Where you at?

The Manor.

Be there in two.

Make it one.

Fuck. Don't do anything dumb.

Define dumb, I quipped before our connection was silenced, sending a shudder down my spine. I scented the air, detecting the faintest hint of forest and ash. Not a soul I recognized.

Stay alert, the damned shadows hissed in my ears a beat before a rumbling baritone filled the hallway in a leisurely drawl.

"*Do* keep me waiting, little Prince. I've all the time in the world."

Stepping around the corner into our gathering hall, my focus snapped to the looming figure *in my mother's throne.* My first thought was our thief, but this intruder was twice my width, lounging nonchalantly on the armrest, spinning a ruby-encrusted dagger between his fingers, its point balanced on his knee. The leather demon mask and the twin swords strapped to his back sent my hackles rising.

"Don't kill the messenger," he greeted, nonchalantly. Tempting as that was, the raw power rolling off him in waves told me he was ancient —and that I was drastically outmatched. Besides, if he intended to kill me, I'd already be dead. Or fighting like hell to stay on this side of the veil.

"That doesn't belong to you," I said, striding forward as if his presence didn't have every bone in my body ready to riot.

"Doesn't it, Princeling?"

What kind of psychopath waltzed into Paladin walls and sat in our Queen's throne? Her mate had killed men for far less.

A low rumble of laughter bounced off the ceiling as he leaned forward, bracing his elbows on his knees. Before I could vocalize my disgust, he sighed theatrically. "Don't feel bad, little one. You're not the only newblood they've hidden our history from. Can't believe everything you read, now can you?"

Of all the ludicrous things ever said to me, no one—not once—had called this seven-foot frame "little."

Chuckling darkly, I rubbed the back of my neck. "I don't think I missed any history classes. Furthermore, I dunno if I had one too many drinks tonight, but I won't be able to take *anything* you say seriously while you're wearing a fuckin' Halloween mask."

"I've grown rather fond of the effects these have."

In an instant, he flitted through the shadows, closing the space between us until dark brown eyes peered through the cutouts in the leather. I matched his height, but the brute force of his frame—his sheer presence—had me doubting my odds.

"I don't have long, so I suggest you listen." His voice was a hiss of warning. "I do believe a pet of mine has taken an interest in your assets."

I said nothing.

His eyes wrinkled in what could only be a knowing smile. The power radiating off this motherfucker made my magic thrash against my ribs. Slowly, he started circling me like a vulture studying its prize. I held my ground, shadows wreathing around me to watch him as his steps landed soundlessly, prodding for information they refused to surrender.

"The Wraith and I have unfinished business, and I would like her returned to me in one piece—with a functioning mind, Princeling."

"Her life belongs to the Paladin heiress," I stated indifferently, though the sweet taste of validation sat thick on my tongue. I was fucking right. "As of tonight, there's a bounty on her head, and I can't say I'm willing to call it off without good reason."

"And what about a debt settled?"

Judging by the wolfish tilt of his head, I did a shit job of concealing my curiosity.

"It would help if I knew which debtor was calling."

A low chuckle sent shadows pouring off him like mercurial beings. My magic roared for release as darkness swallowed the moonlit windows. Eyes darting to his display, I barely made out the illusion of massive black wings.

In some alternate world, he was one of us.

That knowledge did little to still my hammering pulse. My body screamed to run or fight, but the echo of my father's voice held me steady.

Stuarts didn't run.

Knowledge came first.

Reaching for my connection, I was met with nothing but silence.

"They can't hear you, Princeling. Neither can anyone else, so stop wasting your energy." His voice was almost amused. "Your Queen knows. Tell her my offer stands. But I need my prize returned, and unfortunately, time is of the essence."

"I have to admit, I'm disinclined to settle a debt I do not owe," I said, matching his ridiculous formality. That earned a chuff of humor. Damn, he was a force to be reckoned with, and I wasn't dumb enough to start a fight I couldn't win.

"Perhaps a token of goodwill will help?"

In an unspeakably bold—or foolish—move, the man turned his back on me. Either disproportionately confident or underestimating his opponent. I was magically outmatched, but not an invalid. And one hell of a shot.

Leisurely, he lowered himself back into the ornate Paladin throne. "If I tell you where to find your thief, can you ensure your Wings return her to me in one piece after their fun?"

Our most elite warriors bore their angel-wing gauntlets permanently inked into their forearms, a celestial gift from our familiars once earned. Nix, Carr, and our friends had been marked. Poe had yet to grant me mine. What he was waiting for, I wasn't sure.

"What state would you expect us to deliver her in?"

"The price of her crime is a hand per offense."

This motherfucker knew way too much about old customs for my liking.

"Unfortunately, I'll need her sentence postponed. At least until I'm done with her. Or she's of no use to my king."

"And the offer of goodwill?"

"It starts with me leaving you alive to serve your Heiress when she rises next season. And ends with a location. In return, you'll supply me with knowledge of your own."

Dread settled like a stone in my throat. Cold sweat crawled down my spine.

Next season? This motherfucker thought my mother would be dead by winter's end?

Mercifully, my voice was steady. "And what location is that?"

Easing to his feet, he finally sheathed the golden blade at his hip. A twin dagger rested on the other side. Peculiar. Two blades strapped on his back— all mirrors of the other. The shadows knew there was significance in that, even if I didn't.

"The armory nearest the Sisters' Divide. She strikes at high noon tomorrow. A dozen Wings should be adequate, I presume."

High noon. What the fuck kind of Western did I just step into?

"If we apprehend her, how do we contact you?"

"Your Queen knows that, too."

"And if we don't?"

"You don't strike me as suicidal," he drawled.

I supposed I should've expected that answer.

"And the information you requested?"

"The nomads that scattered during the divide of our Mother Hierarchy...where do they gather in your territory?"

Confusion pinched between my brows. Mother. Hierarchy?

Was this asshole Bellpost? Or further rooted? The Knights?

"Mmm. Interesting. So not all youths disregard their heritage," he murmured, evidently responding to my unspoken question.

So, he's a clairvoyant.

"Correct, Princeling." He exhaled, a bored sigh. "Though I've grown tired of our conversation, and our time is fleeting."

"The nomads settled in our Northern Rift, high in the Appalachians."

"Excellent."

He studied me—measuring my resolve. "All debts must be paid, Princeling."

Then, he vanished.

So much for damned wards.

A roar of chatter slammed down the mental line as Carr's panicked voice echoed off the walls.

"*Cy!*"

"Throne room," I barked back.

Taking a steadying breath as that unnatural silence gave way to an entire hierarchy of voices, I glanced up at the moon, its silver glow spilling through the grand cathedral windows.

My mother owed us a mountain of explanations.

Mind-to-mind, I summoned Calypso, both my parents, and our Wings.

NINE
RAVENS
FREYA

Five years ago...

Screams ripped through the night, replacing laughter with terror. Something growled, and my breath lurched forward, heart hammering as I dug into my heels, jerking my wrists until they popped, pain searing up to my shoulders. A low laugh slithered through my ribs as I cried out, yanking against my restraints and kicking out, striking nothing before they wrenched me off balance.

Harsh hands caught my elbows, steadying me just long enough to yank me forward again. Scrambling to keep up, I spat out a curse, colorful enough to earn another low chuckle wrapping around me like smoke.

"Get fucked," I snapped. "Cut it out!"

The screams had gone silent. Then fingers seized my shirt, jerking me onto my tiptoes as that smoky voice snarled, "Or what, jailbait?"

Jailbait. Only one person called me that.

I threw my head forward, satisfaction sizzling through me when I heard the crack of cartilage, followed by a sharp curse. The grip on my shirt slipped as I planted my feet, ripping the blindfold off—only to be caught again. Strong arms wrapped around my waist, hoisting me off my feet.

"I said stop!"

Laughter rang out. Moonlight bathed the clearing, revealing half a dozen *figures in ski masks, shadows pooling around them. My head snapped side to side. Where the hell was Shay? Katie? Someone.*

Shay would never leave me alone. Not willingly.

Panic tightened my ribs as I was tossed like a rag doll into another set of rough hands. These hands wandered, fingers scraping over sore breasts that didn't exist before shoving me away. Once. Twice. Three times I was passed between them, their laughter rising over my hammering pulse. On the fourth toss, I lashed out, driving my elbow into a masked face.

He cursed, throwing me to the ground.

My palms scraped against stone and pine needles as I braced for impact. A dark silhouette lunged, but I rolled, scrambling to my feet. My fingers went to James' knife by instinct, flicking it open in a single motion. Just like August had drilled into me—over and over, until I could do it blindfolded. "All in the wrist," he'd said.

I spun the blade into position, bracing my stance. The boys circled, five feet away and closing in. My breath came hard, my muscles coiling with fire.

"We like our fresh meat feisty," one growled.

"Get. Fucked," I seethed, panting in a weak attempt to catch my breath.

"Just our type," another said, amusement curling his words.

"Crew." I locked eyes with the second tallest, who was still pinching his nose. Darkness obscured his features, but I knew him. I swung the blade at one who advanced, halting him in place. No chance in hell I could take them all. But I'd be damned if I didn't draw blood first.

"I said stop."

"Easy, Jailbait. Nobody's gonna hurt you."

"Real convincing." I took two more steps back, fingers flexing on the hilt as the hair on my neck stood on end. They kept advancing, their movements a slow, methodical press. My skin prickled. There was no outrunning them. Was there?

A raven cried overhead, its throaty call slicing through the trees.

"Crew. Please. This isn't funny."

"Who's Crew?" one mocked from my right as another flanked me on the left.

"Who's laughing?" another countered, herding me toward the trees.

Standing here was a death sentence. If I could just reach the tree line, maybe—

I turned and bolted.

I was the fastest in my class, already training with the high school track team. I pushed full throttle, but they were taller, their strides swallowing the distance. The trees loomed ahead—so close.

An arm snaked around my torso, yanking me off the ground. My blade slipped from my fingers as my ribs compressed in a brutal squeeze.

"Get off!" I sobbed over my shoulder as the air crushed from my lungs. Heckles and taunts rained down, growing sicker with every breath.

Bitch. Whore. Pretty little fuck toy.

I swallowed back a scream. This wasn't happening. Couldn't be happening.

A plan formed, desperate and reckless. I lolled my head sideways, eyes sliding closed as I went limp.

"Hey," my captor barked, alarm lacing his tone as my body slumped.

"What the fuck?" Someone advanced. Crew? His voice was sharp. *"What the fuck did you do?"*

"Nothing," the other hissed. Hands braced my weight. A shake rattled through me, my head lolling the other way. Voices pitched up, their threats shifting into panic.

I exhaled. And stopped inhaling.

My captor spewed a string of curses. *"Lay her down. Dammit. What the fuck did you do?"*

Crew. That was Crew.

As he lowered me, I planted my feet—one crushing his toes into the dirt—and rocketed upright. The crunch of bone filled me with satisfaction. My eyes snapped open onto a horrified face.

Crew.

I grinned. And head-butted him. Again.

The world exploded into chaos.

I sprinted through the group, someone barking to let me go.

"That bitch is crazy!"

Damn straight, you twatwaffle.

The sleeping cabins were too far, but the rec shed—where Chad always kept the keys to the lifeguard's speedboat—was fifty yards away.

I bolted.

Half the distance closed when my instincts screamed. Someone was on my heels.

"Porter!"

I didn't stop.

"Porter! Hey!"

Shit. Too close.

Three steps.

I launched toward the boat. Just one more—

A hard, lanky body slammed into me.

We hit the deck. Keys flew from my fingers, scraping across the wood. Arms wrapped around me, tucking me against his frame as we rolled. I barely registered the crack—

And then we plunged into freezing water.

Down, down, down.

His weight dragged me deeper. My lungs burned, panic clawing at my ribs. I shoved against him, into the darkness, kicking, twisting—

But the world spun, blackness swallowing me whole.

Six weeks before the portals opened...

"CAN YOU HANDLE THAT?" Reyna asked, her gaze locked on me across the breakfast table. It took all my self-control not to blink stupidly as I forced down the scalding mouthful of coffee I'd inhaled in my surprise. The Queen of Bellaton was still watching me, her expression impatient, waiting for my answer.

We'd yet to have another moment alone, and she hadn't bothered to ask about my findings—waiting, I suspected, to get me alone again.

Which meant she either didn't trust her team or simply didn't want them to know everything I had to share.

She'd just used the morning debrief to play back footage of two burglaries—both at greenhouses supplying her labs. These were the sixth and seventh such offenses in as many weeks, further confirming my suspicion that my dear old friends were orchestrating some kind of biological attack. A drug, perhaps. And I had a sinking feeling my most recent strike had drawn them out—unfortunately targeting Reyna in the process.

Clearing my throat, I said, "My pleasure."

"My tools are at your disposal," she replied simply before turning back to Verena, her second-in-command. "Next on the agenda: the strike team. Are they prepared for Thursday?"

Wait, that's it? No further information or instructions? My mouth popped open a beat before my irritated gaze flicked to Brody, who smirked but gave me an incremental head shake.

That's an olive branch, he said through the mental link. *Don't destroy it.*

The fuck?!

I mean, at least she's giving you something. That's progress.

Handle her thieves? Seriously. They look lame.

They had. No shadows. No magic. Just three thieves in standard-issue cat burglar outfits.

It could be worse. They could not *be lame.*

No instructions. No handoff to someone who can show me the other burglaries? She's setting me up to fail. So much for our brief truce. Was this punishment for not reporting in the second I snuck back onto the property?

We warned you she wouldn't be an easy mark.

An easy mark! I balked. *An easy mark would have the common fucking sense not to attempt neutrality in a war against humanity.*

Allying with other resisting hierarchies isn't exactly neutrality.

You're right, my bad. It's fucking idiocy.

Brody audibly snorted, trying—and failing—to disguise it with a cough. Alastair patted him on the back like he'd choked on a grape. Reyna's eyes flicked to him, then to me, without breaking her sentence—something about reports from the West Coast and worsening healer attacks.

I can't argue there, Brody finally admitted. *But we're a little biased, don't you think?*

Biases involve prejudice. Lived experience is tangible proof.

Patience, Alastair chided, though the corner of his lips twitched upward.

Aren clearly forgot who he was deploying, I countered. Patience had never been my strong suit.

Shut up and listen, their brother Ajax piped up.

Okay, soap boy, I bit back. Seriously. Why did he keep that damn name?

Regardless, I did as he asked, bringing our mental chatter to a halt as all our eyes flicked back to life-size Southern Barbie.

"Once the hostages have been through our healers, we'll bring in our mentalists to correct memories and deliver them to the proper authorities," Reyna said before rising from her chair, straightening her chiffon skirt as the others followed suit.

Wait, what? I asked internally, suddenly intrigued.

Talk less, learn more, you punk, Ajax smirked.

Reyna believes she's called to right injustices among humans, Brody explained mentally. *Believe it or not, this little blonde twig is regarded like a saint in many circles.*

Saint Lucifer? I bit out, somehow more irritated that they weren't answering me directly. This time, they didn't laugh.

Her hierarchy uses their gifts to free slaves, Freya.

Blinking, I rushed to stand, sliding my chair into the enormous dining table before whirling to follow the Queen herself. Looking around at the palatial estate, my brow furrowed, unable to shake the morbid irony.

I don't understand, I admitted. *Why live in a place like this if that's her mission?*

She once told me her goal was to bring beauty to something where so much hatred was once harbored. To use what was built for evil to create more love in the world. Have you never read the sign on the gates, Little Wraith?

I thought for a long moment and realized that in all the times I'd driven in and out in my new car this week, I'd never bothered to look at them like they held any significance.

No, I finally confessed.

You're walking on the grounds of Second Chance Ranch.

Ugh. Cheesy.

Or beautiful, you Jaded Jubilee, Ajax interjected.

With a huff, I rushed to catch up with the Commander herself. "Reyna!" I called after her. She paused just outside her office, and I knew from experience that once she waltzed through those doors, she wouldn't be out for hours.

"Miss Porter?"

"Can I visit the sites of the other burglaries?"

"I have videos available. Blaz will see that you get them."

I shook my head.

"That's not how I work. I'm a tangible tracker, like my aunt."

Hard eyes and pursed lips stared me down for a long moment before she gave a curt nod, waving forward Verena, who abandoned her conversation to be at our side. Darius, Blaz, and Montague followed in her wake.

"Blaz," I said pointedly, inclining my head in greeting. "Nice to see you bright-eyed and bushy-tailed. Darius. G," I added, flashing the latter a smile, a little thrill in my veins when the deep brown skin near his eyes crinkled with his answering grin.

Damn, they made men beautiful in the South.

"Darius," Reyna cut in before they could respond. "Miss Porter will require an escort to the greenhouses, in addition to a video review of the prior incidents. See to it she has what she needs."

"Yes, ma'am," Darius said with a nod.

"*After* she completes her lessons of the day, of course," Reyna added with saccharine sweetness. My eyes jammed shut before I could stop them. Ope. There it was. She *was* mad.

"Shouldn't the robberies take precedence?" I offered, but all the testosterone-fueled meat suits stood sentinel, leaving me to my own destruction. "I can't promise results if the crime scenes are tampered with."

"A few herbs and plants hardly require more of your focus than learning what you're up against."

By *up against,* she meant the entire mountain of Middle Realm history she was jamming down my throat every day.

"Now, carry on. You've got a long day ahead of you," she added with a vindictive spark in her eyes before motioning toward my damn tutor.

Nobody rose to my defense.

Dammit, Brody.

"IT'S some kind of drug, I think," I said as Ansel and I tiptoed through the fresh crime scene that afternoon, studying what had been taken, what was broken, and what remained undisturbed. Ansel and Lana had helped Aren lead the first training session with the Hazelharborian witches today, but he'd still jumped over to help me find answers.

"Any indication of what nature?"

"None yet. Damien is digging through the hard drives up in Westerlund." Damien, one of the three Westerlund brothers, was our best contact when it came to technology. The drives I'd stolen from Paladin labs were heavily encrypted, and I didn't stand a chance in hell of breaking through them as quickly as he could. When Ally didn't answer her phone, I figured he was my best bet for a quick resolution.

"He'll fill you in soon." Everything The Old General said sounded like a promise—like he spoke in vows rather than statements. It was oddly reassuring, and I understood how he'd been such a steadying presence for Aren and Alvara for centuries. "How are lessons?"

I snorted, frustration slumping my shoulders. "Reyna thinks that since my lives have been so fragmented, I need a full overview of Nephilim history." When he shrugged a shoulder, I just gaped at him, both of us kneeling to study the movement of one of the dirt spills. "You can't tell me the bitch is right."

"Our enemies are likely ancient, judging by Agamemnon's and Adrastos' power on that field. Does it hurt to dig backward?"

"Why wouldn't she just tell me if she has a suspicion?"

"Much like Aren, Reyna believes in equipping her souls to function fully without her. Should you find information in her absence or after her death, what good is her knowledge to you if you don't have access to it in your own mind?"

"Damn you and your logic. She's just so hateable. Like that pink bitch in *Harry Potter*." My response made one corner of his mouth tip up as we both stood, moving to the next spot our thieves had targeted in the video. "It's just so boring."

"It can't all be boring."

"Wanna bet?"

"*Freya*," he scolded, his disapproval wrapped neatly into two syllables, sharp enough to make me rethink my stance. Centuries apart, and he still had a wicked dad-voice. A tone he now used to challenge me. "Find something of value."

I sighed, mentally thumbing through the archives she'd had Blaz force-feed me. "The wars are fascinating."

He chuckled darkly, shaking his head. "Yes, well. You are your mother's daughter."

"Thank you," I chirped, grinning as I simultaneously wished she hadn't been left behind to babysit our Commander and the hippies.

"Any of them particularly interesting?"

"The Ardensian war with Bellpost was insane. I never imagined something so volatile could even happen in The Middle."

"Ahh," he breathed, quirking his head at the shattered glass front of a now-empty fridge. "The fall of Rome's pyros."

"Did you know there's no record of their royals? There was a picture, but it's just assumed he was their Commander because the painting was hung in their castle in The Middle. But...their history was wiped from existence when they fell." The flash of golden skin and pale blue eyes had me furrowing my brow. "Have you ever heard of such a thing?"

"Before my timeline, I'm afraid. Ardensia was supposedly beautiful. But they're just folktales at this point. You could ask Aren."

"Eh," I shrugged. "He's got enough legitimate things on his plate. No need to add Reyna's homeschooling."

"Fair," he said, smirking. "Do you see...?"

When Ansel's voice trailed off, I narrowed my eyes on the fading footprints across the floor before closing them, replaying the video in my mind. Their focus had been on the plants behind us, only briefly considering those on the opposite side. "Yeah," I breathed as we rounded opposite ends of the row, converging on a plant with only a few missing leaves. "Well. That's intriguing."

"Hmm," he agreed, studying me more than the plants.

"Think your witches could help us out?"

"They've barely agreed to tolerate us, but I can ask."

"Thanks..." I swallowed hard as those silver eyes lanced through me, pinning me to my spot on the floor. "What should I call you? The Old General makes me think of some elbow-patched, stogie-smoking jarhead, so that doesn't work. I mean, there's Papa," I suggested sardonically. His deadpan didn't let me down. "We could go with *Poppi*? Or *Father*? Too old and formal?"

He huffed, looking sheepish, but his eyes bore the weight of our separation, a tangible agony still embedded in his skin. The image of him filleted open ached like a wound still healing in the flesh of my mind rather than my body.

Finally, he breathed, "Dad is fine. Or Ansel, if the former feels disrespectful to the humans who raised you." It didn't. I loved them, was grateful for their incessant rules and open arms, for what they provided for August, James, and me, but...they felt like a memory, where Ansel was real, standing right before me.

"I quite missed being your daughter," I admitted. "I think I'll savor it."

"The feeling is mutual."

"Yes, well," I swallowed hard, choking back the emotion welling in my throat. "Thanks, Dad."

"Anytime, babygirl. What's next?"

"I have a pretty good idea."

"TOOK YOU LONG ENOUGH," I muttered, even as my heart leapt right out my ass. The harsh sun streamed through the treetops the following day, glimmering over splashes of colorful flora and illuminating a lone waiting figure in full Paladin attire. His black mask was pulled up over his nose, hood hanging low so only a strip of skin and his eyes were visible—just like mine.

Well, granted, mine was a bit outdated. And even in the winter, the layers were insufferably muggy this far south.

As expected, the armory was magnificent, though it held no hint of a pathological weapon. Illuminated LED walls stocked every kind of weapon I could imagine. My knuckles were now wreathed in brass, a monkey fist swinging from one hand, pockets all full of goodies, and a semi-automatic strapped across my back. A decent haul. One they likely wouldn't have noticed had I not been terrorizing them all week. But it was the box of data they'd locked behind a steel safe that I was most excited about.

"How did you know where I'd be?"

I held my ground as the figure canted his head curiously, then took slow, meticulous steps forward, assessing me. *Christ, he was tall.* Nearly Aren's height, though the comparison stopped there. Where our Commander, Ansel, Alec, and August were all racked with muscle, this silhouette was long and abnormally lean.

"Wanted women are hard to miss." That rich baritone tickled some distant part of my brain, the southern lilt stronger than Blaz's, but not by much.

"Well," I giggled girlishly, dramatically settling a hand over my heart as I took a step to the side, back toward my car. "As flattered as I am," I drawled in my best mockery of that Southern twang, "I have plans, Stretch."

My confidence faded as the unmistakable croak of a raven ricocheted off the trees a beat before the call was echoed from all directions. A flicker of a memory tugged at my mind—a human memory, fresh from this life. But it couldn't solidify because, as if that had been their signal, half a dozen looming figures emerged from the trees. My head swiveled, tracking them all.

I may have underestimated the value of that lab.

Six silhouettes. One to every side. Twenty yards to the drive, another thirty to the road. Or forty yards back to the water, but I wasn't in the north anymore. Water meant gators, and I wasn't particularly inclined to test the efficacy of my shields.

The wind kicked up around us as my assessment grew grim. If I'd learned anything from my sire, it was that confidence was half the battle, so I just slowly began twirling the steel ball at the end of the rope.

"Can I help you, gentlemen?"

"Well, you see, we were mad enough when we thought you were just looting weapons, but this"—the first figure nodded toward the box in my hand—"presents a whole new problem."

"Who sent you?" A second voice—also male—asked from behind me.

"Nothing but an orphan looking for some quick cash," I said, lifting a shoulder like the thing of value was the weapon on my back.

"Bullshit," a third voice declared, this time from my right...that itch in my brain intensifying.

"Start talkin'," the first demanded as they slowly closed ranks around me. They were cautious, I noted. No doubt waiting for an element to come roaring to life to defend me. Based on the Paladin attire, I could safely wager each one of these assholes had shadows. Hence, rifling through their shit in the middle of the day.

"You caught me," I said, holding my free hand up. "Not an orphan. Though I *could* use some quick cash," I allowed as my plan began to formulate.

Another call between the ravens sent my hair on end, eyes flicking up to realize there were as many birds as men.

Because *that* wasn't disconcerting.

A shiver rocked down my spine, and I did my best to hide it as I took a leisurely step forward. They were assessing, not attacking, which told me they needed something from me before they did away with me.

"We can do this the easy way," the lanky one promised. "Who sent you? Grayshell? Bellaton?"

Scoffing, I said, "You clearly don't know me."

"Why's that?" the second asked.

Thunder rolled, and my eyes shot skyward as a smile curved my lips. "Nobody *sends me* anywhere."

"'M about to send you to meet your maker," the third promised as lightning shredded across the darkening sky.

I laughed, rotating as I set the box of hard drives on the dirt so my hands were free. The birds began croaking, a melancholic song erupting, branches creaking as they called back and forth. As though in warning, two dive-bombed the men below before soaring up and away.

My laughter grew.

"Why are you laughin'?" the second demanded.

"There wasn't a storm in the forecast," I pointed out, grinning. Only the first was wise enough to straighten, eyes darting skyward.

The rest chuckled as the third spoke again, chastising me. "Welcome to the South."

Stretching both hands toward the ground, I breathed in deeply, summoning what little air magic I possessed. The wind began to whistle through the trees as the first and second Paladins wreathed themselves in nebulous shadows.

With way too much satisfaction, I countered, "Welcome to Midgard."

TEN

MIDGARD

CYRUS

Welcome to Midgard.

A shiver shot down my spine, and I jerked my eyes skyward as thunder rolled, the wind tearing at my hood. *Holy shit.* The once-blue sky had filled with livid clouds, heavy with unshed rain. The tempest churned, flashes of lightning turning it a startling purple, each jagged bolt streaking across the bulbous expanse.

Midgard. As in *Earth*—to the Norse pantheon. As in, the domain of the God of thunder. *Lightning wielder.* No. Fucking. Way.

And my men were too busy laughing to comprehend the hell about to rain down on us.

Fuckwits, the lot of them. The 'Wings' my father had *spared* were newly marked—young and inexperienced—namely, my cousins. There were only four ways to become a Paladin: birth, ascending as a Wing's calling, mating in, or surviving the Crucible—a series of three trials culminating in a victorious duel against a Wing to claim their place among us. No one had survived in decades. And yet, standing here now, I wished we had at least one victor among us, because judging by the caliber of imbeciles flanking me, birth seemed a laughably low prerequisite for service. Worse yet, if they died today, their blood would be on my hands.

"*Go!*" I bellowed, as three things happened at once.

Lightning shredded the clearing, bolts raining down in rapid succession. Our cadre erupted into bellows of warning, their shouts mixing with the shocked yells of those barely dodging the onslaught.

The wind picked up, The Wraith's heavy cloak billowing in its wake.

And my shadows hissed for me to *run*. Sixty seconds ago, it hadn't even been dark enough for our shadows to hold enough power to speak.

But it was the victorious spark in her eyes, the slight lift of one covered cheek as my men scattered, and the ravens crying as they dove to shield their souls that had me gritting my teeth—and bolting forward instead of away.

Heat scorched across my back as I dodged a searing blue pillar of light, a yell lodging in my throat. Instinct took over, my shadows wrapping an inky curtain around me the instant the blinding glow passed. Relief settled into my bones as time stilled, the murky shadow realm offering a welcome reprieve from the hell we'd just unwittingly unleashed. I sucked down a breath, taking a single beat to glance at the shredded fabric left in the lightning's wake. My blistered skin glowed an angry crimson beneath.

One direct hit, and it'd be the ugliest kind of death. I couldn't have cut it any closer if I'd tried.

Carr panted into existence beside me, Nix a few feet away, his hood blown back. Both of their winged markings had shifted into black metal guards—combat ready. The three of us exchanged heavy stares before scanning the chaos. The shadows would conceal us so long as we stayed the fuck away from the lightning. But if we touched its evanescent glow, time would return—in the most brutal way—before ending altogether.

"What the fuck?" Carr growled.

Nix's gravelly voice was harsher than usual as he bit out, "Nobody said *anything* about a damned lightning wielder."

"Nobody knew," I snapped, my gaze locking onto her slight frame.

Our third voiced the thought I hadn't dared speak. "That's a lot of power in such a tiny soul."

I turned back to our adversary. She stood casually, one hand outstretched toward the earth as she called the wind, the other mid-flip with that monkey fist—like she'd ever need it. She was maybe five-seven. I didn't even know souls could be so small. But what did size matter when wielding power like that? Who in their right mind would get close enough for her to land a hit when she could fry us like shrimp without even touching us?

"What drives did she grab?" Carr asked, still sucking in air as he assessed the distance between our men and the threat. His heart had to be thundering as violently as mine. He didn't need to see my face to understand the depth of my glare when I turned on him.

Idiot.

"Right," he mumbled. "Hey—uh, Nix? You wanna check it out?"

"You first," Nix scoffed, though he took a tentative step toward her. My eyes flicked upward, tracking the lightning inching its way toward the ground like a God's scalding, white-hot finger, ready to obliterate us the moment time snapped back.

"All three of us, different angles," I ordered. "We've got another—" I glanced at the rods of energy stretching for us, "maybe forty seconds before these suckers hit." Without another word, we split, moving in on her while keeping a wary distance from the lightning's inevitable path.

"Watch your feet," I warned, stepping over a puddle of muck. The last thing we needed was to become better conductors.

Carr drew a blade, eyes locked on her dark, determined gaze. Odds of avoiding electrocution weren't in his favor, but I respected his willingness to take the hit if needed. Nix and I knelt beside her, sorting through the drives, careful not to brush her exposed hands. None were labeled.

"How the fuck would she even know what she was stealing?" Nix muttered, shaking his head.

I chewed my lower lip, wondering the same damn thing as I lifted my gaze to her concealed face. I was about to rip her mask off when Nix's voice cut through my thoughts.

"Are those...?" His words trailed off, and I followed his stare, scowling as I reached for the colorful plastic square beneath the externals.

"Floppy disks," I muttered, equal parts bemused and intrigued. That lined up. Oddly enough. My mother had allied with The Wraith in the late eighties or early nineties.

"What are you after?" I breathed, tossing the disks back and handing the whole box to Nix. "Get those to the truck."

Nix nodded once before vanishing into shadow, shocking the hell out of me with his sudden compliance. My gaze flicked to the unnatural barrier of shadows at the edge of the woods, where a line of harsh sunlight lingered just beyond. Nix materialized at the border, pausing for my nod before continuing his mission. Our elements wouldn't get him to the truck, but at least he had a head start.

"Don't let her touch you," I warned Carr.

His only answer was a sharp dip of his chin, much like his brother's.

With that final warning, I dove for her waist.

And time roared back into existence.

FREYA

THUNDER BOOMED as a body slammed into mine, the brutal collision sending us both careening through the shadows. The world slowed, dark and thick like molasses, before snapping back into full color. I was thrown off my feet as two men emerged from the ether, materializing from thin air. Searing agony ripped through my jaws, hot blood flooding my mouth as my canines burst forward. I hadn't used them since the battle with the Renown, and *holy fuck*, it hurt. That pain eclipsed even the impact of our bodies hitting the unforgiving ground.

His pant of exertion met my pained grunt of frustration.

"Who. Sent. You?" he growled, making a move to pin my arms. A cry tore from my throat as I thrashed against him. A bolt of lightning struck so close that the earth erupted in a violent cloud, forcing my attacker to dive for cover.

A little too close for comfort there, I warned, rolling through the smoking debris and back onto my feet.

Get the fuck out of there, August ordered, his temper dripping from every syllable. He and Ally hovered at the edge of the woods, and judging by Ally's trance-like state, she was guiding his shots.

Working on it, I mentally bit back, but the motherfucker misted from the shadows, his arm snaking around my waist as another lunged forward, knife in hand.

Summoning every ounce of strength, I tucked my legs up before snapping them forward in an attempt to break free—or topple us. Neither happened. Instead, he grunted as thunder cracked, the world flashing a blinding blue that forced me to jam my eyes shut.

"Fucking *stop that!*" my assailant barked. As if in answer, lightning struck in rapid succession, each bolt closer than the last. The one with the blade staggered back before vanishing into shadow.

Blood trickled down my chin, hot and sticky, as I bellowed down the mental line, *A little help?!?*

Use your head, Freya, Ally's ethereal voice drifted through my mind, distant but firm.

Breathing grew harder as he dragged my thrashing, stupidly tiny body away from the hidden armory door. I threw my head back, cracking into his face with a satisfying crunch. His grip slipped just enough for me to twist between his arm and hard body before his forearm pinned my neck. With no other choice, I opened my mouth and sank my horrifyingly painful fangs into his arm. His scream hit like a one-two punch, my mouth flooding with his blood. *Nasty.*

Not what I meant, Ally's bell-chime voice admonished.

And then—without understanding how—I was ten feet away, staring back at him. Blood dripped from my mask, the damp fabric caking against my face. He clutched his arm, crimson rivulets pouring from the punctures in his uniform. Smiling, I wiped the back of my hand over my mouth, irritation flaring at the sticky mess.

Flashes of electricity fired like strobes as the last of his men vanished.

We had the same thought at the same time—our gazes snapping to the now-empty ground where the box had been. My attacker dipped his head in a mocking farewell before melting into the shadows.

"No," I breathed, whirling toward the thick woods. Then, the roar of a truck firing up yanked my attention toward the road. My feet carried me half a dozen steps before it happened again—I simply reappeared beside the street.

Movement.

I whirled left as that lanky frame leapt into the open door of a rolling truck.

I bolted in the opposite direction, pushing this pathetic little body to its limit until I reached my car.

Where the hell do you think you're going? August demanded as I turned the ignition.

Be right back.

What are you doing?!

Good God, how many times had I heard that parental disapproval in his tone over the last decade? August had always been so damn serious—so worried—overbearingly protective, unlike James, who barely gave a shit about his own life, let alone mine. Now, all it did was make me roll my eyes as I peeled onto the road after the truck, mentally inventorying what I had learned.

My opponents couldn't jump, or there wouldn't have been a trace left to follow.

These six wore the gauntlets of Paladin Wings but lacked the skills. Which meant their leader was either inexperienced or didn't posess the influence to demand better men from Reagan. A newblood, maybe? Or he was unreliable, and she didn't trust his intel enough to send real firepower.

As we banked a sharp turn, another possibility struck me—maybe she was already engaged in another fight, her best warriors tied up elsewhere. By all means, this could have ended badly if August hadn't jumped at the opportunity to turn this into a literal smoke show. My illusion of solitary strength had worked marvelously—hopefully buying me some extra caution from these assholes until I could properly ascend.

Still, after taking down two strongholds in a week, I expected *better* resistance. Honestly? It was a little insulting.

My tires squealed across dry asphalt as I shifted gears.

His truck might have been a behemoth, but my car was zippier. At least, that's what I told myself as I floored the gas, my eyes flicking between his taillights and the rapidly climbing red needle of my speedometer. I needed those disks. If they were worth killing over, then they were worth dying for.

Every puzzle piece brought me closer to retribution.

I didn't want to *kill* Reagan Stuart.

I wanted to destroy her.

I wanted to pull apart her life like a *Jenga* tower, one brick at a time, letting her know exactly who was dismantling everything she held dear. And when she stood among the ruins, fully aware of who had pulled the last block, *then*—if I was feeling merciful—I'd fucking kill her.

That bloodlust propelled me forward, speeding down the road at three times the limit, locked onto the black-on-black truck as it roared into town.

The driver glanced in the rearview mirror. I winked before looking lower, memorizing the license plate.

The truck veered onto a side street, pedestrians scattering with screams as it hopped the curb before gunning the accelerator. A plume of exhaust billowed from the tailpipe, darkening my windshield.

Cursing, I followed.

He looped us onto a road out of town—relieving, at least. Glancing back at the chaos we left behind, I sighed. *Great.* I just burned my vehicle, and it was only week one. Too many witnesses. It was useless now.

Without warning, he yanked sideways down a slick decline into a muddy field.

"Fuck!" I slammed the brakes, tires screeching to a stop as I watched him plow through feet of deep mud before crashing into the adjoining cornfields.

"Dammit," I muttered, tightening my grip on the wheel. High-centering my Mazda in a mud pit and dealing with human authorities was not on my bingo card today.

Tapping my screen, I called August.

"Can you meet me at the junkyard? I need a lift."

"Already on our way."

"Goddamn, I love you, big brother."

"*Yeah, yeah,*" he muttered. "Lay low. Cops are scanning for you both."

"Figures. Hey, August?"

"Yeah?"

"I need a bigger ride."

With an exhausted sigh, he muttered, "Do I wanna know?"

"Probably not."

"Get me the specs, and I'll make it happen."

"Don't tell Mom," I teased, for old times' sake.

A warm chuckle crackled over the line. "We'll see."

"In all seriousness, thanks for coming," I added, scrolling through my screen to pull up Brody's burner line. It was time to pay Aren a visit and bring him up to speed. Which, unfortunately, meant I needed a lift—and these two circus freaks needed to get back up north before they missed their mark.

"*In all seriousness*, no problem."

"*Please*," I scoffed, stomping on the gas. "You've got enough on your plate."

"Well. It was more fun than twiddling my thumbs waiting for Kingsley."

I laughed, easing off the pedal before making the turn toward the junkyard. "Well, then, *you're welcome*." Though, somehow, I doubted Alvara—the Angel of Death—left August with much time for *thumb-twiddling*.

ELEVEN

MERCY

ALVARA

"Move, August."

He did. But I was faster.

The sharp jolt of pain that cracked through his ribs on impact with the concrete ricocheted through our bond. It took all my focus not to wince before wrenching his neck back, locking my legs around his hips. August resisted—his strength almost enough to overpower my technique. Almost.

I focused on the stutter of his heart as his breaths turned to grunts. Then he tapped out against my arm.

Tucking my chin toward him, I growled, "Don't you fucking tap out on me. Grayshellians don't yield."

Another failed escape attempt. Another wasted session. I zeroed in on the ragged sound of his breathing.

He was better than this. Stronger. He'd spent months training with Aren, Alec, and Ansel—and he was choosing to hold back now? *Now,* when war was imminent, when our shattered reading gave us nothing in the way of results, and centuries of heartache?

We didn't have time for this.

Freya had granted us a reprieve for the week, and now wasn't the time for another.

Irritation rippled outward as I snarled, "There is no mercy out there— *fight,* dammit!"

The vision of him slumping over my body on the cold floor had me growling as I rolled him off me in frustration. He rasped for air as I got to my feet, anger blooming like wildfire in my chest.

"*You're holding back.*"

"Ally," he rasped, struggling to breathe.

"You won't fucking break me," I barked, storming over to Kingsley's woodpile with half a mind to play dodgeball with logs. "Don't insult me by pretending that's the problem."

The man was impossible.

All week he'd been pulling punches. Whether he'd admit it or not, my mate was afraid of hurting me. Laughable. A little pain was inevitable, but August Porter was years away from outmaneuvering me. I threw a piece of wood into the stove, slamming the door harder than necessary.

"Stop acting like you can't fight me."

He blinked down at me as I closed the distance, the justification already on his tongue, "Ally, I—"

"You're being pathetic," I snapped, pacing in front of him.

His jaw clenched, a deep line forming between those emerald eyes.

"You sound like *him*," August warned, voice flat.

Him. *Adrastos.*

Even with how fractured our reading was, I didn't flinch at the comparison. The boy with black hair I chased through the finest castles had shaped me. Whether I'd known it then or not, his hand was in my creation. Our origins were entwined. His betrayal etched into my very bones.

"Maybe I *wouldn't* if you weren't tempting our fate with him on our heels."

The truth was, I had regretted the words the moment they landed on my tongue, but I couldn't take them back.

Not with the memory of Bjorn bleeding out. Not with Michael's body on the cobblestones. Not with Jacob hanging limp as guards dragged me to the pyre.

He couldn't afford not to listen to me. We had weeks at best to prepare him—just weeks before chaos ensued. And the girl in the gowns, the raven-haired boy from my shattered past? They were gone.

"Stop. Pulling. Punches. It's insulting. From the moment you died in that alley, I've done *nothing* but train. Fight. Kill the monsters that took you. So, don't act like you're something I haven't seen before."

I shoved him. He didn't move, but his nostrils flared.

"There is no mercy in the field. So there is none here. I am your mate, yes. But I'm also your *sire*—and our enemy is coming. So listen closely. Grayshellians don't fucking yield. We win. Or we die."

"You're—"

"Perfectly capable of looking out for myself."

His fear bled through our bond like an open wound, even through the shields he kept up to protect me. I understood that fear—if I'd been soft.

Fragile. But that version of me was long dead, and Aren, Ansel, and Marcus had ensured I'd never be mistaken for prey again.

"Now, *fight*."

"Never thought I'd miss Aren," he muttered, circling.

I didn't smile. "Aren would've painted you black and blue by now."

August's control had improved, especially since our field trip to Louisiana, but his training still had gaps. I intended to close them.

"Still," he said, his voice subdued.

"Are you seriously telling me you can't take coaching from a woman?"

"Don't be an ass, Ally."

"Well?" I threw up my hands. "From where I stand, we are weeks from the greatest war this dimension's ever seen, and you're not taking it seriously."

"It's..." He faltered, gaze dropping. "It's different now. With *you*." His sorrow was palpable as he raked his hand through his hair. "Different," he said again, quieter.

I closed my eyes, steadying myself.

This dynamic *sucked*.

It was easier when I was the medic. Easier to stitch him back together after Aren cracked him open. Being the one doing the breaking? That was new.

"Get out of your head," I told him. "In *every life*, you've been a fighter."

"Always hated it."

"It's an unfortunate necessity."

"When does it stop?"

"When *you* make it stop. You hate it for a reason. Use that. Only you can bring peace."

"No pressure."

"On the contrary," I said, stepping forward, "an entire universe of pressure." I struck in a familiar rhythm, and he dodged, then blocked. Better. But not enough.

"*Get mad*," I snarled. "Get pissed if you need to. But *fight*."

"Ally!" he barked, catching my wrist as I struck for his face. He yanked me into his chest, face twisted in anguish.

"I can't," he breathed.

"Yes, you can." My voice cracked. "You *have to*."

"*Do you know what this is doing to me? This broken fucking reading?*"

I did. Because it was destroying me too. Every attempt, every death. Over and over, like we were cursed to repeat it.

When he realized I wasn't going to strike again, he released my wrist. One hand threaded through my hair, the other cupped the back of my head, drawing our foreheads together.

"I understand now," he whispered. "Why you didn't want to read me until we could do it right. If I have to watch you die in my fucking arms one more goddamn time, it might kill me. Do you have any idea how brutal it is —knowing I've never *once* been enough to save you?"

His eyes—so vivid beneath the buzzing overhead lights—cut straight through me.

"For centuries, I've fought my way back to you, only to be cut short, and now I finally have you. How am I supposed to raise a hand against you—even like this?"

His palms gentled. A scrape across my cheek vanished as healing magic bled into my skin. Subconscious. Loving. I leaned into his touch.

"I know," I breathed. "But I need you to move through this. I need you ready. And since it's just the two of us here, I don't have an alternative."

"I couldn't live with myself if I hurt you."

A snort caught in my throat. "Don't flatter yourself. My idea of a fun Friday night is hitting the mat with Aren, Ansel, and Alec—at once."

"I told you I don't share," he muttered dryly, the corner of his mouth twitching.

"*Ew.*" I laughed, wrinkling my nose. "No, thank you."

A flicker of amused satisfaction crossed his face before he masked it again—like even now, after everything, he still needed reassurance.

Gently, August cupped my cheeks, thumbs stroking the lines of my face. "I finally have you."

"And we'll have to fight like hell to keep it that way. So trust me. There's nothing you can give me that I can't take."

That cocky brow arched, heat licking down my spine as carnal images flickered through his mind—and *my God*, he had plans. My head shook as he grinned.

"You sure about that?" he teased. "I've got a few ideas."

"Jesus, August. *Focus.*"

"I am."

"On survival. Not fucking my brains out."

A slow, wicked curve lifted his lips. "Can't we do both?"

"Debatable." With a huff, I brushed my lips over his before shoving him once. "If you manage to hurt me, I heal fast."

"Slower than you're used to," he muttered bitterly.

"Be as cowardly as you want," I taunted, narrowing my gaze. "But your resistance to the inevitable makes *me* want to hurt *you.*"

He grinned at that—crooked and gorgeous and infuriating. For the first time, I understood why Aren had broken me so many times only to piece me back together. There was something in the instinct. In the drive to teach him to survive. Was it the mate bond? Or simply the pull of guarding a calling?

"Give me your best shot, then," he said, voice low and challenging. "*Sire.*"

When I lashed out, he moved. Fast. God, he was faster, dodging and striking in fluid movements.

"*Yesss,*" I hissed, giddy as our bodies collided and rebounded in a brutal rhythm. One for one, blow for blow—we whirled, ducked, dodged. Sweat prickled my spine as our breathing quickened, our limbs moving in a blur.

I took him to the ground in a spin, but he rolled and landed in a crouch. When I lunged, he was ready this time.

There you are, I encouraged, mind-to-mind, the connection flaring bright.

This—this was peace. My sanctuary. Motion, movement, combat. My body knew the steps. Anticipated his without conscious thought.

Weave, duck, strike.

Long black hair. Blue eyes. A girl dancing on a bar top.

Lunge, dodge, spin.

A smile that sent his pulse racing. A defiant chin.

Block, pivot, feint.

Smooth skin beneath calloused fingers tracing a phoenix up her ribs.

Strike, strike, shift.

The wind on his face. Her legs clamped around his hips. The purr of his bike.

Rain, tears, blue eyes rimmed in red.

Aren's soul twining with hers.

And one word he didn't dare say. *Mate.*

Pain exploded across my cheek as I hit the floor hard, breath knocked from my lungs. I barely caught myself, powers flaring just enough to soften the blow.

But that word echoed louder than the impact.

Mate.

I blinked, disoriented. Not from the hit, but from the vision. From what it meant.

Aren had a mate.

Now. Of all times. After everything.

"Ally!" August dropped to his knees, panic etched into every line of his face. I tasted copper, licked blood from my split lip, and laughed.

"About damn time," I rasped, a feral grin stretching my lips. God, he hit like Aren. I *loved* it. August's answering concern had me laughing as my head spun...and his wide-eyed horror only made me laugh harder.

And then—I lunged.

THE CRYSTAL CRUNCH of snow and ice beneath our boots was the only sound, save the distant hum of rubber tearing across the highway. Still no sign of Kingsley—and it had been a day and a half since we arrived. Not that we could complain. The safe house was stocked with snacks, books, and a ridiculous number of timeless movies. But it wasn't what I'd seen in the visions, and that...unsettled me.

"Aren has a mate?" August asked, still parsing through the chaos from our sparring session.

"I think so."

"'Think' doesn't exactly inspire confidence."

"I'm not sure how else to describe it. She has to be," I breathed. Lately, my visions had lagged—like a glitch in the system. Blurred and imprecise. I didn't know if it was August's immense power beside me, or Adrastos lurking again, veiled in mist and shadow. Hiding. Obscuring.

Regardless, I'd seen Kingsley marching up to the cabin by morning, giving me hell over his brownies. And as cozy as this temporary exile was, we didn't have time for comfort. Too much to decipher. Too little time. Too many alliances we needed *yesterday*.

I blew out a frustrated breath, watching it cloud in front of me, the snow crackling beneath our boots.

"You sure we're not being punished?" August asked dryly, hoisting the axe. It came down with a crack, splitting the log cleanly. He set another piece on the block.

I laughed and tossed him a smile, enjoying how his gaze lingered even as he swung again—crack, *thud*.

"A cozy mountain cabin with your new wife is punishment?"

"*New* wife," he scoffed. "Collectively, how many years do you think we've been married?"

I tilted my head, narrowing my eyes. "Haven't thought to count."

"At *least* the human equivalent of a normal, not-hunted-by-demons marriage, right?"

I snorted. "Probably. It has to be at least a century?"

"Feels longer."

"Ouch."

He grinned as he split another log, the pieces thudding softly into the snow. "I just meant...you feel like a part of me. Like you've always been there. As long as I can remember."

"As long as the visions can show."

He paused, then lifted his gaze. "So. You didn't answer my question."

"No, we're not being punished. Don't you like the snow?"

"Generally? Sure. But after a few weeks in the Florida surf every day? Not so much."

"Fair."

"Freya and the Greek brothers are warm and sunny. Aren's in Santa Bloom. And we're here. In the frozen tundra."

My laughter was cut off by a vision, and I hissed, "Don't grab the blade when you set that down—you'll slice your hand open."

August froze, then shot me a glare. I shrugged, grinning.

"Occupational hazard," I said, tapping my temple.

He smirked but rolled his eyes. "Thanks, babe. I'll try not to maim myself on *the axe.*"

Instead of setting it beside the woodpile, he pivoted and threw it into the target pinned to a tree. It struck dead center with a resonant *thunk*, the handle still vibrating.

My brows lifted. Axe throwing wasn't part of our usual arsenal.

Bjorn, perhaps?

That grin curled slowly across my face. Without looking away from the embedded weapon, I raised a hand. August slapped me a high five before scooping up the firewood. I crouched and did the same, relishing the sting of cold against my palms.

The world had long since surrendered to snow. Light glimmered across the surface like powdered glitter, the sky washed in gray, save for the smear of soft pastels fading over the western horizon. The last stretch of winter clung stubbornly to the mountains, storms rolling in exactly as I'd foreseen.

As we neared the cabin, the air thickened—woodsmoke, roasting meat, and pine. But beneath it all lingered something else. Familiar. Male.

I smirked at August as he scented him too.

"Kingsley?" he whispered.

I nodded, and we quickened our pace. Smoke curled from the metal chimney in lazy spirals.

"How didn't we *feel* him?"

I raised my brows and waited.

August's grin came slow, dawning bright. *That's what he does. That's why we're here.*

I nodded again as we stepped onto the porch. August had a way of storing away little pieces of information for later retrieval. He preferred to rely on me for instant recall—maybe to flatter me, maybe because he liked hearing me talk—but when nudged, he remembered.

We call him the Alias. Freya may be the Wraith, but Kingsley? He can vanish—and he's damn good at making others disappear with him.

Not the Smuggler?

My grin sharpened. *That could work too, I guess.*

August balanced the logs in one arm and opened the door for me. It swung inward with a soft squeak, letting warmth rush out to greet us. The roast filled the cabin with savory spices, my mouth watering on instinct. At least I'd remembered to buy enough portions.

Kingsley sat in the corner, perched in a low leather chair, his brown eyes fixed on the fire. He didn't move. Didn't blink. "If you're going to eat my food and drink my coffee, you could at least call first."

A coal burst in the iron stove, sending sparks popping.

I arched a brow. "I'd be happy to. Do you even *own* a phone?"

At that, Kingsley smiled wryly, brown eyes flicking up to me as he ran a hand over his tight russet curls. "Perhaps our anonymity might discourage visitors."

"Perhaps," I agreed, "if you didn't have a clairvoyant for a cousin."

"Indeed," he sighed. "So. It's time, then?"

My lips pressed into a thin line and I nodded once.

Another sigh. He didn't try to hide the weight of it—shoulders sinking, expression pinched. Kingsley wasn't precognitive, but like Aren, his intuition rarely led him astray. The response had been similar through all of our stops. Nobody wanted a visit from Aren's Angel of Death. If *Grayshell* was asking *for help*, it meant things had gotten dire.

"Alright," Kingsley muttered. "We start tomorrow."

"Thank you." Relief thudded through my chest—not surprise, but that quiet release that came from progress, from checking off one more crucial task before the wheels fell off completely.

"I apologize. I'm being rude." I gestured between them. "Kingsley, this is—"

"August Porter. The prophesied King Calloway himself," Kingsley said dryly, not looking at August's outstretched hand. "Even the game in these woods knows his name by now, Alvara."

"August," I said with a soft smile, "this is Kingsley. Our...elusive cousin of the North."

"Pleased to meet you, Kingsley. Alvara and Aren speak highly of your abilities."

"And of their need for them, I'm sure," he replied coolly, eyeing August's hand like it might carry disease.

"They didn't mention you were a jackass," August said at last, withdrawing his hand, no longer hoping for a formal introduction.

I blinked. Blunt wasn't usually his default. When I glanced over, his face was unreadable, but Kingsley's lips twitched, clearly amused. The tension broke with a chuckle, and a reluctant grin crept across his lightly freckled cheeks. It didn't quite reach his eyes, still creased with perpetual concern, but the air shifted.

And then I felt her.

I turned toward the hallway, a broad smile breaking free. Her power reached me before her presence did—a quiet, steady beacon that pulled warmth from my ribs.

Rosaleigh emerged from the gloom, every step deliberate, graceful. Her cropped brunette pixie cut framed her delicate face, and her ears glittered with gold and diamond stars that climbed the curves. A slender gold moon pendant rested against the creamy gray of her sweater. Purple liner rimmed her soft brown eyes, silver shimmer dusting her lids. The shifter moved like a memory—familiar, regal, grounded. She stared up at me through a fan of lashes, lips twitching.

And then we collided.

Arms around each other, laughter spilled into the hallway as we rocked from one foot to the other like schoolgirls reunited after summer break. When we pulled apart, both men were watching—August amused, while Kingsley appeared to be tolerantly exasperated.

"August," I said, breathless. "This is Rosaleigh. Rosaleigh, this is—"

"Your *mate!*" she shrieked, hands flying to cover her mouth—though they did very little to muffle her excitement. I couldn't help but beam back at her. "Fuck," she squeaked. "Took you long enough, for pity's sake!" She flung her arms around August's neck, hugging him tight.

He laughed, eyes flicking to me as he gingerly returned the gesture.

Kingsley grumbled something behind us, and I glanced back just in time to catch him rolling his eyes as Rosaleigh bounced away and wiped her cheeks with her sleeves.

Still grinning, I looped an arm around August's waist. He mirrored the motion instinctively, pulling me flush against him. His warmth, his breath on my temple—it settled me instantly.

"Rosaleigh, *really?*" Kingsley teased.

She slugged his shoulder without missing a beat, though tears were still streaking her face.

"She waited so damn long," she whispered, pinching the bridge of her nose. "I can't imagine...I'm just so grateful you found each other again."

Her sincerity hit me like a wave. My throat tightened, my eyes stinging. That old ache—grief and hope tangled in a knot—rippled through me. I turned toward August, letting my gaze trace him. The angle of his jaw, the small kink in his nose, the soft curve of his lips.

He smiled and pulled me closer, pressing a kiss to my hair.

Weeks had passed since our reunion, and still—*still*—it struck me like a blow. Crushing and exquisite. Whether it was his emotions or mine overflowing, I couldn't say. But he held me tighter, hand fisting gently at my shoulder.

Rosaleigh sniffled, then turned flirtatious as she raised her brows at August. "A man who makes pot roast for company?"

I giggled as he gave her a rueful smile. "Only what my lady requests, ma'am."

"We've always shared our favorites," she said with a wink, earning a groan from Kingsley and a blush from August.

With a flourish of ring-bedecked fingers, she waved us toward the kitchen. "Come on. Kingsley brewed coffee. I've got Bailey's in the cupboard. Now tell me what kind of trouble you two have stirred up."

TWELVE

VENDETTAS

FREYA

I hadn't had the chance to fill Reyna in on what I'd learned over the last few days, so when I woke to the unmistakable cadence of boots over marble and the too-dim light of early morning, I groaned. Palming my face, I puffed my lungs up with air, succumbing to a vicious yawn as I looked at my watch.

Fuck, it was early. Even for me.

Reyna had scheduled a personal training session with me at nine a.m.—I'd hoped it was just a cover for a private audience. But I had a sinking suspicion that plan was about to get torched. And that was a problem. Not just because I needed to earn Reyna's favor, but because I needed more resources if I was going to drag Reagan down by the throat. And if there was anyone who might *possibly* sympathize with that mission, it was Reyna.

Instead, she had me running laps and dodging hexes like I was some minor annoyance, not the thief she'd sent out to spy on a mutual enemy.

My comment to Aren about wanting to stab her with a fork at "family dinner" was not an exaggeration. There was nothing—and I do mean nothing—more infuriating than being treated like a pawn when the damn board was on fire.

I was still tugging on a boot as I stumbled into the hallway, hair tie between my teeth, laces flapping. It only took ten paces to reach the overlook above the foyer.

Below: fourteen souls, all high-ranking, stacked with muscle, expressions carved from stone. Retribution, then? From the look of them, two covens' lead cadres. More weapons than I wanted to tally, but knowing our own style of concealment, I'd guess fifty at least.

I slid down the banister, landing light, and began weaving through the rigid formation—until a firm hand clamped down on my shoulder, freezing me in place.

Didn't have to turn to know who it was.

"Darius," I muttered, already bristling. That familiar tension pulsed from him in waves—tight control, quiet power, a century of discipline barely leashed. When I looked back, his green-flecked hazel eyes locked onto mine, hard and resolute.

"You're staying."

I narrowed my eyes. "What happened?"

"Complication with a mission."

"I can help." My voice sharpened, frustration already climbing my spine.

"Not this time, kiddo."

"Don't *kiddo* me, D. Where are you going?"

"Don't call me that," he replied, tone clipped. He hesitated for half a breath, weighing something, then exhaled. "Not this time, Freya. Please. Trust me."

Movement behind us caught my attention, and I turned just as Reyna stepped forward to take point. Her long blonde braid coiled and tucked like a crown of steel. Silver and white armor hugged her frame, luminous and cold as moonlight. Sentinels buckled her vambraces—metal wings, like Grayshell's.

"Sound off," she ordered.

As the first soul declared his name and rank, Darius leaned in, hand shifting from my shoulder to my bicep, grip tightening.

"I don't have time to explain," he said, voice low. "Your capabilities are promising, but I can't risk the safety of my souls—or yours—with a newborn who hasn't proven she can jump out of a hot zone."

"I *did* jump—"

"Once," he cut in. "And haven't done it since." His voice wasn't cruel. Just...unforgiving. "When you're no longer a liability, I'll be the first to vouch for you. But not tonight. Reyna will brief you when we return. Stay with Blaz."

Oof. That one landed.

Without breaking my gaze, he turned and stated, "Darius Alexander McCoy, third coven head. Head of security."

"Let's roll, ladies and gentlemen," Reyna commanded, and the double doors flew open.

Darius held my eyes for one long, unspoken beat. I dipped my chin in a stiff nod, biting back everything else I wanted to scream. Then he turned and walked into the morning, his soldiers filing out behind him in disciplined silence.

Blaz sidled up on my right as Alastair mirrored him on my left.

"They'll be okay," Blaz said gently. "My mother doesn't leave a single soul behind. Come hell or high water."

"Yeah, whatever." My throat felt tight. I hadn't meant to care. Not like this. But it wasn't Reyna I was worried about—it was Darius. It was G.

It was realizing I'd started to give a shit about these silver-draped robots. And that was a problem.

This wasn't what I was here for.

But I'd seen what Aren was willing to risk for a few mortals. I'd seen the blood he spilled to protect them. To protect *me*.

And that same weight was building in my chest now.

Goddammit. Grayshellians were already enough to worry about. Toss in the Westerlund shifters, and I was about to drown in people I cared for. I had a mission. I had my own retribution to see through. And yet—

I followed the Bellaton brigade to the porch just in time to watch them vanish.

Leaving me useless. Again.

"If I didn't know any better," Alastair drawled, all accent and a smug smile, "I'd say you care."

"Good thing you *do* know better."

"Attachment isn't weakness, Porter."

"*I'm not—*" I realized my voice had risen, low and sharp. I inhaled. Tried again. "I'm not attached. I'm irritated."

"That you can't go with them?" Blaz asked.

"No," I snapped—then winced. "I mean...*yes*. Maybe. It's going to be hard to win Reyna's favor if I can't even prove I'm useful."

"Surely the infamous Wraith isn't short on creativity," Alastair said, mockingly scandalized.

Creativity. If Aren was famous for anything, it was his terrifying creativity in jumpstarting latent powers.

Maybe I'd been going about this all wrong.

"You're a genius!" I spun and nearly smacked a kiss to his cheek before remembering Alastair towered over me like a redwood. Opting for an affectionate shove instead, I grinned. "And you're going to help me."

He didn't so much as rock on his heels, just smirked lazily. "I am?"

"Yes. You are."

Blaz groaned beside him. "Why do I have a feeling I'm not gonna like this?"

"Because she's *her*," Alastair replied, shaking his head. "What undoubtedly manic idea has rooted itself in your skull now?"

"Help trigger ascension," I said plainly, pulling my hair back and snapping a tie around it. I remembered Aren practically beating me senseless in one incarnation to force my power to surface. He'd always been *much* more amenable when I came in a male vessel, damn him.

Alastair's smile vanished. "Freya…"

"If you don't do it, I'll find someone who will."

"Aren and August—"

"—have enough on their plates right now and couldn't give a flying fuck in a squirrel suit. I can take it."

"That's what she said," Blaz muttered, taking an instinctive step back like one of us might spontaneously combust. Which, honestly, was fair.

"Blaz Gwyne!" I gasped, shocked into laughter. So far, he'd been the picture of calm diplomacy and good manners. I was starting to question whether he was even human.

The impish smirk and the blush on his cheeks sent me grinning. "You *are* a real boy, after all."

"Oh, piss off," he chuckled. "Thought we could use a mood shift. Big guy here looked like you nearly gave him a coronary."

"That's because he's being a baby," I said sweetly, aiming the jab squarely at Alastair.

"Chivalry," he began, lips pursed in protest.

"*Is dead*. Or needs to be. This is survival, Alastair." I turned back to Blaz. "I don't *like* getting punched in the face, but I'll take pain if it shakes the magic loose. You could help too. You don't need power to scare mine into showing up."

Blaz tilted his head. "What do you mean, *scare* it?"

My ridiculous chaperone sighed. "In desperate circumstances, or when an ascension is proving particularly…stubborn, Aren discovered we could—"

"Beat it out of people," I cut in. "Let's not sugarcoat it. It sucks, but it works. And *I'm not made of porcelain*. We heal fast, so who cares? If the world wasn't ending, Aren would've done it already."

"If the world wasn't ending, you'd be in The Middle, and this conversation wouldn't be happening."

"Because August didn't need a few hard shoves?" I snapped. "Aren practically threw everything he had at him trying to bring his memories back. And even now, he and Ally are still dredging."

I stepped closer—not that it made much of a dent, considering Alastair's seven-foot shadow was still looming. "If I fail to ascend before the war hits, we both know what that means."

What I didn't say—what I wouldn't say—was that if I couldn't ascend before I challenged Reagan for her throne, it wouldn't even matter. I'd be dead long before the battlefield.

Dismantling the Crucible's assets, I could handle. That was strategy. That was calculation.

But challenging a Paladin matriarch without power equal to or greater than hers? That was suicide. Even if I won, it'd be labeled treason. Disrespect.

And I could live with that.

As long as Reagan ended up in the dirt. If the Paladins knew the full truth—the treason she'd committed, the dishonor she'd been hiding for the last three decades—they would honor my claim. But *that* required surviving first. And this half-ascended, half-mortal meat sack wasn't going to cut it.

Alastair looked pained, dragging a hand through his ash-brown hair, eyes lifted skyward like he was asking the creator to bail him out.

"You do realize your brother and your father are two of the scariest motherfuckers alive?"

"Oh, please." I rolled my eyes. "August is harmless."

He arched a brow. "Tell that to the Renown."

Okay. *Fair point.*

"Well. He's harmless *to you*."

Still unimpressed, he cracked his neck and muttered, "Fine. But don't say I didn't warn you when they lose their goddamn minds."

Refusing to let him change *his* mind, I threw my arms around his middle and buried my face in his chest as Blaz stared, wide-eyed.

"Thank you. Thank you. Now please—fuck up my face."

"WHAT IN THE *Lord's name* happened to you?" Reyna snapped, her disapproving Southern twang cutting through the stillness like a blade.

Loose strands of blonde hair framed her bruised face, the braid she'd worn tucked into itself now frizzed and battered. Fair skin was streaked with sweat and crusted blood, purple bruises and shallow slices already stitching themselves closed. I bit back the retort *look who's talking*.

After several painful, *unsuccessful* attempts to force my magic to rally, I'd retreated here—her study—when Alastair refused to keep pummeling me. The overgrown paperweight had unceremoniously thrown me over his shoulder, dumped me in the foyer, and taken up residence at the dining table with tea and a twin-worthy scowl. I'd staggered to the kitchen for coffee, water, and whatever would numb my aching pride before taking refuge in Reyna's office.

Now, as she surveyed my wrecked face, her gaze slid to the offerings laid neatly across her desk.

"And *what* are you doing in *my* office?"

"Sparring," I muttered through a jaw that felt like it was still rearranging itself. Fucking broken ascension. Fucking Adrastos. "And delivering your order, Commander." She narrowed her eyes at me. "Mission go poorly?"

"No," she bit out. The tone said otherwise.

"Anything I can do?"

"I have an entire wing full of rescues, Miss Porter. I don't have time for you today."

I blinked. "A wing full of..."

"Rescues," she repeated, enunciating with deliberate disdain.

"Here?" My voice pitched higher. What kind of stronghold just *opens its gates to* strangers? *Traumatized* ones?

"Where would you suggest I take them?" she snapped. "The mortal governments don't lift a damn finger to protect their own."

"I just—uh..." I tried to roll my lip between my teeth and immediately winced. *Right. Split lip.* Alastair.

"How can I help?"

"You can get your ass out of my chair and your trash off my desk so I can attend to what matters. Our personal matters can wait."

The finality in her tone slammed into me like a slap. Throat tight, I nodded and reached forward to gather my things.

"Leave them," she barked.

"What? You just said—"

"I know what I said. Leave them. I'll review what you brought later. Right now, I need to scrub the atrocities I just witnessed out of my mind and call in every favor I have to get those mortals placed somewhere safe."

"...Can I help?"

She studied me for a beat. "Can you mend? Manipulate memories?"

"I can heal the basics. Broken bones. Surface injuries. No mentalist abilities."

After another hard stare, she gave a curt nod and pointed to the door.

Feeling smaller than I had in lifetimes, I slipped into the hallway, following the muted chaos toward the west wing.

And stopped dead.

My hand flew to my mouth, stifling a gasp as horror rooted in my gut. *Children.*

The wing was filled with children—dozens of them. Most hid behind the Bellaton souls tending to them, their eyes empty and glassy, staring straight through the world. That haunted, hollow stare only came from the worst kinds of trauma.

Bellaton souls knelt, murmured, tended. Some kids cried. Some spoke. The older ones described injuries, relayed needs. Others tried to give orders on behalf of the younger ones who couldn't speak for themselves.

Blaz appeared beside me, calm and composed, diving into the scene without hesitation. I blinked away the sting in my eyes and followed.

And as I moved among them—seeing their faces, their wounds, their silence—I felt it.

Shame. Soul-deep and burning. First for the selfishness I'd been drowning in. Then again for my uselessness.

I'd been worried about politics, alliances, and whether Reyna respected me.

And she'd been *rescuing children.*

Then I saw Darius.

He moved quickly through the hall, focus sharp, face grim.

I rushed to him. "Tell me what to do."

He halted, his scowl sliding into confusion. "Did you have a stroke?"

"I'm serious. Tell me how to help. What to do."

"Didn't think I'd ever hear that from your mouth."

"Darius—" my voice cracked, "—I'm serious."

He watched me, the tension between us shifting. "Okay," he said finally. "We need clothes. Someone has to run into town—sizes and needs are here." He handed me a scrap of paper. "We also need tea. Chicken broth. Many were starved as punishment. If they eat solids, they'll purge. Can you handle that?"

"Yes," I said, voice hoarse. "Call me if anything changes."

With a single nod, he turned and slipped beyond the hallway—into shadows, into motion.

When I whirled to head out, Alastair was already waiting. Hand outstretched. Ready to jump.

***

IT WASN'T until late evening—after the victims had been tallied, clothes distributed, healers rotated through, and children tucked into warm beds— that a heavy hush finally fell across the estate.

A haunted silence clung to the walls, trailing after the Bellaton souls as they drifted away in pairs and trios, worn from triage and sorrow. The new watch rotated in, shoulders tight with responsibility. I spotted Reyna retreating from the fray, her posture regal despite the exhaustion carved into her movements. She was pulling pins from her braid as I caught up on silent feet, her long hair falling free around her shoulders.

She was sucking in a breath—tight and pained—when I reached her side.

She flinched, catching sight of me. The moment of relief that flickered across her face quickly vanished behind a glare.

"*What?*"

"I want to help."

"You did," she said curtly.

"*More.* I want to help more."

Those disapproving blue eyes swept over me—bloodied cheekbone, stiff posture, jaw still tender from being rearranged—and she sighed.

"Your magic hasn't even finished knitting your skin together. You've done all your gifts will allow you to."

"I don't just mean tonight."

Her brow twitched. "What *do* you mean?"

"When I've properly ascended...I'd like to help the children."

"When this is all over, you'll be back beside your Commander, ferrying souls between realms," she said flatly. Just facts. But my heart sank anyway.

"Right. But when I'm not...on assignment. When I'm not needed by Aren or called into something with Ally—I want to help. Here."

She studied me for a long, unreadable moment, then turned and resumed walking toward the owner's suite. I fell into step beside her.

"Can I ask you a question?"

"If I say no, won't you ask anyway?"

"Probably," I admitted, keeping pace. "Why here?"

"They need somewhere to sleep. Somewhere safe to heal. And I'm not handing them over to the incompetent hands of mortal systems when I can care for them myself."

"Sure, I get that. I meant—why *here?*" I gestured around us. "This place. Surely the irony isn't lost on you. Frankly, it gives me the creeps."

"The irony," she said without turning, "is exactly why I'm here."

The Greeks had hinted as much, but I needed to hear it from her. I wanted a crack in the armor. A reason behind the woman everyone feared. I wanted to understand.

"Explain."

She stopped so abruptly, her hair whipped around her shoulders as she turned on me, expression cool and blazing all at once.

"I don't owe you that."

"No, you don't," I agreed, holding her fiery gaze. "But I'm asking anyway."

Her jaw flexed. For a long moment, I thought she might just walk away.

Instead, she said, "My first life in the Americas was spent on this very plantation—serving a master more animal than man. My parents bartered their way here from Ireland, hoping the new world would treat us better than the old. But the terms of their servitude...kept extending. A dropped plate. A doctor's visit. Convenient debts."

She looked away, voice still calm. Almost clinical. But rage sparked behind her eyes.

"He took a particular interest in me when I was young. Raped and beat me through my teenage years. Then he caught me trying to flee."

My stomach twisted. I couldn't breathe.

"That monster beat me to death in the yard beneath the mossy oak. I was too young to ascend. I bled out before anyone found me."

Her tone was flat, but her eyes were flint. Controlled. Burning.

"When I recirculated, less than thirty years had passed. That cruel bastard still drew breath when I found my way back here, but his wife had died. So I used the vessel I was born into to do what it was clearly designed to."

She turned her gaze out the window, distant now.

"I seduced him. Slowly. Carefully. Preserving my honor. And when we finally stole a moment alone—scandalous, of course—I slit his throat with a letter opener he'd gifted me."

I swallowed. Hard.

"I generally prefer cleaner methods. But his blood on my hands? That gave me closure."

She straightened, spine aligning as though bracing against memory. Her hands clasped neatly in front of her. Somewhere in the distance, a bird called. Otherwise, the estate held its breath. My heart, too.

"From there, I turned my efforts to freeing as many souls as I could. Evil only holds the power *we* lend it. So, I took his life. Then—with Bellaton's help—I took his land. And since then, I've made a mockery of his legacy. This place? This house? It's freed a hundredfold more than he ever had the right to harm."

My mouth opened and closed twice.

There were no right words.

Then a sliver of a smile—sharp and dry—ghosted across her lips.

"I recognized a past-life vendetta, Miss Porter," she said. "Because I'm still living mine."

THIRTEEN
OLD HISTORY
AUGUST

Alvara spilled out everything we knew—and more pressingly, everything we *didn't*—about what was coming for the world. A hefty silence settled over the four of us as we finished our plates, still gathered around Kingsley's too-small table.

He shook his head, rubbing his thumb and forefinger across his brow. Rosaleigh watched him warily, her lips pressed into a flat line.

With a sigh, Kingsley looked up at Ally. His expression was far from hopeful. "Quite the mess, Alvara. I can't see the way out either."

Ally's eyes weren't glazed with the other—but they weren't entirely present, either. She was looking through Kingsley, scouring his impressions, thoughts, emotional residue. I hadn't realized seers were that common—I just knew Ally was the best. And now, watching her read Kingsley, it was clear how vivid her visions really were.

Kingsley's gift was more like static on a broken signal—snippets of imagery, sudden flares of emotion: fear, fury, retribution. It reminded me of the weeks we'd just endured. Sharp, disjointed. Survive now, make sense of it later.

For a moment, Kingsley studied her face with a look that reminded me —uncannily—of Ansel.

The permanent scowl. The jaw carved from stone. The eyes tight with concern, even when the rest of the world mistook him for unfeeling.

A pang caught me off guard.

I missed the grumpy bastard.

Kingsley's gaze shifted to me. His scowl deepened when he caught the smirk on my face, and I laughed.

"Something funny, Mr. Porter?"

"You remind me of someone."

"*Someone?*" he echoed, arching a brow.

I shot Ally a look, and she mirrored my amusement. "You ever met Ansel Callahan?"

His eyes narrowed, then relaxed, the right corner of his mouth tugging upward. He glanced at Alvara, grin spreading, then chuckled.

"I like him," Kingsley declared, turning to Rosaleigh. "Babe, did you hear that? The great King Calloway says I'm like Grayshell's Old General."

They all laughed—the kind that says there's an inside joke I'll never be in on. Being the rookie in a circle of ancients was getting old fast.

"The General and I go way back, kid." Kingsley lifted his brows. "Insufferable old ass, but one hell of a fighter. Better man to have at your back."

"He's pulled through for us this year," I offered.

"And he'll keep doing it as long as there's air in his lungs. How's he healing?"

"Almost back to himself when we left. Would've been one-hundred percent if we could've made it home."

"I didn't think about him healing on earth time."

"Marcus took him to Westerlund to see if the magic there could help."

Kingsley nodded. "It should. But nothing restores us quite like the home realm."

"How's Lana holding up?" Rosaleigh asked softly. Her voice cracked, just a bit.

"She's alright," Ally said gently. "She hasn't left his side. But Freya's ascension brought them hope."

"Good," Rosaleigh breathed, her shoulders loosening. "They've been through so much, those two."

Her eyes shimmered, and I sent a private thought to Ally.

What am I missing?

Old history, she sent. *I'll fill you in later.*

Kingsley cleared his throat, snapping us back.

"Alright. Enough gossip." He leaned back, an ankle over a knee. I mirrored him, arm slipping around Ally's shoulders as she leaned into me.

She'd been quiet since training, sheepish after losing her cool. I felt the same anger, the same fear burrowing into my marrow. *I get it,* I sent down the line.

She nodded, small but sure.

Kingsley sighed. "Step one—you need to learn how to navigate your Soul Bond. My guess is, your gifts are mutating because of how you draw off each other. Rosaleigh and I are happy to share what we've learned. But we're all we've got. No other pairs like us that we know of."

We nodded in thanks. Ally had known he'd help, but it still felt good to hear it out loud.

"And frankly, I'm offended there was *ever* a question about which side we'd stand on. Whatever's going on between you and Adrastos, or his keeper—that's your business. But Terramyst's neutrality ends where innocent blood spills. *Of course* we'll stand between the Horsemen and the mortals."

He rolled his eyes, and I couldn't help but chuckle.

Kingsley squinted at me. His lips *almost* twitched.

"And what the hell is your Commander doing chasing a mystery book and a *crown?*"

"He trusts my foresight," Ally said. "He's where I need him to be."

I caught the tiny, nervous hitch in her smile. Reached out, brushed my thumb over her cheek—then over the smooth skin where I'd split her lip earlier.

Mate. Aren had a mate. I couldn't help wondering if it was *her* thread that sent him on that mission.

Kingsley continued, unfazed. "Back to the Bond. Until we break whatever's binding your visions, we work with what we've got—which is you. You were channeling power through each other before you even understood what you were doing. That tells me you'll pick it up fast."

He jerked his chin at Rosaleigh.

She stood gracefully, backing toward the hallway she'd emerged from. Her sweater sleeves rolled up, gold-stacked earrings catching the light.

"Think of it like catch. But with elements," she said with a wink. Water spiraled above her hands in shimmering coils.

"Kingsley's an air elemental. I'm water." She twisted her hands, steam curling into a glowing sphere. With a toss, it arced toward him.

Kingsley caught it with a burst of wind, his magic shaping the water like thread between his fingers. It climbed up his arms in elegant spirals, never soaking him—just dancing.

I grinned. Our coven played element games too, but this? This was *art*.

They don't have all four elements? I asked.

Most can wield earth. Beyond that, or shifting, second affinities are rare.

Do they jump?

Short distances. In battle. But they rely on mortal transport. Now, focus, baby.

Kingsley went on, eyes still on Rosaleigh.

"Magic is alive. It *lives* in the body, in the blood—as much as it does in the world. Too much, and it drains us like a parasite. Too little, and we're mortal. Just enough?" He smiled. "And you can do things you've never even dreamed of. Your Bond should speak for itself. Magic should *listen* to you. Between you two? It'll speak fluently."

He glanced back at us. "I assume you haven't been able to keep your hands off each other."

Rosaleigh laughed and settled herself on his lap, energy between them thick and humming.

I stared. So did Ally.

So that's what nauseating *looks like.*

"We're definitely in the honeymoon stage," Ally said cheerfully, not the least bit shy.

"If you keep connecting," Rosaleigh said, trailing her fingers down Kingsley's neck, "there doesn't have to be a *stage*. Mates are a gift—common, yes. But nothing's more precious. Your intimacy—it'll build your power faster than anything else."

Well. No complaints there.

See? Told you we could do both.

Ally's grin widened. *I'm inclined to test your theory.*

Don't have to tell me twice.

Kingsley's voice cut through the haze.

"To be Soul Bound is nearly unheard of." His expression turned serious. "You should be able to lend each other strength when one of you's depleted. Yes, if one dies, the other will follow—but to kill a Soul Bound mate, you have to deplete *both*. That kind of power's hard to match."

That...that was useful. *Very* useful.

"Can you show us?"

His eyes gleamed. "Gladly."

He patted Rosaleigh's lap. They both stood. Ally and I followed.

She froze mid-step, eyes distant for a heartbeat before she grinned.

"Clever, Aren."

"What?" I whispered, lacing our fingers as we followed them outside.

"He's just making rapid-fire decisions without intent to follow," Alvara explained, shaking her head.

"*What?*"

"Triggering visions—testing outcomes, seeing what sticks. One way to save time, I guess."

I chuckled, nodding. She pulled out her phone and started tapping rapid-fire messages while Kingsley and Rosaleigh led the way. I placed my hand at the small of her back to keep her focused as we stepped into the bitter air.

The cold hit like a wall—sharp and skin-stinging, the kind of cold that forced you to be *present*. As we crunched out into the snow-blanketed field,

I turned over what little we'd gathered about Soul Bonds, magic, and the rapidly escalating threat none of us could fully see.

Kingsley finally stopped. Rosaleigh clung to his arm, looking up at him with that starry-eyed affection only a mate could wear.

"For the sake of time," Kingsley said, "we'll start with Rose as your single target. Her power reserve's shallower than mine, so it'll deplete faster."

I didn't love the way he presented her—as if she were a soft, expendable resource. But Alvara seemed unfazed. Rosaleigh nodded, kissed his cheek, and sashayed a dozen paces into the snow, popping her neck as she turned to face us.

"When you're ready," she called sweetly.

In response, fire licked down Alvara's arms, the crackling heat almost lost in the hush of falling snow.

We're supposed to attack her? I asked mind-to-mind.

It's just a game, August. Can you sense her gifts?

I closed my eyes. Focused.

And...nothing. She felt *human*. No echo of soul-bound gravity, no immortal burn. Unlike Alvara—or Aren—who radiated power like their blood hummed with it, Rosaleigh read as utterly ordinary.

Maybe that was Kingsley's advantage. Maybe his people stayed hidden because they *could*.

So, Ally thought, *we empty her well. He wants to show us how to fill it.*

No further instruction needed. We split, circling her as we launched attacks in tandem—fire, air, water. She dodged and deflected with almost bored precision.

Three minutes in, she finally huffed, "Come on, Porters. Is that all you've got?"

Laughing, Ally spun both palms forward, releasing a flaming cyclone toward Rosaleigh's chest. The woman grinned.

It was there, in the far northern snow, that I decided all ascended females were mad.

With a press of her dainty hand through the air, Rose swallowed Ally's fire with a wide-armed sweep that conjured a wall of snow to smother the attack. Water melted in a wave that splashed over our boots.

Icy cold bit through my shoes. Gritting my teeth, I launched a second wave of water, and watched as she wove it seamlessly into her own defenses.

It went on for the better part of an hour. Back and forth, dancing on ice and flame and air. Eventually, I noticed her forms losing sharpness—her smile slipping. Sweat beaded across her brow.

Ally saw it too. Her flames vanished. She rotated a blast of wind that knocked Rosaleigh clean on her ass.

I was winded. Ally was flushed, breath hitching. But we'd barely dented our wells.

Ansel had been right. Grayshell called the strongest to its ranks. Power *drew* power, and Aren was the flame every storm surged toward.

As Rosaleigh scrambled to her feet, magic flickering at her fingertips, she grinned. "Took you long enough."

"I'm fucking frozen," Kingsley grumbled, rising from his perch on a snow-dusted tree stump.

"Serves you right," Rose shot back, then flicked her gaze to me. "Give me what you got, Commander."

Ally's nod sent me forward.

I hurled power—raw, intentional. Rosaleigh braced herself, arms wide. Wind whipped through the clearing, tugging hair and cloaks and every stray piece of energy not nailed down.

The faster I hit her, the harder the current roared between her and Kingsley. The connection wasn't visible, exactly—but you *felt* it. The thread snapping tight between them.

She kept pulling long after I stopped. Eyes closed, breath deep. Power sluiced between them until droplets rose into the air, suspended like diamonds in moonlight. They hung weightless, shimmering.

Rosaleigh opened her eyes. Smiled. Soft and full.

"For souls like you," Kingsley said into the stunned quiet, "with reserves as deep as yours, you could volley your strength between you for days without ever hitting bottom."

The snow glittered like starlight. His gaze cut to Alvara.

"Short of leveling a city," he added with pointed sharpness, "taking out the Great Commander would require an unholy effort. I know it feels like a vulnerability—but done right? This Bond is your greatest strength."

I felt Alvara's energy shift before I saw her face. Her shield didn't drop, but mine did.

Her eyes fixed on a point beyond us—staring through snow into the other. Visions stuttered, flashing like strobes. *Bloodied wolves in a clearing. A woman with black hair on her knees, trembling hands lifted in surrender.*

A man in a leather demon mask stepped forward.

Her throat was slit.

And then—those five cursed words. Always the same, always with that same gravel-choked voice like fire eating through silk.

Hurry up, El. They're coming.

FOURTEEN

COUSINS

ALVARA

My horrified eyes flew to Kingsley, who stood utterly still, gaze fixed on the snow-blurred distance.

"Where?" he breathed.

"A clearing in the woods. They were dying mid-shift."

"There was a woman," August added immediately. "Black hair. Kneeling in the snow."

"Sandpoint safe house," Rosaleigh whispered, eyes wide, flicking between us.

"We can jump you in if you show me where," I said, hand already extended.

Without hesitation, Kingsley grabbed it. The layout and coordinates rushed from his mind to mine. August and Rose fell into formation, each clasping on as we turned back-to-back, power flaring and locking like gears.

Together, we jumped.

Relief slammed into me with the same force as the cold. No screams. Not yet. For the first time in months, a vision had hit early enough to make a difference.

They're coming, Adrastos' voice echoed in my memory.

I scanned the clearing as darkness fell around us like a curtain. Stark trees jutted from the earth, skeletal and watchful. To the east stood a two-story stone cabin, windows glowing, smoke curling from the chimney.

"What are we up against?" Kingsley asked.

"I don't know," I admitted, shaking my head. "From the bodies? Nothing I'd want to fight alone. Can we evacuate?"

"This is where we keep the wounded," Rose said, her voice breaking.

"*Healers*," August growled. *Fucking hell.*

Yeah, I agreed. Aloud, I asked, "How many?"

"At least two dozen last I checked."

"Mortals?"

"A few souls. Mostly braids. Some humans."

"Too many to jump out?"

Kingsley's grim nod was all the answer I needed.

"So, we fight," I said, lifting my chin.

"I'd expect nothing less," August replied, rolling off his jacket, scanning the woods. He turned to Kingsley. "Got somewhere to take the worst off?"

Another nod.

"Then go. Do what you do best. We'll do the same."

The stone-set king locked eyes with my mate for a long beat, then gave a final dip of his chin, grabbed Rosaleigh's hand, and vanished.

"Certainly not the group activity I had in mind," I muttered.

"You have *got* to stop suggesting that," August teased, sleeves already rolled.

Despite myself, I grinned. "And what if I told you that *is* my thing?"

He scoffed. "Only boys share. Men keep what's theirs."

"Mmm. Kingsley's pretty appealing." I stripped off my hoodie, scanning the woods as energy crackled through the air. "Might be fun to fill our tanks together after."

"Don't make me remind you who you belong to," August growled, yanking me into a kiss that shut me up in the best possible way.

"You know I love a challenge," I whispered against his lips.

He pulled back with an exasperated huff a beat before a howl split the distance. "Thinking that's a good thing right about now," he muttered as a half-dozen deer bolted through the clearing, eyes wide, heading for the cabin. "Kingsley have any fighters?" he asked, tracking their path.

"Plenty."

"Where are they?"

I reached into the other and scanned the threads. "He's sending them— or he's about to."

"Can we call backup?"

I already knew the answer. "Aren and the Callahans are with the healers. The Carters are on Westerlund defense. Freya and the Greeks are engaged."

The sharp, warbled howl of a blood wolf cut the air.

"We're severely outnumbered."

"Great," August deadpanned.

"They're not alone."

"*Of course* they're not."

"Something...stronger, lurks with them."

"Yep," he said, popping the 'p'.

Shadows moved at the edge of the trees. I caught flashes from their minds—crawlers skittering low, tormentors slinking behind. And then—

My stomach bottomed out, heart going with it.

A crowned demon. *The* crowned demon. The same from the hospital—Aren, bleeding out on a poison-drenched blade. That flickering hallway.

"A crowned demon," I whispered.

"Like the one that—"

"*Yep.*"

August blew out a breath as thunder rumbled above us, the sky darkening by the second. "Let's roll, baby."

"Give 'em hell."

More howls. Twigs cracked under clawed feet.

"Follow my lead."

August scoffed but nodded. "Learned my lesson. I'll always bet on you, my love."

Those words sank into me like fire into flesh. If they were the last I ever heard, it'd all be worth it.

I turned and struck—blade flashing—an enormous head severed with a spray of blood. I slipped into battlefield calm, instincts syncing with August's. We moved like one, choreographed chaos in perfect rhythm.

A blood wolf barreled toward us, jaws gaping. I threw up a wall of fire, singeing fur, scorching flesh, incinerating the crawlers beneath it in a single blast. Thunder cracked. Lightning followed.

The beast shrieked, crashing to the earth as gore flew like shrapnel around us. A bolt of lightning speared between demons, sending them flying in the same moment I lowered my blade with a satisfying squelch into bone. It shrieked—inhuman, horrible as always. Claws swung wide and I ducked just in time, teeth bared.

Pried my weapon free. Swung again, this time successfully severing the thick spine. I threw my other hand out, blocking a swarm of crawlers that surged for my open flank.

"Ally," August warned.

I turned—followed his eyes.

A blood wolf had slipped past me, headed straight for the house. "On it!"

I jumped, landing between it and the cabin. Its eyes—black and empty—fixed on me, and another lightning volley tore open the sky, scorching treetops.

God, I love that man.

I threw fire and the wolf rolled. Smart bastard. It came again, faster this time, but I missed the neck. *Again.* It was watching. *Learning.*

Kingsley's energy flared with another jump. He was still evacuating.

But my focus was on the beast's snapping maw, drool flying, as a deep growl rumbled from its chest. Another boom overhead sent it lunging. I spun, dodged, and hurled more flames before a scream brought me up short. Human.

Rage snapped through me, and I jumped, coming down on its spine, my sword plunging deep. Black blood fountained as I hacked, again and again, until its head dropped to the ground.

Lightning flashed as more demons surged. As I torched the treeline with fire, I knew it wasn't enough—*we* weren't enough. The crashing of their footsteps was nearly as overpowering as August's livid storm. I could light up the forest, but this was Kingsley's *home*. His people still inside these woods in their shifted forms, requiring precision.

Crack-crack-crack—August's lightning rained down. Some strikes hit true, while other bolts went rogue. Movement to my left. Six humans running for the woods. *No*—

A surge of energy pulled from the same direction, this one dark around the edges, sending my heart hammering as panic wrapped around my windpipe. Crawlers were tracking them.

"*No!*" I screamed, reaching for August—but slammed into his impenetrable shield. My mind lashed out in desperation as lightning fell. A dozen demons—instantly gone...

Along with two humans.

My heart shattered and I reached for the quiet space—where time stopped. Where it was just us. Nothing. Just blood.

Horror curdled my stomach at the sight of burned flesh—that mishap would haunt my mate.

But *nothing* could be more horrifying than the rapid jerk of their scorched limbs as the mangled bodies rose from death.

AUGUST

"Alvara!" I bellowed, her scream slicing through the chaos. A darkness rolled down the mountainside like a dam bursting—heavy and suffocating. The trees seemed to bow beneath it. Terror slammed into our Bond, and I jumped without thinking, tearing through the air toward the cabin.

We'd shared a thousand emotions over the past few weeks, but *never* *terror*. Not from her.

When my boots hit the ground, thunder still growling above us, I didn't know where to look first.

At Alvara, locked in a vicious dance of blue fire, arms flung like wings.

At the fleeing humans, barely ahead of the pack.

Or at the charred bodies with skin split open, twitching like puppets on tangled strings. Bloody. Burnt. Moving in jerky, bone-wrong ways.

Humans and blood wolves alike.

What. The. Fuck.

The corpses won. My stomach churned as their ragged limbs began to move more fluidly, smoother, more purposeful, as if the puppeteer had mastered the marionette. I jumped between them and Ally—ready to defend—but froze.

They passed us.

Not *toward* us.

Past us.

Ally's hand slid into mine, her fire flickering out as we watched in horrified silence. Demon bodies twitched across the snow, rising like insects from rot. Crawlers. Wolves. Many of them headless. Onyx blood wept from the stumps.

"What in the fuck is happening?" I growled, lightning crawling under my skin.

"Necromancer," Ally breathed.

We didn't speak. We *moved*—split and jumped to the humans, gathering them two by two, depositing them inside.

Necromancer. The word stuck in my throat. By the time we reunited, an eerie green mist curled between the trees, thick and wrong. The few remaining demons screeched and scattered.

Gooseflesh prickled my skin. The power in the mist—it didn't just move. It *pulled.*

"Flesh puppets," Ally said, her voice strained. Her fingers gripped mine as her eyes raked the woods. The mist touched the animated corpses, and one by one, they dropped. Barely audible, Ally whispered, "Where are you?"

And like an answer, a man stepped from the trees. He strolled—*strolled* —through the carnage, flipping a charred crawler with the toe of his absurdly polished black loafer. The forest itself bent around him, like it recognized what walked within it.

"Oh, fuck," Ally muttered, eyes locked.

That...was not a good sign. "Ally?"

She tightened her grip, and I felt her shift—subtly, instinctively trying to pull me behind her.

Absolutely not. I stepped shoulder to shoulder with her, anchoring us and reaching for my power. Lightning split the sky, bolts forming a burning circle around him. He halted, eyes flicking to the electric cage.

He was beautiful in that ethereal, ghost-pale way of old souls—ice blond, hollow-cheeked, with eyes like glowing turquoise glass. Alec's age, maybe.

"Who are you?" I demanded, barely keeping my instinct to shield her in check.

"What ever happened to *hello*?" he said casually, a thick Scottish accent curling his words.

I glanced at the nearest body. Human. A woman, face frozen mid-scream, charred beyond recognition. Her burned hand still twitched where he'd dropped it.

"*Hello*," Ally said coolly, her jaw clenching.

I gave her fingers a squeeze. *Who the hell is he? Are we fighting or talking?*

Talking, I guess.

You guess? Ally didn't guess.

I can't read the minds of the undead.

The what?

Necromancers. I can't read *necromancers.*

A jolt of something—understanding tangled with dread—tightened in my gut.

His puppets had *defended* us, not attacked. And in Ally's world, that was enough reason to *talk first.*

"Now," I said, "who the fuck are you?"

Thunder rumbled overhead. He glanced skyward, annoyed.

"If I don't answer, are you planning to fry me like these poor sods?" He nudged the body at his feet with visible distaste. My gut twisted. Human. *I killed a human.*

Ally must've sensed the dread icing over my chest because she lifted her chin.

"I am Alvara, of Grayshell. This is my mate, August."

"Oh, I'm well acquainted with you both." His serpent's smile spread. "We had a rather inconvenient run-in with your masked *cousin*—two blades, big promises. I came to investigate if his stories held weight."

Ally tilted her head. "What stories were those?"

"That the Seer of the North was bonded to the messiah of the damned." A rueful smile curled his lips as he added, "A lightning wielder called *August Porter*. Honestly? Sounded like bullshit. No one's seen lightning since the great King Calloway."

He bent, lifting the woman's scorched hand with two fingers—still wearing a tailored pinstriped suit. Emerald tie. Pocket square. Like a demon walked out of a boardroom.

"But this…" he said, letting her hand fall, "this is worth a conversation."

"You know us," Ally said flatly. "We still don't know you."

"Frustrating, little seer?" he said, eyes narrowing in amusement. "*He* couldn't read me either, if it means anything, and the bastard is ancient."

Ally didn't blink.

"Well?" I pressed.

He sighed. "Kade. King of—"

"The Necromancers," Ally cut in. "Yes. You certainly made an entrance."

Kade shrugged. "Seemed prudent to expedite the slaughter so we could discuss bigger issues."

Howls echoed from the treeline, and Kade flicked his eyes to the sound —then stepped forward, misting into shadow.

He reappeared right beside us. I didn't move. Neither did Ally.

"You are just as magnificent of a specimen as he promised you would be. As are you." Those nearly-turquoise eyes flicked between us. "While our cousin's pitch was…compelling, I'm not eager to lay waste to this realm for his ambitions. This is my home. And as you are the weapon he most craves, I believe we could come to an understanding."

"I'm not eager to ally with necromantic black magic," Ally snapped.

"And that bias is what he's counting on for your destruction, little seer." When he reached toward his chest, our blades snapped up in unison.

He stilled. "Just grabbing my card," he said mildly. "Don't skewer me— I'm not into that kind of foreplay."

Still holding position, he retrieved a sleek black business card and extended it between two fingers. Ally didn't move, so I took it.

Kade's smile widened. "Glad to see not all of Grayshell is allergic to diplomacy."

I glanced at the card. *Psychic Readings*, embossed in emerald foil.

Kade caught my raised brow. "Even kings need day jobs. Burn it if you want to talk—or if you're in a pinch. I'm usually quick to respond."

Howls rose again. Footsteps thundered downslope. Kade's expression finally faltered—shoulders tensing.

"With the utmost respect," he said, nodding once, "I'll take my leave."

Then he vanished, just as dozens of wolves descended on our killing field. Their coats glimmering like silver silk. Eyes sharp. *Massive.* They fanned out across the blood-soaked snow, standing tall as men. Watching.

Waiting.

FIFTEEN
SOLSKIVALL
ALVARA

The largest wolf in the pack skidded to a halt in front of me, mud and dirt spraying as it snapped its massive jaws. Saliva splattered across my cheek.

"*Hey!*" August roared, flinging out a shield that slammed the alpha back.

Before he could step in front of me, the wolf's form twisted mid-snarling leap—and in the next breath, Kingsley stood there, blood-soaked, demon gore streaked across his bare skin, and murder in his eyes.

"You let him go?!" he bellowed, voice raw with disbelief.

I nodded once, breath catching.

"Back off," August warned, stepping between us and giving Kingsley a shove. The King of Terramyst stumbled, then turned on him, jabbing a finger into August's chest.

"The King of the Dead is forbidden in my territory, you insolent child." He whirled toward me again, veins bulging. August's hand shot out, gripping his throat and yanking him back around.

"*I said* back *off,*" he growled, voice low and cold.

The wolves snarled, teeth bared, circling us. A dozen massive shifters we couldn't afford to antagonize—but would fight, if it meant getting August out alive. Kingsley's fury wasn't just righteous—it was fucking dangerous.

"Kade defended us," I said quickly, eyes scanning for Rosaleigh. I didn't trust the necromancer, but killing an unprovoked ally wasn't in my arsenal.

"Kade?!" Kingsley spat, outraged, hurt flashing across his expression. "*Kade's* people slaughtered the Solskari *for sport!*"

"I know." My hands lifted slowly. The images were seared into my memory—light-wielders cut down, Aren calling me in too late to save them.

"Do you? Do you know what it's like to cleave through the corpse of your brother? To *shred* what should be healed, just so they can't reanimate him and turn him against you?!"

"No." My throat burned. Images of Ansel and Alec blinked behind my eyes. "But I can imagine. And I'm so sorry for your loss. Don't diminish that. We're on the same side here."

"My *side* doesn't let *perpetrators* of genocide walk free, Alvara."

A slick ruby blade. A twist. A body collapsing—brown eyes wide with betrayal.

I swallowed hard, eyes dropping.

"Kade was young. Vulnerable to his king. That doesn't ease the injury, but tonight, he defended your *people*. He protected the safe house."

"The price of his trespassing is his head, per our treaty."

"Yes, well, he asked to meet with us. He's not aligned *with Adrastos.* Cool your anger and consider humanity's survival before your retribution."

Kingsley sneered, but August stepped in—this time with a gentler hand to his shoulder.

"*I see you*, brother," he said. "Let's talk. Tell us what you know. We'll consider it before we make a decision."

A reverent hush fell as an albino doe stepped delicately through the wolves. A moment later, Rosaleigh shimmered into her place, blood-splattered chest heaving. She crossed the space, placed a hand over Kingsley's heart, and leaned up until their foreheads met. After one shared breath, he gave a single curt nod.

The wolves melted into the forest, howls echoing through the trees—long, aching notes soaked in a song of deepest sorrow.

"That could've gone better," August muttered, sliding up beside me.

"Could've gone a hell of a lot worse," I replied, slipping my hand into his as we followed the Thornquists home.

Inside, the hearth fire crackled, flickering over gore-streaked faces. We'd scrubbed the blood from our skin, but no one had changed. No one had spoken until Kingsley broke the silence.

"There was no declaration of war," he said, pacing in front of the river rock fireplace. "They just eviscerated them. No warning. No survivors. Pinebarrow and Carroway came to aid, but the only North American responders were Grayshell, Westerlund, and Bellaton. None of The Six. Not even Hazelharbor."

"Autumn sent healers," Rosaleigh added. "She didn't bother to come herself."

August's eyes met mine—and I saw it register. The scope. The magnitude. Maybe for the first time, he understood what we were up against. We were diplomats. *Aren's voice* in foreign lands. But *he* was the only soul who could walk into nearly every camp on Earth and be received as a friend.

"By the time you all arrived," Kingsley continued, voice cracking, "we'd killed King Khaos. After he slaughtered my brother." He cleared his throat. "Thadius' mate was never found. We assumed she was dead. But she turned up *here*—five thousand miles from home—six years later. Brutalized. Strung up on Reyna's gates as a reminder of what happens to their enemies."

"Jesus Christ," August whispered, paling as he ran a hand down his jaw.

"They'd been friends," Rosaleigh murmured, "Thadius' mate and Bellaton's queen. We thought she was lost...but now..."

"I have to assume my niece died with her. Reyna said there was no sign of the baby. I believed her. I had to."

An heiress. Gone. A child stolen before she could rise to claim the bloodline that was wiped from the Earth.

"An entire Hierarchy," Kingsley said, "one that stood for neutrality—for refuge—obliterated. And no one came."

"We've stayed here ever since," Rosaleigh said softly. "Thirty years. Hidden. Healing."

"Not anymore," I breathed.

Kingsley looked up, eyes sharp.

"There's no hiding this time," I continued, knees drawn to my chest by the hearth. "Tonight proved that."

"No," he agreed. "There's not."

His gaze flicked to the little healer—the woman from my vision. The one who would've died if we hadn't intervened.

"I don't trust him," August said, still turning the black business card between his fingers. "But Kade is not his father. You don't have to speak to him. But shouldn't *we* at least hear what he has to say?"

"The blood of the betrayer flows in his veins," Kingsley snapped. "And you think his words are worth hearing?"

My stomach twisted. Brown eyes. Another life. Another betrayal.

"Our blood doesn't define us," I said quietly. Before he could object, I added, "But I don't expect us to ally with a Hierarchy capable of that, either."

"So what, then?" August asked. "Let that kind of power fall to Adrastos? He used headless corpses to snap necks tonight, Alvara."

"I'm saying we wait. We don't answer his call. We watch where he stands when battle comes. Because sweet words and promises mean nothing when blood is spilling."

Kingsley held my gaze, testing me. Then finally nodded. "I can live with that," he said. "But when shit hits the fan, unless he's standing between you and a blade, I'll be the one to put mine in his spine."

AUGUST

As Rosaleigh silently opened the door, I reached out and tapped Kingsley's shoulder. When his eyes met mine, I asked simply, "A word?"

He gave a curt nod, then leaned to press a kiss to his mate's crown. She nodded once—throat working—and turned to head inside. Alvara's emeralds lingered on my face, sharp with unspoken worry. I offered what I hoped was a reassuring smile.

All is well. I'll be right in. The promise passed mind-to-mind, and the reluctant dip of her chin told me she accepted it—though not without skepticism.

Kingsley led the way down the steps and into the snow, hands sliding into his pockets, breath curling in the air. He didn't speak. Maybe giving me the floor. Maybe choosing his words.

I sidled up beside him, eyes drifting to the moon hanging bright and solemn above us. I let the silence breathe for a moment—cold air in my lungs, pulse still settling.

Then I said, quiet but firm, "I didn't want to undermine you in front of your pack or your mate. But I need you to understand—I'll excuse your poor manners exactly once. That woman back there? She might be Grayshell's Second. She might be Aren's Angel of Death. But first and foremost, she is my mate."

Kingsley didn't flinch. He kept his gaze fixed on the woods.

"Her tolerance for your misdirected anger is infinitely better than mine," I continued. "I get it—we stumbled into a raw wound. But I won't justify disrespect. Not toward her. Not from anyone. You pull a stunt like that again, and you *will not* appreciate the outcome."

His head turned, jaw tight.

"Are you threatening me, Commander Porter?"

The use of the title told me we were at least in the same book, if not on the same page.

"No threats," I said evenly. "Just boundaries." I let the next words settle before I said them, clear and without apology. "She doesn't need protection

—she's more than capable of handling herself. But any working relationship needs rules. And mine is Alvara. I'll fight this war because it's the right thing to do. But if keeping her safe from our enemies means watching the world burn, I'll soak it in gasoline myself."

He tensed, but didn't interrupt.

"She's died in my arms too many times. I won't let it happen again. And you—of all souls—should understand the severity of Bonds like ours. What we'll do when the lines are drawn."

Kingsley's brows pinched tighter, gaze distant, but listening.

"If we're going to stand side by side in this, you will treat her with respect. Especially when there's an audience. And in return, I'll do the same for Rosaleigh. I'll lay down my life before I watch her suffer. I'd hope the sentiment goes both ways."

Silence hung for a beat too long. The pine branches swayed overhead, wind rustling like ghosts through the trees. One of Kingsley's wolves glided between trunks in the distance, silver coat gleaming under the moonlight.

At last, Kingsley nodded. "I believe we understand each other."

Relief washed through me—cool, settling. When I turned to face him, his gaze met mine, solemn and steady.

"I apologize for my lapse in control," he said. "And I'll apologize to Ally, too. We've kept this place hidden for years. To have not one, but two enemies show up within hours of your arrival..." He exhaled sharply. "It doesn't bode well for the weeks ahead."

"No," I agreed. "It doesn't. Healers have been under constant attack in our territory."

He nodded, eyes hard. "Ours as well."

"He's hunting her," I said. "The prophesied witch."

Kingsley nodded. In an unexpected level of candor, he said, "I'm not ready for this."

I laughed—low and bitter, the sound steaming in the cold. "There is no being ready for this."

"ARE YOU ALRIGHT?"

I hadn't heard her approach. After my shower, I'd retreated to the Thornquists' porch, watching the moon climb the sky until clouds swallowed it whole and snow began to fall. The quiet had been a balm. But it was her voice that made me breathe again.

"Yeah," I said, though we both knew it was a lie.

In one night, we'd learned more about our Soul Bond than we'd ever dreamed possible—only to be hurled straight into combat. I'd summoned a storm that turned demons into ash, and in the chaos, two innocents burned too. Mortals I was sworn to protect.

Their screams wouldn't leave me. Nor would the vision of them fleeing, just before the lightning struck.

You are just as magnificent of a specimen as he promised you would be...As you are the weapon he most craves, I believe we could come to an understanding.

Bile rose in my throat. I stared out into the blanket of white, the storm's wreckage hidden beneath it like a mass grave.

"You're replaying the necromancer's words?" she asked softly.

"Like a broken record," I murmured.

"Don't let him in your head, baby." But her voice held that same quiet horror. She didn't need to say it—she'd felt it too.

Ally settled beside me, fingers slipping into the curls at the base of my neck. My eyes fell closed, greedy for the comfort. Her touch was the only steady thing in a world tipping sideways.

And that bias is what he's counting on for your destruction, little seer.

"They could be a terrifying weapon," I said, not even sure if I meant Kade or necromancers in general. My voice sounded detached, like it belonged to someone else.

"They could," she agreed. "But at what cost?"

I leaned back in the rocking chair, the old wood creaking beneath me. "It's different. Hearing all their stories. I can't help but wonder...will we be remembered as heroes? Or murderers?"

Her fingers stilled. "What we did in that war camp..." I shook my head. "Was it really that different from what Kingsley's accusing Kade of?"

"The Solskari weren't a threat," she said quietly. "They brought light—literally. They were entertainers. Artists. Joy incarnate. And they were slaughtered. It's not the same."

"But there's still no victory in war. Only survivors." I looked over at her. "We're painted as monsters just for mourning both sides. And even Adrastos had reasons. Justifications. My first regression was Agincourt—I was a victor there. But I doubt the man who ran me through saw it that way."

Ally's brow furrowed.

"In that life, I took maybe a few dozen. In this one?" I exhaled. "It'll be countless. Those two humans tonight—if your visions are right, they're just the beginning."

She hesitated. "Are you saying...do you think we're on the wrong side?"

Her voice was almost a whisper and I flicked my gaze to hers. "You're telling me his words didn't resonate with you at any point?"

"No," she admitted. "I'm not saying that. But his means are wrong," she added quickly. "Stripping their freedom isn't the answer, August. Protecting them is."

I closed my eyes. "And what of the collateral?"

"The worst part of war," she said. "But inevitable. You think you're alone in wondering if someone innocent died in your wake?"

My hands tightened around the arms of the chair. "I never wanted to be a monster. Not in any life."

Her hand dropped from my neck.

"Is...is that what you think of me?" she asked, voice breaking. "After everything I've done?"

"No." I turned to her in an instant, reaching for her hands, lacing my fingers through hers. "Fuck, Ally. You risked your life for my family. For Freya. I'm not talking about the Renown. I'm talking about humans. Collateral. People who have *no* idea what we are, what's coming."

She searched my face, unsure.

"I've always been the blade in someone else's hand," I said, quieter now. "Enacting the will of mad kings and conquering tyrants. Not once did I want to. And now..." I broke off, pressing her knuckles to my lips. The words came slower, heavier. "Now I come back and everyone's looking at me like some prophesied messiah. Born to bring peace. Damned to shed blood. And all I've ever wanted was to be remembered as The Healer. Not for my lightning. Not for what it destroys. Just for the mercy I might leave behind."

Ally stared at me for a long time. When she finally spoke, her voice was stronger than mine. "Don't confuse weakness with mercy," she said. "You're not destined to be harmless, August. Aren and Marcus—they're the best Commanders in the world. Not because they're *less* dangerous than Adrastos. But because they choose not to wield that danger until it's the last option left." Her fingers tightened around mine. "*Let me* equip you. Let me make you the most dangerous weapon on this planet and *only then* can you show the world what mercy looks like."

I huffed a breath and let my forehead rest against her temple. "You sound like Aren."

She smiled, just a little. "I'll take that as a compliment."

"You'd be better at this than I'll ever be."

"Time will tell. But I'm here. You're not alone."

I nodded, voice rough. "Together?"

"Always."

The wind shifted again. Snow started falling in earnest, dusting the porch in white.

"Dressing for the elements wasn't on my list tonight," I muttered, trying to shake the cold from my bones. Ally pressed against me, warm and solid. Her fingers never letting go.

"I hope Freya's doing better than we are," I said.

But I wasn't sure if I meant it as a joke or a prayer.

SIXTEEN

WHERE THE FUCK IS BACKUP?

FREYA

Five years ago…

I Kicked. Hard. Up, I prayed. Hoping I was moving the right direction, even as the burn in my lungs deepened and everything inside me screamed.

Where the hell were his friends? Why wasn't anyone saying anything?

A noise. A shout. A laugh. Anything to anchor me.

But there was nothing. Just the cold, the dark, and the panic twisting up inside me.

I kicked again, even as my lungs spasmed.

Please. Please.

Finally—finally—I broke the surface. Mountain air sliced through the cold and stabbed down my throat. But instead of filling my lungs, I choked. Water surged up and out, purging itself in ragged coughs that left me wheezing.

Limply, I dragged my arms forward, toward what looked like a strip of white. Sand. Shore, I hoped.

Every breath was a fight. My body shook with adrenaline as I hauled myself through the shallows and collapsed, soaked and trembling, onto the bank.

Where were they? Where the hell was he?

Had someone heard me scream?

The silence beyond my gasping breaths was…wrong.

No music. No splashing. No taunting jeers.

I sat up fast, panting, scanning the water. The dock. The boat. The dark expanse that stretched on forever. I knew that voice. I'd heard him.

"Crew?" *I croaked, then louder—rougher—*"Crew!?"

Nothing.

I was on my feet a heartbeat later, slipping on the wet boards as I sprinted back onto the dock.

"Help!" *I shouted.* "Crew, where are you?!"

He might have been a royal douche canoe, but he couldn't drown. I couldn't let him drown.

This couldn't be happening.

I screamed again, shrill enough that someone should come. Where were his fucking friends?!

No answer.

Panic swelled in my chest, expanding like a storm, rattling the cage of my ribs. I whirled toward the lake, eyes scouring the black water for anything— anything—and then I saw it. A glint of gold. Moonlight on a wristband, maybe. Hair.

I didn't think. I dived.

The cold hit like a freight train all over again. But this time, I was ready.

Powerful strokes brought me to him. "Help!" *My hand closed around fabric, then hair. He was face-down. Floating. Heavy as hell. My lungs spasmed as I turned him over, and the effort dunked me under again.*

When I resurfaced, I screamed, mouth full of water, arms wrapped under his shoulders. "Help!"

But no one came.

Kicking furiously, I dragged him toward shore. My body screamed in protest. He was taller than me—lean and long—but deadweight in the water.

"Come on, damn you," *I growled between gasps.* "Stay with me!"

Ten yards. Then five.

I felt the lake bottom under my feet and staggered upright, dragging his body through the muck and weeds. "Thank fuck."

We hit the sand. I collapsed with him, dropping to my knees and yanking him up by the arms, just enough to clear the waterline. Blood and water streaked his face, painting his features in warped color.

"Crew?" *I slapped his cheeks lightly, then harder, panic rising.* "Come on, kid. Don't do this. Don't fucking do this."

His hair clung to his skin in thick, wet tangles. Blood was gushing from a wound somewhere above his temple, streaming down in rivers.

Footsteps thundered behind me—finally. I didn't look up. Couldn't.

I just pressed my shaking hand to his chest, and screamed again.

"HELP!"

Six weeks before the portals opened...

"HELP!"

I jackknifed out of bed, sweat slicking my skin, exhaustion blurring the numbers on my clock as I blinked into clarity. *Not again.* Reyna had worked me to the bone this week—training, missions, and my own private war against the psychopath who slit my throat. The first of the Paladin trials was still in progress, though incomplete until I earned an audience. The second was shaping up. I'd intercepted three scores this week alone and delivered more drives before Wednesday afternoon than most managed in a month.

But...my hair hadn't even dried from my shower.

Had I imagined it? My body felt like lead. I popped my jaw, then rolled my neck. "What the fuck?"

"Help!"

Shit. That was real.

By the time I hit the hallway, I was already running. Blaz was there, fully dressed down to boots and a jacket, his face pale with alarm. His cold hands caught my arms, steadying us both before we bolted down the stairs together.

And then I heard the scream.

Not the pain of a broken limb or the frantic cry of a training injury. This was something else. *Ripping. Ragged.* The scream of death—or birth. But the voice was male, and I was afraid it was the former.

I'd trained with these people. Freed captives beside them. Cut throats and cracked skulls until every hostage was accounted for. Men. Women. Children.

None of them deserved to feel what that voice was feeling.

Blaz and I took the stairs two at a time, skidding into each other as we hit the landing to find chaos erupting as souls came from all sides. The front door gaped open. Blood streaked the floor. Montague was on his knees in the foyer, cradling a writhing, long-limbed body in his arms. Blood matted dark brown curls to an ashen forehead.

Darius.

No.

"What happened?" Reyna snapped as she swept into view, absurdly regal in a robe rimmed in feathers.

"Renown—attacked us," G gasped. Darius screamed again, clawing at his shirt, the veins in his neck bulging.

"Get it *out!*" he howled, tearing at his own chest.

My stomach lurched. He was peeling away his skin. Screaming like an animal. I'd never heard anything like it.

Guys, where the fuck are you?! I begged down the line. *Please.*

Someone sobbed from the hallway—the kind of grief that only came from love.

"Get him inside!" Reyna barked, throwing open the nearest door. Blaz knelt and scooped Darius into his arms, G at his heels as they hauled him into the healer's room. They threw him onto the table, holding him down as he thrashed, his limbs wild, tears streaking his cheeks.

Reyna summoned scissors and shredded through his shirt. What she revealed beneath turned my blood to ice. His skin bubbled like third-degree burns. His veins were black—spidering out from the gaping hole in his chest like rot.

"What curse or blade was this?" Reyna demanded, eyes wide as she turned to Montague.

"I—I didn't see," G stammered. "I heard gunshots, then screaming, and found him like this."

"Bullets *don't do this*," Reyna muttered, already at the wound, her hands glowing.

Darius arched off the table, screaming.

I couldn't breathe. I couldn't move. My mind begged for someone—anyone—with healing magic. *Where the fuck were the healers?*

"Get me a clairvoyant!" Reyna shouted, throwing Darius onto his side, yanking what remained of his shirt away. "No exit wound," she gasped. Her eyes found mine. "Help me."

"Tell me what to do!" I cried, lunging forward.

"Calm him down."

Calm him down?

I dropped to my knees, cradling his blood-slick face in my hands. "Darius. Focus on me. Right here. I've got you."

"Get it out," he croaked, barely audible.

"We are," I lied. "I'm here. I won't leave you."

His bloodshot eyes flicked between mine, dazed.

"We'll patch you up, alright?"

"I'm scared, Freya," he whispered, voice like paper.

"I know," I said, throat burning. "But you're not alone."

Reyna returned with metal and leather. I offered him the bit and he clamped it between his teeth, shaking.

I felt the moment his energy shifted—the moment he began to fade. Reyna did too.

"No, no, no," she breathed.

"Where I come from," I whispered, "this is just the beginning. Energy doesn't end. In one form or another, we go on." I kissed his forehead, already cooling. "See you again soon, brother."

And then Reyna was moving—desperate—climbing over his body and digging into his chest, trying to root out whatever was killing him. Darius groaned, bucking as Blaz rushed to hold him down.

But then his head dropped, going limp.

"No!" Reyna shrieked. "Stay with me, Darius Alexander! You stay with me!"

She pulled something free. A bullet. But it shimmered with a silvery-blue glow, and every inch of my body froze.

"No," Reyna sobbed, hands glowing, pouring healing magic into him. "No no no no—"

I added my power to hers. Others joined. A desperate, united effort. Still, his skin darkened. Veins blackened. The bullet wound began to decay, like his body was being eaten from the inside out.

"Reyna," I said, my voice hollow.

She didn't stop.

"Reyna!" I grabbed her waist, pulling her back. "You can't touch it. You can't—"

When she shoved forward again, I slapped her. Hard. Her head whipped toward me, stunned.

"It's over," I said, panting. "It's over."

She broke like glass, collapsing into my arms. Sobbed like her world had ended—because it had.

The healer arrived too late.

I gave Darius a Grayshell salute with a shaking hand. "See you again soon, brother. Until we meet again."

HOURS LATER, we stumbled out of the war room with a strategy. Reyna had summoned every leader she'd ever deployed. Brody, Alastair, Ajax—they returned to blood-stained hallways and impossible grief.

We were armed. Prepared.

I was cleaning the chamber on one of the pistols Reyna had pressed into my hand when my phone buzzed.

Damien Westerlund.

"D, tell me you've got something."

"It's not a drug," he said in return in that delicious accent of his. "Not entirely."

I squeezed my eyes shut. "It's a bullet. Isn't it?"

"How the hell did you—?"

"Long story," I cut in, rubbing my forehead with the butt of the gun.

Reyna had already declared open season—on the Renown, and her sister's people. If they'd had any hand in what killed Darius, they'd burn with our enemies. I wouldn't stop her.

"Freya," Damien warned, "I don't know what you've stepped into, but be careful. If I'm reading this correctly—"

"He is!" Jason shouted from the background.

"They've built a bullet laced with Reaper's venom. Pierces shields. Keeps eating once it's in."

"As in...*Agamemnon* kind of reapers?" I clarified.

"One and the same."

I saw that glowing slug again. Fuck, I'd never *unsee* it.

"They've weaponized his magic to debilitate ours."

"Freya, you're freaking me out. Are you—?"

"I'm fine." A lie. One of the worst I'd ever told.

"Should I call Aren?"

"It works," I whispered. "These bullets work."

"Freya—?"

"We lost a good man today." *The first of many*, I didn't say. "Find me another location. And update Ally for me, will you? I'll be...occupied."

I ended the call and powered the phone down before he could call back.

If I hadn't already had enough reason to burn the Paladins to ash, selling souls out to the demons would have sealed it.

Motherfuckers.

SEVENTEEN

LITTLE HISTORIAN

CYRUS

Four screens illuminated my cave of an office when my shadows warned me of an intruder. It wasn't the motherfucking time—or place, for that matter. My parents and Mother's Guardians might bend a diligent knee to human evils, but from where I stood, *the balance* was directly impacted by the ravages of human disease. They'd become a cancer on the planet, destroying anything good or innocent in the process.

Don't get me wrong, I was far from some glittering fucking snowflake, but my respect for my Mother's guidance ended the day she denied my request to send her precious Wings after the lowest kind of parasites— thriving in *our* backyard.

Not impactful to the balance.

Bullshit.

Something intrinsically evil had infected human blood, nesting in their governments and celebrities, and magnified by media manipulation. What was the point of being a tool of balance if I wasn't allowed to define what that meant?

To me, it meant defending the defenseless.

There was no way under the stars my mother could predict if one of those children being preyed on would grow up to be the next Einstein, the next earth-whispering prodigy. Yet she still chose policy over protection.

So yeah, my plate was overfull *before* the Wraith came sniffing after the bin of information sitting beside me. Floppy disks. Fucking *ancient*. It had taken me a week to track down a drive that could read the archaic fossils, and now I was filtering through one file at a time, trying to decipher what she was after. Not even my software could identify a pattern.

The moment my shadows sensed him, the hairs on my arms stood on end. *Power.* Heavy enough to make the air thrum.

I didn't bother hiding the scowl that split my face when I hit the key to pull up a screensaver, closing the files I wasn't ready to share.

"Did I stutter, Princeling?" he drawled as his shadows poured into the office like smoke, crawling up the legs of my desk like ivy.

"I don't have time for company," I bit back, voice mirroring his drawl as my thumb ran over my signet ring. The raven wing etched into the silver soothed me more than I cared to admit.

"I'd offer a trade if I believed you could hold up your end."

"A trade?" I snapped, spinning to glare at him—and nearly doing a double take. The bastard was draped across the armchair in the corner like a ragdoll. His limbs barely fit. One hand pinched his temples like he willed away a migraine.

He was exhausted. I didn't need to see his face to know that.

"Are you or are you not targeting the O'Haires?"

Goosebumps crawled down my spine and I just stared. How the fuck did he know that? But he'd already proven he didn't need to be invited in. Clairvoyant. Disturbingly accurate.

"Are you going to continue pilfering my time contemplating how deep my gifts reach, or make yourself useful and take a target off my list by adding it to yours? Should they survive the next drop, their power will double, maybe triple. I'm offering you a favor. Evil thrives in chaos."

He leaned forward, voice tightening. "In exchange, you finally deliver your side of our prior bargain. Perhaps this time, you'll be capable of following my instructions."

"You didn't tell me she was a *lightning wielder*."

He stilled. Fingers stopped moving. Then, quietly: "She *isn't*. In no life has she ever been."

"Then explain the charred skin on my men from indirect hits."

He vanished in a whisper of shadow, reappearing inches from my face. "Hold still," he said, peeling off his gloves.

"You're not my type."

"Hold. Still."

"Since when do psychics have'ta touch anyone to see shit?"

"Since it *already happened*, halfwit."

With a reluctant sneer, I held out my hand. He took it, muttered something under his breath, and went quiet.

His eyes glazed beneath the mask. Then, softly: "Clever, little Wraith."

"That *little Wraith* turned my men into kabobs."

"*Did they die?* No? Then next time bring more than children. And *she* wasn't alone. Quick thinking on her part."

"There was only one masked intruder..." but I'd been grappling with the fact that we were all alive since the night she chased us through our city streets. He made a motion to continue and I smiled, shaking my head. "We're not alive by chance. It was a smoke show."

"If that conclusion hadn't evaded your pea-sized mind for the better part of the month, I'd congratulate you on reaching it."

Scanning his ridiculous black attire and leather mask, I jabbed, "Halloween was three months ago."

"And yet the O'Haires are still breathing."

"You want her. The girl. The one killing our assets."

"For starters."

"This is a recruitment, then."

"An alliance," he corrected. "One I forged with your mother centuries ago. She tossed me a bone a few decades back. I'm calling in a favor. A mutual enemy is rising. Best to shore up the defenses."

I stared him down. "I don't make oaths to faceless men without names."

"Paris," he offered. "You may call me Paris."

I arched a brow. "And what does my mother call you?"

"Ask her yourself."

As though he had summoned her rather than the other way around, the shadows trembled as the energy shifted, and the looming man across from me straightened. That was his only sign of unease or surprise, however, leading me to believe that even my best shot in the dark was fruitless. I'd done some reading after his first visit—between the ink splayed over those pages and my experience with my father, I had a decent grasp on how a seer worked; the closer someone was to the soul wielding foresight, the more details they would receive. The further disconnected the two were, the less they'd see.

While this alleged *Paris* and I had only had a physical encounter once, he left me with the distinct impression he was no stranger to me, even if I had nothing to go off of for him.

Which meant it was time to delegate. Let someone else handle the security risk. Someone like my cousin—unranked, untitled, and hopefully unseen.

Carr had rolled his eyes when I told him about the masked freak in our manor.

He hadn't said no.

Unfortunately for us, the masked man didn't look the least bit rattled as my office flooded with shadows, closing in a perfectly executed ring.

Carr, Nix, Vesper, Orion, my parents—every Paladin within striking distance—materialized through smoke and shadow, our collective power humming like a war drum. My own darkness coiled tight, winding down my arms in sleek ribbons, ready to strike. Only our heiress remained shielded, locked in a safe house under our uncle's watch.

Paris chuckled under his breath. "Your response time is abysmal."

He raised his hands slowly, deliberately, letting the shadows peel away as he laced his fingers behind his head.

"Freeze!" Nix barked, his power launching forward to bind the man's wrists in place. "Don't fucking move."

"Hello, hatchling," Paris crooned, maddeningly calm. "I only intend to show you I mean no harm."

"Reaching for your weapons hardly reads as peaceful intent," my father replied, the iron in his tone sharp enough to slice bone.

But it was my mother who caught and held my attention—her expression stony, her shadows frozen in midair. And then—

"Hello, Heiress," Paris purred, voice rich with something like reverence. "Or I suppose it's now Queen."

The silence crackled. Slowly, Ma lowered her hands, signaling the rest of us to stand down.

My heart thudded. No mental reprimand followed—not because she didn't disapprove, but because whatever game was being played here, she was already five moves ahead.

Beside her, my father's jaw ticked. He, too, retracted his power, though his expression said it took everything he had not to cleave the masked man in two.

We were yielding.

Paladins didn't yield.

Certainly not to masked intruders in our own house.

"Lonan?" Ma asked, voice cold as obsidian.

"Hello, old friend," he said, like this was a reunion over wine instead of an invasion.

"Forgive the intrusion, hatchlings—I needed your Queen's attention."

"A letter would've worked," Orion muttered, stepping protectively between Ma and the masked man.

"If she'd deigned to respond, perhaps," the intruder countered.

"What happened to *Paris*?" I demanded. The name, the performance, the flair—it was all theatre. I wanted the man behind the façade.

He tilted his head toward me, those shadowed eyes glittering. "Ask yourself that again later, little historian."

Nix's growl vibrated the floor. "Orders, Ma'am?"

"Stand down," Ma said evenly, turning away from the door to face the intruder fully. "We have noble company, Nix. Mind your manners."

My stomach twisted.

Paris followed her into the hallway like a guest invited for tea. "Some things never change," he said lightly.

"And some do," Ma replied, her tone grave. "I'm not used to seeing you alone. How's Leo?"

"Dead."

The single syllable landed like a hammer. Orion froze, and Ma turned sharply, disbelief carved into her face.

"My condolences," she murmured, dipping her chin. Her gaze sharpened to a blade.

"When?"

He didn't answer.

Who the fuck is Leo? I asked down the line.

His brother, Ma replied silently. That was all. No further explanation.

Once we were seated in the private meeting room—gleaming hardwood floors, velvet drapes, expensive distractions—Paris sipped tea like he hadn't just forced our shadows into submission. Ma straightened like a blade beside him.

"Well," she said, the Queen now fully ascendant. "You bring news?"

"War is on the horizon," Lonan replied.

"No shit," I bit out before I could stop myself. "Do you have information, or did you just miss our company?"

"Cyrus," Dad warned, leveling a glare at me. *Read the room.*

"Your son is correct," Lonan said. "*Idiotic* to speak so bluntly when outmatched, but correct."

I curled my fingers into fists while the bastard stirred honey into his tea, utterly unbothered.

"I come with a warning," he continued. "And a proposal."

"Oh, by all means," I muttered. "Do keep us waiting."

Ma didn't react. Neither did the masked man.

"The warning is this: regardless of your current allegiance, The Six are aligning with the revolution."

"Hazelharbor?" Ma asked, mask firmly in place. "I find that hard to believe."

"They'll change hands soon enough."

"But that doesn't tell us where they stand."

"To be determined."

"And Kade?"

"More of the same."

"So, *three* of The Six withhold their support," I said. "Three back the revolution."

The pinch in Dad's brow and set of his jaw had me glancing between him and that damn leather mask, loathing his lack of transparency. Dad was uneasy—a feat rarely accomplished. And he'd been that way for days—buried in his thoughts. "*If* the bounty goes unanswered," my father reminded us.

I blinked. "Bounty?"

"Commander Amadeus issued a public warrant," Lonan explained. "A sketch. A head price. He demands Adrastos' death."

The name sparked something—half-forgotten, just out of reach. Some distant corner of my mind stirred to life, like a shadow within awakening.

I should know that name. I *did* know that name.

But the connection danced just out of reach.

"Who is he?" I asked, leaning forward, shadows pulling tight around my hands.

"No one knows," Dad said. His voice was quieter than usual. Tight.

"If we've learned anything," the intruder added, "it's that Adrastos is only found when he wants to be."

My shadows hissed uneasily.

"But do you know who he is?" I asked, voice low.

He didn't blink. "*Who* isn't the question you should be asking, Princeling."

"What he wants is," Ma finished for him.

Paris, or Lonan, or whoever the fuck the grim messenger was, inclined his head.

"You've come to deliver a warning," she prompted again. "So, deliver it."

He exhaled. "The world has fallen out of alignment. Adrastos seeks to restore it. He proposes a new social hierarchy—one where mortals know we exist. One where we rule openly, as protectors."

The room erupted.

"Impossible—"

"Suicide—"

"Utter madness."

"Blasphemy—"

"Enough!" Ma's shadows snapped like whips, silencing the outbursts, wrapping around mouths and throats with deadly precision. "This chamber holds my confidence. One more interruption and it will empty."

All eyes lowered.

She turned back to Lonan. "Continue."

"He believes we've failed. That mortals suffer beneath our silence. That we owe them better. He proposes dominion with mercy."

"And the cost?" Ma asked quietly.

He smiled behind the mask. "A reckoning."

THE WAR ROOM had dissolved into chaos the moment Lonan uttered the word *reckoning*.

Even the Guard fractured into whispered dissent—some intrigued, others enraged, all too aware that the definition of "balance" was as mutable as the powers who enforced it. My parents, ever the anchor in the storm, sat like carved obsidian, unmoving as they tracked every argument volleyed across the table. My mother eventually raised a single hand, and with that, banished all but her king. No further discussion. No input from her commanders.

She trusted this 'Lonan'.

At least, she trusted him enough to be alone with him and her mate in the same room. And I wasn't sure what unsettled me more—his confidence that we would align with whatever vision he'd brought...or her willingness to entertain it without the counsel of her leaders.

So, instead of stewing in that simmering unease, I returned to where this hell of a night had started: my cave of an office. The disks. The hunt.

Which brought me back to *her*.

Valora E. Lamb.

According to the caption beneath a faded photo, that was her name—caught in a candid, all-too-friendly moment between my mother and father. She stood between them, a lanky woman with short dark hair, pale skin several shades fairer than mine, and a posture that screamed nonchalance. The timestamp on the file matched the tail end of the Solskari war—the last time Aren and my estranged aunt had supposedly reached out to my mother for aid that never came.

There was no record of Valora in any of the sanctioned logs. No death certificate. No burial.

Just a disappearance—like mist in morning sun. A vanishing act worthy of a Wraith.

Any tactician will tell you: enemies become predictable. You learn their rhythms, their angles, their fallback routes. Patterns reveal everything.

But it's the ghosts you fear.

The ones who never follow the pattern. The ones who flicker in and out of view, dancing between bloodshed and silence, a trail of wreckage left behind with no footprint to follow.

And maybe that's why I couldn't stop staring at this image. At her. Valora didn't *look* like a threat. Bootcut jeans, a basic button-down rolled to the elbows—she could've been any Southern girl from a backwater town. But the spark in her eyes, the crooked smirk tugging at one side of her mouth...

That was arrogance.

That was *intention*.

And the more I stared, the more certain I became: she wasn't an extra in some forgotten war story. She *was* the story.

Which meant every soul my mother had just dismissed from that war room could now become an asset. If my instincts were right—if Valora Lamb was who I suspected—then I would need all of them.

Because the only way to trap a ghost...is to stop playing by the rules of the living.

Time to build a snare worthy of a Wraith.

EIGHTEEN

SHARDS

ALVARA

"Remember, El..."

A flash of that war tent—his war tent. That arrogant smirk, slouched behind the desk like he already owned the world. Books stacked beside him. A flash of gold lettering on black leather. I couldn't read the title...

Then: blood. Seeping across black marble...

"No, not yet. Focus, El. Remember. I can't do it for you..."

The book again. Black, leather-bound. Gilded title still unreadable. Then, in his hands—my enemy's—as he marched into Grayshell...

Blood again. Spilling like a waterfall...

"El, stop. Focus. Wake up, please." A voice threaded with panic, desperate. But it was another voice that rose clearer in my mind—

"The only thing more powerful than a leader is a martyr. There is no greater boon to rebellion than the death of the beloved. If we wish to turn the tides of any war, the most revered must fall. Or be perceived as fallen."

So, a trick? A manipulation?

I looked up at my father. His long white hair framed lifted cheeks, a silver crown gleaming above his softened expression. The smile he saved for me, when it was just us.

My heart ached. "But...what of that love?" I asked, voice small. "Can a people survive the loss of it?"

"Where love grew," he said, "grief will follow. But it's in our lowest moments that a people unify."

"And if we want to prevent rebellion?" my brother asked—always the *challenger. His hair hung wild, dark waves refusing to be tamed, just like him.*

"Then you crush it before it begins," Father replied without pause. His gaze hardened. "At the first whisper of dissent. The moment a leader begins to rise, you strike..."

"El, please." This time, the voice was hoarse. Cracked with despair...

Then—white. Blinding, colorless white. Endless and consuming.

I couldn't move. Couldn't breathe. Couldn't think.

My heart pounded against my ribs. Shallow gasps of air barely kept me tethered to the veil...

"I am not a man inclined to begging, but I implore you—don't choose that path again. It might just kill me..."

Mother lifted her hand. But no shadows followed. Only pale, trembling flesh...

"Wait," said the voice—fear now edged into it. Grief braided through the lone word...

"R—Reaper..." she breathed, a broken sob...

"No." Just one word. But it shattered...

Then the mob. Faces blurred by rage, descending from all sides. No sign of my brothers. No allies. No escape. She tucked me behind her, trying to shield me—but it wouldn't matter. Not this time.

They saw us as demons. No mercy. Not for what we were...

And then—him. A man too beautiful to belong in a place like this. Silver-blond hair, bone-pale skin, and eyes like dying stars. Eyes I should know.

I shouldn't be here.

Somewhere in my mind, I knew this was an intrusion. But I couldn't pull free. I was frozen, trying to name him.

Those onyx eyes sliced toward the boy beside him—my brother—face curled in contempt. "Pathetic." That voice—like cold steel dragged through ash. He didn't stop glaring at my brother until—

He turned to me.

The instant his gaze found mine, a cruel smile twisted his perfect mouth.

He closed his fist.

Agony crashed over me.

My legs buckled. Knees cracked into a puddle of heat.

Blood.

I was kneeling in blood.

A chill raced across my spine, and I turned—

August. Chained. Hanging by his wrists, his beautiful body flayed from collar to navel.

Skin peeled in strips, wounds deep and wet. His hands hung limp, twisted at grotesque angles. His feet grazed the blood-slick floor, barely teth-ered to this world. His head slumped forward. He didn't stir.

He was—

No. No, no, no. A scream tore free of me, raw and feral...

"El, wake up!"

With Adrastos' final plea, I jolted upright, gasping for breath, my body wracked by adrenaline as if I'd been dragged through fire. The dirk was already in my hand before reality caught up to me. Heart hammering, I scanned the darkness, my mind still half-trapped in that vision.

"Ally?" August's voice, rough with sleep, grounded me.

I twisted to face him, relief crashing over me like a wave when I saw his groggy form blinking into the dim room. I closed my eyes and inhaled, letting the here and now settle into my bones.

"I'm okay," I said, though the ragged edge of my voice gave me away. August pushed upright, bracing on one arm, and reached to brush my hair from my face, his calloused fingers soothing along my cheek. His curls were tousled from restless sleep, his brow creased with concern.

"I'm right here," he murmured. "You're okay. We're okay."

I nodded, trying to reorient to the present. Kingsley's guest room. The rough-hewn walls. The clean scent of pine and smoke. The silver glow of the winter moon peeking through snow-fogged windows.

I tossed the dirk onto the bedside table with a metallic clatter and pressed the heels of my palms to my eyes, willing the pressure away.

"We need that goddamn book," I muttered.

"Anything on the crown?" August asked gently.

"No." I dropped my hands, resting my elbows on my knees. "I still haven't seen it."

"Okay," he said with that unshakable calm of his, his hand skimming up my calf in slow, grounding strokes. "What do you know?"

"He kept pushing me to focus. On the book, I think." August tensed, jaw locking, but he didn't interrupt. "He had it with him—before—when Agamemnon took me. But I can't remember the title."

"You can't see it in the vision?"

"It's always blurry," I whispered.

"We should tell Aren." August reached for his phone, but the second his hand left my skin, panic surged. That white expanse. The scream. The chains. My hand shot out to catch his wrist.

"Wait," I gasped, voice barely more than a breath.

His eyes snapped back to mine.

"We'll tell him," I vowed quickly. "But please...just stay."

Understanding dawned in his eyes as he set the phone down and gently pulled me into his arms. I melted into the solid comfort of him, his warmth grounding me as his shield slipped beneath my skin, sealing me in the safety of his presence.

My fingers traced the familiar lines of his chest, each rise and fall of his breath a lifeline. His hand slid beneath my shirt, warm and protective over my spine, while the other cradled the back of my head.

"They're coming for us, August," I whispered. "And I don't know how to stop them."

"One step at a time, baby," he said, brushing a kiss into my hair. "Your plan is a good one. We just have to see it through."

I nodded, but the images kept flashing—his body hanging, blood pooling beneath him.

"I have to add a caveat."

August stilled. "What kind of caveat?"

"If something happens to me, you can't go after Adrastos' keeper."

"Excuse me?" August asked flatly, tone implying I was either joking or daft.

"His keeper—whoever pulls his strings—there's a power there that I don't recognize."

"You saw him?" he questioned, his hold on me tightening as his fingers speared through my hair in firm strokes. When I nodded, he added, "You don't know him?"

"No. But I feel like I should." It was that same eerie familiarity as the music box on the battlefield, niggling at the back of my consciousness. Something so simple I should recognize it, but couldn't, no matter how hard I focused. "This soul...he feels like death."

"Like Kade?"

I pursed my lips, running my fingers across the soft curls of hair over his chest as the steady thud of his heart soothed my own. "Not quite. This is different, somehow. And I...I think Adrastos fears him, at least judging by his tone."

"And you expect me to let you face him alone?" he demanded, hand stilling on my lower back.

"No," I said, shaking my head. "I expect you to trust me to see a way out."

"Ally—"

"You are what the world needs to secure this win. Not me. You." I leaned in, grazing my lips over his, our breath mingling. "Which means—no matter what happens—you follow the plan. Understand?"

Every agonized goodbye over centuries hunting for each other stared back at me as he said, "You are mine, Alvara Porter. And we're doing this together." His hands came up to cradle my face, one spearing into my hair so he could position my head.

"You have to listen—"

"I can't promise that, Ally."

"You're the hope, August. The mercy. They'll follow you."

His pain cracked open and spilled between us, raw and furious. "You are mine. We're doing this together."

Tears pricked behind my eyes. "Then promise me. If it's me or the world—"

"It's you," he cut in, voice ragged. "Every time."

Then he rolled us, pinning me beneath him as his mouth found my throat, his hands burning hot against my skin. And I let him claim me, silencing the storm inside me with his devotion, his desperation, his love.

Because I knew—if it ever came down to a choice...

Neither of us would survive it.

"August," I panted. I meant it to be a reprimand, but it came out a plea —and like the damn deity he was, he smiled against my skin. Breathless and accusatory, I managed, "You're a beautiful distraction."

"Is it working?"

"Maybe...but we—should talk," I said, voice dissolving into a breathy whimper as I rapidly forgot why that mattered. His mouth, his hands—he wasn't just touching me; he was unmaking me. The bastard chuckled, wicked and unrepentant.

"You're mine, Ally. You're not going anywhere I can't follow." With that promise, he closed his mouth around my breast again, his grip tightening around my throat—not harsh, but commanding, claiming. And then his other hand slid down my torso, slipping beneath my silk shorts, and that was it. My surrender wasn't conscious—it was instinct.

In seconds, he had his fingers working my clit, coaxing me into writhing beneath him as he lapped at my breast like a man starved.

"August," I breathed again. He hummed in approval, his grip tightening on my neck just enough to make me dizzy with need. I dropped my head to the pillow in wordless surrender, letting my legs fall open as he dipped lower, spreading my slick arousal over my entrance before easing a finger inside me.

Pleasure speared through me, hot and immediate, and I arched into him, silently begging for more. August took his time, readying me with those precise strokes, and only when I began to rock against his hand did he release my throat, his palm sliding down to tweak a nipple before shimmying out of his low-slung sweats.

My mouth watered the moment his cock sprang free—long, hard, and already glistening.

"Mine," I whispered, wrapping my hand around his thick length and bringing him to my lips. His breath caught, then released in a choked sound as I traced his tip with my tongue. Our eyes locked—his gaze emerald fire as I slid him into my mouth, slowly, savoring the taste, the feel, the weight of him.

I took him deeper, swallowing past the urge to gag, loving the way he groaned—deep and guttural—like I was dragging it from his soul. His fingers tangled in my hair, not demanding but reverent, encouraging me with each stroke of his thumb against my temple.

"Baby," he rasped, his voice a prayer. Every moan, every shiver that rippled through him sent heat coiling low in my belly. I pressed my thighs together, desperate to ease the ache.

But the sound that escaped me—muffled and needy—snapped something in August.

His eyes flew open, burning with possessive hunger. One hand slid to my jaw, tilting my head as the other swept my hair behind my shoulder.

"You're so fucking gorgeous," he breathed, gaze flicking downward as I slipped a hand between my thighs. A growl rumbled from him as he caught my wrist and pulled it away. "That's mine. Are you wet for me?"

I could only nod around his length, taking him deeper, craving the way he cursed and trembled.

"Fuuuck, Ally. You take me so good. But you want me between your legs, don't you?"

My desperate hum was all the answer he needed.

He pulled free of my mouth with a pop, shifting his glorious body over mine, kissing me hard as he stripped my clothes in a blur of motion. Then he was there, lined up and braced above me, his forearm cradling my head, our breaths mingling.

"Please," I whispered. I didn't even know what I was begging for anymore. Release. Escape. More of him. All of him.

"Anything," August promised, sliding inside inch by aching inch.

Pleasure bloomed hot and full as he began to move, slow at first, deliberate, reverent. My body arched, stretching around him. I clutched at his shoulders, my mind going blank from the overwhelming ecstasy of it.

But just as rapture neared, something cold and cruel twisted in my mind—a memory, a warning. Anything, he'd said.

How many terrible things could be born of a vow like that?

"Eyes on me," August ordered gently, his hand pressing between my breasts to ground me. "Stay here, baby. You stay with me when I'm inside you."

I nodded, blinking away the ghosts, anchoring to the warmth in his voice. He smiled—slow and breathtaking—and I gave him a tentative one in return.

"Good." He slid his hand between us, thumb pressing against my clit in steady, delicious circles. "Now give me what I want, Ally."

"God, August!" I gasped, biting my lip to muffle the cry as heat ignited in my spine and shot through my limbs.

He chuckled low, the sound vibrating against my lips. "Can you be quiet, wife?" he teased, and then slammed into me, stealing my breath and any ability to reply. His thumb circled harder, faster, and when my orgasm detonated, it was his name that filled my throat.

I just couldn't let it escape.

NINETEEN

STORKS

AUGUST

We were a pile of sweaty, tangled limbs, panting into the softly glowing guest room of Terramyst's king, and there was nowhere on the planet I'd rather be. Ally's hair fanned out around her in a rich brown halo, strands tossed every which way. Her fair skin was painted a delicious shade of pink, and the lips I craved with every incessant beat of my heart were bee-stung and parted as she caught her breath. Our lives may have collided when I was at her mercy, but with every reading that took us deeper, I realized this life was unique in that. My mate was right. Whether I wanted it or not, every incarnation came with two constants; brutal, bottomless bloodshed, and the soul so pure and bright she outshone the darkness.

I wasn't sure what I'd done in my first life—or what it was about my creation—that had granted me a gift like her to circle back to, but it was in her solace that I thought the rest of this hell might just be worth it.

"Mmmm," Ally purred softly as the pads of my fingers continued their dutiful patrol of her curves. I didn't want to believe this life was just as damned as the rest of them. But if it was, I wanted to remember the lines of this warrior's body so deeply that she was written in the marrow of my next one when I woke.

A smile threatened my composure as gooseflesh pebbled to life in the wake of my touch, and I guided that chill up between her breasts and over her collarbone, satisfaction curving my lips as her ribs expanded in a wanton breath before I swept the rogue strands of hair from her face. She was teetering that line of ecstasy between sleep and wake, her body so sated not even her mind was whirring when I finally stroked a petal soft touch over her eyelids, down her cheek and over the bow of her lips. A soul as fierce as Ally, trusting me with this level of vulnerability, was a gift I would not be taking for granted.

I would worship at this woman's altar after erecting the damn thing myself. There was nothing she could ask of me I wouldn't break my back to give her.

Nothing...except for *that*. Her plans might take us to the ends of the earth, but in no universe could I carry on if we were cleaved apart again. Some fates are truly worse than death, and *her* back in our enemy's hands...

As I memorized the subtle give of her swollen lips beneath my thumb, I decided once and for all, that was the one reality I couldn't live with. If our enemy was mad enough to strike that particular match, I'd burn this realm to ash myself.

"THIS GUY? REALLY?" Kingsley asked a few mornings later, tapping on the headshot he'd just slid across the wood table with a sigh. Ally leveled him with a glare that I hoped knocked his ego down a few pegs before ignoring him altogether. We'd spent the last few days testing the water, breaching an unspoken pact between all clans that humans could not know of our existence in the pursuit of preparing them for the war to come. But humans were a stubborn breed, dedicated to remaining so deeply steeped in their cognitive dissonance that the knowledge of creatures more powerful than them didn't seem to settle well. Not even for Ally.

"We've had minimal success thus far." That was her understatement of the year, unfortunately. Thus far, our only victory was that we'd been able to contact more than half of Grayshell's globally deployed souls, and they were righting their affairs before heading to Chicago to report in to Marcus until we found our damn door. "The visions show Mr. Mori is our best bet from Japan, and I have high hopes for Lochlan, but our odds are truly stacked against us at converting most bureaucrats. Their need for control will supersede the good of their people."

"And Adrastos has people on the inside," Kingsley deduced. Correctly, if the visions were indicative.

"He wouldn't be much of an opponent if he didn't," I stated simply. "The bastard was right about one thing, though." When Kingsley's gaze flicked to me, I explained, "Adrastos believes that humanity has, by and large, given up. The bureaucrats will hear what they want to hear where power is the prize. Our enemy will use that to their advantage. Meanwhile, the populace is so beaten down..." my words wandered off, and I shook my head. "They are so blindly inured to the system that, should our enemy possess their governments, they will defend their own impending enslavement. They've lost too much of their courage to fight for anything beyond what they think they know."

"So...are you saying we've already lost?" Rose asked tentatively, her eyes round with the kind of bone-deep terror of someone staring down death itself.

I guessed that's what it had felt like for me lately, too, if I was honest. Problem being, these souls would look to me to guide them through it. "No," I said, eyes dropping to the table where I rotated an empty cup in my hand. "I'm saying our enemies have been planning this for centuries, and if they have infiltrated the human world as deeply as we believe they have...we are in for an uphill battle."

"Don't Aren and Marcus have braids in the system as well?"

"Yes they do," I assured. "And they have them trying to sift through suspects, but even if we can turn politicians our direction, I don't think that's how we win this."

Alvara's face morphed into the same scowl she wore while outmaneuvering Adrastos the first go around. "This resistance is going to be from the ground up, or not at all."

"That sounds...promising," Kingsley growled sardonically. Ally was startlingly quick to forgive his temper in my opinion, but I couldn't deny he'd minded his mouth since. Still surly and generally unpleasant to be around, but he had our back in this, albeit begrudgingly. It had grown quickly apparent Kingsley was *begrudgingly alive*, though, so I couldn't take it too personally.

"So, how do we connect our people and theirs?" Rose asked from where she braced herself on the edge of the table, brown eyes trained on the images splayed across its weathered surface.

"We show them who we are," Ally said simply.

"We expose ourselves?" Kingsley's tone turned disapproving. "Holding out hope for a better explanation than that."

"They're going to know soon enough," Rose pointed out. "Inevitable, really, once Adrastos and his keeper make their move."

Stomach growling, I eyed the tower of muffins our wives had prepared, wondering if we'd actually break our fast at some point. Training these last days had been harrowing at best, the readings damn near bringing me to my knees every time we tried to break past the wall in our history. The Bond seemed to have a mind of its own, and didn't seem eager to bend to our wills.

We'd risen at dawn. While the coffee percolated in a gurgling worn out machine, Rose and Ally warmed the kitchen baking muffins and whipping up lemon poppyseed pancakes that smelled divine. I fried up a pack of bacon to the sound of their chatter, only for all of it to get set to the side when Kingsley slapped a newspaper down on the table.

Attempted explanations for not only the mysterious 'tectonic shift' we'd left in the Rockies, but also the recent weather anomalies consumed the headlines. Whoops. My bad.

Worse yet, conspiracies were already getting out of hand online—the most concerning of which regaled the stories of the old gods, and the fact that perhaps those lost tales weren't so lost after all.

Those realizations led to an animated discussion over Grayshell's proposed strategy moving into the coming war. Human safety—an inevitable byproduct of their authority's compliance with our proposal—was a top priority, followed shortly by preserving as many natural resources as we could.

Attempting to silence the complaints of my hunger, I nodded in agreement before explaining, "There will come a day—not so far from now—where our existence will be common fact. According to Ally's visions, there are two outcomes. Either we will be demonized and prosecuted, or worshiped like gods. If souls aim to oppress them, then all souls must be punished alongside those at the helm of the revolution. It's there that we can make a difference. As their defenders, we will at least plant the seed that we're not all the root of their problems."

"Right," Ally said definitively. "Our best bet is making sure we're prepared to differentiate ourselves from the Renown, or whoever else these assholes acquire. We need a presence that's undeniable. A cut and dry divide between dark and light, so that they can correlate the difference and know we're here to help. Because..."

"The witch trials will be back," Rose deduced.

"Only, it's a shoot first and ask questions later situation," I pointed out, shifting back in my chair with a huff. Ally and I might've run circles around this conversation but it didn't mean any of our allies had the same chance to process.

"Good thing bullets can't touch us."

"They can," I countered, earning two sets of narrowed brown eyes.

"Or they will be able to soon," Ally amended. "I've seen it, and it's going to get unspeakably ugly. They've...weaponized reapers venom, as far as we can tell. Freya saw it in action, and it's not a desirable death."

"What do you mean?" Kingsley asked, drawing out each word as if keeping a rope on that temper I'd born witness to.

"Slow. Agonizing. According to Freya it eats the skin alive from the inside out," I said. I went on to explain everything Freya had reported to us. The ongoing plea of Reyna's man to 'get it out' was what seemed to catch his attention the most.

"What if you did?"

"Get it out?" Ally guessed, or read, I was never sure which. When the king nodded, she sucked down a breath. "I don't know. I haven't seen them in malleable visions and—luckily—haven't encountered one in person, so I'm not sure. Perhaps if it goes clean through, you can avoid it leaching into your system?"

Irritation etched across Kingsley's perpetually solemn face as he asked, "Like lead poisoning?"

"Maybe? Your guess is as good as mine until we can get our hands on one."

"Why are we worried about allying with the humans if there's a weapon like that in the hands of our enemy? Shouldn't that take priority?"

"Freya and Bellaton are hunting for it now," she reassured.

"No offense, but I'm not putting my faith in a newborn."

"A newborn with divine memory," I said, trying and failing to avoid feeling defensive of the soul that chased me through lifetimes to fulfill her vow to my mate. Freya wasn't just my sister, anymore; the connection of finding another soul mate in our group had roared to life on that killing field. "She's lived many lives and has a record of most of them."

"So, how can we help?" Rose interrupted cheerily before Kingsley could snipe back, clinging to some semblance of her enthusiasm despite the circumstances. She waved her hand, and the plates of food hovered over to the table, settling with subtle ceramic clinks. The clouds finally moved past the sun, freeing its warmth to radiate down through the windows into the cozy space, the light settling over Ally's luminous skin.

"Keep your eyes up. Help us talk to human leaders. Mostly though, we have to understand this bond before the horsemen descend, or I don't see this ending well for us..." Ally's eyes drifted off into the other, her ribs ceasing their movement mid-inhale. My shield had remained properly spooled inside my chest today, so I could watch the vision clear as day as it rushed through her mind.

Running through the heart of a city, fear coursing through her veins as rapidly as the rivers of sweat across her skin, the healer banked towards the hospital. There would be help. Magnolia said there was help there.

She dared a glance backwards, sobbing as she saw what she fled from. Tight on her heels stood a skeletal demon, its frame a cross between an onyx stag and a man, ribs jutting out, and hands tipped in blood soaked talons. The mutated face was topped with a crown of antlers, the comparison halting as it opened its mouth to roar and revealed rows of jagged teeth. She screamed as the beast caught her, gutting her in one motion with those enormous horns.

Ally's hand flew to her mouth, eyes wide as they locked on me for a beat before she was moving, rushing for her phone where she'd left it across the room.

"With all due respect, what the fuck was that?" Kingsley asked, scowl directed at her back, clearly irritated he couldn't see whatever sent her launching for her cell.

"Mortiferous Nóchtaithe?"

"Christ," Kingsley groaned, running a palm over his face. Nausea roiled in my gut, nerves bristling. I had seen it in her mind; the beast peeled right out of a nightmare. But logic was warring hard with what the vision had presented. Alvara's mind was thrumming—she had decided to research the beasts, and hadn't even made it to Kingsley's computer when the visions began whirring through her head with the information we'd find. "Because hell hounds and blood wolves weren't enough, we just needed to add more nightmares to this mess."

A muffled thud jerked all of our attention to the front door right as it opened—all, except for Ally, of course, who kept her eyes in the other world. Cold rushed through the little room, stealing the air from the space, but relief washed over me. Something like a sense of coming home as I laid eyes on Alec and Fae, both bundled and red nosed, snow sliding off their boots beside the black backpack he had evidently dumped on the deck.

"I'm sorry." Alec blinked before clearing his throat, eyes narrowing to slits. "Did you just say we're hunting the *Lethal Night*?"

"Actually," Fae interjected, stepping forward to wrap her arm around his as she continued, "given the state of the world right now, that tracks."

Rose burst out laughing, rising from her chair and heading straight for the little blonde to wrap her in a collision of a hug, right as Ally pulled herself from her psychic download. Rose had just inclined her head in curiosity, when a smirking Ally prowled up to her sister, wrapping her in a much gentler embrace. Alec's narrowed eyes flicked to her face, the dip between his brows deepening.

"You know." A clever smirk curled his lips like smoke as the accusation flew from his mouth. Ally grinned, biting her lip as her eyes flashed to mine, and I suddenly felt like the only one out on a very important secret. "How, dammit?" he demanded before spluttering, "*When?*"

Ally's smile broadened. "I'll give it to you, you guys did really good the whole time you were in Westerlund. I almost dismissed it in the dreams."

"But we decided to come to see you," he said as a knowing gleam settled over his expression, eyes rolling sardonically.

"But you decided to come to see me," she confirmed, smiling sweetly and tucking a strand of hair behind Fae's ear with so much care, she could have been a—

Knowing slammed through me, leaving me feeling rather daft, and about a million other unfortunate combinations of self deprecating emotions. "No!" I looked between the two of my friends, whose lips were twisted with cocky smiles. "No way!" I said again, eyes locking on Alec's as his face split in an ear-to-ear grin. He gave me a nod, right as Kingsley picked up on what our mates had noticed immediately.

"Yeah, soooo, if we don't stop Adrastos and The Horsemen in the next seven months, things are going to be infinitely more complicated." Fae said cheerily, wrapping her arms around the women to her sides. The most sincere smile I'd seen on his face softened the permanent furrow between Kingsley's brows as he stepped forward to clasp Alec's forearm in a brotherly handshake.

"Congratulations, Mr. Carter."

The moment his arm had been released, Alec flung himself towards me, and I crushed him in a bear hug. He set his head on my shoulder and a wave of uncharacteristically candid emotions slammed through me in a suffocating rollercoaster—hope, joy, fear, grief, love—as he tried to process what in the hell this would look like.

Would he live to meet his son, or daughter? To support Fae through childbirth?

Fear wrapped around my windpipe, overwhelm crashing in a relentless cascade. I just gave him a pat on the back, trying to be reassuring. I'd never been great with kids, never really thought much about them, at least, not with Layla. And I certainly hadn't thought about what all of this madness would mean for bringing one into the chaos.

Something was underlying Alvara's apparent calm. Like a serpent, it slithered along the edge of her mind, leaving an oily feeling between us. Dread coiled in my gut as I found her eyes, and I pressed against her shields, which remained obstinately in place. She'd gotten better—infinitely better—since we'd been cradled in these mountains. But it was there, in the set of her jaw below the false smile, the way she lifted her chin, like Freya defying the giants.

She didn't like the thread ahead of us, had just decided to fuck the odds, and change it herself.

I could feel it in her aura, as much as she tried to hide it for Fae. But Alec wasn't stupid—was nearly as attuned to her as I was—and his expression fell as he noticed her stance, head bowing for a heartbeat before he slapped that cocky grin back on his face to protect his mate.

"So, where are we headed?" he asked, a touch too cheerily as he returned to Fae, slipping his arms around her waist. It was then that I saw it, wondering how I had missed the color in her cheeks, the faint glow to her skin, the usual flicker of hope in her eyes stoked like a flame.

"Field trip to SoCal, I'm afraid. But we're not to intrude on Aren's thread. Not yet. We'll let him and Nathara's allies handle them until we're absolutely crucial. We just need to get close enough to capture one of these things."

"I think the word you're searching for is *kill*," Alec snarked, raising a brow.

"No," Alvara said on a sigh, "I mean capture. We need to figure out how to turn them back before we kill them."

"The...demons?" Rosaleigh didn't bother to hide her horror, her eyes wide.

Alvara chuckled. "According to the lore, these monsters are a result of a curse upon susceptible mortals. If we can reunite them with their mortal souls before we send the demons to the after, they might actually find rest."

"You realize you sound insane, right?" Alec blinked pointedly twice, earning a sly grin from Alvara as she turned the full weight of her attention on him.

Blinking in bewilderment, she said, "Is that new?"

I snorted, reaching forward to snatch her hand, and dragging her over so I could wrap her up, needing to touch her. Long since realizing there was no changing this woman, or talking her out of something she'd made her mind up about, I just resigned to feel her, to know she was with me here and now. Safe. As safe as one could be when they were about to go hunting enormous, man-eating demon beasts.

"Welp. If we're Nóchtaithe hunting, we're going to need imbued steel. Ally, do you still have that collection of Solskari blades?" Kingsley asked as he turned for the back hallway. She *grimaced* as he vanished down the passage. Actually grimaced.

On the tale of his boisterous laughter, Alec mumbled, "Oh boy." I was about to ask what I was missing, but saw the answer in their minds.

"What's *the shop*?" I looked between my companions as Ally palmed her face.

"One of my safe houses," she muttered, eyes going fuzzy as she thumbed through the threads.

"*Welp*," Alec clapped his hands before bending to hike up their bags in the same motion. "Have fun with that. We'll settle in."

"What's the shop?" I repeated, confusion and irritation flaming in my chest as he marched inside, his eyes locked on our remaining host.

Ignoring me entirely, Alec asked, "Got room for two more, Rose, darling?"

"Kindly fuck off," Kingsley's voice trailed from the back room, earning an eye roll so big it must have hurt from his mate.

"Upstairs, second door on the left," she said cheerily, ignoring his surly denial, and pressing a kiss to Fae's cheek as the two of them passed her.

Glancing from their backs, to Rose's bemused expression, to Alvara's... *embarrassed* one with no further sign of explanation, I asked, "Why do I feel like I'm walking into an ambush blind?"

The laughter that trailed back from the stairwell wasn't particularly encouraging, but neither was her face as Ally lifted her sheepish eyes. I'd been to countless safe houses—Aren's many favorites, Ansel, Marcus, and Alec all had bottomless getaways.

Slowly, reality crept into my bones as I realized that I had yet to step into one that belonged to my mate.

"Why haven't you taken me to *your* houses?" As heat crept into her face, a cheeky smile lifted my own. Because what on earth could be so humiliating that the motherfucking angel of death looked this mortified? "Oh," I chuckled, grinning as I said, "this is too good."

"I have it under control," she grumbled. When I only hiked my brows, my suspicions immediately confirmed, she scowled at me, ignoring the Carter's cackles of amusement from upstairs. Alvara in her element was a Goddess among mortals. But Alvara battling embarrassment was the kind of endearingly adorable I'd rarely witnessed. She squirmed where she stood, massaging her wrinkled nose as I burst out laughing.

With more force this time, she barked, "I have it under control."

TWENTY

TREASURES

AUGUST

My mate did, in fact, *not* have it under control.

"Oh man," I breathed, trying to swallow the laughter bubbling up in my chest. "Ally," I said in mock reproach. "You need help."

"I do not."

"You absolutely do."

"I do not. It's fine. I have it under control," she said for the half a dozenth time, and I wasn't entirely sure if she was trying to convince me or herself. How had nobody told me about this? The amusement won out, bursting from me in a rumble that earned an elbow to my gut. Somehow, her discomfort only made me laugh harder.

"You're a *hoarder*."

"Am not."

I motioned to the surrounding chaos. The warehouse—because let's be real, that's what it was—was tall enough to house an airplane hangar, and its contents spilled from every container and pile. Chandeliers hung from metal rafters, and what looked like a rusted antique plane hovered from cables in the far corner, suspended above endless shelves of trinkets and knick-knacks.

"Is that...is that *Pocahontas*?" I tilted my head at the smooth planes of the statue. The carving rose to my sternum, expertly crafted, though most of the color had long since worn away.

"Matoaka," she whispered reverently, uncrossing her arms as she stepped forward, fingers grazing the whittled braid of hair, eyes sliding closed. "Mortals like to dust the atrocities of history under the rug, romanticizing the crimes of humanity. But they can't hide it all—not really. And she…" Her lids fluttered as she sifted through the stories behind the piece.

I turned, giving her space to sort through the echo. Dust-coated treasures lined every inch of the place. How did she carry so many stories in one space?

On the end of a long, satisfied breath, Ally's eyes opened. "She brought me strength when I ran out. In the face of the darkest atrocities, she reminded me to keep getting up. Gave me a purpose—to defend. To right what I can for those who can't."

I squinted at a sepia photograph, the frame cheap, the paper cracked with age. "And them?"

Ally smiled, laughing softly. She wet her lips before saying, "Pechey, Chaplin, Jex-Blake, Thorne, Evans, Bovell, Anderson."

"And you remember them because…?"

She sighed at my ignorance, but as the story began playing through her mind, my fascination only grew.

"The Edinburgh Seven paved the way for women who wanted doctorates in the UK."

The next image tugged at something in the back of my mind. A woman in a blue dress with white sleeves, adorned with rosebuds. I scowled, a far corner of useless knowledge rising.

"Don't think too hard, Porter."

"I should know this one."

"You should," she agreed. "Should I let you suffer or put you out of your misery?"

"Who is she?"

"Flora MacDonald. I have mixed feelings, but you can't deny she had moxie."

As we rounded a corner, I watched her fingers trail gently from one object to the next, inhaling the stories as they rushed through her mind. I stopped when I reached a towering stone sculpture. The oriental styling was obvious, though I couldn't read the language. My eyes caught on the axe in her hands.

"Fu Hao—also known as Si Mu Xin," Ally supplied, catching my pause. "First known female military leader. Queen, priestess, general. Shang Dynasty. She was so legendary, they thought she was folklore…until they found her tomb."

"Estelle would lose her mind in here."

"Probably," she said with a nervous giggle. Then she was off again, pointing out favorite pieces—women who inspired her or shaped her craft. Boudica. Jeanne de Clisson. Joan of Arc.

"When did you start this?" I gestured around us.

"The first time Ansel knocked me out in the ring."

I winced involuntarily, the memory of Aren's merciless training still fresh.

"It started with small tokens—things I could hide in Grayshell to remind me to keep getting back up. Eventually, I collected anything I couldn't bear to lose." She paused, a mischievous glint in her eye. "Legally, of course."

"If I asked you to define legal?"

"I'd probably backpedal and say *ethically*."

"That's my girl," I chuckled, leaning in to kiss her cheek. As I pulled back, my eye caught on an antique piano in the corner. Goosebumps rose along my arms.

I stepped toward it, fingers tracing the keys, then the delicate Victorian design etched along its side. Layla. Nightmares. Alvara. A cluttered thrift shop. My gaze flicked up to Ally, who was braiding her hair, lips curled in a satisfied smile.

"Is that—?"

She drew a breath. "We were days behind you. For months. Always just a beat too slow."

"Christ," I murmured, tapping out a melody. It was slightly out of tune, but tolerable. I remembered the piano—dust-covered in a salvage shop.

"I was losing hope I'd ever catch up. Couldn't explain why failing you felt like dying. Maybe it was Adrastos stirring things up, but...I saw you once before. Did I ever tell you that?"

I shook my head.

"New York. Marcus called me in to assist the local Commander. I felt you calling me. I slipped away after the mission, followed the pull, but it led me to Coney Island, and you were—"

"Down on the beach," I finished, smiling. "I couldn't sleep, so I snuck out of our hotel room."

She laughed quietly. "I remember watching you. Wishing you'd turn around. Furious I couldn't find your mind. I blamed the city."

"What pulled you away?"

"A healer went missing in Chicago. One of Eloise's friends. The whole hierarchy was searching for her. I couldn't be sure you were *the* calling. Couldn't breach your shield, I guess. But when Jason and Damien called for backup, Marcus sent me in."

She ran her hand over the piano, clearing a trail through the blanket of dust. "When this thing showed me you playing in that store...I realized I'd missed the mark."

"Not that protecting friends is ever a mistake."

"No," she agreed quickly, eyes softening as she turned to me. "We brought them home. And we found you in the end. That's what matters."

My hands slid beneath the hem of her shirt, palms warming to her waist as I drew her close. Our hips brushed a beat before our mouths met. I wanted to feel every inch of her—wanted to peel away every barrier until nothing stood between us.

"You know what matters now?" I breathed against her lips.

She shook her head, nose brushing mine, but the way her body pressed into me said otherwise. The shift in her scent hit a second later—sweet and heady—and I wrapped her braid around my fist to angle her mouth, deepening the kiss.

"Six thousand square feet, and nobody's around to stop us."

"The blades can wait a little longer," she whispered, smile wicked in her voice.

FREYA

"DID YOU DO AS WE ASKED?" Ansel paced in front of me, his calm betrayed by the fact that he couldn't keep still. His presence in Bellaton was as much a comfort as it was a concern. As much as I needed more time with my family, things were escalating—and not just here. A magnificent beast was stirring, the clock ticking down with every bated breath. Even the humans were noticing.

Per The Old General's instructions, I'd ditched all my mortal tech, plus every stone and totem from both Grayshell and Bellaton. My clothes were old gym scraps I wouldn't miss when I burned them on our return.

"You can't let her touch your skin after this. Are you okay with that?" he asked. Unease prickled up the back of my neck. Keeping secrets from Ally hadn't been on my bingo card this year. Secretly dismantling Reagan's legacy to bypass the Crucible, expose her for the snake she was, and take her throne—that was heavy enough.

"Yeah. But Reyna has everyone on the ground tonight, so we've gotta be quick. The last of her troops are rolling in for the meeting."

"Good," he said. "We're going to need them. And I'll have you back before the meeting. At least she can still call her forces home." He turned on the ball of his foot, flipping his cigarette case open and shut as he thought. "Of all my regrets in this life—of which there are many—not finding you sooner, and not calling our troops home before that duel...those are the worst."

"I'm home now," I said, swallowing past the ache in my throat. "And you couldn't have known we'd be cut off. Even Reyna's history books don't have record of something like this. In all my ascensions, I've never seen anything like it." His stoic expression pinched slightly as he studied me—subtle enough that I probably only noticed because we were growing familiar. Wordlessly, he nodded, sliding the tin into his back pocket and opening an arm. I stepped in, wrapping mine around his waist.

"You ready?"

"You gonna tell me where we're going?"

"Somewhere you can only find if you've been there before."

"Because that's not ominous," I muttered. His earlier explanation had already been cryptic enough—something about a place Ally couldn't see. Something Lana needed me to witness. A huff of amusement escaped his chest, and I grinned, tightening my grip a little before he jumped us out. The familiar twist in my gut had me wrinkling my nose and sucking down a breath, fighting the urge to vomit.

"Some treasures are best kept secrets," he muttered as I staggered a few paces away to regroup. Still a bit peaky, I righted myself...and stared.

A shack—for lack of a better word—stood maybe a hundred yards away, looking more like a tetanus trap than a treasured stronghold. Dust-caked windows gaped like broken teeth, and a rusted lightning rod creaked in slow, uneven circles as a bitter breeze sent sand skittering past my boots. The siding was patchy and warped. Boards sagged on crooked nails. A rusted-out sedan sagged under a half-collapsed carport, and above the back door, what looked like a Russian assault rifle had been mounted.

"I think your definition of 'treasure' and mine are wildly different," I muttered, nose wrinkling. A tumbleweed wouldn't have been out of place. Just for dramatic flair, I mimicked that classic Western whistle and spun in a slow circle.

Melted snowbanks gave way to rusted-out car skeletons and debris-strewn hills. Tires, broken bottles, busted crates. The opposite hillside was mostly bare, except for an overgrown dirt road and an RV that looked like it had been stepped on.

Something moved. A tan bunny darted through the rotting boards of what might've once been a garage, then sprinted toward a garden enclosure, its little white tail disappearing beneath a fence. A horned skull hung over the gate's remains, and below it—"Are those snake skins?"

"If you hang 'em up, their friends don't tend to come calling."

"Charming," I said flatly. My stomach twisted for entirely new reasons. "Dad, what is this place?"

"Come on. I'll show you." With a nod, Ansel shoved his hands in his coat pockets just as a brutal winter gust slapped my face. Suddenly, the Spanish moss curtains of Bellaton didn't seem so bad.

I hustled after him around the corner—again, using the word "house" generously—where a metal box with a hand crank sat waiting. Ansel blew into his hands before grabbing the crank and working it in smooth circles.

"Generator?" I asked as he worked it, nodding at me as we both turned our backs against the cold. "How endearingly...mortal," I mumbled as shivers won the battle with my stubbornness.

"It's just for the locks and porch lights." A moment later, the thing hummed to life. A porch light buzzed and flickered on under the sagging roof. Ansel exhaled a puff of breath, smoke curling into the cold air, then jerked his chin toward the building. I followed him to a metal screen door, which opened with an ear-splitting screech.

The second door was in slightly better shape—flaking paint, electronic keypad. "The plot thickens."

"You'll see," he said, keying in a code and angling his shoulder so I could watch. Then he pulled a pocketknife from his jeans and popped it open. "Life hack," he muttered, slicing a neat line on his forearm and watching the blood well. "Draw blood from somewhere other than your hands if you're expecting a fight. Hollywood always gets it wrong. Straight across the palm—like enchantments demand undue inconvenience. Bunch of bullshit."

Smiling to myself, I watched him drag the blade over a rune on the threshold. I didn't bother telling him I'd learned that from him in our first life together. Divine memory was bizarre that way.

When he spread his blood over the final rune, the seal glowed faintly gold. The door creaked open with a prolonged protest of neglected hinges.

I don't know what I expected inside, but I wasn't ready for the dust. Or the stench. Or the possum-sized rat that bolted across the floor and out the door.

"Did you bring me here to murder me?" I joked, though Reagan's betrayal crept to the front of my mind. My spine straightened as I scanned the space—one hallway, two doors, a fridge growing horrors of its own, and a stairwell I could only assume led to the basement.

"Not funny," Ansel growled, heading straight for said stairwell. Dust clouds puffed under our steps as we descended the nightmare carpet.

"How old is this place?" I asked.

"Older than your last life," he wagered. "Come on."

"Of course. Why wouldn't we walk into a murder basement?" I muttered, eyeing a suspicious splatter on the wall. Rust. Hopefully.

When we reached the door at the bottom, Ansel turned to me. A somber burden carved into his features, eyes dropping to his boots in that way a doctor would before they proclaimed the death of your loved one.

Voice feeling rather brittle, I tentatively asked, "Dad?"

"Not everything we do, we do because we want to," he said. "Okay, kid?"

"You're freaking me out," I admitted, my chest tightening. Was this some fucked-up torture chamber? The hidden underbelly of the only hierarchy I actually believed in?

"Aren and Ally have a relationship built on trust. They back each other's plays. She leaves him trails through time, and he follows because they communicate freely."

"Okay?"

"But early on in this life, when she was still catatonic after..."

"Losing Michael," I finished, watching his expression crack under the weight of it.

"Yeah." He took a steadying breath and re-sliced the mark on his arm, the skin already starting to knit together. He scooped up the blood with his thumb, deliberately showing me, then drew a cross over the metal door and brought what remained to his mouth. "She wasn't talking, but we started to understand her gifts. And," he paused, head shaking, gaze heavier now, "one night, somebody took her."

My breath hitched. He held up a finger, asking me to wait, and opened the door.

This one didn't creak. The hinges were smooth, and a warm gust of air swept in, lifting my hair.

"Or we thought they did," Ansel corrected, stepping into a chamber of pitch black. Without hesitation, he kept walking, and fluorescent lights hummed to life along the ceiling. I turned in slow circles, mouth falling open as an endless hallway gradually lit ahead of us.

"She'd gone *home*—maybe looking for answers, maybe for some piece of her mate—only to find it burned down. Nothing left of her mortal life but ash. According to her reading, a man in a demon mask set the fire."

Goosebumps erupted down my arms. I didn't know if it was the story or the creepy ass hallway that felt so damn haunted. I glanced behind us, watching the lights flicker off as we moved forward, the path gently sloping deeper into the earth.

"While she was missing, while we hunted with Griffin and Yvaine— *Alec and Fae* to you—Marcus, and Saraya, we started to grasp her potential. We knew she'd become the gift any Commander would kill to claim. The hierarchy's greatest asset. But also...a liability. You know what she is as a reader. How quickly her mind dissects everything. Have you ever encountered a mentalist?"

He looked over his shoulder. Our footsteps echoed down the concrete corridor, and I swear the air got heavier with every step.

"I've read about them," I said, remembering Reyna's study and the refresher I'd done just days ago. The opposite of Ally's gift—where she drew knowledge from the world, mentalists could implant it, deeply and in detail.

"Between mentalists and Aren's near brush with the reapers, we decided we needed strongholds. Just in case. Because great knowledge comes with immense power...but also immense vulnerability. If your mates fall into the wrong hands, so many of our secrets—*Aren's* secrets—live in her mind. And all that stands between them, and exposure is her will. And that infamous 'fuck you' attitude she's known for." He paused. "But spite only takes you so far, kiddo."

I nearly walked into him when he stopped abruptly and pushed open one of the metal doors.

My breath caught.

Massive overhead lights clicked on, illuminating a cavernous space larger than Grayshell's great hall. I blinked at the rows—no, *acres*—of tables stretching down what looked like the world's most absurdly oversized cafeteria. Hidden beneath a hill in the middle of bumfuck nowhere.

"Aren has a theory," Ansel said, stepping inside, "that for every power born into this world, there's an equal and opposite."

"So if Ally's that strong—"

"Then her counterbalance is, too."

I saw him then. Our enemy. Standing beside his brother, cold and regal.

"Twin powers," Ansel continued. "Usually with opposing aims. If Aren's right, there's another reader out there—or a mentalist—"

"Who could extract everything from her if she were taken," I finished, arms wrapping around myself, hand hovering near my mouth.

Ansel turned, leading us back out into the hall, chin gesturing toward the door we'd entered through. "Lana and I were already outsiders," he said, voice careful now. "We volunteered to be Aren's secret keepers."

"But you're his assassins. That makes you targets. Shouldn't this have gone to someone less visible?"

The question rushed out of me like a waterfall. But his answer—his crooked smile, the flicker of pride in his eyes—nearly knocked me over.

Without breaking stride, he hooked his mouth open and back, revealing the edge of a molar that shimmered silver-blue.

"People underestimate healers," he said with a shrug. "But who needs to raise a hand if you can carry a curse?"

He opened a door on the opposite side of the hallway. Fluorescents flicked on, revealing an enormous training ring. Racks of Grayshell uniforms lined one wall. Weapons filled three others.

"Like a cyanide pill." My voice was hollow as the weight of it sank in. My soul parents had suicide pills. *In their mouths.*

Ansel ran a hand over one of the punching bags and turned to face me. "You're a secret keeper now, Freya. Grayshell lives in you."

"*Why?*" My voice barely made it out.

"Because according to our second, none of Aren's Seven have more than a fifty-fifty chance of surviving the first wave. Which means...we need fail-safes. This is one of them."

My heart clawed toward my throat. Panic did a quadruple fucking backflip in my chest. I'd just found them—I couldn't lose them again.

"You and Mom have to get through this."

He gave a faint, tired smile. "We have no intention of leaving you, baby-girl. This is just *a precaution*. The Deadly Seven's version of writing a will."

"Aren set this up?"

"He...advised. Said historically, they've been necessary." Careful words for a strategic choice. Even if Ally saw that conversation, she wouldn't go digging out of respect. Jesus, this was so fucked. "Your mother and I did the rest."

"Who else hasn't let Ally read them?"

The corner of his mouth twitched, and he turned toward the wall of firearms, golden light illuminating the display like an art exhibit instead of a weapon cache. "Bash. But we lost him last year. August killed that demon, at least, so there's that small mercy. Eloise Westerlund. Their daughters. Your warden," he added with a snort. Reyna. Of course she was a secret keeper. Christ, there was no title more fitting. "They had to be people—"

"Ally didn't interact with regularly," I deduced, the implication sinking into my stomach like a stone. He nodded, pressing his thumb to a screen beside the wall. An interface lit up, and he tapped through a series of commands before gesturing me forward.

"But you gave her blood," I said, breath catching. "On the killing field, you gave her your blood to read—so she'd know about me—"

"Freya." His voice was gentle as he caught my hands.

"Did you compromise this place? Does she know? What's the point of secret bunkers if you gave it all up just so she could find *me*—"

"Freya," he said again, slower this time, squeezing my hands. "Ally's gifts were compromised."

"She still read you," I insisted. His crooked smile made me question everything I thought I'd seen on that field.

"Give your old man a little credit," he said with a low chuckle. "Back when Ally was human, her accidental readings were like highlight reels. You know what mortals think about when they're dying? They replay their best moments. Their greatest regrets. Their sharpest memories. She read their final thoughts, babygirl. Only what they carried in that moment."

My eyes flicked between his as the truth settled in.

"We tested the theory a couple times, over the centuries. When she was depleted. She didn't know we were doing it, but she only ever saw what they saw. Ally knows what I chose for her to know. What she *needed* to know...to get you out of there."

My lip wobbled. I stared at him—this warrior who'd built a life of sacrifice and silence. A man who had put oceans between himself and his only family to protect the rest of us. For centuries. How unspeakably lonely.

"What now?" I asked, once I could trust my voice not to crack.

"Now, we scan your biometrics into the system, and I show you around. If shit hits the fan, Freya, you get our people here. Should something happen to Ally, you bring *August*."

There were worse fates, I supposed, than joining their ranks as a secret keeper. At least this way, the three of us would have each other—just like Ally, Aren, Alec, and Fae did. Like August did now. Maybe my timing hadn't been an accident. Maybe I'd come back to shoulder the burden with the ones who carried it best. And the fact that he chose to share it with me?

That was everything.

I nodded, throat too tight to speak. He glanced at the screen, and I lifted my hand. Ansel chuckled and guided me over to the reader, scanning my prints.

"Now," he said, fingers flying across the keys. "While the system's doing its thing—what was it you said you needed our help with? Ally has Aren and me meeting with mortals all week, but tonight is yours."

I flashed him a watery smile, scrambling to pull the mission back to the front of my mind.

Reagan. Right. Reagan was going down—before the horsemen opened the gates. And if I had to burn every thread she'd ever woven to do it, so be it.

"Reyna says Reagan's son is obsessed with history. *Our* history, specifically. But apparently he's not above collecting rare items and tomes, mortal or otherwise. Think anyone in the coven has something that might lure him out if I dangle the right carrot?"

Ansel studied me for a long moment, weighing something behind his eyes. The machine chirped softly, and he dropped my hand and entered another command.

"I can think of a few things we've picked up over the years," he said at last. "But first—are we getting the carrot back?"

"I make no promises," I said, grinning. "But I'll do my best."

With a wry smile, he turned back toward the door. "You gonna tell me why we're baiting her kid if you're not planning to use him as leverage?"

The black leather of my gloves creaked as I tightened my grip on the arms of the metal chair. Round and round, I rolled a strawberry-flavored hard candy across my tongue, eyes locked on the psychopath tied to a matching chair across the interrogation room. Chin dipped, mask up, I watched Nix lower into a squat, two Wings flanking the perp as he screamed behind a blood-soaked gag.

Luckily, the masked man's tip about O'Haire had panned out. Unfortunately, that meant I had to deliver on my end—and he didn't strike me as the patient type.

I had to admit, it was a refreshing change not being on the receiving end of my cousin's brutality. Watching him stalk the metal table of instruments, pacing like a tiger about to pounce, was almost enjoyable. Mother might not have sanctioned these side missions, but our Heiress had. And if I didn't know better, I'd say the smile in his eyes meant Nix was enjoying this.

"If I take out your gag and you scream, I'll pluck your fucking teeth out one by one," he said flatly, pliers dangling from his hand. "Your whining hurts my head. Things that irritate me don't get to keep existing. Got it?"

The wide-eyed bastard nodded frantically, whimpering around the gag. Nix yanked it free and offered a bottle of water—more mercy than he deserved, and a waste of plastic, if you asked me. After wiping a mix of blood and spit from his face, Nix stared him down and repeated the question.

"Where are the kids, man? Simple transaction—save your life, give me a location."

The beauty of Nix's warped view of balance was that it kept him flex-ible—especially if it meant dishing out some justice. He'd never admit it, but the way he lit up around my cousins' kids told me the dickhead might actu-ally care.

And while we might not have known what to do with a bust the size of the O'Haire ring, luckily enough, I knew of a rather uptight pain in my ass that might.

Not that it mattered. This piece of shit wasn't walking out of here. Nix knew it. I knew it. And judging by the pinch of Spencer O'Haire's brow, *he* knew it too.

"I-I d-don't know anything," he stammered, eyes darting from Nix's hooded face to ours. Still squirming in his restraints, wrists rubbed raw. Nix pressed a hand to the bullet wound in his leg, and O'Haire squealed like the pig he was.

"I swear, you've got the wrong guy!"

"Hear that, Nightwatch?" Nix said, head tilted, voice mockingly bright. He turned just enough to meet my gaze. "Got the wrong guy."

I sighed, glanced at the clock, and rose slowly from my chair. My eyes stayed locked on the target as I strolled toward the table of instruments, rolling the candy in my mouth. I grabbed a crowbar without ceremony, crossed the room—and swung.

Bone shattered with a sickening crack. His hand, still bound to the chair, caved under the force of the blow. Nix flinched back just in time to dodge the blood spray, but no one else moved as the perp screamed.

The crowbar still in hand, I crouched beside Nix, resting the bar behind my shoulders. O'Haire writhed and whimpered, the sound grating against the steady drip-drip-drip of blood hitting the tarp-lined floor.

I shifted the candy again, cracking its center. Too-sweet syrup spread across my tongue as the man's agony painted the air.

Somewhere along the way, the whispers started.

That the heathens in *The Rougarou* could find people.

Could *help*, if you were desperate enough to track them down.

That the tattooed blond in the corner booth—the one in the black jacket —could bring them home. One way or another.

That's how, on a stormy October evening, a girl so slight a stiff breeze could carry her off slid into the booth beside Carr and me. Early twenties, maybe. If she'd had more weight on her, she'd probably look younger.

She was shaking. Pale. Scared. But she still handed me a photo—two beautiful blonde girls, their faces trembling in her grip.

Blue eyes. Tan skin. Dimples. The older one was *maybe* sixteen, if the precision of her hair and makeup was any indication.

Sisters.

Her sisters. Snatched from the front yard of their foster home.

Which meant no one was fighting for them.

She showed me the doorbell footage before I could say no.

Broad daylight.

Motherfucking.

Daylight.

Police had no leads. Not since the lead detective turned up skinned and frozen in a warehouse meat locker.

I told her I couldn't help.

Sent Wings to get her home safe.

Kept the photo though.

Now, with what was left of the candy tucked between my cheek and molars, I let the crowbar drop from my hands. O'Haire flinched, dead eyes watering, blood still pooling beneath him. Slowly, I reached into my coat and pulled out the photo, holding it up between two gloved fingers.

"Tell me again that you don't know Sadie and Ashley," I said, voice low, lethal. "I fucking dare you."

THE SHADOWS DROPPED us on the front lawn of *Luminark Manor* the next morning, just after it was all over. The collective flap of wings and deep croaks signaled a dozen ravens returning to their trees as our familiars let down their guards. Poe trotted along beside my boots, giving a throaty *tok* that I took as approval. My theory was confirmed when I raised my arm and he landed, glassy eyes twitching as he studied my face.

"All good, buddy," I murmured, stroking his sleek coat. That was all he needed—he launched into the air to rejoin the others at their perches along the perimeter.

We crossed the ward line without a word, and once inside, Nix was the first to speak. "So, what now?"

"Now, I owe Calypso and Lonan turns with a ghost."

"You're still on that?" he scoffed, already stripping off his cloak and the blood-streaked shirt beneath it as we filed into the prepped locker room. A pile of evidence dumped in the center tarp was growing by the second.

"You got a better explanation for Uptown, shithead?"

"Look, princeling, I know you like your fairy tales, but we've got actual fish to fry."

I deadpanned at his use of Lonan's less than flattering moniker and yanked my own clothes up and over my head, tossing them in the pile as somebody behind us started the showers. Growing up, Charles and I begged our mother to tell us the old stories. Back then, I'd thought it was about our obsession with lineage—our ancestral claim to the Stuart crest, the noble bloodline we were meant to defend. But really, I think it was just one of the rare ways the Queen acknowledged we existed.

We lived for the tales spun in blood and shadow, but one story fascinated us most: the *Brothers of Blackthorn*. A tragedy, sure—but buried in it was the promise of the Obsidian Crown. Crafted centuries ago, lost in translation and time, but one truth endured: *he who possessed it would become Keeper of the Veil.*

And it was the promise of that title that led to our downfall.

My brain was already scrambling when Carr mercifully cut in.

"Yeah? On that note—how's your intel on our masked intruder looking?"

When Nix's eyes hardened, I chuckled, unbuttoning my pants. "That's what I thought."

"Our Queen trusts him," Nix growled—but the current beneath the words didn't sound like confidence.

"You saying you do too?" Carr asked, scowling as he peeled off his gloves and eyed the blood lining his forearms.

"I'm saying that should be enough."

"Because hierarchy leaders have never been bonded, forced, or coerced into compliance," I muttered, stepping into the showers as a few of the Wings rolled up the tarp for incineration.

Our routine was surgical. We stepped into our stalls and scrubbed like hell—every trace of blood, sweat, and magic gone. Never forget your fingernails. Be meticulous with your hair. Some dumb fuck skipped that step a few years back—got convicted on residue. We didn't let him rot, but burning an alias to fake a death is a bitch. I never skipped my hands. Nix said it was overkill with our gloves. I said fuck that. Some stains stayed with you—literally and otherwise.

"We called a meeting with The Six. Grayshell and Bellaton are both hunting this ghost. They say he's English."

"Then call Pinebarrow, or Carroway, or Seasmith. Not my fucking problem," I said, shampoo dripping down my face.

"And if war breaks out?"

"That depends on the tip of the scales, doesn't it?"

"War always tips the scales," Carr pointed out—surprising me. "Look, brother, I know you're pissed. I know the four of you have shit to work through—but Nix is right. We need to think."

By "four of us," he meant the Paladin royal family. Yeah. We fucking did. Dad knelt to Mother no matter the cost. Cali—brilliant as she was— didn't give a shit about anything beyond her lab, despite being next in line for the throne. And my mother? Preached balance. Practiced selfishness.

"Did I just have a stroke? Nix was right about something?"

I didn't need to open my eyes to know my sister had entered. I dunked my face under the stream, finishing the rinse, as Nix cursed and shoved his citrus body wash back onto his shelf.

"Fucking dammit, Cali. Shower. Privacy. Ever heard of it?"

"Don't flatter yourself, Nix," she shot back. "And I see being clever was a one-time thing. I'm here for my brother."

"Great timing," I muttered, turning off the water and catching the towel she tossed. She stared at the ceiling while the other guys scattered, heads down as the three of us wrapped towels around our waists.

"Little hypocritical, don't you think?" Nix grumbled. "If we walked into *your* locker room, you'd order a lashing."

She flipped him off, unbothered. Her gaze found mine, and a smile curved her lips. "I approve," she said simply.

I narrowed my eyes. "Of what, exactly?"

"Your plan to ensnare the Wraith. I like it."

A slow smile tugged at my mouth. "Good."

"Someone wanna fill me in?" Nix snapped, sulking like a toddler.

"If you had a say, sure. But as it stands—get the fuck out," Calypso said, jerking her thumb toward the door.

"I'm one of your Wings."

"And you'll do what I say. Right now, I need my second and third. You're dismissed."

I didn't bother hiding my laugh as Nix glared and stomped off. His scowl lingered at the door.

"Feel better?" I asked.

"Loads," she chirped, sitting on a dry bench. "Also, Mom and Dad are off meeting with The Six."

"Ahh," Carr and I said in tandem, exchanging looks as we headed for the door. With our parents gone, Cali *was* the executive power. That meant the plan was greenlit—for the next couple hours, at least.

"How long do we have?"

"They just jumped. Two hours. Maybe three."

"That's enough."

Her grin turned wicked. I gave her a look as we headed down the hall. *"What are you doing? Why are you* smiling *like that? You look like a psychopath."*

She cackled then flashed me her *I-know-something-you-don't* grin that meant either glory or doom. No in-between.

"You know what else is enough?" she said smugly. "Two hundred and twenty-five thousand dollars."

I froze. "You're shitting me."

My sister just beamed. "You got it, Cy."

"Got what?" Carr asked. "Somebody catch me up, please?"

"We put a bid on the Shield of Saint Ascalon. Showed up at a private auction. Mortals didn't know what they had—we got it cheap."

According to our lore, the Paladins came out of the great divide, where the mother hierarchy fractured into twelve smaller factions, set to disperse throughout the known world. They served the crown until the church corrupted from within, at which point our ancestors opted to serve the balance instead.

Along the way, the mother hierarchy's treasures had gone missing. Our history books. Our relics. The documentation of our royal line. The Middle Realm grew sick, and somehow our stories went with it, leaving her descendants to piece together what we could from the scraps left behind. The Shield of Saint Ascalon belonged to the first Paladin, allegedly imbued with his power, with a sapphire enchanted to defend the weak. Lost for centuries. And now it was coming home.

Carr blinked, impressed. "Damn." He clapped me on the shoulder as he passed, still shaking his head when he paused outside his door, one hand on the knob. "It's a damn good day, brother."

One less monster in the world. Dozens of kids safe—Sadie and Ashley among them. And a relic returned to our line.

"Yeah," I said, almost scared to say more.

"I'll see you in the war room in ten."

"Relish in your victory later," Cali said, winking. "Today, we move players on the board."

"Thanks, sis," I muttered, ruffling her hair before heading to my room.

Music on.

Systems online.

I pulled on clothes while my software updated, scanning the web for anything up my alley. Just as I tugged on my socks, a notification popped up. Email. I reached out and tapped it open.

Bank confirmation: my security questions had been successfully changed.

Stomach bottoming out, I yanked on my boots.

Not today, ghost girl.

An ethereal gust of preternatural wind woke me the day after our first fruitless field trip to California, but when my eyes opened into the gloomy gray space, four vacant walls greeted me.

Ally, where are you, baby? I asked mind-to-mind as I sat up, painfully aware of how tight my hamstrings were after demon hunting the prior evening. That had been the more exhilarating pastime, as our days had been spent attempting to secure human alliances and encountering disbelief and crippling distrust more often than not.

"Ally?"

Resounding silence was my answer. Even after opening the bedroom window, the muffled isolation of snowfall was my only greeting. With a sigh, I pulled on my pajamas and a pair of combat boots before padding out into the hallway and down the stairs. The last lingering flicker of the fire in Kingsley's metal stove was my only form of company, and it was dancing in unnatural movements, spindly limbs stretching and curling like a ballerina made entirely of flame.

Ally?!

Fear skittered down my spine, but I silenced it, closing my eyes and holding out my hands as I'd so often watched my mate do—sensing, probing—even as our bond burrowed deeper, gently tugging at the karmic thread binding us together.

She didn't tug back.

But intuition had me glancing out and to the left. On silent feet, I snagged my jacket from the coat rack by the door before creeping out and down the porch, where—sure enough—steady footfalls broke the glimmering crust of late winter snow. Three sets, to be exact. Stretching my magic, I found them. Like a distant tug on that invisible line—a song meant only for me. Following their trail, I ventured into the blanketed darkness, intrigue and concern warring in my chest. Why weren't they answering mind-to-mind? What on God's green earth had drawn them out into the frigid morning?

The world had gone gray again inside this mountain valley; the clouds grazing the earth in a foggy hug that chilled my lungs with every breath. Allowing my flames to spark in my veins for warmth, I looked up and around, studying the crystalline layer of hoarfrost coating each branch and pine needle as I entered the perimeter of the forest at the far side of Kingsley's property.

What felt like an eternity later, my steps slowed as I spotted Ally—dressed in nothing but her silky pajamas—standing in eerily immortal stillness, staring out over the sunken snowfield of a frozen pond.

"Ally? Baby?" I breathed, unsure why I felt such an intense instinct to stay quiet. A subtle shushing sound drew my attention to where the Carters huddled beneath the bowed branches of an evergreen, wrapped in a fluffy fur blanket. A small flame flickered in front of them, dancing in that same peculiar pattern—as if her magic was conducting them without her awareness.

"No, mate," Alec whispered, shaking his head adamantly.

But it was the hard set of Fae's jaw and her furrowed brow that had my attention darting between them, then back to Ally—and around the surrounding space.

Her eyes were locked a million miles away, staring into the other with such blind fixation that I couldn't help but study her, silently closing the distance. She didn't so much as shift. Didn't flinch. Didn't adjust her weight or her deep, steady breathing that spoke of sleep. But her eyes...they were twitching. Lids fluttering at an impossibly fast pace—like she was seeing everything at once.

I reached for her mind, terrified I'd find her trapped in one of those sweat-inducing nightmares that robbed her of peace—but Alec's shield snapped forward, coiling around my own with the viciousness of a boa constrictor.

Anxiety had me looking sidelong, earning one simple shake of his head, his expression uncharacteristically serious.

Opting to trust his judgment, I made my way over to their makeshift camp where they'd cleared the ground of snow and ice with magic. Settling beside Fae, I smiled weakly when she lifted her fur blanket like a wing in offering.

Anxiety chewing a hole through my windpipe, I ducked beneath it, nodding in thanks before the three of us...watched.

The gentle glow of rising sun beyond the thick canopy of clouds and forest turned the frozen lake into a softbox, a glow gradually filling the space as she continued to stare—only the puffs of breath solidifying before her proving she was alive and not carved of the mountain itself.

Mentally, I reached out, tapping against Alec's shield, relieved when his eyes flashed to mine a beat before he dropped his walls and let me in.

What is this? Is she sleepwalking? I asked quickly.

Kind of, but also, no.

Very helpful.

I do try. He chuckled softly, and we both looked back to where she stood, watching her breath cloud and dissipate. *She's...entranced in visions, for lack of a better explanation.*

I don't understand. I've never seen her do this.

I have, Alec assured, though something foreboding lingered in his voice.

Albeit, only once, Fae amended.

When?

When she read Aren, Alec said. *In the beginning.*

Painfully, I peeled my gaze from her to look at them. My friends. The shield and the Goddess. Alec's amber eyes carried a kind of agony I was afraid to ask about.

It nearly broke her, Aphaea thought softly, shaking her head. *Thousands of years of bloodshed, loss, and grief—what Aren endured as a mortal alone would be enough to drive most to madness. But in the centuries since...*

He's lost everyone he's ever cared for, Alec said. *Over and over again. We've all been ripped from him—sometimes we circle back in decades, other incarnations take lifetimes. But he's spent centuries in complete solitude. Staying steady for his Commanders, then for his people. Grayshell has risen and fallen. Great wars have devastated our numbers more than once. And he was always left to survive the aftermath. Alone.*

His father was a monster, Fae said. *Abused them all.*

Sold them like cattle. Aren was beaten, defending his sister when men came to take her. His father meant to sell her. Aren volunteered instead, insisting his strength and experience with a blade should fetch a higher price. His mother tried to save him. His father killed her. Right in front of him.

*Then came the Colosseum...*Fae's thoughts drifted, her eyes lifting toward Ally. I blinked hard, the burning behind my eyes building.

Why? I thought gently. *Why would he let her live all of that through him?*

He tried to warn her, Alec explained. *But Ally wouldn't hear it. She believed she could handle it. It took years for him to trust her enough to let her in. I think...he believed himself a monster for a long time. And she didn't want him to be alone in that. She wanted him to have one person who knew everything—and still loved him.*

We were all back, but...

It was dark, I said. *More than he should've survived.*

Our Commander may be feared now, but the man knew nothing but abuse, Fae whispered. *Soldier, then sacrifice, then slave. Flesh traders. The unthinkable—*

Her voice broke.

Beaten, assaulted, branded, used as a whore for the nobiles, Alec continued. *He killed one of his lanistae—his handler—but they broke him for it. Threw him in with* lions *as execution. Bastard survived.*

When he was finally free, Fae thought, *he beat his father to death with his bare hands.*

Then he tried. He really did, Alec added. *He ascended, but...he's lost every lover.*

Every friend.

Every confidant.

Leader.

Second, and third.

Again and again.

It wasn't until Ansel and Marcus returned that he let anyone back in, Fae explained. *It took time. But we convinced him he didn't have to carry it all anymore.*

With every word, my chest grew tighter. *She lived all of that. At once. Through him, but still.*

She wouldn't let go, Alec said. *Ansel and I tried. We tried to break them free, but she's too damn strong. Aren was locked in there with her, and...He* shook his head. *Tears just started pouring from his eyes. Her eyes looked like that. This feels just as heavy.*

I couldn't watch, Fae confessed, her voice steeped in shame.

Ansel and I tried to stay, but even we lost our stomachs. Me, more than once, Alec added.

How long has she been out here like this? I asked, breath like lead in my chest. *Where was she locked now? In pain? Or was she finally seeing true visions again, like she'd begged the threads for?*

My eyes drifted to the others. *She'd read nearly everyone in the hierarchy—only a few had refused to let their Second inside their story. Which meant...she carried it all.*

Their grief. Their pain. Their shame. Their secrets.

It lived inside her.

I'd known her "gift" felt like anything but. But hearing Aren's story made it *real*.

Jesus Christ.

I dunno, mate, Alec said. *We woke a few hours back, found her tracks, followed them out here. She locks in like this during readings—but she's not reading anyone now, so...*

My gaze snapped to Ally. The rapid twitch of her eyes. The way her hands hung at her sides, fingers slightly curled—

As if she was holding someone's hand.

I'm not so sure about that, I thought, horror rooting in my gut. *Were you able to get through her shield?* I asked, suddenly breathless, needing to know she was okay.

Just for a few seconds at a time. The images are like strobes—moving too fast to make sense of.

I was on my feet before I could stop myself, heading for my mate.

August, Alec warned. *I know none of us want to see her in that kind of pain again—but if you interrupt this—visions or reading—you'll break it. Like your reading on the field. Only fragments will remain. And she'll have to relive the worst of it just to get to the rest.*

How long did it take to read Aren? My pulse spiked. I yanked off my coat, a cold sweat soaking through my shirt.

Alec shook his head. *Days, mate. Days.*

I'm supposed to leave her out here for days? I snapped. *In the damn snow?*

That's what she needed from us for you, he admitted. *We failed to give her that. It never felt like the right time. That was a shitty call. Aren agrees. Please don't ask me to fail her again.*

I met his pleading eyes, then looked back at her. I'd likely peeled the top layer off my bottom lip from biting it before I finally nodded.

She won't freeze—her flames won't let her, right? I asked.

Alec shook his head. *She's a phenomenal pyro, mate. With anyone else, I'd worry. But she's got this rookie. Let her work.*

"Fuck," I exhaled, nodding, and walked to the edge of the bank— anchoring myself in the steady whoosh of her blood pumping through her heart.

FREYA

THREE DOORS, twenty first-floor windows, one enormous glass pane in the drive-thru. Four cars in line, one woman at an ATM, five civilians, six employees, one vault. Two body cams, one hacker, five of us on comms, and as few minutes to work with before response was inevitable.

Had I intended to work with a team to check off my incognito Paladin trials? Not in a million years. I mean, as long as I was the one orchestrating and redirecting the money from the corrupt to the needy, it should fulfill the rules. Beyond that, was it kinda nice not flying entirely solo?

Yeah. Yeah it was. Even if (especially because) Blaz Gwyne was equal parts thrilled and terrified to be included on an op.

"You're sure about this?" Blaz asked for the millionth time, straightening the collar on his black leather jacket as we sat side by side in the tinted SUV.

"Ally hasn't called to tell me we fucked the plan up the ass with a cactus and no lube, so yeah, I think we're alright."

"Jesus Christ, Freya," Brody mumbled from the front seat, his eyes widening in the rearview as he fought back what had to be a smirk. He thought I was funny. He just didn't have the balls to admit it.

His brothers, however, both burst out laughing.

"This still seems like a dumb way to get arrested," Blaz muttered, shaking his head as he stared out the window at Cyrus 'C.' Stuart's bank.

To my other side sat Tessa, Marcus Westerlund's daughter. Just like her predecessors, the shifter's electric blue eyes sat in stunning contrast to her warm brown skin, dozens of breathtaking braids pulled into a sexy high pony. Evidently, when her uncle wasn't available, Tessa was a close second in the computer-whiz department.

"Well with that attitude, of course it is, silly," I said, plopping the fedora over his head. "But everybody's gotta pop their cherry at some point, and you said you wanted to help."

"If you're not calm, cool, and collected, you'll blow this whole thing," Tessa pointed out, glaring his way as her fingers flew a million miles a minute over her keyboard—eyes locked on coded gibberish I'd sooner tattoo on my ass than understand.

"Stand tall." I flicked his chin up. "Shoulders back." A playful shove. "Attitude mellow," I added, miming smoking a joint.

Tessa snickered, shaking her head.

"You're *just* withdrawing some cash. Your assistant called ahead. You remember the plan."

"Couldn't she just transfer it out?" he asked, glancing between Tessa and the bank entrance.

"I could," Tessa agreed, "but Freya's right. We don't want a trail. I'm good, but I'm not that cocky. I can't fathom the Paladins don't have someone better."

"In short, cash is king," Brody added helpfully, earning a snort from soap boy where he sat in the passenger seat with his boots on the dash.

"So why don't you do it?" Blaz shot back. I leveled him with the glare that deserved.

"Because while Brody is too sexy for his shirt, the man belongs in a museum."

"Rude."

I ignored the giant. "He's over seven feet tall and, at best, looks like he's in his early thirties."

"Again, *rude.*"

"You're nearly the same age as your cousin, and according to your mother, the two of you look alike."

"Blond hair and hazel eyes hardly make me a doppelgänger," Blaz grumbled.

"But add some ink illusions," Tessa tapped his knuckles, where her father had enchanted look-alike tattoos based on intel from Reyna's spies, "and some tacky fashion choices, and you're golden."

"But if we sit here any longer, that'll raise suspicion, so either shit or get off the pot," I said, blinking pointedly.

"Ohhh," Blaz groaned. "I'm gonna regret this."

"That's the spirit." I slapped his back, then leaned over to unlatch the handle and kicked open the door. "Now, move your ass. I'm with you every step of the way." I tapped my earpiece as Tessa hoisted her laptop, showing him his body cam feed. I quickly decided I would keep her. It was rare to find another female who carried the same chaos I was born with.

"You owe me," he growled, stepping out of the SUV and straightening his slacks.

"This is going to work," I said, returning his glare when he tried to laser-beam me into surrender. "You love me and you know it." I blew him a saccharine kiss before shooing him away and slamming the door closed.

"Pop. His. Cherry?" Brody asked from the front seat.

"Eh." I shrugged. "He'll get over it. Now hush—I promised him we'd listen. We're sure this ID will work?" I triple-checked with soap boy, who was allegedly a convincing forger. He flipped me off, and I burst out laughing.

"Alright. Any objections? Speak now or forever hold your peace."

"I can hear you, you know?" Blaz snarled—then cleared his throat. Was it an absolute Hail Mary pass—throwing Reyna Gwyne's mortal son into the role of conman?

Hell yeah.

Did I think it would work?

Abso-fucking-lutely.

Was I having way too much fun pushing this kid out of his comfort zone? Yup.

Besides, his mama and her crew were busy hunting the fuckers who killed Darius, determined to reverse-engineer their reaper venom bullets before all-out war sent everything sideways.

"Yes. Now be a very good boy and open the door for the people ahead of you. Thieves don't have manners, and they *definitely* don't hold doors."

"Lord forgive me," he muttered before straightening and jogging ahead to open the door for the arm-in-arm couple across the lot.

They dipped their heads with a pleasant thank you, and I watched Blaz step inside behind them.

I glanced at Tessa's computer. I had to admit—doing this with tech was a lot more fun than doing it without.

"See? You're doing great, kid. Keep your head down like you're checking your phone. You've got a camera at your three and nine."

Blaz did as instructed, scrolling his phone as the line moved forward.

"Doing great," I murmured, smirking when Tessa shot nervous electric blue eyes my way. I shrugged, covering my mic to hiss, *"Isn't he?"*

"We're about to see," she whispered back. "Still want me to drain the other accounts as soon as he's out?"

"Yeah," I said, grinning like an idiot. Revenge tasted sweet in every flavor, but my favorite kind was the slow and steady dismantling kind—with a sprinkle of pain-in-your-assery. "But not a minute sooner."

"Obviously," she said dryly, popping her knuckles. Sometimes I wondered what it would be like to work with my brain instead of my hands. Then I had moments like this, where it took everything I had *not* to bolt into the building after him.

"Retie your shoe," I murmured. "Don't answer—just kneel. Let the guy who came in after you go ahead. You're going to the teller on the right."

Much to my satisfaction, he did. And continued to, throughout the entire transaction—seamlessly reciting the new security answers we'd programmed.

I was starting to think we might get out scot-free when Tessa elbowed me in the ribs, manicured nail tapping the screen. The alley camera showed two men—faces shaded by rat-pack hats, collars popped—approaching fast, and pissed.

"Don't run," I warned. "But we gotta go. We've got company."

"On it," Tessa said, passing me the computer and untangling herself from the cords. She ran delicate fingers along her cute laid edges to smooth them, then turned and swiped Ajax's coffee right out of his hands.

"Hey!" he barked, but she was already gone.

I hadn't planned to put Tessa in anyone's path—but she was the only one who wouldn't need to stick around. Much less likely to show up on camera later.

Plus, she was gorgeous. Killer body. Nice rack.

Men are men.

"Steady, Blaz," I murmured, watching him move through the lobby at the same pace as the men in the alley. "Not too fast, but don't slow down."

Tessa made a beeline down the sidewalk, pulling out her phone. I flipped back to the overhead cam, unsure which angle would be best. She was speed-walking—head down, braids swaying, coffee rising to her lips just as she slipped between the buildings—

And collided directly into the taller man.

He spun, hands out to catch her. The cup must've burst—judging by the puddle spreading at her feet. Outraged, she flung her hands, shaking off the coffee. Her head snapped up—pissed.

Right until Stretch grabbed her arm, apologizing with his other hand.

She resisted. Then relaxed. Shook her head. Glanced at her shoes.

Oh my God.

Was he flirting with her?

They really can't help themselves.

The car door whooshed open and I jerked my head up to find Blaz sliding in beside me.

"Get in," I hissed, waving him forward as he climbed in, pale but upright. Brody still watched Tessa's little scene unfold.

She shook her head, waved the men off, and continued down the sidewalk.

When she crossed the street and slid in next to me, she was grinning—expression all feline.

I couldn't help but wonder if she took after her mother or father when she shifted.

"God damn," she said, fanning herself. "They make them pretty in the South."

"Cheers," I chuckled, handing her the laptop.

The three of us bumped fists as Brody began a smooth, reasonable victory crawl out of the parking lot.

"To correcting the balance."

TWENTY-THREE
CRUCIBLE
FREYA

There's nothing quite like a thief's high, but seeing Blaz hyped up on adrenaline and talking a million miles a minute was a close second. "You thought of everything, you evil genius—how did you work through the cameras so quickly?"

"Practice," Tessa said simply, shaking her head, but her lips were just as curved as mine. "Lots of practice."

"You get a knack for evaluating surveillance over time, but everybody's gotta start somewhere."

"I'm not sure Reyna would particularly approve of the direction this conversation is taking," Brody said from the front seat as he rounded the last corner onto her street.

"Cockblocker," I jabbed, rolling my eyes as I passed Tessa the final cord —now neatly wound—and she tucked it inside her bag.

"No cocks were blocked in the making of this heist," Blaz interjected, sending both Tessa and me into a fit of giggles.

"You've got a long way to go before we'll classify it as a heist, kid," I chided.

"Besides," Tessa added, "if you're clever, you'll mimic your mentor over here and be in and out without causing a scene."

"It really is the way to go," I encouraged.

"Always so humble," Alastair grumbled from where his long-ass legs were cramped into the back seat.

"Certainly not something anyone's ever accused me of."

"You sound like Alec," Tessa pointed out.

Grinning, I said, "I'll take the compliment."

"Whoa," Brody's sudden tone had us all craning for a view of whatever he was seeing through the windshield.

"We didn't have a strike scheduled," Blaz breathed as we took in the litter of teens on the front lawn, Reyna and her inner circle weaving through them, healers busy in what looked like a designated injury line.

The high abandoned us as quickly as it struck. The second Brody rolled to a stop, we were flying out and around the hood. Reyna's eyes locked on mine, and she jerked her chin in silent summoning. Tessa, Brody, and his brothers jumped to her side, but—for once—there were no taunts or smirks sent my way as Blaz and I jogged over.

"What is this?" Blaz demanded, taking in the thousand-yard stares of a mostly female cluster of mortals. "We didn't have a unit deploying—"

"Sure as shit didn't," Reyna said, pursing her lips. "Woke up to a late Christmas present, it seems."

Reyna's "Flying Squad" had returned home over the last few days, filing in and all demanding justice for Darius with equal levels of fervor. To my surprise and utter delight, all her titled heads of coven were women.

Like their leader, there was a shrewdness to Reyna's squad—unrivaled by any other unit I'd seen in my many lifetimes. Words like knives, eyes just as sharp, they didn't give me the impression I'd get anything past them either.

Two of her coven leaders—sisters named Izzy and Makena—came down the stairs carrying cases of water, the mid-morning sun glimmering over their radiant mahogany skin and springy curls. Reyna's girls came in every shape, size, and power ranking—the only common denominator was an inhuman perfection that rivaled their queen's. The kind of beauty that left men dumb and women meek. And judging by the way they all carried themselves, they fucking knew it.

Makena broke left, handing her case to Montague with a nod before turning back for the estate. Her sister cut right, stopping at the healer's table before whipping a blade out and flaying the case open like a salmon, passing the bottles out herself.

"No idea who brought them in?" I asked, gaze scraping over once-young faces, now stripped of innocence—some bruised and ashen, others eerily preserved.

Reyna shook her head, a strand of golden hair falling loose from her braided updo. "Just this," she said, holding up a Polaroid with a crease down its center, the corner bent. When she turned it, I narrowed my eyes at the messy scrawl, goosebumps ghosting down my arms. Déjà vu.

Sadie and Ashley Johnson, followed by an address.

When I lifted my gaze, I had to turn to find Blaz, already climbing the porch steps with his phone in hand.

"It's on the Paladin side of the divide," Reyna said, drawing me back to her and correctly predicting my first question.

Three more of her Flyers descended the stairs in elegant dresses, the redhead at their center giving me a slow once-over before a cocky little smile stretched her cheeks.

Yes, you're prettier. No, I don't have fucks to give.

Diverting my eyes, I studied the girls in the photo again.

"Are they…" I glanced through the softly murmuring crowd, but Reyna hiked her thumb over her shoulder toward a healer who was tending to two girls.

"Accounted for? Yes," she confirmed.

"Do you mind?" I nodded to the Polaroid, relieved when she handed it over. At the very least, I could take it to Ally, see if she could read it and glimpse our unsuspecting hero.

"Thanks."

"Tell me where it leads."

"Yes, Commander."

My show of respect didn't go unnoticed, that spider's smile creeping up her face just before she cleared her throat.

"Alright. You're not paperweights. Make use of yourselves."

Between the order and her shooing motion, we dispersed into the recovery effort. Tessa stayed glued to her side, and as they waded into the gathering, I caught her next question.

"Do you know where you're taking them all? We have room in Chicago."

God, I *loved* my fucking family.

"NO PROBLEM, August. Please let me know when she comes out of it."

I'd called him later that evening, hoping to borrow our Second for a lightning-fast reading on our Freedom Santa. He brought me up to speed—human delegates were being obstinate, there was no progress on the book or the diadem, the bond was fucking finicky—and then told me about Ally's current preoccupation.

Jesus. She sounded terrifying.

"Yeah," he breathed, trying to project strength with a steady voice and trusting words that didn't fool me for a second. "Will do."

"August?"

"Yeah?"

"She's gonna be alright. You know that, right?"

"Trying to."

"Trust your wife, big brother."

"It's not her I don't trust."

I frowned, about to push back—what the fuck was that supposed to mean?—but he wasn't having it, quick to cut off my train of thought.

"Who—"

"Anyways. Gotta go, sis. Stay safe."

"Yeah," I breathed, but the line had already disconnected.

I was undoubtedly missing something, and I needed to get to the bottom of it. But as fate would have it, G came around the corner, lacking his usual exuberance.

Not that I could blame him. He'd been Darius' right hand for years.

"We got intel the Renown are moving tonight," he said in greeting.

I gave a quick dip of my chin. "Where at?"

"That's why I'm here."

Chuckling darkly, I guessed, "*Also* on Reagan's side of the river?"

Montague blew out a heavy breath, nodding solemnly, as if that barrier was actually going to keep us from getting what we needed. The image of Darius clawing at his poisoned flesh lit fire in my ribs, and I nodded, standing from the armchair I'd occupied during my depressing chat with August.

"Give me an hour to prep—"

G shook his head, the rare refusal freezing me mid-step.

"You gotta roll out now, Porter."

Narrowing my eyes on his haunted browns, I nodded. "Okay. Let me run to my room and get changed. I'll be down in ninety seconds."

He dipped his chin, rolling his full lower lip between his teeth with clear discomfort.

"Reyna sent a Paladin uniform up to your rooms."

It was only as I moved past him that his hand latched firmly around my arm, halting me in the threshold.

Pain ricocheted in those dark irises.

"Be careful, Freya. I don't wanna see that twice."

CYRUS

THE VIEW from the top spire of *Luminark Manor* had always been my favorite. Something about trading shadows for clouds of Spanish moss and a bird's-eye view of the grounds. Maybe it was getting above whatever creepy lingering souls haunted the top floor and into the sunlight.

Or, the petty, vindictive, scorned prince that I was, it was the fact that Ma fucking hated me being up here.

Round and round, I turned the origami star the Wraith left behind in my safety deposit box between my fingers. *Cocky little shit.*

Today had been the storm to end all storms.

Like her moniker promised, there was no trace left behind after folklore's ghost wreaked her havoc. My account hadn't been the only one emptied. Mom, Dad, and Calypso's personal accounts at our primary bank were drained to the dregs.

We had reserves, of course—but it was still an infuriating blow.

My firewalls had crumbled like fucking clay in the sun—all but one final line of defense guarding our offshore accounts.

And Bellaton was out in full force. Our shadows across the river came scurrying back with the fear of death in their eyes.

Which meant someone had stomped on Reyna Gwyne's pedicured toes hard enough that she was out for blood.

Not good.

But the bitch didn't stop there.

The IRS served us audits on *three* of Ma's most lucrative above-board businesses. *The Rougarou* got hit with a health violation—not inaccurate, but a pain in my ass regardless. Mortal repo men—with miraculously forged documentation—swiped *two* of our SUVs.

And to top it all off?

Calypso, Carr, and I spent our afternoon quelling tempers at *La Lune Noire* due to a "freak cyber glitch" that overbooked every. Single. Room. The lobby was a chaotic mob of exhausted, hungry, increasingly pissed-off travelers with nowhere to stay.

It was as if only international trips got rerouted into the glitch—every last one of them had endured at least fourteen hours of travel to get here.

In addition to the hundred dejected guests we were scrambling to accommodate, our reviews plummeted from a wave of one-star ratings claiming we had bedbugs, leaky pipes, and—*my personal favorite*—ghosts.

There wasn't a nicer hotel south of Manhattan, and *lilyloo98271* could kiss my pasty fucking ass for claiming otherwise.

As it became more and more apparent that these compound inconveniences were a brilliantly orchestrated dismantling of our livelihood, the star in my coat pocket started burning a damn hole through the silky lining.

God.

Fucking.

Damn her.

Well-organized causes were a prerequisite for balance.

Causes required resources—i.e., funding.

Funding required proper income and, more often than not, a way to launder that income.

She wasn't just here to burn Paladin down.

She was gonna do it with fucking flare.

The fact that no one had a single goddamn lead worth chasing was on me—and our people were starting to resent the failure.

Needless to say, it was a two-cigarette kind of day.

Which was what brought me here—lurking on the rooftop while the estate below filled with equally aggravated Wings, all busy putting out metaphorical fires like their lives depended on it.

I was taking a long drag when I spotted my father materialize beneath the great oak in the front yard, head down, shoulders tense as he marched toward the porch. Blowing out a long stream of smoke, I stubbed the cigarette out on a shingle and slipped into the shadows, gliding down to the front steps behind him.

"Dad."

Everything that needed saying landed heavy in that one fucking word. To my relief, he hesitated—then turned, the exhaustion in his pale face etched into every line. He jerked his head toward the barn. I nodded, and we both misted into the world between worlds.

"You alright, son? Long day."

"Yeah," I said flatly. "What aren't you telling me?"

"Straight to the point. Always been like your mother in that way."

My face must've twisted into a scowl without me realizing, because his turned scolding. "Meant it as a compliment."

"She hasn't exactly been forthcoming lately."

"She's spooked," he said—an excuse that fell flat.

"And hiding things from our fucking family."

"Cyrus—"

"Don't, Dad. You can't convince me any of this is coincidence. You're both hiding things. Taking intruders into private meetings. Refusing to shoot straight about strategy or intent in the war that's coming. Where, pray tell, does the balance lay?"

"You deserve explanations," he said, that soothing tone meant to placate a child. It did nothing for me. "But allow us to get our story straight."

"The truth doesn't need straightening," I snapped, barely keeping my temper leashed. "What happens if something happens to you and Ma? Calypso and I are just supposed to clean up your messes with no idea who we're even dealing with? Mysterious debtors show up and we just pay without proof? A royal family unprepared to defend the throne. This shit doesn't make sense."

Dad stared at me for a long moment. His chocolate eyes had always been darker than mine—but tonight, they were just as tired.

Finally, he gave a short nod. "Five minutes, Cy."

Needing no further prompting, I said, "Tell me about Valora Lamb."

Long seconds passed. He didn't tell me to fuck off—but the way his eyes stayed locked on mine, hard and assessing, made the silence drag.

"She saved your mother's life on the wrong side of the river. A tentative alliance became more. They were inseparable—for years. She just...fit, Cy. Fit here with us. Just as ruthless. Just as scrupulous. Hell, her fighting style would put the Northern assassins to shame."

"She was like a sister to your mother, Cy. Became her second-in-command."

That brought me up short. An ache pressed behind my eyes and I itched for another cigarette.

"Outsiders can't claim rank," I snapped. My gut told me there was more to this than he was saying.

"Right. *Outsiders.*"

"She was no Paladin."

"Not in the beginning."

My brows winged up and I took a step back. *Perplexed* didn't begin to cover it.

Dad huffed, pacing a tight circle before slumping onto a hay bale with a long sigh.

"You telling me she survived the Crucible?"

"First in a century—"

"And no souls have survived since," I finished for him, turning to pace the opposite direction as the pieces began to click.

Paladin law was murky to outsiders but blunt in execution: all could be forgiven, save for treason against your own. If a leader wasn't fit or if blood had been spilled without cause, there were trials and duels for that. No one was untouchable, but no Paladin was to be harmed without consequence. The balance came first—but harming your own? Execution.

There were only three ways for an outsider to be protected under the *Knight's Accord*:

Mated to a Paladin.

Sired by a Wing.

Or brave enough to petition for the Crucible and survive the ensuing series of trials testing both their allegiance and skill set. It culminated in a brutal initiation ceremony—a duel with a trained Wing. Most weren't daft enough to attempt it, and even fewer survived. It took most souls at least a year to complete. Which brought me to my next question.

"Where was she from?" i.e., what hierarchy created a thief or assassin so fierce she not only left—but survived the Crucible?

"She never knew," Dad said, sorrow mixing with something like fondness in his eyes. "Ascended alone—no known sire. Stumbled into a battle with the demonic Renown, saving your mother by fate alone."

"I don't—"

"Believe in fate," he finished. "I know. But you do believe in time. And you're running out of that before your mother comes looking for us."

"Did she kill her?"

The recoil to that question had me reassessing everything. His scowl carved a deep V between his brows.

"God, Cyrus, no. Your mother loved Valora. More than I was comfortable with."

Coming from a man who shared his mate with six goddamn Guardians, that actually surprised me.

"They were inseparable."

"Then how the hell did she end up on the east side of the river?"

He was already shaking his head, rising to pace again. "Val had a calling. Said she could feel it—but couldn't find it. We gave her our best trackers, but no one found a trail. She went a little mad, Cy. Kept saying she had a vow to keep. One night, long after witching hour, she left. Never came back. Your mother was *rocked*, son. Don't ever accuse her of something like that again. She didn't get out of bed for months after Val was killed. The Guard kept up appearances so the people wouldn't know how bad it was— but she wasn't right. Hasn't been the same since."

My theory dissolved on contact. I groaned, dragging my hands over my face.

Back to ground zero. If Ma wasn't behind Valora's death, then what else had angered her enough to make our lives hell now? It didn't make sense.

"Got any other murder accusations to fling around, or are we done here?" Dad asked, insult bleeding into his tone.

"The big man on the security cameras the day before Uptown burned. Was that who I think it was?"

A long breath. Then a curt nod.

"What the fuck," I muttered, turning in a tight circle before glaring down at him. "The strongest Commander this realm has ever seen strolls onto Paladin property and you don't think that's something your head of security should be privy to?"

"He came as an old friend. Didn't seem relevant."

"Fucking hell, Dad. *What did he want?*"

"Commander Amadeus came to see where we stood in the coming war."

"And?"

"I told him I didn't know. And that our queen wouldn't see him."

"Why?"

"Because it's the truth."

As luck would have it, that was the last bit of truth I'd get tonight—because Vesper and Portia came flitting inside, both out of breath, sparks dancing in their eyes.

"What?" Dad demanded.

Portia's box braids swayed as she stepped forward, chest heaving, eyes landing on me.

"The Renown are moving, my Prince. They have more of the cursed ammunition."

Surprise lifted my brow as I rose to my feet. "Take me there. Now."

She stretched out a rich amber hand. "Yes, Your Highness."

AUGUST

A GENTLE SQUEEZE on my shoulder had me jerking awake. I hadn't even realized I'd started to drift off—still sitting at Ally's feet, head in my hands, elbows braced on my knees.

Some guard dog I was.

I blinked up to find Kingsley staring down at me with that permanent scowl of his.

"Eat," he ordered curtly, handing me a steaming bowl of...*stew*. My mouth filled with saliva at the savory aroma of meat, herbs, and spices.

Blowing out a breath of relief, I reached up and accepted the offering with a quiet, "Thank you."

A grunt was his only reply as Terramyst's king turned his focus to my mate, his sorrowful eyes scanning her face—those haunted emeralds still trained somewhere far away.

"No change, I see."

"No," I agreed quietly, shaking my head as I cradled the soup in one hand, inhaling the rich scent. The spoon settled into my stiff fingers, and I practically moaned when I brought it to my chapped lips.

"Damn, that's good."

"I'll pass the praise to the chef," he said flatly.

"Extend my gratitude to Rose as well, please."

"Least we could do," he replied, still watching Ally like he could will her back to us with enough focus.

My vigil hadn't been entirely solitary—Alec and Fae had come and gone, as had Rose and Kingsley. Around midnight, half a dozen of their wolves had padded down to settle around us, keeping silent company while I took the chance to relieve myself, wash up, and grab coffee before rushing back with a thermos in hand.

The sun rose, and the pack melted back into the woods with the blanket of darkness, leaving us in that lonely kind of silence that only two people could make feel endless.

And with every hour Ally stayed locked in her visions, my prognosis worsened. Nothing good could come from being stuck there this long.

The color in her cheeks was fading, my anxiety was tightening like wire.

Kingsley seemed to notice the same thing. "She's flagging."

"Yeah," I breathed.

"Why?" he asked, curt and sharp, irritation spiking down my spine.

"It's been at least thirty-six hours of this kind of energetic output."

"Right. But you're not pulling on your reserves."

"No...?" I answered, earning a look that said I was one dumb son of a bitch.

"Feed her, August."

I stared at him, still wolfing down the soup like a starved animal. He shook his head.

"Jesus. You two really are new to this whole Bond thing. You can funnel your power into her without her needing to channel it. That's the whole point, Porter."

"How?" I asked, already rising to my feet. If there was anything I could do—*anything*—I'd do it.

"Soul Bonds weave two souls together. You can draw off or lend power at will. Once you've practiced, you don't even need to be near each other to do it. Just find the weak point in your own well—that's where she begins. Or at least, that's how ours works."

I held the bowl out to him and nodded when he took it. Wiping my mouth with the back of my hand, I nodded again. "Okay."

"Breathe, Porter." I did. "Center yourself. Connect with your power. I'm sure it feels infinite, judging by how you register to the pack."

Chuckling darkly, I muttered, "Was that a compliment, Commander?"

"Just stating fact. Focus, August—she needs you."

I nodded, closed my eyes, and sucked down a breath of frigid air. I dove into the well of power at my center, hunting for that weak point in the wall.

Nothing.

"I can't feel her," I grumbled, anger bubbling fast beneath the surface.

I was so fucking sick of feeling useless.

Sick of being a liability. Sick of living with the truth that in no life had I ever been enough to save her. It had to be different this time. *I had to be different this time.*

"Where is she, dammit?"

"You're in your fear, August. That's the death of all power. Settle yourself and call to her—not mind-to-mind. Let your magic talk."

"Trying," I growled.

When another long beat passed and still no progress, Kingsley huffed.

"Look. Can you picture her in the throes of passion?"

My eyes snapped open, lip curling back with a growl I barely kept in check.

He raised his free hand, unbothered.

Fuck, I felt like a lunatic.

"Connect with her there. The way your magic and hers intertwine when you're intimate? That's the same current you tap into now."

I held his stare, heart pounding.

He chuckled, setting the bowl down in the snow by her feet and backing away with both hands raised. "I'll leave you to it. Don't touch her—you jostle her out of that *trance*, and we're screwed."

Jaw set, I turned back to Ally and studied her face.

I thought of her lips beneath mine, the way her body melted in my hands, the breathless moans I pulled from her. I thought of her laughter. Her head thrown back in my Jeep, the sun lighting her face. Her smile, soft and full, as she ran her fingers over Estelle's antiques.

I closed my eyes and reached into the space we shared in the depths of midnight. Relief slithered through me the moment I felt it—an ember flickering in the dark.

Christ. Relief was a sweet fucking thing.

Slowly, I opened the wall between us. Elation poured through me as my magic rushed into her.

Her lungs expanded in a sudden gasp, like she'd just broken the surface of a deep, black ocean.

There.

Just like that, our energy flowed freely.

And I watched in real time as her color came back, her breaths deepened, her shoulders eased.

She siphoned only the top layer of my magic—just enough to refill her well.

Holy shit.

TWENTY-FOUR

THIRTEEN?

FREYA

My gentle triple tap on Reyna's study door sounded deafening in the now-empty hallway, nerves dancing in my belly as she cleared her throat inside.

"Reyna?" I called softly, hand settling on one of the blades at my hip, ears straining. Wetting my lips and pushing down the sting of hierarchy differences, I raised my voice as I knocked again. "Your Majesty?"

Something like a gasp slipped through the door. Goosebumps raced up my neck.

Oh man. This could go so, so badly.

Knowing that—and unwilling to risk her being in some kind of jeopardy—I drew a blade just before silently pushing the door open and slipping through the smallest gap I could manage.

One Bellaton queen. One open window. Two rippling curtains. Desk. Chair. Armchairs. Bookshelves. An empty wall behind the door I'd just moved through.

My tally came up clean, but it wasn't until I swept around the desk to check the cubby beneath that I finally felt at ease enough to slide the dagger back into its sheath.

"Reyna." This time her name came as a demand, unease settling in the pads of my feet and making stillness elusive.

She was hugging herself—toned arms wrapped tight around a pale blue nightdress with lace-trimmed cap sleeves. An audible whoosh of air filled her ribs just before she turned sharply to face me.

My heart sank as her throat bobbed and the painted lines of her mouth twisted with her sob.

Oh man.

Heists? Robberies? Steady sabotage of an enemy? All in my wheelhouse.

Processing emotion with healthy coping mechanisms? Soooo fucking not.

Per human tradition, I blamed my soul mother.

"I'm sorry," I muttered, gently closing the study doors to protect her privacy. "I can wait outside."

"No," she bit out with a jerky shake of her head. She sucked in a breath, cheeks puffed before exhaling through pursed lips. "That won't be necessary. I didn't expect you'd check in before leaving."

"Thought I ought to pay you that diligence."

"An unexpected turn of the table."

I chuckled, nodding, but clenched my jaw as a silvery trail glimmered behind the tears streaking her cheeks. She rushed to wipe them away, sniffling as she turned to face me and straightened her dress.

The woman had been a vault since the moment we left the healers' room after Darius' death—chin high, orders sharp, leading every strike against the Renown herself. This was the first crack I'd seen.

Forcing myself to close the gap, I softened my expression, holding her watery gaze as I said, "It's okay to feel, Reyna. I'm a wretched example, but that's what I've been told. He was a good man."

"One of the best," she murmured, nodding shakily.

I thumbed her dress strap back onto her shoulder where it had slipped, swiped a tissue from her desk, and held it out—all while my stomach squirmed at the idea of admitting how much my heart had been aching too.

Instead, I said flatly, "Just...don't let your crown slip. You're too...*relatable* right now. It makes me want to like you."

A watery laugh escaped her, lips twitching as she swiped the tissue under her eyes, smudging away mascara. "Can't have that now, can we?"

"Certainly not," I said, widening my eyes in mock horror as I stepped back to lean against the office doors.

She folded the tissue neatly and repeated the motion under her other eye.

"So, G tells me I'm Renown hunting tonight," I said, glancing at her dress. "But judging by the lace, I'm guessing you're not coming."

She shook her head, brow pinching. "Blaz and Montague are concerned I haven't slept since—" She swallowed instead of finishing the sentence. I understood more than I'd like to admit. "They say my mind will be compromised."

"Probably a good call," I offered, not pointing out the obvious.

She sniffed irritably, straightening her spine and lifting her chin. "Idle hands do not serve me well."

"Now *that*, I believe."

With a half-hearted chuckle, she tossed the tissue into a gilded waste bin. One last sniff, a roll of her neck, and she squared her shoulders, eyes hardening as she looked at me.

"There she is," I said, grinning.

"I want you in and out of there tonight, Freya," she ordered, gliding behind her desk and into her chair like a ribbon folding into place. She bent to slide open the bottom drawer. "If I had faith in anyone else crossing the river and returning undetected, they'd be going in your stead."

Metal and plastic clunked as she rummaged. I tilted my head, trying to see what she was fiddling with.

"Avoid conflict like the plague," she continued. "I've got shadows ready to bring you home the instant you cross back over. Your chaperones are unaware of this particular adventure—I don't think they'd approve much."

Also known as: You're on your own, kid.

I smiled. "Always did work better alone."

"Had me fooled," she replied, that spider's smile returning. She sat up with a triumphant, "*Aah!*"

"What's that supposed to mean?"

"You've complimented my team well this week, Miss Porter. For someone determined to run off on solo missions, you work in a unit marvelously. My coven heads and the Flying Squad all agree."

Well, that stopped me cold. I looked down at my freshly polished boots, then traced the gold filigree in the pale blue carpet.

"As it is, should you land yourself in trouble you can't get out of..."

She held something out.

"...burn this, and I will come calling."

A lone black feather twirled between her fingers and I fought a smile.

"Flying Squad, huh?"

"I do live for a double entendre."

"Yes, well. That won't be necessary."

She stepped around the desk, expression hardening again into the mask of the Bellaton Commander. "You'll take it because I order you to. And because I owe your Commander a debt I'd rather repay sooner than later."

"You—?"

"Story for another time, Miss Porter," she cut me off. Which was beyond unfair, considering she'd just tossed an entire grenade into my curiosity.

If Reyna owed Aren a debt, why had I been sent here? Couldn't he have called in the favor himself?

Of course, he wouldn't. The man didn't even use his gift to command *our* people, let alone manipulate someone's will.

Her eyes skimmed my face, then she gave the feather a little shake. "Time is of the essence."

I rolled my bottom lip between my teeth, eyeing the dark sheen. Raven feather, by the look of it.

With a nod, I took it and tucked it into my jacket pocket.

"Freya." Her voice stopped me at the threshold. I turned, head tilted just enough to catch her tone. "In and out, do you hear me? No trouble. Not tonight."

Cyrus

Through the realm of mist and shadow, twelve Wings and I took our places outside a dilapidated warehouse in Old Town. Flickering exterior lights revealed brick walls crumbling in more places than not, mottled with black mildew, green moss, and vines that wove around corners and ducked through the mortar.

On my count, I ordered, double-checking positions. *First goal is the ammunition. Second is their leader—take them alive. Understood?*

Understood, came their collective reply.

Good. Rattle the cage.

Rattle the cage, they echoed, energized. That was what we did. Dark beasts thought themselves infallible—untouchable—caged in golden bars of their own making. As Karma's executioners, our job was to make it tremble before we robbed them of the illusion of safety. Subtlety was not the assignment.

*Five. Four. Three...*My countdown faltered as movement flickered across the rooftop of the neighboring building. So brief I almost dismissed it —black as the night around us.

Sound off, I ordered, tension coiling up my spine.

Nix, position one.

Carr, position two.

Portia, position three...

The roll call continued. All the while, I scanned that building, waiting. Watching. The shadows hissed out and away, skimming across the gravel rooftop—but came up empty.

A trick of the eye?

Still uneasy, I glanced at my watch as the twelfth soul confirmed position. Poe, sensing my unrest, launched from his lamppost perch and circled the block, wings silent as sin. When he returned with nothing to report, I gave the all-clear, trying to shake the tightness between my shoulders.

I'd lost my damn mind.

Cyrus, on point, I reiterated. The shadows churned in anticipation.

With a murmured protection spell, I gave the nod, and chaos descended.

There was a specific flavor of satisfaction in watching the Wings dismantle a line of opposition. Before the Renown had time to react, we were inside—shifting through vents, emerging from darkness, blades catching light as bodies hit the floor in a rhythmic percussion of death. A symphony of justice. One soul at a time, we cleared the space.

Still no cursed ammunition.

I pressed deeper. Someone in this place had that elixir loaded into a clip, and I'd make Calypso's month bringing it back. Her cloud backups held some of the data, but this—the sample—was what she really needed.

On your left, prince, the shadows warned.

I ducked on instinct, slipping into a lit room no one had dared enter yet. An axe whistled past where I'd stood, and I lunged, blade sliding through a Renown's Achilles before I rolled and came up with steel in both hands.

Seven. Seven enemies, one of me.

Perfect.

I struck low, dodged high, drove a blade through one brute's belly and yanked up into his chest. Just as I evaded one, three more descended on us.

There.

A flash of blue.

The tallest bore a firearm with a glowing blue magazine, and with no shadows to retreat into, there was no choice but to fight and attempt to keep his men between me and those bullets.

Good plan in theory. Only, the next had a garrote around my neck in seconds.

Motherfucker.

My stab barely slowed him. His grip tightened as I clawed at the cord, scrabbling for air, stars flaring in my vision.

"Cy!" a voice barked in warning.

I twisted, jerking sideways, but my eyes locked on the big guy as he raised that cursed weapon—aimed dead center at my chest.

And my captor shoved me into the line of fire.

With a final wrench, I ducked sideways, jammed both arms up, and flung myself free. I was still gasping when another knocked my legs out. The world tilted and I collided with the floor, crushing the wind out of me. Boots soared past me as I rolled, spluttering—

A shadowy figure was sprinting across the rafters.

A Wing? That was our black uniform, but...the proportions were off. Small. Lithe. Fast as hell. Was I fucking hallucinating?

Still choking, I dove for the enemy with the cursed weapon. Like a goddamn bird, that uniformed figure dropped from the ceiling, and their boots collided with his skull.

We all went down in a tangled pile, my hand locking around the Renown's wrist while the lithe figure rolled and snatched the weapon, training it on our enemy.

"Clear!" echoed around us as the others finished the sweep.

Panting, "You good?" I turned toward my supposed Wing—

Gone.

Weapon? Also gone.

I spun, found the rafters empty, and my heart slammed into its cage.

There—nearly to the far side. The figure sprinted across a beam, Paladin uniform flitting behind her.

I hoisted my gun up and fired in rapid succession. The rounds ricocheted off her shield, but I swore she *flinched*. Which meant she knew exactly what those bullets in her hand could do.

"Wraith!" I barked, scanning frantically, and deciding the corner offices built into the far wall would be my best bet as our team opened fire.

Hopefully, they'd at least be distracting enough to slow her down. I bolted across the open space as she scampered through the open rafters above me. Leaping toward the wall of the office, my boots pushed off the siding as my gloved fingers clamped onto the sharp corner of the office's roof decking. With one great pull, I was on my feet, ducking under the railing to sprint across the plywood, dodging outdated HVAC equipment. Meanwhile, the Wings stopped shooting—probably concerned I was now in their line of fire.

"Stop!" I shouted as she vaulted up, and vanished through the hole above.

Fuck me.

Shouts echoed—at least two of my Wings were in pursuit. I leapt after her, cursing my height as I lumbered across the beam and cleared the skylight. I hit the rooftop, breath tearing from my lungs. Panting down thick gulps of air, I did a full three-sixty.

Nothing.

No trace. No sound. No shadow. Panic prickled through my chest—until the shadows tugged left.

There.

Three buildings over. Her figure leapt wide, graceful as a dancer in mid-flight. I followed into the realm between, traveled through shadow, and stepped into place just as she landed. She screeched—in frustration, not fear.

I caught her mid-momentum, sending us toppling over. I twisted and my shoulder slammed into the roof first as I curled instinctively to shield her body, the weapon skidding across gravel as I clung to her delicate frame.

What the fuck am I doing?

I rolled again, reversed our positions, shoved her off and drove my boot into her sternum.

She hissed—feral, feline, and vicious.

Vaguely, I recognized Carr yelling my name from the warehouse roof, but I was too busy scrambling to my feet to answer. In a mad dash, I dove for the weapon, dropped the mag into my palm, pocketed the ammo in two practiced motions, then slammed the empty mag back into place and spun, training the weapon forward. I was betting it had one round in the chamber.

My eyes swept the now-empty rooftop as I fought to catch my breath.

Anybody got eyes on her? I demanded mind-to-mind.

Negative. She's in the wind, man, Carr replied, his focus on me palpable.

Did you fucking see that? She just vanished, Nix added, surprising me.

Jumper? I guessed.

I don't think so, Carr thought. *She dove off the building like a fucking bird. I shifted down as fast as I could, but she was just gone.*

Goosebumps rose along my neck.

Then: soft rubber soles on asphalt.

I spun, sprinted for the opposite edge, and caught the tail end of her black cloak fanning out around a building's corner.

Find her, I snarled down the line, misting into the in-between as the Wings followed. *She doesn't leave the city, do you hear me?*

You have the Reaper's gun? Carr pressed.

Yes, but that was our ghost. She takes precedence. The heiress and our debtor both had stakes in her capture.

You're certain? Nix scoffed. Even mind-to-mind, I wanted to throttle him. My pulse ached in my throat as I moved feather-light through the streets, gun low.

The city mercifully slept, save for the occasional car. My senses burned with adrenaline.

Maybe I was fucked in the head, but the fact that she'd just vanished into nothing made the historian in me smile. It would've been disappointing if she didn't at least attempt to live up to the legend behind the moniker.

Pretty fucking certain, I muttered, checking an empty alley, shadows coiled to strike. *We need her alive,* I reminded them. Human targets bored us. But this? This was a real fucking hunt. My fingers twitched.

My eyes jerked skyward at the throaty cry of a raven.

She's yet to leave, Poe seemed to warn before he vanished again. I cursed when the next street up buzzed with nightlife. Clubs, bars, streetlights washing my shadows across the concrete.

I hesitated at the corner—that's where I'd go. Disappear into a crowd of bodies, laughter, and lust.

Firearm hidden at my side, I moved. We couldn't get too close in uniform without suspicion. I kept my mask up, guessing she'd shed hers. Probably ditching her Paladin gear in some bar bathroom as I stalked the sidewalk.

At your back, the shadows hissed—too late.

She hit me like a launched missile, slamming us both through the nearest shop window. Alarms shrieked. People screamed. I tucked my chin, eyes shut tight.

We hit the floor with an impact that ricocheted down my limbs, pistol skidding from my grasp. She popped up like the nightmare she was and slammed a forearm into my face.

I grabbed for her, yanking her away from the gun.

Rolling, I shoved up—but she hauled me back by my fucking jacket. I kicked hard, but agony flared as her blade tore through my ankle tendon with a vicious, growled, "Kee-*ahh.*"

Tears blurred my vision and I roared, flinging her into a brick column. Her head cracked back into it with a promising *thud.*

Panting, I struggled up, but my leg refused my weight as fire raged in my nerves.

Feral fucking demon creature.

I limped toward the reception desk. Scouring the shattered glass, where it glimmered in the flashing red alarm lights, I found our prize against the wall. I dragged my ruined leg toward it.

She released a blood-curdling battle cry and leapt onto my back. My knee buckled, and we hit the ground.

Then—teeth. Right where my neck met shoulder.

She just fucking *bit* me.

I bellowed, reaching behind us and wrapping her hood around my fist to heave her over my shoulder, my skin screaming as she *tore* through it. She landed flat on her back with a sob, mask torn where she'd bit through the damn thing. *Again.*

"Fuck!" I snapped a hand to the wound. "Rabid vampire bitch!"

"Get. Fucked," she wheezed, staggering upright. She vanished, reappearing beside the pistol. "Oh, fucking *finally!*" she cried, snatching it.

I braced.

But she didn't aim. Not at me, not anywhere.

She was frozen. Eyes brazenly locked on her hand, where shadows curled up her arm, she studied it like it was new.

"Wicked," she breathed, glancing back at me with victory in her eyes.

Then she winked—and vanished.

I stumbled through the broken window, dragging my useless leg through clinking shards. Civilians were filming. Others clearly reporting the altercation to the cops.

Two Wings sprinted up, eyes wide behind their masks. They hauled my arms over their shoulders and whisked me away into shadow.

We solidified a block from the river. Up ahead, our thief flitted short bursts forward—*jump, jump, jump*—just far enough to stay ahead.

"Orders?" Carr panted.

"Get me closer."

We dropped behind her. Our shadows surged forward, forming a billowing wall.

I raised my gun and aimed at the streetlight giving her cover.

"Valora!"

Had my eyes not been zeroed in on her, I would've missed her involuntary twitch in my direction before she caught herself.

Gotcha', ghost girl.

Vindication filled my veins a beat before she vanished again, reappearing at the top of the bridge.

Two shadows joined her. A blink later, they were gone.

Stolen by the night.

TWENTY-FIVE

SUICIDE

FREYA

"What were you thinking?" Reyna barked, her lacy dress fanning out like a cape as she whirled around the healer's room. I loathed this place—hated stealing breaths of air where Darius had taken his last. But I needed my face put back together. Ergo, *hell.*

"This is not what I meant when I said in and out undetected," she snapped, waving a manicured hand in my direction.

"Do I get bonus points for pretending to care?" I bit out, but winced when her healer dabbed something fiery on the wound in my back.

"Mind your tone," Blaz growled from the far wall, looking sleep-rumpled and only halfway conscious. And okay, yeah, maybe snapping at a hierarchy queen wasn't smart—but *everything* hurt. And the bastard I'd fought had emptied his magazine, leaving me one single round to send in for diagnostics.

Worse? I'd defended him. Some twisted instinct had kicked in before logic caught up. Too many damn years fighting to protect people.

"Your *thieves* were about to scuttle away into the shadows with the weapon. *I* got it. Case closed," I repeated, jamming my eyes shut so I didn't snarl at the healer still plucking glass from my shoulder.

"Aren would—"

"*What?*" I yelped as a jolt of pain iced through my nerves. I glared at Reyna. "Aren would *what,* Commander? The man is guarding an entire legion of the world's most competent healers—*thousands* of them. He and Nat are embedding them into every hierarchy for the coming war. He's chasing down fragments of Alvara's visions, negotiating with humans, and prepping centuries of allies for the war to end all wars. Trust me, a few scrapes on a voluntary pawn aren't making his priority list. Nor should they."

Reyna snarled and dropped into a chair in a rumple of satin and lace. Her glare could've split steel. "The second the Paladins descended, you should've returned to the estate."

"And miss our last chance to intercept that weapon before Alvara says the war begins?" I asked, keeping my voice level. My camisole clung like a second skin, suffocating me. There was pressure building behind my eyes—maybe from that Paladin or just from being here, listening to this damn lecture.

Everything ached.

A shot of whiskey, an ice bath, and a long sleep were calling my name. In that order.

"You're reckless."

"This isn't news. Aren's well aware my methods are unconventional."

"You could've been killed."

"*And Darius was!*" I snapped, yanking my shoulder away from the healer still at work.

Reyna stiffened as I waved the man off. I gritted my teeth and pulled the bloodied tank top over my head with a hiss of pain, relief trickling in once I was down to just a sports bra and leggings.

Somehow digging my own fingers into the hellscape of my back wasn't nearly as aggravating as sitting still while someone else did it. The soft clink of shards into the steel bowl eased something in me.

"I have no right to grieve him as you do," I said, voice tight, "but I knew one thing—he was unfailingly *good*." *Clink.* "He didn't deserve the death they gave him." *Clink, clink, clink.* "And over my dead body will that loss be in vain."

Reyna held my gaze, then glanced over my head—at her healer, I assumed—before abruptly grabbing the alcohol and dousing my shoulder, neck, and ribs in one brutal pour.

My bark of pain turned into a hiss. I gritted my teeth, breathing hard as my back spasmed with sight-stealing agony. Blaz jolted forward—though what he planned to do, I had no idea.

"If your pride won't let you accept help," Reyna snapped, "at least have the sense to sanitize, you thoughtless barbarian."

"The real question," I said, breath ragged, fingers carefully skimming my ribs, "is whether Damien can work with so little venom."

"If anyone can make something from nothing, it's that man."

The admiration in her tone didn't go unnoticed. I nodded, flinching as I dug out another shard. *Clink.* "Then we better hope he has another trick up his sleeve. Because they were preparing for something, Reyna. And it doesn't bode well."

The desperation I'd seen in that Paladin's eyes when he fought for the ammo—he hadn't looked like someone guarding it. He looked like someone trying to *take it*. Which begged the question: was this weapon stolen? Were they running the same op we were, trying to get ahead of a deadly Renown secret? And if so, were we sabotaging a silent ally?

"Do you ever intend to tell me why you're here? Why you're hunting my sister?" Reyna finally asked, the v between her brows practically etched into stone. My gaze flicked to Blaz, who mirrored her expression—like the question had never occurred to him. Hurt flickered across his face before he buried it.

"You'll know when my plan works."

"And when is that?"

"Soon," I promised. "I can't say more."

"I should send you back to Aren."

"It wouldn't change anything." Not entirely true, but the pieces were already in motion. If everything played out right, Reagan would watch her empire crumble through her traitorous fingers before I forced her hierarchy to kneel—and I'd march into this war with two hosts' worth of souls instead of one.

Truth be told, I was starting to like the Bellaton queen. Even if she was infuriating to answer to. It made keeping this secret that much harder.

But two souls are one too many to trust with a plan.

I glanced at the healer. "I'm sorry for snapping at you, Carlton. I shouldn't have taken it out on you. Would you still be willing to check this?"

To my relief, he gave a sheepish smile and stepped forward, closing the distance.

"Where did it go?" Reyna asked softly, her gaze fixed out the window.

"Where did what go, Your Majesty?" I murmured, eyes falling shut as Carlton's magic ran a cool, soothing circuit over my pulverized skin. The title still felt like marbles in my mouth—outdated and infuriatingly formal.

"The money you two stole," she said, flicking her gaze between us, disapproval written in every line of her posture.

I grinned. "To a more worthy cause."

The silence that followed cracked when a gravel-toned voice called out, "What in Sam Hill happened?"

Jesus—I hadn't even heard them come in. But there they were. Ansel and Alana Callahan, leaning in the doorway and looking thoroughly unimpressed. You didn't become Grayshell's assassins by accident, I supposed. But still.

My soul mother's jaw was ticking so violently it was a miracle she didn't have TMJ. My heart grew wings, but got lodged in my throat, making speech impossible.

Reyna straightened like a wilting flower spotting sunlight. Formality seemed to be the only thing holding her together. "Would it be too much to ask for an announcement before you enter my home?"

"That depends on whether you're capable of keeping our calling safe," Lana said, striding into the room, eyes pinned on me with barely veiled retribution.

"Apologies. Smelled her blood," Ansel offered, like that made it okay. As if souls were nothing more than beasts tracking their wounded. To drive the image home, the Old General added, "You know how it goes."

Reyna inhaled slowly, tightening her robe as though it might restrain her irritation. "Mr. and Mrs. Callahan, you both look well."

Lana huffed and brushed my blood-matted hair away to examine the newly healed skin beneath. Ansel dipped his chin in acknowledgment and said, "We come with news. Perhaps you'd be more comfortable in business attire before we deliver it, Queen Gwyne?"

Ass kisser, I thought. And if I wasn't mistaken, Lana's lips twitched. But Ansel kept his chin lifted, gaze pointedly above Reyna's neckline.

"Very well," she replied curtly, arms still tight around herself like she'd caught a chill. "My son will escort you to the study."

WHEN BLAZ CLOSED the three of us inside Reyna's office, my soul parents finally relaxed. Lana's gaze softened with that uncharacteristic gentleness she reserved just for me, her mouth pinched as she scanned me for injuries Carlton might've missed.

"Body aches, but I'm okay," I assured.

"Fucking Adrastos," Lana muttered, biting her lip.

"I don't think this one was his fault," I said with a laugh, gently pushing past her to wrap my arms around Ansel, burying my face in his chest. I exhaled into the comforting sound of his rumbling chuckle. "Hey, old man."

"Good to see you, babygirl."

"Can you two focus?" Lana snapped. Never one for sentiment.

"An hour in the Middle would set you right as rain," Ansel explained, studying me with a little more restraint than Lana—but his chrome eyes were sharp.

I was already shaking my head. "We don't have time for that. I'll be fine. Promise."

"And what, pray tell, was worth spilling your blood this time?" Ansel guided me to one of Reyna's armchairs, settling in beside me.

"I was going after the reaper's bullets. We're trying to figure out how they're making them before everything goes to hell and we have no way to defend ourselves." My words froze Lana mid-step, her back to us as she stared into the night. But Ansel's expression barely changed—just a subtle narrowing of his eyes. A tell I wouldn't have caught if I hadn't studied him for a lifetime.

"What went south?" he asked.

"The Stuart boy, I believe. He was after it too."

"Your prior report implied he was the one distributing it," he said clinically, concern taking a backseat to duty. In a world of chaos, his steadiness was a godsend.

"That was my hypothesis."

"Did tonight change your prior conclusion?"

Scratching the back of my head, I replayed my encounter with the Wings and their ringleader. "It might've," I admitted, the words more question than conclusion.

"Walk me through it," Ansel said. "We'll see what adds up."

So I did. In painstaking detail. Because the truth was, I needed eyes on them. I needed a face to go with Cyrus Stuart's name, beyond the haunted hazel eyes behind his mask. And more than anything, I needed to know whether they were the ones crafting those soul-slaying bullets—or if my old friends were hunting the monsters responsible, same as us.

I finished with Lainalei and Makena scooping me off the bridge and getting me here. Then I pulled my eyes from the dark estate and locked onto the steel of Grayshell's right hand. He clasped his silver tin between still fingers, the corner pressed against his lips as he thought.

"You hesitated," he said flatly, no accusation—just truth.

"No, I—" But shaking my head wasn't enough to dissuade him.

"You hesitated in the rafters. Again in the shop. You had the gun. You could've killed him, taken the magazine, and run. Why didn't you?"

To my immense relief, there was no judgment in his tone. Just quiet, infuriating accuracy.

And he was right.

I didn't want to admit it, but he was right.

Some frail, traitorous part of me couldn't bring myself to deliver that kind of death. Not again. Not like Darius's.

"Your soft heart will get you killed," Lana chastised. I couldn't argue with her. It always had.

A sword pledging loyalty to my king.

Mercy where I should lend none.

Again, when I trusted Reagan.

The image of my calling's body flashed through my mind—the blank emerald eyes, the thunder-split sky above him.

Guilt twisted deep in my gut.

"I don't know," I finally admitted, the words dragging across my unwilling tongue like glass.

Lana didn't miss a beat. "If you're still categorizing a grown man with blood on his hands as a child, perhaps Aren was foolish to deploy—"

"It's not that," I snapped, rising from my chair to pace. "He's ascended. He kills for them. He's collateral."

"Then *what?*"

"I..." My voice trailed off as my mind drifted back to that warehouse. The advantage had been mine. I was above them before the shadows poured in. I'd turned, inexplicably, just in time to see him materialize from the dark—ducking low, fast and fluid, slipping free of the blade meant for him.

My heart...twisted. Twisted with fear that wasn't mine.

As the others swarmed and robbed him of his cover, as that glowing gun aimed for him—I was already moving. Sprinting across the narrow beam before I'd even made the choice. No plan. No certainty I'd reach him in time. Only that paralyzing, unshakable sense that if I didn't, something irreversibly catastrophic would happen.

Fate weaves its own golden threads—braiding soul to soul over centuries, through lives, through blood and dust and time. None of it accidental.

That thread had yanked me forward, sent me diving from the rafters like a living blade to intercept a bullet that wasn't meant for me. Even then, I hadn't known why.

"Fate," I whispered.

"And was it 'fate' that had you coming back here?" Lana asked, more softly now, exchanging a glance with Ansel that was one part worry, one part warning.

I nodded.

"Aren told us you'd open Pandora's box if given the opportunity. Is the prince related to Pandora, by chance?" Ansel asked mildly.

My throat tightened, my entire body aching for sleep. I couldn't lie to them, so I didn't. I nodded again.

"Why did you accept this mission?"

Reyna's presence just outside the door made me hesitate. But that same soul-deep thread that had pulled me off that beam lifted my chin now.

"I intend to destroy Reagan Stuart."

"Now?" Lana demanded, her voice flat with disbelief. "Freya, we're on the brink of catastrophe. What the hell are you thinking?"

"That I was betrayed—and only justice will quiet what's left of my soul."

"That I can understand," she said slowly. "But think. The last thing we need—what Grayshell *or* Bellaton need—is to give Reagan more reason to turn the Shadows or The Six against us. Aren's peace is tenuous at best. So long as that bitch wears the crown, we're suspended in the space between alliance and war."

"Which is why she must fall—to a successor."

"Her death will martyr her. You think Calypso will be more likely to ally if you murder her mother in cold blood?"

"Maybe if she's exposed. If the Paladins see her betrayal."

"They won't care what she did to *you*, Freya."

"No," I agreed. "But they'll care if I try her under Paladin law. If she killed one of their own without a trial, they'll condemn her themselves."

That was the moment Reyna entered, pushing through the study's double doors. All three of us turned to her as she stepped inside, tension slicing through the air like a guillotine. Lainalei and Blaz followed, silent sentinels at her back.

"What you're proposing is suicide," Reyna said, her flyer's eyes wide even as she moved with that same eerie grace, gliding to her desk like the news had knocked the air out of her.

"Not if you know how to survive the trials," I said evenly, watching her brace herself on the edge of the desk as though the force of my intentions might knock her over.

It had been decades, but I remembered The Crucible like I remembered the battle that bought my family's freedom. And all this chaos I'd sown in Reagan's kingdom? That had been strategy—every last piece of it, a carefully deployed illusion.

"Nobody survives The Crucible," Lainalei breathed, following Reyna like a too-pretty sentinel, red braid trailing down her back.

"Bullshit," I muttered—just as Lana barked the same.

Ansel shook his head. "That's categorically untrue."

"Okay," Lainalei amended, "So few survive we haven't heard a name in centuries."

"There was one," Reyna murmured, eyes never leaving mine. "A few decades ago. She didn't last long after, though."

"*She* didn't have the gift *I* do now," I said, swallowing the smile threatening to rise.

"Humility?" Lainalei shot back.

If my brain hadn't been too busy sorting what to share and what to bury, I might've paused to appreciate her sarcasm. The only universal language.

Ignoring her, I met Ansel's eyes—and watched them shift with dawning understanding.

"Both times you bit him, you were able to jump after," he deduced.

When I nodded, he shook his head—not in reprimand, but in wonder. "If we can get you to the Middle, you'll be a threat like none other."

At last, I let the grin come. Because if I could ascend, I could execute Reagan for her treason. And I could challenge Calypso—the lab rat—myself. The board was set. The players were moving.

"Is someone gonna fill me in?" Blaz asked, his eyes locked on mine, swirling with something that hovered between hurt and panic.

On a sigh thick with pain, Reyna announced, "We're in the presence of a long-lost legend."

TWENTY-SIX

USURPERS

CYRUS

Every nerve ending screamed as I lowered into the copper basin on shaking limbs. Fully submerged in ice and gelatinous healing salve, I sucked a breath through clenched teeth. Still panting, I looked up at Carr, perched on a marble bench built into the ceremonial site.

"She's a siphon," I gritted out.

Unfortunately, it wasn't Carr who answered.

Nix barked an incredulous laugh. "Right. And I'm the fucking King of Avalon."

"Mock all you want, Nix, but I've thought this through." I forced myself to breathe around the frigid temperature, willing my body not to seize. "If I'm right—and I usually am—"

"Glad to see the ego's intact."

"She's even more dangerous than I thought."

"Dangerous?" he scoffed, stripping off his tac gear and letting it fall beside Carr's bench. "I think you're confusing a threat with a gift that's gone extinct." One gold iris flashed as his hard stare landed on me, his mouth curled in a smirk as he shrugged out of his vest and dumped it next to his cloak and mask. "Do you realize how many folktales you've tried to resurrect this month alone? You're nostalgic for a time we weren't even alive for."

"Maybe," Carr cut in as I closed my eyes and tried to adjust to the cold. "But if he's right, then the old stories are right too."

"And if she can steal magic, that changes *everything*," I added, voice steadying, though hoarse.

It tracked. The infamous Wraith—known for stealth and sleight of hand —with the ability to rob and temporarily embody a soul's magic, tapping into their reserves with the enthusiasm of a high school sophomore at their first keg party. How dangerous she was depended on the limits of her gift. Some siphons needed only proximity. Others required touch.

She'd jumped and wielded shadows only after she *bit* me—no doubt getting a mouthful of blood—and even then, she only jumped short distances. Which meant physical contact was the trigger.

Slightly less threatening.

Unless she was a newborn...

In which case, she hadn't even scratched the surface.

Did our masked intruder know? Lonan didn't strike me as the type to chase useless relics, which meant he probably knew exactly what I'd been sent to retrieve.

"Let's humor your delusions for a second," Nix said, dragging me back to the present. "Say you're right. The slippery little bitch *is* a siphon. What's she gonna do first?"

"Destroy us," Carr said grimly, glancing at his brother as he stood and began pacing the edge of the basin.

"She doesn't have to," I countered, catching Carr's conflicted look. "It could be worse. She could be a reaper. Something happened last time— something personal. She's out for blood. But if we can make it right, pay the price, maybe strike a deal...maybe there's potential."

"You've lost your mind, cousin."

I ignored him. "With a gift like that, she could rewrite the balance of power."

"For or against us," Carr said, leaning back with his palms braced on the bench. My wounds were starting to tingle—my leg a wildfire of nerve endings as the magic did its work.

The Middle was the only place I'd ever felt peace. The skies above hung in perpetual gray, like a storm forever threatening but never breaking. From the sacred west garden, I could see the glowing fields stretch all the way to the castle—a sharp black smudge on the horizon.

"I think Uptown's smoking remains make it pretty clear it's the latter," Nix said, pulling my eyes from the spires back to his grimace. "So what's the plan, Cyrus? She's made her intentions clear. She wants to break us. You gonna roll over and give her the hierarchy?"

"Our best bet is to neutralize her before she figures out what she is."

If she'd been fully in control, that jump wouldn't have surprised her. Neither would the way *my* shadows writhed on her skin.

"Sure. Obvious deduction, *Sherlock*."

"Got a better one?"

"Maybe don't repeat history. *Clearly* your plans have worked out great so far."

"The plan *will work*. Siphon or not. We bring the Wraith in on Valentine's Day. We've already seeded intel through the lower ranks—someone'll leak it to Reyna, and to her."

"Perfect. Trouble from two sides."

"Nix, will you shut the fuck up for two seconds and let the man plan?" Carr snapped. "She sliced through his Achilles tonight. Legends have died for less. Let him breathe while the pool does its work. Cy, you must be in a grip of pain."

"Cakewalk," I muttered, sinking deeper into the copper. The burn gave way to the sharper prick of nerves waking up. "We're living through history, Nix. Like it or not, we need to fire on all cylinders. Lonan wouldn't be bartering if she wasn't valuable. Now we know why."

"You little freak. For as long as I can remember, you've had these illusions of grandeur bouncing around your head. But that's your problem, isn't it?"

"*Nix—*" Carr warned, straightening.

"You think Paladin is supposed to be some fantastical kingdom of vigilantes. But we're *not*. We're balance keepers. This is why your mother doesn't take you seriously. Why Poe won't give you Wings. Your head's too far in the clouds. You'll get yourself killed because you hesitate when you shouldn't—all because your mark reminds you of a fairytale."

"Nix. Shut the fuck up," Carr said again. But I wasn't looking at him.

I stared only at Nix as he froze beside the pool.

"She responded to 'Valora.' She *is* who I say she is."

"You're trapped," Nix insisted. "Trapped in the mind of a little fucking kid who can't come to terms with the fact that they failed—and something terrible happened."

"*Don't,*" I growled, my fingers white-knuckling the basin. Frost crackled in spiderwebs under my hands.

"If you'd been a little more grounded—just a little more down to earth—Charles would still fucking be here—"

Shadows lashed forward. The strike knocked him off his feet before his own power could snake from his body. He rolled back to standing, but I had him in the air before he could regain his footing.

"Say his name again," I growled, tightening the noose of shadow around his throat. My grip trembled with the memory of my little brother—his screams as they tore him apart, the searing pain of my own forced ascension, helpless to save him.

My fault. My fault. My fault.

All because Charles wanted to win our mother's favor by unearthing history, and I didn't have the spine to tell him no.

"And I will strike you dead where you stand," I hissed. "As I recall, you didn't stop us either, Nix. *You* were the oldest. Just as liable as I was. But don't forget—we *both* saw the Oracle. *You* were weighed and found wanting. We *both* know how this ends."

Because in a kingdom ruled by balance, power was the metric that mattered. And mine was superior.

Despite Poe's lingering hesitation keeping me from my gauntlets, the Oracle had already spoken.

If strength alone determined succession, I—not Calypso—would be the next Stuart on the throne. The only thing keeping her ahead was the matriarchal enchantment. And Calypso had never wanted the crown anyway. She was content in her labs, happy among her beakers and equations.

Leading negotiations? Balancing power? Navigating the thorns of the throne? That was all deadweight to her. Which meant she'd lean on me more than she'd admit. That dependency would make the crown look weak. And a weak crown meant a vulnerable hierarchy. It had plagued us both since we were ranked.

The only grace? We worked well together.

We'd prepared for this—for our line to be tested. Which meant if our insufferable cousin opened his mouth one more goddamn time, I'd be forced to silence him.

Without another word, I rose from the tub, unbothered by the fact I'd stripped every bloody scrap of clothing before stepping in. Water dripping down my skin, I crossed the soft, luminous grass and stopped in front of him.

"Just when I thought you might've grown into a half-decent Wing, you open your fucking mouth and remind me you're still the same piece of shit you've always been." A memory flashed—Nix's hands on a body he had no right to touch—and I inhaled sharply. "You might wear Paladin gauntlets, but mark my words, Nix. You will kneel before your prince—or I'll have those Wings carved from your flesh."

"You'd never...get it past...the trial," he choked, lifting his chin in defiance even as my shadows coiled tighter around his throat, his own magic useless against my grip.

"Everyone has skeletons," I said quietly, thumb brushing the raven on my signet ring. "Lucky for me, your closets are shallow. And I've always had a talent for digging."

I stepped closer. "If you really think I've lost my mind, then stop whining and *challenge me*. Call a meeting. Demand a trial. Only a coward insults a naked man soaking in a medicine bath. You a coward, Nix? You know what the hierarchy thinks of men without honor."

His mismatched eyes locked on mine. Behind the fury and fear, I saw it—something deeper.

Hatred.

Resentment.

That same slithering snake of betrayal we'd sensed as kids but never had the words for.

With a huff, I released him and turned my back on my mother's newest Captain of the Wings.

———

THE DULL THROB of an oncoming headache rang in my ears the next morning as I nodded along, only half listening.

Like nails on a chalkboard, the mortal woman's voice droned in my ear. "Mr. Stuart, we cannot thank you enough for your generous donation. You truly don't want any credit? We could name the new wing after you—"

"That won't be necessary," I said, rubbing slow, tight circles into my temples.

She *donated* it.

The bitch siphoned our funds and funneled them into four separate organizations.

Mine had—allegedly—gone to a boarding school for troubled and disadvantaged teens. What was I gonna do? Reclaim the money? Tell the school to return a few hundred thousand dollars meant to help kids escape generational addiction?

Calypso's funds were worse. Experimental treatments for children with cancer. We couldn't take the money back even if we were heartless enough to try. And legally? There was no way Valora Lamb had pulled this off without cover.

This wasn't about the money anymore.

This was personal.

"I believe it will be," the woman chirped. "Oh! We could have you appear at an upcoming gala—"

"The only insult you could offer, Miss King, would be wasting a dime of that money on a *party*," I snapped. "Use it for the kids. Equip them. Give them something stable. Not some bullshit soiree for the egos of the upper class."

Silence stretched on the line. Then, a sheepish, "Oh—of course. No disrespect intended. I just thought—"

"I apologize, but I have a meeting," I cut in, ending the call before she could backpedal further. I tossed the phone onto my desk and buried my face in my hands.

Game. Set. Match.

And she knew it.

I'd spent the night in the Middle, healing from the Wraith's ambush, flanked by my two sulking cousins.

Nix had brooded in his chambers, doing his duty in silence until sunrise, when I could safely return to the mortal realm.

The day had offered nothing but headaches since.

Dragging my palms down my face, I pulled out my phone and fired off a text to Calypso.

> CYRUS
>
> Can you meet me in my office at La Lune in fifteen?

> CALYPSO
>
> Kinda in the middle of something. How about forty?

> CYRUS
>
> Make it fast, Cal.

> CALYPSO
>
> Yeah, yeah.
>
> Be there ASAP. I just gotta wrap up this test.

> CYRUS
>
> Thanks. See you soon.

With that established, I sighed, downed the last gulp of my black coffee, and thumbed through the remaining files on Valora Lamb. Once it was clear I'd sucked every ounce of marrow from these drives, I grabbed my phone again.

> CYRUS
>
> Can you talk?

Three dots appeared. Vanished. Reappeared.

Then my phone rang—an old photo of me and my mother lighting up the screen. A relic from before everything had gone to shit.

Her voice came breathy, unfamiliar only because it had been too long since it sounded like that. "Cyrus, darling, what's going on?"

I blinked, leaning back to double-check the caller ID.

Yup. Still her.

So what the hell was she high on? "Ma?"

"Yeah, baby. What's up?"

My heart sank. She sounded like the old her. The version of my mother from before Charles. Before I fucked up so badly, we'd never recovered.

The her that fucking gave a damn if I lived or died.

"I, um..." I swallowed down the nostalgia tightening my throat. "I gathered some intel. I'd like to run it by you. I'm in the office. Could you spare fifteen?" A light laugh crackled through the line. I winced, then asked, "Are you with Dad?"

"And the Guard, baby."

Ew. Damn me. "Gross, Mom. TMI."

"Get your head out of the gutter, Cy."

"Born and raised there, so technically not my fault."

She laughed—*actually laughed*—before saying, "I can be there in fifteen."

"Good. Bring Dad."

"Are you okay, son?"

"Yeah."

Lies. I was anything but okay. I was chasing a ghost. One with brutal aim, if the ruined tendon in my leg had anything to say about it.

My asshole cousin had somehow advanced in rank. I was only his superior by blood—and the Oracle's word.

And my brother's screams were still stuck in my skull on a cruel, endless loop.

"Fine," I added quietly.

"We'll be there soon."

"Soon" turned out to be closer to thirty minutes than fifteen, but punctuality had never been a Stuart family strength. I'd hated it since I learned to read a clock.

My mother entered the room with a softness I hadn't seen in years, a gentle smile lifting her cheeks as she stepped inside with Dad close behind —and Orion trailing them like a loyal hound. Evidently, my appetite for multiple partners came from her, though I couldn't exactly relate to my father's...generosity.

Guilt twisted in my gut. She looked happy. Relaxed.

And I was about to ruin that.

Cyrus Stuart: ruining bliss for twenty-two years and counting.

"Cy," she murmured, her palm brushing over my cheek.

I missed this version of her.

Missed it until I remembered what she probably had to take to *be* this version. My gaze flicked to Dad, but he seemed calm. At ease.

"Hey, Ma," I muttered, accepting the hug she offered with all the enthusiasm of a frog offering a ride to a scorpion. Her moods were just as volatile.

"What's going on?" she asked, lowering herself onto the couch between Dad and Orion. I dragged my office chair closer with a metallic clank, then turned it backward and straddled it.

"We had a run-in with our thief last night."

"Nix reported it," Dad said, the easy smile he'd worn slipping away. His posture shifted into something sharper, more regal. The king taking the reins.

"How detailed was that report?"

"Concise," Ma replied. "Just said you got what you went for, despite a scuffle."

"*Scuffle*," I scoffed. I tugged my neckline down, revealing the new scar seared across my shoulder. The effect was immediate—her body froze, eyes darting from the wound to my face.

"Vampire?" she demanded. Her voice lost its warmth, tone hardening into the Paladin Queen.

"Siphon," I corrected, bracing for impact. But instead of outrage, she and Dad exchanged a heavy glance, sinking deeper into the couch as if the word physically weighed them down.

"Cyrus—" Orion started.

I lifted a hand, cutting him off. I had to stomach my parents' opinions—as both their son and subject—but their Guardians didn't get the same courtesy.

"There's more," I said. Dad's fingers slipped between hers, tightening, like he could keep this peaceful version of her anchored a moment longer. "The thief responded to the name Valora. I don't think she meant to—but she did."

"That's not possible," Ma snapped. *Ah. There she was.* The Queen again.

"I have a theory," I said, taking a breath. "You're not gonna like it, but I need you to hear me out. If she's targeting us, we have to assume there's strategy behind it. And I need as much intel as possible on your old Second."

She stiffened. But I pressed on. "I get that you don't wanna acknowledge this. But she's been attacking in a *pattern*—precise, brutal, strategic. Let me protect this family. Let me do what you asked me to do."

Silence.

Nothing.

Neither of them said a word. Which told me *everything*.

What the hell had they been doing last night that made *this* version of them so...quiet?

"What trials did she select for her Crucible?"

The Crucible consisted of three trials, followed by a duel. Any nominee could select from over a hundred options in the Accords. In my twelve hours of forced solitude, I'd had plenty of time to think. And the more I studied her movements in the present, the more familiar they seemed. Too familiar.

"Hearthkeeper," Dad murmured, eyes drifting far away. "Shadowed Path. And Illumination."

Fuck me.

"Okay," I said slowly. "How'd she complete them?"

"Her Trial of Illumination culminated in exposing a conspiracy. A usurper in the line. She was skilled at infiltration and deception. That one brought her to the Guard's attention—and the Council's."

"It's rare to survive the second," Orion added, his gaze sharp on me.

"Which did she complete next?" I asked, already knowing I'd hate the answer.

"For Hearthkeeper," Dad said, "she smuggled food and medicine to imprisoned Paladins behind enemy lines. Eventually planned their escape."

I frowned. "Then why does no one know her name?" Someone like that should've been a legend.

"She wasn't one for the spotlight," Ma said softly. "Preferred her actions stay unsung. But we knew. Of course we did."

"And the final trial?"

"She completed the Shadowed Path by entering an abandoned crypt in the old country," Ma continued. "It was rumored to be cursed, but she didn't care. She went in to retrieve an ancient relic of Bellpost proper, and braved the labyrinth alone. She brought it home."

"What relic?"

"A trinket," she said. "A ring from the Hadrianna line."

"But she knew it could buy peace with The Six," Dad added. "So we used it as an offering. It worked."

"The Council's been secure since," Ma said.

Expose corruption.

Restore balance.

Reclamation.

Those were the themes of Valora Lamb's trials.

And now they were the very blueprint of her vendetta.

TWENTY-SEVEN

THE DELEGATION

AUGUST

"Help me."

The whimper was so faint my sleep-deprived brain almost missed it. I blinked, trying to clear the exhaustion from my eyes as I scanned our group—Alec, seated beside me against a tree trunk, his gaze locked on Ally with lethal stillness, and half a dozen Terramyst wolves lying nearby. Ally was still in the other realm, but for the first time in days, her brow furrowed in distress. The first sign of emotion we'd seen.

"Did she—"

Alec answered with a single nod.

It was probably the longest I'd ever gone in any life without speaking to him. We'd exhausted every topic in the first forty-eight hours—Adrastos's escape, the odds our souls were intact, whether we could keep protecting Fae without pissing off a powerful earth-wielder who wasn't ready to be benched—and had promptly gotten our asses handed to us.

I cracked my spine with a stretch and crouched, dry throat working to swallow as I watched her.

"Please. *Help me.*"

The second plea had me on my feet. Alec was a heartbeat behind as we closed the distance. One of Kingsley's wolves raised its enormous head, snowy coat shimmering under the moonlight.

I crouched in front of her, every instinct begging to pull her out of whatever madness had taken hold. She'd been drawing from our bond for days, and as I shot Alec a look, I signed *shield's up*, using the language he'd been teaching me. Grayshell and Westerlund used it before our mental bond was forged, and though we'd stopped asking questions, it was comforting to feel my shield ripple and know Alec was reinforcing it.

"No," Ally gasped, tears welling, voice breaking. "*No.*"

I glanced at Alec again, silently asking for answers, but he only shrugged, just as lost.

"Ally."

"No, God, *please* no."

"Ally," I said again, more firmly. "I'm right here, baby. I've got you."

Her head turned toward me, but her gaze was far away—like she was staring through me. Her broken voice whispered, "Aren."

Jaw tight, I looked to Alec, who was already dialing his phone, stepping back to get a signal. She blinked, dazed, then stared down at her nightgown —then at the clip of my knife in my front pocket. She snatched it with frightening speed. Before I could react, she flipped it open and sliced her arm.

"*Yo!*" I barked, heart slamming into my ribs. I lunged, but she dropped to the ground, bloodied knife in hand, eyes glassy as she began painting symbols into the snow.

"One hundred and eight. One hundred and eight thousand to three," she muttered, drawing 108k across the icy ground. One of the wolves stirred, shifting to better see her movements. "One-oh-eight. Three. Three thousand two hundred and forty." She scrawled again, then hissed in frustration when the blade was clean.

I dove as she moved to cut herself again, knocking the blade aside without touching her skin. She whirled on me, canines lengthening.

My wife *hissed* at me. Jesus Christ.

"Aren's okay," Alec said, rejoining me—but his voice trailed off when he took in the scene. I couldn't tear my eyes from her as I summoned a blanket and slowly stood. Ally dipped her fingers into her wound, drawing again in blood.

"One-oh-eight. Three. Three thousand two hundred and forty. Book, crowns, seven pieces. One-nineteen!"

Please tell me you've seen this before, I said mentally.

No, mate, Alec answered, voice grim.

"Seven pieces. Seven pieces. Three!" she screeched, jamming her thumb into the wound before drawing a trembling crimson 3 in the snow.

"Ally," Alec breathed, his terror echoing my own. No sign of his usual bulletproof humor.

"Baby, I'm going to wrap you in this blanket, okay?" I said, moving slow as her wild eyes snapped to mine, then back to the ground.

"Three. Three," she panted, tears streaming. Ally shook her head frantically, tiny jerks of panic coursing through her. Her gaze locked on mine, desperate. "Three. *Three?* Please *help me*," she sobbed.

"I will," I promised, though I had no damn idea how. "Just let me get you inside, okay? You can write it all down. Tell us everything."

"Three," she whispered, her hoarse voice shattering me.

She didn't flinch as I gingerly wrapped the blanket around her. Her skin burned hot, no doubt from the fire churning inside her, but she let me cover her completely. I couldn't risk her touching us now.

"Book, crowns, seven pieces. The lost queen is calling. Stop! Calling, calling, *calling*."

I looked to Alec—his mouth was open in horror, amber eyes glued to her trembling form. Blood dripped from her arm to the snow, stark against the crystalline white.

Praying I wasn't making a mistake, I pressed a hand to her back and jumped us to Kingsley's safe house.

The quiet shattered as we burst through the front door, Ally screaming, "Help me! Please. Three. Three. The queen comes calling."

Three stunned faces turned toward us, frozen mid-breakfast at the table.

"Clear it," I snapped.

They moved instantly—grabbing dishes, magicking away what they couldn't carry.

"Something to write with?"

"Uh—" Rose bolted upstairs. Kingsley was faster. He yanked open a drawer, ripping it off its tracks in his haste, and tossed me a carpenter's pencil.

I caught it and gently placed it in Ally's hand, steering her away from the bloodied wound and toward the table.

"Paper?" Kingsley barked, vanishing before anyone could answer. But Ally wasn't waiting. Her eyes locked on the empty table and she lunged, pencil flying in frantic, jagged scratches that made me wince.

I'd be buying the Thornquists a new table.

"Which witch, which *witch*, three, two, four, zero. *Three!*" The blanket slipped off her shoulders, her trembling hand clenched to her chest. "Raven locks. Raven locks. Black and blonde. They hunt. Eyes like water. Blue, blue, *blue*. Tightrope—*stop moving!!*"

We did. All of us. I was pretty sure Alec and Fae stopped breathing. Kingsley froze mid-step as he reentered the room.

"Commander at the helm, always shifting, shifting, *shifting*," she growled. "Commanders at the helm, united. *With me*, he says. Three. A raven cries, three. Prince of many names, a book, a crown, a raven *cries*. Shifting, calling, *shifting*—STOP SHIFTING!"

Ally rocked on her feet as her words crumbled into sobs. She crouched on the table, squeezing her head between her hands, eyes jammed shut.

"Mate, mate! Too fucking late. Through the gray she calls him. Broken, he rises."

Her eyes flew wide as she began drawing again, desperate, unintelligible shapes rapidly scratched and colored in. "Don't let go, just don't let go. *Stop fucking shifting!!*" she shrieked, slamming her palms into her forehead.

I staggered back, as if a few feet of space could ease the hell she was drowning in.

"A bear. A bear—bring him back, dark one. White, white, and *white. It burns!!*" Her trembling hands moved to her eyes, pressing hard before her scream splintered into a piercing cry no soul should ever have to make. *"Make it stop! Make it stop! Please! Help me."*

"Fuck this," I growled, stepping forward to pull her into my arms.

But Ally was faster—she always had been.

One hand flung out and we were all shoved back, force radiating from her as she screamed, "Don't touch me! Too much, *too much.*"

Tears spilled as her fingers resumed their frantic motion, eyes darting too fast to follow.

"Make it count. Make it count, make it count," she whispered. And I stood there, helpless. Unable to guide her through this nightmare but refusing to look away. Refusing to leave her alone.

Kingsley huffed and stormed outside, Rose on his heels. Alec and Fae slipped quietly onto the porch so Fae could cry without waking Alvara.

The sun set. Rose again. Ally's prophecies spread across the walls, the table, anything that would take pigment. Mangled bits of charcoal littered the floor. Her pale hands were smeared black like patchwork gloves.

At last, her weary eyes met mine. She whispered, "August," and collapsed into my arms.

I WOKE to the sharp edge of hushed whispers and the weight of hunger clawing at my ribs. Gingerly, I slipped from bed, blinking hard to get my bearings. Judging by the cotton in my mouth and the ache in my limbs, we'd been out for a while.

Despite the tension thick in Kingsley's safe house, I felt the first stab of relief in days.

Ally's color was back.

Her hair fanned around her in rings of silky chocolate, framing her face like a halo. Her brow was smooth. For the first time all week, there was no tightness in her cheeks, no cursed trance pulling her away from me.

Was this what she would've endured if the reading had gone as planned? Would she have been trapped in the hell of our memories for days, clawing through the chaos of King Calloway's twisted truth?

If we tried again, would it break her?

I sucked in a breath, ribs loosening as I watched her chest rise and fall in steady rhythm. Reluctantly, I turned toward the murmuring voices.

"None of this was planned for," came a hissed whisper—Alec, I was almost sure.

Kingsley's sharp retort confirmed it. "*Three*, Carter? Three threads that don't end with the world burning?"

"I trust Ally," Alec replied, steady as ever. If I hadn't already known, that would've been enough to prove he was the best friend any soul could ask for. And coming from someone who grew up glued to Sam and James, that was saying something.

"Same," Fae chimed in, sing-song but sincere.

"She's rarely wrong," Rose added.

I crept down the hallway, skipping the second stair to avoid the telltale creak.

"But when she is," Kingsley snapped, "it's catastrophic."

My brow furrowed.

Thankfully, his mate wasn't one for ambiguity.

"It's unfair to hold that against her, love. What happened with the Solskari wasn't Alvara's fault. Aren answered our call faster than anyone, and summoned her. She rained down hell—for us, for them."

"Seers are for the living," Fae added softly. "Necromancers walk the line. They're veiled from the other."

"Right. So what if *they* side with Adrastos and his keeper?" The voice was male, soft, unfamiliar.

Another answered before I could place it. "She can't account for participants who aren't in the threads."

"It's not a science," Alec said. Only someone who knew him as well as I did would've caught the irritation in his voice. "She's doing the best she can."

"And even then, it's not good enough," Kingsley barked. A heavy thud followed—palms on wood.

Yeah. That was enough.

I gripped the leash on my temper tight as I stepped into view. "She's a soul, not a God. The fact that she suffers so severely to give our people even the slightest edge? That's more than enough."

The room fell silent.

Way more than four pairs of eyes turned toward me. One pair—cerulean, bright and sharp—belonged to a stunning woman whose features mirrored Marcus and his brothers. Skin a lighter shade of amber, maybe, but unmistakably Westerlund.

The energy coming off her was more telling than anything. Familiar and foreign all at once.

"I assume you're a Westerlund?" I asked.

She nodded, offering a gentle smile, her braids swaying with the movement.

I turned to the others.

A woman perched in the windowsill, limbs folded into the narrow space, skin a ghastly pallor. Pale hair fell in a sheet to her waist, and her eyes—icy blue, almost translucent—locked onto me with open assessment.

Beside her sat a man so impossibly symmetrical he had to be a Soul. His light tawny complexion all but glowed in the sun now streaming through the windows, giving him an ethereal quality that spoke to hours spent in the Middle.

At least, it did—right up until he smiled. Fine lines broke around his light brown eyes as he dipped his chin in greeting. If Rosaleigh was joy personified, this man was her male counterpart: the same bright complexion, the same dark hair and eyes.

Brother, maybe?

A dozen new faces studied me as carefully as I studied them. Some dipped their chins, others bowed like they'd been waiting for a deity. I ran a hand over my jaw, scrambling for how the hell to start this particular conversation—lucky for me, Fae had her own plans.

She danced her way over, blonde hair swaying, and looped her arm through mine like she had the day we met before turning to the room.

"August, these are the leaders of the sovereign Western hierarchies. This is the first branch of your...*delegation*, if you will. This is Kalma, of the earth wielders," she said, motioning to the lanky woman with snow-white hair. "Tieran is Rosaleigh's brother, a fellow shifter from farther north."

Canada, then.

That sunburst smile flashed across his face again as he offered a wave-salute hybrid.

"Sable and Onyx hail from Northern California. Water wielders." She gestured to two women who looked like they hadn't seen daylight in years, matching green eyes watching me intently.

"Ajéí, her mate Kai, and their son Otto," she continued, motioning to a trio at the breakfast table clutching coffee cups like life preservers. The matriarch, with wavy black hair falling to her waist, had a youthful face that belied the age in her eyes. It was to her both males turned for cues—subtle, instinctive.

And so it continued, Fae introducing each newcomer in turn.

"Guys, this is The Great Commander."

"August," I corrected quickly. "Porter."

"Do you believe your mate will see another way through?" Ajéí asked, her amber-flecked eyes flicking to me.

"She's still resting after that...trance. I haven't discussed it with her yet, and I don't feel qualified to speak on it until I do."

"Very diplomatic," Tieran said, head tilting slightly as he studied me. "But if you were a betting man?"

I met his gaze, unwavering. "I'd say Ally is rarely wrong. If only three threads lead us forward, then those are the threads we follow."

A chorus of murmurs rose as the souls conferred among themselves, until Sable cut through the noise.

"And the common denominators—can you make sense of them?"

"Some," I allowed. I'd spent the last forty-eight hours following along the best I could, watching her write, rewrite, cross out, circle, connect notes to columns and margins. "Others, not so much."

"Give us an example," Onyx pressed.

To my relief, Alec appeared beside me, pressing a hot mug into my hand. I downed a scalding mouthful of coffee and let my eyes drift across the Thornquists' now-vandalized cabin.

"There are consistencies in the threads she's marked victorious. One is the fulfillment of the prophecy Adrastos laid out for her. We have to acquire all six pieces to stop the rise of the four horsemen."

"Great Commander, Angel of Death, Fertility Goddess, Warrior, Witch, and Wraith," Tieran recited, clearly briefed. "Right. He named all but the Witch and Wraith."

"We're still no closer to identifying the Witch. But judging by her notes, Ally may have narrowed it to one of two. The Wraith, at least, allies with us."

Even if she was up to something on her own that kept shifting her threads like a live wire.

"And what about this raven's cry?" Otto asked, adjusting the collar of his leather jacket. He had his mother's onyx hair and the same inquisitive eyes.

"Your guess is as good as mine," I admitted.

"Multiple hierarchies have ties to the bird," Alec added. "We don't know if she meant it literally yet."

"I did," croaked a hoarse voice behind us.

Alec, Fae, and I whirled to find Ally standing on shaky legs, now wrapped in my sweats and hoodie. My heart lurched.

She looked pale. Fragile. Chilled. How long had we been out? Evidently long enough to summon a full diplomatic court.

"Ally," I breathed, rushing to her—but faltering before I could touch her. I didn't know if she could handle contact yet.

She nodded—saw my hesitation—and closed the space herself.

We crashed into each other's arms.

Relief slammed into my ribs like a hand reaching into my chest and setting my heart gently back in its hollow cage. Without her, I'd been half-dead.

I buried my face in her hair, the bridge of my nose burning. "I fucking missed you, little nova."

Something between a sob and a laugh rasped out of her, broken and hollow, but her arms tightened around my waist anyway.

"You never let go," she whispered into my chest, turning her face to rest it over my heart.

"Never," I promised. And I wouldn't. My mate might be a force of nature—the storm to level all storms—but she was mine to withstand.

She inhaled deeply, maybe anchoring herself in my scent as I was in hers, then turned to face the sea of eyes...though she didn't let me go.

"I'll answer all of your valid questions," Ally said with a near-convincing attempt at humor, "but first, I need to eat before I sprout fangs."

Laughter rippled through the room, and to my relief, the Souls moved quickly—clearing space, fetching plates. Tieran pulled out a chair for me to guide her into. Onyx poured coffee. Kingsley slid into the seat beside hers, slicing fruit just as Alec arrived with a platter of bacon. Rose brought donuts.

Only once Ally was seated, shoveling food between her chapped lips without apology, did the next wave hit.

The Souls hovered like panicked bees around an injured queen, speaking all at once.

"Ally, where is Commander Amadeus at a time like this?"

"You saved my sister in Cabo. We'll answer when you call."

"Alvara Goldman, Death's Angel—what do you foresee for my hierarchy?"

"What's the raven mean?"

"What is 'white and white and burning'? It's circled three times. That sounds absolutely wretched."

Alec tried—bless him—with a jabbed, "Awe, come on, that just sounds like a beach vacation."

"Aren's six saved my hierarchy. Where you lead us, we follow, no matter the end."

"Are there really only three threads that lead to victory?"

"What do we do with the necromancers' offer to ally?"

"You mind your own fucking business, that's what," Kingsley growled.

"You and Aren saved our entire coven. We'll answer your call."

"Take it easy," I rumbled, my voice low and dangerous as sparks skittered over my raised hands. "Let my wife breathe. Let her eat. Then, for the love of God, *speak one at a time."*

Mouth full, Ally looked up at me, amusement flickering in her eyes.

Everyone laughed—but I didn't miss the way her shoulders dropped when the crowd retreated, settling into seats. Giving her the space she needed.

We were in for a long fucking day.

It was Alec's inevitable mental voice that finally put a smile on my face.

Just another Wednesday, then?

TWENTY-EIGHT
WORSE ODDS

ALVARA

The unmistakable blanket of pine and snow wrapped around my senses once the last Soul left. I tipped my face up to what would likely be the final snowfall of the season—perhaps my last snow in this life. Fat, fluffy flakes kissed my skin before dissolving just as quickly, and I fought to silence the persistent hissing of the other, still tugging at the edges of my mind.

There had always been a madness looming just beyond sight.

It was the curse of a seer.

The very real probability that we could see *too much*—slip into the depths of insanity.

Like a phoenix, something new rose from the wreckage. A creature born from ash: sightless, incoherent, a vessel for terrifying predictions the homeland called an *Oracle*. Nothing more than a mindless conduit between this world and the Fates, their words rarely understood. All that anchored them to reality was the rotating line of power-seekers, kneeling and offering their blood to be ranked and measured. Something in the transaction kept the Oracles lucid—like they fed off the magic in those drops of blood.

My ultimate nightmare was to end this life as one of them—an Oracle.

Incapable of making sense of the threads myself. Subject to others' interpretations.

When I first read Aren centuries ago, I'd thought myself close to the border of madness. Naïve. That anguish hadn't even scratched the surface of the hell that followed: watching a hundred-thousand threads unspool on a loop, each difference so minute it barely registered.

One hundred thousand and eight potential futures, to be exact.

Only 3,240 probable realities where this realm still contained life beyond microorganisms. Where some sliver of what we called humanity *survived*. I used that word loosely—those lives existed in servitude, enslaved by a so-called "greater race." Demons posing as royalty, free to conquer, brand, rape, and bend survivors to their will. It was suffering no creature deserved.

Only 119 threads where humans survived *and* sovereign Souls still drew breath—but not here. In those, we were banished to The Middle, forced to seal the portals for good, praying humanity could survive without us.

Fifty-seven where we still walked between realms.

That idea alone made my stomach turn. Souls weren't energy meant to be contained. We weren't made for cages.

Three.

Three slender threads where the world was made anew and humanity lived in a state still worth enduring—though even then, it came with rebuilding.

And one—one thread of genuine victory.

One where the Horsemen were stopped before their rise.

One where united hierarchies flew a single banner and brought a great power to heel.

There were consistencies, of course, in the 119 threads the Western Delegation deemed "acceptable" outcomes of the war. Fewer still tied the final three together. But in every one of those...all the pieces of the prophecy knelt to August.

Only, there was a hole in the vision. A glaring blank space, like a missing puzzle piece. A *seventh* part. Adrastos had withheld something—and I was more furious with myself for being surprised than at the bastard for keeping secrets.

Of course, that twisted fuck hadn't given me all the pieces.

Of course there was a mystery piece on the damn board. And now I'd have to beat it out of him—or find it myself.

Aren always led at August's side. Always at the helm of the conflict. Always steering us through.

Two souls with opposing gifts—death in one, life in the other—sealed the portals in the final inning. Their appearances differed as starkly as their magic, save for haunting blue eyes: one aqua, one husky blue. Where one went, the other followed. Even through the darkest threads.

It had taken combing through hundreds of outcomes before I realized I was watching two of Hazelharbor's beloved healers. Not random witches. One of them was bound to the Commander.

I couldn't bear to entertain Aren's innumerable threads. Too many ended in heartache. The bile rose in my throat just thinking about them. I'd already purged my stomach for ten straight minutes this morning.

In every victorious thread, we had both a spell book and a crown—tools to contain and channel an immense power.

In only one did my coven survive intact.

But there were losses we could survive and those we couldn't. Even if it was the last thing I did, I had to ensure Freya, Aren, and Fae survived long enough to finish this...beside *him*.

That goddamn, cock-sucking, arrogant fucking shifting shadow bird.

In none of the "acceptable" threads could Adrastos die before we sealed the gates. *Not one.* Losing him meant losing everything.

And despite all the atrocities he'd committed, I wouldn't get the justice I craved. Couldn't tear his heart from its cage. The knowledge left a scream boiling in my chest.

There was nothing *just* about that monster surviving while my family was torn apart.

I sensed August before I heard him—the warmth of him brushing the periphery of my mind, like a lover's hand across my thoughts. A few moments later, the crunch of his boots broke the sheen of ice layered over the snow.

I opened my eyes to watch flakes dance across the blackness. Without a word, he slipped his fingers into mine and turned his face skyward to join me.

Seconds passed. Or hours.

Then, softly, he cleared his throat. "What are you keeping tucked against your vest, love?"

Of *course* he'd noticed.

Of course, he knew me that well.

My tells were as blatant as neon signs these days.

I'd broken down the threads. The delegation had debated each scenario, weighing the cost and merit of every outcome. Whatever distraction had tied up Adrastos long enough to grant me space had bought me the time I needed to deliver the odds to our allies. And now, they'd carry that information far and wide.

But there was one truth I'd kept for myself.

Because *I* was the one who'd walked those paths. I'd nearly crumpled under the pressure of all I'd seen.

Fate marked *me* to carry that weight.

And if they knew—if *he* knew—it would open new pathways. Dangerous ones. Deviations from the outcomes we still had a chance at.

So I tucked that truth close. Against my chest. Just for me.

I stuck out my tongue and caught a few oversized flakes. The frozen tickle drew a smile across my face. Sled races with Aren and Alec. Ansel's low, begrudging laugh. The sting of a perfect snowball to the face. The weight of August's body over mine, his hips pressing into me for the first time...

Most of my joy had lived in the snow. And now, knowing how fleeting it truly was—

Every memory felt all the sweeter.

Seeming to remember our only Christmas together, August huffed a breath that bordered on a chuckle before giving my hand a gentle squeeze.

Fighting back the truth threatening to spill from my lips, I studied him —my breathtaking mate. The man who'd stayed out here in the freezing cold to stand guard over me for days. The man who wouldn't—*couldn't*—submit to the reality I was about to lay bare. Who would fight like hell to rewrite it. The man who'd chased me through lifetimes.

Being cleaved into twin, gaping wounds wasn't new for us. But somehow, that made the words that much more bitter on my tongue.

Silver lined his eyes as he studied the tears welling in my own, and August's expression crumpled in pain—as if he knew what I was going to say before I did. As if he were drawing in his last breath.

August Porter, the Great Commander, my mate in all incarnations, dove for me. His beautiful, calloused hands cupped my face, cradling me in his palms. His desperate lips found mine in a crushing collision, as though he could kiss hard enough to erase the reality before us.

As he poured all the unsaid things into that kiss, painting stars across my vision, I realized: there is no crueler fate than the star-crossed lover.

The love that's doomed from the start.

I breathed my question against his lips, throat tight. "Do you remember Zeke?"

He nodded, silent. I whispered my story nearly as softly as the snow falling around us.

"Decades ago, I spent a summer in the Arizona desert with him, before he met Livvy. Poor bloke was trying to teach me earth magic—something about how it pertained to desert flowers." August's thumb stroked a barely-there pattern over my cheek, his nose brushing mine in a quiet rhythm. Back and forth. Back and forth.

"I am completely useless in a terrarium," I murmured. "Turns out my skill set is more blunt force than delicate bloom."

He said nothing, only whisked away an errant tear before it could fall.

"One night stands out most."

"Not sure I like this story," August breathed, aiming for humor despite the hollow ring behind his voice.

I chuckled anyway. His need to make me smile in the face of devastation was one of the most beautiful blessings of my life.

"Have you ever heard of the night-blooming cereus?"

When he shook his head, I swallowed down the emotion climbing my throat.

"They're beautiful. Like a daffodil crossed with a magnolia." My eyes drifted closed. I could almost feel the velvet of the petals on my fingertips—but I reached instead for the map of his forearms, tracing each proud tendon with reverence. "They bloom once a year, in June. The *smell*, August—God, I'll never forget it. They open just after dusk, but wilt before midnight. By morning, they're gone."

He brushed the hair from my face with so much gentleness it could bring me to my knees. His eyes pleaded with me not to say it. Not to destroy the fragile bubble we'd built these past few weeks.

"In all my years, in all the countries I've walked, I've never seen anything so breathtakingly delicate," I whispered. "Sometimes, the most cherished, most memorable parts of life are the treasures that have no chance of lasting. I never really understood why I loved that night so much. But I get it now. It's the double edge of mortality that makes life so precious."

"Don't, Ally," August rasped, voice serrated. "Please. I am begging you."

Steeling myself into the role of Grayshell's second, I forced my voice into compliance, delivering the truth I hated with every fiber of my being.

"There are no threads that end well for us. In every outcome where humanity is spared—*we* are the price."

AUGUST

WHOOSH, *whoosh, whoosh.*

The world had long since vanished, leaving only the steady thrum of blood in my ears. Mouth suddenly bone-dry, I shook my head. I would've spoken—said something, anything—but my lips refused to form words. Finally, I managed one. "No."

"I'm sorry," she breathed, eyes pleading as I kept shaking my head, panic coiling around my ribs, my throat, the weight of it threatening to crush me.

"We'll find a way. We'll make one ourselves. I'll carve it out of fate's cold, dead fingers if I have to."

Lip wobbling, Ally looked up to the flurries of snow above us, her voice softer than the flakes. "Not this time."

"There's always another thread, baby."

"Not this time." Her certainty was sharp enough to slice me clean through.

Jamming my fingers through my hair, I turned to pace. My hands had nowhere to go, so I shoved them into my jacket as I carved a trench into the snow.

Fuck this.

I spun back. My wife—my goddamn mate—stood staring into the snow like it was some kind of benediction. Like she was *ready*. That resigned serenity on her face made something primal scream inside me. She'd accepted this. This...martyrdom.

"You're just gonna stand there like that?" I demanded, heart hammering in my chest, the pulse echoing like a million boots marching across stone. Loud. Steady. Promising suffering.

"It's peaceful, isn't it?"

"Maybe?" I stared at her, waiting for the punchline. "I'm too busy panicking to think about it, if I'm honest."

"There's no point in panicking, August. Death is the lone inevitability."

"Sure. For mortals. But we're not mortals, Ally. Aren has avoided that bucket for nearly two millennia."

"One and a half."

"Same difference."

"I mean, technically—"

"Ally!" I barked, my voice tearing through the sacred silence of the snowfall. The quiet that followed was somehow worse—deafening—as I stared into those round, tear-bright emeralds. "What are you doing? And I don't mean watching the snow. I mean standing *there*, acting like this fight is over when it hasn't even started."

"I'm...I'm processing, August. I—"

"Processing? Fine. Process. Adjust. But you can't stand there and tell me that after watching you slip through my fingers in agony more times than any sane soul could count, you're just...giving up."

Her chin quivered, eyes watering, something frantic bubbling just beneath the surface. The first signs of a boil.

Good. Because I was *breaking*. And I needed her to *care*. Needed her to need me as much as I needed her—because the thought of being cleaved apart again, of either of us moving on, of new lives with new lovers, only to die before we ever truly *lived*...

No.

Just...no.

I opened my mouth to tell her all of it when she whispered, "It is what it is."

Whoosh, whoosh, whoosh.

Oh God, I was gonna puke. A tidal wave of hot saliva flooded my mouth as nausea climbed. I pinched the bridge of my nose, breathing hard through the sting. "No."

She stepped toward me, reaching out. But the second her fingers grazed mine, I stepped back—ripped away. The scream in my throat burned. I wanted to beg. Threaten. Call Aren. Plead with him to command her to *fucking fight*.

Her gaze dropped. Her chest heaved. That boiling point rose.

Good. *Push her.*

Because I was falling apart.

But then she said, "August, you have to see reason—"

"No." I turned and paced, finally giving in to the *rage* boiling in my veins.

Alvara was the most incredible leader I'd ever known—*too* incredible. Always the one to fall on the sword. Always putting her people first. But *we* —as mates—we were the beginning, middle, and end. And she didn't get to throw that away.

Trying and failing to soften my tone, I said, "No, Ally. *You* see reason. Look at me." When she didn't, I crossed the space, lifted her chin between my thumb and finger. "Look at me, baby."

She did. Eyes locking with mine, twin galaxies of grief and fire. I'd never wanted to hurt her—never wanted to be the cause of her pain in a world that already demanded everything from her. But silence had bought me nothing.

Because I was losing her.

And of all the torments I could endure, that wasn't one of them.

"I can't do it, Ally. Not again."

"We go out together this time," she whispered. Like that should make it better. Like that should make the agony *easier*.

"No."

"Stop being so fucking selfish!" she snapped. Her hands flew to her mouth, staggering a step back, like she couldn't believe the words had come out.

"*Selfish?*" I echoed, almost relieved by the fire in her voice. It was better than apathy. Better than surrender. At least it meant she *cared*.

"Yes. Selfish."

"You know what's *selfish*, Ally? Giving up on your mate. The soul the universe *weaved* specifically for you. The karmic equal who could never love another the way *they* love *you*. And you're standing there, telling me that's *disposable*? That we just toss it away?" My voice cracked. "What if we don't find each other next time?"

"We will," she murmured, more to herself than me. She turned to pace, wringing her hands against her chest.

"Fuck that," I snapped, lunging to grab her arm and pull her back into me. "Stop running from me."

"I'm not—"

"Bullshit. I just found you."

"*I* just found *you!*" she sobbed, her voice finally cracking wide open. "Don't forget *I* was the one who watched your body burn, Michael. I was the one who lost my mate when you didn't ascend—and lived to tell the tale. *I* was the one who endured nearly three centuries alone while I just waited—"

"And you don't think that's exactly why I refuse to give up?!"

"—while you circled through lives, living and loving and fucking, and I was *alone*, August. For centuries. I couldn't stomach looking at another because I'm yours. I've *always* been yours."

"Then fight for me. *Fight for us,* dammit. What are you thinking?"

"I'm thinking there's an entire realm of souls impacted by this outcome, and I can't place my own happiness above their survival."

Whoosh, whoosh, whoosh.

Chests heaving, we stared each other down—her with stubborn resolve that this was the only path, me with the full force of defiance.

"Fuck the threads, Ally. Damn them all. I'm not letting you go. Not again."

"Selfish," she breathed, and the word ripped the air from my lungs. I scrubbed my palms over my face.

"Answer me this," I said, struggling to keep my voice even. Every nerve in my body buzzed, every instinct screaming to grab her and never let go. "Were there threads that gave us a happy ending—but you cut them because someone else lost theirs?"

Her lips parted, surprise flashing in her eyes as her spine straightened. I let out a hollow, humorless laugh.

"And what about *their* choices, Ally? You really think anyone we love—anyone in the hierarchy—wouldn't honor you the way you're trying to honor them?"

"It's not the same."

"How!?" I snapped. "A life for a life. The only difference is you got to watch the options—and now you're choosing *for them.*"

"I could never—"

"And you think Aren *could?*" I cut in, her flinch like a physical blow. "He's on there, isn't he? That death toll you're so obsessed with avoiding while you *happily* toss mine on the pile."

"It's not the same," she whispered, the color draining from her cheeks.

"Because you're somehow not as valuable?" My voice cracked with frustration. "I think I can speak for the coven when I say: bullshit. Lana and Ansel would've thrown themselves to the wolves for you on that field—not just because they fucking love you, but because you're the bulwark between our people and annihilation. Alec would throttle you just for suggesting otherwise."

"Stop," she ordered, voice sharp with command.

"I'm just getting started." I stepped closer. "Right now, it's just you and me, baby. You might be our Second, but right now, you're *my mate*. And for all the love you give our people, they love you back just as fiercely. You've spent your whole life protecting them—but when it matters most, you won't give them the dignity of choosing for themselves."

"I couldn't live with myself—"

"So dying is the easy way out?" I cut in, hard.

"Cheap shot."

"Am I *wrong*?" I challenged. "Prove me wrong, Ally. What future scares you more?" I gripped her shoulders, trying to break through. "The one where someone loves you enough to choose your life over theirs? Or the one where you rob us of the masterpiece our maker *crafted* for us? Where's *my choice*, Ally? Where are *our* threads? What happens to the hierarchy without you watching their backs?"

"I can't see past the point of our deaths."

I froze. Every muscle locked, vibrating with the urge to explode.

"So...what you're saying is, you don't even know if it works."

"What? No, I—"

"You *can't* see past the point where we die. So, you have no *idea* if it even works."

"The best odds—"

"Fucking hell," I muttered, fingers raking through my hair hard enough to sting. "You're so busy sacrificing everything for everyone else that you haven't even considered this might all be for *nothing*."

"The others will finish it."

Shaking my head, I dragged a hand across my jaw, pacing in a tight circle. "No."

"There's more, August. And you have to promise me you'll make it count. My price goes beyond my life..."

The image she failed to block out of her mind hit me like a gut punch. Bile surged. My hands clenched into fists, one swiping hard across my mouth.

My wife. The martyr.

Blinking back the sting in my eyes, I growled, "No," and turned toward the wards. Her energy rose behind me, swelling with frustration, vibrating off her like static.

"Dammit, August, where are you going?" she shouted, boots thudding behind me as she followed me up the stairs.

"Out," I huffed, flinging open the cabin door—and nearly barreling into Fae, who was channeling water into Kingsley's plants with wide, startled eyes.

"We're in the middle of a conversation."

"From where I'm standing, you won't even *have* a legitimate *conversation* about this. So how can we be in the middle of one?"

"Oh shit, mom and dad are fighting," Alec whispered—*loudly*. Ally flipped him off. I didn't even look at him. Didn't care. Every last one of my fucks was accounted for. And the woman who owned them? She was about to hurl herself into hell.

"August!"

"Nope," I muttered.

"*August*," she hissed through gritted teeth, chasing me up the stairs while Alec and Fae whispered God knows what behind us. I pushed through the cracked door to our room and went straight to the closet, ripping off my clothes as I moved.

I needed to hurt *something*. Someone. Preferably whoever was responsible for even *suggesting* Ally should die.

God, what I'd give to get my hands on Adrastos right now.

I'd just grabbed my battle blacks when Ally strode in, yanked them from my hands, and hurled them onto the bed.

"Look at me."

"I am," I said flatly, shoving my jeans to the floor. "And I see a woman so terrified of being loved as deeply as she loves, she won't even let her family try."

Gaping, Ally watched me cross to the bed and yank on my Grayshellian armor.

"Where are you going?" she demanded.

"I need to hit something," I growled, shoving my arms through the sleeves.

"Not an answer."

I dropped onto the bed and shoved my feet back into my boots. "Has yours changed?"

She didn't respond. Just stared, nostrils flaring, jaw clenched.

"That's what I thought."

"So tell me, August—" Ripping off her shirt, Ally hurled it to the floor. I turned toward the door, afraid if I *looked* at her—really looked—I'd buckle. My need to touch her, hold her hips, kiss and cherish her, would smother my fury. "—who are we sacrificing then? If I find a thread where we survive, who dies in our place? Who falls on blades I could absorb?"

"I don't know. But it's not just our choice to make, is it?" I strapped Solskari daggers into their sheaths, the steel humming like it shared my unrest.

"Yes it is," she snapped, her voice edged as she stomped into her boots.

I glanced down at her untied laces and scowled. "What are you doing?"

"Going *with you,* dammit. Isn't it obvious? We do this together. *Always.*"

"You say that, but I don't think it means the same thing to you as it does to me." I shoved open the door and barreled down the stairs, shaking my head as she cursed under her breath behind me. The moment I cleared the wards, I jumped—just as stubborn hands latched onto my arm.

Our boots hit asphalt for all of a second before another twist of space dropped us back into snow. Only...this wasn't Kingsley's.

It was the lake house.

"What are you doing?"

"Fighting, dammit. Who's running now?"

"Don't be cute."

"I'm not. You want a fight, August? Here I am. Away from prying ears. If you want to go nuclear on a nest of Mortiferous Nóchtaithe, we can do that. Later. After we're on the same damn page."

I barely held myself together. "I don't want to lose you."

"I don't want to leave you either, dammit."

"Then *don't.*"

"I'm not sure we'll have a choice. But tell me—honestly—who would you kill, August?"

I recoiled at the question. "That's not the same."

"But it is. Isn't it?" Her voice was so calm, it hurt. "*That's* your solution —let someone else die. So who do we trade for our lives? Alec, just as he's about to become a father?"

"Stop." I staggered back, as if distance could protect me from the image of Fae in mourning black, clutching their baby.

"Ansel? Finally reunited with his daughter. Aren? He just found his mate after millennia of solitude." She stepped closer. "Who goes?"

"I won't choose for them. But you shouldn't either."

"Freya?" she pressed, driving the knife deeper. My pulse spiked.

"No—"

"It would take more of them to pay the same price. And even then, I don't know if all of them together could pull it off."

"Then give them the choice." My voice cracked. "Just...*give them the choice.*"

"No." She stepped close, pressing a hand to my chest plate, over my heart. I wrapped my fingers around her wrist, holding her there. My other hand cupped her cheek, sliding along her jaw.

"This is my burden. Don't you see? That's why I have this gift. Why no one else does."

With a ragged breath, I slid my hand up to the back of her neck and lowered my forehead to hers. Her scent, her fingers drumming against my armor, steadied me.

She slowed her rhythm like she could sync my pulse to hers.

Then she tilted her head, our lips a breath apart, like she was asking permission. As if the weight of our future fractured the right to simply take what we wanted.

That broke me. So, I took the kiss.

I scraped my fingers through her hair and pulled her in, claiming her mouth like it could anchor us to *this* reality.

When she pulled back, her voice was a whisper. "Fuck the odds, August."

"We've faced worse," I rasped, grazing my lips across hers. Her eyes lit as the warmth of her surged into me. "We make our fate. Promise me."

She rose on her toes and pressed her lips to mine more firmly. My resolve faltered. Because if she was right—if our days were numbered—then *this* was what mattered most.

Gravel in my voice, I swore, "We'll make it count," and backed her toward the lake house.

The second the door clicked shut behind us, Ally's hands were already undoing the clasps on my armor, her gaze burning into mine. Our mouths collided with frantic need—hungry, urgent, desperate—as her fingers wrenched off my scabbard and sent it clattering to the floor.

We were in this together, no matter how cruel the ending. And we'd cherish *every second* in the meantime.

With each kiss, each drag of lips and tearing of clothes, we made our unspoken vows.

"Mine," I snarled as her pants hit the hardwood.

"Yours," she promised, leaping into my arms. I caught her instinctively, always in sync, her legs wrapping around me as I turned and slammed her against the door. "Always yours, August." Her voice caught on my name as I drove my cock over her entrance, then thrust deep inside.

The way she took me in—utterly and without reservation—shattered me. This bond might be cursed, but her willingness to carry it...her determination to claim me through it...destroyed every defense I had left.

"The damned devil himself couldn't keep us apart for more than a few centuries," she whispered as I stilled, buried in her, fighting for control.

When I started to move, hard and deep, she gasped—head falling back, hands threading into my hair, nails scraping my scalp.

"No matter what dimension I wake in next," she panted, "I will find you, August."

She cried out as my rhythm built, pleasure twisting her features into something *sacred*. I couldn't look away. Couldn't stop chasing the way her body broke for me.

"Ahhh—August!"

"Yes, baby. Say it again."

"*August*," she moaned, over and over, our names mingling with the frantic slap of skin. Her eyes dropped to where we were joined, and suddenly flames erupted down her arms.

A ribbon of blue fire curled around us, licking at my skin without harm. I might've been immune to her gifts, but our house was not. I flicked a hand, dousing the flames before they spread—but not before they seared her shape into the door.

"Oh fuck," she panted as I spun her off the wall and slammed her back down on my cock.

Ally wrapped herself around me, feet braced against my back, driving herself onto me with brutal force. Her head fell back, body shuddering with every thrust.

"Fuckfuckfuck—" Her eyes rolled back and I squeezed her ass in warning—eyes on me, little nova.

Emerald eyes locked on mine as her body bowed, the pleasure breaking over her like a wave.

"August," she whimpered—right before her orgasm tore through her. Her flames surged, her pussy clenched around me, and I came on a growl through gritted teeth, our releases crashing together. I only slowed when her fire finally flickered out.

Sweat-slicked and gasping, we kissed like we were drowning.

Then, breathless, she gave me her final vow. "We...make it...count."

TWENTY-NINE
CHAOS AND MARBLES
ALVARA

When I told August we had to make our sacrifice count, I meant it in the fate-of-humanity kind of way. We needed to line up every consistent piece, every domino, to ensure that when our final strike landed, it *meant* something. That it moved the needle. That if we lost, our people would still have a shot at winning the last inning.

August, however, took it in two directions—yes, secure a strategic victory for our side, but also check off as many shared dreams as possible while we still had time.

In just forty-eight hours, he'd argued with human representatives, met with the Eastern Delegation, and whisked me off to his three favorite beaches and their accompanying restaurants. Apparently, most of August's favorite human memories revolved around food. I wasn't complaining. His list made me think of mine, though. We'd missed football season, but I could still drag him to a hockey game—something simple, human, frivolous. The kind of joy that made you yell for no real reason.

Somehow, in the same breath we were strategizing how to draw out Adrastos, we were also planning our one and only Valentine's Day.

Because...we *did* need to draw him out. For some Godforsaken reason, he was essential to winning this thing. Thanks to the Magic Bond I'd gained when we emerged victorious, if I could just get him within mental range, I could bend him—at least partially—to my will. His vow was to serve August upon our victory. Maybe that vow was the only reason he'd survive the war's finale.

"Cheesecake or tiramisu?" August's left-field question yanked me out of my spiral. I blinked down at the training ring inside Terramyst's massive terrarium-style hall.

We'd made it to the Middle after Kingsley addressed his people and put it to a vote. We were the first outsiders to step foot inside their castle since Thadius's mate, more than a century ago.

"What?" I asked blankly, dragging my gaze from the sparring souls below.

"I'm planning a theme for our date," he said at rapid-fire speed—same as everything else lately, like he thought he could cram more into the time we had left. "There's this place in Manhattan with the best manicotti in the country—"

"Why not just go get the real deal?" Alec, nosy as ever, appeared beside him, arms crossed, watching the ring. "Ooh, or a good Cornish pasty," he said, giving his fingers a chef's kiss. "Can't beat the real thing. Kinda like chowder. Either get to the coast or don't bother. Am I right?"

"Can you two think with *anything* besides your stomachs?" Fae demanded, coaxing pink flowers to bloom along the banister with her outstretched hands while she observed the chaos below. Like Grayshell, Terramyst's training style was either structured matches or all-out chaos. Today was the latter.

"Occasionally," Alec said with a grin, "I like to think with my dick."

"Jesus, Alec," I muttered, eyes closing as I huffed a reluctant laugh. Ansel would have a coronary.

"As evidenced by your mate's current state," August added smoothly.

Fae elbowed him. "I expect absurd remarks from Bozo over there—but *you*?" She pouted, dragging her voice into a baby lilt. "My sweet wil' rookie?"

The vines near her swayed toward her like they'd finally found their sun in a world without one. Smiling, Fae extended a finger, and I swear one of the blooms nuzzled it. As flames bent and curled to me, plants had *always* loved Aphaea.

"Oh come on, babe," Alec teased, his grin stretching wider. "You walked right into that one."

"Just because someone sets the ball doesn't mean you have to spike it."

"I prefer a gentle fondle."

August snorted. Fae rolled her bright blue eyes and turned to me, leaning her back against the railing, silently begging me to help her.

They might've been idiots, but they were *our* idiots. And I had a feeling Alec was being extra ridiculous to offset the anxiety radiating off August and me. He could play the fool all he wanted, but the man was sensitive as hell and always keyed into the people around him. I couldn't bear to tell him the truth of it. Besides, I'd missed their babble. Desperately.

So, I pulled in a breath, forced a smile, and shrugged.

Fae huffed but continued. "My idiot mate is right, though—why not get the real thing? There's this pub in Wales with the most *divine* Shepherd's pie—"

Her words cut off as a vision slammed into me.

Adrastos. Standing on a black sand beach beneath low-hanging clouds, staring into the frothing sea.

I threw up a hand, halting the conversation, watching.

He turns toward a jagged hillside and stares up at the perilous ascent toward crumbled ruins. This place holds pain—deep, ancient pain. Grief that long-since calcified.

"Get the real thing," I breathed, locking eyes with August.

Something tugged at me from that vision. Something *familiar*. A long-forgotten ache stirred in my chest, amplified when I looked at my mate.

We'd planned to train with Kingsley, then walk through the Terramyst Forest to the vanishing sea. But a different tide was calling.

Where are you? The question pulsed through me, a desperate attempt to reach down whatever twisted line bound me to my enemy. But the link still only worked one way. I couldn't send thoughts back. Not yet.

Still, I wondered—if I went overseas, would it change? Would *he*?

It might not work. It might not be how we bend him. But maybe...

"Of course."

"Gonna fill us in, Al?" Alec asked, tilting his head and chomping into an apple from—who the hell knew where. He wiped his wrist over his mouth. "You're doing the creepy, muttering-to-yourself thing again."

"Adrastos is English."

"*Uhhh*, yeah." The *duh* practically dripped from his tone and the lift of his brow.

"Of course we're not finding him. We're looking in the wrong places." I stared down at the ring, heart thudding. "What if...he went *home*?"

"Okay, right, I'm picking up what you're putting down. But where is that, exactly?" Alec asked. "I know the UK's not huge, but it's still a lot of ground to cover. So...where's home?"

Home. The word planted a pit so deep in my belly it ached.

Home...as in Grayshell.

Home as in...*why* couldn't I remember where we *actually* came from?

The accent, yes. The crashing waves and *his* laughter echoing off stone walls? The begrudging smile of a cruel king without a name? Yes. But beyond that—just flickers. Black marble. The nightmare thread. Nothing more.

"Dialect was the Queen's English, I think?" Fae offered. I nodded. If we'd heard his true voice, yes. Southern England. It was a place to start.

A groan followed by a loud *smack* pulled our attention back to the mats, where Kingsley had just disarmed and flattened one of his trainees. I opened my mouth to speculate—

—and another vision hit me like a sledgehammer.

From silence to tsunami, they came roaring back, brutal and vivid.

Aren, dancing with the dark-haired witch.

Aren, shoulders sagging.

No. No, no. Slow down. What the hell went wrong this time?

Because in that solitary, hail-Mary thread—our only true victory—his mate, the girl with darkness in her veins, had stood beside him in the final battle. *She* was the key. I just had to figure out how to get her there.

Which was easier said than done. She wasn't exactly...cooperative.

Eyes shut, I tuned out the others placing bets on the matches below and focused.

Valentine's Day. Jesus, August must've rattled something loose in my brain. It was the perfect excuse. Sappy? Yes. But maybe it would work.

We were talking about England when the vision flared. Did I need to send him there?

The girl rolls her lips, shakes her head, nervously working a silver ring around her finger. A closed door.

Fuck. Okay. Um...what did she like? Chinese?

The door shuts.

Pizza?

She saves pizza for Fridays. Raincheck, Commander.

Sushi?

She just had it with friends, and besides—nothing to wear to someplace nice.

Fuck me. Okay. Um. Mexican?

She briefly considers a burrito, then rejects him. Still no outfit.

With a growl, I centered myself. What if her friend—the blonde—helped her get ready? Picked out a dress?

Her mouth falls open. Black roses in hand, she steps aside to let him in.

Yes. That was something. I dove deeper.

She laughs—pink behind her like a halo. God, she's pretty. All soft lines and that rare, blinding smile. He wants to taste her—

Woah-kay. Focus. TMI. What's next?

A movie?

Too much anxiety in crowds. Santa Bloom has no low-key options. Date ends.

Hard pass.

Something fun. Memorable. They had that teacher-student dynamic— maybe he could teach her something. Skydiving?

She recoils like he proposed to throw her off a cliff. Nope.

Bookstore?

She's on a book-buying ban. He offers to pay. She bites her lip, fiddles with her rings, and shakes her head.

No dice.

Dammit, this girl was impossible.

Snapping my fingers, I dug deep for something...romantic. Had I ever *really* thought about romance outside the occasional novel I stole from Fae or Lana?

Dancing was out—they'd already done that. But...

Ice skating?

She clings to his arms, eyes wide with fear and wonder as he glides backward. Old-school romantic music hums in the background. She blinks up at him, dazed, lips parting as he presses her into the partition—

Sweet baby Jesus in the manger, yes.

When I opened my eyes, all three of them were staring at me with identical raised brows.

"Were you just..." August trailed off, confusion etched in his features.

Alec stepped in without missing a beat. "Manipulating Aren's romantic life?"

"Maybe?" I said, pushing off the banister and heading for the stairs.

"*Who the hell is she?* Why are we setting Aren up with some witch? Why is she scared of literally everything fun?"

"Come on, Alec."

"No, but for real. Answer my questions."

"Maybe after I kick your ass in front of all the Western shifters."

<hr>

AFTER OUR COOLDOWN and healing session in the Middle, I fully intended to call Aren the second my boots hit the earth. At least I did—right up until I had my phone in hand and every single outcome...

Vanished.

Gone. Like smoke. Like someone had pulled the thread right out from under me.

I stopped so abruptly that August walked straight into my back, both of us scrambling to stay upright.

"What the fuck," I breathed, my chest hollowing. My hands flew to my ribs as if I could hold them together.

"Ally?" August asked, his voice dipped in concern, like he knew something was *off.*

"It all changed." The words came out thin. Barely audible. "It's gone."

"What?"

"Aren's threads. The second I went to call him...it all changed."

August gently turned me to face him, widening his stance until we were eye to eye. Behind him, Alec and Fae peeked around his broad shoulders like concerned meerkats.

"And these are crucial components?" he asked.

I nodded as dread churned in my stomach. Of all of us, Aren's threads were the most volatile but...why had they vanished?

I tried to focus on the girl instead, to make sense of her decisions. Nothing. Not even a name.

Until—there.

Aren, arms spread wide, that grizzly bear grin in place as he booms, "Magnolia!"

Oh shit, we were with them in that one.

I tried again to zero in on her—names usually helped clarify things—but still, nothing. Just static where her future should be.

Impossible.

I didn't understand...

I shifted tactics, checking whether we'd see him if we jumped west. He was with the witch—*Magnolia*—or would be before we arrived. Florida? The Naples house was *sacred* to us. Our only true Earthbound sanctuary. For him to bring her there?

Oh, fuck. This had to work.

Scowling up at the others' questioning expressions, I grabbed August's hand and jumped without another word.

The instant my boots hit the ground, the threads tumbled around me like marbles down stairs in a chaotic cacophony I immediately regretted.

Swallowing hard, I braced myself and lifted my hands to read the townhouses in front of us.

"What happened to not interfering with his thread?" August hissed, tugging my wrist as he shot a wary glance between me and the house.

"We're not."

"Umm. Sure smells like we are," he muttered. A quick glance through his thoughts confirmed—Aren's scent was everywhere.

What if we told him in person?

Nothing.

Had Ansel tell him?

Still nothing.

Fuck. Fuck!

What if...Ansel and Lana helped—but made him think it was his idea?

Like a half-illuminated bulb, the thread flickered back to life.

I was going to develop an eye twitch. No soul was meant to meddle in this many fates at once. And Aren...Aren's survival meant more to me than almost any other. His happiness?

Priceless.

Which begged the question—what kind of temperamental chaos was I sculpting here?

So far past irritated I couldn't see the line anymore, I stomped up the steps to the townhouse and flung open the door.

I barely made it two steps inside before Ansel appeared, arms crossed over a fitted black tee.

"Um...hello? What's happening?"

Tears pricked behind my eyes the moment I saw him. That gravel-edged voice, the scent of home—of him—washed over me in a wave. My teacher. My friend. *Alive.* Not a prisoner of war. Not a broken shell after months of torture.

I'd seen a thousand brutal ends for the people I loved. But this? This hit me like a sucker punch.

And the threads were so damn fragile I didn't even dare hug him.

Stop shifting, I growled in my mind. Literally growled—like a mutt snarling at God.

Mad. I'd gone mad.

"Hey, hi, how are you?" I chirped, zipping around the room like a tornado, deliberately not touching a single thing. Not a table. Not a dust bunny. Nothing. "Good? That's good."

"What are you doing here, Ally?" he asked, silver eyes narrowed. But behind them—anxiety. I tapped his mind, and his walls dropped.

He *was* worried. Not just about me—but Freya. She was across the country, and the last time he saw her, she was still healing.

I wrapped my mind around his in response. The closest I could come to a hug.

"What?" I squeaked, voice several octaves too high. "You don't recognize a meddler when you see one? I learned it from you."

"Somehow, I doubt that," August snorted—right as Lana came sauntering around the corner...in bunny slippers?

A blush rose to her translucent cheeks as I blinked between her pink feet and her wide-eyed expression.

"Is that a cat?" I barked, eyeing the spotted brown and black furball in her arms.

She glared and pulled him protectively against her chest like I'd try to confiscate him.

Never was one for cats. Or most animals, really.

"Nat's familiar," she snapped. "He likes to hang out over here when she's gone."

"Mmhmm."

"Fucking *rude*, Ally!" Alec bellowed, stomping up the stairs behind us. I squeezed my eyes shut. What in the seventh circle of hell were they doing here?

"Just felt like having an impromptu family reunion, and you left us?!"

"It was pressing," I grumbled as he wedged himself between me and August.

Fae made a beeline for Lana's feline companion, but I snatched her arm mid-reach.

"Oh," Alec added, casually saluting Ansel and flipping off Lana, who returned the gesture without hesitation. "Hey guys!"

"Don't. Touch. Anything," I barked. "This thread is balanced on a goddamn blade, and it likes to teeter even when I'm not interfering. So *do not*. Touch. Anything."

"Do you need a good lay, sister?" Alec deadpanned, glaring at August like it was his fault before rounding back to me. "You're extra cranky today."

"*Oh my God!*" I groaned, pressing my palms to my face as August muttered something unintelligible and Lana snickered into her coffee.

"Shut up. All of you. Look—we're not supposed to be here."

"So why are you?" Ansel asked, clearly unimpressed. "It's your damn plan we're following."

In predictable harmony, Lana chimed in, "We were having a perfectly lovely morning."

"We were just going over your notes for the emissary meeting tomorrow."

"We're not staying," I said quickly.

"What?!" Alec's eyes bulged, blinking like I'd grown a second head.

Maybe I had. Maybe the trance had broken something. Maybe this wild-eyed madness was all that remained.

This felt like Grayshell's most chaotic rendition of *Who's On First*. Nonsense volleyed between us while no one understood a damn thing. I wanted to laugh and cry at the same time.

Laugh, because, my God, I missed our family.

Cry, because there were emissaries to contact. Strings to pull. A counterweight bastard to trap into an alliance. And Aren's Deadly Seven were bickering like middle schoolers.

This was the problem with sneaking in under the radar.

As Ally, the meddling sister, I had zero authority.

What they needed wasn't Ally.

They needed Alvara Porter. Second-in-command.

"*Focus*, Alec," I snapped, standing straighter. "If your presence was prudent, you would have been invited. We can't stay. Being here interferes with too many threads still in motion. And I've got a hell of a lot on my plate, which brings me to this—" I met Ansel's eyes and widened my own for emphasis. "I need *your* help."

"Kinda figured," Ansel muttered, lifting his mug for a slow sip of what smelled like black coffee. His gaze swept over the four of us, then darted toward the open front door.

Voice tight, I said, "I'm going to give you a *very* specific list of instructions. And you cannot miss a step. Okay?"

THIRTY

TICK-TOCK

FREYA

Of all the ways I'd died in past lives, none were as shameful as getting beaten to death by a Southern Belle *Barbie*. Alas. First time for everything.

Groaning, I rolled onto my back and blinked up at the ornate ceiling of Reyna's ballroom. "That all you got?" It would've sounded tougher if I had enough air in my lungs to do more than croak. The next thing I saw was a too-pretty face with livid blue eyes and blonde hair glaring down at me.

"If you challenge *my sister* like this," Reyna snapped, disgust curling her lip as she vaguely waved at, well, all of me, "your death will be swift and humiliating. You'll bring shame to Grayshell and Bellaton alike. I won't have it. Now get up."

Ah. *Now* I saw how she and Aren had been a thing. Jesus Christ. Saints and angels. I really needed to finish ascending. Now that Reyna understood the urgency, she was more willing to help, but still refused to take me to the Middle. Claimed she'd triggered plenty of ascensions right here on these mats. Doubtful. I highly doubted any of them had been stuck in an eighteen-year-old vessel. And try as she might, Queen Reyna Gwyne was not more terrifying than Agamemnon with his mammoth hand around my throat.

This body was just too damn young.

Still, I staggered to my feet, stepping into a fighting stance—not that I could defend myself. I'd taken worse beatings. On second thought, as shadows slithered around my body, trapping my arms and binding my throat in silky ribbons, maybe not. Reyna squeezed, and I gasped. A flicker of power sparked deep in my core, and I thrashed, trying to draw on every last drop of adrenaline.

In the corner of my mind, I heard my phone ringing.

"It's Ally," Brody called from the edge of the room.

"*Gahhh*," Reyna snarled. Her shadows dissolved just as fast as they'd formed, and I dropped to my knees, coughing. Brody clicked the answer button while she huffed, "I wasn't *actually* gonna kill her!"

Snickering, I grabbed her outstretched hand and hauled myself up. But Brody's face had gone pale, his eyes bouncing from Reyna to me. Without a word, Carlton and another healer stepped forward, running hands over my limbs and lifting bruises and scrapes from my skin. Nothing major. They'd have me good as new in a minute.

But I couldn't look away from Brody as Ally's voice poured through the phone at hummingbird speed.

"We're on our way," he vowed, summoning his armor in a snap. His brothers followed suit, weapons materializing in the space of a heartbeat. Eyes locked on me, Brody said, "Aren's in trouble."

My stomach plummeted. I was already moving forward when he raised a hand to stop me.

"You can't even jump, little Wraith."

A fair wrist appeared in front of my face, a line of red seeping from a fresh wound. The scent of iron hit the air. Blood.

Reyna's blood.

Reaction one? Disgust.

But as Brody barked orders and Reyna shook her sliced open wrist, I lunged. Careful not to pierce the skin with my canines, I clamped my mouth over the bleeding wound and drank. The magic hit hard, my stomach flipped, and I swallowed it down.

"*Go*, damn you!" Reyna barked.

I didn't stop to question the weight of that gift. The four of us sprinted outside and hit the jump point in the yard. Brody's hand clamped over mine —and then we were gone.

The city rooftop snapped into focus. Broad daylight. Exposed. Minimal cover.

Three men in creepy-ass masks.

Ansel, Marcus, Aren—already armed.

But something was wrong. Shadows curled along the concrete. Shadows in broad daylight? What the fuck?

Wide-eyed, I glanced at Aren. He sent a single thought down the line.

Get the emissaries out.

Judging by the frantic heartbeat behind us, I didn't have to go far to start. The jump was *easy*—Reyna's power thrummed in my veins like an elixir I could get used to.

The sharp-dressed man hiding in the elevator raised his pistol. I disarmed him in a blink, raised a hand, and said, "I'm Aren's," before jumping us out onto the street below. He retched on landing, but there wasn't time for sympathy. I shoved his half-curled form toward the road and barked, "Get to the park. I'll get the rest."

In any other situation, I might've felt bad. Instead, I shoved the pistol back in his grip and jumped.

How surreal—war raged floors above us, and down here? Not a ripple. Mortals laughed by the coffee pot. Answered phones. Oblivious to the blade swinging above their heads.

Michael, help us.

Eyes scanning, I searched for any way to speed this up—and found it. I jumped, yanked down the fire alarm, and hissed as blue ink sprayed across my hand.

"*Fire!*" I bellowed into the eerily calm lobby, wiping the ink on my jeans. That's when it hit me: none of us grabbed masks. If this was caught on camera, our faces were done.

"*Go, go, go!*"

What floor? I shot down the line.

Thirteen, Brody sent back.

I was already in the air.

My stomach dropped as I landed. Too many mortals. Too many lives. They sprinted for the stairwells, panic rising like a tide.

There's no burden worse than choosing who lives or dies. But Aren's order rang again: Get the emissaries out.

Fuck me.

I jumped into the glass conference room where Brody was herding them, flung my stolen shadows like smoke-laced ropes, and coiled them around their bodies. Seven. My magic pulled tight, strained—but held.

I yanked them close and jumped, dropping them beside the first guy in the park. His eyes were locked on the building.

Once. Twice. Three times. I jumped back and forth, dragging clusters of screaming mortals into the shaded grass. But I felt the power thinning, slipping.

No. No. No.

God, I could do this for hours—if I had my own well.

Fuck it. One more.

I landed hard on corporate carpet, lungs seizing, the sound of evacuating chaos crashing into me.

Get out, now! Ansel's voice snarled in my mind.

My mouth went dry.

I...I can't leave them, Dad. I—

Now!

That wasn't my father. That was the Third of Grayshell giving an order.

I scanned the floor one last time. A woman clutching a baby. A lunch pail hanging from her elbow.

Shit.

I sprinted. Wrapped my arms around both her and the baby and jumped. We hit the ground harder than before, my knees screaming at the impact. The baby burst out crying as the woman staggered to her feet, eyes wide, staring back toward the building.

"My...my husband. *My husband!*"

"Fuck."

I leapt again.

Inside, a confused-looking man with too much belly and no neck was yelling into the now-empty office. Terrified Reyna's magic had run dry, I bolted for him.

"Here! *Run!*"

His eyes met mine. I snatched his hand. The world twisted—like we fell through the floor and rose through the grass—and landed.

Holy shit, we did it.

The woman dropped to her knees, weeping. The three of them folded together, sobbing in the grass as I stood there panting.

The sound of my name caught my attention, and I jumped to Ansel, the last ember of power flickering through my fingers.

"Here. Fine," I gasped. "I've got to take Reyna more seriously during training. Hard to follow a *Barbie,* but—"

BOOM.

I hit the ground in a crouch, hands flying to my ears. Ansel's arms wrapped over my head, shielding me.

We watched in mute horror as the building crumbled.

A plume of dust and debris blasted into the city.

No.

We were out of time.

CYRUS

ENTIRE WORLDS WERE on the brink of war, and still, the underworld kept on fucking churning.

Truth be told, I didn't mind it here so much. Humans were so locked into day-to-day survival they didn't notice their world teetering on the edge. Mortal wars. Attacks on American soil. The clock was ticking, and they were too busy to care. Arms deals, drug drops, corner hustles—business as usual. Like ants oblivious to the magnifying glass overhead, they scurried through their routines, unaware of what was coming.

But we felt it. The shadows hissed and stirred. The balance shuddered. My heart pounded like a war drum. The snow moon would rise tomorrow—Valentine's Day, tail end of Aquarius, mercury crawling out of retrograde. The short version? On a scale of one to ten, we were *so* fucking fucked. I pictured a clown juggling chainsaws in a category four hurricane. Minus the laughter.

Ma had called a war room to sort out the chaos and where to focus while we still had time. But for now, I was waiting for Carr at *The Rougarou*, thumb tracing condensation down the side of my glass.

"Cyrus," Melody purred, sliding into my booth. "Where've you been, Prince?"

"We've missed you at *La Lune*." Carissa's perfume hit me before her voice did. I should've checked on them after Uptown, but they hadn't crossed my mind. I wasn't one for relationships. A few family members, fewer friends—that was enough. The hierarchy kept my plate full.

"Been busy," I murmured, still drawing through the droplets.

"Busy chasing ghosts." Nix's voice was like getting socks for Christmas. Wet ones. That smelled like mildew and shame. Nothing good ever came of it.

"Ladies," I sighed, nodding. "You remember my cousin."

"Nix, you look good," Carissa said, already scooting toward him. Four words and she'd banned herself from my bed. Shame. I hated finding replacements.

"Ca-riss-aah," he drawled, sleazy as ever, rolling up his sleeves to flash those damn wings. "What's a girl like you doing in a rat's nest like this?" His eyes cut to me, then to Melody's cleavage where it spilled from her tank. "Better question: what are you two doing without *me?*"

"Avoiding STDs, I'd think," I muttered, draining my beer. The girls giggled and Carissa leaned into his side.

"What was that, little cousin?" Nix smirked, arm sliding around Carissa's waist, hand landing on her thigh. Making a show of it, like a kid grabbing someone else's toy.

"You're like a dirty fucking penny," I grumbled. "Instead of luck, you just make everyone wanna leave."

"Big man scared of a little competition?" He squeezed her thigh, watching me like it would get a rise.

"Just what my night needed—secondhand embarrassment," I said, brushing a kiss to Melody's temple before motioning for her to slide out. "Nothing says desperate like drooling over your cousin's leftovers."

Nix laughed, but his ears turned red. "What do you say, ladies—wanna set your stakes?" he asked.

"I've never had to persuade a woman into bed, Nix. Not about to start now."

I stood, tucked Melody's hair behind her ear, and offered her my seat. "You know where to find me."

"Cyrus, *don't go*," she whined. "We came for *you*."

But I was already turning, the noise of the bar falling away as every nerve lit up. Combat focus. A hum in my bones. Something—someone—had stepped into the room.

Where are you?

I couldn't see her. But I could fucking feel her.

Every inch of me could feel her. I nearly jumped out of my skin when Carr dropped a hand on my shoulder.

"Hey, man, sorry I'm late. You okay? You look...peaky."

"Pesky ghosts again?" Nix laughed.

"Somethin' like that," I muttered, stepping around Carr and praying the universe was listening.

The place was almost entirely Nephilim. That mortal frame shouldn't have been hard to spot. I moved through the crowd, every sound too loud, pulse thundering in my ears. I turned in a circle, scanning for new faces, just as a flash of red vanished through the front door.

Without thinking, I bolted out into the parking lot, lungs heaving, adrenaline flooding my system. Three bikers rumbled onto the road. The redhead—gone.

"Cy, what the fuck?"

I turned to Carr, still panting, sweat trickling down my temple.

"Thought I..." My voice trailed off. I scanned the lot, the road, the building. Nothing. "Saw something."

"Okay...but we gotta go. Your Ma's meeting's in half an hour. Last briefing before the ghost trap."

THIRTY-ONE

THE BEGINNING

ALVARA

August's beautiful Valentine's Day date would've been a lot more fun if I wasn't juggling the fate of every soul I knew in the palm of my hand. Chaos was unfolding all around us, and it felt like every thirty seconds I had to fire off a new text.

We'd tag-teamed with Kingsley and Freya to flush out a Renown nest after an Adrastos lead turned out to be a bust. Since then, I'd been busy keeping our allies afloat.

Marcus was about to get ambushed by those second hierarchy assholes wearing crowns.

Freya was in for a world of pain—but she came out okay in every thread. And something *needed* to happen there for her to bring in the numbers we saw in our best-case scenarios. I had Brody on standby, wrapping up his own to-do list.

My Hail Mary trip to England yesterday, hoping to bait Adrastos, did absolutely nothing. Now, the visions were down to blurred colors and the occasional middle finger. Motherfucker.

Aren was the hardest to leave alone. Our bond made it impossible not to obsess over his every move. His date night was flickering through my head like a damn strobe light.

At seven-thirty, August finally plucked the phone from my hand with a sigh.

"Ally. Baby. Love of my lives. Is anyone we love dying?"

I scowled.

"Will any of these messages change the final tally?"

Pouting, I crossed my arms like a sulking child.

"Then I am *begging* you. Not even for the whole night. Just...give me one hour. An undivided hour with my mate, on what might be our only Valentine's Day."

"You're right," I whispered, eyes burning at the weight of it. "Oh my God, I'm so sorry."

"Don't be sorry. You're saving the world. It's *expected*. But just...*be* with me, okay?"

Blinking back tears, I squeezed his hand and looked around for the first time all evening. He'd done it. Planned the perfect night for us—and I hadn't been present for a second of it. Not the Broadway play, not the drive, not a single word he'd said.

Fuck. Me.

August looked sinful in a sleek black suit, his hair tamed for the first time in months. My dress was stunning—some ungodly expensive fabric that dipped and hugged in all the right places, making my long, lean frame look deceptively feminine. For once, I actually had a shape.

Low lighting set the mood, candles flickering off single-stem roses in slender crystal vases. A man and woman sang opera softly on the far side of the room. A plate of manicotti I hadn't even noticed being delivered sat in front of me, steaming and garnished.

Smiling weakly up at August, I whispered, "You're right. It's perfect. Thank you, baby."

"*You're* perfect."

I shook my head, gaze darting away from his. "A perfect mate wouldn't have to be a martyr."

"I'm not giving up," he said gently. "We'll find another way."

"Maybe," I murmured to avoid the fight. But there was no other way. I'd looked. A hundred-thousand times, I'd looked.

We were the price.

Not me.

Not August.

Us. *Together.*

To keep myself from breaking down entirely, I cleared my throat. "Did you look at the wine menu?"

Only to see two glasses already on the table.

"Oh. Oh, August," I lamented, jamming my eyes shut. "I'm so sorry."

He lifted his glass with a forgiving smile. "It's a Barbera. Server said it pairs with the dish." He took a sip, then added more softly, "Listen, baby, I fully intend to plan your meals and spoon-feed you for the next four weeks if that's what it takes to keep that brilliant mind of yours working. But..." He swirled the wine and stared into it for a beat. "I know it's selfish, but I just want one last night to remember. One more night to memorize your smile. To feel your body in my hands when we dance. To drink your laughter like the finest French wine. To see that little happy dance you do when you eat."

Blood rushed to my cheeks.

August set the glass down and reached across the table to take both my hands.

"And you're right. It doesn't matter. No matter how many times these demons beat us into the after, hell itself couldn't keep me from crawling out of the grave to find you. I will always find you, Ally. In every life. In every form. And if that makes me a selfish bastard for wanting to memorize this one while I still can, so be it."

Heart in my throat, cheeks burning, I nodded as tears streamed down my face.

"I love you," I whispered. "It sounds so simple after all that"—I motioned at him with a teary laugh—"but I love you, August Porter, and I don't think I'll ever get to say it enough."

We both leaned across the table at the same time. His hands cradled my face, lips brushing mine before our foreheads touched.

I wanted to stay there forever. Wrapped in August. Soaking in his breath, his cologne, his warmth.

Naturally, the devil himself rose to make sure that couldn't happen.

That swaggering, lilting bass cut through the air, rolling over my nerves and bringing us both to our feet in a heartbeat. "As deeply as I loathe interrupting such a tender moment, I do believe you summoned me, Princess." Adrastos turned those brooding brown eyes on me, a smarmy grin spreading across his face. "Hello...sister."

FREYA
Five years ago...

I MUST HAVE SCREAMED *for help half a dozen times as I traced his ribs and positioned my hands for compressions, just like my brothers taught me. On the fourth heave of my bodyweight into his chest, Crew puked up a mouthful of water, eyes flying wide as he turned onto his side and heaved.*

"Oh, thank fuck. Holy shit. What the fuck, Crew? Jesus, Mary, and Joseph." The string of profanity poured out faster than the water coming out of his lungs. The footsteps were closer now—so much closer—but still, I yelled for them.

When Crew finally collapsed onto his back, smacking his head into the sand and writhing as he gasped for air, I leaned forward. I wiped blood from the side of his face, dabbing the stream from his nose with my soaked sleeve before pressing my hand to the gash on his forehead. It needed stitches—split clean through his brow and slicing into his cheekbone.

The contact earned a gruff wince, but he didn't pull away. His breathing was rough, uneven, but the relief rushing through me was pure and blinding. He looked like hell. But he was alive. And some vindictive little monster inside me screamed that it made no sense to care—and yet I'd never known a relief like this.

A mess. But alive.

His wide hazel eyes wandered to my face, the effort to focus clearly costing him. Chest rising and falling hard, his brow furrowed in frustration as he forced out one hoarse word:

"Why?"

I didn't get the chance to answer. Flashlights blinded me, shouts filled the night, and counselors rushed in. I scrambled back, falling onto the ground and tucking my knees against my chest.

One of the camp counselors knelt beside me, moving toward my face with an alcohol wipe.

Crap. Maybe she'd said something—I couldn't hear past the blood pounding in my ears. When I brought my fingers to my cheekbone, they came away red. I blinked, dazed, just before the sting of the wipe set fire to my skin.

Someone settled a blanket around my shoulders. Someone brought warm tea.

But as supplies arrived, and questions were answered—it was me Crew kept looking back to.

Five weeks before the portals opened...

ALVARA

Don't kill the shadow prince.

I STARED at Ally's last message—timestamped over an hour ago—before clicking the button on my smartwatch to shut it off. What the hell was she smoking? Why would I kill the shadow prince now? I'd already had my opening and didn't take it. Why the sudden warning?

But the second-guessing was short-lived. Ally didn't say things unless she was sure. And that knowing, awful pit in my stomach told me everything was about to go sideways.

Valentine's Day had been packed. Intel from Damien confirmed that Dad and Aren got their hands on more reaper's bullets after the Renown ambush on our human emissaries. He was demanding fast results now, especially with Mom's run-in fresh on his mind.

I'd spent most of the afternoon casing Luminark Manor—the Paladins' main stronghold—to check for changes over the last thirty years. Rumor had it they were moving classified lab contents tonight, and while I was more than ready to fuck up their plans, Damien finally thought we had enough to act.

A proper night's sleep sounded orgasmic.

Sighing, I climbed out of the sexy truck August had replaced my burner with, slamming the door shut. I straightened at the sight of Lainalei and G on the front porch, her head resting on his broad shoulder. G had one corded arm wrapped around her in quiet comfort. The crunch of gravel under my boots was the only thing that made them turn.

"All well?"

"Evenin', Miss Porter. Far as I know," G replied, as Lainalei's expression soured.

"Anything I can help with?"

"No, ma'am. We're, uh...I haveta say somethin' at Darius' service in the mornin' and I needed an ear."

"He trained us both," Lainalei added curtly. I wasn't sure when I'd gotten on her bad side, but I clearly had. "Not that it's any business of yours. We were just swappin' stories."

Get it out!

I nodded, throat tight, resisting the urge to shut my eyes against the image that wouldn't stop haunting me. "I'll leave you to it," I said, voice nearly cracking. This was war. There was no space for grief—not until it was over.

"G'night, Miss Porter," G said amicably, offering a small smile. I clasped his bicep in passing before heading inside, kicking off my boots and dragging myself upstairs.

The house was unusually quiet, most lights dimmed. Evidently, G and the firedrake weren't the only ones feeling melancholy today. That, or I was the only pathetic soul without a date tonight.

As I turned the corner, something felt *wrong*. So wrong that my body reacted before my brain could. I dropped into a crouch, drawing the blade from my boot, pulse hammering in my ears.

Guys. Where you at?

Crickets. Nothing from Brody or his brothers. Ally must've had them out on a mission. Which meant I was alone—with the feeling that someone was watching.

Ally's text blared in my memory as I crept down the hallway.

The moment I opened my bedroom door, a scent hit me. Spicy orange, almost like Pinesol. The kind that sent flashbacks tearing through my spine. Roaming hands. Taunts and jeers.

I shook my head, trying to stay present as I moved in a methodic sweep.

Every ounce of warmth drained from my blood when I reached the back of my bedroom door.

Painted in red: *You're not the only one who can play this game, and it was only a matter of time before you got sloppy. 8:00. Come alone or he dies.*

Breath hot in my chest, I reached for the folded paper pinned to the door. They'd been inside the estate. *Inside the estate.* How had no one sensed it?

My stomach dropped as I opened the note and saw the surveillance photo.

Blaz. Coming out of the bank, profile barely visible between the brim of his hat and his popped collar.

"Blaz," I barked, louder than intended. "Blaz!"

No answer.

I sprinted across the hallway and slammed my fist against his door—but it was already cracked open.

Empty.

The room was a mess—two broken lamps, one cracked glass pane, an open window. No sign of an assailant. I dropped to a crouch, checked under the bed. Nothing. Cleared the bathroom and closet. Nothing.

The scuffle had been contained in the bedroom—and he was gone.

"Blaz!" I shouted, flying back into the hall. Footsteps started sounding through the house. Shouts. Doors opening. "Intruder in the estate! Intruder in the estate! All hands to your fucking posts!" I roared, cutting through the chaos as people sprang into motion.

I slammed into Reyna's door and rushed to her bedside. She blinked up at me groggily—scowled, then froze when she really saw me.

"What?" she demanded, already moving faster than I could form a sentence. Her eyes locked onto mine, sharp and knowing.

This was *my* fault. My fault he'd been involved. My fault if something happened to him.

He wasn't even ascended. He had no way to defend himself.

I looked into Reyna's face—not the queen now, but his mother. A mother who'd already lost her partner. Who'd just lost her closest advisor. Who couldn't lose anyone else.

No words could cover the guilt choking me, so I went with facts. Cold, sharp facts.

"There's been a breach," I said. "They took Blaz."

CYRUS

THE COPPERY TANG of iron coated my tongue as I thrashed against the hands trying to drag me off a dead man walking.

"You selfish fucking prick piece of shit!"

I tore free from Carr and Calypso, lunging for Nix. That insufferable grin turned my vision red. We collided for the fifth fucking time, the bastard dodging my first blow and landing an uppercut to my gut before I drove him to the hardwood floor of the Manor. We rolled, tumbled—again.

Same queen.

Same trainers.

Same fucking tactics.

I could've shot out the lights. Dropped us into the dark and torn him apart in the shadows. But there was something far more satisfying about beating that pretty-boy face in with my bare fucking hands.

Pain was registering somewhere in the back of my mind—his hits were landing—but I couldn't stop long enough to care. Every grunt, every hiss I ripped out of him was a balm to the writhing panic inside me.

"You ruined everything," I spat between clenched teeth. I dropped low and drove my shoulder into his chest, sending him stumbling into the wall. A framed oil painting clattered to the floor just before I jammed my forearm into his throat and pinned him there.

"*Cy!*" Calypso barked. "You can't kill him!"

"Bullshit," I snarled. "That's *treason*, Nix. You just fucked us all over to prove a fuckin' point."

"You don't—" He gasped for breath, clawing at my arm, bloody spittle flying as he ground out, "—have the fucking balls to finish this."

"There was a sting planned *tonight*, you fuckin' idiot. Winning a war takes *plans*."

"She'll come," he growled.

"With the might of Bellaton at her back, you dim-witted psychopath. *You just declared war.*" I slammed my fist into his face again. Blood spilled from the split in his brow. Hands clawed at my arms, trying to pull me off him, but it only added fuel to the fire.

"I will carve those motherfucking wings off your arms before I dishonor your bird by killing you while you wear them," I panted, still shaking with rage as Carr gained enough leverage to yank me away.

He shoved himself between us, his own split lip and swelling cheekbone screaming for attention. His burning sapphire eyes locked onto mine like *I* was the threat now. Behind him, Portia and Orion were hauling Nix backward, the traitor still grinning through his bloody mouth.

Crossing the river was bad enough. But entering Reyna's estate? Taking *her son?*

He'd lost his damn mind.

When Carr was sure I was focused, he snapped, "Enough!"

Calypso slid between us before I could move again, her wide eyes scanning my face. Then she cupped it gently. "Cyrus. Stand down."

I wrenched away from whoever was behind me, chest heaving, breath ragged. I pointed straight at Nix. "You have no idea who you just fucking unleashed, *cousin.*"

"Can't be afraid of ghosts in the South," he shot back.

"She's not a ghost, dammit—she's a fucking nightmare. And *she* spared *me* last time, not the other way around. Legends don't grow out of thin air—they're the stories told by the sons of bitches lucky enough to survive them."

"Keep your dick in your pants."

"You'll be lucky if she leaves yours on your body once she finds out it was you who took him."

"When'd you become such a pussy you're afraid of a little girl?"

"When I read about the massacre at Dunvallach in sixth fuckin' grade, you nimrod."

Calypso visibly paled. Carr's expression twisted into something between fear and intrigue.

"*And* the thief of Bellpost. The haunting of Carroway. The Pinebarrow fires. No hierarchy's ever wronged the Wraith and walked away clean. Now we've got a masked man willing to trade high-level intel just to keep her alive—and you think she's a fuckin' *campfire story?*"

To stop myself from throwing another punch, I turned, pacing toward my healer as she hovered over Blaz Gwyne's unconscious form.

My baby cousin.

Nineteen. Not even ascended—and he still drew blood before Nix cracked his skull.

Fucking stars.

Fucking retrograde.

Fucking *family.*

My voice finally leveled as pain registered like a delayed slap. "You just wrote a check the entire hierarchy can't cash, Nix. And mark my words—we'll hold you accountable when the dust settles."

As if summoned by fate, the alarm blared. I scoffed, pulling my mask from my back pocket as everyone else did the same.

"You better pray Calypso makes it out of this," I told Nix, "or your precious queen will spike your head to the gate for good measure."

Shouts echoed through the Manor foyer as I bowed my head and steadied my breathing.

When they came through that door, I couldn't be Cyrus. Couldn't hand over Nix and hope they'd call it even. Not now. Not after Paladin blood hit the floor.

They couldn't see the cracks in our walls. The Wings had to appear unified. Which meant I had to become the monster my title demanded.

Growling, I turned back toward my baby cousin just as all hell broke loose.

I'd just heaved Blaz off the couch—held him in my arms like an over-sized infant—when my worst personal demon rounded the corner, dressed in a full Paladin tac suit and hooded cloak. Each hand gripped a gore-soaked blade. Wakizashi, maybe.

But it wasn't the blades that caught me. Not the gore. Not even the red Paladin battle stripes painted across her eyes.

It was the stance. The stillness. The tilt of her head like she was listening forward and back at once. And the eyes—

Glowing *red*, locked on me.

THIRTY-TWO

UNPLEASANT COMPANY

FREYA

"Come, little Wraith. We just wanna talk."

Two of them stepped forward like they meant to seize me—and I reacted on instinct. Grabbing one, I yanked him through his own momentum and slammed the two together with a sharp crack. One collapsed. The other clutched his face, swearing violently, blood blooming between his fingers.

"I wouldn't do that," I warned sweetly, every word steeped in saccharine venom.

The closest one's eyes flared with anger—then stuttered. *Mismatched eyes.* Blue and amber. My focus nearly slipped as memories pulled taut.

A third man stepped forward.

I struck before he reached me—two fast slices across his torso dropped him to his knees. I lunged behind him, twisted his arm, and jerked him upright. My blade pressed to his throat, his back arching painfully against my grip.

"Give me Blaz Gwyne."

The one with heterochromia lunged. I shifted the blade higher, angling it over my captive's carotid.

Everything stopped.

Perfect. He was valuable. Or sentimental. Family, maybe. I didn't give a shit which.

I shot a roguish grin at the mismatched man and leaned close to my hostage's ear. "Something tells me I chose my prize well."

"Fuck off," the man in my arms growled—but wisely, didn't move.

"Easy, *easy*," a resonant baritone drawled.

It came from the man holding a bloodied, unconscious Blaz.

"And you are?" I batted my lashes, keeping the knife pressed to skin, my gaze flicking to the leader prowling forward. The others were shifting around me, closing in. I felt their movements like changes in air pressure. But I didn't flinch. Didn't breathe wrong. Didn't let my attention drift.

"None of your concern."

"You're here. Holding *him*. That makes it my concern."

As my eyes swept over his lanky frame—Wing-less, tattooed arms, fabric hood, and brooding posture—I knew exactly who I was looking at. Cyrus Stuart.

"That's one of my best," he said, nodding to the man at my mercy.

I snorted. "Sure you want to admit that? Doesn't say much for your standards." A cracked laugh slipped free. "Not exactly intimidation material."

"I'd like it very much if you released him."

"I'm listening."

"We give you Blaz. You stay for a chat."

"Mmm, afraid I'm booked."

"Simple inter-hierarchy negotiations," the prince insisted. "I just wanna talk."

"Then you should've sent an invitation."

He half-shrugged. "You for him. Easy trade."

Canting my head, I studied him. Studied the twitchy one beside him, likely ready to explode. Then I leaned into my hostage and cooed, "Hear that, poppet? You're not the main event. Just me."

"Go to hell," he spat.

"Very well. You first." I jerked him forward sharply—and the effect was instant. Several Paladins flinched. So did the one to my right. Even Cyrus nearly dropped Blaz.

"*No!*" came the collective shout.

I grinned. "Good news, poppet. Maybe you're not so useless after all."

"Mr. Gwyne was not authorized collateral," the prince growled. "The perpetrator will be punished. The Stuarts did not approve a breach of treaty."

Even from this distance, I could see the pinch in his brow, the way he seemed to beg me to believe him.

I looked around. The Manor hadn't changed much. Newer furniture. More art. Same cold palette—just cheerful enough to depress *Wednesday Addams*. Two exits. Too many windows. One hearth fire. Nine Paladins in total. Three in uniform. None fully masked. They didn't look like they were expecting me, so this wasn't a trap. But that didn't mean they wouldn't exploit it.

And of the three in uniform...only *one* had blood on it. My gaze locked onto the mismatched eyes again. Chest heaving. Gaze flicking between me and the hostage.

"So then," I asked lightly, "why isn't he home?" No answer. I leaned the blade tighter against my hostage's throat. "Uh-uh-uh," I tutted when they stepped forward. The blade pierced fabric. My hostage hissed.

"Does Reyna know?" Cyrus asked carefully, taking a step closer.

"I *said*," I enunciated, smiling like the blade in my hand wasn't already slick with blood, "Give. Me. Blaz. Gwyne."

Ally had told me not to kill this bastard—but Saints, was it tempting.

A smaller Paladin edged forward, hands raised.

"You have no honor," I snarled. "He's a *child*. Innocents aren't collateral."

"But the man in your arms is?" Cyrus challenged.

"That man's about to be a father," a woman said.

"Sounds like his fucking problem. There are no innocents where ascended Paladins are concerned."

She flinched—but tried again. "We return Blaz. You let *him* go."

"Now," I barked. "I have shadows out front. You'll take him out to them. I'll follow."

"Okay," Cyrus agreed, voice calm but cautious. He moved slowly, deliberately, his eyes never leaving mine. "Now take your blade off my man."

"*After.*" I pressed the blade harder, grinning as iron laced the air and my hostage hissed through clenched teeth.

The power I'd stolen on the way in buzzed through me now, settling deep in my limbs. I could almost welcome it—almost—if not for the problem it posed.

Because it wasn't enough.

A sick, primal hunger stirred as I smelled blood and wanted more. Wanted his power in my veins.

Wanted to break the pact I'd made before this began.

I smiled at him, slow and sharp.

"Hurry, little prince," I whispered. "Your friend smells delicious."

The expression that flashed in the prince's eyes hovered between fear and revulsion—and I grinned as he vanished outside with Blaz in his arms.

Too easy.

I turned my gaze on the one still in my grasp. "You next, handsome."

His mismatched eyes flicked to the woman nearby, like he needed permission. My laugh burst out in a breathy whoosh. "Calypso, I assume?"

She didn't answer, but I saw her then—those haunted hazels framed in the slit of her mask. I stood ten feet from the heiress herself. And I couldn't capitalize on it.

This mission was to bring Blaz home. Nothing more.

Bitter with wasted opportunity, I changed tactics. Dragging my hostage upright, I trailed my blade across his tac gear, leaned in, and whispered, "Sorry about this." Then I plunged the blade into his shoulder, careful to miss his subclavian artery.

His scream had the desired effect. When I yanked the blade free and kicked him into the arms of my new target, two Paladins lunged to catch him.

Family. Interesting.

I bolted after the prince, boots pounding the foyer floor and launching me down the steps. Marble echoed behind me—pursuit already underway.

I'd just crested the steps when Reyna's eyes found mine, her son in her arms. Her mouth opened to call my name—

Two Flyers vanished into smoke.

A body slammed into me and darkness swallowed the world.

Twisting, wrenching, shifting pressure—and then we dropped.

When my boots hit solid concrete, I slammed them down, rearing back so my skull cracked against bone. My heel came down on a foot; my elbow drove into a gut. The man cursed, folding in half.

I spun, blade in hand, chest heaving. He raised his hands in surrender, three more stepping out of the smoke beside him.

"Easy," he said again, extending an arm to hold back his companions. Bright eyes locked on mine.

I reached for the well of stolen power and jumped—slamming straight into a shield. A ward. I was locked in. Eyes darting, panic rising, I took in my surroundings: a looming warehouse. No windows. Concrete everywhere.

"I suggest you let me out before I paint the floor scarlet."

"*Easy*," he repeated. His voice was silky now, low and assured.

The hair on the back of my neck prickled. More of them. I didn't need to look to know.

When I lunged, I bent through shadow, slicing forward.

He jerked back—barely. My blade grazed his chest, carving through fabric and skin. A thin line of red bloomed.

"This how you usually request an audience?" I snarled, blades flashing.

"This how you grant one?" he gritted out, dodging every swing with infuriating precision.

Then, to my surprise, he dropped his weapon—some unimpressive little OTF knife—and raised his hands, palms down, feet light.

"When you threaten Paladin lives," he said, circling, "you're lucky to draw another breath."

He snapped for my wrist, trying to lock my elbow. I dropped the blade to avoid a reversal, hissing. My other blade sliced across his arm—but he was already retreating. Fast. Graceful. Like shadow incarnate.

Footsteps pounded toward us. I dropped and rolled, landing on my feet as two more males appeared, sizing me up.

"You really live up to your moniker, don't you?" Mismatched Eyes muttered.

"Sure, *now* you fucking believe me," the prince growled.

Infighting. Noted.

"So pleased my reputation precedes me," I said sweetly—and struck, slicing a shallow cut across the kidnapper's chest.

My second strike didn't land. Shadows snapped tight around my wrist, yanking me back.

I bit down on a cry, snarling, "You'd think you'd be smart enough not to learn the hard way."

"Teeth!" the prince barked.

The shadows disappeared. Mismatched Eyes dropped his hold and shoved me away, panting.

I cackled, though the sound was breathless, ragged.

This was bad. The warehouse was massive. A mock living room on one side, training ring on the other. Two doors, plus the roller. No windows. Two immediate opponents. More closing in.

I was standing in New Uptown. Had to be.

"We were just gonna bring you in for a little chat," one said—voice brittle, fragmented.

"How'd that go for you?"

"Messier than anticipated," the prince admitted, right as the man I'd stabbed stepped closer, hand still clamped over his shoulder wound.

I couldn't get to him—not with these two in front of me. Not with shadows crawling at the edges of the room.

"Sounds like poor preparation," I muttered—and moved. In a blink, I dropped into shadow, reappeared behind the kidnapper, hooked my shadows around his neck, and slammed him to the ground.

Fucker was faster with the element, his power hitting me like coiled silk—ribbons of force locking my wrists.

I gritted my teeth and shoved back with everything I had, but my power had already shifted back to its default.

Wind. Useless, panicked fucking wind.

"Perhaps," the prince said, crouching low. The blood splattered across his face wrinkled with his expression. "But I'm not the one pinned in my enemy's base."

I gathered the stolen shadows again, slamming them into Mismatched Eyes and yanking him into a chokehold. My legs locked around his waist, and my arms wrapped around his throat.

He thrashed.

I gritted my teeth tighter. My eyes flicked to the others—weapons, positions, spacing.

My professional assessment?

Fucked. Fuckkity fucking *fucked.*

Regret clawed its way up my throat. I should've let Reyna plant the damn tracker.

With a roar, I shattered the shadows restraining me and flung the two closest Paladins aside, their boots skidding over concrete.

"Eh. I've faced worse odds."

"No doubt."

"You going to let me go," I ground out as my captive struggled beneath me, "or have you tired of your men and brought me here to dispatch them?"

"Feisty little shit."

This voice was female—cool, amused. Another shadow sauntered up beside the crouched leader. She had deep brown skin, long braids spilling from either side of her hood, and a dangerous kind of stillness. Two more women flanked her, all of them watching me like they had time to kill. Like the man clawing at my arms and writhing between my thighs wasn't seconds from blacking out.

Unbothered, Cyrus nodded toward us. "Though it pains me to admit this embarrassment and I share blood, should you spill his, there'll be no stopping the war you're starting. I'll petition on his behalf—for your sake—to let him go."

"I'm gonna need more than that, *Cyrus*," I hissed, tightening my hold. His asset groaned, the air tanging sharp with copper. "I'm not *the Wraith* by accident."

Cyrus raised a hand—somewhere between protest and promise.

"You have my word: we'll send you on your way alive and unharmed, if you release him in the same condition." He gave it a beat, then narrowed his eyes. "Do we have an accord?"

"*Like our last one?*" I gritted out. My breath came fast, body trembling with the fight. I scanned my odds and opted to bargain with his humanity instead.

The man in my grip started to go limp. I squeezed harder and growled into his ear, "That's for Blaz, you piece of shit." Then I shoved him off.

He hit the ground like gelatin and someone swore. I barely had time to scramble to my feet before a body slammed into mine. My blade skittered across the concrete with a metallic shriek as I was tackled down.

I thrashed, catching at a mask. Hands struck and seized, pinning my wrists above my head, the heavy body bore down on mine, weight and heat and rage.

Cyrus.

His mask was askew, revealing a brutal scar cutting through his brow and down his cheekbone. My breath caught as confirmation sliced through me.

Oh, hell. Pinned, heart pounding, I forced a snarky smile onto my face as he wrapped one hand around my throat.

"Harder," I choked out, eyes wide.

"Jesus H. Christ," the second woman muttered. I might've laughed—if I could breathe.

I jerked my knee up, aiming for his balls, but someone threw themselves over my legs, slamming my joints back to the ground.

"Cal!" Cyrus barked.

A slighter-framed woman rushed forward with—*fuck me*—a glowing blue syringe in hand.

All humor vanished.

I lost it—thrashing, bucking, shoving with everything I had. But he was twice my size. His grip on my neck was steel. His other hand yanked my head to the side. And 'Cal' stabbed me.

Terror surged. The memory of Darius's brutal death flashed behind my eyes.

"We had a deal," I croaked as the world started to tilt.

"And we still do." Cyrus's voice was calm. Cold. "I never said *who* I'd release you alive *to*. I believe Lonan is expecting you."

My heart nearly beat itself to death in its cage.

Lonan.

The name cracked something inside me. A nightmare made flesh. More merciful than only the devil himself. And the way my buried magic stirred confirmed the worst.

That ancient bond was still alive.

Some debts don't die with you.

"Get fucked," I spat.

A rumbling chuckle followed me into the dark.

AUGUST

"HELLO...SISTER."

"You are no brother of mine," Ally muttered under her breath.

I glanced around—no reinforcements, no signs of an ambush. We'd both marked exits coming in, but I checked again, even looking up. Nothing. Still, I didn't like it. After yesterday's attacks, subtlety wasn't exactly in their repertoire.

And yet, this bastard just waltzed up to our table like a damn waiter—button-down shirt, black denim, smug as hell. Judging by the arrogance in his smile, he knew we wouldn't put him down. Not here. Not now. No matter how desperately we wanted to.

"Pity we don't get to choose our family," he drawled. "Me, for instance—I'd have selected a sister wise enough to know she was being watched. And courteous enough to invite her brother to sit."

"And I'd have chosen a brother with an ounce of honor," Ally snapped.

Adrastos chuckled low and dark, the sound curling under my skin like smoke. He spun a chair around and straddled it, acting like the fucking guest of honor.

A thousand years. More than a millennium since that life. The one where they were children together. Where I watched from a distance as the girl I loved was promised to someone else. A life we still couldn't fully grasp—no matter how many lives we lived, no matter how hard the world begged us to remember.

The torture of the readings had revealed only three things:

I loved a girl so far above my station it could cost me everything.

She loved her brothers most ardently.

And her death was so brutal, Alvara puked the first time she saw it.

White-hot fury lit my veins as Adrastos stared at us with expectation—like we'd fall in line. Like he was still the brother she once adored. As if he hadn't buried that bond centuries ago.

He reached for Ally's glass and lifted it to his lips with theatrical flair, eyes never leaving mine. "Hmm. Barbera?" He clicked his tongue, then motioned toward the chairs across from him.

Only then did I feel the pressure of watching eyes—whether his people or human civilians, I couldn't tell.

Every. Fucking. Fiber. Of my being itched to kill this slimy bastard. Fuck the witnesses. He should be bleeding out right now.

Ally didn't hide her fury. She reached down, tore open the slit in her dress, stepped out of her heels, and kicked them beneath the table. She looked ready to carve him open with the steak knife still resting in front of her.

It was all I could do to keep breathing.

She dropped into her seat, still glancing around the restaurant—calculating, seething.

"Before you skewer me," Adrastos said mildly, "do consider the celebrities dining in the back. Paparazzi outside. A rather inconvenient time to expose yourselves, wouldn't you say? And you know how cornered animals respond."

"What are you doing here, you spineless, slimy coward?" Ally asked, voice low and lethal.

He turned to me with mock interest. "You look like a man who knows what's good here."

"We're not staying," Ally snapped, practically lunging across the table.

I dropped into the seat beside her, arm sliding around her waist like a warning. "Are you here to negotiate the terms of your bargain?"

"Something like that." His eyes flicked to me again, that same smug grin that made my fists itch.

I anchored my hand to Ally's hip and tried to keep the red out of my vision.

"Why so glum, Mr. Porter? You should be thrilled with your little arrangement."

"And you should be dead."

"Evidently, *someone* thought otherwise." He gave a careless shrug. "I can see my presence isn't welcome."

"No shit," I bit out.

"And yet...your wife has been so persistent in her attempts to reach me."

"You couldn't respond through the same torment you always use?" Ally snarled.

His eyes landed on her, suddenly more somber. He wet his lips, visibly choosing his words before settling on just one.

"No."

Ally blinked, stunned. The rage returned quickly, hotter than ever.

"Excuse me? Heinous dreams. Wretched memories. All in your wheelhouse. You've sent us warnings."

"Have I?" His lips curved into a sly smile.

"Don't toy with us, Adrastos," I snapped.

"Couldn't have been me."

"Fuck right off," Ally fumed.

"Such language," he tsked. "So much effort to lure me out...and no useful questions when I finally oblige. Seems your education under Amadeus left something to be desired. I would've thought he taught you to seize opportunities. Leaders ask questions, don't they, Ally?"

"Too busy deciding which of the three hundred ways to kill a man I'll use," she said sweetly.

Adrastos smiled wider. "If only that were an option, Princess."

Questions. I had a million. Beginning with the life we shared...ending with was Alvara right?

Fuck it.

I dropped one brick from the wall I kept between us.

His eyes snapped to mine—lupine brown, wary, not triumphant. I let the question hover at the edge of my mind.

Is there no happy ending for Alvara this time?

His jaw tightened. For a second, he looked like a man in mourning. When his gaze met mine again, he gave a nearly imperceptible shake of his head.

Not anymore. Not one she's willing to pay the price for.

The world buzzed back into focus as my mental shield slammed into place.

Ally was mid-rant, spitting a colorful series of epithets and accusations.

"Well," Adrastos said, rising from the chair with practiced indifference. "Apologies for the intrusion. I was just in the neighborhood. Thought I'd drop by. You two really do make a picturesque pair. Excellent restaurant choice, by the way. Divine. The only trouble is, they seem to entertain some rather...*undesirable* company, with a knack for theatrics. I'd recommend ordering dessert rather hastily, if I were you. Then again, clearly, I'm not."

"Where the hell do you think you're going?" Ally nearly shouted. "We're not done here. There's a debt to be paid."

"Sorry, *sis*. That would require my physical manifestation."

He stood—and Ally moved with terrifying speed, grabbing the steak knife and slamming it straight *through* his hand.

It passed clean through, lodging into the table.

"He's an illusion," I breathed, ice spreading down my spine.

"*Yahtzee*," he drawled. "Pretty damn good one, if I do say so myself. Took me centuries to perfect."

"He can't be far," Ally murmured, already grabbing her coat. I threw a hundred-dollar bill on the table and bolted after her.

His parting laugh chased us toward the exit, ending in a sing-song:

"Don't miss the finale!"

THIRTY-THREE
BLESS YOUR HEART
FREYA

A familiar, fiery pain tore through my shoulders, arms aching, back spasming as I blinked into the warehouse—dimly lit, just enough for shadows to thrive. But none stirred in my veins. For that matter...no sign of magic stirred anywhere.

Well, fuck.

The cool sweep of fan-driven air hit my now-bare face, the fabric mask drooped around my neck like a scarf.

Double fuck.

They knew my face. My name wouldn't be far behind—if he hadn't already recognized me.

It was a fight to breathe—lungs constricted, ribs screaming with bruises. I looked up at the chains they'd used to suspend me, bare toes pressing uselessly against chilled concrete. Not enough slack to lift the weight from my wrists. But the chains were thin enough that I smirked.

The best thing about this new body? Everyone underestimated it.

"That's gonna leave a bruise," I muttered, blinking up at my bleeding skin and wincing at the rusted shackle.

"You're awake. What a *joy*."

That southern lilt—I'd heard it before. Less swagger when I'd had their man pinned by the throat.

The woman from earlier. *Calypso.*

Her hooded, masked face was suddenly inches from mine, hazel-brown eyes flicking over my features as she raised a water bottle with a straw to my lips.

I jerked my head away.

"No more of your poison, witch."

"Just water." Through my periphery, I caught her raising a hand like she was swearing an oath.

Fatigue pulled at my eyelids like an anvil, every inch of me aching like I'd been hit by a bus. A metal door clanged open, the rubber soles of boots echoing through the space.

Calypso's gaze sharpened. "Come on, be a good girl, and maybe he'll let you down."

"Fuck. You," I growled.

"You're a charmer, aren't you?" she said. When I didn't answer, she shrugged. "Well, by all means, just *hang around* until he's back."

Har. Dee-har. Har.

I HAD no idea how long I'd been there. My arms were long past numb. The pain in my back had melted into full-body tingling. Every breath crushed my lungs a little more.

There was a plan forming in my head. Problem was, I was unarmed, outnumbered, and magicless.

Being without it was worse than standing naked under a spotlight.

Which wasn't far from the truth—these fuckers had stripped my cloak and weapons. An empty tac suit was about as helpful as a wet napkin. They'd even taken my boots and the blades hidden in them.

Though she'd tired of my incessant questions, Calypso hadn't moved from the couch in what felt like hours. Feet up, flipping through a fucking newspaper like we weren't playing a high-stakes game of cat and mouse.

"Who the hell reads a paper these days?" I asked as the chains rotated me in a slow, creaking spin.

"Oh, do *shut up*," she muttered without looking up.

"You know, I don't think I will."

But then the door creaked open again, and a group of Paladins strode in. My stomach dropped as I scanned their silhouettes, hunting for the demon mask Lonan had been besotted with.

Seven fabric Paladin masks. No demon. My breath eased—until it stuttered again at the sight of a familiar silhouette breaking from the group and striding toward me.

Oh, shit.

Cyrus Stuart.

Son of Reagan and Ciaran Stuart. Prince of the Southern Paladins. My personal nightmare. He stopped just outside headbutt range, well within my personal space, a smug glint in his eyes. He dragged his gaze over my suspended form like I was some prize cow at market. Each slow step around me felt like a strip of skin peeled away. He paused at my side, where my mobility was most limited—smart bastard.

I could feel his breath on my face as I tilted my chin and gave him the most feral grin I had left. My mouth tasted like iron, my lip split, my neck throbbing like hell. God, I had to be an absolute mess.

Whatever they'd drugged me with had a base of reaper's venom—less toxic, but no less effective.

Was this what Agamemnon dosed Ally with?

A blade slipped free from a sheath at Cyrus's wrist. My gaze dropped to the ace of spades etched into the metal near the guard. Maybe I would've appreciated the humor if I wasn't seconds from screaming.

I sucked in my gut as the dagger hovered over my belly. Somewhere, Aren had a lesson on mentally preparing for pain. On surviving torture. I tried and failed to recall it.

Cyrus smelled like cedarwood and leather, like campfire smoke and clean tobacco. The scent bit at my senses as he pressed the dagger's tip against my stomach and dragged it slowly upward. Between my breasts. Over my clavicle. My heart thundered.

He flicked the knife until the edge bit into the skin just over my artery. Then used the flat to lift my chin.

"As much as I enjoy my women smiling in chains," he whispered, his mask brushing my ear, "you're a bit young for my taste."

Revulsion burned in my gut. "You're disgusting."

"And you, pretty girl..." he purred, the blade guiding my face back toward him, "are insane."

I narrowed my eyes and laced brown sugar into my voice. "Yeah. But you already knew that. Comes with the reputation."

If I didn't know better, I'd swear he was smiling beneath the mask.

He shook his head and said, "If I unlock you, will you try to sterilize me again like a rabid animal, or can we talk like civilized beings?"

"I've been called many things in many lives," I said, smirking, "but I'm not sure civilized was ever one of them."

"No, I don't suppose you were, were you, Valora? Souls focused on civility make particularly pathetic Paladins."

His use of my old name iced my veins. So, the rumors were true—he was as clever as they said. But hearing it confirmed? That tightened the noose. If he figured out what my strikes were *actually* meant to do, this would get infinitely harder. Assuming I could get out before Lonan arrived to collect on the debt.

My stomach twisted at the thought.

I resisted the urge to glance up at the guards—no need to tip my hand.

Instead, I shrugged, nodding as if genuinely evaluating his statement, even though the motion ignited fire across my upper body.

My hands remained numb, magic refusing to surface. I could *feel* it, a distant echo far beneath the skin—but there was no answering pull, no surge. Magic lived in the blood. And with no blood flow...

Oh, this was going to hurt like a bitch.

"Hello, Pot? Meet Kettle," I drawled, grinning—though my confidence wavered when my canines didn't descend. Damn, that vial was potent. I wondered if a mouthful of this bastard's blood might counter it.

"If you unlock me," I offered sweetly, "I solemnly swear to be a *very* good little prisoner."

"I'm sure you would. Is that why Lonan was willing to bargain to bring you in? What do you owe him, little one?"

I swallowed—*audibly*—as a glimpse of sparkling obsidian stone flashed in my mind. His chuckle went dark.

When it was clear I wasn't answering, Cyrus took a hammer to the silence himself.

"So. *Valora Lamb*, back in the flesh—albeit with a bit of a downgrade in vessel." His brow arched as he looked down his nose at me.

Damn tiny fucking body.

I must've flinched, because his cheek lifted in amusement beneath the mask.

"Don't be too hard on yourself. We can't choose who we come back as."

He lifted a gloved hand, slow and deliberate, to trace the faint scar across my cheekbone—mirroring the brutal line on his own face. So he *had* recognized me, even after all these years, even with the acceleration from my partial ascension.

I snapped at his fingers, teeth bared, but he flinched back just in time.

"Feral fucking demon creature," he muttered, rubbing his gloved hand like he could feel the ghost of my bite. Murmurs broke out among his guards —uneasy, half-laughing. Probably his coven.

"I'll give it to you," he said, "the destruction you leave in your wake is... disproportionate. From what I understand, you've always known how to make the most of shitty circumstances. What I *don't* understand is why you're so hellbent on being a pain in my ass."

"Unfortunate side effect of you being born to the bitch queen."

His knife bit into my neck.

I arched away, but he followed, his snarl curling like smoke between us. "You will watch how you speak about our Queen, or you will choke on your screams as I carve your tongue from your mouth."

Low laughter made a round through his men and Calypso perched on the back of the couch, another woman draped across her lap. Intriguing.

"Ahh, come on now, *Crew*," I said softly, batting my lashes as I dropped the bomb. One of the Paladins—the one I'd stabbed, I thought—straightened from the wall. His arms fell from their cross, hands loose at his sides. Calypso did the same.

Satisfied, I turned my attention back to Cyrus.

His eyes had gone hard. Dangerous.

"You wouldn't want to add to your karmic debt now, would you?" I asked, voice velvet-edged.

"Can't say I know what you're talking about. I am aligned with the balance."

"Not. *Yet*." I plucked each word like a guitar string.

His citrine-flecked eyes churned with fury as we locked gazes, the air buzzing between us.

"Has the universe told you what you'll have to do to pay off those debts?" I asked, smiling wider. He looked ready to snap, his chest rising and falling hard with each breath.

So, I winked. Then turned to Calypso. "Hi, Cali, darling. Nice to see you. Sing anything good lately?"

She straightened. The woman lounging in her lap glanced up, tense. I dragged my eyes to the one I'd stabbed—the one who'd protected Cyrus the most.

"Carrson Landry, right? I liked you better as the runt of the litter."

Before he could react, I looked to the uneasy one—the kidnapper—with mismatched eyes.

Tonguing my canine, I grinned. "That would make *yooou...Nix* Landry. Didn't recognize you without two black eyes and your face taped back together."

Nix moved.

His hand struck my face before I could brace, my head snapping sideways with a crack.

"Stupid bitch," he growled.

Through the blur, I saw Cyrus shove him hard. "What the fuck, man?"

Nix had always reeked of little man syndrome—like those dicks with lifted trucks and metal balls on the hitch. I'd always assumed he was the one groping me in the woods that night, but never imagined I'd be face to face with him again.

I blinked tears from my eyes, laughed maniacally, and spat blood at his feet.

"Bless your heart," I said in my best Southern drawl. "Sweetie, was that supposed to hurt?"

"Keep runnin' your mouth and you'll be spittin' teeth."

I widened my eyes in mock terror. "Best hurry, now—your comebacks are just as wretched as your reflexes."

"Cyrus," he barked, glaring at the man still watching me intently. "She's worm food. You ending this, or am I?"

"You afraid I'll tell your mother what you really did all those years ago?"

"Shut your fuckin' mouth," he snapped, turning back to Cyrus. "She's a liability. A loose end is better off cut."

I gasped, slumping into the crook of my arm, wailing, "Oh no! Whatever will I do in a world without your glittering personality?"

Cyrus muttered, clearing his throat, "To be fair...her odds of survival probably rise with each of your demands."

"What the fuck does that mean?"

Carrson stepped forward, hands flexing at his sides, eyes trained on his hothead brother.

Close now—so close.

One. More. Push?

"You're really giving me all four inches, but it's just not getting the job done, is it, buddy? I'd think you were used to this response by now."

The *slap* came as expected—though that didn't dull the agony. My neck howled as my head snapped sideways, vision blurring with tears. His fists pounded into my ribs like a drumline, and my body swung, air crushed from my lungs.

Lucky for me, my reflexes didn't need vision.

I wrapped my legs around his waist, yanking him closer, and slammed my forehead into the bridge of his nose with a satisfying crunch. Bone and cartilage cracked under the blow. Before I could sink my teeth in, his forearm caught me across the face and flung me back.

Note to self: elbow to the face? Zero out of ten—do not fucking recommend. As satisfying as that busted nose was, I needed more than a splatter of blood. I needed a *mouthful.*

I dragged my toes across the concrete, trying to slow the swing of the chains, coughing out blood and spit as I wheezed, "Oh, *there* you are, princess."

The asshole lunged—but Cyrus was faster, slamming into him as two more uniforms charged in.

"She's not ours to break!" Cyrus barked. "Fuckin' hell, Nix."

A short scuffle followed, my name tossed like a curse in the chaos.

Still gasping for air, I snickered as they dragged Nix off, snarling with bruised pride.

Once on his feet, he barked, "I'm cool! Don't fuckin' touch me." They might've set him down, but they didn't back off—two bodies firmly planted between him and me.

"Just *had* to poke the bear?" Cyrus growled, storming back toward me.

"Wouldn't want the poor thing to trip over his ego again, would you?"

"Dammit, Freya," he snapped, yanking his hood down and tearing off his mask.

God.

Damn.

Ascension wore Cyrus Stuart like a perfectly tailored suit.

The asshole was gorgeous in that rugged, bad-decision-on-a-motorcycle kind of way. Not someone I'd bring home to meet my mother, but fuck if he hadn't grown up well. Fair skin tinged with Southern sun, golden hazel eyes that looked straight through you, and a jawline etched with stubble. His long blond hair was mostly tamed into a messy man bun at his nape—though a few strands had escaped in the melee.

Unfair. Karmically unjust.

"*Shucks*, Crew," I drawled. "Didn't know you cared."

"Don't flatter yourself. I'm the only one allowed to piss Nix off that much."

"You always were a territorial bastard."

"And you were always a damn pain in the ass."

"Guess you should've known, then."

"Guess so."

"Bit hypocritical, don't you think?"

"*What* is?"

"Making those girls share you, but you won't let the rest of us have any fun. Almost like you're compensating for something."

A ruinous smile spread across that infuriatingly pretty face. "And what, pray tell, would that be, Freya Porter?"

I sighed, slowly dragging my gaze down his frame and back up to his face. "You grew up nicely," I said flatly.

He narrowed his eyes. "Was that a compliment?"

"I would never."

"Of course not."

"I see you're still waiting on that frame to fill in, though."

"I see you're still waitin' to grow the fuck up."

I shrugged one screaming shoulder. "Small size came in handy infil-trating Uptown." Something flickered behind his eyes at that—agitation, maybe. His lip curled before he could catch it. Smirking, I leaned in for the kill. "*Oof.* Sore subject? I'll try another. How's mother dearest? Still prancing around like Lonan's little bitch, or did she finally get off his leash?"

Something deeper flashed—pain, maybe—before anger roared back in to smother it.

"I see we're declining the invitation to civility," he hissed.

"Your chance for civility ended when you let a scorpion ride on your back, *Crew*."

"Big words for a *little woman* hanging from the rafters."

I laughed, the sound unhinged and breathless. "I thought Paladins traveled in sixes," I said, nodding behind him. "Not eights."

His scowl carved deep lines—then vanished as Cyrus whirled.

Chaos erupted.

The two tallest shadows I'd clocked earlier turned on their uniformed companions, LEDs blasting to life overhead. Shadows scattered. The room exploded into a melee.

I swore, my grin vanishing as pain surged.

Curling my body toward my wrists, I climbed the chains—arms trembling, muscles screaming. My hands were barely functional, and each pull made me want to sob. But I forced them to move.

Thank you, Aren. Thank you, August. Thank you, Brody and Reyna, for every sit-up and Russian pull-up you ever made me do.

The clang of combat echoed through the steel walls as blood hit the floor.

I climbed.

My abs were on fire. This would end one of two ways—and both were going to hurt like hell.

I climbed until my numb fingers could take no more, then, whispering, "Fuck me," I let go.

And for three glorious seconds, I was flying.

Cyrus

FREYA.

Fucking.

Porter.

Anyone but her.

The one soul I owed a life debt to was the same I'd been tasked to deliver to a man I knew nothing about.

Her mask had done its job, perfectly hiding the pale scar on her cheekbone—one that mirrored my own. A shared reminder of the night me and the boys went too far. We'd been cocky little shits, high on the blood in our veins, convinced the Wings were ours for the taking. Titles destined. Power assumed. Our inflated pubescent egos left us blind to consequence.

She'd had every right to leave me in that freezing lake. But our thirteen-year-old victim had risked her own neck to go back in when I didn't come up. She saved my fucking life. And I'd just repaid her by poisoning her—injecting her with venom that left her powerless.

Once Cali's drugs turned the Wraith docile, we manacled her tiny wrists and suspended her before daring to strip her weapons. If there was one thing I'd learned about this infernal demon, it was never to stand within reach of her with anything she could use.

I shoved back her hood, releasing a spill of short red hair. My heart clawed into my throat, disbelief the only thing keeping it from breaching.

Then Cali yanked off the mask.

No more doubt.

"Well. I'll be damned," Cali breathed.

"Holy fuck," Carr muttered, pacing. Nix stepped closer, but I shot out an arm to block him.

The last time we'd seen Freya Porter—in that music camp—we'd terrorized her. She'd snapped, slashing wildly with a knife she had no idea how to use but a soul fierce enough to wield it anyway. Nix had taken his opportunity—too eagerly. Even then, I'd noticed her. The way people whispered jailbait behind closed doors made more sense now, knowing a soul had inhabited that porcelain body.

But Nix's words, his hands...they'd been wrong then. They were wrong now. I wasn't about to let him cross that line again.

This woman had survived The Crucible. Maybe a lifetime ago, but part of her still bore the Paladin insignia.

And without her, my parents would've collected a corpse that summer, not a son. Not an heir to punish for his disgrace.

What Lonan did to her was Lonan's problem.

A life saved. A debt paid. Imbalance, righted.

And maybe, if I played this right, I'd settle whatever cryptic deal my mother had made with the masked man.

Then I could pretend our paths had never crossed.

That Bellpost's ghost had never resurfaced.

But then she woke up.

And those eyes—bottomless jade green with a ring of hazel—locked onto mine. Recognition. Promised retribution.

She tracked me with every movement...right until the world exploded.

Flash-bangs erupted. Lights burst. Steel clanged. Shouts filled the air. The warehouse spiraled into chaos.

Portia lunged for Cali and Jo, hauling my protesting sister out the back. Carr and Nix moved fast, shielding me and the girls.

But then—I heard it.

A scream. Not just sound, but a full-body rupture. It punched through my chest, lit every nerve on fire.

I spun around and found Freya on her knees, clutching her arms, chains broken above her.

"Fuck," I breathed, just as she launched to her feet.

Eyes blazing, she sprinted for the door.

The two men fighting my coven moved as one—one scooping her into a fireman's carry, both vanishing a second later. Right through the wards like a knife through damp tissue paper.

The guards bolted, but I barked, "Yield!"

They froze, skeptical, but I held firm.

"They were jumpers," I said. "They're gone. We need to get back to the Manor. Clean up after Reyna's Flyers threw a tantrum on her behalf."

It was weak. But maybe just enough to maintain the balance.

The next time I saw Freya Porter—

I would owe her nothing.

THIRTY-FOUR

TESTING ME

ALVARA

'The finale' greeted us in the goddamn street. *Cheeky fucking bastard.*

He had to be close—*so close*—to project a full-scale illusion that moved furniture. *That* meant he could use telekinesis, which meant if we moved our asses and tracked him down, I had a shot at pulling him under the thrall of the Magic Bond we'd wagered.

Only, our sprint out of the restaurant ended as abruptly as a dive off a pier into shallow water.

"Get down," I barked as we rounded the first corner.

To my eternal relief, August didn't question me. Not anymore. Not when it really counted, at least. He dropped and rolled without hesitation as cursed bullets sheared stone from the wall. The silenced cracks sent pedestrians screaming, bolting down the street, but we were already moving —splitting to divide their targets.

We came face-to-face with two men of Renown.

Moving as one, August and I engaged them without a word, dropping both in seconds before backing together—me scouring the sky for that damn oversized shadow bird, him scanning the alley.

"Clear," he breathed.

"Same," I muttered, disappointment leaking into my tone.

"Where'd he go? Can you feel him?" August asked as I stripped the Renown's weapons, dropping one glowing magazine, then another.

"Motherfucker," he growled when I held them up. For good measure, I slammed the mags back in, holstered one weapon, and passed him the other.

"Damien better work fast."

"Will he finish in time?"

"In the victorious threads? Yes."

"Ahh, good," he said with a chipper tone that rang completely hollow. "Where are you, Adrastos?"

As if summoned by the name, a chill settled through the alley. August exhaled, closing his eyes in resignation as we braced for whatever wickedness was about to descend.

"Bullets are a last resort?"

"More useful in Damien's hands than these motherfuckers'," he agreed.

"What was that field trip you were craving? Lethal Night hunting?"

He chuckled, shrugging off his coat and folding it neatly over the building's fire escape. His fingers made quick work of the shirt buttons, tie slipping free, sleeves rolled to expose glorious, veiny forearms that made my mouth go dry.

Blood heating, I palmed my blades. He caught my expression and arched a brow, amusement flickering across every inch of his face.

"Are you—"

"Shut up," I scoffed, stifling laughter as the temperature dropped another ten degrees.

"You are a peculiar kind of woman."

"Violence and vascularity turn me on," I said, wetting my lips and cracking my fingers. "Sue me."

He was still laughing when the first wave of crawlers slammed into our shields.

Annoyed, I assessed what little energy I had left after the trance and decided to trust my hands and good old-fashioned combat.

You low, little nova?

Nothing I can't handle, I promised, blades already cleaving through the chest plate of a venom-fanged, furry fucker. I discarded the corpse and struck another before August's mental voice came again.

Draw when you need to. Reserves are decent.

A brutal squelch followed, and I heard the thud-thud of a decapitated body hitting the ground.

I nodded, not bothering to answer—too busy fighting off two of the beasts at once. I'd never been bitten by one and didn't care to learn what the greenish hue of their saliva meant.

So, I was thinking about our situation, August pushed into my mind again, just as I lost patience and unleashed my flames like arrows—once, twice, three times.

Little busy, babe.

Right, but we never really came to a conclusion. We need a gameplan. As flattered as I am that you find my violence delicious—

Panic tinged my movements. I struck two more, flames whipping wide, devouring them like snacks.

Pre-fucking-occupied here, I snapped.

When are we not?

Touché. Maybe after we finish this?

I sighed, annoyed that my well was still painfully low. So I pulled on August's.

His power filled me like the glide of his calloused hands over my collarbones. A shudder rolled through me as the flames grew—our energy merging in an intoxicating, seamless flow. Like a tantric dance, our bodies and power undulated together, tracking the demons through alley after alley until we reached the pulsing center of their dark pull.

One look from August. A nod.

I pushed the door open and grimaced. *Of course*—a dark stairway, plunging down into shadows.

Sensing ahead, I found a few dozen more, but nothing strong enough to shake my confidence.

We descended, steady heartbeats echoing in the dark, the chill intensifying with every step. Then a portal flared across from us—and from it stepped a crowned demon.

My spine stiffened as its black eyes locked on mine before the others even noticed us. Its bloody sneer pulled wide.

I didn't wait. I pulled on August's well and loosed fire into the open basement.

Flames consumed everything. August caught the stragglers, wordless and methodical, dismembering whatever slipped through my wall of heat.

But my focus was locked on the crowned motherfucker—the memory of Aren's agony fueling every strike. We carved our way through rows of crawlers until my blade met the demon's.

Pain echoed in my skull like a memory, but this time I had August's shield. I yanked it forward, wrapping it around me—a wall between me and the second hierarchy nightmare.

Strike for strike, we danced in a firelit ring. Its talons clawed at my shield, power reaching for my mind—but August held strong. Impenetrable. Towering.

And in its hollow eyes, I saw it—fear.

Satisfaction surged, and I drove my sword up and through its chest, striking where its comrade had impaled Aren. A screech tore through the air, onyx blood spraying as the flames receded.

August moved in behind me.

This had to be the last one. At least, I prayed he was the last.

Its frantic gaze flitted from August to me—and then it said it. The same word they all did when they saw us together.

"Impossible."

"In the flesh, motherfucker," I snarled, twisting my blade, watching the light drain from its eyes. And then—

Witches running, screaming.

A wall of horned demons descending.

Gold and ruby. The crescent moon framed by wings.

Aren, smiling fondly down at Magnolia.

Me, wearing the diadem, channeling power.

Aren, outnumbered in a burning building. Masked Renown. Horned.

"No," I breathed, snatching my cell and dialing. But I froze, phone halfway to my ear.

I couldn't place the images. Couldn't tell if they were hours or days away.

"Oh, that looks promising," August muttered darkly.

I turned back to the portal, which glowed an eerie blue.

"Aren," I whispered, the visions still pouring in—dozens, no sequence, no clarity.

"Go," August ordered. "I've got this."

FREYA

ANSEL AND LANA were waiting when Brody set me on my feet on Reyna's front porch. The Old General was beside me in a heartbeat, his calloused, scar-flecked hands reaching for mine where I cradled them against my chest.

"Jesus Christ, babygirl—you broke both your wrists."

"Got out alive, though," I said halfheartedly, wincing as Ansel sent healing light into the joints. Whatever they'd injected me with...now that the conflict was over, there wasn't an inch of my body that wasn't screaming in pain.

"That was ballsy as fuck, little Wraith," Brody said, rotating his sword arm.

Soap Boy—aka Jax—stood beside him, eyes locked on me with stern, brotherly disapproval.

"Thanks, Jax," I breathed.

He lifted his chin.

"I knew I'd been practicing my ragdoll impression for a reason."

A begrudging chuckle slipped past his lips, but he didn't say a word—

just crossed his bulky arms. The man had tossed me over his shoulder and hauled my ass the hell out of Dodge the moment he reached me.

We hadn't even made it two steps into the estate before a blonde blur collided with me.

Reyna.

Reyna Gwyne, Queen of Bellaton, buried her face in my shoulder as I hissed in pain and pulled my hands free with a grimace.

"You are one crazy bitch," she breathed in a rush. "How could I ever thank you? Christ have mercy, Freya Porter, look at you. You're a damn wreck."

"Gee. Thanks," I deadpanned.

"Come inside and sit with the healers."

When she peeled away, barking orders like a whirlwind, a legion of healers appeared beside the exam room. I stood there blinking, momentarily dazed as I glanced between Brody and my parents.

"You have my sword," Reyna declared. "And those of my people. My allies as well. I was goin' to tell you in this week's meeting, but fuck formality. You're a psycho—but you're my kind of psycho. And if Aren trusted you to bring Bellaton home, that should've been enough from the start."

"Reyna!" I gasped.

"What?" she snapped. "You saved my son, Freya Porter. I think that earns my loyalty, don't you?"

"I saved *my friend,*" I corrected. Blaz's title had jack shit to do with it.

"Lucky man, to have a friend like you," she said, her eyes shimmering. I shifted my weight. If she cried, I might actually die.

"Where *is* Blaz?" I asked, following her cautiously into the side room.

"Here," he said, hopping off the counter with a grin. "You came after me," he added, like it still surprised him.

"Duh," I grumbled as he crossed the space toward me. "No hugs, please. I'll squeeze the shit out of you later. Can someone put these back together first?"

I would've lifted my arms if I had the strength. Didn't matter—Reyna's healers descended at once, and Blaz guided me into a chair as their hands lit up against my skin.

"How's your head?" I asked, eyes locked on him.

"Good as new," he promised. "Thanks to you."

Tingling magic soothed through my extremities. Everyone Reyna had on-hand fussed over me, but my gaze kept drifting back to my soul parents, where they stood with a strange mix of relief and tension. As the bruises and welts faded from my skin, I finally got a clear look at them.

Ansel had...a telescope?

Yep. A telescope. Strapped to his torso like a quiver.

"What in the hell were you two up to?" I asked.

Unflinching, Lana answered, "Valentine's Day," like that explained everything.

"Just felt like...stargazing?" I pressed.

Ansel smiled fondly and tucked Lana against his side as he told me about their traditions. One after another, story after story spilled out as the healers worked. My pain dulled. My body calmed.

And somewhere between the memories and the magic, I realized something. I didn't really know them. Not anymore.

So much time had passed. So many lives had filled the space between. I had to relearn my parents. Relearn who they were. How they laughed. How they loved.

Before I knew it, I was in Ansel's arms. He carried me up the stairs, Blaz rushing ahead to throw open my chamber doors and straighten the duvet.

Ansel laid me down gently. The last thing I saw was his soft, chrome gaze.

The last thing I *felt* was Lana's fingers sweeping my hair from my brow, lulling me into sleep.

THE TRILL of a telephone dragged me into the moment. Eyes heavy, I opened them just in time to see Ansel lean forward in the armchair beside the bed, yawning as he checked the screen. His brow pinched. Then he swiped to answer and tapped the speakerphone.

He didn't say a word before Aren's voice blared through the line.

"All three of you. Egyptian Theater in Old Town. Sixty seconds. A dozen of them. Save the coven."

"Godspeed, brother," Ansel said, rising to his feet.

He pocketed the phone, then barked, "Lana."

My soul mother jolted awake on the bed beside me, and before I could process anything, I was *moving*. Flying off the duvet. Thank fuck my boots were still on and my filthy tac suit was mostly intact.

I sprinted to the cabinet and yanked out my weapons.

As Ansel relayed the orders, he glanced at me once—sharp and assessing. Then he pulled a pocketknife from his denim, dragged it across his forearm, and held it out.

A silent offering.

I closed my lips over the wound just as the energy twisted and swelled.

And then we jumped—straight into the heart of oncoming chaos.

Cyrus

At no point in history had Luminark Manor fallen into such disrepair. Shadows wrapped around the spires and porch railings in their mercurial forms, scouring the grounds for any remaining intruders. The familiars were in an uproar, their haunting cries piercing the night as our boots hit the lawn.

Hand-stained glass lay in shattered pieces across the floor, too splintered to reassemble. Inside, the walls echoed with fury—voices ricocheting off every surface.

This will mean war.

What was Cyrus thinking?

A sacrifice. She will require a sacrifice to preserve the treaty.

Who approved a strike against the queen herself?

They didn't know the half of it. The worst part was that they were right. This was on me.

As head of the coven, it was my responsibility to know everything that moved under my roof. A failure of one of my souls was mine to answer for. And as Calypso's second, I couldn't afford to have rogue agents starting wars on my watch.

We'd be lucky to avoid one now.

Shoving Nix between the shoulder blades, I stalked after him into the manor.

"You have one goddamned job, Nix—protect this family. You jeopardized *everything* tonight."

"Maybe if you bothered to communicate with your leaders, we'd feel represented—"

"It's not your job to *feel* represented. *Fuck your feelings.* It's your job to follow orders and defend this family. To defend the balance. That means keeping peace between our side of the river and theirs—not starting an inter-hierarchy incident."

"Didn't take long for the Queen's favorite to run home with his tail between his legs."

"Oh, I'm sorry—did your plan involve you swooping in to save the day after you cracked like a fucking egg?"

"I'm just saying, you must be awfully bitter you let your prize get away."

"*My* prize?" I scoffed. "If Lonan requires payment for tonight, I'll gladly offer your head in her stead."

"What's he even want with that bitch? She's underpowered, undertrained, and undersized."

"She still managed to escape. And not before rearranging *your* face," I muttered as our boots crunched over broken glass. Paladins rushed to reset the manor around us. We needed a mender. We needed *a miracle*.

"Fuck off."

"*Guys*," Cali cut in sharply. "You sound like petulant toddlers. Bite your tongues before the Queen hears you bickering."

"It's bad enough Nix revealed there's infighting to the Wraith," Jo said, unusually irritated.

"They're right," I growled. "We don't need the rest of the hierarchy knowing this coven's a goddamn disaster." I leveled a glare at Nix. "Can you bandage your pride together for an hour, *cousin?*"

"It's not *my* pride I'm concerned with."

"Right. Must be exhausting watching me clean up your messes all the time. Shouldn't be hard to earn respect with all that natural talent, right?"

"Careful, Cyrus," he warned, turning on me instead of making himself useful.

I met his eye and flashed my most winning smile. "Or *what?*"

"Boys," Cali hissed, trying—and failing—to wedge herself between us.

"Let's not forget who earned their Wings and who didn't," Nix said. "I'd hate for Reagan to bury her *second* golden boy."

Rage pulsed behind my ribs.

Charles. The Obsidian Crown. My obsession with history. My brother's death, thrown at my feet like a weapon.

"I was just thinking the same fucking thing," I said quietly. "Only difference is—I have the brass to back my claim. Do you?"

"*Cyrus,*" Calypso snapped, shoving a hand against my chest. I stepped back, placating her, but my smile stayed locked on Nix. I tracked the clench and release of his fists, watching his face wrinkle into a snarl as his breathing picked up.

"You testing me, *cousin?*"

I dropped the smile. Adrenaline hissed through my bloodstream. There were actual problems to solve, and yet here I was, *welcoming* a fight.

I was sick of Nix's mouth. Sick of his whining. Sick of his lust for a birthright he didn't have the balls to claim.

"If you ever find your spine," I said, voice low, "name the time and place."

His amber eye flared—pupils narrowing as fire sparked behind them. Satisfaction was a balm to my livid soul.

I'd just wrapped an arm around Calypso to haul her behind me when he swung. I ducked low, sidestepped, grabbed his arm, and yanked him past me—delivering him promptly into an antique chair.

"Stay down."

Shadows erupted from every direction. Nix's lunged for me as mine did the same, but Calypso's burst between us like a bomb. She flung Nix's chair screeching back against the wall as I stumbled, catching my footing.

"Enough, you spoiled fucking brats," she snarled.

Her shadows swallowed Nix's like a snake, binding him to the chair. A single tendril pressed against my chest in warning.

"Next one to throw a punch greets the sun at the whipping post. Do you fucking read me?"

"Yes, Heiress," I said flatly. I smirked at Nix over her shoulder, daring him.

His lip curled, but then he glanced at Calypso—and dropped his gaze.

"Good. Now away, both of you," she said, waving us off. Her shadows retreated like loyal subjects. "There's a mountain of shit to do, and you're standing here fighting like children. We got bested. Get over it. Set things right. Brace for the impact tomorrow. Our people are watching you, idiots."

They were. And some pathetic whisper of shame fluttered through me.

When I looked around, the entire coven was behind me—including his brother.

With a furious huff, Nix pushed out of the chair and stalked past me, muttering, "This isn't over."

"Counting on it, *buddy*."

Only when his storm cloud presence passed through the archway did the room breathe again. Cali tracked his retreat. Thea Blair from Vesper's coven darted after him.

Stupid. Reckless to provoke him here. Of all places. But I was fuming.

All of this—every ounce of it—because I shared blood with the worst Wing in history. What the fuck had Eris been thinking when she gave him that ink?

I'd demand answers from Poe when I saw him next.

Calypso laid her hand over my chest, feeling the fury hammering inside me.

"He's dangerous, Cy," she cautioned gently. "Angry enough that we sit in the line of succession and he doesn't. One day, you're gonna push him too far—and I won't be here to stop it."

"Then he better fucking *finish it*," I muttered.

"I need you, little brother. Don't forget that."

"*Prince Cyrus!*"

"*Heiress!*"

We both turned as Portia and Sidra skidded to a stop, their cloaks fanning out around their boots. Breathless, both women knelt.

"What happened?" we asked in unison.

"Healers," Portia panted. "Up in Appalachia. Under attack. We just got their S.O.S."

My eyes met Calypso's. I dipped my chin—and stalked after our rogue cousin.

"What are you doing?" she called after me.

"Praying that, for once in his life, Nix will do his fucking job."

THIRTY-FIVE
END OF THE ROPE
AUGUST

Turns out, I did not have it under control.

The glowing blue portal in the corner was, evidently, a tiny gate to the underworld. Or at least, that's what I decided after a few dozen nightmares came pouring through it. When Ally reentered the fight, breath finally returned to my lungs.

"You okay there, rookie?" she teased, decapitating a crowned nightmare before it fully emerged from the threshold.

"Just saving you some *fun*," I grunted, kicking the body back into the tear between worlds.

Ally was still pulling from our shared magic—her own well dangerously low after the week from hell she'd had. Not even our time in Terramyst had fully refilled it.

"Thanks, baby. You know bloodshed is my love language."

I snorted and ducked a blade, twisting back as it missed me by inches. They were adapting now—emerging ready for us. I grabbed the nightmare's arm and yanked it forward. Ally cleaved through it in one brutal chop.

"Any idea how to close this fucking thing?" I asked, just as a shrieking banshee-type creature barreled through.

Ally summoned a fireball with what little magic she had left and hurled it at the open maw pushing through the portal. The space went still. Spinning light pulsed at the portal's center, throwing harsh shadows across the floor.

"Working on it," she panted, trying to slow her breathing. Her eyes began to glow, scanning the perimeter of the gate. She was preparing something, drawing deeply from the well. How exactly you closed a portal to hell, I had no idea.

"Goddammit, big brother," she muttered, "could you send me something useful for once in your fucking life?"

"Let's not invite the devil to dance right now."

"If he could close Grayshell, there's a way to close this."

"Sure. Yeah. I hear you, baby. But if he was gonna help, he would've stuck around."

"I have a sinking suspicion his hands are more tied than ours."

"Sympathizing with the enemy now?"

"Not sympathizing. Analyzing."

"Okay. I can live with that—wait, what are you doing?"

I reached out to block the hand she was raising toward the gate.

"Maybe I can glean something from it."

"Maybe. Or maybe you'll get sucked into whatever hell pit these things are crawling out of."

"Only one way to find out," she said with a shrug. But the tension in her face betrayed her nerves. As she reached out a pale hand, I grabbed the other. If she was going, I was going with her.

Fuck me.

Unease churned in my gut. The moment her finger grazed the ring of light, three things happened at once:

A deafening crack tore through the air.

A blinding flash of light stole my vision.

And Ally's hand was ripped out of mine like it had never been there.

I blinked furiously, heart pounding as I tried to find her in the now-dark basement.

Panic surged—but only for a breath.

Then I heard her voice. "Fuck."

She was slumped against the far brick wall, rubbing the back of her head. Relief flooded my lungs.

Then the visions took her.

White-blue flames. Hands outstretched. A scream as magic was ripped out of her and the portal closed.

An Irish pub—engulfed in flames just before it exploded.

Weeping women. Dozens of them.

A golden theater, full of smoke and screaming, the curtains ablaze.

The raven-haired and blonde witches, clinging to each other—both of them bloodied.

Aren, sun-kissed and beautiful, crying as he met Ally's eyes.

"When?" I asked.

"Now," she breathed. Her horrified gaze snapped to mine. "It happens now. Minutes at best." She fumbled for her phone, then cursed. "No bars down here."

"Go. Warn them." I yanked her to her feet and glanced over my shoulder at the pulsing portal. "Quickly, though. I don't think this is over."

She nodded, already typing, already moving.

An inhuman chorus of screams echoed from the chasm.

I drew the last of my blades and turned to face it, wishing more than anything I had my armor—and a goddamn bow.

A great horn sounded. My stomach dropped and every inch of my skin pebbled with gooseflesh.

Alvara

AT SOME POINT, you have to admit when you're at the end of your rope.

I'd warned as many allies as I could before August was overrun by sheer numbers. Then I returned to his side—back where I belonged—to fight with my mate.

Hours. Endless hours.

We held the line. Just the two of us.

As it had always been. Me and August against the world.

No matter which ally I called for, all were occupied—or about to be.

Was this how it ended?

The portals would stay open, and from them a ceaseless torrent of demons would pour. We'd be trapped fighting at the gates forever. An eternal stand. A slow bleed into exhaustion.

Eventually, someone would slip. A hand would falter, a ward would fail, and these monsters would tear through to humanity.

Battlefield calm had long taken over. My movements flowed smoother, more precise. Every slash and flare of magic perfectly choreographed. Our rhythm held the tide—for now.

How many of them were there? Portals, just hemorrhaging enemies into our realm.

August didn't say it, but I could feel it: he was low. Even his seemingly bottomless power was dwindling under the weight of endless combat.

Cursing, I leaned into the vision and embodied the sensation at its core. I threw my arms wide and pulled—*hard*—channeling every flicker of strength I had left.

"Ally," August panted.

"A little more," I breathed. My arms trembled as I pulled on the tether between us, flinging the gathered energy into a great arc of flame. I became the phoenix from the vision—gold and orange and light. I inhaled the white-hot inferno at the center of our well and dragged the borders closed. Bit by bit, I sealed the tear in the world.

Something was burning. Singeing like parchment tossed into flame. But I couldn't stop.

I *wouldn't* stop.

There would be other gates to close—dozens, maybe hundreds. This was only the first.

My power shuddered. I drew again—deeper. Into the marrow.

But the gate was too vast. Too strong. Its gravity unbearable. It would swallow us. Drag me straight into hell. My joints popped as fire exploded across my skin, magic erupting in some final, desperate attempt to hold the line. My shoulders threatened to dislocate under the force.

Someone was screaming.

Me, I realized—*I* was screaming.

Screaming as I gripped the edges of the gate and pulled. Screaming as August and I together cauterized the damn tear in the world. And then— finally—it vanished.

The portal snapped shut and I collapsed.

My knees hit the ground. My hands let go. The world spun and stars sparked to life behind my eyes.

Just for a moment, I thought.

I just needed to rest my eyes for a moment...

My body hit the floor. Blurry vision slid sideways to find August— sprawled out beside me. Terror gripped my chest. My spine refused to hold me up.

I blinked hard, trying to see if he was breathing.

Had we broken?

Slow, meticulous clapping broke through the haze. Terror prickled up my limbs, and a dark ring slid into my vision—black dress shoes, suit hem, gleaming leather.

Adrastos?

I tried to ask. My mind screamed at my lips to move, but nothing came out. A loafer hooked my shoulder, rolling me flat onto my back.

My eyes fluttered closed.

"Brava, Alvara, darling," came a drawled voice. "Truly. I'm impressed. Though I must admit, you lost points on the landing."

My last glimpse of the world was slicked-back blond hair, aqua eyes... and a curl of green mist.

FREYA

WHEN OUR BOOTS hit the ground, Ansel gripped my arm to keep me steady. Lana sprang into motion, a commanding bellow ripping from her throat with the authority of a battlefield general.

"Get out! Get out now!"

I tore my mouth free from Ansel's arm and dragged a breath into my lungs—my first full inhale in what felt like hours. Magic tingled at my fingertips as I met his silver stare. One nod and he peeled away, moving fast.

"Are you deaf?!" Lana shrieked. "Move your asses! *Now!*"

I wiped my mouth with the back of my sleeve—only then registering the eyes on us.

Women. Dozens. Wide-eyed, stunned women outnumbering their male counterparts twenty to one. It wasn't until they spotted the two familiar Grayshellians in their midst that the witches fully grasped what our presence meant.

Panic ignited.

"The nearest gate is two blocks over," Ansel barked as chaos erupted. He turned to the cluster of witches and shouted, "Run! Get to the door!"

Gasps and screams meshed into a frenzied wall of sound. The witches bolted for the entrance, and Lana and I stayed behind to usher them through as Ansel sprinted toward the front of the building to lead them out.

There were humans too, I realized with no small kernel of horror.

But it was the Hazelharborians we were here for—all healers. We'd need them soon. Their energy shimmered with some ethereal blend of laughter and light, unmistakable even before the hierarchy crest tattoos registered in my scrambled brain.

When the building shuddered, I locked eyes with Lana. She swore, throwing her arms wide as she cast her shield. I did the same, grateful Ansel had shared his well—at least I could be of some fucking use. He was barking orders at the front of the theater, though we couldn't make out the words.

How many? I asked, reaching out mind-to-mind.

Didn't say, Ansel replied sharply.

Great, Lana bit out.

Shimmers of light flickered through the space as more shields rose—witches protecting each other, slipping out one by one. Relief carved through my chest.

"Good, ladies, now run!" Lana barked, the words layered in her unique brand of affection: rough-edged satin. She liked these girls. This mattered to her.

With that fact searing through my mind, I turned toward the splintering sound ripping the space in two. A jagged crack carved through the gilded plaster, splitting the wall. Bits of drywall crumbled and fell.

Demons had never had much taste for my blood—usually kept their distance. But as gnarled arms punched through the crevice, shattering the ceiling, I figured that truce was over. I rolled my shoulders until my back popped, twisting my neck side to side. The second crack didn't come from me.

I glanced at Lana. She grinned—a sharp, serpent's smile.

Like mother, like daughter, I thought.

Prove it, halfling, she teased, blades singing free with that telltale shnick.

Loser buys dinner?

Bacon-wrapped filet mignon?

Deal.

Cackling, I charged the demons clawing their way after the fleeing witches. Adrenaline roared through me—old and welcome. We dismembered the first wave with practiced ease, our Grayshellian blades biting through flesh and bone.

And God help me, I moved like her. The soul who first gave me breath. Who poured her blood into my veins.

Lifetimes lost. And still, our blades fell in synchronized rhythm—a lethal dance of mother and daughter cleaving through the abyss.

When the final body fell, the last of the witches fleeing with Dad, I panted, "Ten."

Lana's smile wasn't a pretty thing. The woman was preternaturally beautiful—harsh lines, striking angles, and that shorn blonde hair—but her grin? That was predatory. And right now, victorious.

"Fifteen," she said breathlessly.

"Fuck," I laughed. We backed our way down the aisle, eyes sweeping the ceiling where more monsters clawed their way through the breach. But we weren't here to exterminate. We were here to ferry souls.

Reluctantly, we turned to follow.

Flames climbed the heavy maroon curtains flanking the stage. Lana and I cast out air, drawing it back to choke the fire as we retreated.

Get clear, Ansel ordered mind-to-mind.

We moved. No hesitation. We bolted from the scaled nightmares and sprinted after the witches. Jogging at the rear of the group, I scanned the shadows for more demons. For Renown. For Adrastos.

Too easy, I said across the link. *I don't like this.*

A diversion, perhaps? Ansel mused, guiding the witches down an alley. A girl with dark russet skin stood by the door, her palm bleeding as she pressed it to the runes embedded in the stone. As I scanned the group, I noticed—most of the witches were brunettes. A few redheads. A couple of fake blondes. All of them heartbreakingly beautiful. Like Reyna's girls.

Must be, Lana agreed. *Where the fuck are Mags and Aren?*

The alley shifted—gravel tumbling as though the world tilted. Pebbles rolled and power pulled from the way we'd come. Lana and I turned, stepping into position between the witches and the billowing darkness.

Three figures emerged from the smoke. Not paladins—at least not in any uniform I recognized. But the moment they lifted their faces, my blood turned to ice.

Demon masks. Leather stretched into grotesque snarls, horns curling skyward.

Lonan.

I'd only ever seen one soldier with a mask like that. If he was here—if *he* recognized me...

My stomach turned. My breath stuttered. Sweat beaded across my forehead and trickled down my back when they charged.

I forced myself forward, feet leaden with dread. Death itself sang in their shadows—sweet, alluring. For a second, I almost gave in.

Then: Light. The alley burst with it, and the shadows recoiled like rats from flame. Lana and I raised our blades, bracing as the door behind us flared blue. The witches filed inside. All we had to do was hold these fuckers off long enough to get the witches to safety—to protect the healers of the realm, on the eve of its greatest war.

Hold steady, Freya, Ansel's voice echoed in my mind.

But then they shifted, moving amongst mist and shadow, they materialized, singling us out.

One-on-one.

I raised my blade just in time to block a vicious blow. It rang through my bones. Crying out, I parried, lithe and focused, the scuffle of the alley fading into white noise. Onyx eyes peered out from behind the mask—gleaming with satisfaction.

Then he barked, "This one comes alive."

"Like hell," I muttered, eyes raking over dumpsters, piles of trash, and discarded furniture, wishing for something—*anything*—more effective. My twin blades suddenly felt laughably naïve, like trying to paper-cut a stallion and expecting it to drop.

Remember your training, Ansel demanded. Though I knew he was fighting his own battle, I could've sworn his hand ghosted down my arm, guiding it through the motions. On instinct—or command—I shifted and struck, drawing blood with the precision of an asp. I recoiled before the beast could react, my blade having cut deep into the thick flesh of his neck. Dark blood seeped between his fingers.

Good. Finish him.

He roared, a gloved hand flying to the wound. But when he swung, I ducked beneath it, using my smaller frame to slip around him. He turned—too slow. My blade punched into the vulnerable space beneath his arm, armor thin under the pit. Some ancient reflex had guided me there. I retreated fast, evading the next blow.

Dropping to one knee, pain shrieked through my body as I drove the blade up through tendon and bone. The beast collapsed with a startled cry, his enormous frame buckling. His throat went easily after that.

Panting, I watched him topple sideways onto the asphalt.

"Holy shit. It worked."

A delighted snort burst from Lana before she could stop herself. I looked up and realized they'd both been watching, their own opponents dead at their feet.

"Well met, Freya Porter," Lana said, breathless. "You're truly back, darling. You always did make the big fuckers dance before they fell."

"Evidently," I exhaled, letting the flood of relief wash over me. My eyes swept the alley—mercifully empty now. We'd done it. The witches were safe. My pulse calmed just knowing we'd managed it.

I glanced to the still-open gate, then back to Lana. "Did you think I was a mirage?"

"I think we've both been fighting an ongoing state of denial," Ansel admitted, smirking. He tipped his chin toward the gate. "We prayed for your return for centuries, babygirl."

"It's a relief to see you in true form."

My eyes were absolutely *not* stinging. I was *not* about to cry. Nope. Not happening. "Where we headed?"

"Aren said the Middle, so we'll start there. If we've beaten him back, we'll need to find him. Call Ally. Get a feel for things."

I nodded, though my heart clenched at their outstretched hands. I needed to get back—to form a plan. Now that the Paladins knew my identity, surely Cyrus and Calypso had already reported back to their parents.

Groaning as I stood, bones aching, I muttered, "These healers...can they replace knees?"

Ansel huffed a sound so close to laughter I couldn't help but smile. We stepped through the gate into Hazelharbor—which, at that moment, felt like a gilded wing of Hell.

Keening cries and ragged sobs met us. A woman with glassy brown eyes sagged with relief when she saw us, her shoulders dropping as a breath whooshed from her chest.

"We were about to close it," she whispered, grief carved into every word. Her gaze flicked between Ansel, Lana, and me.

"Thank you, Kari," Ansel said with a nod as the gate sealed shut behind us.

One of the few males stood beside her, grief pouring off him like smoke. He was the stark opposite of the woman—where she was dark-skinned and overtly feminine, he was willowy, pale, and sporting purple hair. Kari smiled gently as his jaw tensed, his eyes locking on Ansel with a silent promise of retribution.

"What now?" she breathed.

"File inside and get a headcount," Lana ordered curtly. "We need to know how many souls made it through before the night is over."

"On it," Kari replied, slipping past the stunned circle of women. All eyes were on Ansel, looking for direction. And he gave it—flawlessly.

"Wes, reinforce the wards. Something bigger is coming. No one gets in or out anywhere but this gate. Lock it down." The purple-haired man nodded and disappeared.

"Tana, prep the infirmary. I expect more injured soon." A Latina girl nodded and took off running.

To the blonde watching her go, panic painted across her face, Ansel said, "Brooklyn—gather your seers. I assume I won't have access to mine, or she'd already be here."

One by one, he assigned them tasks. Missions. Purpose. He knew their names—*all of them*. And judging by the clarity that returned to their eyes and the precision with which they moved, they trusted him implicitly.

Grayshell's Old General.

"Where are the gingers?" Lana muttered, scanning the group, the line between her brows deepening.

"Where the fuck is Aren?" I added, stomach knotting.

Ansel jerked his chin toward the side of the room, and I followed his gaze.

There.

A familiar mountain of a man wrapped around a curvy little woman. The way they clung to each other—like life preservers in a hurricane—made me feel like a voyeur. I looked away, throat tight, and followed Ansel through the crowd.

The Callahans moved differently—Lana slicing between souls with razor focus, Ansel *among* them. He offered glances, touches, comfort. In three minutes, he had the whole room running like a well-oiled machine.

God, I wished I were more like him. Loved and respected so swiftly. Their trust in him was so natural it was like they'd been following his lead their whole lives. He didn't flinch from their tears or fear. He faced them. Moved slowly, methodically, filling need after need with quiet steadiness.

I could barely keep up.

A blade of grief sliced through me and I pressed a hand to my mouth, breath catching as I watched these women—their sobs. Their stories. Their *loss*.

They spoke of demons in leather masks.

Like Lonan.

Were they connected? Lonan and Renown? Did one serve the other?

He was cruel enough. Vindictive enough.

The room softened, voices lowering to murmurs. The witches numbed beneath the weight of trauma, their hands still moving on autopilot.

And I kept returning to *her*.

Petite. Blonde. Blue eyes fixed on the marble floor like she could see straight through it. Through three rounds of healer check-ins, she hadn't moved. Not even to cry. Even the woman who'd been wailing to the gilded golden ceiling had calmed long enough for her sisters to sedate her.

But not the little blonde.

Had anyone even checked on her? I had little time to dwell on it, because a familiar, enormous frame blocked my view. Aren's eyes landed on me, heavy with a burden I didn't recognize.

"You okay, kid?"

Nodding, I swallowed thickly. "Yeah. You, Commander?"

"I'm alright. Did Ally talk to you?"

"No," I breathed, eyes scanning the broken souls around us. But it was the black-haired witch moving between the huddled clusters of survivors who held my attention. She moved like the eye of a dark vortex, the grief curling inward around her as if she *pulled* it in—absorbed it. Commanded it.

A strange instinct surged, fight-or-flight kicking hard in my chest. Something about her...A scent? A flicker in the air? It tugged at a memory I couldn't reach.

"She's magnificent, isn't she?"

I blinked and looked back at Aren. "What is she?"

"Their heiress. Or...she will be, soon. She's a shadow walker."

I opened my mouth to say 'that's no shadow walker', but he cleared his throat and rubbed the back of his neck.

"Look, Freya, I know Reyna's had you busy..."

For a second, I nearly told him. That Reyna was helping us. That maybe the weight on his shoulders didn't need to be carried alone. But I couldn't. If he knew, he'd pull me out—reposition me. And with Cyrus now aware of who I was, it was only a matter of time before he figured out *why*. I couldn't risk losing time. The window was already shrinking.

So I stayed quiet.

"I hate to add more to your plate," he said instead.

"Aren," I chided gently. "Anything, old man."

His lip twitched, but it didn't reach his eyes. Fitting, given the circumstances—but disheartening all the same.

"I need you to take over the hunt for the diadem. Magnolia—the heiress—got us intel, including a few possible locations. It's in the possession of one of The Six. I've never met him."

"You want me to ask for it?" I asked dryly, though my attention was snagged by the statuesque woman alone in the corner. She wasn't even *blinking*. Was she breathing?

"Magnolia will get a feel for the council's stance at their next meeting. Alvara thinks The Six are riding with Adrastos. Minus Nat, obviously."

And hopefully not the Paladins, if I had any say in the matter.

"I was thinking it's more of an 'acquire it first and beg forgiveness after we win' scenario."

I nodded, eyes still locked on the silent woman. "Get me the details. I'll have it to you before the Equinox." Or die trying.

"Her friends say the thing belonged to Rhiannon Hadriana. The last Bellpost queen."

I blinked, stunned. A diadem. *That* diadem. Whether Aren knew it or not, he'd just handed me my final Crucible trial. And I knew where to begin. I just had to find a way to right a wrong in the process—maybe trace the bloodline, reunite it.

A fresh wave of despair cut through the room, prickling along my skin. My hands itched for something to do.

"Let me know if you need a team. You'll have our best."

"Right. Thank you," I murmured—but I was already moving.

My feet carried me across the room, straight to the source of that anguish. The paralyzed soul. I dropped onto the bench in front of her, breath catching as her eyes snapped up to meet mine—and magic burst outward from her like sunlight. It kissed my skin, just as warm, smoothing scrapes and bruises without even trying.

"You alright, little one?"

She scowled, sitting up straighter, not bothering to hide her once-over. "Who are *you* calling little, *Thumbelina*?"

Chuckling, I raised my hands in surrender. "Name's Freya. I'm Ansel and Lana's soul daughter."

She studied me for a moment, then nodded, extending a tan hand. "Blythe Briar."

"You were in their coven? The girls who were killed?" At her nod, I said quietly, "You have my deepest condolences. Can I do anything for you?"

"That depends," she said, voice crisp. "Can you jump?"

I scanned my reserves—fuller than they'd been since the war began. A few hours in the Middle had done more than I expected.

I nodded. "Where do you need to be?"

"Somewhere I can remember how to breathe."

PART 2
THE PAWN'S ASCENT

THIRTY-SIX

BAD BLOOD

AUGUST

Tap, tap, tap.

Everything ached. The hammer of my pulse was a steady assault against my temples, clear down to my fingers and the tips of my toes. Even my stomach seemed to vibrate with each beat.

Tap.

My mouth was so dry I nearly choked, the lingering residue of ash poisoning every attempt to draw in air.

Tap, tap.

A groan wheezed out of my throat as I shifted, mind working double time to locate the muscles required to move. The world was both an ice-enveloped river and an inferno, sweat trickling down my forehead, back, and chest.

Tap, tap, tap.

What in the hell was tapping so obnoxiously?

Eyes stinging, I tried to open them, but they felt glued shut. Panic nipped at the edges of the calm I'd managed to maintain so far. I brought my hands to my face and found a sickly crust over my eyes—like the goop that layered them when I had pink eye as a kid. Scraping it from my lashes, I tried to summon water, but not even a drop manifested. Growling, I jerked upright, wiping furiously, fighting the compulsion to claw.

"Take it easy, Commander. You're safe," a woman said, her voice threaded with a thick Scottish lilt.

"Where am I—who are you?"

"My name's Cairis. You're at Morrieth Hall, one of King Kade's estates, my Lord."

My head spun as memories returned. Demons—endless demons. And Ally...drawing power from my chest like a jumper cable gone wrong as she fought to close the gate. Did it work? I couldn't remember.

Another memory flickered. Me—realizing we'd empty our well before the onslaught stopped. The silky linen feel of a gilded business card between my fingers. Flames curling around it.

I should've been in a panic—should've held on long enough to see if Kade had answered. But instead, I felt...oddly calm. The woman with us seemed maternal, if I had to guess. But I needed to fucking *see*.

"August," I rasped, clearing the gravel from my throat as someone—I prayed just Cairis—shifted nearby. I pressed my mind out, but it came up empty, a livid throb slicing clean through my temples. "Please. Call me August."

A warm chuckle filled the space, closer now. "He said you were different," she noted, not unkindly, as she pressed a warm, damp cloth into my hand. "How about we settle on Mr. Porter?"

"Good enough for me," I muttered, sensing Ally beside me, her breaths still deep with sleep.

"For your eyes, Mr. Porter. You've been burning up for more than a day —move slowly."

With no better option, I pressed the cloth to my lids, welcoming the heat as I tried to orient myself. I could feel muted sunlight on the left side of my face, likely filtered through a windowpane.

"How long was I out?"

"Nearly forty-eight hours, my Lord."

"*August.*"

"Apologies, sir. Your mate's just there, and she's deep in fever. We've been monitoring her, but she should be fine in another day or two."

"We don't have that much time," I muttered, relief and anxiety tangling in my gut as the glue finally gave way and my lashes parted. "We need to get back."

"I understand, Mr. Porter. But you burned through the last of your magic—both of you were bone dry when he brought you to me. Damn quick thinking, calling him."

Burn that when you're ready to talk. Or if you're in a pinch. I'm usually pretty quick to respond. The last conscious thought I'd managed to summon before the world went dark. A damn miracle, in hindsight.

It was a good thing we could trust the son of a monster.

Or could we?

We were alive. Cared for, apparently. The bed beneath me was plush.

The estate quiet, though I could sense more than one set of footsteps below. *Upstairs, then?*

Eyes finally peeling open, I dropped my hands into my lap, blinking into the warm white light. Cairis was a deceptively maternal figure—plump, ivory-skinned, with rosy cheeks that pinched at the corners of her pale blue eyes. She couldn't be far off from Aren's age. She tucked a strand of blonde hair behind her ear, fair lashes fluttering as she dipped her chin.

Feeling confident the woman dressed like porcelain china wasn't a threat, I surveyed the room. One window. Vacant blue sky beyond it...and a raven perched on the sill, cocking its head as if studying me right back. It shuffled a few feet and pecked at the glass.

Tap, tap, tap.

Emerald wainscoting split black walls that rose to an exposed wood ceiling. The space was open and airy, the comforter beneath me a rich green. Ally lay tucked beneath it, her lips parted, breathing heavily, skin still wan. I resisted the urge to clean the gunk from her eyes and let her rest. Whatever we'd burned sealing that gate—it had cost more than advised. But it worked.

When I reached over to brush the hair from her face, a vision slammed into me like a snare around the throat.

She yanks the knife free, stumbling backward. Alec looks down at the gaping hole in his chest before collapsing. She turns to flee—flee the murder of her best friend—but stumbles, a sob tearing up her throat. Her gaze locks on Aren's cold, dead body. Green fletching. His eye.

Her fault, her fault, her fault.

She screams, saliva flying. Her trembling fingers wrap around her neck as Ansel's voice rings out. "You'll kill us all, Ally."

"No."

"One by one, you'll spill our blood to save your own."

"No! Please! Ansel, you have to believe me. I would never."

"But wouldn't you? Wouldn't we all? To save our mates? That's what August asked you to do, isn't it? Sacrifice us to stay with him?"

"I can't! I won't, I swear."

"And if you must?"

"Please, God, no," she begs, rocking, sobbing. "Please, Ansel. Tell me what to do."

"Make it worth it."

"What? How?" she gasps, but then her mouth opens in another scream as she lunges for him, too slow to stop the dark line stretching over The Old General's throat. Rich crimson seeps from the gaping wound as his eyes roll back in his head and his knees buckle. Screams fill the hall as Lana and Freya throw themselves over his body.

I yanked my hand back like I'd touched a stove, lungs seizing as I snapped back to the present. The give of the bed. The steady rhythm of her breathing. A nightmare. Just a nightmare.

"My Lord?" Cairis's voice was careful, concerned. "Are you alright?"

I didn't answer. No—I wasn't fucking alright. Were those the dreams that woke her night after night? The ones she refused to talk about? Did she ever know rest, or was it always haunted by the deaths of our family—by blood she believed was on her hands?

Smoothing the crease between her brows, heart stuttering at the heat radiating from her fevered skin, I whispered, "How long has she been like that?"

Cairis's pale eyes softened. "Since the king found you, my Lord."

Two days. Ally had been trapped in that nightmare for two whole *days*.

With a quiet exhale, I nodded and gently settled the cloth over her eyes, hoping to clean the film before she woke.

"Ally, baby," I murmured. "Wake up, my love. It's just a dream. We're safe. You're safe."

She stirred, a whimper escaping before she jackknifed upright, hands flying to her eyes. Embers fizzled along her fingers but died out just as fast.

"Ally, I'm right here. You're okay." Her shoulders dropped an inch, breath deepening.

"You burned out, m'lady," Cairis added gently. "That's all. You're safe."

Ally's body locked up again, chest heaving as she oriented. "I have a washcloth for your eyes," I offered, placing it in her hand. She needed some control—something that felt like a choice, this far from her comfort zone.

Her emerald eyes had just landed on me when a knock interrupted.

"Come in," Cairis sang, before either of us could respond.

The thick oak door swung open, and Kade stepped inside.

"Oh, thank the fucking saints. You're both alive."

Ally stiffened beside me. Her face twisted—half terror, half fury.

"I can face most opposition," Kade continued, "but Aren has never been on that list. I'd like to keep it that way."

"Smart man," I said, forcing a smile. I slid from the sheets, noting we were still dressed in our filthy 'date night' clothes—which was probably for the best. I suspected Ally might actually ignite if strangers had changed us.

"I take pride in very little, but that sentiment from King Calloway might top the list," Kade quipped. He pulled an embossed card from his pocket and tossed it onto the comforter. "To replace the last one."

Tap, tap, tap.

His aqua eyes flicked to the window, frowning. "Eris?"

Tap, tap, tap.

"Thanks for the hospitality," I muttered, watching him smile down at Cairis, who bowed her head.

"I did say to call in a pinch," he muttered as he crossed the room and unlatched the window. The raven hop-hop-hopped inside, fluffing as Kade ran a finger along its feathers. It rumbled contentedly, eyeing Ally—then me. "Glad you listened—though a wise man may have reached for the card sooner," he added the last bit as the bird flapped its enormous wings, landing on his outstretched arm.

A wise man may not have reached for the card regardless, Ally snapped into my mind, her voice tight.

Westerlunds, Terramyst, Bellaton, Hazelharbor. All under attack. Alec and Fae were with Kingsley. Freya and the Callahans out west with Aren. Who was left, Ally?

Had it been a gamble? Yeah. But it worked. When I realized what was coming at the end of that well, it was that—or black out in a demon-infested basement, praying someone tracked our phones before the enemy did.

Sensing the tension, Kade offered a grin and raised one hand, almost playfully dismissive. "Breakfast is on the first floor, in the dining room. Join me. We can talk." As he turned, the raven gave a disgruntled rumble, watching us as he disappeared through the doorway. "For what it's worth, I'm glad you're well. We have much to discuss," he called back.

The silence that followed was awkward and heavy.

"There's a washroom just there," Cairis said, clearing her throat. "The king had fresh clothes washed and sent up—you'll find them on the counter beside the towels. I imagine you'll want to properly rid yourselves of the gore."

Ally's gaze softened. "Thank you," she said simply, and slipped from the sheets.

ALVARA

August called Kade.

Kade.

The King of the Necromancers.

The sworn enemy of our *friend.*

Some toxic, twisted sensation roiled in my gut. The moment the door snicked shut behind him, I whirled on August. "What were you thinking?"

"That we were out of options and about to pass the fuck out in that hellhole," he replied unapologetically, stepping wider so we were eye-to-eye. "Who knows what would've found us there, powerless to stop them from slitting our throats—or worse."

"Hell of a roll of the dice, August."

"And one I'd take again. Kingsley didn't exactly behave like a king when we arrived, and he hasn't earned my loyalty beyond the loosest kind of alliance."

"We need—"

"His numbers," he cut in. "I know, baby. But what if Kade was sincere in his offer to fight beside us? What are *his* numbers worth?"

Ignoring the question I certainly had no answer for, I hissed, "He manipulates the dead." I huffed a breath, trying to think. My energy was too depleted for the visions to offer even a whisper of foresight. "I don't think there's a darker magic on the planet."

"Maybe not," August said, scraping his hand through his ash-flaked hair. "But it's worth feeling out. An enemy of my enemy is my friend."

"Until he's not," I snapped, rubbing at my chest as I fought the urge to pace. "What happens if the more advantageous match is Adrastos and his keeper? Or he sees an opportunity to seize power with us in his palm?"

"Then we cross that bridge when we get to it."

"We are in *his home*, August. Powerless. What was your plan if he betrayed us?"

To his credit, my mate didn't flinch. "Between demons and a soul, my money was on the soul. He might preside over death, but he seemed just as eager to protect this realm as we are. I took a chance."

"A big one."

"But it got you to safety, *and I'd do it again*. We *will* do it again—a thousand times over before this war ends, Ally. How many hierarchies exist in this world? How many are we going to have to trust before it's over?"

He had me there. And he wasn't done.

"I know their absence in your visions makes this alliance harder to stomach, but can you *please* do what you're always begging me to do?"

"And what's that?"

"Trust me. Follow the plan, even if you don't like it. I didn't come up with a backup because I felt we'd be safe here. I believe he means what he said. He wants a partnership. And I know that puts us on thinner ice with Kingsley, but I think Kade will do what's right when it counts. And I think Rose loves you too much to let her mate do something that would harm you. Including reigniting a war."

Before I could stop it, I smiled, the expression hesitant as warmth touched my cheeks.

"Why are you looking at me like that?" August asked warily.

"Because the Great Commander unites all hierarchies under one banner. And I'm looking at you and..." My words faded as the truth settled. "I see him. Right here."

"There is no victory without tremendous leaps of faith."

"No," I agreed quietly, though anxiety still coiled in my belly. "There's not."

"A wise woman showed me that."

With a sigh, I nodded. "She must be pretty brilliant."

August's answering smile could melt glaciers. "Oh, she is," he promised, pulling me close and pressing his lips to my forehead. With a sly pinch to my backside, he added, "Now, we should go make a friend."

WASHED and dressed in clean clothes—thankfully free of demon guts—we stepped from the washroom and called Aren to assure him we were well. We were met by a jubilant Cairis, who bowed deeply before ushering us out.

Visions or not, the staff's respect felt genuine—or they were masterful liars.

The estate was a labyrinth of grand halls and ancient decor. Eventually, we arrived at a wide stone archway. Cairis stepped aside to reveal a massive trestle table covered in cascading blooms and delicate greenery. The thirty-foot windows were draped in rich emerald. It was breathtaking.

"I don't think we're in Kansas anymore," I murmured.

August chuckled, but a low laugh beat us both to the punch. We turned to find Kade lounging at the head of the table on a throne-like chair—crafted entirely of skulls and bones.

A shiver rolled down my spine.

This was a diplomatic meeting. I'd asked Aren and Ansel to endure worse. I could manage a little discomfort.

"Good morning, Mr. and Mrs. Porter," Kade said, standing and gesturing to the seats beside him. "Please, join me. Mira, make sure our guests have all they need."

A petite woman hurried forward, cheeks flushed as she met August's eyes. *Same, sweet girl. Same.*

"Coffee or tea, m'Lord and Lady?"

Still drained of power, I couldn't press into her soul—not that it would matter. Necromancers were notoriously difficult to read.

"Coffee would be great, thank you. Black."

"Of course. And for you, sir?"

"Same, please."

"My pleasure."

"Thank you, Mira," August said, dipping his chin. Her face turned crimson.

We took our seats, and August laced his fingers through mine. "Thank you again for rescuing us."

"It's been a long time since I hosted hierarchy royals," Kade said, lifting his mug in salute. "Didn't think I'd live to see the rise of King Calloway. An honor."

We mirrored the gesture. When we lowered our glasses, he asked, "Now that you're awake, shall we dance around formalities, or dive right in?"

"Let's get to the meat of it," August said, matching Kade's relaxed posture. For a heartbeat, I saw the businessman in him. Calm, cool, collected, and prepared to negotiate. It was...hot, for lack of a better word.

"Excellent," Kade agreed, his smirk infectious.

"Does your proposal for an alliance still stand?"

"You think you'd be breathing if I served Adrastos?"

"That wasn't an answer," I bit out.

August squeezed my hand, subtle but steady. He had this.

Kade nodded slowly. "You're right, Mrs. Porter. My apologies. I'm out of my comfort zone here."

"Because The Six will side with Adrastos?"

He nodded again. "Because my father left shoes I have no desire to fill. But I can't blame the clans for seeing him when they look at me."

"Kingsley Thornquist is one of our most trusted allies," August said. "I was always a handshake kind of man. But we're past that now. Lives hang in the balance. So tell me, how do we know your words aren't hollow?"

"I knew Terramyst would cling to history."

"Thirty years isn't exactly ancient," I pointed out, watching his jaw tense.

"No, but my father's crimes belong to the past. I understand your friend hates my family—truly, I do—as any dutiful brother would be bound to. But my father..." He trailed off as Mira returned with our drinks. "Let's just say Khaos was not known for diplomacy. But I am not my father." His gaze landed on me with the force of a blow. "You, of all people, know what it means to rise above the sins of the past."

"What's that supposed to mean?" I asked flatly, my finger tracing the edge of the mug's porcelain handle as the image of that cruel king's smile flickered in my memory. August's thumb traced the back of my hand again. A silent reassurance that I wasn't alone.

"Only that your gifts likely grant you more empathy than most."

Still. Unreadable. He knew something. I could feel it in my bones.

"Sure," I replied. "I understand carrying the blood of a betrayer."

"But Kingsley's wounds aren't some sin to wash away," August interjected, clearly pulling the attention back to him. "Children died," he added, voice low. "*Babies* thrown from rooftops. Six years later, their queen was found hanging from a garden gate. If you were reigning, who was responsible?"

"I don't know. But it wasn't by my command."

"I'd hope not. That would be unforgivable."

The tension lingered.

"I fought in the last stretch of the Solskari war," I reminded him. "It was *genocide*, not just an assassination of the royal family, which would have been horrific enough. We fought undead with survivors, while your hierarchy hunted their blood."

"Then let us atone," Kade said. "Let us face the demons together. With necromancers at your front lines, you'll never run out of soldiers. We only ask for rest and refuge between shifts. Adrastos sees our value. Without us, your people will bleed."

"They'll bleed regardless."

"But *more* without our numbers—without the gifts we possess."

Fighting beside corpses made my skin crawl. But corpses couldn't feel. Couldn't suffer. Maybe...

August blew out a breath so burdened it weighed down the air between us. "If we accept, how do we know you won't switch sides when the tide turns?"

"Intend to lose, Commander?"

"War always has losses. But I intend to stand with my allies when the dust settles."

Kade smiled. "Then treat me with dignity, and my loyalty stays. I'm not an easy man to sway."

His attention shifted to the window as food arrived. August thanked the servers before returning to the matter at hand.

"We have an understanding. For now."

"For now," Kade echoed. "And perhaps I can prove my loyalty with a gesture of good faith?"

"I think—"

I raised a hand, halting August. Kade's teal gaze snapped to mine.

"There's a woman—Magnolia Green of Hazelharbor—about to request an audience with The Six. I can't disclose her aim, but she has Aren's blessing. She'll write within days. See that she gets a meeting. Quickly."

Amusement danced behind Kade's eyes. "I can't guarantee the outcome."

"That wasn't the request."

His grin sharpened. "I'll see that your witch gets her meeting."

THIRTY-SEVEN
COMMON GROUND
FREYA

When Aren assigned Rhiannon Hadriana's diadem—the supposedly illustrious heirloom of a once-beloved Bellpost queen—I assumed tracking down information would be simple. After all, how difficult is it to find information about royals? Their egos ensured they were well documented, and the fanatics that followed them bent over backward to preserve every detail.

Hell, according to Reyna, the Hadriana bloodline had been one of the most deliberately curated weapons on the planet before her death.

Her...*death*. Where—*allegedly*—a queen so powerful they'd crafted a ruby-encrusted diadem—crown, tiara, *circlet?*—as a conduit for her magic, was murdered...*by mortals?*

The math wasn't fucking mathing.

Which was spectacularly disastrous, as beyond that, we had nothing. The revised Bellpost tomes held no mention of their rightful ruler, and neighboring hierarchies focused almost exclusively on her husband, Koa—AKA 'the cruel king' or Koa the Conqueror—and her father before that. Her name was barely more than a footnote, sandwiched between the men who dictated her legacy.

Ahh, to be a woman.

My fingers drummed against the thick book beneath my arms as my eyes blurred from one too many hours hunched over Reyna's library table like a shrimp. Straightening, I sighed and locked onto a pair of bright caramel eyes and a shock of messy blond hair.

"Want a lolli?" Blaz asked halfheartedly, popping his sucker out of his mouth and twirling it like I needed a visual aid.

"No, you *child*," I scoffed, shoving his feet off the table. He just snickered.

"What? Gotta keep the brain working. No sugar, no worky."

Gesturing to his casual sprawl and the abandoned books on his side of the table, I pointed out, "You're not doing much in the way of work, by the looks of it."

"I was waiting for you to come up for air."

"Sure."

"I *was*! You had that look about you—the one my mother gets when she's so focused she'll rage if you interrupt her."

"Do us both a favor and slide your blade across my throat the next time you contemplate likening me to your mother."

With a snort, Blaz shifted the book from his lap onto the table with a resolute thud, then slid it in my direction. "Pages are missing."

"*What?!*" I barked, lunging forward. "I'll be damned."

Sure enough, multiple pages had been torn clean from the spine. The section before discussed the fracture of the mother hierarchy into twelve smaller pieces. The section after mentioned a dwindling family line. Everything in between was gone.

Some deep crevice of my brain itched in protest. I thumbed to the back of the book and flipped through the glossary. As suspected, the line of succession should've been listed in the missing section. A snarl slipped from my throat. I pressed my fingers to my ears, trying to dispel the sensation of something crawling in. Unsolved puzzles made me twitchy, but a whole bloodline torn out of recorded history?

Fucking monstrous.

Worse yet, Bellaton's original souls were direct descendants. If anyone should have had proper documentation, it was them.

"This is all your mother had?" I bemoaned, still rubbing at my ears. The world muffled and roared back in alternating waves.

"They're hard to get in the first place—the fact her predecessor had them is a miracle."

"Fuck."

"*What was that?*" he teased, cupping a hand around his ear. I fought the urge to rip the sucker from his mouth and hurl it at the wall. In what I could only assume was an asinine impression of me, he said, "Aww, thanks, Blaz, for showing me the library." Switching to his own low tenor, he nearly stole a smile I didn't feel like giving. "Why, you're so welcome, darlin'. Anything for my friend." Then, pitching his voice into a ridiculous falsetto and fanning his face, he declared, "Why, Blaz, *you handsome man,* you've gone above and beyond."

I rose from the table, ignoring the Scarlett O'Hara theatrics.

He snickered, then followed lazily after me, books in tow. "I just *must* rush to win you favor with the queen!"

"Your impression is terrible."

"And *you're* in a *terrible* mood," he noted, accepting the books I practically hurled into his arms.

He'd grown since I'd been here. I half-wondered if he was creeping along the world's slowest ascension.

"Losing will do that to a woman."

"You don't look like you've lost much from where I'm standing," he retorted, trailing me with long, easy strides as I led us out of the library. My gaze scanned the hall ahead, tracking for threats on autopilot.

"I wouldn't classify my last interaction with the Paladins as a win."

"Eh," he shrugged, drawing my attention. The soft fall of our steps was the only sound in the corridor—most estate-dwellers were deployed or on perimeter duty after the Paladins' little stunt. "*You're* alive. *I'm* alive. Mother's negotiating a price for the treaty violation. I'll call that a win."

Reyna's study door was cracked, but I knocked anyway. Her answer was immediate.

"Come in. Ahh, what are you two up to?"

"Research for a mission," I said, dipping my head respectfully as we stepped inside. "I'm hoping you can help."

"I'll do my best, but I've got a meeting in—" she checked her wristwatch "—ten minutes. Hit me."

"What do you know about the survivors of the Hadriana line?"

Pale blue eyes blinked twice before she seemed to shake off the surprise. "Not much."

"How is that possible? You all descend from Bellpost proper."

"Before my lifeline, I'm afraid, Miss Porter."

I froze. "You were hellbent on teaching me all the tenets of hierarchy politics, but you don't know your own ancestral line?"

"No one does."

"*What does that mean?*"

She shrugged, delicate shoulders rising. I hadn't realized how loud my face was until she added, "Don't narrow your eyes at *me*, Freya Porter. You're the only one in this room keeping secrets."

Ignoring the barb, I asked, "How does a royal line *vanish?*"

"With intention," she said simply.

"Care to expand?"

"Bellpost's core value metric was *honor*. I'm not sure what happened when the hierarchy fell, but I'm sure it wouldn't have garnered much in the way of *that*, based on the curse that crumbled their Middle Realm."

"Again. What does that mean?" I pressed breathlessly, a familiar serpent of fear winding around my ribcage and squeezing tight. A hint of knowing crept into my mind, but for once, I really, really hoped I was wrong. Reyna's eyes narrowed imperceptibly—more in study than accusation. I stood my ground, even as Blaz dumped the books onto her desk with a clumsy *thunk* and sighed in exasperation.

"Why so curious?"

"The lineage is missing from your library."

"As it is in all archives."

"Why do you say that so casually? That doesn't *bother* you?"

"Of course it does, *don't be ridiculous.* But what am I supposed to do? Their hierarchy fell long before my first life. The curse corrupted The Middle, and for centuries the world believed they'd all died in the fires that ravaged their Earthbound lands. It was only in the last century that their heir emerged from the woodwork to fill the empty seat at the table of The Six."

"What fires?" I demanded, shaking my head when Blaz pulled out a chair for me. He motioned for me to sit. With a huff, he took the chair opposite his mother and watched as I began to pace. The cogs in my head churned with the subtlety of rusted gears forced into motion after too many years of stagnation. Reyna, however, looked equally intrigued and horrified as she shook her head.

"Their estates burned—all records, all the libraries with them. Everything was destroyed by a fire that burned like midnight, save for the few tomes now circulating. Even those seem to have been...altered."

"Like the pages being torn out?"

"That seems to be the rarity. Some files are redacted, others...read like forgeries. Whatever happened in that hierarchy, someone didn't want the world to know."

"Only cowards shy from the ugliness of history," Blaz said, almost to himself. The words crept from him like a memorized lesson. Judging by the subtle quirk of Reyna's lips and the finger she held up to ding an imaginary bell, I assumed I was right.

"Very good, son."

Fear settled like a flock of locusts, making my skin itch as my mind whirred with theories. But it was Aren's mission that forced the words out. "What do you know of Rhiannon's diadem?"

Another shake of her head. This time her thin lips pursed in an expression of condolence, like she sincerely pitied my lack of answers. "Not a lot. Only what's in that book on top. It was crafted out of pure power to harness and control Rhiannon's magic," she explained, her tone as calm as reciting a grocery list. "She'd been bred to be invincible—the perfect breeding mare for a powerful king—but they hadn't anticipated how much magic would course through her veins until she ascended and couldn't control it. The diadem was their attempt to funnel it for her."

"What came of it?" Aren had said the current surviving King had it, but I certainly wasn't about to earn an audience with Moros Balaskas. My last interaction with Bellpost involved me scooping a treasure out of a tomb for Reagan Stuart—so I doubted I'd be particularly welcomed on his doorstep.

"Nobody knows. It was lost to history when the curse claimed the kingdom. They're just as locked out as your souls are."

"Can you think of anything else?"

Reyna's lips curled inward before she sighed, shaking her head. "Only that it had a counterpart."

Every. Single. Hair on my body *upended*. A tickle raced over my skin as gooseflesh pebbled to life. My lips parted as an image stirred—of a crown woven of midnight, spirals of star-flecked obsidian stone that hissed promises of power in a thousand whispering tongues. Even now, centuries later, the memory turned my stomach.

There was a reason Lonan had demanded Cyrus deliver *me*, not my corpse—and I wasn't ready to face that reality yet.

"Did your parents ever read you *The Brothers of Blackthorn*?" Blaz asked, as casually as if discussing the weather. When I shook my head, Reyna offered a small smile, maybe sensing the turmoil now roaring in my veins. None of my parents had shared the fable in any form...but I knew how it ended.

Seeming to tiptoe into dangerous territory, Reyna cleared her throat and gently clasped her hands atop the desk.

"Well, the gist is that there were once two brothers who wielded shadows and death. One a reaper, the other a mender. Together, they brought their people to unimaginable power, ruling with fear and respect that demanded allegiance. But the peace of the Highlands was fragile, and war brewed between their hierarchy and Bellpost. To end the bloodshed, they did as all kings did."

"He married off his daughter," I guessed.

"Bingo," Blaz said, eyes alight with the tale. *Rhiannon*. Even my mind barely dared to whisper her name, as though it were something sacred to keep hidden.

"For their wedding, the first brother presented his bride with a gift," Reyna explained. "An obsidian crown unlike any other—secretly forged by his brother as a gesture of goodwill. But the truth was hidden in the crown's shadows."

Blaz scooted to the edge of his seat, hands growing animated. "The brothers imbued it with their own magic, weaving spells into the stone so it would pull the wearer's strength into the shadows themselves. They believed they could subdue even the greatest powers—he who owned the crown would become Keeper of the Veil, the wearer's power funneled through it to feed their reign. Once worn, it couldn't be removed until the second brother's rightful heir came to reclaim it. Only to this heir would the crown submit."

"But the bride somehow sensed the nature of the offering and refused to accept the gesture, burying it away where it was lost to history. The brothers began to hunt, but the loss drove a wedge between them. The first brother became so consumed by ambition that he betrayed the second, turning to dark magic in pursuit of the crown's power."

Reyna cleared her throat and straightened her spine. "Some say the second brother was so heartbroken by the betrayal, he vanished into the shadow realm, taking the truth of the crown with him."

"Others whisper that the first brother killed the second in his outrage," Blaz added with scandalous enthusiasm.

I cleared my throat in turn, unable to shake the chill turning my skin to ice. "You uh...wouldn't happen to have any drawings or paintings depicting the crown, just for curiosity's sake?"

"Not here—I have a copy of the fable at our home in the French countryside, but I haven't read it in years. I just remember that it was impossibly black—somehow absorbing the light around it as though it intended to snuff them out, and—"

"Glittered with starlight," I finished, my heart racing.

"Yeah," Reyna said, canting her head. "How did you know that?"

"History is long, Your Majesty." And mine was longer than most.

"Countless have tried and failed to find the Crown—its allure just as appealing as the diadem you're hunting—but all have failed. One a relic of light, and the other of darkness, in honor of balance."

"Hell," Blaz interjected. "A couple of Paladin kids went after it a few years back—one of my cousins was killed in their attempt. Charles. He was only sixteen."

My gaze snapped to his in equal parts shock and disbelief. Pieces clicking into place, I rocketed upright, nodding toward Reyna as I breathed, "Thank you," and turned to rush from the room.

Her voice trailed after me as she hollered, "Where are you going?"

"To visit Damien Westerlund."

"Why?" she called in disbelief.

My bare feet coasted over the cold floor as I rounded onto the staircase. Would it be certifiable to seek out the son of my enemy—not to mention my adolescent bully—to pry through his vault of a mind? Probably. But the man's life was dedicated to history, and something about those hazel eyes when he realized who I was told me Crew wouldn't hurt me.

Cyrus. Not Crew.

Whatever the fuck his true name was, he might've been a jackass when we were kids, but he never seemed...malicious. Not really. It might've been a gross overestimation of his character, assuming he would've gutted me when he had the chance if he was going to, but I had a feeling he wanted to hurt me about as much as I did him and Cali.

Ipso facto: not if he could avoid it with his honor intact. Maybe it was the life debt he owed, or maybe he was less of a garbage human being than the teenage asshole I'd known.

After all.

He was the only one to check on me after that...incident.

With a sigh, I called over my shoulder, "I already arranged our counter-strike. Now, I need a peace offering."

THE FOLLOWING EVENING, guilt gnawed at my stomach as I ignored all of Mama Porter's messages for at least the tenth day in a row. I knew I needed to reach out—the woman had raised the three of us with loving arms and tender words, and deserved more than being abandoned by her children one-by-one. But she felt like a vision—a fragment of a memory. And with everything going on, it never felt like the right time.

It certainly didn't now, as I listened in on the raid while the cops tore apart the warehouse Nix had taken me to.

Flashes of red and blue strobes lit up the street, panic rising as fire trucks blared sirens a few blocks over, clearly en route.

Fuck you, Reagan. And fuck you, Nix, you perv. Replace that, *mother-fuckers.*

Hefting the weight of my cross-body bag on my shoulder, my boots scuffed over the sidewalk as I glanced back to the screen in my palm.

Alvara. Some mother hens could not be ignored, and I scowled as I opened the message, sighing as I read.

> ALVARA
>
> Good work tonight. Deep breaths. He doesn't hurt you.

> FREYA
>
> Doesn't or didn't?
>
> Past or present, Ally?!

> ALVARA
>
> Look up.

The road ahead was clear, save for the rush of cars and the hiss of tires. Look up? I glanced skyward, up and around, spotting nothing except the hanging sign of *La Lune Noire,* and the distant red light of a security camera.

I'd made it. The hotel was the Stuarts' new cover for all things illegitimate, but I'd yet to actually step inside.

The heavy thud of sprinting footsteps perked my ears, and I glanced over my shoulder as the sensation of being watched prickled up my neck. Fighting my body's reaction to adrenaline, I kept my breathing even, turning back to the road ahead as a man with dark hair in a slick suit turned the corner.

Face a mask of contented indifference, I met his eyes, offering a soft smile that he reciprocated immediately. As our paths crossed, I lengthened my stride, suddenly aware of eyes on my back. Human or camera was yet to be determined, but I was certainly being watched.

The warm light from the hotel lobby spilled onto the sidewalk as sunset claimed the city. I hopped inside, bypassing the irritated-looking front desk girl as she argued with someone on the phone in rapid-fire French, in favor of a beeline to the brass elevators.

If I hadn't been aware of who owned this place, I likely would've found it beautiful. Regal, even. All sweeping bronze curls and rich, moody accents. The perfect vibe for one of those new-age speakeasies or cigar lounges.

I glanced up at the camera at the end of the hallway, flipped it the bird, then smiled as the clock on my watch ticked down. Just as it hit the quarter hour, the camera light turned off.

Right on time.

Ansel always said that walking this quickly was 'moving with intention.' Just fast enough to look like you'd be pissed to be interrupted, but not so rushed you'd draw attention. Petrified to be locked in one of those ornately carved brass traps, I rounded the lobby and resisted the urge to sprint down the long hallway to the fire escape stairs.

Certainly not my favorite place to encounter a conflict, but if I could bottleneck adversaries in a doorway, I'd have a slight advantage. The appeal, of course, was the lack of surveillance—something I fully intended to exploit, as security had likely already raised the alarm.

Relief washed through me as the thick metal door slammed shut, echoing off the concrete walls a beat before I broke into a run. The weight of the drives suddenly seemed infinitely heavier as I bolted up flight after flight, cursing Calypso and Cyrus both for choosing the top fucking floor.

Pretentious assholes.

My breath scraped hotly up my lungs by the time I reached the seventh level. I peered through the window down the hallway. Was it a law that even boutique hotels had to have creepy-ass hallways? Because for fuck's sake, nobody actually likes that looming patterned floor, do they?

Eyes tracing the suite numbers, I counted: 740, 739, 738...

My ears strained for sounds below—sirens blocks away—but I shoved them aside, searching for anything more pressing. Hearing nothing but my own pounding heart, I abandoned the bag in front of Calypso's door—at least, according to the directory Tessa had tapped into for me.

Step one, complete.

Step two—get to the opposite stairwell in case anyone saw me enter the first, and get the fuck out.

I made it about a quarter of the way down the hallway before a door flew open and a leather-clad arm reached through. Before I could dodge, his firm grip wrapped around my elbow, yanking me back through the threshold and sending me tumbling into a dimly lit...sky palace, for lack of a better word.

It was the most open-concept hotel suite I'd ever seen.

Not *suite*, I noted as I spun on my heel. Based on the art and well-loved belongings haphazardly strewn about, this was a home.

I fought the yelp in my throat as my attempted turn was overpowered, lashing out with an arm that met immediate resistance as a broad hand seized it and pinned it to my side.

With a snarl, I snapped my gaze to raging hazel eyes.

THIRTY-EIGHT
RETHINK THAT
CYRUS

CARR

Security is down. Nothing but static. Last recording
was Freya Porter flipping us off. Do you have Cali?

"Are you *insane?*" I ground out, yanking her roughly into my space. Freya's eyes widened as she looked up at me, mouth parting before she masked the surprise. I dragged her further inside and slid the deadbolt shut.

"What the fuck are you doing here?"

"Get out of my way," she snapped, glaring at the door like she could eviscerate it with will alone.

"What in the hell are you doing here?"

"Leaving your heiress a little gift," she said.

Holding her livid gaze, I backed her toward the wall, trading my grip on her arms for a hand around her throat. "If you hurt Cali, I will tear you limb from fucking limb. What did you do?"

"I assume she's been missing her data," she purred, lifting her chin in defiance despite the pressure. Cocky little shit. I leaned in, and her hands flew to mine, trying and failing to pry free.

"I didn't hurt her, Jesus Christ," she hissed. But she wasn't fighting me—not really. No fury, no biting. Just calm defiance. It made me hesitate.

Breath burning in my lungs, I stared down at her—those sincere jade eyes with hazel rings locked on mine. She was just as I remembered. Tiny. Feisty. Entirely unruffled. Grinding my teeth, I let her go and took a step back.

"*Why?*"

"Because we've gone through every scrap of it," she said, rubbing absently at her throat. "And while I appreciate the serum's formula, it requires reaper venom to work. Which means we need one alive—and by my lab's report, Cali hasn't made an antidote yet."

I said nothing. But a whisper inside me insisted I owed this woman my life. Damn me.

"If our seer is right, we have a month before war descends," she continued. Dad had said as much in council yesterday. "I thought a gesture of good faith might get me a head's up if she solves it."

"Why the fuck would I do that?"

"You didn't arm the Renown."

"No shit." We might have sovereign rules, but we'd never arm those bastards—Nephilim twisted by demon magic. Most fell slowly. Some chose damnation. They hunted souls and mortals alike. I wanted no part in aiding that war.

"And by my count, you're just as antagonized by their presence in your city as we are in ours."

"Do you have a point?"

"The point, Mr. Impatient, is that whether we like it or not, we're facing the same enemy in four weeks."

"And you think I give a shit about you having the antidote *because...?*"

"Because you owe me."

"*Owed,*" I corrected, even as my body disagreed. "Past tense."

"Excuse me?" she blurted, then let out a cruel laugh.

"I *ordered* my men to yield in that warehouse. How else do you think you're breathing? We're even."

"You think *my escape* nullifies a karmic debt?" She cackled like a cartoon villain, shaking her head. "Nice try, prince of shadows."

"A life for a life. We're even."

"Even if your actions had been substantial enough to qualify—*which they weren't*—I've saved you twice."

When my mouth opened to argue, she held up a finger, a smug fox's grin curling her lips—lips I shouldn't be looking at.

...With the Renown. Shit. She hadn't run from me. She'd run *to* me—leapt from the rafters and tackled that bastard off course when he had cursed rounds pointed at me. She'd stayed until I was clear, then vanished with her quarry.

Freya fucking Porter had saved me. Twice.

"Ahh, there it is," she said as realization no doubt flickered in my eyes. "So this is how it's going to go."

"You bitch," I breathed, drawing my blade. She responded just as fast—

tiny frame flying forward as she pressed one blade to my throat and the other...

She grinned, canines dropping. "If you want to keep your sack attached, I suggest you rethink that."

My knife met her throat in turn. Her chin lifted with swagger, like she was daring me to tempt fate.

"You like to study, I'm told. Allegedly there's a brain worth rivaling under that pretty face, but I've yet to see the proof."

Fighting a growl, I held her gaze. Lemon and sage filled my lungs. Sweet, too sweet. Mouth-watering.

"That's what I thought. So, Mr. Historian, tell me—what happens when we ignore karmic ties to another soul?"

When I just glared, her grin widened.

"They grow louder. More demanding. Screaming for release. *Balance.* Until they're satisfied...or you're dead. But balance isn't always eye for an eye. It's flexible. Depends on the mercy of the claimant—and what they most need."

"What are you doing here, Freya?" I demanded again, not flinching as the tip of her blade nicked through my jeans.

"I've come to make a deal, prince of shadows."

"What kind of deal?"

"One that will satisfy both debts."

"Explain," I said, lowering my knife from her throat and dropping it to the floor with a metallic clatter in a sign of truce. I had more. She knew it. She didn't care.

Her blade flattened against my jugular. The other pressed harder.

"You help me acquire an artifact for my Commander, and I clear your life debt."

I studied her. This woman had fucked with my life for weeks, threatened everyone I cared about, and now she had me by the balls—literally—offering some half-baked deal. Returning Cali's data, if she even had, wasn't enough.

Not even close.

"What kind of artifact?" Voice flat, I stared down at her, gaze dropping as she dragged a sharp canine over her bottom lip.

"Rhiannon Hadriana's diadem."

I blinked. Twice. That's how long it took for cold fear to wrap around my throat. I staggered back. Freya let me, lowering her weapons but not sheathing them.

With ice in my veins, I asked, "What are you playing at?"

"It's needed to secure victory against Adrastos."

"And you think *I'm* gonna help you steal my mother hierarchy's relic?"

"Yes."

"After everything you've done?" I growled. "You break into *my* home and expect that I'll—"

"You live in a hotel so I'd hardly call it breaking in."

"—drop everything and *help you?* Don't fucking play semantics."

"Door was wide open," she said, all wide eyes and sarcasm.

"Well, I'm thrilled to disappoint you. Ain't gonna happen."

"Of course it is," she said sweetly.

"The fuck are you talking about?"

"Do you want to be rid of this debt or not?"

"Nah, I think I'll keep it," I said, narrowing my eyes. "Rather than face Moros Balaskas."

Recognition flickered in her features, but she didn't back down. Her gaze flicked around, scanning the room, correctly concluding I was alone.

"Scratch my back, I'll scratch yours. A buddy system. But instead of friendship, we're bound through trauma."

I snorted. She'd lost her mind. Cute, pint-sized, and overly optimistic. "Highly doubt that."

"What if I told you I know where the Obsidian Crown is?"

Every muscle in my body froze. Even the shadows inside me recoiled. Charles' screams echoed in my skull.

My voice was barely a breath. "How do you know about that?"

"What if I told you I can get it for you?"

I was too numb to be angry.

Boots pounded down the hall. Nix and Carr's voices filtered through the door.

"What kind of demon are you?"

"The kind that will do *anything* to secure victory," she said with a wicked smile.

"Cyrus!" Nix's voice trailed in—panicked?

Freya didn't glance back. Her stance stayed ready, like she expected to be attacked.

"Tick-tock, Stuart."

"You're bluffing," I snapped.

"Why do you think your mother is on Lonan's leash? You're not the first Stuart to try and fail."

"Bullshit." Mom always said it *was a prison.* A warning.

Freya laughed—low, feminine, chilling.

"One time offer, Prince. If I leave, that's it."

"You walk out there, the Wings will be on you."

"You have a balcony," she deadpanned, tone dry.

"You can't jump or fly, so how's that help you?"

"*You* don't have to *see*. Just believe. Based on what you've read, do you really think I don't have more tricks up my sleeve. Now. Are you in, or am I out?"

The Crown. The Keeper of the Veil. Of course, she knew how to get it. Years of obsession had consumed our childhood. A vow to find it. Charles...

Dad's words echoed: *Valora conquered the Trial of The Shadowed Path...brought it home.* A relic from a cursed crypt.

Expose corruption.

Restore balance.

She'd already started. Already out-smarted the magic.

Reclamation.

"The crypt," I breathed.

She smiled devilishly and sheathed her blades.

"Well done, Prince," she mocked, striding inside like she owned the place.

"One last question."

"We'll be lucky if we have the time."

Carr's call came again. "Cyrus!"

"The Crucible. You're trying to complete it again, aren't you?"

"By now you should know—I don't *try*."

"Not an answer."

She peered through the curtains, hand on the deadbolt. I could knock her out, gag her, hand her over.

But the idea of Lonan touching her delicate throat...

"Wait."

"No time, gotta go."

She opened the door. I rushed to her side to close it.

"You'd be the death of me."

"Hardly," she snorted. "Her precious golden prince?"

"You burned Uptown. Killed our men. *My* men. Allying with you makes me a traitor."

Her mask slipped for the first time, then worry flickered. "Cyrus. I very intentionally use non-lethal blows. They're still *my people*. I didn't kill anyone."

"Two souls died Uptown."

"Not by my hand." She studied me. "You really didn't know."

"Who then?"

"A question for a different time."

Nix slammed his fist into the door again. "Cyrus!"

"Answer me," I said, grabbing her arm.

"You first."

If she could get the crown, maybe I could reclaim something. Prove Charles had died for something real.

"Yes," I said—before I'd even processed the full weight of it.

Treason. This would be treason.

Her eyes searched mine, scanning between them before giving one nod. Before I could respond, Freya was already moving. She eyed the bathroom, and its desperate lack of exits, her teeth digging into that full bottom lip. She glanced toward the neatly made king-size bed.

"Nice," she breathed, yanking her sweater over her head and discarding it onto the ugly patterned carpet.

"What the fuck?"

"Did you think I'd actually go out the window? You live in the *penthouse*, Crew. Be so for real." Even as she said it, she pulled her tank up, exposing chiseled creamy abs beneath, my hands buzzing in response. "Come on, playboy." She rushed for the bed, telekinetically tossing the pillows aside and throwing the curtains closed.

"What the fuck do you think you're doing?" I hissed, hoping my voice was low enough the Wings in the hall couldn't detect it.

"Getting busy, *obviously*," she snipped. But she was moving—disheveling the sheets, plopping on the bed as she yanked her boots off and threw them at me. I dodged the first and caught the second, shaking my head and muttering curses under my breath as I chucked it under the bed, kicking the first along with it. Understanding dawned, and my mouth fell open in shock. Insane. The woman was insane.

Freya was back on her feet as I closed the distance, stripping the leather jacket from my shoulders to drop it beside my espresso bar and kicking off my shoes. Another rattling knock banged against the door.

"*Dammit, Cyrus! I'm coming in!*" Carr warned.

"Fuck off!" I snarled back. "*Busy, motherfucker.*"

A weighted pause. "Are you alone?"

"No!" I barked back as Freya fucking Porter—jailbait, in the flesh—*climbed into my bed*. That iconic flash of red had me snarling, "Your fucking hair. You couldn't have been a brunette?"

She snorted but curled her fingers to beckon me forward. Shaking my head, I lost my damn pants and launched onto the bed to the thunderous knock of Nix as he bellowed epithets.

It wasn't hard to swallow her tiny form beneath mine, yanking the blankets up and over my back as my body went to war.

Betrayer. Traitor. Defector...

Hunger.

White-hot need ate at my spine as my eyes scoured over a perfect female body—petite and tight, all muscle and subtle curves, with the world's most elite tits, crushed into a bra I itched to unlatch.

Keeping my eyes locked on hers, I growled, "You're fucking insane."

"And you're honor-bound," she snapped back. But she didn't miss the way my eyes scraped down her exposed torso, or how I lingered on her breasts. "Enjoying the view, Prince?"

I scoffed as another fist slammed into the door. "Don't flatter yourself, *Wraith*. You're not my fucking type."

"Whatever helps you sleep at night."

"*Busy!*" I called over my shoulder. Freya tossed another pillow aside, knocking over the desk lamp in the process and smiling at the ceramic clink as it hit the wall.

"Rude."

"The fuck is this?" She scowled, gripping my shirt and yanking it up. I scoffed and shifted so she could jerk it over my head. Her eyes skimmed over my chest, a coy smile curling her mouth.

Absolutely not. She wasn't gonna come up with the worst cover known to man, then check me out while I played along. Flipping her over like a prop, I ignored the way my blood heated at her shocked laughter. Like the glitter of a lake, it seemed to draw me in. I pushed her torso down into the mattress and draped my body over hers, straddling her legs. I wrapped her hair into my fist, concealing it the best I could, yanking her face back over a shoulder until our foreheads met. I groaned as the door burst open, grinding on her ass as my mouth claimed hers, effectively blocking her from view. Heat exploded through my veins, her taste invading my senses as she stiffened beneath me before going pliant.

I didn't have time to think about how my magic hummed beneath my skin, or the ten degrees my temp climbed. Didn't get to think about how much I liked the feel of those silky auburn strands.

When the handle cracked into the wall, Freya cried out, and I fisted her hair tighter, keeping her in place and praying I was shielding her completely. I didn't risk turning my head. "*What the fuck?* Get the fuck out!"

"Cyrus," Nix protested.

"*Door.*"

"Cyrus!"

"For fuck's sake, Nix, I said *door*."

"We're hunting for The Wraith."

"Do you *see* a damn ghost?!" I demanded through gritted teeth, rocking against her in a mock-thrust.

"She called us in. Warehouse is toast."

"*Get out!*" The anger in my command wasn't feigned.

I turned back to her as their feet shuffled away, accusation warring with the fucked-up chemical reaction her body had on mine.

"Sorry," Carr muttered, and I heard him turn to leave.

And then my lips were jammed against hers, rough and bruising as I ground into her again. My calloused palms scraped along her ribs and squeezed her hip, dry humping her ass. When the latch clicked, I pulled our mouths apart, glancing over my shoulder. Chest heaving, I let her up, watching as she slowly righted herself.

"Fuck," I muttered. "What's wrong with you?" My eyes scraped over her skin again as she twisted back to face me.

"Bite me," she growled, shoving me away with that disproportionate strength of hers.

I chuckled darkly, the corner of my lips quirking. "Careful what you ask for." Lunging, I wrapped a palm around her jaw, crushing her cheeks. "You do realize how stupid that was, right? A lesser male would take advantage of what you just offered."

"And I'd slit their throats before they tried," she mumbled through squished lips.

Anger burned through me. Not just at the hell she'd put our hierarchy through in the last month, but at her recklessness. Her tiny frame might make her fast, but three-on-one were terrible fucking odds.

"Big bark for a little dog."

"Big fight, too."

"Of that I am well the fuck aware," I snarled, phantom pain shooting through my Achilles. I shoved her face to the side before slipping off the bed and marching over to my pants. "What happened to a truce?"

"The truce is for *you*. My quarrel has only ever been with *Reagan*." She flung Ma's name off her tongue like a mouthful of rancid fruit.

"And yet it's *my* life you're dismantling."

"Temporary inconvenience, I swear."

"How am I supposed to trust you while you attack my family?"

"I never said you could." Her gaze hardened. She didn't cower—just lifted her chin. "One bargain, and we go our separate ways with clear karmic ties. That's all I'm offering. You're bright enough to find what I want. And I have something you need."

Have. Present tense. She was *in possession* of the crown—or confident enough to act like it. I shifted off the bed, bent down to snatch her sweater, and tossed it back before glancing over my shoulder.

"Midnight tomorrow. A mile north of the bridge, where the river meets the marais."

"Absolutely not," she laughed—but the sound was humorless. Instead, a skitter of fear ran up her vocals.

"Awe, is the infamous Wraith scared of a swamp?"

"A swamp? No. The fucking dinosaurs that live *in* the swamp? Absolutely. Do you know the bite force of an American alligator?!"

"Gators don't just wander off to attack humans, Freya."

"Not a chance I'm willing to take."

I threw my head back and laughed. The feral demon creature would take on an entire coven of trained Paladins—*including Wings*—but was afraid of swamp critters. I couldn't make this shit up.

"Bellaton side," she amended, and I rolled my eyes. "There's a cemetery not far from the bridge where the Bellatons have their mausoleums."

"That's a death trap."

"Literally," she said, rolling her eyes in exasperation. When I wasn't envisioning strangling her, she was fucking funny. Because of course she was.

"I mean it, Freya, I can't cross over. Reyna will kill me."

"Is that what you told yourself when you brought her those victims?"

A laugh skipped off her lips when I scowled back at her.

"Don't look like I ghasted your flabbers. Who else would deliver an entire group to Reyna without a word?"

"Does she know?"

"No. I didn't see a point in ruining your street cred, *Crew*."

"Fuck," I groaned, fighting to keep my balance as I yanked on my boot and she did the same. "Why shouldn't I kill you right here and now, and be through with this?"

"You and I both know you don't want *that* kind of debt, don't we? Midnight tomorrow. I'll come alone. You do the same. Trust me, I want witnesses to this bullshit alliance as much as you do. It's an unfortunate necessity. Nothing more."

"Fine."

"*Fine.*"

"Wait for us to leave. Gimme three minutes to get them out of here and then get the fuck out. Don't take the alleys. *We own this block.* Get to the main road and jump back to your Queen."

"She's not my queen."

A snort was my only response as we both yanked our clothes back into place. Buckling my belt, I breathed, "You've got brass, little one, I'll give you that. But you're playing a game with no clue who's on the board. You can't win. They will eat you alive, and I'm not gonna stop them again."

"I can handle myself."

"Maybe." I picked up my jacket. She'd certainly held her own thus far, to my entire hierarchy's chagrin. "But maybe not. I know what my men do to playthings, and it's not fucking pretty."

"So change that."

"Our only rule is to not upset the balance. What they do within that is their fucking prerogative. Like I said, you're safer to keep a wide distance."

"Nice cop-out," she spat, yanking her sweater back on.

I smirked, straightening the collar of my jacket. "Nice ass. Now *that*, I would do."

She narrowed her eyes on me. "Thought I wasn't your type."

"You're not. But I'm not that picky. Pussy is pussy."

"*Gross*," she muttered, wrinkling her nose—reminding me so much of that thirteen-year-old girl every kid at camp thought was adorable. That teenage girl I tried and failed to hide my soft spot for, right up until she saved my fucking life.

"Oh, I'm sorry, did I offend the delicate sensibilities of the *nightmare* hellbent on destroying *my life?*"

"Get fucked," she jabbed back.

I jerked my head toward the door behind me. "Three minutes."

THIRTY-NINE

DISOBEDIENT PRINCE

FREYA

I thought the South was supposed to be warm. No trace of that Southern heat lingered when the bitter, damp cold sank into my bones the next night.

Aren had always preached arriving early—first to the location meant first to understand the terrain, to detect hidden threats, to take control. But as a shiver rolled through my ribs and my lips trembled, I cursed whatever sadistic deity decided forty degrees could exist with sixty percent humidity.

I leaned against a marble mausoleum—newer, judging by the lack of mildew and grime. Death never bothered me, but even I was a little unsettled by how close it loomed here. The sense of *other* pressed in on all sides.

A gust of wind—not wind, *shadow*—heralded Cyrus' arrival. I turned just as he materialized.

And froze.

The shadows coalesced into *forms*.

Plural.

Not *alone*.

Carrson Landry stood beside him, looking about as thrilled to see me as I was to see him. His fingers hovered near his weapons. I'd already palmed a blade, gripping the tip for a throw—only to watch his hand close around the hilt at his hip.

Cyrus dropped a hand over his cousin's to stop him.

Both wore knee-length peacoats with popped collars, no Paladin masks. Not that it mattered. Cats were already out of the bag.

I scanned the area, fast, sweeping from one direction to the other. Mercifully: empty.

"Just us," Cyrus said curtly.

My eyes snapped to his and anger surged.

These weren't the trouble-prone teens every girl at music camp had gawked over. These were weapons—trained, sharpened, and sanctioned by one of the cruelest hierarchies on the continent. I'd do well to remember that. Even as I stared into those familiar eyes.

"We had a deal," I snapped. "Had to bring your fucking lapdog?"

"It's my honor to serve my *prince*," Carrson growled, voice as low as his tolerance.

"A prince incapable of keeping his mouth shut."

Cyrus stalked forward as I pushed off the wall, the two of them subtly shifting to stay between me and the other.

"Given the current climate between my hierarchy and Bellaton, Ma decided I needed a damn *bodyguard*. In no small part thanks to your fucking attack yesterday."

He gestured toward Carrson. "You have yourself to thank for the mother hen."

"And the great Prince of Paladin couldn't shake a tail?" I sneered.

Carrson grinned. "A Wing has one purpose above all—*protect* our *royals*. Even when they're little bitches about it."

Cyrus tilted his head toward his cousin in a slow, exasperated motion. Didn't even bother to glare.

"Untie your knickers, Carrson. I'm not here to hurt him."

"Could've fooled me."

"*Please.* If I wanted either of you dead, you'd already be rotting in one of these pretty stone boxes."

Carrson surged forward, but Cyrus caught his collar and yanked him back. They locked eyes—probably having one of those irritating silent conversations—and turned back to me. Carrson still looked like he wanted to punch something.

"You can trust him," Cyrus insisted as we closed the distance.

"Trust is a fool's luxury I won't be affording."

"Fine. *I* trust him. That's enough."

"*For who?*"

"It'll have to be—unless you'd rather deal with Nix."

We stopped just outside of arm's reach. He was sincere. I could tell. But I was outnumbered, and that fact gnawed at the back of my skull.

Bullshit. This whole thing was bullshit.

I shook my head, stepping backward, needing to get out of portal range. "Deal's off."

"Wait," Cyrus breathed, lunging.

But I was faster. Until black ribbons of shadow whipped up my arms—not tight enough to harm, but more than enough to block escape.

"Let. Go," I snarled. My borrowed shadows stirred, ready to counter—

But he *released me*. Hands raised in that universal gesture of surrender.

"Moros Balaskas holds the diadem. At his personal estate."

"No shit. You'll need more than that."

"It's in his vault. Air-locked to prevent fire destruction. If you get trapped inside, you're as good as dead."

Well. That was notable. Not that I was about to *say* so.

Carrson shifted uneasily, his eyes scanning the perimeter like he fully expected me to spring a trap.

"Not. Good. Enough."

"Oh, pump your brakes, *Speed Racer*," Cyrus snapped, flicking his imaginary tail like a cat in full pissy glory. "I have more, but you've given me jack shit on your end."

"You promised *information*. I promised an *object*. Not your involvement in retrieving it. You'll get what you need to know—which is *nothing*—until the diadem is in my Commander's hands."

"What the fuck would *Reyna Gwyne* want with Rhiannon's diadem?"

Carrson's assessing gaze flicked back to me, but I smirked, swaggering a step back. My shadows curled up around me like lazy smoke.

"Like I said. She's not *my* queen."

Cyrus stepped forward again—like something in him couldn't help it. "Then who is?"

"I serve no queen."

My shadows surged, cloaking me in mist—until he lunged again.

"Freya, wait. *Please*."

Carrson's side-glance was sharp. He'd heard the desperation, too. And he didn't like it.

I froze.

Cyrus stepped under a shaft of moonlight filtering through mossy branches. Breath fogged between us. Shadows curled around him, but he didn't use them. Didn't try to hold me. Just *looked*.

So.

I waited.

He swallowed. Loudly.

The key to besting any enemy was knowing where their armor cracked. I'd thrown a ruthless shot about his *dead brother*, and it had hit home.

"Your words were clear," he said, voice level—but eyes pleading. "But I'm asking anyway. The crown. It last appeared around the end of your—Valora's—timeline. A few years later, there were whispers of one final light wielder. That's what the records in Ma's archives say. Were the events coincidental? Or connected?"

The last Solskari death. I shook my head. "Regrettably, after my lifeline."

"That wasn't an answer."

God, I hated that he was smart. Hated that he could read the space between the words as easily as I spoke them.

"I can't provide answers I don't have."

"But you know where the crown is."

"I do."

"Were the light-wielders guarding it?"

"Why are you asking?"

I could feel Carrson tracking every word, but I didn't take my eyes off Cyrus.

A muscle in his jaw feathered. He looked down. Looked back. The air shifted as understanding clicked into place.

Some glimmer in my mind whispered one word. *Mercy.*

Clearing my throat, I guessed, "*Charles* thought the two were connected."

Carrson flinched. Like hearing the name made him ill. His hand wrapped around Cyrus' wrist like he could anchor him to the present.

Voice low but steady, the prince replied, "The answers to today's problems almost always have mirrors in the past. History is *cyclical*. Damned to repeat itself until we learn."

He pointed upward. "Sol—the God. He was just a Solskari. A king with too much power. Death erased his people."

"You're telling me the Grim Reaper wiped *light* from the world?"

I studied him, watching for cracks. He just stared back—longer than I liked—and something unfamiliar stirred in my chest. I fought to crush it.

This wasn't a place for emotions.

Only logic. And leverage.

Finally, Cyrus said, "I suspect death is no more an element than we are."

"You sound mad."

"Notice you said *mad,* not *wrong.* Which means that even if you won't admit it, some part of you knows I'm right."

"*Orrr,* I don't wanna piss off the insane."

Ignoring me entirely, he pressed on. "We might know little, but we *do* know this: Death doesn't act without preamble. The Solskari genocide must have been triggered by something that pissed him off."

King Khaos. Ruler of the necromancers. He'd emerged from solitude to rally surviving Bellpost descendants—and wipe the Solskari from the planet. Cyrus was taking his hierarchy's interpretation of the tale quite literally.

"Every war has a catalyst. Like, maybe, the theft of one of his objects of great power."

"The Solskari war was already raging when I last served your mother."

"Right. But how long before you came here did you steal the crown?"

I stepped back as if his words had formed a noose around my throat. "Are you...Are you insinuating that I caused Khaos to wipe out an entire bloodline?"

"No!" he blurted, stepping forward. "But if you unearthed it—moved it —in your last life, maybe he sensed that. Where did you find it?"

"There was an entire ocean between me and that war."

"That didn't answer the question. Where was the crypt, Freya?"

I stayed silent.

Cyrus exhaled, jaw tight. "Fine. Don't answer. But the pieces line up. The last light-wielder was killed on Reyna's side of the divide. Five years later. *After* Valora Lamb."

"By every historical account, no Solskari were spared," I countered.

"Right. And history's written by the victors."

"And you honestly believe there was a survivor."

The silence that followed was thick as the fog rolling between the tombstones. A chill skated over my arms.

"A woman kissed by sun, but coveted by death will escape the collapse of a kingdom."

"I don't appreciate riddles."

"Not a riddle. A prophecy."

But not Alvara's. Hers came woven with more structure—more bite. Or...at least, they did now. But Ally hadn't been the only seer in play thirty years ago.

"Ciaran?" I asked.

He nodded, expression stony as he sighed. "Months before the attack, their queen announced she was carrying an heir."

Pregnant. They'd butchered everyone—women, children, even souls not yet born.

"She claimed a daughter would continue the bloodline. A soul named Anastasia. Only, the queen was found—"

"Dead. Five years later," I finished, nausea creeping in with the memory. "Again. *After* my lifeline."

"Right. But where is she? The most powerful line of witches in the world vanished overnight, and Anastasia just disappeared?"

"Apparently starlight only burns so brightly."

"*What else* would've drawn Khaos' wrath besides the crown?" Cyrus asked, eyes sharp. "He had to be the wielder. Didn't he?"

I didn't answer. I couldn't.

And he noticed.

"Rumors say Bellaton hunted for her. But found nothing. Now we face a Commander more shadow than man—more death than life—building his army. Grayshell's already hunted one of his generals. A brother who died as a Renown."

Agamemnon's roar echoed in my head. The memory of his blood—rotten, rancid—still turned my stomach. I remembered the sound of August's blade cutting through his spine, remembered the way the body fell.

I fought to stay present. To keep my face from revealing any of it.

"*All* this time," Cyrus went on, "I've wondered if Death was hunting for the crown...or the princess. Unless, of course, they're connected."

"You think he's looking for some long-lost heiress named Anastasia?" I scoffed. "*Seriously?*"

"Ironic, I know. Maybe the name was intentional."

"Ridiculous is more like it." I massaged my temple, trying to sort through his theory. The image of my brother doing the same when solving complex equations made me lift my head. Freaky.

"But were they?" Cyrus asked. "Connected?"

Swallowing, I met his gaze. "I'll give you an answer when one's given to me."

He nodded, clearing his throat like it cost him something to ask. "And this Commander Adrastos...do you know anything of him?"

Goosebumps lifted along my arms. My mind flicked to the brothers—one already corrupted, the other slipping fast. To those demonic, hollow masks.

"Why not ask Lonan?" I asked. "His men wear the same masks."

That made Cyrus tilt his head, thoughtful.

"Meet me here," I said finally, "same time, day after tomorrow. But bring something useful next time—schematics, coordinates. Something I can *implement*."

"Fine."

I started to turn, but he stopped me.

"One more thing."

I paused, eyes narrowing.

He seemed to debate whether to speak. The words sat heavy on his tongue. "Don't let your skin touch it."

The warning took a second to land.

"You telling me not to touch the crown?" I asked slowly.

He didn't answer. Just held my gaze.

"Thanks for the heads up, Prince. But uh...I've punched this ticket before. And the ride sucks *every* single time."

His only reply was a single nod.

I stepped back—slow, deliberate. Keeping my eyes on both of them.

His observations had raised more than my hackles. I'd need to run everything past Alvara. Or Ansel. Someone who'd had boots on the ground when Solskivall burned.

As for Grayshell's hunt for Adrastos?

Wherever the bastard was hiding...he was doing it well.

And if we'd learned anything since the battle—it was that he wasn't hiding alone.

FORTY

BURNOUT IS A BITCH

ALVARA

We spent *three days* negotiating the alliance with Kade and his advisors and gaining a clearer understanding of his current forces. Not that his men would be short on bodies to work with in a matter of weeks. The thought had bile rising in my throat. An invisible clock was ticking down toward the end of the world as we knew it, matching each beat of my heart.

Three days spent evaluating where his covens were stationed and how quickly they could be called in. Three days understanding how their power worked and who his strongest wielders were.

Three days we *didn't have to lose.*

When our combined well finally filled enough to jump from Morrieth Hall on the fourth morning, we headed straight for the Westerlunds, where they were hosting a handful of our refugees on their upstate horse ranch. As much as I loved Rose, my ability to let my guard down here would be immeasurably higher.

We landed in the pasture just outside the wards, my knees nearly buckling from the impact. I couldn't remember the last time I'd emptied my power so completely.

"Noted," August breathed, steadying me with a hand on my elbow, even as he wavered. "Don't risk hitting the bottom of the joined well."

"Burnout is a bitch," I agreed, straightening my spine and pressing through the ripple of the wards.

It was beautiful here. He couldn't have designed a respite more different from Aren's cozy cabin. Where the Chicago loft and Manhattan flat were sleek and modern, every inch of this place looked like a postcard.

From the dual-winged farmhouse, to the distant outbuildings for guests and staff, to the wood barn marked by the Westerlund crest—all of it framed by the rolling mountains of New York.

Like Ansel, our eastern brother liked to work with his hands to unwind. Some bittersweet part of me wondered if any of us would ever know the meaning of *respite* again.

When Aren and Marcus reunited in this life, they'd quickly agreed that leading our hierarchies differently than other Commanders made sense. Two centers of command for a legion of like-minded souls might've seemed unorthodox—but I'd never been more grateful for the merger that gave us a second home. A second leader. A forged hierarchy with proximity-based mental connection—life-saving on the field.

They'd decided that advantage outweighed the risks—after centuries of fighting side by side. I'd never expected to wish they'd connected the Middles too. Never thought the idea of more internal voices would sound appealing. But compared to the silence I was stuck with now? It did.

We'd barely made it ten steps past the wards before the red farmhouse's blue door opened in the distance. The calamity of Marcus' dog pack brought a smile to my face as they howled their way across the field to greet us. One by one, souls filed onto the wraparound porch, waving. Marcus, Eloise, and their daughter Tessa came out first, followed closely by Damien and his son.

Even from this distance, Marcus missed nothing. His wave faltered midair, hand lowering slowly as he tilted his head in that way that meant he'd seen too much already.

I'd say it's nice to see you both, but you look like shit, Marcus said down the line, his rumbling mental voice landing like a hug I didn't know I needed.

Gee. Thanks.

I heard him and Damien laugh before Marcus added, *On our way.*

A sharp whistle sounded. August and I trudged up the path in silence, too exhausted to speak. The gallop of hooves soon followed—two magnificent horses barreling across the pasture. Lord, they were stunning. One peeled toward Marcus, her white coat gleaming in the morning sun. The speckled one veered toward us.

"Escort by horseback?" August asked, amusement slipping into his voice.

Sighing, I muttered, "Marcus loves the classics."

A wordless weariness settled between us, my shoulders finally beginning to relax for the first time since Valentine's Day. Miraculously, our hierarchy had remained unscathed. Hazelharbor, not so much.

The draw between August and me felt just as fluid now as it had in the beginning. That should've tipped me off. I should've realized it didn't feel like *my* well emptying. The mistake was amateur, and irritatingly so. One I wouldn't be repeating. I glanced up at August. He was scanning the northern mountains like they might hold answers.

I could've lost him. I'd pulled every ounce of energy from him *without backup*. No one to fish us out if it went wrong. August had improvised, sure, but it still felt like dumb luck that King Kade had taken us in.

The pounding hoofbeats drew my focus forward again, and I tried to smile. Judging by Marcus' expression, I wasn't doing a great job of it.

The speckled mare—an Appaloosa, maybe—had waited for her rider before approaching. The two horses now stood side by side, evaluating us like we were the ones being tested.

"Well met, sister," Marcus rumbled, stopping before us. "Brother," he added with a curt nod to August, who returned the gesture.

But Marcus' eyes settled on me again, sharp as ever. "You wear defeat poorly, Ally."

"I can explain—"

"No need." He waved me off, sunlight gleaming on his rich amber skin. "Come get what you came for. Do you even remember how to ride?" His white mare snorted in agreement.

I glared at him, catching August's barely stifled grin in my periphery. Marcus didn't bother hiding his own, one brow raised in challenge.

"Hello, pretty girl," I murmured, approaching her carefully.

Marcus wasted no time. He fed us, then jumped us into the Middle to replenish—a gift I could never repay properly. After a twelve-hour coma, with our wells fully restored, my stomach finally yanked me back to the land of the living.

Peeling my eyes open, I spotted August in the corner of the chambers Marcus had loaned us. His hands were braced on a dark wood desk, eyes scanning a map of the hierarchy's territories.

"Fifteen thousand," he muttered, a crease between his brows.

"Hmm?"

"Fifteen *thousand* Grayshellians are still unaccounted for."

"Oh," I breathed. The weight of it sank deeper into my chest. I needed fifty of me to even begin fixing all of this. "I've been trying to focus on the ones we *have* found."

August rubbed the back of his neck, wincing. "Me too. But *fuck*."

"Most show up in the acceptable threads, if that counts for anything. I have faith they're okay."

"And in the less favorable ones?"

"We don't restore communication in time."

"Aren *has* to find our way back into Grayshell."

"I know," I said, my feet finding the warm floor. Twisting, I popped my spine in at least three places before repeating the motion on the other side. Without another word, we dressed and made our way back to the bustling Westerlund grand hall, hugging familiar souls and shaking hands along the way.

When at last we reached the hall, we were greeted by an entourage of expectant Grayshellians and Westerlund souls alike. Boisterous laughter and the murmur of voices danced with the clatter of silverware on porcelain.

Or...at least it did until they noticed us.

The expansive wood tables fell silent as eyes turned our way, August's hand finding mine as reverent voices whispered in chorus.

"The Great Commander."

"That's him."

"August Porter—that's what Marcus called him."

"Mated to the Angel of Death. Can you imagine the power ranking for their *children?*"

Benches scraped against the stone floor as the room seemed to rise in unison. My eyes went wide as, one by one, the souls knelt.

August's grip tightened on mine. I gave what I hoped was a reassuring squeeze.

The only time I'd witnessed mass kneeling like this was beside Aren, and even then, it hadn't been this...overwhelming. My throat tightened, heart racing as I tried to parse the flood of thoughts pouring in. Most were filled with gratitude. Others...less so.

Marcus was right. They're really going to stand with us.

The Angel of Death!

He doesn't look like much.

Oh good. The bringers of war.

We will rise together.

It will be an honor to fight beside souls so bright.

He's just a newborn.

He'll only be a puppet for the Deadly Six. For the Commanders.

"*Seven,*" I corrected stonily, eyes locking on the cynic in the back—the only one who'd remained seated, his chin dipped, brows drawn in wary assessment.

The room froze. Several faces drained of color.

A familiar voice slipped past the din, weaving smoothly between the mental bonds like it'd sidestepped them entirely. *Nice opening, sis. Gotta scare the shit outta them right out the gate, don't you?*

Good morning, Alec.

Smiling faintly, I snapped my shields into place before the crowd's collective curiosity could flatten me.

"We are now the Deadly *Seven*. August ascended as *my* calling. Therefore, he is as much one of us as any of the rest. We fight as a coven."

As if on cue, Alec, Fae, and Ansel stepped forward from the crowd. A familiar voice piped up from my right, still chewing through a bite of breakfast.

"I-mean, I'mma just ignore that you're not counting me." August tensed beside me as Freya slid off her bench, yanking a hoodie over her head that was at least three sizes too big. "Deadly Eight just doesn't sound as cool."

"Please stand," I said, pleading with my eyes now. "We've fought together for centuries. August may be an answer to prayers we didn't know to send up yet—but we're still just Grayshell. Rise."

They did, but instead of returning to breakfast, the crowd surged forward.

August's eyes went wide as he instinctively tucked me behind him, jaw tightening as dozens of hands reached for him.

They're excited, baby, I assured.

They're touching me, he replied, mental voice tight as soul after soul laid hands on him—first his hands, then his shoulders, until there was no room to breathe. The rest placed hands on their nearest hierarchy-mates until the entire room was linked, heads bowed in reverent unity.

"Lord, we ask you to bless this young man with strength and wisdom. We thank you for sending us a leader worthy of..."

Tears welled in my eyes as August's went round, his Adam's apple bobbing hard, mouth parting as the voices rose in solemn prayer. I knew I should look—should take in the sight of our soul family praying over the man who held my very being in his hands—but I couldn't.

When the souls let go, August remained frozen, speechless. His eyes found mine. One hand rose to his mouth as if trying to hold something in.

His shield cracked, light spilling through the seam where our walls touched. His voice slipped into my mind, thick with emotion.

I'm not who they think I am.

But you will be.

You sound so certain.

That should reassure you. These are your people now, August. They believe in you.

It's me believing that's the problem.

Only one way to start, I thought, shrugging.

Out of the pan and into the fire.

I chuckled softly and squeezed his hand. *The qualified aren't called,* I reminded him. *The called are then qualified.*

"You alright there, rookie?" Alec asked cheerily, as if we hadn't just witnessed something extraordinary. When August only nodded—still dazed—Alec stepped forward, arms out like a bouncer parting a crowd. Ansel mirrored him silently, that little curl on his lips unmistakable. It widened further when Freya wedged her tiny frame in beside him, joining the effort.

I couldn't help wondering what the hell she was doing here—relief blooming when my vision answered a heartbeat later. *Oh, this should be good.*

"Alright, alright," Alec said, ushering the crowd back with spread arms. "I know he's positively spectacular to look at, but back it up, people."

Laughter rippled through the group as they drifted back toward their seats.

"Let the man breathe."

I gave August's hand a final squeeze, and he nodded, clearing his throat and stepping forward.

"I uh..." He wet his lips, dragging a hand through his hair. When he tried again, his voice was magically amplified, casting calm across the room. "I'm not sure what to say to that, other than an unequivocal *thank you.* I uh...I don't feel worthy of the faith you just placed in me, but I swear on my immortal soul—I will do everything in my power to earn it."

Freya

TO NOBODY'S surprise but my own, Ally didn't even blink before whipping her Scottish dirk out from between her boobs—without me even asking. Sometimes, having a psychic for a sister-in-law was convenient in my oh-so-humble opinion. Titty knife and all.

I weighed the blade in my hand, balancing it on my fingers beside Ajax in the cemetery as we waited for Cyrus the following evening. The knife dated back as far as any of us could remember—*Saoirse* far. And I needed something from my first life for one of the enchantments.

The golden prince's face dropped the second he and Carrson material-ized on the outskirts of the twisting wrought-iron fence, eyes landing on the giant beside me. "What happened to *alone?*"

"You get to use the buddy system, but I don't?"

"Double fucking standards," my grumpy chaperone muttered, voice uncharacteristically flat. Without even looking, I raised my hand and smirked when he high-fived it.

"Cyrus, Soap Boy," I said, motioning between them. "Soap Boy, this is Cyrus Stuart, Prince of the Paladins, and his lapdog, Fluffy."

Carrson dropped his gaze to his obscenely shredded torso, then glared. I was ninety-nine percent sure Ajax was smirking as he gave a two-finger salute.

"A—"

"Jax," I cut in quickly, not wanting any tie back to Grayshell. Patting Ajax on the back, I added, "This is my brother, *Jax*. We've been nomadic for a while now, but he refuses to lose the accent."

My gargantuan battle buddy rolled his lips against his teeth—annoyance or humor, unclear—before forcing the least convincing smile in human history and grumbling, "Pleasure."

"*I'm sure.*" Oh look—sarcasm *was* universal. "Carrson Landry." He dipped his chin in a well-worn gesture of formality, but no one moved to shake hands. The whole thing felt like a suspected-but-unconfirmed leprosy convention.

I popped my lips to break the awkward. "Did you bring something useful, or are we just freezing our asses off to burn calories?"

"No *hello*? I'm hurt," Cyrus bit back.

Turning to Soap Boy, I chirped, "Hello, how are you? Good? Good, glad to hear it. *Me?* Oh, I'm fine. Just freezing my lady balls off because this idiot wants small talk." I smiled sweetly at Cyrus. "Now that we've got that out of the way—can we move on? I have a memory foam mattress screaming my name."

Cyrus deadpanned, mercifully cutting to the chase. Thank baby Jesus.

"I found your schematics. Still working on coordinates."

"Good, so he can be taught." I waved him forward, hand extended. He pulled a skinny rolled poster from his backpack with the flair of a swordsman—then, instead of handing it to me, slapped it lightly against his palm before lowering it to his side.

"You get the coordinates for the diadem once the crown is secure. These, you can have tonight—but I have a condition."

"Oh, *goody*."

"Well, two, actually."

"Color me shocked," I deadpanned, earning one of his patented irritated glares.

"Are you capable of holding your tongue for thirty fucking seconds, or would you like assistance?"

"Mmmm, will report back." I twirled my fingers theatrically. "Do carry on."

His jaw flexed. Then, glancing at Carrson, his face softened before sliding to Ajax...and finally to me.

"I wanna come."

When silence loomed with deafening finality, I burst out laughing. "I feel obligated to take a drink just so I can spit it in your face."

"I'm serious."

"I know it's shocking, but so am I."

"Listen. I've studied the crown since I was ten. Charles was the first to connect it to the Solskari. And I have a sneaking suspicion your grand adventure takes place in my mother hierarchy's original territory. I wanna help. Maybe all those years of study can be useful."

"*You*...want to assist *me*?"

"Don't make this a fucking thing."

"Me?" I balked. "*I'm* not the idiot trying to convince the woman he's tried to delete from the planet twice—"

"If I wanted you dead, you'd be dead."

"—and kidnapped once—"

"*Technically,* that wasn't me."

"—that he wants to follow her into a cursed. Crypt. *In the old country.*"

His solemn face twitched into a smirk that threatened to become a smile. "I mean...who wouldn't want to come along for that ride?"

"I assure you, there will be no riding of any kind."

"You're the one that said you'd already punched this ticket."

"And you conveniently missed the part where it *sucked* every time!"

"So let me help you," he said flatly, like the outcome mattered far less than his insistence implied. "If it's a Bellpost crypt, I'm sure shadows would come in handy at least once."

"I'll siphon from Bellaton's queen before I go. Thanks."

That brought him up short. His eyes widened slightly. "Reyna...my aunt lets you *siphon* her power?"

"Thus far, I've yet to be told no by any of them. Turns out when you save their heir, they get *very* accommodating. If you want to help, you can donate that way, poppet. Your power was the sweetest."

"First—ew. Second—no. *I'm going.*"

"You know," I drawled, shooting him a withering glare. "I've seen this movie before. Didn't care for the ending."

"*Huh?*"

Rolling my eyes, I snapped, "Keep up, Cyrus. Paladin word doesn't mean monkey shit after how my last life ended."

"*About that,*" he said carefully, tugging his hands from his pockets to hook them into the collar of his leather jacket. "You haven't exactly been forthcoming about what happened—or why you've got it out for Ma."

"That's, frankly, none of your business."

"You're making it my business."

"Are you going to stand here and bicker, or hand over my goddamn schematics?"

"Sure. If you've agreed that I will act as your second for this mission."

"Quite the demotion you're giving yourself."

"The end justifies the means."

Resisting the urge to snarl, I said simply, "No."

"Why?"

"I've always worked better alone."

Cyrus hiked a thumb toward Jax. "*He's* going?"

"That's different."

"I can't see how."

"Have fucking mercy. We doing this all night?" Carrson groaned, lunging forward. "I'm gonna lose my balls to frostbite at this rate, Cyrus." He snatched the scroll and pointed it at me like a drawn sword. "*You* want these." A sharp thwack across Cyrus's chest. "*He* wants to honor his *dead* fucking brother—"

"Such a diplomatic speaker," Cyrus muttered, eyes flicking skyward.

Carrson was undeterred. "—by completing the mission that *killed him.* The man ascended hunting this crown. For fuck's sake, Freya, *have a heart.* I once watched you climb sixty feet into a half-rotted tree to retrieve a nest of baby birds after my idiot brother killed their mother with a slingshot. You bottle-fed them until the camp counselors promised to bring them to the *bird lady—*" He threw up angry air quotes. I was too caught up wondering how the fuck he knew about that to care about the attitude. "And you insisted on going with them to make sure they didn't just dump the nest in a bush. We all fucked around too hard and nearly got you killed, and you *still* dragged this unconscious dumbass out of the water. So don't stand there with your ascended bravado and pretend you're impervious to why he wants this."

With a huff, he crossed his arms, the scroll tucked under one elbow. I just stared back, stunned. That dull, wordless sensation had me frozen.

"Don't look so shocked, Freya," Cyrus drawled, though his eyes were fixed on his boots.

"Just...didn't think any of you noticed me back then. Not until that night."

"Everybody noticed you, Porter," Carrson bit out. "Why else would we all have had a collective aneurysm when you were the one strung up in our rafters a few nights back? You think our coven just lets a hostage stroll out the goddamn door?"

"I just thought—"

"That was rhetorical," Cyrus cut in, rubbing the back of his neck before lifting his gaze. There was something unusually sincere in it. "One bargain. To clear a life debt. But if you give me this, I'll trade you a vial of my blood before you go after the diadem."

I wrinkled my nose. "I'm a siphon, not a vampire. That's not exactly a cocktail."

"No, but it's a key. One that could unlock limitless potential. If you're infiltrating a Bellpost stronghold, you'll need the shadows. Take it or leave it. Buddy system, remember?"

"Bonded by trauma," I muttered. My gaze dropped to my boots before flicking up to Ajax, who raised his hands in the universal symbol for *leave me the fuck out of this.*

The Paladins' expressions were unreadable, but their eyes told a different story. Sapphire blue, and warm citrine, both full of ghosts.

They'd changed in the last five years. *Charles* had changed them. Whether for better or worse, I hadn't decided. But if my plan worked—if Paladin belonged to me by the end of next month—these two dipshits would make or break my coronation. If I won my duel and Cyrus and Carrson backed me, I had a feeling Cali might abdicate rather than take me on. Maybe that was a wild assumption. But she didn't exactly scream *queen material.*

The Guardians had to die. Unless their bonds were more sentence than honor. That was a given. But if I could preserve any of the ruling members, it would save me a hell of a lot of grief.

Throwing them a bone...might not be the worst idea.

Something golden shimmered faintly in the air—just at the edge of my sight. Like a glimmer of the web of fate. Again, it whispered that word into the cold, dark wind.

Mercy.

With a long-suffering sigh, I said, "On one condition."

"What. Now?" Cyrus bit out.

"I'll be real with you. I don't fucking trust you."

"The feeling's mutual."

"Good. So you won't mind my proposition."

"My hand in marriage was spoken for decades ago, I'm afraid."

Yeah...to me. Not that I was about to tell him that. Gross.

"Business proposition, jackoff." When Cyrus just crossed his arms and sighed like I'd asked him to donate a kidney, I wet my lips and continued. "A Magic Bond."

"Who the fuck is mad now?"

"Just for the duration of the job. Once we're home safe, we're all free and clear. But this way, we're magically compelled not to harm each other, lay traps, or assist any outside parties with ill intent. No acting on behalf of Lonan. No breathing a word about the mission or destination to *anyone* else. We are all bound to do everything in our power to bring each other home safely. The Bond will dissolve once we're back from the Crypt, and not a moment before. Our window is noon GMT—sun at its peak. We leave here by five-thirty sharp. Oh, and one more thing—Freya Porter will hold the highest title and command for the operation."

Cyrus and Carrson exchanged a long, meaningful look.

To my immense relief, Jax said absolutely nothing.

The Prince of the Southern Paladins exhaled like I'd asked him to give up his firstborn, ran his palms down his face, and finally gave one reluctant nod.

Wordlessly breaking the stand-off, all four of us stepped forward, clasping forearms—bodyguards linking over our hands like one big knot.

A thief with ink on their hands was a bold choice. I took full advantage of Cyrus's rare gloveless condition, eyeing the hooded angel and inked shadows on his arm. I arched a brow and rotated his hold to reveal a brutal blade etched into his forearm, its seraphim wings detailed and biblically accurate. A chain looped the angel's neck, and eyes were inked into the wings of the dagger.

So *that's* what we missed when Blaz's illusions masked him. *Whoops.*

Cyrus's ensuing deadpan made it clear he didn't appreciate me memorizing his tattoos. Too bad.

I closed my eyes and whispered the incantation. My forearm burned as the bond sealed, and we all recoiled with the enthusiasm of someone who'd just grabbed a flaming pile of horseshit.

A Celtic knot had branded itself into my skin, encircled in a braid. Each of our initials marked a quadrant.

Clasping my hands in front of me, I rocked on my feet and looked up at the two of them. "The game is set. May God have mercy on your souls."

FORTY-ONE

THE CRYPT

CYRUS

"Fuck, I hate that feeling," I muttered as we landed on the rocky black shores of the English coast. Travel by shadow was infinitely less jarring—but shadows couldn't carry us to the opposite side of the planet.

"You get used to it," Carr said, slapping a hand between my shoulders and giving me a little shove forward.

Freya, evidently done waiting, was already halfway across the beach. Her stone-faced companion simply motioned us after her. Not about to walk ahead of us. Smart man. Not that I'd pull any shit today. Not that I *could* even if I wanted to—with the brand burning on my forearm.

The irony was, they didn't need the insurance.

From the time I could read, *The Brothers of Blackthorn* had been an obsession—one I shared with a brother close enough in age we might as well have been twins. The idea of a relic corrupting our friendship had always felt laughable. But in his absence, I'd realized how easily power could've sunk its talons into one of us. Just like it had the brothers.

Carr jerked his chin at Jax, and I nodded—too tired to argue with a cousin hellbent on 'protecting' me. Eyes fixed on the woman who'd shredded my life into ribbons over the last four weeks, I followed her across the crunching pebbled shore.

She hadn't said where we were landing, but far to my left, the teeth of jagged stone ruins jutted from the earth—cathedral-style arches and blown-out windows marking the bones of an old castle. Ahead, on the crest of a hill, a church leaned into the wind, half-swallowed by earth. To the right:

crumbling spires, lone stone slabs—the ghost of a village, long buried in history.

*Could this be...*Carr's train of thought drifted, but I could feel his mind turning. It looked like Bellpost. Proper. She hadn't hidden it in a crypt—

She'd hidden it in *the* crypt.

Just under their noses for all this time.

Holy shit.

You could say that again.

Ho-ly shit.

"Hurry the fuck up!" Freya barked from midway up the cliffside stairs, her short auburn hair whipping in the wind. Pale skin, piercing gaze—she looked like she belonged to the land itself. "Trust me, our time here is limited before we have very unwanted company, and the clock started ticking the second we rattled the wards."

I quickened my stride. "You hid it *at* Bellpost?" I asked, disbelief leaking into my voice.

"Sometimes the most obvious places are the ones most overlooked."

"Fucking hell."

"Also," she added, "if you hide something where they've already searched, they're less likely to go back."

"Most people know better than to disrespect the dead," Carr muttered.

"*Most people* suck," Freya said, breezing ahead. My smile was involuntary.

The familiar cry of ravens cut through the wind. We all glanced toward the cliffs, silence falling hard as we climbed. Only once we emerged between the walls of black rock onto the rolling green did anyone speak again.

"Drink," Freya ordered, tossing a slim water bottle from her pack and watching us with a wariness that said she'd rather toss us off the cliff. "Last chance to turn back."

"You'd like that," Carr grumbled.

"Not a chance," I promised.

She shrugged. "Your funerals."

"If *you* can survive it, *we'll* be just fine."

She arched a brow—*you know jack shit*—and twisted the cap back onto her bottle.

"Hypothetical awareness isn't the same as experience, Prince boy."

"Only one way to gain that."

"Fine. Don't die. It fucks up my plans. Not irreparably, but still."

"I'm touched," I said flatly.

She shook her head, turned, and resumed our trek. The scrape of wards across my skin sent a shiver down my spine. From the dilapidated church roof, a murder of crows took flight, and the already-frigid air dropped colder. Two babbling black streams—one from the castle, one from the church—merged beneath our path.

"The first floor is the easiest," Freya said, glancing back. "Don't let it lull you. The whole place is enchanted. Your ancestors were fond of mentalists, and their gifts are laced into every chamber."

"Yummy."

She whipped her head around and stabbed me with a glare. I smiled. Irritated, she turned back. "There are trap doors everywhere. Touch *nothing* without my say-so. Once we hit the second chamber, you'll see illusions. They get worse the deeper we go. They can't hurt you—but they'll make you *wish* they could. You'll be shitting your pants before we hit the third layer."

"Highly doubt that."

"I'll remind you of that when you're changing your drawers. Until then, shut the fuck up and listen."

"I don't remember you being this bossy."

"*I* don't remember *you* having a death wish."

"Valid point." I gestured for her to go on before she knocked me the fuck out.

"These illusions show you your worst nightmares, Cyrus. Your darkest thoughts made real. I can't see what you're fighting—and you won't see mine. But whatever you hear—screams, demon voices, pleas for help—it's not real. Not unless *you* make it real."

"Um. Come again?" Carr asked, for once too focused to sound like an asshole.

She sighed and turned to face us. "The second your fortitude cracks, the illusions *solidify*. What you believe becomes your reality. Staying alive means staying in control. I don't care what language you need to say it in— your mantra for the next hour is: *Not* real."

She held our eyes, her chin high. Firm.

"Carrson, I'm putting you on watch."

"*Excuse me?*"

"I could be a goddamn tour guide at this point, but sure, let's pretend I don't know what I'm doing."

"I came to protect my Prince," Carr snapped. "Not stand outside like a dog."

Raising her hand like a soldier taking an oath, she recited, "*Freya Porter will be the commanding rank and highest title for the duration of the operation.*"

Then she turned and started climbing toward the church. "Carrson, you're on watch. Jax is coming with me and Cyrus to hold the gate if we don't get back in time—he's got strength but no shadows. *You've* got shadows. I need someone I can trust to warn us if company shows up."

Well. That sounded...promising.

"Cyrus comes with me," she added, "because it's his goddamn prize—and because I don't trust him out of my sight for more than a heartbeat when I know what demons live in his mind."

"You don't know shit."

"Maybe. But I've used this crypt in my last three lives, so I know what it can conjure. And it's safe to say your odds are better with me than without. So. Last offer. Only you can determine if you're strong enough to go in, face what waits, and come back out alive."

She stopped just before the church steps, eyes locking on mine with a silent plea for honesty. "So. *Choose.* Coming or staying?"

Carr thought what I was already contemplating. *It's going to show you Charles.*

Yeah.

Can you handle it?

Fuck no. *Don't have a choice, do I?*

I can go in your stead.

And face your mother's death? That's no better.

Maybe. But that's my burden.

No. I shook my head. *This is my weight to bear. I'll bear it.*

Out loud, all I said was, "Coming."

Jade irises caught mine and held. Freya sucked down a long breath before finally nodding. She didn't look away until I shifted on my feet—then turned her attention to Carr.

"Any sign of trouble, you blow the metaphorical horn. It takes more time than I'd like to get the fuck out, and while shadows can move freely, *we* won't be able to conjure once we hit the depths. If we're not back in an hour, we're probably dead, so just send shadows to check. *Do not* come in after us."

"Guard the doors. Mind the clock. Got it."

"Good lap dog." She rose onto her toes and stretched out a delicate arm to pat him on the head.

I laughed as Carr jerked back, scowling at her hand.

"Now, *watch*," she demanded, pointing back toward the beach.

I swear to every god, he muttered internally—but he turned.

One hour, cousin.

Make it fast, he pleaded.

"You two, with me. Clock's ticking," Freya called, checking her wristwatch.

For someone with such tiny legs, she made damn good time. I rushed after her into the gloom of the old church.

The interior was...anticlimactically *charred*. Every surface blackened, crumbling. The only real light came from shattered windows and a gaping hole in the roof. I wanted to stop and study the decayed statues, the scorched altar—but I stayed close to my personal demon as she led us up the grimy stone steps, stopping in front of the massive crucifix.

She crossed one arm under the other, bracing herself, eyes on her watch. Expression unreadable.

"Just...felt like a quick prayer break?" I asked, irritation bubbling up at her refusal to explain anything.

The wind whistled through the rotting boards—an eerie chorus moaning in the dark. Freya stood motionless, as if carved from stone.

"Shut up," she bit out.

Jax's eyes widened, his raised brow hinting at humor. He said...nothing. Literally nothing. What a desk lamp. Why the hell did she bring him? A statue would be more helpful.

Just as her watch hit noon, she lowered her arms, hands hovering near her weapons. Overhead, the sun crested the jagged hole in the roof, casting harsh, angular shadows across the dais.

Before I could open my mouth again, she was already moving.

A blade manifested in her hand, and without a blink, she sank it into her forearm.

Every single movement was precise, deliberate.

She moved like something timed to a rhythm I couldn't hear—a machine more than a monster. Calm. Calculated. Controlled. She stepped up to a golden goblet on the altar and pressed on her wound, coaxing blood to pour into the cup.

My breath caught.

Ribs cinched tight as a circle of runes appeared on the stone floor, glowing an eerie blue. To my immense relief, Jax also flinched—at least a dozen symbols had lit up around us. Freya held her hand out, and Jax sealed the wound without even looking at her.

She turned slowly toward the stone wall, which now groaned forward, as if leaning to meet us.

And finally—*finally*—my brain caught up.

I'd been too preoccupied. Carr. Treason. Survival. I hadn't stopped to register what I was standing in the middle of.

The girl who pulled me from the lake five years ago? Just a vessel. A shell.

The soul inside her was lore made flesh.

Her auburn hair shimmered in the light as mechanical cogs clicked to life behind the crucifix.

My breath lodged somewhere under my sternum as I realized: I was standing in the presence of a legend.

The wall began to lower.

Click-click-click-click.

The sound reverberated through the stone floor and up into my ribs. Freya didn't look back. Feet planted. Jaw tense. She drew a dagger from the sheath at her side and faced forward.

"Eyes up, buttercup."

With a thunderous boom, the wall disappeared into the floor, revealing a yawning black archway. Freya sighed—so dramatically it might've been a chore she'd been nagged into, rather than a legendary crypt. She swiped a torch off the wall, sneering at the cobwebs that came with it.

"Can you conjure flames?" she asked, tone clipped, eyes flicking to me with clear irritation.

I shook my head and she sighed again—this one even more put-on.

"Great. Well. This should be fun."

Jax lit the torch with a snap of his beefy fingers and passed it to me as Freya grabbed a second and third.

A low, guttural groan echoed off the walls below us, every nerve in my body snapping to attention. My heart kicked up. I summoned my shadows into my palm, about to deploy them to scout ahead, when Freya's hand clamped down on my wrist.

"What did I say about not touching anything?"

"Not even in the shadows?" I asked, incredulous.

"*Especially* not in the shadows, Prince."

"I don't understand."

"And that," she said sweetly, "is why I'm leading this op and you are not." She turned to the tunnel—a spiraling staircase so steep and narrow I couldn't see more than four steps before it vanished into curve and shadow.

"There are monsters in the shadows not even *you* want to play with. And I promise you—they loathe intruders. You may heed their warnings, but do not send your ribbons out."

"Awesome."

With that sunny little warning, she began her descent—torch raised, blade at her side.

Don't die, Carr's voice muttered in my head.

Love you too, asshole.

Suddenly my job doesn't seem so bad.

You dick.

Hey, I offered, he defended. Even over the scuff of boots on narrow stone, I could hear his laugh. The warmth of it lingered in my chest—for a heartbeat—until the walls around us groaned.

Dust rained down as a massive grinding sound filled the air. The light trickling down behind us dimmed…then disappeared.

"That was the door, wasn't it?" I asked flatly.

Freya scoffed. "*What?* First carousel ride from hell? If we live, maybe you'll start making better life choices."

"Doubtful."

Jax snorted behind me, his heavy footfalls dragging. "I'd feel better if I knew how to open it back up."

"Pull down the sconce I took the first torch from. It'll open—but it takes just as long."

I smirked to myself. "How very *Scooby Doo* of you."

My comment earned a chuckle from behind, and another scoff from ahead.

"Fuck, I didn't *design* this hellhole—I've just played the game before. Survive long enough and you start learning the cheat codes."

"This is your idea of an *accessible* hiding place?"

"No, silly. Who in the hell hides cursed items where any Joe Blow can grab them?"

"You gonna pack your shit now that Carr and I have been here?"

A humorless laugh floated back as something clattered across the ground. "No."

"And why not?"

"Because most people don't survive this place."

Jax exhaled hard. "Nice, Freya. *Real* nice."

"Well?! It's effective, isn't it?"

"Christ, have mercy."

"I'm not even Catholic, and I have to echo the sentiment," I muttered.

My head snapped up at the sound of a prolonged *moan*—followed by a rush of frigid wind. I went still, listening. It sounded like…the earth shifting. A resonant rumbling so deep my bones vibrated, my skin prickling with goosebumps as the shadows begged to race ahead.

But the steady flicker of Freya's torch held my focus.

I was following The Wraith into an enchanted crypt. *Me.* The kid from the library. The prince with blood on his hands and his head in the fucking clouds.

I was following a folklore nightmare in the flesh—to prove Charles hadn't died in vain.

He'd been right. *We'd* been right.

This was like a Celtic kid waking up to find the fae on their front lawn

—and being insane enough to walk into the mushroom ring and tell them their true name.

Every logical part of me screamed to turn back. But I couldn't.

There was a core truth in every story about this particular succubus:

She got what she wanted. Repeatedly. Until someone finally killed her.

Deeper we went. The chill worsened, until our breath clouded the air. Then she stopped.

Her head tilted back—and mine followed.

Skulls.

An entire wall, at least fifteen feet high, built of human skulls. Bones lined the base in a neat, haunting border. The wall curved into a round tunnel overhead like the maw of something ancient and buried.

Reading about ossuaries was one thing. Standing inside one, surrounded by the remnants of my ancestors—still humming with traces of old magic—was something else entirely.

Freya held her torch right. We both turned to the dead end, littered with tokens. Coins. Stones. Charms.

From somewhere deep in the crypt, a ghostly melody began to hum. Like the echo of *other*—like the way it felt back at Luminark.

Freya didn't move.

I reached out, resting a hand on her shoulder. She jumped, scowling at me like I'd grabbed a live wire.

"You alright?"

"Yes. Just...preparing. This body is different. I'm still acclimating."

Newborn.

Was that something she'd meant to share?

"Come on. Let's get this over with."

"Not exactly what I'm used to hearing on a first date."

"Really?" she chirped. "I assumed you'd be used to that by now."

"*Burn*," Jax muttered. His heavy steps had gone eerily silent since we'd entered the chamber.

"Alright, history buff," Freya said, elbowing me in the ribs. "Pay attention. I'm not doing this for you again."

She jerked her chin toward the far end of the crypt. We raised our torches—light flickering over the walls—until the bones gave way to stone.

"Holy shit," I breathed, stepping ahead. My eyes raked across every ornate carving.

Behind me, warm orange flickers bloomed. I glanced back—Freya and Jax were lighting the sconces.

The floor was a mess of janky concrete tiles, some jutting at odd angles. Staggered marble columns supported an archway beyond. Faded light poured through, revealing the outline of something massive.

I didn't care about the bones anymore.

My attention was fixed on what had to be the King's crypt.

Torch raised, I crossed the space. Harsh shadows stretched and leapt. My gift stirred—but not in warning so much as curiosity.

In the center of the room, five marble steps between me and an enormous sarcophagus. Just beyond it, an archway rose like the mantle of a giant fireplace. And perched above it—the all-seeing eyes of Death himself.

Carved into the mantle were the Latin words:

Nullus immunis ingreditur. Nullus onere solutus egredietur.

No one enters unscathed. No one leaves unburdened.

The earth gave a deep, resonant rumble, and I blew out a breath—but held my position.

"Oh look, he *is* a good boy," Freya said, so saccharine I was developing diabetes. She lowered her torch to a groove at the perimeter of the floor, and I watched in fascination as flame ignited across the border—spreading like gasoline-fed fire. Foot by foot, the trail lit up until two massive stone bowls flared to life beside the opposing archway.

"I am way too elated to give a shit about your perception of me. We're standing in the crypt of King Koa, aren't we?"

She gave me a glare, tongue pressing into her cheek. "You say that like he deserves your reverence."

"Reverence? No. The man was a monster. But fuck me—this place is insane."

With a roll of her eyes, she waved me forward. "Go look. Just don't touch anything."

A chill coasted over my skin as I took the steps two at a time and stopped at the edge of the massive marble casket.

"What do you wager the Umbrabàs is in there with him?" Koa's legendary sword—said to cleave souls from bodies, no matter their origin. Mortal. Spirit. Demon. With an ego like his, I'd bet good coin he insisted it be buried beside him, just to keep it from other hands.

"The *what?*" Freya asked, clipped—clearly impatient with my awe. Her focus was already shifting toward whatever came next.

"Big sword?" Jax guessed lamely.

Why were the big guys always so *incredibly* thick?

I sighed. "Big sword."

Blowing out a reverent breath, I leaned over the sarcophagus—careful not to bump it—and squinted at the inscription.

Audaces fortuna juvat.

Fortune favors the bold.

"I know I'm interrupting your wet dream," Freya called, "but unless you'd rather Jax escort me the rest of the way—"

Reluctantly, I straightened, glaring at her. "That tongue of yours is going to get you in trouble one of these days."

"Don't I fucking know it," she muttered.

Her eyes locked on the wooden door set within the archway. Rigid posture. Jaw tight. Whatever lay beyond that entrance wasn't exactly a cakewalk. The second chamber. The illusions. That's what she'd warned about outside.

I didn't want to leave. My curiosity itched to explore every corner.

"I could spend weeks in here and not see everything," I muttered, staring up at the fractured stained glass dome overhead. Charred vines crept through the cracks and down across the columns, tangling near the gate.

"Whatever gets your rocks off, you psycho. I, for one, would like to get the fuck out of here at your earliest convenience."

She turned and hefted her backpack off her shoulder. "Okay, Jax," she said, breath tight. "I need you to put these on."

She ripped open the flap, pulled out old-school plug-in headphones—and a fucking *Walkman*.

A *Walkman*.

"You wanna talk about fossils?"

Who the hell had a *Walkman* anymore? She ignored me entirely, keeping her eyes on her brother.

"*No matter what you hear*, you do not move from this spot. If the gate closes, we're all trapped. Got it?"

"What kind of psychological-warfare psycho are we playing right now?"

"The master himself," she said, jerking her chin at the sarcophagus. "Do not move once I open that door—not unless I come to get you, you have to defend yourself, or—" she held up a mechanical kitchen timer set for an hour, "—*this* goes off. If it rings and we're not back, assume we're dead. Make a break for it."

"I'm not leaving you here."

"And if you come in alone, we're all toast. This is a trial of fortitude. You will not break. For the next hour, *nothing* beyond this gate *is real*. It'll try to convince you otherwise. The only reason you move is if that door starts to close. In which case—" she pointed, "—I beg you to use every one of those ridiculous muscles to keep it open until we're back."

The tick in Jax's jaw said he hated every second of this plan. But he nodded.

Then—without a word—he drew his blade, set it over his heart, kissed the back of his hand, and held it out to us in a silent salute.

And something in me shifted.

My heart kicked hard in my chest as a realization surged through my blood.

Grayshellian.

The Wraith was *Grayshellian.*

No wonder she was such a tactical pain in the ass. No wonder she moved like a machine. She'd been trained in that school of brutal loyalty and death-before-failure precision.

I looked at her. Eyes cold as steel. She returned the salute—then flipped her blade into a ready stance and *kicked* open the wooden door.

Torchlight illuminated a stone tunnel, the floor sparking with a ripple of flame that danced along the carved edges, stretching endlessly into black. A rush of freezing air and hissing voices slammed into me like a semi-truck.

I blinked—

And opened my eyes to the bloodied, sneering face of my baby brother.

FORTY-TWO
YOU FUCKING DRAGON
FREYA

A chill ghosted over my spine as I came face to face with the usual demonic bullshit—the walls rumbling, a bone chime competing for dominance—as I looked back at...me.

Me. Covered in blood, crimson dripping from the blades at my side, eyes glowing red. Nice touch. I had to hand it to them. This illusion had deep rings beneath her eyes, lips stained a red too specific to be anything *but* blood. Harsh shadows amplified The Wraith's skeletal cheekbones as a sneer curled her lip.

"Well. Look who the cat dragged in. If you aren't just as pathetic as I remember."

Clearing my throat, I stepped into hell, hesitating only when I noticed Cyrus was frozen just outside the threshold.

"Oh, pretty boy doesn't stand a chance, does he?" the demon-me drawled, satisfaction dripping from her voice. It was mine, but not mine. Too breathy. Too seductive. But she was right—Cyrus was frozen, the color draining from his face.

"Hey!" I barked, jerking my head toward the infinite decline.

"Not real," he breathed, eyes flicking from me to the empty space ahead. I shook my head and waved him forward.

"They get worse. If you can't separate the illusion from reality now, swap with Jax. I say that with more respect than you've earned. This shit isn't for the faint of heart, Cyrus."

A witch's cackle tore from The Wraith, her head canting in a serpentine motion as she mocked, *"Poor wil' prince. So much guilt in his black heart.*

And you—did you bring him here to die? Couldn't bear to do it yourself? For someone lacking a killer instinct, people sure fall like dominoes in your wake."

I pulled my eyes from the curse and focused on Cyrus. He was staring blankly forward, Adam's apple bobbing, but then he nodded. "'M good."

"Alright." We began a steady march down the hallway. All the while, the bitch with my face wouldn't shut up.

"Every life you've touched, you've ruined. Reyna's next, isn't she? And that boy of hers—what's his name again? Blimpy?"

I clenched my teeth but didn't respond, keeping our pace steady through the tunnel of bones.

"Guess it doesn't matter. You'll spill his blood before he can do anything significant anyway, won't you? And then his cousin will be next? Cousin— hah!" She threw her head back, hood falling to reveal hair soaked in red, like she'd bathed in blood. *"That's rich. Do you want to kill Reagan or fuck her? Because this is some kinky ass shit if that's the case."* She gestured between Cyrus and me.

Cyrus, who was rapidly losing color.

"Hey," I repeated. "Eyes on me."

He nodded, then muttered, "You weren't fucking kidding."

"Best not to kid about the underworld, darling. They don't like it."

His snort did monkey shit for my nerves. "So. Back at camp, you played guitar. You still do that?"

"Uh...seriously?"

"Yeah," I chirped as the flames flickered around us. Dark spirits despised few things more than being ignored. There's no power in invisibility. "You were good."

"Fuck, I haven't played in years."

"You should make time. I mean...assuming things go our way. Music holds people together through the darkness. My brother plays."

Another maniacal cackle. Dark Freya got right in my face, breath thick with the tang of sweet iron. *"Ahhh, August Porter. The Great Commander. He's damned too, you know? He'll never make it. Too good. Too pure. He'll crush like a flower petal when the fighting gets real."* She balled a bloody fist, opened it to a palm full of ashes, and blew them in my face.

I closed my eyes rather than flinch.

"That guy?" Cyrus asked skeptically, hitching a thumb over his shoulder toward Jax.

"Another brother."

"Got a few of those?"

"You could say that."

The Wraith scoffed. *"And none of them will remember a damn thing you've worked so hard to do, will they? Too busy cleaning up your mess, as always."*

"Blood or Soul?"

"Both." My torch flickered, a gust of wind carrying the low, resonant rumble of things better left unnamed.

"Ugh, I hate this part."

"You don't say," Cyrus said, straightening his spine.

"Lesson number one, Prince of Night. I oversell nothing."

"I'm picking up on that."

We stepped into the second tomb—this one all black marble, vines consuming every inch. Why couldn't they have buried this woman with her damn crown on? Knocking out two birds with one hellscape would've been too easy, apparently.

A high-pitched ringing filled my ears and I jammed my eyes shut like that might keep the sound out.

"You never win, you know?" That husky Southern lilt hit like a fist. Cyrus stiffened beside me. Never in my life would I have predicted the *son* of *Reagan Stuart* serving as my anchor point. But there he was—the rhythm of his breath, the steady beat of his heart—suddenly the only thing I could trust.

I glanced sideways and found Reagan.

Exactly as I remembered her from my last life—long blonde curls falling to her waist, bright swathes of fabric braided through. She held a curved blade in one palm and grinned before slashing it across The Wraith's throat, cackling as she fell.

"Hell, you never even make a difference," she told me. *"Not even projection-you is good enough to change anything."*

"Not real," I breathed aloud, gripping Cyrus's bicep and tugging him faster through the depths, around the second sarcophagus. He didn't stop. Didn't ask to look.

"You can incarnate a million times, and you'll never be enough to beat me!"

"How uh...how much farther?" Cyrus's voice was steady, but I heard the edge in it. Same edge I felt in mine.

"That's the second. We need the fourth."

"So far, my pants are still intact."

I laughed. *Really laughed,* glancing up at him in surprise.

He looked more likely to puke than join me, but his lips twitched.

Conn materialized as we passed through the next archway. I resisted the urge to look back. We were only halfway. No point in measuring distance when I knew how deep this went.

"You only had one job," he said, eyes like knives. *"Saoirse trusted you to look after me."*

"She never wins," Reagan told past-life August conversationally. *"All she knows how to do is sacrifice the people around her. You. Your queen. She'll do it again, you know?"*

"You'll kill us, Freya," August said as he appeared beside Conn, the three of them hovering backward, blocking my view of the pathway toward the catacombs. *"You've always been too fucking selfish to just stay out of trouble."*

Aren came next. *"I told you not to open Pandora's box, Freya. But here you are. Fucking him."*

I flinched before I could slam my eyes shut. "Not real."

"Not real," echoed Cyrus.

What personal hell was he walking through right now? The death of his brother? The collapse of his hierarchy? They were surely preying on the fact that I was helping pull it apart at the seams. Picking up on my anchoring game, Cyrus asked, "How the fuck did you find this place the first time?"

"I was hired for a job."

"A job you failed," ghost-Reagan hissed. *"Kin slayer. Betrayer."*

"Naturally."

"Sometimes it's easier to tuck things in plain sight."

"This is anything but that," Cyrus muttered.

"Okay," I laughed. "Sure. But they hired me to steal a Bellpost relic. So why not bury it where the rest of their stories rot?"

We came to a halt at the last chamber—simpler, made of bones. Small braziers flickered down each of the eight spider-leg halls branching from the vast circle.

"Did they bury the architect in here?" Cyrus asked.

"I dunno. Why?"

"So I can resurrect his ass just to send him back myself."

I huffed a half-hearted laugh and pointed down the correct path. "You're doing great. Honestly, I'm floored."

"Sure, talk him up before you get him killed," August snarled, his eyes flashing red like the Wraith's had. Cyrus followed my lead, and both our paces quickened.

"You're incapable of keeping anybody safe."

"Stay steady. We're almost there."

"Just a typical Tuesday morning walk."

"You often keep skeletons for company?"

"Obviously," he drawled. "They're the only companions that don't annoy me."

I snorted, thumbing at my knife as the specters closed in, hurling the ugliest parts of my lives in my face. Every failure. Every fear. Every bone-deep realization. They preyed on it all. August. Ally. Ansel and Lana. The Porters. All dead—and the corpses only grew more grotesque the deeper we went.

I clenched my jaw and repeated my mantra.

"Okay, here we go," I breathed, pulling down a sconce that triggered a creaky trapdoor.

"*Oh, good.* Deeper into hell."

"You *volunteered*, might I remind you?"

"No need. I am well fucking aware. As a matter of fact, I'm scheduling my cat scan when we get back."

"Book me one too, will you?" My eyes flew over the vacant wall, scanning—*there*. An ancient, rust-covered key, half the size of my palm, rested on the third row. I swiped it, wiped grime onto my pants, and headed for the ladder.

Cyrus snatched my elbow.

"We gotta go, dude. One way to your precious crown, and that is *down*."

"You rhymed," he complained. "And I'm going first."

"Fine by me. Expect the worst."

"Stop that."

"Tit for tat."

"Lovely," he muttered. "I broke her already."

He vanished down the hatch. I clambered after him, maneuvering down the short ladder into the darkest chamber yet—only our torches giving us light.

Boots on solid ground, I hoisted my bag over my shoulder, unzipping the back to slide in the goddamn crown the moment I got my grubby hands on it. The illusions, mercifully, didn't follow.

The final chamber was all coffins. Stacked like building blocks, row after row. All but one—hollow. A mystery I never solved, though I'd since used it for...we'll call it *storage*. I checked my gloves to make sure no skin was exposed. Good. I blew out a heavy breath.

"Things usually escalate once I take something from the vault."

"Yeah, but can we run this time?"

"Through the dark? I mean, sure. But watch your step, 'cause I'm not coming back for you."

"Noted. Me neither."

"So long as we have an agreement."

The key slid into place with a clunky scrape. I gave it a quick twist and a great mechanical click vibrated through my hand. I yanked it free, coughing on dust and God-knew-what as Cyrus raised his torch for a better view.

"Fuck me, that's a lot of gold."

"Most of it's cursed, so don't get too excited," I mumbled, running gloved fingers over my collection until I found the wooden box at the back.

"Who the fuck steals cursed gold?"

"Past-life me. Settling a beef with pirates."

"You really are something," he muttered, mostly to himself.

All the while, voices kept whispering epithets in my ears. Just to make sure I never had to return, I popped the lid, revealing a glimmer of black stone and starlight. I snapped it shut and slid it into my bag.

A deafening animal roar yanked me upright.

Cyrus spun, torch raised.

Holy shit. The illusions were never shared.

Not good.

I straightened just as his light cast across the end of the hall. Two crab-like creatures scuttled forward, flanking a man in a demon mask.

Please don't be real. Not real. It's not real.

"Not real," Cyrus whispered—just before the knife hit him square in the chest.

He staggered. Eyes wide. Mouth open. His name tore out of me in a ragged scream a beat before the next blade took him to the ground.

Raw, inexplicably soul-deep fear wrapped icy talons around my chest and squeezed. I lunged for him, yelling, "*Cyrus!*"

His head cracked against the stone, the torch rolling away. His hands found the blades in his chest.

"No! Don't!" I screeched, diving to his side as my own torch flickered feebly on the floor. My knees hit stone. The man in the mask was gone, but the crab-creatures were still click-clacking toward me.

I looked back—blood coated Cyrus's lips. His hazel eyes locked on mine. "I'm...scared...*little wraith.*"

I lunged to stop him from pulling the blades free. My hands hit his chest—and he *dissolved.*

Dissolved into *spiders* that skittered up my arms, toward my throat. I screamed, frantically batting them off. Their bodies hit the ground with sickening thuds as I scrambled backward.

"No," I breathed aloud as the truth hit me.

Cyrus—the real one, judging by the heat of him and the way his knees cracked as he dropped beside me—slid across the floor. His hands cupped my face, forcing my gaze to his citrine irises where they caught the flickering torchlight.

"*Not real!*" he barked, his fierce stare capturing mine. "Focus on *me*, Freya. *Me. I'm* real."

"Not real," I whispered, eyes flitting between his. But my thumb traced the scar we shared. Real. He was real.

The spiders didn't vanish. They solidified. Crawling up the walls, a few falling to the floor when a deep groan rattled the space.

"*Go!*" I shouted as horror bloomed in my gut. I'd just killed us both. "*The door!* Get the door!"

But it was already slamming shut.

CYRUS

"*Fuckfuckfuckfuckfuck!*" Freya was *flying* to her feet and across the hall, muttering an ongoing string of expletives as she grabbed my hand and yanked me with her. The walls shook with the rumble and click of ancient mechanisms, dirt and debris raining from above. A screeching sound snapped my attention upward as she scrambled up the ladder.

"*Freya,*" I warned, watching as the top row of skulls retracted into the wall, revealing a dark void.

"I know," she breathed, throwing herself against the trapdoor. A growl tore from her throat as she gave it everything she had. We were already fucked. I reached for the shadows, but they were locked inside a black stone cage.

Unable to conjure. That's what she'd said.

Fuck. Me.

"Come on!" she growled, shoving against the door. I climbed up behind her, locking her in against the ladder, pressing my hands to the trapdoor. Together we pushed, arms trembling.

"Is there another way?" I barked, fear climbing into my bloodstream despite every ounce of Paladin training. We were taught that fear was the soul's parasite. But this? This was survival.

"There has to be—"

A wall of water slammed into us, hitting the side of my neck and face, nearly throwing us off the ladder. I grabbed Freya's tac suit and held fast, shoving myself between her and the torrent. Her breaths came in quick, controlled pants as she wiped water from her eyes.

"Think, Freya!" I shouted, blinking through the relentless torrent. Already, a solid six inches had collected on the floor. The spiders that had solidified out of nowhere were now crawling across the skulls beneath the arch of water, all moving toward the end of the hallway. "There has to be another way up!"

"Yes, but you're not gonna like it."

"What else is new?"

"Good point!" She swung around the ladder, splashing down. I followed, stunned when she darted back to the treasure trove and started tossing weapons. A bow. A quiver. Knives. A rock?

No time to think on that one as she tucked it away, because she slammed the vault shut, turned the key, and broke into a sprint.

We nearly slammed into the wall as she banked right. I followed, taking a wave of water straight to the face.

"The gates will all begin to close!"

"I am *not* drowning in my ancestor's crypt!"

"I don't care if your fucking pants ripped!"

She sprinted toward a twelve-foot wall with a ledge above it. No shadows. No wind. No time. Just cold stone and rising water.

Freya turned back to look at me, scowling at whatever she saw. "We are not dying today, Prince."

"We need to climb up?"

When she just nodded, I gauged the distance, the roar of my blood in my ears beginning to beat the thunderous downpour into submission. Impossible. At least for me.

"There's not another way?"

She shook her head. "Up and out."

"I won't reach it once you're up there."

"Come on, I have a plan." She grabbed my shoulder. "Lift me?"

"So you can leave me here?!"

"Life for a life, right?" she said, but I remembered the way she'd screamed my name before the spiders materialized.

My name.

I tucked that away for later.

"Nice, Freya. Drowning wasn't on my list of desirable deaths."

"It's just hyper-aggressive hydration! You'll be fine. But fucking hurry."

Water up to my calves, I bent and boosted her up. She scrambled over the ledge, laid flat, reached—

But I was right. She couldn't reach me.

"*Go!*" I shouted. "Call us even."

Her brow furrowed, insulted. But she vanished in the next breath.

She left. She actually fucking listened.

Some fucked up kind of relief washed through me—after all, it was my debt we were clearing, not hers—but it lasted only a heartbeat because the water was climbing. Some book I'd read said drowning was a peaceful way to go once you stopped panicking—like a natural high.

Nope. Not willing to find out.

"Think, Cyrus."

I sloshed backwards, ran and leapt—predictably came up short.

"Fuck," I muttered, scanning for anything, anything at all. "Think, Cyrus."

"*Or fucking pay attention*," Freya snapped from above.

I looked up and found a dangling rope.

"Please tell me that's fastened to something heavier than you."

"Get fucked. I'm stronger than I look."

"*And half my weight.*"

"Run and jump. Do it like you fucking mean it."

"Freya!"

"Cyrus! Hurry up before I leave you for the spiders."

"You're insane!"

"*Well aware!*"

I ran through the sloshing water, jumped, grabbed the rope, and climbed.

Screeching stone. Cracking bone. Hands scrambling for the ledge.

Freya grabbed my tac suit and hauled me up and over. She threw her bodyweight backward, and we collapsed, stacked on the platform. The heat of her breath was a welcome ghost across my cheek as her eyes searched my face.

I rolled off her, scrambling to my feet. I extended a hand, relieved as fuck when she took it, letting me haul her up.

"You *just so happen* to have rope in that bag of yours?"

"Always come prepared," she said, straightening and nodding ahead into the looming darkness. There were no torches up here, and we'd both discarded ours before climbing. In near unison, we grabbed our tactical baton flashlights from our belts. I exhaled when they clicked on, beams slicing through the dark to reveal another passage—and an identical wall. Spiders crawled across every surface.

"Small mercies," she muttered, jerking her chin forward. I made it five feet before the light caught a looming shadow. I turned, flashlight beam catching on a massive stone reaper statue, sword braced over its chest. Behind it, a death mask had been carved into the stone.

"*Faster*," Freya snapped. I bolted, and the hair on the back of my neck raised as I took in the statues lining either side.

We sprinted the fifty yards, then scaled the ledge the same way as before. She dropped her bag and tossed down the rope without hesitation, bracing herself.

Fuck, for a tiny thing, she was disproportionately strong.

By the third ascent, I finally asked, "Is the Angel of Death watching your threads?"

"Fucking Ajax," she muttered, snatching up her flashlight as we bolted for the fourth climb.

I huffed a laugh, pausing to hoist her up. "Don't know how I didn't see it *sooner.*" The last word came through a grunt as I lifted her overhead. I made a mental note to start joining Carr and Nix in their training.

"Weeks of intention, that's how," she growled, pulling herself up and over.

"So?" I yelled up, backing into a run and leaping to grab the rope.

"*Yes!*" she barked, voice strained as she took my weight. Freya threw herself backward, heels sliding over bone as I scrambled up. Together, we collapsed flat on our backs, sucking in breath as the sound of rushing water finally faded.

"So, there's a way out of this then?"

"That's what I'm clinging to. She's usually good about warning us if we might die. But even the best seers miss shit."

"Yeah," I muttered, rising to my feet and sweeping my flashlight forward into pitch black.

"No more ledges?"

"No more ledges," she confirmed, but her tone was far from reassuring. She reached into her pocket and fished out the *rock.* With a furrowed brow, I mirrored her as she knelt, cocked her arm, and tossed the stone like she was skipping it across a lake. It clanked loudly on the floor, bounced forward, and then…nothing.

She exhaled, stood, and grabbed my hand. "Stay behind me."

"What?"

"No questions. Just commands."

"No wonder you were best friends with my mother."

She stopped short. I nearly collided with her before she turned to glare up at me.

I raised my hands in surrender, chuckling. "My bad. Not the time."

"*Asshole,*" she muttered, resuming her careful march. We caught up to the stone, she knelt again and repeated the throw.

"What exactly are we testing for?" I asked.

"Trust me. You don't wanna know."

I followed her as she slid the stone across the floor again. "I'm just saying, maybe it's time to find a different place for your treasure trove, you fucking dragon."

"You coming back down here to help me move it?"

"Hell no. But I'll rent the moving van."

"A generous offer," she scoffed, lips twitching. Another throw.

"Seriously, what kind of lunatic does this more than once?"

"The kind with a habit of acquiring things other people want."

"Like *what?*"

"Oh, I dunno, maybe a *crown* that siphons power and funnels it to an overlord?"

"Did you die hiding that, by chance?"

"What?"

"I just don't remember any stories about you being a siphon. Wondering if you died holding the damn thing and stole its power."

"Interesting theory," she said—right before the floor *snapped.*

Freya froze, mouth and eyes wide. "Go," she breathed, body rigid.

"What?"

"*Go!* Dammit, Cyrus, *run!*"

"You didn't leave me. I'm not—"

A rumble of stone cut me off, a slow hiss silencing us both.

"Run!" she barked again—just as a blur of darkness came straight at me.

I raised a blade, but faster than seemed possible, Freya threw herself between me and it. Bone crunched as the two collided.

Her scream cleaved the air.

FORTY-THREE
SILVER LINING
CYRUS

"What the fuck is that thing?!" I barked as Freya rolled backwards, springing upright like a goddamned cat. It had been a blur of shadow and gnarled bone, without much else. She'd...saved me. *Again.* What the actual fuck?

"Don't know. Don't care. Make it dead, please," she panted and crouched low, her canines elongating as she drew a new blade—hers had gone flying. She brought the weapon up into a defensive stance.

Canines.

I tried to pull on my magic, but nothing answered. We were close to the surface, but not close enough. My own teeth elongated, a burning pressure searing through my jaw as my eyes locked on—

"Holy shit."

"Yeah," she huffed.

The beast rose to its full height—shadow, exposed sinew, twisted bone. Its spine arched unnaturally, taloned fingers bent at grotesque angles.

"Split ranks," she ordered, pulling another knife from the sheaths on her ribs. For once, I had no snark left. Slowly, I slid the bow off my back and began sidestepping. The creature's eyeless skull tracked us in a serpentine motion, its jaw opening into a broad, jagged snarl.

"Fuck me," I muttered.

"No thanks," she shot back, a beat before she rose and threw. The creature *roared*, the sound slicing through my skull and spine. Both blades hit—no hesitation, no mercy—but the damn thing surged forward anyway.

While its attention was fixed on Freya, I nocked an arrow, aimed, and prayed. Released. Missed.

Freya's scream cut through the din, visceral enough that I felt it like a blade to the ribs, like I was the one with a slash over my chest.

Fuck this. I aimed again. This one landed, embedding in its shoulder.

It screeched at an inhuman, skull-splitting decibel that had me clutching my ears, collapsing to my knees as pressure crushed my skull. Blood hit my lips. My vision blurred, but I saw as Freya went down.

The thing backhanded her, sending her flying as her head snapped back.

Something fractured inside me, and I roared, leapt to my feet, and loosed another arrow. The thing charged. Another arrow sank into its chest. Too close for ranged shots, I flipped my grip and swung the bow like a staff. It shattered against the creature's skull.

I scrambled, drew daggers, and slashed across its throat. Black blood gushed, but it struck again—missed. The thing collapsed with a wet thud.

And just like that, it was over.

"Holy...fuck," I panted, chest heaving, heart a war drum in my ears. A roar echoed from the chamber below, and my gaze snapped to where Freya lay crumpled.

"Freya!"

Dead sprint.

Knees in the dust.

My chest warmed when I saw green eyes blinking up at me, dazed but focused. She was alive. Suddenly, that was all that fucking mattered.

Fuck me, why did I care? If the Wings or the Guard got their hands on her, she was as good as dead anyway.

"You're...bleeding," she croaked, her hand reaching to swipe the blood from my lips.

"Look who's talking," I muttered, pressing against her split brow with one hand while the other braced her side. Blood soaked through where her tac suit had been ripped, revealing torn ivory skin.

Her lids fluttered.

"Absolutely not," I growled. "You're not leaving me in this mess."

"Would serve you...right," she whispered, but a new round of howls was fast approaching. I slipped an arm under her shoulders and hauled her upright. "No time," she wheezed.

"Get up," I ordered, securing her pack to mine and throwing her arm around my shoulders. Her whimper of pain hit me like a knife to the gut— her agony somehow mine to bear in this hellhole.

"Ribs," she croaked. "Think it...broke a rib."

Jaw clenched, I scanned ahead. A flicker of light reignited my focus.

"Come on. Almost there. You've gotta be a pain in my ass tomorrow."

She made a pathetic little noise—half laugh, half sob—and stumbled with me. Another screech chased us down the hall. I tightened my grip, drew a blade in my free hand, and sped up.

We reached another rotunda, this one smaller, a cracked glass roof letting in a haze of daylight. Five tunnels.

Freya was losing blood fast, basically dead on her feet until I jostled her. "Focus, Porter. Which path?"

She blinked dazedly. Those pretty lips parted as she looked between them and nodded. "Second to the left."

I hauled her forward, praying she knew what she was doing. Her feet barely moved, her near deadweight slowing us too much.

I bent and scooped her into my arms.

Panic surged when she didn't protest.

"*Freya?*"

"Hurts," she breathed.

"I know. Focus. We're getting out of here," I promised, even as the snarls bounced up the halls and echoed through the rotunda behind us.

If those fuckers caught up, I'd try to bottleneck them at the entrance, but that'd only buy time. And Freya...

Freya wouldn't last long.

Silver lining—no one would have to bury us. We'd already picked our grave.

I snorted at the fucked-up thought and pushed on. Her breathing too shallow, her body limp.

I adjusted my grip, tucking her head against my chest, shielding her as I picked up the pace.

She whimpered, and I gritted my teeth as pain echoed through my chest.

"Don't bitch out on me now, little Wraith," I muttered. "We gotta run, yeah?"

"Fuck me," she whimpered.

"Maybe later if you're a good girl."

"*Ew,*" she muttered, but her grip tightened around my neck. I took that as the only consent I could count on. We shifted into a jog. She tensed, but didn't complain. I wanted to sprint—put miles between us and whatever that was—but she was already halfway to unconscious.

"Historians always get it wrong," I muttered, mostly to keep her awake. A distant gray light came into view. This space looked...bigger. Brighter. Another chamber?

"*What?*" she mumbled into my shoulder, her voice shredded with agony. It lit something violent in my chest. I wanted to burn this whole place down for her. Fuck history.

"They say you're notoriously light on your feet, not dead weight."

A breathless chuckle, and equally reedy response: "Remind me...to stab you later."

"Deal. Just stay awake."

"*You* stay awake," she whispered.

The screams behind us crept closer. I grimaced and shifted my hold.

"Sorry about this," I muttered, and before she could protest, I tossed her over my shoulder and broke into a dead sprint. Her stifled cry hit me square in the gut, but pain meant alive. That was the only metric that mattered.

Every step was torture. Like her torment was bleeding into me—like I could steal the damage if I just held her tight enough.

The magic here was fucked.

Fuck Koa. He could go to hell. Whoever built this labyrinth of torture could follow. Fuck Freya for stashing her secrets in a goddamned crypt. Fuck the demons guarding them. And fuck whatever vision of me had broken her so badly she lost her grip on reality.

If I made it out, I was demanding answers.

Just ahead, a ripple of power flickered over my skin—too familiar.

Wards.

Thank. Fucking. God.

Magic surged in my veins. Shadows peeled out like unleashed beasts, racing down tunnels ahead and behind us.

We burst into a vast chamber carved entirely of obsidian stone. I ducked us out of the archway's line of sight and slowly bent to lay her down. This was not Rhiannon's tomb—this one gleamed with gold instead of vines. Carvings sprawled across every inch of black marble, shimmering like starlight in the dim rays filtering through a cracked dome.

The shadows whispered—*beasts diverted, took a wrong turn.* Relief rippled down my spine.

My eyes swept over the inscription carved into the wall:

"*Equites nati ex duobus regibus umbrarum quattuor. Quando virtus manifestat, magicae mors promissio in venas eorum cantabo. Quattuor animae regnabunt super omnes.*"

A prophecy. *The* prophecy?

I fumbled for my phone and snapped a photo.

Then turned back to the girl who'd saved my ass—again. I cupped her face, coaxing her half-lidded gaze to meet mine.

"Almost there?"

She nodded faintly, lips curving into the ghost of a smile. Just then, a wave of magic rolled over us—Carrson. Were we past the hour mark?

Where are you?! His voice boomed in my mind.

Third circle of hell, but alive.

Something ain't right, man.

Demons. Trying to get to you before they do.

Hurry.

No shit.

A spark hit. I looked down at Freya. This was my chance. If I dragged her to Ma right now, I'd be untouchable. A legend. The bastard who bagged the Wraith.

The idea made me sick.

I drew my blade across my forearm and crouched beside her, holding it out in silent offering. Her eyes snapped to mine, flying wide.

"Don't look so shocked. I promised you a vial, didn't I?"

"No glass tubes?"

"Didn't bring one." Shadows coiled around my boots, squirming, uncomfortable with what lurked beneath. "*Now*, Freya. We gotta go and I'm not a pack mule."

Her jade eyes narrowed, suspicion flickering behind them. Like she thought I'd yank it away. That pissed me off more than I wanted to admit.

She leaned in hesitantly, disbelieving eyes locked with mine, lips brushing against my skin. Lips I remembered—kissing me like she meant it. Her fingers tenderly curled around my forearm. She moved carefully, almost reverently. Her sharp inhale was the only sign it was working.

I looked away. Needed to. If I kept watching this beautiful creature, I'd—

Her mouth lifted. She ran her tongue over the cut, then swiped it with her thumb. It sealed with a whisper of heat. Disgust and arousal warred in my chest.

Goddammit, Cyrus.

I stood abruptly. "Better?" I asked, voice too sharp.

She nodded slowly. "Thank you. You didn't have to—"

"It's nothing," I cut her off. "Can you walk?"

She drew a breath then nodded again. Good enough.

I shoved her forward, falling into step behind her as my shadows slipped ahead to scout. We ran through the tunnel, past the third crypt—I didn't even think to look for a name.

A few minutes later, we hit another rotunda. This one had eight paths.

We were almost free. Nearly out of this fucking nightmare.

Freya didn't hesitate—leftward path. We bolted. The glow of Koa's tomb rose ahead, blindingly bright, just as screeches split the air behind us.

I shoved her between the shoulder blades. "Go! Faster, Freya!"

The shadows screamed—*Run. Run. RUN.*

She surged forward, footfalls frantic.

Ten paces. Talons scraped bone and stone behind us.

Nine. She looked back—eyes wide.

"GO!" I shouted, the sound swallowed by a guttural roar behind us.

Eight, seven, six—

The hair on my spine lifted.

Five. Four. Three.

"Get down!" Jax bellowed from the archway.

Two. Hot saliva splattered my neck.

One. Jax stepped aside.

Freya turned—but I was faster. I dove, wrapping her in my arms, twisting to take the impact. Something massive and snarling lunged. A flash of teeth. An inhuman scream.

The marble floor cracked my ribs but I rolled, covering her, pressing hands over her ears. Our faces inches apart. Green eyes heavy with something unreadable.

Breathing. She was breathing.

I jolted upright. Jax fought the first beast, but a second was barreling through.

In a snap decision, I unleashed the shadows—wrapped them around the great stone coffin lid. With a groan, it slid back, revealing gold and ruby gleaming inside.

I lunged, yanking the sword free as bones disintegrated.

Whirling, I swung the blade, cleaving through the second beast in one blow.

Jax staggered back as the gate slammed shut. The rest crashed into it from the far side in a series of thuds and screeches. Shadows recoiled and retreated—into Freya where she stood by my side.

She exhaled. "Jesus Christ." Her eyes met mine. A frantic laugh escaped her lips.

I blinked, then snorted, unable to suffocate my disbelief. That did it— she doubled over laughing, shoulders shaking with pure, unfiltered relief. It was contagious. I slid down the tomb wall and let the laughter come, the black blood-slick blade of Umbrabàs across my lap.

Jax surveyed us like we'd lost our minds. "I will not pretend to understand what you two just survived. Judging by that *thing*, I don't want to. But let's get the fuck out of here. This place gives me the creeps."

All I could do was throw my head back and laugh harder.

Freya

"SUNLIGHT HASN'T FELT this good since I escaped prison in my fourth life."

"Jesus," Ajax muttered as Cyrus burst out laughing again. Neither of us could do much except collapse into hysterics as we climbed the endless staircase and finally emerged from the church.

"Could that grand adventure have *gone* more terribly?"

"Probably," Cyrus replied, dragging that damn sword behind him. *Fuck you, Koa, you genocidal psychopath. That sword never looked that good on you.*

"I sure as shit don't want to see how that would go," I muttered as we passed Carrson, who looked at us like we'd both grown second heads. I felt about as insane. What. The fuck. Was that?

"Nice try with the stones," Cyrus said, casually hiking the enormous sword across his shoulders like he'd been born with the damn thing. "Pretty fuckin' clever, but we'll need another system before you come back."

"We?!" I asked at the same time Carrson did.

"Tell me you don't want help outsmarting *that* shit," he said. "Please."

"You sure you're not the one that hit your head?"

"Somebody shut the fuck up and tell me what's going on," Carrson demanded.

"Oxymoron," I sing-songed, resisting the urge to skip—barely. And only because my ribs wouldn't survive it.

There were many highs I'd chased in my lives, but surviving by the skin of your teeth? That euphoria was hard to duplicate.

"What did you call me?" Carrson balked as we crossed the grassy plain. I burst into another round of giggles.

"We can't both shut up *and* fill you in—it's an oxymoron," Cyrus explained dryly.

"Thanks for the vocabulary lesson. What happened? Why are you both beat to shit and covered in demon filth?"

"Long story," I said between breaths.

"Long staircase," Carrson countered.

"Touché, Landry," I replied, feeling one bird shy of the nest. Was that the saying? My marbles were somewhere back on that third floor.

"The first two layers went fine," Cyrus began as we moved single-file down the cliff face.

"The third is where it got tricky," I explained.

"You gonna tell me why the fuck you screamed my name?"

"Not like that," I muttered to Ajax, who snorted and shook his head.

"Wait. What?" Carrson asked, glancing back at me before wisely focusing on not dying during our descent.

"You died," I said flatly.

"What?!" Cyrus blurted, instantly sobered.

"Yeah. There was a Renown in a demon mask and a couple crawlers. You turned to face him, and he threw a blade. Hit you square in the heart. You dropped, and I dove to stop you from pulling it out. You said you were scared, and *that's* when I broke the rules and engaged with a specter."

The unspoken reality came down between us like a curtain call at the end of the night.

I'd broken protocol because I thought *he* was dying.

Not even I could rationalize that one.

The Magic Bond didn't compel us to sacrifice everything—it demanded we protect each other to the best of our ability, not at all costs.

Step by step, the pregnant silence deepened until our boots crunched against gravel. Back on the beach, I faced the uncomfortable reality that as soon as we jumped back, this alliance was over. We'd survived. That was it. We'd done what we came to do.

So why was my stomach twisting when victory should be swelling in my chest?

We grabbed hands, and Ajax took us home.

When our boots hit the damp cemetery grass, we released each other. I met hazel eyes that were suddenly too distant. Burdened. Forcing a smile, I dipped my chin. "Midnight tomorrow for the coordinates?"

"Yeah," he said, voice flat—somehow hollow.

A prick of unease went up my spine, but before I could turn, he grabbed my wrist. My gaze snapped to the contact, then up to his face.

Cyrus wet his lips and unshouldered my pack, catching it as it slid forward before holding it out to me.

I shook my head. "Take it. It's yours."

"Not until the coordinates check out. Bring it back when you return with the diadem."

"What?" My voice jumped an entire fucking octave.

"The deal was, I get the crown when I help you get the diadem. Keep it as collateral. I know you've got it now."

I was *frozen*. In a huff, he raised my hand and shoved the pack into it while I just stared at him.

"Cyrus—"

"*Well*. Isn't this a surprise?"

We turned to find Nix, a pistol outstretched...with a glowing blue magazine locked on *me*.

"Nix," Carrson warned, stepping forward. "I know what this looks like, but it's not what you're thinking."

"Stand down," Cyrus ordered, walking slowly forward, subtly placing his body between me and his cousin. "We reached an accord."

"An accord?!" Nix barked. "You just handed her—whatever's in that bag—and met alone on Reyna's side of the divide!"

"To negotiate a ceasefire, I agreed to meet her on neutral ground."

"Neutral?!" Nix's voice cracked with rage. His eyes didn't even register Carrson or Ajax moving to block me. Not until Ajax pulled me behind him did his focus snap to mine.

"This bitch is an enemy of the crown. You *jumped* somewhere with *her*, Cyrus. Fraternization is treason—fuck you *and* your accord."

"*Nix*," Carrson warned again, drawing his blades.

"Lower the gun and I'll explain," Cyrus said. "Stand down. That's an order."

But Nix was already gone, the rage now steering the ship.

"A dead enemy, and a dirty Stuart. I'll be a fucking hero."

I knew, then, how this was about to go. My stomach rose into my throat. Wind whistled through the cemetery trees.

I lunged for Ajax.

Too slow. It was daylight. I'd only siphoned shadows, a kiss of ice, and life force from Cyrus. No burst of wind could shove him aside fast enough if that gun went off.

Ajax gripped my hand, ready to jump right as Cyrus lunged.

CRACK!

Ajax staggered, giving a grunt before stepping toward Nix as my ears rang.

Crack! A blood-curdling scream tore from my chest as I lunged for him, horror icing my veins as Ajax crumpled.

Crack!

The world exploded into fire and agony.

FORTY-FOUR

FATE IS A RAGING BITCH

CYRUS

"A dead enemy, and a dirty Stuart. I'll be a fucking hero," Nix sneered—my instincts shoved me forward before I could think. Carr released his blade as he bolted for him.

The first shot fired, and my vision flared red a beat before we collided.

Carr lunged for the gun as my fist slammed into Nix's face.

He discharged again.

Freya's scream pierced my chest—and the motherfucker fired again.

The world went silent.

High-pitched ringing filled my ears as fire exploded in my chest, and I dropped to my knees.

Pain blurred everything. I couldn't breathe—*fuck,* I needed to breathe. I was gasping like a fish on dry land, hands digging into the ground as heat flared behind my ribs.

Cyrus!? Calypso's voice crashed through the bond, thick with terror. I'd called her the moment Nix advanced—she and Jo were already getting dressed, on their way—but she must've felt that shot. Felt my pain.

Hurry. One word. All I could cognitively send.

I fell forward as Carr yelled something that looked a hell of a lot like *you stupid son of a bitch,* then slammed the butt of the gun into Nix's skull.

Once.

Twice.

Three times before the bastard went limp.

So...time really did slow down when you were dying.

I managed to roll over, dragging in a breath that tasted like blood and fire—and saw her.

Wide, stunned green eyes. Glossy with shock.

Ajax was pushing to his feet, wincing—but unharmed. *Kevlar.* He was wearing Kevlar.

But Freya—

No.

Terror cracked through me like a whip. I dragged myself across the dirt on hands and knees, unable to stand. The pain was fading now. And when I looked down, my chest was intact. Which meant...

"Cyrus!" Carr dropped beside me, hands clamping my shoulders and shoving me upright as he searched my body for the wound.

But my eyes were locked on *her.*

Freya. Paralyzed. Her gaze found mine as understanding clicked.

"No," I breathed—horror carving through me like a blade. I would've torn my heart out of my chest and handed it to her if it would've kept her here.

"Her! Freya!" I shouted at Carr, grabbing for his shirt, begging him to understand what I didn't know how to say.

It was impossible. Improbable. But there she was.

And I was so utterly, thoroughly fucked.

Light burst from her chest and she arched off the mud, hair falling back in a wave of crimson as her eyes rolled into her skull. Then came the scream, shredding me from the inside out.

If any god was still standing, I'd give them my soul to make her pain stop. And what the fuck was happening to me?

I was beside her in the next breath, knife in hand, tearing through her suit. She was choking on those screams. Carr dove in beside me, helping rip the fabric away.

The energy tilted—then Calypso's voice cut through like a whip. "Move!"

Carr scrambled back as my sister hit the ground at my side. But I couldn't look away from Freya. Couldn't see anything but her. Couldn't breathe until she did.

Her eyes fluttered open and locked on mine, her chin trembling.

"You're okay," I said hoarsely. "You're going to be fine. Jo and Cali will fix this."

"Cyrus," my sister breathed. Something about my skin. I didn't register it. Couldn't.

Freya's hand lifted from the ground—pale, shaking. It fell toward me, no strength left to reach.

I snatched it up, cupping it between both of mine, bringing it to my chest.

"Real?" she mouthed.

I nodded frantically, flattening her palm over my heart. "Real. I'm *real*."

She nodded—just barely—as Cali and Jo hit the dirt across from us.

"What the fuck happened?" Cali barked.

"Nix shot her," Carr snapped. I still couldn't speak. Couldn't look away from the black bleeding from the wound through her veins, defiling her creamy skin. "Reaper's bullet."

"I see that. How long?"

"Sixty seconds? Maybe less."

"Thank fuck," Jo muttered, pulling something from her bag. "We have to get it out."

Jax lumbered to Freya's side, still looking a bit stunned. I couldn't help but hate him for not putting her in the vest instead. But when her glossy eyes found his and started to stream, all I could do was watch as he knelt by her head, broad hands coming to cradle her face.

Jo shifted into motion, leaning over her with a light directed at the wound, barbaric tool in hand.

Freya bucked off the ground, her agonized scream snapping my mind into action. I tore my knife from its leather sheath, tossing the blade aside before stripping its case off my utility belt.

"You're alright, Freya. You're gonna be fine," Jax echoed when she sucked down a breath, but her gaze flicked back to me.

I held up the sheath, jaw clenched. She gave the smallest nod, and I pressed it into her mouth.

"Freya, I need you to hold incredibly still, do you hear me?" Jo said. Another nod. "Three, two, one."

Freya bit down hard as Jo moved. Her hand crushed mine with staggering strength—and it was the greatest gift I could've asked for. Because it meant she was still breathing. I didn't have time to question why. Not when Jo was digging the bullet out and holding her glowing hands over the wound.

Freya met my gaze.

My fault.

My fault she was on the ground. My fault I hadn't reached the weapon.

My fault I hadn't realized why I couldn't hurt her.

Why she kept saving me, to her own detriment.

Fate is a raging bitch.

Jo exhaled a breath of relief and fell back, her hands trembling. Only then did I inhale. I held onto Freya like she might vanish. Closed my eyes and counted all the ways this could still go wrong—and everything I'd have to do to make sure it didn't.

Jo passed her palm over Freya's forehead. Her eyes slid shut, head lolling.

"Carr," I rasped. His head snapped up, jaw tight. "Get Nix to the brig. No one talks to him until I get back."

Jo turned on me. "Somebody better tell me why I just pulled a goddamned slug out of our enemy in broad fucking daylight inside a cemetery."

I met her glare, lifted my chin. "Because she's my mate."

The silence hit like a shockwave.

My sister, naturally, was the one to say what everyone else was thinking. "Oh, *fuck.*"

"CYRUS."

I blinked into the gloom of The Middle, straightening in the armchair I'd occupied for the better part of thirty hours. As I wiped the sleep from my eyes, my heart stuttered at the bold black ink now covering my arms.

Wings.

Poe had marked me before the coven even answered our summons. Cali had even called home Elinora—our most trusted truth-sayer—to ensure we could manipulate the narrative to land in our favor. Every member of the coven had studied the markings with reverence before diving into the plan. I couldn't blame them. I had no idea how many times I would stare at these feathers before it would finally sink in that they were mine. That Poe had offered not just his blessing—but the ultimate token of faith. He'd waited all this time to be sure I would earn them.

My job now was proving him right.

It had been twenty-four hours of healing baths in the Middle, tinctures, and pleading to a universe I wasn't even sure was listening before Jo finally said Freya was out of danger and deep into ascension. Only then had I slept —and apparently, three meager hours were all Poe needed to weave his magic over every inch of my skin. The implications of that were...vast. And they would not be inconsequential.

"Cyrus. It's now or never." Carr's hand tightened on my shoulder, but his gaze remained on Freya, who slept soundly, a pinch of concern in his brow. Given what I was about to face, I couldn't blame him. There may be no place for fear in a Paladin's heart—but there was always room for preparation.

"Protect her," I ordered as I stood, locking onto those warm sapphire eyes.

"Do it yourself," he shot back—more a demand than a retort. My chest tightened. Nix might be an asshole, but Carr's allegiance would be a double-edged thing. Yes, he had my back—but at what cost?

"He is your brother," I said gently, hoping it landed softer than it sounded in my head.

"And he wove his fate. See that he faces it."

Jo entered the room, as though summoned by our shared purpose. I'd always admired Jo. Her mind was a sharp match for my sister's, but it was her gentleness that set her apart. Healers were rare behind Paladin walls—gentleness even harder to come by. But somehow, she managed both.

Her chocolate hair was woven into an intricate braid, a few strands framing her tan face as she studied Freya's sleeping form. I couldn't help but do the same.

I didn't know how the hell to process this.

I had a mate.

Not just any mate. The woman who had saved my life—not once, but three times.

Maybe I'd repaid the last debt by dragging her out of that hellhole, but life debts meant nothing once eternal bonds were forged. *This* was why we'd hesitated to strike the final blow. Why we kept showing up in the same goddamn places like magnets destined to collide. Our souls had known long before we did. She might feel differently when she woke, but from everything I'd read, that tether would remain—whether we wanted it to or not.

Again and again, fate would draw us back together like a moon pulled by gravity.

In this life, or the next, this soul would be mine. Whether that became a burden or a gift was now up to us.

While most mate bonds evolved into romance, it wasn't a requirement. The bond tied us together regardless, into all eternity.

The stunning redhead ascending in my sheets was my other half.

And if I didn't move quickly, she'd be executed before she even woke.

Jo held her hands over Freya's chest, light blooming from her palms as she checked the vitals she'd monitored on the hour since the wound stabilized. She didn't look at me, didn't need to—but when her head turned, she nodded.

"I have her. Go rattle his cage, Prince."

Karma was coming for Nix Landry. I just prayed I was enough to deliver her.

The grand hall was full when Carr and I strode through the double doors, the hinges creaking. Chattering Paladins grew so silent it was deafening—my ears grasped for the steady rhythm of breathing, heartbeats, anything beyond the impenetrable shields they'd all snapped into place, cutting me off as I marched toward metaphorical gallows.

My eyes found my mother's, where she was braced in her throne with a clear view of the circular platform now raised in the center of the room, as though she sat on the precipice of battle. Dad sat beside her, eyes distant, jaw tight, fixed out the window of Luminark Manor. On her other side, Calypso stood with her spine long, exuding royalty, already a queen in the making.

The council sat below the dais in a semi-circle, a nod to Luna, their expressions a blend of apprehension and excitement. After all, it wasn't every day two souls in the line of succession were accused of treason.

As we closed the distance, I locked eyes with every one of them.

This was my hall.

My hierarchy.

My people. And soon, they would realize it. Even if it took a motherfucking spectacle to get there.

As we approached the royal dais, I glanced sideways and spotted Nix beside his father, that cocky smirk just begging me to knock it off his face. Juno wore a mask of indifference, but his eyes held the weight of a father who knew his son was on thin ice.

Carr and I bowed to my parents, who silently nodded before we moved to our places—me standing beside Cali, Carr two steps behind and to my right. Once we were hidden behind the seated front row, I adjusted my jacket sleeves, ensuring they covered my new ink.

The doors swung shut behind us with a kind of finality fit for a colosseum. My mother sighed, then cleared her throat.

"We are gathered today in evaluation of two accusations of violations of the Accords."

A murmur rippled through the gathered witnesses. Cali's fingers found mine at our sides, hidden behind the council chairs. I gave her a reassuring squeeze but kept my eyes forward, trying to embody the prince our people deserved. Mother cleared her throat again, like the words physically hurt. I'd love to see that emotion actually directed into giving a shit about us when we weren't on trial, but I guess a flicker of distress was better than nothing.

"Captain Nix Landry, please present your claim to the council."

He rose, turning over his shoulder to smirk at me, arrogance etched into every step as he swaggered to the raised platform at the center of the broken circle.

That shit-eating grin stretched as he lifted his chin. "I accuse Cyrus

Stuart of fraternizing with an enemy of the Crown, harboring a threat to the hierarchy, and allowing that enemy to infiltrate our ranks, thus endangering us all." He turned toward the council, brow furrowed in righteous anger. At least the bastard meant what he fucking said. There was no hesitation in his claims, though I'm sure watching me fall would be his idea of a wet dream. "Our so-called prince brought a Grayshellian spy into your inner sanctum. This isn't just treason—it's betrayal of our brotherhood. A desecration of the laws I have sworn to uphold."

He crossed his wrists over his right shoulder and bowed his head in a Paladin salute. A low ripple of unease passed through the room.

Mother's jaw flexed, knuckles white on the arms of her throne. "Cyrus Stuart, you've been called to the platform."

I turned to Cali. Our eyes locked a beat before she gave the slightest nod of dismissal. I almost smiled.

I fucking loved my sister.

When I stepped onto the stage, a hush fell. I circled slowly, head high, cataloging the faces around me. Who looked outraged? Who looked uncertain? Who might be swayed? I found a pair of wide, uneasy eyes and dipped my head, offering a reassuring smile.

"I assure you, the integrity of our ranks remains intact. I've done nothing but uphold our laws. Yes, Freya Porter hails from Grayshell—but prior to her ascension, she fought under the Paladin banner." My eyes met my mother's. She'd already molded her expression into a wrathful mask. She'd absolutely rip me a new one later. "Freya entered a petition under the Accord of Oath—"

"That's a lie!" Nix snarled, turning sharply to face me.

I slid my hands into my pockets to avoid fisting them. "—which, as you know, protects all souls seeking to complete the Crucible, regardless of origin. To harm her would be a direct violation of the Knight's Accord."

"I object!" Nix shouted, flinging a hand toward Ma. "Section Four, Code Three, Point Four of the *Knight's Accord* clearly states that any soul seeking a Crucible must present their petition to an acting royal. Your Majesty, did you authorize Freya's petition without notifying the Wings?"

"No," Ma replied coolly. Her eyes cut briefly to mine—sharp and clear. A warning. Get your shit together.

"If our queen didn't allow the petition, then who did?" he demanded triumphantly, glaring in my direction.

"I did," Calypso said calmly, standing beside our mother.

It took every ounce of self-control not to grin up at her, to keep my face schooled into the same indifference modeled so perfectly by our parents across from me. She turned to Carr, tipping her chin in silent command, and he rounded the dais with the paperwork to prove it. Paperwork she had happily signed—and predated by a calendar week to match the day our parents were absent. Jo had cast the charm to dry and age the ink just enough to make it convincing.

"An heiress-apparent acting as regent in the absence of the Queen has the authority to sign a petition."

Another wave of murmuring unrest swept through the onlookers, their gazes shifting between the three of us as Calypso raised her head.

"While Nix claims to defend our hierarchy, he violated the very laws he swore to protect when he disobeyed a royal command, harmed a petitioner protected by the Accord of the Oath, and fired a reaper's bullet—a weapon *I* designed, reserved for enemies of the Balance—outside our territory. This is after a prior violation of the treaty dividing us from Bellaton. If treason lies anywhere, it's with the Captain."

Voices of agreement echoed across the chamber. Our people knew what Calypso was studying. Knew the cruel death the reaper's bullet inflicted. And to use it on a petitioner protected by the Accord?

My cousin wouldn't walk away with his Wings—if he kept his head.

Some dim corner of me flinched at the idea of spilling his blood, but the image of Freya writhing under reaper's venom had my jaw clenched tight. If her pain in the crypt had sloughed off into me, it was nothing compared to *that*.

"She's covering for him!" Nix barked. "You can see they've orchestrated this. I've been set up!"

He set *himself* up the moment he shot my mate. The moment he knocked out our cousin and dragged him across the divide as blackmail, in direct violation of my orders. The tension between us had been building for years. I just hadn't expected it to break under my mother's rule.

"If you're so convicted," I said, turning to meet Nix's glare, "then call a truth-sayer. Simple problems require simple solutions."

"Like we can just summon a truth-sayer," he scoffed, rolling his eyes.

Still holding his livid stare, I smothered a smile and lifted my voice. "Elinora, would you do us the honor of moderating the rest of the trial?"

"Elinora is currently—" Nix began, but his words died as she rose from her seat and moved toward the dais in her royal purple priestess robes.

His disbelieving glare turned to me, heavy with accusation.

You planned this.

"Present," Elinora said silkily. "It would be my honor to preside, if it is the will of Her Majesty."

Ma looked at me one more time before giving a curt nod and leaning back in her seat, legs crossed, relaxing into her elbow like she meant to enjoy the show. "Proceed."

Elinora bowed her head reverently before stepping between us. Nix and I moved to either side, giving her space. She steepled her fingers to her chest, her eyes fogging white as she began.

"Cyrus Stuart, did you bring a Grayshellian into our sacred ground?"

"Yes," I breathed, voice steady. "Under the laws of the Crucible."

"Did you know of her allegiance to Grayshell prior to granting her protection?"

"I knew of her desire to complete the Crucible, and the efforts she was taking to prove herself. Her heritage was brought to my attention less than an hour before Nix shot her."

"And was she acting as a spy or agent of Grayshell during her time here?"

"No," I said firmly. "Freya seeks to prove her worth under Paladin law. To reclaim her honor as a Paladin soul."

Elinora's milky, unseeing eyes turned toward Nix, who clenched his jaw.

"Did you knowingly fire upon a petitioner under the Accord of Oath?"

"No," he snapped, shaking his head. "I didn't—*and don't*—recognize her petition. She's an enemy of the Crown."

"Whether you recognize it is irrelevant," Calypso called from the dais. "The law stands, no matter your feelings. Your prince told you he had an accord with her, and you told him, and I quote, 'fuck you and your *accord*,' and *shot her* anyway."

Chairs screeched as the chamber erupted. Raised voices, panic, betrayal like smoke clinging to every breath. I kept my mask in place, but Nix saw it. The twitch of my mouth. The gleam in my eye. Rage flared in his as Ma's voice cracked across the noise, demanding silence.

Only when every soul was seated did Elinora continue.

"Captain Landry, were you given a direct order by Cyrus Stuart to stand down?"

"Yes, but I—"

"Yes or no?" she interrupted sharply.

Nix's eyes found mine, promising retribution. "*Yes.*"

"Did you disobey Prince Cyrus' order and fire upon the petitioner?"

"I did what I thought was right!" Nix roared, turning now to appeal to the crowd.

"And in doing so," Calypso said smoothly, stepping down from the dais with regal precision, "he violated the Accords and disobeyed a direct command from a superior title. We can all agree—these are treasonous acts."

Chills ghosted over my arms as Elinora tilted her head, her voice growing breathy and strange—otherworldly.

"Why did you risk the sanctity of our laws to protect her, Cyrus?"

I shifted, eyes falling to my boots before lifting to the dais. My parents. The council. But it was Portia's deep brown stare that held mine—steady, commanding. There was something like fear in her gaze, even as she jerked her chin in a silent order to answer.

"Freya Porter is my mate."

Gasps cracked across the hall like thunder. Color drained from Ma's face in real time. I thumbed my signet ring, studying the veins in the marble floor, then met her gaze again. And nodded.

Calypso let the chaos burn itself out before stepping forward—between us and the council, between us and Orion, the heart of judgment.

"Under the Accord of Blood," she said, voice ringing clear, "a mate is as sacred as our blades. To harm her outside of a council-sanctioned duel is treason in itself."

Nix didn't speak. The tips of his ears were cherry red, his face blank with something like disbelief. He looked at me like I was a stranger. And maybe I was.

Because something *was* happening to me.

Even if I didn't understand it yet.

"The Prince speaks truth," Elinora intoned, her vision clearing. But the people already knew. My victory had been cemented, every step of this trial choreographed to end exactly here. Freya would be safe, no matter what came next.

That was all that mattered.

"The punishment for breaking your oath is the stripping of your Wings," Ma said gravely. But her gaze drifted—watching her brother, Juno, to see how he'd react to the guillotine now hovering above his son's neck.

And Nix...closed his eyes. In resignation. Nix never—*never*—backed down from a fight.

"Or a trial by combat," I said quietly.

His eyes snapped open.

"Let the betrayer decide."

"Cyrus," Calypso hissed, whipping around to glare at me. This hadn't been part of her plan. Not by a long shot. But it was sure as shit mine. This motherfucker—blood or not—was going to get someone killed eventually. And his honor would be more intact in death than without his Wings.

Nix scanned the chamber as it unraveled around us. A prince in a duel was serious business. To kill a prince might earn you rank—but no one would trust you after. No one would *respect* you.

He would lose. Or he'd win and live as a pariah.

To decline was dishonor.

"I accept," he said over the growing roar.

Cali clapped a hand over the bridge of her nose, visibly reining in her fury. If I survived, she was going to beat the ever-loving shit out of me.

Carr stepped forward with my weapons, and I moved off the platform to meet him. I unbuttoned my jacket, shrugging it off in one fluid motion.

And the crowd lost it.

Because Poe hadn't just given me *gauntlets*.

He'd inked enormous wings across my back and down my arms—bold, black, divine. I hadn't yet tested them in combat, but I had a feeling they were more than just a flex. This kind of familiar's mark hadn't been seen in centuries.

I reached back to strip off my shirt and hand it to Carr, baring the rest of it.

Chaos erupted. Souls flew from their seats. Even Ma had risen, eyes wide, descending the dais in stunned silence.

But it was Elinora who said what they were all thinking.

"Harbinger of Glory."

FORTY-FIVE

HARBINGERS

CYRUS

"When?"

Every soul in the chamber hung on Ma's single-word question. "When I saved her."

She tongued at a canine, then nodded so slowly it felt like time itself had halted. Dad stayed a few steps behind her out of deference, but his gaze seared into mine.

Her voice rang out clear for the crowd: "And who is your champion, Prince?"

"I fight for myself."

"*Cyrus,*" she bit out, horror cracking her regality. "Princes do not fight their own battles."

"Maybe," I allowed. "But Kings do."

Her bright blue eyes turned pleading. And for a moment, I considered her. To lose one son before ascension was a cruelty few survived. To lose another—this young—was a burden I had no intention of saddling her with. But Nix was, and always would be, a liability. A weak point Calypso couldn't afford to inherit.

And Poe chose *me.*

I cannot lose you, she whispered in my mind.

You choose an inopportune moment to show it.

Her brows pinched—just for a breath—and then her mask snapped back into place.

Nix is a trained Wing, with more experience.

And I'm the son of Reagan and Ciaran Stuart.

Dad stepped forward, resting a hand at the back of my neck and bringing our foreheads together.

He's a bull in an arena, he said mind-to-mind. *Easy to anger. Easier to distract. Nix always leans on strength, but don't mistake that for an empty mind. He tracked you with that girl. He wouldn't have accepted unless he had a plan. Don't let him get under your skin.*

Thank you. The balance will choose the righteous victor, I replied, trying to project more confidence than I felt.

Then my mother was gone, the Queen in her place.

She straightened her spine, brought her arms up, crossed her wrists over her chest, and bowed her head in a warrior's salute. Dad followed suit.

With one final glance, she turned to face the gathered crowd, voice sharp and clear. "The rules are simple. One weapon. No magic." She looked back at me, eyes unreadable. "The balance will choose the righteous victor."

Nix and I turned from our parents and stepped onto the platform, blades raised. Anticipation silenced the room.

We paced forward, clasped winged forearms, and bowed our heads.

A muscle ticked in Nix's jaw as I murmured, "May the light falter on your blade."

"May the light falter on your blade, *cousin*," he returned.

At least the last thing we said would be in honor. A blessing from the shadows. It was there—in those mismatched eyes I'd known my whole life—a flicker of gratitude that I hadn't stripped him of it.

We backed to our respective corners, and I scanned the crowd. Most wore the same careful neutrality I'd expected. Calypso looked ready to storm the ring and kick both our asses. Carr crouched at the edge, my belongings clutched to his chest, elbows on his knees, fists pressed against his mouth.

If anxiety had a face, it was his. A coiled spring waiting to release.

He'd be the only one I'd grieve. He would lose either way.

A ripple of awareness skated over my skin. The shadows whispered in a million voices, a spectral chorus of wisdom and warning.

I closed my eyes, centering myself. Then turned to face my opponent.

We held the same style blade—the raven hilted knives we'd forged ourselves in the Rite of Steel, when we ascended.

Same defensive stance. Same goddamn stubborn blood in our veins.

There was a reason royals didn't duel.

"Begin!" Mother's command cracked like a whip across my shoulders.

I held my ground, and homed in on my target as the world fell away.

Nix charged. Guard fist first, then the blade, curving on the third strike to slit my throat. I dodged, backpedaling, blocking the final swing before lashing out. Strike for strike, we mirrored one another. The tension in the room coiled tighter.

Then my blade glanced off his pec and he hissed in pain.

"*First blood,*" someone murmured.

A growl rumbled in Nix's chest.

The spark in his eyes burned brighter—part irritation, part renewed focus.

Then we moved.

For such a bulky bastard, he was fast, and with our mirrored reach and shared training, neither of us could land a clean advantage. Fatigue, not finesse, would decide the victor.

Most duels didn't last this long.

I finally landed a solid blow to his face. His head hadn't even snapped back before he swept my leg out from under me. I hit the ground hard, rolled just as quickly, narrowly dodging the follow-up strike.

Relentless as ever, he adjusted mid-lunge. I blocked with my boot, kicked him back, and scrambled to my feet.

Momentum was both his strength and his downfall. I let him get close again, dodged, snatched his arm, yanked him forward. Growled as I struck for his kidney.

He barely evaded it, crimson blooming beneath his ribs.

Panting, we squared off, then he charged.

Left, right, right, dodge, block, kick, dip, attack.

Each breath was punctuated with two strikes. Faster. Harder. Steel clanged. The hiss of agile footwork wove between grunts and sharp inhales.

The next blow would draw more than blood.

It would draw judgment.

Pain slammed through my skull as his forehead crashed into mine, staggering me back. I choked on a breath, blinking away stars, arms rising just in time to parry his next combination. The floor spun beneath me.

Nix's fury coiled through every muscle as he charged again. I could barely breathe, vision swimming with black spots.

Too slow.

A dull, cold pressure punched through my abdomen with the force of a hammer. My body jolted. My mouth fell open as I realized his blade had struck true—driven deep. Shock stilled everything. I blinked, a guttural sound clawing up my throat as my blade clattered to the stone.

Gasps cut through the haze like razors over my pride as a searing heat spread up my side, liquid warmth running across my skin. A feminine cry pierced the fog—Cali's—sharp with disbelief.

Someone moved in my periphery, but my focus stayed fixed on Nix. I shoved at his chest, grasped at the hilt lodged in me, even as he leaned in, driving it to the guard.

Fuck, that would hurt later.

Nix slammed forward, his free hand closing around my neck as he pressed our faces together in a cruel parody of my father's embrace.

"All this over some cunt who *hasn't even accepted the bond*, cousin?" he growled.

Breathing through the fire licking up my insides was a battle in itself.

"She's fucking pretty," he continued, twisting the blade as he pulled it upward, "but is she worth this?"

"No!" *Cali.*

I wanted to look—wanted to find her—but I was trapped in this moment. Trapped with him.

"She'll be prettier on her knees," Nix snarled, "with her lips around my cock."

Red flooded my vision. More than the blade. More than the pain. *That* was the strike he meant to land.

He needed to break me.

I couldn't let him.

Agony pulsing through me, I anchored myself. Training fell away, leaving only instinct. I leaned into the pain with an agonized groan. Let my body go slack. *Let him* think he'd won.

The world vanished. All that remained was the blade, and the bastard.

"I'll take good care of her," he whispered—vile promise thick with implication.

That would be the last thing my cousin ever said.

With a roar of fury, I cracked my forehead into his. Bone crunched, and I slammed into him, dropped my shoulder, and drove him back. Ducked low. Snatched my blade.

For the first time, *I* advanced.

The world narrowed to a tunnel, my vision locked on *Nix*. Blood poured down his face as he scrambled to defend.

Each breath was a furnace.

Each strike a war drum.

He tried to retreat, but I was rage incarnate—driven by something larger than anger. Larger than pain.

Larger than him.

Snippets of strategy flickered through the fury. Every strike landed harder than the last, my body screaming to stop. But I didn't—*couldn't.*

He'd fed the fire. And now I'd burn him with it.

Freya didn't have to choose me. I had already chosen her. Whatever form that took—bonded or not—her soul was mine.

The universe didn't make mistakes.

Rise, mighty ruler, came the omnipresent voice—male and female, dark and light, Poe and something beyond. *Our people watch you bleed, Prince. Do not let them think you weak.*

Nix dropped low to strike, but I was faster. I twisted over him. By the time I straightened, he was back on his feet, sucking wind, but too late.

I struck—my blade biting into his side. He tried to block but missed, a growl of pain erupting from him.

Next: his wrist. I seized it, twisted, and drove my knee into his gut. His blade clattered to the floor as I raised mine overhead.

He caught my wrists with both hands. We grappled, foot to foot, strength against strength. I hooked his leg and brought him to his knees. The blade inched closer to his throat with every heartbeat. Our groans of effort blurred with the crowd's roaring silence.

"Yield!"

Disbelief simmered through me. One more inch and it would be done.

"Cyrus, I *ordered you* to yield!" *Mother.* Her voice cracked through the storm cloud of my fury.

I hesitated, blade trembling in my grip, eyes locked on Nix's. Anger was a tangible entity, peeling free of my soul as I wrenched away, booting the motherfucker in the chest, toppling him over.

I whirled toward her, chest heaving, blood dripping from my blade.

"*It is my right!*" I bellowed. Murmurs of outrage sparked flames around me—fitting. Their sense of betrayal validated the fire of my own. Paladins did not yield in a sanctioned duel. We did not extend mercy. We won, or we died. I threw a livid arm out toward Nix, where he was fighting his way onto hands and knees. "You rob me of my victory's *honor!*"

"And he will live with this shame," she snapped, steel in every syllable. "Your strength, Cyrus Stuart, is not in taking life but knowing when to spare it. The traitor will live in dishonor, but his death will not be *your* burden."

Weak.

Even now, she made me look *weak.* After everything.

After Poe's declaration. After a duel fought with blood and fire.

In front of the council and our people—she stripped me of the justice I'd earned.

If I hadn't already been sure I hated my mother, I *knew* it now.

Anger in every stride, I moved to Nix, bent down—pain screaming through my gut—and yanked my blade free. Sheathed it. Raised his overhead, basking in a roar of victory.

I straightened, spine tall, turning to let them revel in this. Let them *know*. Their Prince would defend what was his. And should enemies cross him, mercy would *not* come from *me*.

Nix didn't deserve even a glance.

I turned toward the council, sweat stinging, wounds screaming.

Twelve stone faces stared back.

I met each and every one of them. Then I stormed off the stage.

Mother's voice followed me, cutting through the din as I fumed, barely able to breathe.

"You do not get the gift of being a martyr, Nix Landry. You have dishonored your coven and your blood. Your days will be spent in exile for the next hundred years."

Or maybe it wasn't fury making it hard to breathe. Maybe it was the fucking stab wound.

I needed to get to Jo.

THE ARMCHAIR in the corner of my room was going to have a permanent imprint of my ass if this girl didn't wake up soon. Jo had patched me up, and between her and the Middle, all I really needed was a nap. It pissed me off to no end that Nix would probably get the same if they granted him access before shipping the fucker off.

Across the room, Jo flipped through a superhero comic like this was any other Tuesday. Carr walked in looking more exhausted than I felt. He and Cali had followed me to the Middle the moment my mother dismissed the gathering, but something bitter had rooted itself in his expression.

"What?" I snapped. I'd had enough for one day.

"The Six have summoned a conclave."

I stared at him. "What the fuck for?"

"No idea." He shrugged, but there was nothing casual in his voice. "Cali's occupied. Your mother expects you to attend in her stead."

"My mother can get fucked."

"You want to tell her that, or are you asking me to do it? Pretty sure only one of us walks away from that conversation."

"Fuck her."

"I know, man, but listen. That was all very public. If we were worried about infighting with the Wings before—what happened today, after Poe named you Harbinger, is about to split the whole fucking hierarchy in half."

"Good." Let them split. Let the cracks show.

"You say that now, but what about when Cali inherits this mess?"

"Fuck," I groaned, closing my eyes like I could will the world to vanish.

"Go, Cyrus."

"But Freya—"

Carr glanced her way, his expression softening. "If you're implying Jo and I would let anything happen *to your mate*, I swear on my life Nix stabbing you will be the high point of your day."

I snorted, curling forward to brace my elbows on my knees, massaging the throb in my temples. "Thought she was a pain in your ass."

"She is. She'll probably be worse now. But my loyalty's to you. Until you say otherwise, she's mine to protect too."

I held his eyes for a long beat. Then I sighed and shook my head.

A mate from a rival hierarchy we'd just defended with our lives and still didn't fully trust.

A cousin exiled and fuming, who'd never stop trying to prove he deserved a second chance.

A mother who saw her son named a glory-bringer and then stripped him of honor in front of our people.

A council threatening to tear itself apart over a war none of us chose.

Yeah. *Fuck me.*

Three Stuarts, stone-faced and silent, sat at the marble table in the neutral estate The Six used for conclaves.

Normally, they met quarterly—unless something urgent arose. This felt urgent.

More likely, it would be as slow and stupid as every other council meeting: posturing, politicking, and everyone chasing the same drug—control. Three hierarchies had already whispered about seceding from the covenant. But unraveling the old magical contracts would require sacrifices few were willing to make.

This time, it was King Kade of the Necromancers who'd called us here. No one knew why.

Kade *never* called these things. Hell, he barely showed up.

Then again, Moros was worse. His so-called hierarchy was a shadow of a memory—a few dusty descendants clinging to a title with no realm left to rule. His votes were symbolic at best, arbitrary at worst. I wondered if he even knew I now held his psychotic father's sword.

One by one, the hierarchies arrived. The fourth door to open was the one that made me turn.

She walked in like shadow wrapped in silk.

The power around her was *wrong* in all the right ways—coiled, ancient, bone-deep. Not loud, not flashy. Lethal. A red dress hugged full curves with a femininity most souls didn't dare wear. Not my type—but Carr would trip over himself.

My shadows stirred and...*knelt?* As if a queen was in their midst. Like a goddess among men, she wore death like her skin as she lifted her chin—not in deference to the leaders gathered, but in defiance of them.

I liked her instantly.

My power tugged toward her like it had already decided on my behalf, and when I glanced at my mother, her head was tilted in that predator's way—watching, calculating.

The men around the table squirmed, but it wasn't reverence. It was fear. They couldn't see the balance, only the threat. They had no idea what she was. Just that she could end them.

And for once, I didn't mind serving a matriarch. Not when it made me sharper than the idiots around me.

Who is the goddess in red? my mother asked, voice slicing between me and Dad like steel through silk.

Life. And death, Dad replied, as if that explained everything.

Hell, maybe it did. She wasn't a Reaper, or a siphon. But whatever she was, it coiled through the room like a serpent—and I didn't have a better word for it.

She met my eyes, and a chill danced down my spine. Teal blue and electric.

Nathara followed behind and took the seat beside her, confirming my suspicion—Hazelharbor's new second.

Ceremonial introductions followed. Moros, unsurprisingly, was absent. I'd hoped to charm an invite to his estate to advance my search for Freya's diadem but no such luck.

The newcomer? A healer named Magnolia Green. And as luck—or fate —would have it, she was the reason we were here.

"Well," Kade said, slicing through the noise, "Dr. Green, you have the floor, as requested."

All eyes shifted to her.

She stood calm, unyielding. Her tattooed fingers laced, and chin lifted. She reminded me of Freya.

When the room went silent, she said, "I motion to repeal the Guardianship Law for Matriarchal hierarchies."

Chaos descended like a storm nobody saw coming. Voices exploded across the table. Men shouting over one another, too small-minded to even let the witch talk. Tradition gripping their throats like nooses snapped taut.

My mother stayed silent—studying Magnolia like a puzzle piece she'd half-suspected existed.

You'll vote in her favor, I asked, mind-to-mind. More statement than question. I turned, staring at both my parents stony faces.

Calypso had begged us to leave the council for years—for the freedom to love who she wanted, when she wanted. She was twice the soul and three times the mind of anyone here.

But if she ever took a male to bed after the magic marked her Heiress, that soul would be bound by law, their fate sealed.

Fucking archaic.

That enchantment should've been gone generations ago.

My mother was quiet for an eternity before finally replying.

Yes.

FORTY-SIX

THE WRAITH

FREYA

A silky-smooth cloud cradled my bare skin, and I nestled into the warmth of absolute bliss. Tugging the plush comforter up to my chest, I buried my face in it. So stinking cozy. My body actually felt rested—for the first time in... God, when had I last felt balanced? I couldn't remember. Certainly not in the last six weeks.

Inhaling deeply, I soaked up the scent—cedarwood, leather, and... *tobacco.*

I jackknifed upright.

My hands flew out to steady myself, fingers sinking into the softest comforter I'd ever touched in my life. Gasping, I took in the unfamiliar room. Enormous stone walls, an art collection that would make most curators weep, an entire wall of perfectly straightened bookshelves. Opposite that, four cathedral windows framed a soft gray light.

Disoriented, I blinked rapidly, then looked down at my body.

That was definitely not a tac suit.

I was wearing someone else's silky cami and a pair of cute boyshorts—and *were my boobs bigger?*

What. The. Fuck.

Had my biceps gotten more defined, or had I lost my mind?

And Jesus—were those my quads?

Blinking, comprehension hit me like a slap. I bolted from the bed and sprinted to the windows, clapping a hand over my mouth as I stared out at Paladin's Middle Realm.

Oh. Holy. Shit.

I twisted, stretched, squinted.

"Why *the fuck* am I still small?" I barked, scowling at the same damned perspective I'd always had. Nothing had changed. Or...everything had?

Big nap. Big, healer-induced ascension nap. And *oh my God—that asshole shot me. What the fuck. What the* actual *fuck?*

A sting on my scalp made me realize I was about to rip my hair out—I was already tearing my fingers through it like a madwoman.

I spun around when someone knocked on the door, reaching instinctively for weapons that weren't there as the massive black double doors creaked open.

"Freya?" asked a familiar husky voice, careful and soft—as if *Calypso-fucking-Stuart* was tiptoeing inside her own castle.

"Um. Present," I blurted like a total imbecile.

"Oh, thank the Saints—you scared us to death."

Hah. What?

The Paladin princess stepped inside, shutting the door with a gentle click. Her smile was sweeter than I deserved, and her steps slow, measured. She stopped near the end of the bed, leaving plenty of space between us. Not nervous. Just...respectful.

"Where...I'm sorry, but where's Cyrus?" I asked.

"You're probably freaking out," she said with a grimace, easing down onto the mattress.

"Uh...yeah. A little," I admitted. Where were my weapons? I promised Alvara I'd bring back her dirk. *Alvara—*what the hell was wrong with that woman?! *She let me get shot?!*

"Understandable," Cali said. "Jo was here until a few minutes ago, but they needed her Earthbound to attend to something. I hope you don't mind me covering for her. He doesn't want you alone...for obvious reasons."

Sure. Understandable. The feral demon who tore his life to bits probably shouldn't be left unsupervised.

My thoughts snagged on Jo.

Jo, the nimble-fingered healer—soon-to-be consort to Calypso—who dug that goddamned reaper bullet out of my chest with metal tools of death.

"Oh, this is so fucked."

"Everything kinda hittin' at once, darlin'?" Calypso asked, voice gentle.

"You could say that," I breathed, a hand flying to cover my mouth. I turned and paced toward the window, bare feet sinking into the most luxurious golden rug I'd ever touched. Of all the hierarchy realms I'd seen, this one was the most beautiful. Cascading fountains. An ornate rose garden maze. The healing baths...

Oh.

Images flickered behind my eyes. Cyrus lowering me into some copper pool of goo—healing salve, my clearer mind now corrected. Bit by bit, the pieces clicked into place, and dread sank into my stomach like a stone.

Calypso, furious, barking orders.

Pain. Endless, soul-rending pain.

Golden-hazel eyes stricken with agony. A metronome heartbeat under my fingers.

Cyrus...claiming me as his mate. Offering absolution.

Oh God. He'd meant it.

My heart bolted. Like it could outrun what had happened—what was *still* happening.

Cyrus and Calypso, cleaning the blood from my skin.

Jo and Calypso, guiding me into the clothes I now wore.

Long stretches of darkness, interrupted by citrine eyes watching from above a book he wasn't reading. A quiet gathering of Paladins at the foot of the bed.

Talking about me.

Lying for me.

Fuck me.

"Where is Cyrus?" I asked again, this time sharper—my voice one thread from unraveling. I turned—and found myself face to face with Calypso. She'd stepped closer without me noticing, now holding two cups of coffee, lifting one toward me.

Behind her, a gorgeous espresso bar gleamed—copper and warm wood, with a milk frother to boot.

Last time I saw this woman, I was strung up in chains. She'd watched like it was a chess match.

"I added something stronger," she said. "Seems like it's gonna be a long morning."

"First—thank you," I said, accepting the mug and sniffing it deeply. No way I wasn't checking it first.

She grinned. "If I was gonna poison you, we'd have just left that bullet in your chest."

"Touché." I took a long sip. Bailey's. Definitely Bailey's. A warm, blessed burn followed. So—Reaper bullets could be survived, apparently. If you got to them fast enough. I didn't want to know how many hadn't.

"Second—why are you being so nice to me? Third—how long was I out? And fourth—*where is Cyrus?*"

"First, you're welcome. Second, because I always liked you. After you ransacked my labs, you returned *everything*—and your notations were wildly helpful. Genuinely. Unconventional, but effective. After Cyrus filled me in, I chose to forgive you," she said, rapid-fire, her breezy Southern cadence somehow making it all harder to absorb. "As for three—you were healin' for about twenty-four hours. Then you dropped into an ascension sleep for another sixty."

Sixty?

"Cyrus didn't wanta' leave you," she added, "but if the plan's gonna work, he had to act quickly."

"Plan?" I asked, gulping down mouthfuls of the burning liquid. Sixty divided by twenty-four was…God, I was not awake enough for math. Just over two, plus one for healing.

Three and a half days.

I'd missed *three* days.

As if realizing it flicked a switch, my body suddenly screamed in protest—my stomach trying to crawl up my spine in search of food, my throat dry as the damn Sahara.

"Start with coffee. Let me summon Cyrus—he should really be the one to explain everything."

"You know, I, uh…" I set the cup down on an antique side table, head spinning. My heart pounded. If Reagan got her hands on me, I was twelve kinds of dead. I needed out. *Abort mission.* Finding a door home with Aren suddenly sounded like the greatest idea I'd ever had. Better that than getting my throat slit. *Again.* "I should be going. Really. Thank you—so much—for, uh, not killing me, for the clothes, and the *coffee.*"

"Freya." Her voice softened. Sympathy carved a fine line between her brows. "Cyrus went to great lengths to ensure you're safe here."

"Right," I muttered, more scoff than statement. Great. I mirrored her careful calm and tried for sincerity. "I appreciate it—truly—but I need to go home. Trust me, you don't want my brother banging down your door looking for me."

"Jax? He's been brought up to speed."

That name didn't track. A throb of confusion pulsed in my temple. Jax? *Ajax.*

Oh God. They didn't know about August.

"I have to warn you—Cyrus doesn't offend easily, but if you puke on his Persian rug, that might do it."

"What?" My voice cracked at least an octave too high.

"You look a lil' peaky," she said, making a face. "Try sittin'. Head between your knees."

"I had a stroke."

"What?"

"That's what this is," I declared definitively. "I'm having a stroke. It's fine. I'm *fine.* I'll just—uh—be going so I can die at home. Thanks!"

She called my name, but I was already moving, throwing open the door—

—and slamming into a wall of...man back.

Big. Broad. Impossibly still.

Carrson stood like the King's damn Guard, gaze shifting over his shoulder with all the warmth of a glacier.

"Oh look," he said, dry as dust. "It wakes."

"Morning, Fluffy. Mind pointing me to the gate?"

"What?" he snapped, blinking.

"She thinks she needs to leave," Calypso explained, suddenly at my side, making me jump so hard my heart probably lodged itself somewhere near Carrson's kidneys.

"Stop doing that!" I barked. She looked genuinely confused. Slightly offended. "The just-appearing-out-of-nowhere thing. It's terrifying."

"Oh," she said, laughing. Then to Carrson, "Anyway. She wants to go home."

Carrson's eyes went wide. Outrage flared. He glanced down both ends of the hallway, then turned and grabbed my arm like I was a misbehaving toddler.

"Hey!" I barked, wrenching back. "Touch me again and I will bite your hand off. I'm starving."

"We have *food*, you savage," he growled.

"Look, *Lassie*, I am four days deep into a fever dream from hell and four days behind on plans that cannot afford to be meddled with, and it is time for *this* pain in your ass to go annoy someone else. Got it?"

I swore to God, the two of them blinked at me like synchronized sloths.

"Is she serious?" Carrson asked.

"It would appear so."

"After everything Cyrus fucking did to protect you? Are you kidding me?"

I practically squeaked, "What? Look, we entered that crypt—"

"Not the crypt, you colossal jackass," he snapped. "The man has bent over backwards to keep you safe. You don't just run off—"

"Excuse me?" I snapped, heat exploding behind my eyes. "Listen here, *Shilo*, I don't know who you think you are, but nobody tells me what to do. People who try? It ends *badly* for them."

"Oh, will you please *shut up*?" he bit out, knuckles whitening where his hand hovered over his blade.

"I don't think I will. Tha—"

"*Freya!*" he barked, the sharpness of it cutting clean through my tirade. I went still. "Listen to me. Cyrus had to act fast to keep you here and not in a cell. You get that, right?"

I looked around again. Took in the room. The art, the espresso bar, the castle-sized bed.

And it hit all at once—what he'd done. What they'd *all* done.

Calypso stepped forward, her voice gentler than his. "What my cousin means is—we know this is overwhelming. Ascension's hard even when you *choose* it. But Freya—Cyrus defended you. He stood in front of the council. He *dueled Nix.*"

The floor disappeared.

Vision spun.

Chest tightened.

Head pounded.

Heart raced.

Fear dug into my ribs with its claws and tried to rip out what little calm I had left.

When I finally managed to speak, my voice barely existed. "Is he—?"

"He's fine!" Calypso rushed to say, stepping closer. Concern darkened her eyes. "He won."

Why did those two words hit me like a punch to the sternum?

Relief geysered up, unbidden and unwanted. My eyes stung, breathing shallow.

I didn't even *like* the bastard.

So why did I *care* that he was still breathing?

The relief soured quickly into guilt.

"Nix is..." My gaze shifted to Carrson. He didn't look grieved—just pissed.

"Exiled," Cali said, concern yielding to a flicker of anger. "*Mother* forced Cy to yield, but *he won*, Freya. Gloriously. It was dicey for a minute —always is with a proper match—but he came out on top."

My hands gripped my head, as if that could hold the information inside. "I think I sit now."

A breathy laugh escaped her as she guided me to a settee beside a coffee table stacked with treats.

She was being nice. But there were few things I loathed more than feeling like someone's punchline. And if she wasn't Cyrus' sister—and hadn't just kept me from falling off the edge of existence—I might've punched her square in the throat.

This *wasn't* funny.

Nothing about this was *funny*.

I was vaguely aware of her gently pressing my head between my knees, rubbing my back. Vaguely aware of Carrson growling about what the fuck was wrong with me, and Cali scolding him for being an insensitive asshole. But the toilet bowl that was my brain was already spiraling. Fast. And I was the captain of this shit-boat circling the drain.

Because my killer's *son* was my mate.

My killer's. Son. Was my *mate?*

No.

Nope. Nope. Hard pass.

I hadn't clawed my way back to this realm for a reunion. I'd come to return the favor—end the one who ended me. Reagan Stuart had broken the most sacred of the Accords, and I was going to hold her to it. I didn't give a damn if fate had decided to play matchmaker in the meantime.

Reagan Stuart. Must. Die.

"*Freya.*"

I did not crawl out of Satan's asshole of a crypt for giggles and a good time. No. I'd finished two of my trials. I'd reclaimed a relic, at great personal cost, and returned it to the bloodline. And the first trial—the one that started in Uptown—still wasn't done. I needed that platform. Needed to take back what was mine. Assuming the oracle believed I still had the power to do it.

God. What if I didn't? What if this body hadn't *grown* the way it should've? Could a soul come back weaker?

"*Freya...*"

To my knowledge, reincarnation meant upgrades. More power. More gifts. More knowledge. There was no fear in death because every rebirth carried forward a sharper blade. But now my chest was pounding, fingers tingling as ice roared through my veins—and something else. Slithering. Familiar. Serpentine. Power I hadn't felt in years, rippling under my skin like a beast uncaged.

"*Frey—*"

If I couldn't win—*couldn't beat her*—then all of this was for nothing. I'd have to run. Abandon everything. Tell Ally, tell Aren...and disappear into the North. But even then, they'd hunt me. I'd secured Bellaton, but that was just one piece of—

A thunderous crack shattered the room.

My head snapped up, hand flying for the metal tray on the table. Fight first, process later.

Cyrus stood in the doorway, hazel eyes wide and locked on mine. Panic radiated from him.

Then I heard the thuds.

Cali and Carrson were on the floor. Crumpled. Motionless.

I shot to my feet.

"What the fuck—what's happening?" I choked out.

Cyrus was already moving, pushing through some invisible wall with his eyes squeezed shut like he was in agony. I backed up until the bed hit the backs of my knees, heart hammering as I looked between the two fallen bodies.

"Pull it back," Cyrus gritted out.

"What?"

"You're...draining them," he gasped, staggering as his hand clutched at the armchair for support.

I blinked. No. No, I—

Oh, fuck.

Siphon.

I was siphoning. *Stealing* their power.

"No." It came out as a gasp—a feral, cornered thing with too many teeth and nowhere to go.

Cyrus stumbled toward me, hand flying to his ear like something inside had burst. "I won't...let them...*you're safe,*" he wheezed, his hands suddenly cupping my face, as if by touching me he could force stillness into the storm. "You have to stop. Find a safe *space.* Anchor yourself, Freya. Or you'll kill us." He cradled my cheeks, his hands warm and disproportionately gentle. His skin, too pale.

His thumb stroked the scar we shared, even as the color drained from his face.

I shook my head. "I don't have one," I whispered, panic unraveling every breath. "There's never been one."

Not in this life. Not in any.

No safe space. Only war zones.

I reached for the edges of my power—but there were no edges. Just a vast, endless abyss. I couldn't find the border. Couldn't draw it in. Couldn't—

"I—" It was a whimper. A broken, breathless plea as I tried to pull away, tried to keep my skin from leeching the life from his. He was fading. His legs wobbling. I didn't know how to stop. I didn't know how to—

Without warning, his hand dropped to the back of my neck, and he dragged me forward, slamming his lips onto mine.

FORTY-SEVEN
FEELINGS–GROSS.

FREYA

The world fell away, and in its place was heat—and the pliant demand of Cyrus' mouth opening mine.

He was the heart of a hurricane—direct and relentless—until my defenses collapsed and his fury poured in. He was shadow and demand, and the crackling finale of a summer bonfire all at once. Every synapse slowed, zeroing in on the scrape of his stubble, the press of his mouth, and the way directive fingers gripped my neck and wove into my hair, wordlessly ordering me to submit.

My panic melted beneath the intensity. Before I could think or feel or *breathe*, I was kissing him back—my lips following every coaxing, commanding movement. My hands fisted in the lapels of his peacoat, yanking him closer until the length of his lean body pressed flush against mine, all cedarwood and leather and heat.

Bit by bit, his touch soothed the jagged edges of my overloaded mind. I felt the machinery start clicking back into place beneath the scrape of his teeth and the grounding squeeze of his hand. Then I was breathing again. My power—my out-of-control magic—spooled into my chest, settling behind its walls. Brick by brick, with every flick of his tongue and drag of his lips, Cyrus reassembled the shield I should never have dropped.

Only when I could take in proper lungfuls of air did he ease back. Our foreheads remained bowed together, breaths syncing in the stillness.

"I'm sorry," we panted simultaneously.

His apology was a rough rasp that didn't sound the least bit sorry. Mine was a breathless plea for forgiveness—for the lapse in control that nearly wrecked us both.

"No," I blurted. "*I* lost it. I should've known better than to let my emotions boil over like that."

"I shouldn't have touched you."

"I just got so overwhelmed. I should've slowed down, found a place to—"

"I didn't know how else to get you to—"

"Think," we finished together.

Cyrus exhaled a huff, leaning away slowly. His full lips were kiss-swollen, his long hair mussed. I hadn't realized I'd tangled my hands in it until my fingers lost their grip. He raised his palms in surrender and backed toward the settee, sinking onto the cushions. I lowered onto the bed, my shoulders finally loosening.

He rubbed the back of his neck, tongue skimming a canine as he fought a grin. "My bad."

"No. *Thank you,*" I said quickly. "You saved me. *Oh my God—Cali and Carrson!*"

I shot up, but he raised a hand before I could move.

"They'll be alright. Just...knocked out."

"I'm so sorry."

"Don't be. I should've been here." His brows rose. "Plus, now I've got ammo against Carr indefinitely."

"If *he'd* kissed me, the reaction would've been very different."

A smile tugged at the corner of his mouth. He nodded. "Yeah. Maybe."

"I should go," I murmured, brushing my fingers across my tingling lips.

"We need to talk."

"I was afraid you'd say that."

"But first," he said, nodding toward my chest, "you have to burn some of that off. Or you can try to funnel it back—if you don't think you'll hurt them."

"I've never had this gift before," I admitted. "I feel like I should call Aren or something."

"I figured. I've been reading up on siphons the last few days while you slept. Whatever we're doing, we need to hurry. Magic *hates* being bottled up—it'll force its way out when you least expect it."

"We?"

"I think the last few days have made *we* pretty essential. Don't you?"

"I got the Cali and Carrson *Reader's Digest* version. Care to fill me in?"

"Only if you eat something while I do."

"God, yes," I breathed.

Cyrus nodded, watching me—either scanning for fissures in my control or taking in the changes. Maybe both. I had to look like hell. I silently vowed to find the nearest bathroom and reclaim my dignity.

"I think I downed three days' worth of food in one sitting when I ascended. And mine didn't even take as long as yours."

"Is it a race?" I shot back, earning a twitch of his lips.

"There she is. I was wondering how long it would take for the pain-in-the-ass to resurface."

"First—rude. Second—I could eat."

"I'll get you something. Then we'll talk. After that, we've gotta siphon some of that energy out—or you're not gonna like the results." When I nodded, he did the same. "Bathroom's through the black door by the bookshelf. Towels are in the first cabinet on the left."

"Are you saying I stink?"

"What would you say if I was?"

Wrinkling my nose, I muttered, "Sounds about right."

"Would it kill you to say thank you?"

"Probably."

"Go. Clock's ticking."

I nodded and scurried away like a damn mouse—then froze, grimacing at the sight of his souls crumpled on the floor.

"I should..."

"I've got 'em," he said. "Go, Freya. You're in for a bitch of a wake-up call. Take a minute."

ABOUT AN HOUR LATER—SHOWERED, dressed in clean clothes they'd left out for me, and nauseatingly full after shoveling down everything Cyrus put in front of me—I sat dumbstruck on his luxurious sofa while he watched me from the seat across the room. Sometimes he studied me. Other times, he just stared out at the Paladin grounds like the weight of the world was still on his shoulders.

For someone so devoted to avoiding the emotions of life...I was *drowning* in mine.

Denial had led the charge, right up until he described what he felt in the cemetery—how viscerally my pain had echoed through him. And some part of me, deep in the soul that had once died under his mother's blade, *believed him.*

Every time I opened my mouth, confusion yanked my tongue back down. Cyrus, having said all he needed, seemed content to sit in the thick, suffocating blanket of *what the actual fuck.*

The Prince and his coven had ensured my autonomy when I couldn't.

They'd defended me. He'd strategized with a truth-sayer. Fought his own cousin in trial by combat to defend both my honor and his own. But he'd also forged documents naming Calypso as my Crucible sponsor—something I hadn't even *thought* about since assuming Reagan's endorsement still stood.

This was...better.

And worse.

Worse, because I'd only intended to implicate Reagan in both my prior and current recruitment—so that she alone would face the hierarchy's scrutiny.

Better, because the Accords had changed in the decades I'd missed, and there was a high probability Cyrus had just saved my mission by condemning Calypso alongside me should I fail. It was only the fact that he'd spoken and acted for me—without even asking—that had temper poisoning the gesture. Not that I could claim I'd have thought of a better solution that quickly. He'd reacted fast after I'd unintentionally backed him into a corner.

Gratitude. Anger. Terror. Resentment. Endearment. Each emotion took a swing at me like a bat to a piñata, and I knew it was only a matter of time before the mess inside came spilling out across the carpet.

Emotions always sent *everything* sideways. They had no place in strategy or war—and yet I was drowning in them as I tried to process what I'd missed and what was still left to do.

The truth was, war was coming. And I needed Cyrus's army at my back when it did.

Reagan couldn't be allowed to lead the continent's largest legion of shadows into the next era. Alvara had tried her best with Pinebarrow and Carroway, but both had overseas territories to protect. We had Bellaton, yes —and their blades were sharp—but they had half the shadow walkers. Knowing Adrastos thrived in the dark realm made my personal vendetta feel practically strategic. And if Ally and August's source was right, The Six would likely back Adrastos—all except for the Necromancers and Hazelharbor, who'd become a target the second they stood against the majority.

No. I couldn't *afford* to feel. Couldn't afford to navigate from this place of panic and fractured loyalties.

Cyrus would probably hate me when the truth came out—bond or no bond. That thing between us had already bent the truth, already kept one or both of us from striking when we should have. His hesitation in Uptown. Mine in those rafters. Even as kids, we'd instinctively protected each other from opposite sides of the war.

I felt his gaze on my profile like a strike of heat against my skin.

Was there chemistry between us? Undeniably.

But that didn't erase the mission. It didn't change the fact that the war ahead would take more than either of us was ready to give. Adding another vulnerability to the list would be unspeakably foolish.

Straightening, I said, "Okay. Thank you. For everything. You've shown me more kindness than I deserve. But...I need to go home, Cyrus. We both have a lot to process."

"As our fates are now permanently interwoven," he said evenly, "don't you think that's something we might wanna do together?"

"Why? It's not like you signed up to be shackled to me any more than I did you. Unless you've got some record in one of those books of yours proving this is reversible, I'm not sure there's much left to discuss."

His jaw flexed, those bright hazels sparking with something untenable, and I braced for the backlash.

"You think I wanted this?" His laugh was humorless, a rough scrape through his chest. "Believe me—if there'd been a way out, I'd have taken it before you even opened your eyes. But there's not. And even if there was... with everything you did to earn your place here, you're telling me you'd take it?"

"You don't know what you're talking about."

"Don't I? You're telling me you're not replicating your trials from your time as Valora?"

"I never said I wanted to complete the Crucible."

"And your deflection was answer enough." He crossed one arm under the other, elbow raised so his knuckles rested against his mouth—a posture I'd started to recognize as his thinking stance. "I think you *will* finish this. Whatever *this* is. And at least now, Cali and I paved the path for you to do it well."

"You have no idea what you just did."

"Then tell me."

I was already shaking my head, eyes on the mouth I hadn't stopped thinking about since he kissed me. "Believe me—plausible deniability is your friend right now."

"It would be. If this were about human authorities." He leaned forward slightly. "But you're stepping onto the territory of the Queen of Paladin. So hear me: leaving me in the dark does nothing to protect either of us. I've claimed you publicly as my mate. That makes you mine to protect."

I tried to soften my voice, my expression, my tone along with it, but some bitter concoction of fear and frustration laced every word. "Ahh, but see...you can't protect me from this."

"You're right. If you declare your petition publicly, you're bound to face the final step."

"The duel."

"And I can't interfere once you do."

"I'm *already* obligated to finish."

"Right. And why is that?" he asked, voice chilling.

"Beyond your clearance."

"So, you are here as a spy."

I let out a humorless laugh. "Aren doesn't need more spies. He has them everywhere he finds value."

"Impossible. We don't have Crucible-blessed souls in our ranks—and how else would they get here?"

"Hmm...how else do Paladins earn their blades, young Prince?" I stood, sighing when he did too.

"We're not done here."

"Look, Cyrus." I stepped around him, toward the souls pulsing uncomfortably under my skin. "Like I said—I appreciate what you did. But I didn't ask you to risk your life for me, and you're not obligated to keep doing it."

"Oh, but I am," he growled, grabbing my elbow and freezing me midstep.

His stare was so sharp, so piercing it sent my heart tumbling down a flight of stairs.

"Let go of me."

But he didn't. He pulled me in closer, shaking his head. "You're acting like this bond is some kind of mistake."

"That's not what I said," I snapped, dizzy with the force of his nearness and the scent of him. It was unfair. It was *cruel*—that fate had marked a man I couldn't have as the one I was meant for.

Had I done this? Had Reagan? Had that damn marriage contract she drafted a decade before he was even conceived tampered with his threads?

If fate had a face, I would cheerfully rearrange it with my bare fists. If only to wipe away the hurt I couldn't unsee in his eyes.

Because I fucking cared.

"You didn't circle the wrong answer on a test, Freya." His voice dropped low, laced with fire. "Like it or not, I'm not something you can erase from your lifeline. And you? You're etched into mine."

"You didn't choose this. We don't even *know each other*, Cyrus."

"I know enough."

I scoffed. "So now you're going to profess undying love after one disastrous grand adventure?"

"Who said anything about *love*?" he bit out, annoyance sharpening with every pushback I gave. "I've always known my role. My duty. My honor. But let's not forget—*you're* the one who stormed into *my world* and tore it apart. I should hate you."

"Should?" I breathed as he stepped closer, crowding into my space. "You don't?"

He rolled his lips against his teeth, slowly shaking his head. His grip didn't ease on my arm. "Can't. *Apparently*. And I have a feeling neither could you. Not *then*, even when I deserved it. Not now, when you know what I am. There's a reason for that."

"I never pegged you for a fate person."

"I'm not."

"Then why are you bending so easily?"

"Because some things are bigger than us. And I'm not so egotistical I can't recognize when the Universe is moving."

"The universe has bigger fish to fry than our doomed romance."

"Mates can be platonic," he offered, with a shrug so indifferent I almost believed it.

I shook my head. "I can't channel my soul group mates' feelings, and we're already nauseatingly interdependent."

"Whatever this is, it's not that."

"Then why can't I hear you in my head? Aren't mates connected like hierarchies?"

"Only if they accept the bond. I thought you were the experienced one."

"In *life cycles*, not mates. Obviously. I'm as new at this as you are."

Finally, he let go, raking his fingers through his hair. My gaze dropped to his lips as he wet them—traitorous instincts reacting to every damn detail. What kind of aphrodisiac was this bond?

"Just let me get this out. I'm not a verbal fucking processor."

I raised my hands, signaling surrender.

"All those roles—prince, shadow, Crew..." He arched a brow, and I thought of that teenage boy leading his pack with quiet detachment. "They were all chosen *for me*. Every decision made by others. Which coven raised me. Which I led. My roles with the Wings. When I could speak. When I couldn't. Cali and I learned to work within those lines while bending them to suit ourselves. But I chose you, Freya."

"The *bond* chose *for* you," I said flatly. No point pretending otherwise.

He was already shaking his head. "No. I punched Nix that night and chased after *you*. Because it went too far, and you were scared, and I needed to know you were okay."

I remembered how violently he'd turned on the docks—how he took the impact. Just like on the rooftop. Just like in the crypt. Whether he realized it or not, the bond had likely guided every one of those moments.

"Again, when you proposed our bargain."

"You chose *the crown*."

"You would've been the more valuable prize."

"I never said you had good judgment."

"And I chose you in that crypt."

Damn it. Valid. He didn't have to stay behind. Didn't have to fight for me. But again—

"The bond—"

"Didn't *make me* stab Nix on that platform. Didn't make me twist the truth and *claim you* to protect you from my mother. Those were my calls. And I'd make them again. I got my Wings, by the way."

The bitter words cut deeper than intended. My eyes dropped to his arms as he reached for his coat. And then—

He shrugged out of it, revealing feet of glorious ink.

I stepped forward before I could stop myself, grabbing his wrist and turning it. He let me.

My fingers traced the feathers inked up his arm, and goosebumps chased in their wake. His wings swallowed his old tattoos, all except the hooded angel on the back of his hand. Awe stirred in my chest.

Sweet baby Jesus. I wasn't the only one who needed to see the Oracle.

This could change...*everything.*

Paladin lore told of a leader who would bring a golden age. One marked by wings etched from spine to wrists.

Reagan and I always believed it would be an Heiress.

"Are they...?"

"Yeah. My whole back."

I met his gaze and regretted it. His eyes were a breathtaking storm—fury and conviction brewing in equal measure.

"How did Cali take it?"

"Like I said. Whatever this is...it's bigger than us. She sees that." He took back his arm and smoothed his shirt. "I've studied too much for too long to pretend it's not connected. I don't have to *want you* to see that we're tethered. I didn't even have to *like you* to know I wasn't worthy of Poe's endorsement until I chose you over myself. Over my honor. So hear me when I say, I will keep choosing you, Freya. Even if you hate me for it."

FORTY-EIGHT
BAPTISM BY RAIN
ALVARA

FREYA

Maybe next time I'mma get shot, give me a head's up, mmmmkay?

ALLY

But did you die?

FREYA

multiple middle finger emojis

ALLY

That's what I thought.

Okay, so Freya wasn't the only Porter chapped about my lack of interference—but where this war was concerned, it seemed the more I directly meddled, the worse our odds became. Letting our people choose their own threads remained the best shot at landing on the right one. Adrastos had finally fallen silent over the past week.

No dreams of him or our memories.

No vision tennis.

The clarity was both refreshing and alarming. Refreshing because I'd almost forgotten what it was like to cast threads without someone jamming their oversized fingers into the weave. Alarming, because...where was he, if not terrorizing *me?*

With clarity came conviction. Had I interfered, Freya would have returned to us a hollow caricature of the woman we knew and loved—Bellaton at her back, but loyal to Reyna. That wouldn't be an issue, except for the fact that the Queen would swoop in the second Grayshell showed weakness. And it would. Sooner than I liked, no matter which thread we ended up in.

Whatever Freya's plan was, it was uniting the river-split hierarchies for the first time in centuries.

And she needed their prince at her back to do it.

There were threads ahead where she failed—but not in the one I'd chosen not to touch.

August and I had been plenty occupied, anyway. Between Kingsley, Alec, Marcus, and Aren, the four of them had drafted us a brutal training schedule focused on honing our gifts now that the Bond was in play. With twice the power behind my mental punch, I could force memories into minds at ten times the rate and accuracy—without even *touching* them. The problem? I tended to overload people, and they passed out.

Like *Alec*. Currently laying at my feet.

I nudged him with my boot, grimacing as he rolled limply onto his back, brow creased even in sleep.

"Sorry," I whispered, annoyed that I felt like a newborn all over again.

On August's side, drawing from my well amped both his shield and his ability to alter emotions—like Alec's. Except if I was honest, my mate was better. Which was helpful, considering Alec's very pregnant wife was *very* anxious about him volunteering as our guinea pig. August kept her dreamily calm as she grew Marcus a winding vine of bold fuchsia blooms that had already swallowed half his trellis.

Kneeling beside Alec, I tapped his nose, borrowing a pinch of August's energy to jolt him awake. Alec slapped at my hand like a fly, blinking up at the perfect prairie afternoon.

"You always did have a shocking personality."

"*Boo*," I said. "If you start cracking dad jokes before the baby's even here, we're gonna have beef."

"The grass-fed kind?"

Rolling my eyes, I yanked him to his feet. "I swear to God, Alec."

"You might wanna stop that. Pretty sure it's in the commandments."

"I should've left you a ground potato."

He chuckled, rubbing the back of his neck like he was ready to go again. "What's next? You showed me fire animals and—"

"Nothing," I cut in, shaking my head. "That's enough for one day."

"I dunno. Can you do it without melting my brain yet?"

Grimacing, I shrugged. "It's harder than I expected."

"That's what she said."

"*Oh my God*, Alec!" I shoved him in the chest. He staggered back, laughing like a lunatic. "Will you grow up?"

"So I can be as boring as the rest of you? I don't think so."

"For fuck's sake."

"Have you ever thought about that phrase?" he asked as we turned for the house. August was reading on the porch swing, Fae crooning to her new plants. In the west pasture, Marcus and Eloise were tending to their horses —sickeningly adorable, as usual. Somewhere in the farmhouse, Damien and Tessa were grumbling about failing to catch Adrastos in their nets. "Well?" Alec nudged when I didn't answer.

"No, I can't say that I have."

"It's just funny, isn't it? Like—the fuck is possessive of the sake. For *fuck's* sake. The sake belongs to the fuck. But that raises the question of sentient fucks, and that's a whole other philosophical rabbit hole."

"Have you been diagnosed yet?"

"Like *your* brain doesn't run down bunny trails?"

Sure. Mine just...ran darker. "So the fuck owns the sake."

"There's my girl!" He threw a fist in the air. "Knew you were in there somewhere."

"Watch it," August warned from the swing. Possessive August really did things to me he shouldn't have.

"Oh come on, rookie. She's like—a best friend. Like a loyal doggo, if you will."

August looked up at last, expression flat as he stared straight ahead.

Laughing, I said, "Comparing me to a dog didn't win you any points back."

"Tough crowd today."

We split up at the porch and I stepped up to join August, where he swayed in the chilly breeze, flipping another page.

"You ready?" I asked.

"Just about. You?"

"For a night with you? Always."

The smile he gave me barely reached his eyes, and it twisted something in my chest.

After everything—the staggering welcome, the warmth of this place—it was jarring when August experienced his first full-blown hierarchy rejection. The Aegis were a moderately sized hierarchy of healers—smaller than Hazelharbor, but better at battlefield medicine, where the witches of the west relied on terrain and controlled environments. We needed every healer we could find. But the threads had been divided on which way they'd go.

And our visit had been...

Less than welcoming.

To put it nicely.

He'd been a broody little storm cloud ever since.

It was one thing to know that human delegates were resistant to allying with the same creatures poised to wreak havoc on the world—or to know a hierarchy was choosing to stay neutral, or simply refusing to respond. But it was another thing entirely to be turned away when all you were asking for was help healing the wounded.

Alec hesitated halfway through the doorway, popping his head back out. "Where are you two off to?"

"Concert in Manhattan," I said brightly, hoping the reminder might lift August's mood. "There's a pianist he loves performing with a ballet. The whole theater's lit by candlelight, with aerial artists suspended over the stage—it should be magnificent."

"Hmm."

"What?" August asked flatly. Almost...irritable.

"Nothing. Just. You've been going on a lot of outings lately."

"Got a problem with being a patron of the arts?"

"Of course not. But, I mean...didn't you hit up a hockey game the other day? And literally go to Italy the next?"

"Got. A *point?*" August growled, snapping his book shut and pinning Alec with a look that told anyone with two brain cells to *shut up*. "Some of us actually believe in romancing our women, Alec. She's endured more lives with me than anyone should have to—she deserves to enjoy whatever the hell she wants."

"I wouldn't call them *enduring* you," I muttered, half affronted, half touched. "You're the love of my lives."

His expression softened instantly, those agonizing eyes revealing far too much as he stepped toward me. "And you're mine. In *every* encore."

Nodding, I leaned in, resting my forehead against his and drinking in his heat. "Come on," I whispered. "You always love me in that little sparkly dress."

"I do," he said, brushing a kiss across my brow and jerking his chin toward the door. I turned to lead us out through the bustling farmhouse, but I could still feel Alec's gaze boring into the back of my head. His walls had slammed up—hard and sharp like stone—and my stomach twisted.

AUGUST

SAM

Hey, bro. Missing you.

AUGUST

Miss you too.

JAMES

Sure, when it's you, he'll answer.

AUGUST

Sorry, been busy.

SAM

You at fault for the weather anomalies?

AUGUST

I plead the fifth.

SAM

LMAO I knew it. You fucking psycho.

JAMES

Dammit, big brother. You just lost me twenty bucks.

SAM

I expect it on my desk in the morning. And one of those frappes

JAMES

Kiss my ass.

How are you, man? We've heard jack shit in months. How's your beautiful bride?

OBJECTIVELY, this was exactly my scene.

Or...it had been. Back when I was human.

But during the concert—one of the most acclaimed pianists of our generation playing alongside a full ballet, candlelight flickering across the theater—my skin felt numb. Our days before the portals were thinning, and with every one spent, the threads frayed. Every strike chipped at the armor I'd worked so hard to rebuild, and I could feel myself burrowing deeper into the quiet despair.

James' last message echoed in my mind: *How's your beautiful bride?*

Not great.

Not really.

Even with Adrastos finally falling silent, Alvara was still haunted. Still carrying the weight of lives she couldn't save. Still believing her lack of interference might as well be wielding the blade herself.

I wasn't asking her to simply choose a better thread.

In her heart, I was asking her to *murder* our *family*.

And that burden—it was unspeakable.

She straightened in her seat as the dancers dipped and spun with impossible grace. The music soared, but I couldn't look away from her. Creamy skin aglow against the shimmering fabric hugging her muscled lines, Alvara was a vision in black. She didn't wear much makeup but always knew exactly what to highlight—the high arc of her cheekbones, the bridge of her slender nose, the bold curve of her lips. In a theater filled with rapt patrons, it was the candlelight on her that held me still.

I watched shadows dance across the mouth I'd memorized in every life. Watched her eyes spark with delight at every plucked string and drawn bow. I watched, until she turned and caught me, smiling like I was the only other soul in the building.

When I leaned in to kiss her, the world shrank to that moment. That warmth. That scent of late summer.

Naturally, that's when her body tensed.

She turned sharply, scanning the space behind us, panic flickering in her eyes as they locked with mine.

What is it, love? I asked, mind-to-mind.

I didn't see them coming. Her confusion rang clear, brows pinched as her heart spiked. *Something's wrong.*

The air chilled. I was standing before she was, prepared to snap the neck of whatever fresh nightmare had decided to interrupt *this* night, of all nights.

Someone's here...watching us.

Her eyes combed the crowd, then flicked up toward the balcony. Whatever she sensed, it was enough to have her moving—fast.

She strode down the aisle with purpose, weaving past feet and knees as best she could in heels. I stayed within reach, unwilling to let her out of sight as she pushed through the theater doors and out into the bustling street.

The city hit us like a wave—honking horns, screeching tires, rushing crowds. We both looked, left and right, for the disturbance.

I found nothing. But Alvara stilled.

Her eyes were closed. Hands raised slightly. Then, slowly, she began drifting left through the crowd.

And there they were.

Amid the blur of New Yorkers, one woman stood perfectly still. Silver hair spilled to her ribs, cruelty etched into the slant of her smirk. Beside her stood a man, just as unsettling. Navy jacket with gold embroidery. Pale, statuesque. They looked like mirror opposites—male and female, carved from the same mold.

Unmoving.

Unnatural.

Watching.

Ally was shifting before I was, drawing two blades with a growl as she shoved through the crowd. The woman turned with a serpent's smile before slipping, unhurried, into the nearest alleyway. The man beside her, stone-faced and silent, followed without a word.

We rounded the corner seconds later to find the alley empty. Ally charged in anyway. Her eyes were wild, scanning every crevice, every rooftop, every shadow.

"Who are they?"

"I don't know."

"You didn't look like they were strangers. You've seen them before?"

"In the dreams," she admitted breathlessly. She dropped to one knee in the center of the dark paving stones and picked up a black feather. Straightening, she stared up at the vacant night sky and blew out a shaky breath. "Fuck. It's him, August. In the dreams—he's the one who tortures you both. He's the one who saw me. Who knew I was there." She spun in a slow circle, scanning rooftops, clouds, anything. "Are they just taunting us now?"

"I don't know, love."

"Who *am I*, August?" Her voice cracked, raw and small. "Where did I come from? Are they all as wicked as my brother?"

I had a sinking suspicion that Adrastos might be the reasonable one of the bunch. If Agamemnon was the bar, we were in trouble. "Still no name?"

"No," she whispered. "Whoever wove the bind was powerful. Way stronger than me. I'm in over my head, and I know I'm supposed to be your second and help rally a strategy, but I'm *drowning*, August." The sky broke open, an icy rain pelting our skin, but she didn't flinch—just tipped her head back and let it hit her.

"Baby, you're not *supposed* to be anything for me other than what you are."

I plucked the feather from her fingers and tossed it aside so I could fill her hand with mine. I pulled her in close as the emergency exit of the theater clanged open behind us, a wedge of yellow light slicing across the alley. An attendant stepped out, lit a cigarette, and squinted at the storm like it had personally wronged him.

"Perfect timing," I murmured, glancing down at her. Rain streamed across her cheeks, darkening her lashes. Slowly, I began to sway to the faint music drifting out the door.

"What are you doing?" she asked, voice barely audible over the storm.

"Dancing with my wife."

"But August, *the rain—*"

"Didn't bother me on that battlefield. Not about to stop me now."

Her lips trembled before curling into a smile that lit her from within. She leaned into me, head resting against my chest as we rocked together in the cold. I would've given anything to freeze time—just keep her there, warm against me, the beat of her heart syncing with mine.

We moved through that sliver of calm carved between chaos, the two of us alone as the downpour erased everything else. The chill soaked through my clothes, but it was clarifying—a jolt of sharp reality.

"It doesn't matter," I said.

"What doesn't?"

Mind to mind, I whispered:

Who they are. Who you were. You are mine, *Ally. You are the second-in-command to Commander Aren Amadeus. The sixth ascension of Grayshell's third coven. The Angel of Death. Your past lives don't define you. This one does. And anyone who thinks otherwise can answer to me.*

She huffed a quiet, broken laugh and nodded. "I love you."

"I love you too, little nova."

And then we danced.

We danced right there in the alley—just us and our lone, disinterested audience—as rain turned to sleet and soaked us down to the bones. We danced through grief, through fear, through the remnants of what we'd tried to forget. Every spin and step, every stolen kiss, poured something back into us. The storm cascaded into all the fear I'd been collecting until it was so diluted it no longer had the strength to paralyze.

By the end of the third song, when the door clicked shut behind the attendant, we finally slowed, clinging to the only thing that mattered.

Then we jumped.

Hand in hand, we portled back to Westerlund Estate, sprinting across the pasture in soaked shoes, laughter spilling from Ally's lips. We leapt onto the porch, burst through the door, breathless and euphoric—

And stopped cold.

Every member of our coven—minus two—sat waiting. Their grim expressions sucked the air from the room like a record scratch. Mug in hand, Marcus looked up from the head of the table and raised a pint toward the empty chair beside him.

"Sit." Less invitation than command.

I glanced at Ally. She swallowed hard.

"Did we lose someone?" I asked, tension clamping my spine. "Freya? Aren?"

A chorus of shaking heads was my answer.

"Then why do I feel like I just walked into an intervention?" I muttered, kicking off drenched loafers and squeezing her hand.

"You always were good at calling a spade a spade," Alec said, jerking his chin toward the table.

"Ansel. Lana. Good to see you," I said stiffly.

"*Mm-hmm,*" Ansel grumbled, thumbing the torn wrapper on his beer bottle.

"I don't really feel like sitting," Ally said, unclipping her soaked curls and running her fingers through them.

"Does it look like we give a shit?" Alec snapped. "Let's just get this over with."

"Alec," she warned, sharp and low.

"Don't 'Alec' me when *you've* already given up."

"I haven't given up," she countered. "We're working our asses off to get everything ready before it all goes to hell, and if you'd been around the last six weeks—"

"It's not your effort I'm questioning," he cut in. "It's your resignation."

"You think we can't recognize a bucket list when we see one?" Marcus asked, his eyes cold, locked on Ally.

"*Guys,*" she scoffed, shaking her head—but she didn't deny it. The silence that followed hit harder than any admission. My post-storm clarity faded under the weight of their stares.

"Ally, sweetie, please," Fae said, softer now, pulling out the chair beside her. "We deserve to understand what you're thinking."

I looked at Ally. And I saw it—the hollow ache we'd just danced away flooding back in.

Reluctance was etched into the set of her shoulders, her fists curled tight in the folds of her dress as she finally closed the distance and sat. I did the same, taking her hand while accepting a beer from Marcus with a grateful nod.

"What did you *do*, Ally?" Ansel asked gruffly, leaning forward to brace his forearms on the table, still peeling at the label like it might tell him the answer.

"Nothing any of you wouldn't have," she said simply.

"Explain," Marcus ordered, voice all big-brother authority.

Ally ignored the untouched wine in front of her, stood, and leaned across the table to swipe Alec's whiskey instead. She knocked it back in one gulp before slumping into the chair with a long-suffering sigh.

To my surprise, she actually explained.

Everything.

Well—almost everything. She kept the truth of her origin-life's connection to Adrastos close, but laid out the rest: the threads, the odds, the spiraling futures. And one by one, everyone at the table fell silent, staring at their glasses with glum faces.

Alec blew out the breath we'd all been holding. "Jesus, guys," he muttered, leaning forward until we were braced elbow to elbow around Marcus' table. "You've just been carrying that on your own this whole time?"

"We doled out roles accordingly," she reassured.

"I'm not talking weight distribution. I'm talking emotional bandwidth, for fuck's sake."

"The *sake* belongs to the fuck," Ally mumbled.

"What?" Lana asked sharply. I saw so much of Freya in her now, it was surreal I'd never noticed the resemblance before.

"Nothing," Ally whispered—but her glossy eyes found Alec's across the table. He offered a crooked, agonized smile in return. "I didn't mean it as a snub," she said, voice thin. "It's just...*a lot*. And Fae and Alec are happy." She didn't explain why, and no one pressed her. "Aren *just* found Magnolia. Freya has a chance with her shadow Prince. And I just..." Her voice cracked. A lone tear rolled down her cheek.

I had to fight the instinct to reach out and brush it away.

"Vulnerability's a bitch," Alec muttered, his voice gentler now.

"It is," Ally agreed, her chin trembling as more tears spilled. "But I just wanted everyone to be happy. Just for a moment. Before it all comes crashing down. Is that so *wrong*?" Her shoulders shook as the sobs overtook her. "I just...I love you all so much." She wiped at her eyes with the back of her hand, even as Fae sniffled and mirrored the motion.

"I would do *anything* for you," she whispered. "I hope you know that."

"Ally, sweetie," Fae sobbed. "We love you too, you know? You've shown us every day since you woke up, baby."

Ally nodded, voice hoarse. "I just want you safe and happy."

"I know, honey. But...this is war."

"No one expects you to save everyone," Ansel said quietly, shaking his head. "That *you* do..." his words trailed off, and The Old General tipped his head back and pinched the bridge of his nose.

"Well, it hurts like a mother," Alec added dryly, and the weak laugh Ally gave sounded like a release.

"Did we fail you, Alvara?" Ansel asked. "It was never supposed to be you, facing the world alone in the end."

"You know we have your back too, right?" Alec said, more serious now.

"I know." Her voice was barely above a whisper. She took a shuddering breath, blew it out, and clasped her hands tightly on the table. "But I couldn't live with myself if I didn't do everything I could to protect you."

"Well, that's bullshit," Lana snapped, glaring. "We deserve a chance to save ourselves, don't you think?"

"Seriously," Alec added. "It's been a while since I went out in a ball of fire. Feels overdue."

"Stop it!" Ally laughed—wet and shaky—but still launched her spoon at him. "That's not funny."

"I'm *still* traumatized," Ansel grumbled, flicking a glare at his brother.

"So," Marcus said, steering them back, "you said in the best threads, Aren's always with the Heiress?"

Ally nodded. I passed her a tissue and winced when she blew her nose like a foghorn.

"*Magnolia,*" she confirmed once she resurfaced with a watery laugh.

"But you only ever see Mags *with* Blythe or with Aren?" Ansel asked.

"There are no threads with just one or the other."

"Interesting," he murmured, thumb drifting over the sticky adhesive remnants on his bottle.

"And you two have got to give them space this week," Ally added, color rising in her cheeks. "Trust me, I don't want to know it either, but they're going to be physical. I love Aren, but if the man could shield me out *a little,* that'd be really nice."

"*You're* one to talk," Alec jabbed.

She flipped him off without hesitation.

"Why do you think we're out of the house?" Ansel said, smirking.

Lana buried her face in his shoulder. "Think three hours is enough to let them burn it off? I miss my bed."

"I dunno," Alec said. "The guy's got centuries of blue balls."

"Oh, gross," Ally muttered, wrinkling her nose.

"Tell me he's wrong," I added, laughing as Alec shot me finger guns.

"You think you'll be able to pick up Magnolia's threads in person?" Lana asked, mercifully redirecting the train wreck.

"Maybe? At this point, your guess is as good as mine."

"Only one way to find out," Alec said, shrugging.

"One week," Ally agreed. "We reconvene in Santa Bloom in *one* week."

FORTY-NINE

RANK

FREYA

"So?" Cyrus asked the next day, pushing off the railing as I came down the front steps of the Oracle's house.

"So?" I echoed, brow raised.

He rolled his eyes and shoved his hands in his pocket as he released the most aggrieved sigh. "I got my confirmation. You?"

Translation: he was, in fact, the Harbinger of Glory, which came with a power-up he absolutely did not need and a direct line to Poe whenever he felt like dialing in.

"I got what I needed," I said, nodding. Understatement of the year. I wasn't Alvara-level or anything, but I had over twice the power Reagan did. Now I just had to figure out how to use it before it stopped mattering.

Pushing Calypso and Carr's power back into them had taken so much focus I broke into a cold sweat. And I still botched it. Carrson kept shooting daggers at me while his teeth chattered from the ice in his veins, and Calypso kept trying not to scratch her skin off from the fire under hers.

Honestly? Kind of hilarious. I felt a little bad for Cali—she'd been unnecessarily kind. Teenage me should've chilled on resenting her just for being popular.

My phone buzzed against my hip. I pulled it out and winced when I saw the screen: *Mom.*

Guilt had been riding shotgun for days now—maybe from nearly dying and being yanked back to life by the son of the woman who killed me—but who could say? Either way, I hadn't checked in with the mortals who raised me. In one year, their eldest son had dropped off the grid, bailing on an engagement we'd all been invested in. Then their middle child climbed in bed with the now-ex-fiancé. And their youngest kid—hi, that's me—got swept off to a "specialty trade school."

Ascension made all of it feel more like hallucinations than memories. And if August felt the same...that left them what? Just down two kids?

I swallowed hard, dragged in a breath, and answered the call—fully aware Cyrus was watching me like I was a new species. The man analyzed everything. It was infuriating.

"Hey, Mom!"

"*Hey, Mom!?*" I cringed at the screech. "Glad to know you're alive after months without so much as a word, Freya Porter, so help me God."

"I know, I'm sorry. It's been...*wild* here."

"Look, I'm all for liberation, or whatever it is y'all do in the south for fun, but do your thumbs work?"

"Yes, my thumbs work," I muttered, hanging my head. Was Cyrus—oh my God. He was *grinning* at the sidewalk.

"And I guess your number didn't change? Did you drop your phone in the bayou or something?"

"*Mam,*" I quacked.

"*Where* the hell *have you been?!*"

"Studying," I said emphatically, eyes flicking to Cyrus with a pointed look. "And passing tests."

Not technically a lie. He snorted as he opened the passenger door for me. I flipped him off before stepping into the truck, grinning despite myself.

"Are you even listening to me?"

No. "Sorry, Mama, got distracted."

Silence. That eerie, preternatural, pissed-off-mom silence. "Did something cute go by?"

I pressed my lips together as Cyrus slid into the driver's seat beside me in one smooth motion. "Maybe."

"Freya Lynn Porter, you better not pull an August on me."

"I solemnly vow not to run off and marry the first pretty brunette I see."

Cyrus glared at me as he turned the ignition. It was a physical battle not to smirk.

"So. What's going on? How's school? Do you have friends? Your dad and I were talking about coming for a visit."

"Uhh—it's really not a great time. I've got...midterms. Totally swamped."

Cyrus pulled into traffic, then gave me a look. "Midterms? In February?"

I covered the mic. "I will kill you."

He snickered and turned back to the road. "Just saying."

"Wait. Who are you with—are you with him now?!"

"What? No, just some limp-dick asshole in traffic."

"Freya. Sometimes I worry we damaged you with how much you swear. It's like we raised you in a locker room."

"Actually, studies show swearing is linked to higher IQ."

"I'm teasing."

"I know," I said, smiling. "Listen, Mama, I gotta go. I've got class. But...I missed you. Just wanted to hear your voice."

"Well, fuck, I was hoping to talk."

"And you wonder where I got my mouth."

"I never said that. I said *we damaged you*."

"Thanks. That's exactly what every kid wants to hear."

"I love you, my little sailor. We're booking tickets."

"What? Mom, no! It's not a good time."

"Oh no, going through a tunnel—*chzatchzi*—can't hear—*chzaca*—"

"Mam," I quacked again.

"Oh hey, we're back. Have you heard from your brother?"

"Not in a bit," I said, side-eyeing Cyrus, who could definitely hear every word. "Last I heard, he's doing great." Okay, so last I actually heard, Ally had drained him bone-dry and he woke up in the lord of the dead's house. But Mama didn't need to know that.

"I'll have to wrangle him into a visit too. Oh! Maybe he and Al—"

"Hey Mom, I just walked into class and the teacher's glaring. Love you, 'kay byeeeee." I hung up fast, lips pressed to my teeth as I shifted uncomfortably in my seat, acutely aware of the death glare coming from my left.

"What was she about to say, Freya?"

"Nothing."

"You hung up like she lit you on fire."

Oh, to be so on the nose, and so far away. "I just wasn't sure how to get her off the phone."

"Uh-huh." He shook his head as we approached the bridge. "You know this whole arrangement only works if we can trust each other."

"See, that's your first mistake."

His glare sharpened as he pulled onto the shoulder. "I'm risking my neck for you, Porter. The least you could do—"

"Is finish what I started," I cut in. "And I will. So, there's that."

"I can drive you across."

"And rack up another treaty violation? No. Go home, Stuart. Let me talk to Reyna before you stir the pot." Besides, I needed *space*. The last twenty-four hours had been one craptastic headline after another. And now I had to show up at Bellaton and inform Reyna and Blaz that I'd woken up as their enemy's mate and pray they didn't rescind their alliance.

"Besides. I can jump now. Remember?"

"Yeah, yeah. Fine. I'll wait for your call."

"Good."

"*Fine.*"

Backing away from the truck, keeping my eyes on the broody blond in the driver's seat, I threw up a middle finger. He returned it, smirking as he turned the wheel and pulled away.

What the actual fuck had I gotten myself into?

I crossed the bridge on foot, tucked into the woods, and jumped to the Bellaton estate. This was going to be...*something.*

I let out a sigh as I stared up at the massive colonial façade, counting guards, scanning the patrol paths—only to freeze when I spotted two cats perched like sentries at the top of the porch.

Since when did Reyna have cats?

My phone buzzed. Again. Determined to be the death of me. I pulled it out, stomach tightening at Ally's message:

ALVARA

Whatever your plan is, wrap it up by the equinox.

CYRUS

Before I even pulled into Luminark Manor, a trio of ravens soared overhead. My eyes landed on Poe before he spoke.

Trouble brews, young leader.

Of course it did. *What kind of trouble?* I growled back.

I suggest you hasten.

Muttering epithets, I leaned into the throttle, kicking up dirt as I tore down the driveway.

I didn't bother turning off the ignition. I launched out the driver's side and sprinted for the porch. Raised voices reached me before my boots even hit the decking.

"Because I have nothing to say!"

"My, she speaks." *Oh good. Cali poked the dragon.* Dread twisted low in my gut.

Aside from that meeting with The Six, I'd successfully avoided my mother like the plague she was. But a screaming match between her and Calypso? That was a disaster the hierarchy couldn't afford.

"And here I thought you'd sulk indefinitely like a scolded child."

"And *I* assumed you weren't so heartless as to humiliate your own son in front of the entire Council and all of leadership."

"I'd hardly say Cyrus was humiliated—he fought well."

"And you *robbed him*, Mother!" Cali snapped as I pushed through the cracked door. "Stuarts are *supposed to* stand on honor, and you stole a victory he rightfully earned."

"I was protecting the balance."

"The balance, or your ego?" Calypso's voice sharpened like a blade. "Because I'm starting to think there's no difference anymore. If there were, you'd have trusted your son to finish what Nix started, instead of sparing the worm."

Shit.

I padded on silent feet across the entryway and found them nose-to-nose in the library, framed in front of one of the tall arched windows like a war painting. Cali's fury mirrored our mother's, down to the fire in her eyes. Only our father's coloring set them apart.

"Watch your tone," Mom snapped.

"I could say the same," Cali replied, cutting and cold. "Or I fear you'll find yourself standing before a court of slaves rather than subjects. I'm not the only one who saw your hypocrisy for what it was."

"You forget your place." Power rose like a tide.

I leaned into the doorframe, watching carefully. If this escalated, I honestly didn't know who would win. Cali preferred her lab to the sparring mat, but our mother hadn't worn a cloak in years—she'd grown comfortable wielding others as weapons.

"My place? What is that, exactly, Mother? You raised us to believe *honor* and *discernment* were our greatest assets—shortly followed by ruthlessness. But God forbid we use those to hold you accountable."

"There are some consequences a queen's rule can sustain, and some it cannot."

"Your *son* had the gall to challenge a Wing for treason. He stood his ground. Proved his case. Offered Nix the dignity of dying by the blade—and you pulled that *bullshit?*"

"One outcome would have preserved our family's rule. The other would have sparked insurrection. Spilling my nephew's blood—the Captain of the Wings—for doing what he believed to be his duty would've lit a fuse."

"I didn't see you interfering on *my* behalf," I drawled, pushing off the frame as both women turned livid eyes on me. "Guess the death of their prince wasn't consequential enough for you?"

"I've got this, Cy," Cali snapped.

"I have to agree," Mom said coolly. "You're interrupting a conversation not meant for you."

"Oh, by all means, keep yelling. Let the *entire manor* listen in." I crossed the threshold. "Like the duel didn't already raise enough red flags, now you two are staging a spectacle."

Mom flicked her wrist and the door slammed shut behind me. "The two of you played your cards well. But don't be so arrogant as to think I can't see a trap when you set one. Don't forget who taught you to wield words like knives. You've both loathed your cousin for years."

"Because he's a sociopath with no concept of consequence, *Your Majesty*," Cali shot back without flinching.

Mom's neck flushed a mottled red, but Cali was beyond caring.

"He shot that girl with no thought for who she was or what that would do to your Prince—our Prince—in direct defiance of orders."

"And now he pays the price. If a century on his knees doesn't teach him humility, perhaps it will teach you patience. I believe he can still be... refined into an asset."

Nix's words on that stage had me thumbing at my signet ring. "Wouldn't count on that."

"You've set a precedent," Cali hissed. "That we can be disobeyed without facing the consequences laid out in the Accords."

"She's right," I drawled flatly. I was itching to burn energy, to *do* something. Maybe a brawl with Reyna's guard would've been a better use of my afternoon.

Mother turned that scorching gaze on me, but froze at what she saw.

"You feel cheated." Her voice softened like silk over steel.

"What gave it away?"

"Mercy is not weakness, Cyrus. It's the ultimate form of control."

My blood turned to ice. As for my sister? Nothing but fire. "The blade might be gone, but I assure you, his wound still bleeds. Were you showing mercy? Or were you making sure *he* remained beneath your heel?" Cali flung her hand out toward me.

I cocked my head, but she wasn't done.

"You need the Harbinger of Glory leashed to your throne, is that it?"

"Enough!" Mother moved so fast I didn't see the strike—just the crack as Cali's head snapped back.

I was in front of her before the sound finished. Shadows hissed at my fingertips, and the rage in my chest ignited like dry kindling.

"*Mother.*"

"Remember whose blood gave you the power you now hold," she said icily.

I held her stare, even as every part of me screamed to turn, to check on Cali. But I knew better than to show weakness in front of a predator.

"I think Poe might have something to say about that."

"I've entertained your petulance long enough," she snapped. "I'm not asking again, Calypso. You *will* bring The Wraith in for a formal declaration."

"I assure you," I said, "no one will be *bringing her* anywhere she doesn't choose to go."

Her eyes flared, shadows coiling. "You would defy your Queen?"

"Your need for an heir brought me here," I said slowly. "But the *universe* brought me to Freya."

Cali's hand settled lightly on my shoulder in silent reassurance. She was still standing. Still fierce. My heart finally unclenched.

"She has her endorsement," Cali said. "And that's well within the bounds of the Accords."

"You barely *know her*," Mother spat. "You defend a woman who's waged war against our people."

"We defend a woman who's saved your son's life more times than I can count."

"You're making a mistake."

I arched a brow. "No. I think we're just fixing yours."

"*Now* you look like a Grayshellian!" Brody boomed proudly, throwing his arms wide as I finished the last of Reyna's drills. She'd run me through every medical test in the book before dragging my ass to the field to see what I could do with this thing.

"Except for the fact that she's still...*petite.*" All things considered, that was probably the nicest way Reyna could phrase it.

"Not the size of the dog in the fight, Mother," Blaz drawled from where he lay sprawled in the sun, shirtless and smug in the balmy return of that Southern sixty degrees. Reyna considered that, lips pursed, before deciding not to answer. Long enough to concern me.

"Yes?" I pressed, unwrapping the tape from my hands and relishing the sting left behind.

"Your strength against the Renown will be draining them before they can get anywhere near you," she noted.

"Agreed."

"You'll be...like a power bank for your coven," Blaz pointed out, like that was the most fantastic position a girl could hold. His phone lit up briefly before he slid it into his pocket, expression unreadable.

"Just what every girl dreams of being," I said airily. "A life-size battery."

"But think logistically, Freya. You beside your brother—*the shield*. He keeps them at a distance, and the ones who break through get drained. You redistribute their power to the souls inside the shield. You're a hell of an asset."

"Very good," Reyna said, smirking at her son. "While we're entertaining strategy, what do you expect Adrastos to do next?"

Blaz took a beat, tilting his face toward the sun as he thought. "He hit Grayshell first. Why?"

"We're the strongest hierarchy of warriors on the continent—no offense," I added to the Queen as an afterthought.

"One of us still has our Middle and the other doesn't, so I think that speaks for itself," Reyna shot back snottily—but the brow waggle labeled it play.

"I'll still kick your ass," Brody said, smirking over at her. Reyna *blushed* and rolled her eyes.

"Agreed," soap boy echoed.

"Right," Blaz said, unbothered. "But they didn't just *hit* Grayshell—they decimated your method of communication when they locked you out of the Middle. Oldest trick in the book: divide thousands of souls from their Commander and covens."

"Divide and conquer is tried and true for a reason," I muttered, tearing more aggressively at the adhesive and wincing when it pulled skin.

"How many of those souls have been deployed for decades? How long will it take to get information passed along? Sure, if the world falls under attack, they'll return to your territory...but Adrastos—or whoever's pulling his strings—rendered Aren's superpower useless in a day and scattered the biggest threats of retaliation. Either they rebuild...or find a gate in."

"Kay, you're making me queasy," I muttered, shifting on my feet.

"Sorry, but it's true. I think he's gonna hit hard and fast—everywhere at once. If past strategy tells us anything, it's that what worked here will work again. Smash them to pieces, cut the line home."

My analysis had led to the same conclusion—and Alvara's visions echoed it. But for a nineteen-year-old who'd never seen combat? "I'm impressed."

"What else?" Reyna asked, standing tall now, full Commander mode. "Let's look at it from a psychology standpoint."

"Adrastos bargained with Commander Porter using honor as leverage. It was a mega-duel between hierarchies more than opponents."

"Which makes you think of..." Reyna prompted.

"The Paladins."

"Okay. What else?"

I thought of that day on the field. The way he'd paused battle to call August forward. "He likes a spectacle."

"A propensity for theatrics?"

"Maybe," I said, thoughts drifting. "That lines up with Aren's suspicions. He and Ansel think Adrastos will make a move too public for humans to deny."

"So...city centers, stadiums, concerts, parades," Blaz guessed. "Gatherings with too many witnesses to mind-wipe."

My temples throbbed. Oh, this was a nightmare.

"All coming from different angles," I finished, heart picking up. "Tell you what, kid. If I can't reach Ally, I'll look to you."

"Gotta find a purpose somewhere," he muttered.

I grinned at him. "You'll ascend. Just...stay alive long enough to."

"That's the part I'm worried about," he said, shaking his head as he tilted that bronzed skin back toward the sun. "I feel like a sittin' duck."

I SLOGGED up the stairs hours later, exhaustion weighting every bone, but gratitude wasn't far behind. This body was *incredible*—little, but mighty. Quick as an asp. The last six weeks of struggle vanished the moment Brody fired an arrow and I caught the damn thing. The ability to draw off anyone I chose was a kind of asset I'd never dared imagine.

A notorious thief returned to rob souls of power. A little on the nose for my sense of humor, but fitting. I could appreciate it.

I made it to my room, snagged a change of clothes, and showered. By the time I padded back out in pajamas with my tac suit folded in my arms, a strange warmth still hummed in my chest. Not just physical. Everything felt lighter.

Some days are so...warm? I didn't have a better word for it—like floating on hope for the first time in months. Bliss, maybe.

I sat at the vanity, setting my gear aside and snatching the vintage silver brush. Each stroke through my cropped hair gave me space to think. Run tomorrow's priorities.

Then—shadows stirred in the mirror, curling beside the window like night dripping into the room. I dropped the brush, snatched my blade off the desk, turned, and launched it as they solidified.

The second knife was already in my hand when *Cyrus* deadpanned, "You missed."

I arched a brow. "Did I?"

Turning to face him, I was acutely aware these booty shorts were no better than underwear—and the oversized Guns N' Roses tee had swallowed them whole. He closed his eyes, releasing a breath more snarl than exhale.

I followed his gaze to where my knife had pinned his coat to the wall.

"This was expensive," he growled.

Relief that he wasn't a psychopath here to kill me gave way to something more bitter. Irritation, sure. But also that twisted, cold slide of terror—unreasonable, unearned...and very much still there.

"And you can afford to have it fixed," I hissed, storming toward him with my second blade still pinched between my fingers. "What the fuck are you doing here?" I whisper-yelled, smacking him square in the chest the moment I got within range. Stupid. So fucking stupid.

And why the hell did he look irritated *with me?* He was the uninvited, entirely unwelcome house guest. Reyna would kill him on sight—or worse, use him to blackmail his mother, who'd probably let him die before conceding defeat.

"*Freya,*" he bit out.

"I can't believe you—" Another shove, this one sending his shoulder blades into the wall. "—thought showing up *here*—" I punched what was promptly declared a too-firm bicep. "—was a good idea!"

"Freya," he sighed.

"How stupid can you be? Do you know what Reyna would do if she—"

He growled under his breath, snatching my wrists in his broad hands and pinning them between us.

"Would you stop?! It's like getting beaten by a kitten."

"Tell that to your Achilles."

"It healed just fine."

"*Answer me.*"

He flashed a crooked grin that tugged left, but his flat, unreadable eyes killed the act. "I was just *dying* to see you and couldn't stay away," he said mockingly. "Is that what you wanna hear, Porter?"

"No, you asshole. I want to know why you're in the heart of Bellaton territory after Nix nearly started a war, and I told you to wait for my goddamn call."

I shoved again, and he chuckled low in his throat—then abruptly shifted his grip, anchoring one arm and wrenching me around with the other. My back hit his chest, my arms crossed tight over my own ribs. A chill skittered up my spine as he lowered the scruff of his cheek to my ear.

"Technically, *I* was the one who suggested waiting for your call," he murmured, breath ghosting hot across my skin. "And *you're* a hell of a lot more pliable with your guard down."

He shoved me forward, and I whirled on him, heart thundering. Brows lifted, he looked skyward like he was begging the heavens for patience, then reached down and yanked my knife from the wall—and his jacket.

Holding it up, he glared at me. "Rude."

Rolling my eyes, I sauntered forward and plucked it from his outstretched fingers. "You know what's rude? Appearing in someone's bedroom like a fucking poltergeist." On that note, I was absolutely altering the wards on this room because what the actual fuck. I turned on my heel and marched back across the space. "So," I snapped, flicking my fingers to cast a bubble shield around us. "Why are you here?"

His eyes flicked toward the ceiling, mouth ajar like he could *see* the spell. "Fuck, you learn fast."

"I *remember* fast," I corrected, turning to face him and plopping into the armchair beside the balcony. "I was just waiting on my damn power-up, thank you very much."

"Right," he muttered, wincing as he shrugged off his peacoat.

"Focus," I said, snapping my fingers like I was training a particularly stubborn dog.

"Just a long day, okay?"

My eyes narrowed. "M'kay. And why aren't you with Fluffy?"

"*Freya,*" he growled, hurling his coat onto my bed as he lumbered to the chair beside mine.

"You look like shit."

"Gee, thanks, ma moitié," he drawled.

"I did not miss needing to translate insults in two languages, let me tell you." That earned the smallest of smiles as he crossed one wrist over the other and planted them on his forehead, leaning back until he overflowed the chair like a grown man squeezed into a kindergarten seat.

"What the hell happened to you, anyway?"

"My mother."

My blood simmered. I huffed, tugging my shirt lower over my thighs even though his eyes were closed. "What *now?*"

"Cali and she got into it, and—like an idiot—I jumped in the middle. We both ended up running gauntlets all day."

"Jesus," I breathed. I'd only run a gauntlet once in my Paladin years, during battle prep: one soul against six Wings, or a Guard team, on repeat with no rest. Just wave after wave until you either collapsed or bled out or begged for death to come quicker. Officially, it was a training exercise. Unofficially, it was punishment via performance.

Clever, really.

To fail was dishonor. To fall and not rise before the next wave? Dishonor. To do anything but fight? Dishonor.

So, essentially, she wanted to humiliate them—then remind them who they served.

"Nice. Very maternal of her."

"*Mmf,*" he harrumphed, and as I studied his profile, I realized he was rapidly fading—each breath slower than the last.

"Cyrus," I said, quieter.

"Hmm."

"What are you doing here?"

Heavily lidded hazels found mine. He licked his lips. Gave a half-shrug. Shook his head like it weighed too much. "I dunno, okay?"

His eyes fell closed. He gave a great lion's yawn, and damn it all if I didn't smile. That wasn't good.

"Cyrus," I hissed. "You cannot fall asleep here."

"I know, 'm not sleepin'...jus' restin' my eyes."

Another monstrous yawn cracked across his face as he crossed his arms over his chest.

Muscled. Inked. Arms. And my God, if those wings didn't transform snackable morsels of man into something truly worth salivating over.

Jesus Christ, Freya. Pull yourself together.

Attraction to this man was not something I could afford.

CYRUS

I woke tangled in Bellaton blue, stiff as hell and cradled in scratchy sheets that reeked of disuse. Blinking hard, I shoved the blanket away and scrubbed a hand over my face, wincing at the angle my neck had endured.

What the fuck had I been thinking?

Crossing the river. Slipping into my aunt's territory like a damn shadowspawn. I'd lost my ever-loving mind.

But every time I closed my eyes, I saw that masked bastard with his hands on *her*. And that thought—just that thought—had short-circuited every ounce of logic. I'd needed to see her. Make sure she was safe. Then, maybe, I could finally sleep.

Apparently, I had. A little too well.

I cleared my throat and forced my limbs to cooperate. Sitting upright felt like a full-body negotiation. My surroundings were stark. Bare. Sterile. Like the room itself had been scrubbed of personality. No photos. No trinkets. Just weapons, neatly arranged and ominously gleaming. A room prepared to be abandoned at a moment's notice.

Of course. Freya Porter didn't settle—she survived.

She stood pressed between curtain and wall, completely still. Dressed head-to-toe in black, every weapon strapped on. The only reason I'd even spotted her was because my shadows nudged me toward her presence. Otherwise, she could've been a ghost.

But my mind betrayed me—flashing back to the moment I entered this room and found her in an oversized band tee, one shoulder bare, all lean muscle and carved legs and shower-rough hair.

She looked different now. Sharper. Brighter. Ascension had carved something feral and precise into her face. And those legs...

Fuck.

Guilt soured the thought. I'd come here seeking peace. Instead, I'd stolen hers. Whatever threadbare trust we'd spun in the crypt, it hadn't held. The only thing that hadn't changed about her was the heat in those jade eyes.

But this time, when she looked at me, something in them softened.

"You okay?" she asked quietly.

I nodded—useless, lying motion. Truth was, I didn't know. Maybe she'd been right. Maybe this bond was a weakness. She made me vulnerable. And I couldn't afford *that*.

"Mother is demanding you make a formal declaration for your petition."

"Ahh," she exhaled, gaze turning back to the window.

"Calypso refused on your behalf."

"Oh?" Her arms wrapped around her ribs. "I'm sure that went well."

"About as well as you'd expect."

"Hence, the gauntlets?"

Full armor. Full speed. No breaks. In front of a crowd, of course. A public lesson in obedience from a woman who'd weaponized shame.

"Yeah."

"I'm sorry."

I snorted, hunched forward with my elbows on my knees. My hands hung useless, fingers too sore to even curl. "Wasn't your idea."

"Still."

"Look, Freya...I gotta ask. What the fuck happened between you and my mother? Why does she want you so badly?"

"Nothing," she said. Flat. Fast. Eyes like shuttered windows.

"Clearly. My mistake," I bit out. "Just assumed between the blood on the walls and, you know, dismantling the hierarchy, something might've gone down. Something worth avenging."

Her throat bobbed, but she stayed silent.

"Was it Lonan?" I pressed. "You said he tried to get Mother to fetch the crown. Did she send you to do it for her?"

Still nothing. Not even a flinch.

"That's what it feels like. Like all these pieces fit if I just had the last few. I couldn't stop picturing him showing up, taking you—"

"Aww, *shucks*, cowboy," she cut in, but the words had no teeth.

"Don't overestimate Reyna's shadows," I warned. "They're easier to navigate than you think—if you know how to use them."

"*Clearly*," she muttered, sighing like the conversation had exasperated her. Coming here was a mistake. Two steps forward and three steps back. "Lonan doesn't scare me. Not anymore."

"That's not an answer."

"I was betrayed, Cyrus."

She turned to face me then, gaze dead flat, like I hadn't watched her burn half her life to the ground to claw justice from its ashes.

"By someone with security clearance high enough to know about a calling," she said tightly, "and the op I was running to track him down. I finally got good intel. Showed up. He was already dead. Throat slit. Obvious signs of a struggle."

Her jaw clenched. I didn't breathe.

"I searched every inch of that safehouse. Found a raven-hilted blade I recognized. Then I arranged a meet with your mother, but instead, I got my throat slit, and the last thing I remember is sinking into the muddy river on the divide. I don't know what drowned me first. The water or my own blood."

"You'd already beaten the Crucible?"

"And earned my Wings," she said. Cold as stone.

Fuck.

The first Accord protected shadow magic. The second—the blood. Our brotherhood. That law extended to callings. Mates. Sacred ground.

If she was telling the truth, we had a traitor. In the highest ranks.

"Who was the calling?"

She laughed. No humor. No warmth. "You wouldn't believe me if I told you."

"Try me."

"You need to leave," she said, turning her back again.

"Freya—"

"You've been a perfect gentleman. But you have to get out of here before Reyna or her flyers find you."

She'd armed up for *me*, hadn't she? Stood watch while I slept.

Didn't matter. What mattered was the thin blade of dawn slicing through the sky.

Bellaton would be waking soon.

"You're gonna train your magic with Reyna?"

"Started today."

"Good. Not too much at once, okay?"

"I know my limits."

"Not in this body, you don't," I argued. "Take it slow."

"Careful, Cyrus. You sound like you care."

Because I fucking did.

What else would've driven me to devour every scrap of lore about her kind? What else kept me digging through records trying to find anything about Lonan, tracing his links to the crown, trying to map every threat before it got near her?

But I didn't say any of that.

Instead, I warned, "Your well might be infinite now—but your body isn't. The vessel will burn out before the power does."

"*Great.*" She jerked her chin toward the sun. "Now, move your ass."

FIFTY-ONE

THE DEDICATION OF A QUEEN
CYRUS

The funny thing about a Commander's compulsion was that as long as my intention was to comply, the magic would leave me alone.

I *intended* to report back to my mother whenever I returned from seeing Freya. Therefore, the command left me alone while I slept in her room, planning to ask questions. If I could sincerely twist my plan to fit the confines of her order—say, if going to *The Rougarou* made my mark more likely to talk—I could buy myself time. It only became a hindrance once I no longer intended to uphold it. Intricate magic. A colossal pain in my ass when I dragged my half-asleep carcass back to Luminark Manor and couldn't go home. *Home* didn't involve reporting the instant I had intel from Freya.

Gritting my teeth, I glowered up at the gothic mansion that held my nightmares in the palm of its spindled hand. My feet dragged forward against my will, and with a sigh, I marched in of my own volition. No point letting her magic haul me in like a prisoner when I could at least hold my head up.

She was...less than pleased to learn Freya had no intention of reporting in, but before she could fully explode, Gio—the Wing-Lieutenant—interrupted. Since we hadn't replaced Nix as Captain, I was standing in for now. Given the political mess around Nix's dismissal, the Council wanted to exploit the vacancy with their own candidates. I didn't mind Gio, but I needed to consult Poe before anything moved. I couldn't stop a formal challenge, but I could try to prevent unnecessary bloodshed.

Mother reluctantly dismissed me to keep the peace, and two hours of

Council bullshit later, any fantasy of a nap was obliterated. When my shadows tugged me downstairs over a 'disturbance,' I braced to deal with her latest tantrum—and instead found myself facing hard brown eyes.

Lonan.

Unmasked.

My shields slammed into place so fast I wasn't sure I'd ever peel them back. Fuck this motherfucker.

Quickly, I cataloged what I could: tanned skin, strong bone structure—Mediterranean, maybe?—onyx hair, brown eyes ringed with shadows so deep they looked bruised, and a five-o'clock shadow that didn't seem intentional. This man was exhausted. And livid.

Goody.

"I see you ditched the costume," I stated flatly.

"I see *you're* still empty-handed."

"Wasn't expecting you," I shrugged. "Far as I'm concerned, our deal ended on Valentine's Day." His jaw ticked, but I continued. "I went to a helluva lot of trouble to catch your thief. Summoned you. You didn't show. *She* escaped. Not my problem." I halted in front of the dais, my arms crossed, shadows trailing ahead to scan the room.

"Why do you believe I intend to possess such a weapon? She's a slippery little thing. But I suspect you know that better than most." His gaze raked over me. A slow smirk curved his lips as if he'd found something worth noting.

"What would you do with her, if I turned her over?"

"That, I fear, is above your pay grade."

"And *that*, I fear, ends our working relationship."

"Are you telling me you're not a man of your word, *Prince* Cyrus Stuart?"

"I'm telling you my mother might bend a knee, but I won't let Calypso do the same. We don't pay debts we don't owe. I'm done being a blade with no idea what I'm cutting."

His smile spread as he crossed one arm under the other and rubbed his jaw. He tilted his head, studying me. "I'm impressed, hatchling. Your shields have improved. All it took was proper motivation. You'll find I'm... similarly motivated."

"Not following."

"Does she know?"

"Mother? I can't say she's noticed I've been training more."

"Not your mother, wiseass," he scoffed. "Freya Lynn Porter. *Grayshell's Wraith*. Does she know the two of you share a bond?"

I kept my expression neutral, though magic itched under my skin. "I thought you had all the answers. You tell *me*."

"If you're as clever as I think, she knows what's necessary. No more."

"Sounds like a solid plan."

He nodded, smug. "I'd like a private audience."

"The Queen isn't taking—"

"Not with your Queen. With you."

I raised a brow. "As opposed to this block party?"

"You and I both know the walls have ears."

"I don't go anywhere without the Wings. They don't take kindly to being cut out of conversations they deem important."

"You'd risk critical information falling into the wrong hands?"

"If I ever found someone threatening my people, they wouldn't live long enough to regret it."

"Except for The Wraith. And Nix. He's still out there, isn't he?"

My jaw clenched. "Not my call."

"And yet you speak as though you carry the authority." He descended the dais, step by step, until we stood eye to eye. "I'll be honest, little historian—I'm out of time. And patience is in even lower supply."

"We have that in common," I muttered, on edge with how close he stood. His presence made my skin crawl.

"I think you'll find we're not so different."

"I sincerely doubt that." My hand found the raven-hilt.

He grinned. Fucking *grinned*. "You remind me of myself. Less... damaged, maybe. But just as ruthless. Just as arrogant, clever, volatile. Your weak point is your strength: your sense of duty. It might be the very thing that costs you everything. As for The Wraith...I just want to speak with her."

"You sure like the sound of your own voice."

"She has something that belongs to me. I want it back. Time is running out."

"Ask nicely, and maybe I'll pass along the message." I let my fingers settle around the blade.

"What do you think she'd do if she knew the lengths you'd go to for her?"

"Probably call me a damn fool."

He chuckled. "Yeah, that sounds about right. I ask because I wonder the same thing. Both of us are bound to women with no intention of returning the sentiment."

"Not sure if you're fishing for condolences or if I should offer congratulations."

"In your position, I'd go with the latter. But not all souls with counterparts have souls left to offer. Count your blessings, hatchling."

"This is starting to feel a little too *Yaya Sisterhood* for me."

He cocked his head. "Your shields have improved, *Harbinger of Glory*. But they're not impenetrable. I see your dedication to her. You want to protect her. I want her to return my Crown—because without it, my bonded is in danger you cannot fathom."

When losing a battle to a clairvoyant, the trick was to feed them just enough truth to protect your hand. "Are you telling me you want *my mate* to enter a cursed crypt and retrieve the Obsidian Crown for *love?*"

"Love is a luxury monsters like us never find. We didn't choose our bonds. We didn't choose the absence of a real connection." The more he talked, the more distant his gaze drifted, his thumb brushing over the inner crook of his arm where it crossed over the other. "But you've vowed to protect Freya Porter even if she hates you for it. My begrudging bonded will never even know what I've done to keep her and her family safe. From one man in a corner to another, throw me a line before we're both too late."

"That's not my call to make." Besides, this asshole just opened up at least a dozen more questions for my *begrudging bonded* and provided little in the way of answers.

"Hurry, prince of shadows. I will not ask again. I never intended to make an enemy of you or your people, but it is a sacrifice I'm beginning to consider."

"I don't respond well to threats."

"Good thing I'm not making one. Just stating facts. Alliances require clear communication. Here's mine: I'm out of time. She has my solution."

"The Crown's a prison. What the hell do you intend to use it for?"

"To control a wildcard."

"Who do you serve?"

"The balance," he said, that wolfish grin returning.

"You've allied with Adrastos?"

"I'm not in the position to ally with anyone. But the mission...it resonates. Time will tell if his allies are true."

"You wear the same masks."

"Do I?" That smile widened. "Where do you think they come from?"

"Lots of clans wear battle masks."

"Disappointing. I expected more from you."

"What happened to clear communication?" I snapped.

"When it matters, I deliver. For example, a Queen afraid of losing her crown is more dangerous than any warrior." He smirked. "Ask Jeanne d'Albret how far a mother will go to protect her daughter's reign—oh...wait, *you can't.*"

Jeanne d'Albret. Queen of Navarre. Died right before the St. Bartholomew's Day Massacre. "Catherine de' Medici's involvement was rumor. Jeanne died of tuberculosis."

He backed away, shadows rising like mist around his boots. My own bristled in response.

"*Interesting*," he murmured. "Rather convenient, how that plays out, don't you think? While I'd love to hash out semantics, I've somewhere to be, and so do you."

"What's happening?" I called as the shadows rose.

"Nothing I'm at liberty to discuss." He scratched his face—just below his eye—and my blood ran cold.

Freya.

"I'd be heading east, if I were you."

FIFTY-TWO

THE THIRD

FREYA

As far as I was concerned, there were four levels of tired. Level one—everyday, 'need a reset' tired. Level two—'pulled an all-nighter for midterms and six shots of espresso in Irish cream might help' tired. Level three—'I might puke, pass out, burst into uncontrollable laughter, or punch you in the face, and fuck you for asking' tired. Level four—I am dead to the world after battling to save my people.

Today was firmly a three-point-two-five.

Staying up all night watching over a sleeping Cyrus after training all day might've been a mistake, but I wouldn't have been able to sleep if I tried. Big, insane idiot. What the fuck was he thinking?

My eyes, mouth, and throat were all perpetually dry no matter how much water I chugged or how many bottles of saline I rained into my eyeballs. Blaz's relentless optimism made me want to throttle him. And the schematics Cyrus had gotten me were as frustrating to read as humanly possible—intentionally, no doubt. Still, I was fairly certain I'd mapped at least three ways in and out of the vault.

So when Montague burst into the library, wide-eyed and out of breath, all I could do was glare at him.

"What?"

"Reyna...needs you," he panted, a broad hand on his hip. "Attack...in broad daylight."

"*What?*" Blaz and I barked in unison, flying from our chairs.

"Demons maybe? Dunno. Some kind of dark magic."

"Where is she?" I demanded as the three of us ran into the hallway.

"The Andrews farm."

"Stay here!" I barked at Blaz, who snarled something in protest as G and I bolted into the yard and past the wards. His hand engulfed mine, and then we were jumping.

When our boots hit the dirt, my heart stuttered.

Horses galloped past us at breakneck speed, the reason obvious as my eyes scanned the burning red barn and white farmhouse. Ranch hands scrambled to free the animals while others tried to contain the blaze—no sign of help on the horizon.

But my attention pulled behind them.

To the wall of black drifting through the air like ash.

Wrong, my magic screamed. *Wrong, wrong, wrong.*

"What is that?" I breathed as we both started running toward the darkness.

"We don't know!"

Carrion and rot filled the air, my stomach turning as we closed the distance to the sound of horrified screams. A gust of rancid wind blew my hair back—and that's when I looked up.

Birds. So many birds.

Ravens and...impossible shadow birds.

Seven of them, each drawing on elements. The Flying Squad was airborne.

My theory was confirmed when two enormous shadows dove for the ground, transforming into Lainalei and Makena before they hit the dirt. The earth trembled as they summoned walls of clay in stabbing shards toward...something.

Something I couldn't see beyond the ash.

The closer we got, the worse the reek became. I threw my hands forward, shoving a wall of air through the darkness, sending it rushing across the field. As the debris cleared, a chill raced up my arms.

One figure stood within.

As tall as Alvara, the woman was at least six-three, her moon-white hair blowing in the breeze. She turned with preternatural grace that sent my nerves screaming. I staggered back when her eyes met mine—wholly black, with no whites. Black veins spread from her eyes and neck, climbing her arms like a disease she welcomed.

It looked like the poison from a reaper's bullet—but she was alive, unbothered, and *smiling*.

She lifted her face to the sky and breathed in, drawing power from her destruction. That's when I understood the ash. Every blade of grain she touched withered, died, and disintegrated into soot, blown away on the wind.

Like skin infected by reaper's venom.

Oh, not good.

Reyna's flyers didn't hesitate to exploit the opening. Both charged as three more birds dove.

"Can you stop her!?" G barked, snapping me back to myself. I blinked. *Okay, focus, Freya.*

"I don't know," I breathed, but threw my hands forward, launching tendrils of power.

"Can you *try!?*"

"What the fuck does it look like I'm doing?!"

My gift sensed everything *but* her. Shadows, ice, water, earth—every element brushed the fingers of my siphon. Everything except this Goddess of destruction.

She walked through the field, hands destroying crops with every touch, drifting toward Lainalei and Makena like they were an afterthought.

Only when Lainalei let out a battle cry and spun forward, blades flashing, did the demonic bitch engage.

Each block looked...effortless, even as she fought Makena on the opposite side.

My eyes locked with G's. We were both thinking the same thing.

Not good. Not good. Not *good.*

My boots crunched onto the decaying earth, every step lifting charcoal into the air.

Where the fuck was Alvara? This shit was right up her alley.

The bitch moved with alarming fluidity. Lainalei and Makena grunted with effort, already pushed to the defensive. Dread pooled in my gut, and the warning on my lips came too late.

She clamped a hand around Lainalei's throat. Her other arm threw a shield so violently it sent Makena flying. She slammed through the mud, sliding a good twenty yards before skidding to a stop. A screeching bird dove from the sky as Lainalei's hands clawed at the grip on her throat. She was lifted off the ground, feet kicking.

Then the bitch's lifeless black eyes locked on her face—and Lainalei let out a soul-rending cry as her body turned to ash.

Montague and Reyna's horrified screams cleaved the air as we skidded to a halt, frozen.

Lainalei's body dropped—and disintegrated, drifting away like powder on the wind.

That fast.

Seconds, at most—and a trained flyer was...*poof.* Gone.

What. The actual. Fuck.

Fear jolted white-hot through my veins as my mind reached for connection—nothing. No mind-to-mind links here. No way to call Ally. Just me, this bitch, and my brazen insanity.

Anger tunneled my vision, and I threw my knife with lethal precision. Or it would've been lethal, if she hadn't turned and caught the damn thing.

She flipped the blade, that serpent's smile stretching as her gaze dragged slowly up to mine. Then she pocketed it.

Ahh, hell no.

Planting my feet in the dirt, I anchored myself in the iridescent light of Grayshell, preserved in memory, and *pulled*—hands carving through the air like talons. I locked onto her...power?

Death. She felt like death.

I didn't want that sickly, boiling oil inside me. But what was the alternative? Nobody could kill her if I couldn't neutralize her.

Reyna materialized beside me, chest heaving, eyes wild as she scanned the field. "Don't let her touch you."

"Thanks for that," I snapped, jaw clenched.

I refocused, searching for the epicenter of her magic. A ball of energy pushed against my palms as I closed them, arms shaking with the effort of stealing what wasn't mine and forcing it away from her.

Still, I pulled. G and Makena charged, hurling spears of earth and ice, but she batted them aside like toys.

Her eyes never left me. Twisted bitch was enjoying this.

"Keep her occupied," Reyna commanded, leaping skyward and shifting in the same breath.

Yeah. Sure. No problem.

My skin screamed. The agony of holding this writhing mass of darkness beneath it was blinding. It had to go *somewhere*. But what could handle this sickness?

My body answered: *nothing*.

Which gave me an idea.

"Fuck me," I growled, sprinting *toward* her. She tilted her head, serpent-like, curious. Those onyx eyes stayed unblinking as I clenched my teeth and yanked on G's earth magic, binding the darkness into stone shards and hurling them at her.

She *smiled*. Flicked her hand. My makeshift weapons shattered mid-air, thudding into the dirt like chunks of sod.

Fuck.

"Move!" I screamed. "*Mine!*"

Relief cracked through me as G flipped back and Makena shot upward, shifting into shadow. With everything I had, I hurled her corruption back to her. She hissed, shielding against the blow—and the field blackened further around us.

Wall after wall, boulder after boulder, I turned her power into weapons. Just as I drew my short sword and stepped into range, the psycho hissed. Like a fucking snake.

Her body writhed and stretched, expanding in both width and height until she blocked out the sky. I stumbled backward, fell on my ass, scrambled up and *bolted.*

Oh, fuck. Fuckity, fuck, fuck.

Plan aborted.

I sprinted toward the open field, stalks snapping as a slithering, muscular body thundered behind me. I glanced back—and immediately regretted it.

Yep. Giant snake. She'd turned into a *giant* fucking *snake.*

The fangs were half as long as I was.

Wide-eyed and frozen, I watched her coil.

"What now!?" G barked.

I just shook my head, reinforcing my shields—not that they'd help.

"Run!" I yelled, following my own damn advice. With a bit of distance, I paused to breathe—just in time to see her mouth yawning open and lunging.

I yelped, shifting through shadows, cursing myself for not drawing more. I solidified ten yards to the right just as her jaws hit the earth. The impact shook the ground, sending me stumbling.

She reared back, twisting. An endless coil of glistening black scales churned up dirt, those void-black eyes locked on mine. Decay spread outward, devouring the field.

We were so dead.

I tried to jump—slammed into a shield or ward—and kept running. Reyna's shadow birds dive-bombed, their talons swiping for her eyes, but even they wouldn't touch her. Death pulsed outward, blade by blade.

I sprinted with everything I had, a sob breaking loose as an enormous shadow swallowed the sun.

I braced a beat before a wall slammed into me. A deafening snap rang through my body like a death knell, my ribs protesting the impact.

Then I was rising. Up, up, up.

The ground dropped away beneath me, and the horror below sharpened.

I twisted in the *arms* that held me—and found myself staring into livid citrine eyes.

Cyrus

"WHAT THE FUCK WAS THAT THING?" I bellowed, red clouding my vision as my arms locked around her too-small body. Way too fucking close. I wasn't sure whether to thank Lonan or knock him out next time I saw him. Thanks for the heads-up, but what was with the last-minute interference?

"What the fuck are *those*!?" she shouted back as I descended and deposited her on the ground.

"Poe really said go big or go home," I muttered, flinching as she jerked out of my hold and spun to face me. Her wide jade eyes scraped over the massive, thirteen-foot gold wings now stretching from my ink.

"You have actual *wings*," she gasped, the hazel-gold in her irises shimmering. "You can fucking fly!?"

"We can gush about it later—how do we kill that thing?"

"Your guess is as good as mine."

Fuck that. "I'm getting you out of here."

"Over my dead body."

"*That's* what I'm avoiding."

"I'm not *leaving them*."

"There's a thirty-foot fanged monster devouring the ground and you expect me to let you go back!?"

"It's cute you think 'let me' is in your vocabulary."

"Freya!"

"*Cyrus!*" she snapped, her voice laced with more venom than I ever wanted aimed at me. "There are innocents. I am not abandoning my team."

"*Fuck*," I growled, pacing as I retracted the wings, startlingly light and responsive, folding in like an accordion. Her eyes flared.

"Since when the fuck can you fly!?"

"You're oddly hung up on that."

"Well...*yeah!*" she squeaked. "Can you answer the question so we can move on and not die!?"

"Since—apparently—my mate was being chased by a *goddamn basilisk!*" I barked. "Now focus. What the fuck is that thing?"

"She was a soul—or I thought she was—but her eyes were black like a demon's. Her touch turns things to ash."

"Excuse me?"

"Yeah," she breathed, eyes glazing as she looked past me. "One of Reyna's flyers...she just...she's gone. Like fucking sand in the wind."

"Don't touch the demon snake," I muttered as something heavy shifted the earth.

"Please avoid that."

"Noted. What else?"

"That's all I've got. She swatted away our counterattacks like we were playing with sticks."

"You can't siphon her?"

"Wow!" she gasped, lobbing a blade over my shoulder. "Cyrus! I hadn't thought of that!"

"So that's a no."

Her eyes went wide, and then she was diving. "Move!"

Not needing a second warning, I wrapped my arms around her and launched skyward just as the colossal beast lunged.

"That's certainly handy," she panted as I banked left. "But you have to put me down!"

"Like hell."

"Cyrus, you can't fight if I'm in your arms. I have a plan."

"Fucking bond," I snarled, then dove, wings snapping out to stop our descent. "Now what?!"

She bolted a few steps, catching her balance. "You attack from the air."

"I don't have shadows."

"Wind and ice, then," she barked, yanking her phone out.

Seriously? "That better be for reinforcements."

"No, I just felt like ordering a goddamn pizza. *Jesus Christ, Cyrus.*" Her eyes tracked something past me, and I turned to find the massive beast swarmed by a conspiracy of ravens mid-shift—ice and stone spears launching before they dissolved and regrouped.

"You *will not* get close to her."

"I'll do whatever the fuck I have to. I'll siphon from the base—relay to Reyna's flyers that I need eyes in the sky."

"If you die out here, Freya, I'll bring you back just to kill you myself."

"Counterproductive, but noted."

The air...rippled. Not twisted—shuddered. And then they appeared. Soul after soul. All muscle. All radiating power strong enough to make lesser men shit themselves.

Grayshell.

She'd summoned her coven. No other explanation. They assessed the battlefield with collective sighs, as if this thirty-foot snake was just another Tuesday.

One looked unhinged, grinning as he summoned a bow. The woman beside him looked like Aphrodite's statue—soft features, wide-eyed awe. I spotted Ajax beside two men who had to be his brothers. But the last pair—hand in hand—strode forward without hesitation.

"Oh, what fresh hell is this?" the woman demanded, cracking her neck with indignation.

The male lunged for Freya, enveloping her in a hug that almost earned a growl from me. Until he pulled back and scanned her, head to toe, in that overprotective sibling kind of way.

"What the fuck, kid?"

"That's the general consensus. Catch up after?"

"Yeah," he agreed, their eyes going distant together. Then they moved—jumping across the field without another word.

Freya looked at me. "Be my eyes in the air?"

There'd be time for questions later. I nodded, pushing off and soaring above the monster's head.

Right as the sky darkened.

Rattle the cage, motherfuckers.

AUGUST

OH, *Aren's gonna be so pissed he missed this,* Alec said down the line as he took position on the far side of the field.

You can take him back a fang, I replied, drawing on the power of the sky, darkness swirling as my irritation deepened. Seriously? Man-eating, earth-decaying serpents, now?

The thing reared up, its head swinging from side to side as it assessed the circle tightening around it. Alec lit his fire, dipped his first arrow, and took aim just as the beast zeroed in on him. The Greeks mirrored him from the opposite end of the field.

Flames erupted along Ally's arms. Without a word, she glanced at Freya—who, of course, grinned like the batshit lunatic she was. I felt it then, the subtle sensation of a leak—no more than the pull of blood drawn, but just as vital—as she tapped into our bond, inhaling so deeply her eyes fluttered shut.

Ready? Ally asked, her gaze flicking between the beast and my sister.

Bring it on.

The field exploded into motion. Everyone shifted at once. Alec loosed arrow after blazing arrow, dodging a set of mucus-coated fangs that nearly clipped him. Freya's winged prince dove, spears of ice flying from his hands. Ally raised her arms, sweeping them outward to ignite a perimeter of twenty feet in searing flame.

The sky cracked open, thunder bellowing as I called lightning again and again, bolts tearing downward, each one closer to impact. The ravens made me nervous—the Paladin even more so, knowing how tight his bond to Freya ran.

I couldn't risk driving through the earth with so many of us spread across the field. And try as I might, I'd never been able to force them to fly again.

Irritated, I grabbed my bow—but a scream snapped my head to the side just in time to see the serpent's tail lash out, sending a woman flying. I threw out a hand to slow her fall, but dropped to my knees when she disintegrated into ash. Her terrified face burned itself into my memory.

A moment later, the snake dove, fangs first, straight into Fae's shield. It struck the wall of energy with a shuddering thud, water weeping up from the earth around her. Its tail lashed again, this time narrowly missing Brody, who crept forward, sword in hand.

Oh, absolutely not.

Rocketing to my feet, anger clouding my vision, I shouted, "Retreat!"

The Grayshellians obeyed instantly, Bellaton on their heels. Cyrus twisted into a dive, wings snapping shut as he shot straight for Freya.

My focus narrowed to the serpent as Ally's flames surged white-hot and blue, weaving between souls as the creature thrashed back. I shaped bolt after bolt, guiding each strike down from above, gritting my teeth as the snake's jerky movements kept it just out of reach. Glowing scars marred its iridescent black scales. Sweat slid down my temple as Ally's fire forced it back, the heat rising into the air. It screamed—a high, piercing sound that would haunt my dreams for years. And then it dove again, straight through the wall of flame, targeting Freya as she called her own lightning down—less precise than mine, but enough to force it to veer.

Now! I barked mind-to-mind.

The souls unleashed hell. Alec, Brody, and Ajax rained arrows from above. Fae cracked the ground beneath us, slamming massive plates of clay together to trap the serpent's writhing body.

But it was Cyrus who launched himself between the beast and Freya, wings flaring wide, arms stretched like a living shield.

I'd blinked—and suddenly he was holding an enormous golden blade. The snake reared back with a shriek so loud it rattled the sky, then recoiled, its body folding in on itself as a woman emerged at its center, arrows jutting from her shoulder and thigh.

Then the shadows swallowed her whole.

Cyrus vanished after her, a storm of ravens diving into the darkness behind him.

The rest of us stood panting, stunned. One by one, the ravens returned. A blonde woman I assumed to be Reyna Gwyne met Ally's eyes and gave a small, grim shake of her head.

But it was the man with the gold wings who held my focus as they vanished—seemingly absorbed into his tattoos—while he moved straight for Freya.

FIFTY-THREE
ENEMIES
CYRUS

"You okay?" I demanded the second my boots hit dirt in front of Freya, where she stood staring at her hands, panting.

"Fine," she breathed, dropping them into fists at her sides. Her eyes lifted to mine. "You?"

"Yeah." I could feel the eyes on my back, their animosity about as subtle as a spear to the gut. Unfortunately for them, I was fresh out of fucks after whatever the hell *that* was. Eyes locked on hers, I snatched her wrist. She half-heartedly resisted, and I raised her arm, gingerly peeling her fingers open. She hissed, and my stomach clenched. Livid red blisters covered her palm all the way to her fingertips.

"That doesn't look *fine.*"

"It's nothing," she insisted, pulling her hand back just as footsteps crunched through the grain behind me.

"It's not nothing. You channeled too much power too quickly."

"Giant. Snake," she bit out, daring me to make a scene in front of everyone.

"Let me help you."

"What, are you a healer now?" she shot back, cocking a hip and brow with a flash of defiance.

I glared and took her hands anyway, holding her uneasy gaze as I summoned the softest breath of ice. I blew a plume of frost over her seared skin.

Her moan of relief lodged itself straight in my memory vault. The tension it carved out of her shoulders...the way her lashes fluttered closed...

it stirred something primal. And that possessive monster that woke in my chest? Yeah, not going anywhere.

"I told you," I muttered, shaking my head as I exhaled again, gentler this time. "Your body will burn out before your gift does. The more power you channel directly, the faster it'll wear you down."

"Directly *channel?*" she echoed, eyes narrowing.

"You can either act as a conduit—let magic flow from a source, through you, to a wielder—or channel it directly. Conduit's safer. Slower burnout. As long as the wielder has a well big enough to take it."

She blinked, her lips parting. A flash-fire of emotions tore through her expression—understanding, betrayal, fear, resignation—all there and gone in a heartbeat. Her voice stayed flat. "Makes sense."

She rolled her lips, then snapped her gaze over my shoulder. I turned, feeling the heat before I saw them—the warrior couple standing close, weapons still in hand. The man looked like he was weighing whether to light me on fire. Cold calculation. Familiar eyes.

Freya lifted her hands in surrender, visibly annoyed. He lunged forward anyway. White light flowed from his palms over hers, and I watched the skin smooth and heal.

But Freya was only looking at the woman beside him, whose emerald eyes shimmered.

"I never meant to shackle you," the woman breathed. "I didn't know what we were."

"I know," Freya said softly.

"*You!*" Reyna's voice cracked across the field like a whip. I turned as she stalked toward me, eyes blazing. Ice frothed over my fingers, a spear coiling beneath my skin. Freya grabbed my wrist, trying to pull me back, but I held my ground. The warrior couple stepped between us, casual but protective.

Behind Reyna, two scowling Bellaton soldiers flanked her, and the rest of the Grayshellians watched with wary tension.

"Who do you think you are, crossing the divide!?"

"Cyrus Stuart," I said flatly, holding a mirroring set of my mother's fucking eyes. "*Prince,* actually."

"I know exactly what you are, you Paladin bastard."

"Reyna, I can explain," Freya blurted. "The meeting we scheduled—"

"And here I thought we were aligned, Miss Porter," Reyna snapped, slicing her off. "When were you planning to tell me you were climbing into bed with the enemy?"

"It's not like that—"

"I'm not interested in lies from traitors," she snarled. The more furious she got, the thicker her twang became. Just like my mother. The male warrior stepped forward, his partner's hand bracing him. I beat him to the punch.

"You will *not* speak to her as if she is below you," I growled.

"I take no orders from my sister's progeny—or Paladin filth."

"Then you'll see exactly how volatile we're bred to be."

"Oh, *shit*," said the russet-haired archer, circling cautiously with his bow still in hand. "Look, I know there's some family dysfunction unfolding, but can we maybe focus on the giant snake that just ravaged a field?"

Reyna ignored him. "You are on Bellaton land—"

"Your Majesty, if I may," one of her men said. Tall, lean, brown-skinned, with careful eyes. She didn't look at him, her glower firmly planted on me, but she didn't stop him either. An officer, maybe? "He might be on the wrong side of the river, but he saved Freya's life. And *mine*. He fought well."

"Um. Guys?" The tremulous voice drew every head. The blonde Grayshellian stood at the field's edge, terror etched across her face. "It's spreading."

We bolted toward her. All tension dissolved as we stared at the blighted field. The ground, beyond the scorched border, was decaying—just like everything the snake touched.

"Impossible," the first warrior breathed.

"Unless we're all hallucinating, apparently not," the archer muttered, kneeling to examine the line of desecration as it crept forward.

"It's like..." he whispered.

"A blight," Reyna finished, crouching beside him.

The pyro stepped forward, tossing her hands wide. A perimeter of fire roared into life, consuming the infected ground in a burst so hot we all stumbled back. I raised an arm against the heat. But when it died down, the decay kept creeping.

"Oh, fuck," Freya and I said in unison.

I threw ice. Still, it spread. Everyone tried—fire, wind, shadow, lightning —but nothing stopped it.

The pyro dropped to her knees, setting her hand to the earth. Her mate pulled her back only when the blight reached her fingers.

"Anything?"

She shook her head. "I can't *see*."

"Okay," said the male warrior—Freya's brother, apparently. "Anyone have any clue what kind of magic this is?"

Freya's gaze snapped to me. I shook my head, hating the helplessness that followed. I glanced around—fire, lightning, visions, the archer, the siblings...

"Holy shit," I breathed. "You're the deadly six."

"Seven," the archer muttered absently, "but three are missing."

"Eight," Freya grumbled.

"It'd be eight if the *eighth* intended to stay," the female cut in, stepping forward. "I'm Alvara. This is my mate, August—Freya's brother—and the Carters." She nodded toward the archer and the blonde. "Alec and Fae. You've met Ajax. Those are his brothers, Brody and Alastair."

"Holy shit."

"Yes, yes, fangirl later," Freya said, patting my chest. "Someone fix the food, please."

"I am forced to concur," Reyna grumbled.

"Fix *the food*," Alvara repeated slowly, her eyes snapping to August.

"Famine," he said grimly.

"Oh, fuck," Alec muttered. "The third? How'd we miss the first two?"

"No one said they're not already here," Alvara whispered, voice tight.

I looked around at all the stunned faces. "Sorry—did you just say...as in the third *Horseman?*"

"We're currently hypothesizing as much," Alvara said, striding along the ragged line of blight with steady, purposeful steps. Her brows pinched as her eyes slid shut, and when she turned back to Alec and Fae, apprehension was carved into every inch of her. She was beautiful in a way that felt more myth than mortal—unreachable, like the idea of light. Under her breath, barely audible, she murmured, "A tracker who is...a fertility Goddess will push against the third."

"No," Alec said flatly, slinging his bow across his chest with a snap of finality. "Ally, absolutely not."

"I cannot *see*, Alec," she said softly, shaking her head. "Whatever this is...it's drilling through the whole plan."

"No." Firmer this time. No room left for debate. August stood behind him, arms folded, one open palm pressed to his mouth like it might muffle his instincts.

"Will one of you have the common decency to fill the rest of us in?!" Reyna demanded. Even I found myself agreeing with her—begrudgingly. I nodded, jaw clenched.

"Fae is one of the prophesied pieces Adrastos was trying to bring to life," Alvara explained, still watching the curvy little blonde. "She was meant to counterbalance the Third Horseman."

"She's *pregnant*," Alec snapped, his glare landing like a curse on Reyna. "She can't afford to burn that bright."

"Darling," Fae murmured, laying a hand over his shoulder, "if we don't stop this, there won't be a world left to raise them in. Even if Aren gets us home, living trapped in the Middle is no life at all."

Alec stepped in front of her like a shield, both hands planted on her shoulders. "No, baby."

"She has a point," August said reluctantly, his voice heavy.

"August," Alec hissed, spine curling inward, pain etched in every line of his face, a flicker of betrayal in his eyes. "Don't."

Fae touched his jaw, her voice soft but resolute. "Babe, I've got this. No coincidences, remember?"

Alec looked like he might launch her over his shoulder and sprint for the hills. His arms folded, then dropped. He palmed his jaw, paced in place. Finally, he gave a single nod, his eyes only for her as the group collectively exhaled.

I stayed silent, but my gaze drifted toward Freya. She didn't so much as glance at me. But imagining her in Fae's position had my nerves scraping raw. Fae, however, was unbothered. She strolled forward, eyes sweeping over all of us.

"How many of you have innate earth magic?"

Reyna. Her dark-skinned partner. Ajax and his brothers. Alvara, Alec, and August all raised their hands. Freya started to lift hers but paused when Fae shook her head gently.

"Naturally occurring, sweetie," Fae clarified. "No point draining one source to charge another."

Freya nodded and stepped back, her expression pinched.

"I need you around the perimeter. On my mark, push your magic through the earth and command it to grow."

No questions. They moved fast, circling the tainted earth, dropping to their knees.

Fae pulled Alec down by the neck and kissed him once, fiercely, before mirroring the others. She raised her hand: *three, two, one*—and slammed both palms into the dirt. Her eyes shut. The others followed suit.

For a moment, nothing. Then—green bloomed. The edge of the blight fought back. Growth strained upward, only to falter. For a heartbeat, I feared it wouldn't work. But slowly, grotesquely, the rot began to curl, like worms writhing beneath the skin of the earth. Bit by bit, the darkness retreated. Blight turned to soil, then sprouted.

"*Yes*," Freya breathed, and I turned to see tears glossing her jade eyes. Her lips parted, reverent. Then, suddenly, her hand caught mine.

Tight. Desperate.

I didn't hate it.

I stood as her anchor while we watched a miracle claw its way free.

Fae rose. Arms outstretched like a maestro. Her hair whipped in a sudden breeze as she began to sing. The sound was ancient. Something older than history. Words I didn't recognize—chanted, sung, lifting into the sky with her power like an offering.

Agonizing minutes passed. The eight of them fought rot with root and rain and hope.

And they won.

"IT'S the same damn song and dance," Alvara said later, pacing in front of a makeshift command board and rubbing the edge of her collarbone like it burned.

"She was testing our response," August deduced. The others—all of them, even the ones who hadn't spoken a word—nodded.

The Grayshellians moved like extensions of each other. Like me, Carr and Cali. Like wolves bred to fight side by side. It made me wonder how Adrastos ever landed a hit.

"Fine," Reyna snapped, folding her arms. "But that still doesn't explain why my nephew violated the treaty, crossed the divide, and *just so happened* to stumble into you."

"It wasn't coincidence," I said. "I had a tip."

"From what source?" she demanded.

"Lonan."

Nothing. Not a blink. Just polished silence.

Freya, however, flinched like I'd slapped her. "What do you mean?" she whispered.

"He visited. Demanded I turn you over."

"Who the fuck is Lonan?" August growled, sparks arcing off his hands as emerald eyes promised retribution. For the first time, I wondered who'd win in a fair fight.

"Easy," I said, lifting my hands slightly. I was outnumbered—badly—and sitting alone on a bench while the room simmered around me. "He's an ally of my mother. But he's no friend of mine."

"How does he factor in?" August asked, shifting his attention to Freya. His mate never looked away from me.

I suddenly, achingly, wished the Bond was open. Wished I could just *show* her.

"Can you picture his face?" Alvara asked, voice sharp with suspicion.

Freya shook her head. "He's always masked."

"He was," I said. "Until tonight."

"What?" she choked. "I've *never* seen him unmasked."

"He seemed desperate."

"Can you show us?"

"Draw him?" I asked, irritated. "What, with the stick-figures they taught us in espionage electives?"

Alvara smiled. Sweet. Vicious. "That's the slow way."

Right. *The reading.*

"Yeah, *no.* I'm not submitting to *that.*"

"Hiding something, Stuart?" Reyna asked, her jaw grinding.

"A great many things. But that one's none of your business."

Freya ignored the back-and-forth. She bent and rummaged through her satchel, surfacing with a napkin and a piece of charcoal. Images of teenage Freya covered in paint splatters, or with fingers stained black struck me in the chest.

"You're an artist," I said dumbly.

"Gold star," she said. "Now talk, and let the rest of them work their own magic."

The walls around us were covered in a web of images, maps, articles. Reyna loomed near them, scanning for patterns. I got maybe five features into describing Lonan when Alvara's eyes went molten.

She marched across the room, tore a paper from the chart, and smacked it onto the table.

"This him?" she hissed.

I picked it up. Scowled. My stomach sank. The name scribbled below the sketch turned my blood cold.

Lonan wasn't the enemy's pawn.

He *was* Adrastos. He *was* the Commander half the country was hunting.

And he'd stood in my throne room just hours ago.

I didn't have to say it aloud. Ally read it on my face and turned, livid, toward Freya.

"What do you owe him?"

FIFTY-FOUR
FICKLE POLITICS
FREYA

The implications of Cyrus' confession, coupled with the reality that past-life me may or may not have weaseled out of a bargain with the bastard we were all hunting, sent the gathering into chaos. The underlying fear that Reyna wouldn't play well with others was confirmed as she dug in her heels —and her nephew went...startlingly quiet.

His hardened eyes flicked between them, jaw set, elbows braced on wide-set knees.

When August had demanded how Cyrus hadn't pieced together who Lonan was, he bit out, "I was a little busy being blackmailed to recall your perp's description, and then he implicated Freya was in trouble. I will not apologize for prioritizing getting to her over *your* war."

My chest gave an irritating squeeze, something obnoxiously similar to a heart palpitation. He'd come for me. He'd risked the treaty for *me*. And gave zero shits that it pissed off his aunt to do it.

"In a matter of days, it will be your war too, whether or not you want it," August warned, dissolving my temporary lapse in sanity. *Focus, Freya.*

Voice flat, Cyrus said, "I cannot speak for my hierarchy so long as our queen stands. Aside from a vague-ass description, I didn't know what Adrastos looked like."

"That bounty went out *weeks* ago," Alvara snapped.

"And you know as well as I do my parents have no interest in disseminating Aren's propaganda to our people."

"Propaganda implies you don't believe our report, Stuart."

"It implies the *Queen* doesn't. I didn't say where I stood."

Reyna jumped in. "You're seriously telling us you didn't see the wanted poster?"

He deadpanned. "Do I seem like a man who wouldn't leverage that kind of intel if I knew The Resistance's most wanted just popped into my fucking throne room?"

"It isn't in a Paladin's nature to do anything that doesn't serve them," Reyna said bitterly.

For fuck's sake.

"Cyrus isn't his mother," I snapped, still irritated she hadn't bothered to hear me out. So much for winning her fucking favor. "He proved that the day he chose my life over his own."

"Don't delude yourself into thinking he saved you for anything noble, Miss Porter." Her glare could've burned a hole through steel. "He promised you to that monster."

Cyrus stayed silent, but his eyes burned with loathing as he stared her down.

"He had ample opportunity to turn me over when I was unconscious for *three* days, under his care. If he were going to pay the debt, *that* was the window."

"Or you're too foolish to recognize when he's lulling you into complacency."

"Your theory has more holes than Swiss cheese." Why the fuck was I defending him? He could handle himself just fine. Hell, I didn't even trust the man, Mate Bond or not. But he'd given me no reason to believe he meant me harm—and today, he'd risked his neck...again.

"And your karmic *baggage* is hiding his true intentions," she retorted. A wall of defensiveness rose in my mind, logic be damned. Cyrus flexed his hands where they hung between his knees, unfiltered hatred seething toward Reyna.

"What the fuck do you think I owe you?" he intoned, voice level but ice-cold. "I just gave you all the information on your man. A little gratitude would be nice."

He wasn't wrong. The words were strategic—nothing that implicated him. Lonan had first appeared masked in the Luminark Manor throne room and offered to clear Reagan's debt in exchange for me—hence the Wings' determination to bring me in alive. His mother's familiarity with the masked man confirmed what I'd seen in her court. And Cyrus had summoned him on Valentine's Day, during the trap they'd laid after Nix kidnapped Blaz—but he didn't show. Probably too busy orchestrating synchronized attacks on all our allies.

Reyna didn't care. "If you'd been useful *intentionally*, perhaps."

"*Enough*," Ally and I snapped at the same time.

"For pity's sake, Reyna, he's a new soul. He's saved Freya three times this week *and* challenged his cousin to protect her." Ally tilted her head in feline scrutiny. It made me squirm. Cyrus, however, held her stare like a fucking stone statue. "I agree with Freya. What's more pressing is what Adrastos intends to do with this Crown."

That finally shifted the room's focus. Theories flew, but my eyes stayed on Cyrus where he sat, scowling at the floor. His mind churned—clearly. And Ally, based on that earlier dig, now knew my true intentions behind completing the Crucible. The problem? Adrastos revealing himself had undermined my authority. Who would trust a thief indebted to the enemy with the power of a throne?

Even my coven might balk.

And Cyrus...he might honor the Bond now, but once my true intent came out? No. He was Paladin to the core. Not even a supernal Bond could outweigh duty and honor. Keeping my distance was the only strategy. When I hurled my challenge at Reagan's feet, he'd change his tune—and I wouldn't blame him. He might even place himself between me and his mother.

And that was a blow I couldn't afford to feel.

I didn't come this far just to quit.

As if he sensed my thoughts, Cyrus looked up—warm hazel eyes meeting mine. Imploring. Every line of his face was carved from granite, like he was trying to say something I was too blind to understand.

Eleven leaders surrounded him. One exit. No allies. Of course he was uneasy, anger rolling off him in waves. But he'd stayed. Stayed to make sure I was safe—even knowing Reyna's wrath was coming. He'd cut off August's protest to defend me like I was his to defend.

And now he sat watching his rivals strategize a war he had no say in, both of whom wanted to move him like a pawn on a chess board. Leaving would look like guilt—or betrayal. Staying forced him to endure every barb like a live wire.

I had no business caring that he was in a no-win scenario.

Irritated that I did, I shoved off the wall.

I needed Aren. Or Ansel. Someone who could put Reyna in her place for once. Cyrus deserved better.

And it took every ounce of willpower to stay on the opposite end of the room instead of taking the seat beside him.

"Getting some fresh air," I muttered, though no one bothered to hear me as they debated the implications of Adrastos willingly burning an alias.

The chilly mountain air was enough to fill my lungs, but the still-shining sun took me by surprise. We'd been running verbal laps inside for so long, I expected the darkness to have claimed the day.

"*Mrrp.*"

The happy little sound dragged my gaze down to a black cat perched on August's front step, his eyes drilling holes into me. Raised voices still echoed from the house, so I hurried down the stairs and scooped him up, carrying us both toward the water. He purred against me, the sound reverberating in my chest as I toyed with the bell on his collar.

For as long as I could remember, cats found me when they needed comfort—or maybe they sensed when I did. This one burrowed into my palm like he already knew which of us needed it more.

A few minutes passed before he gave an affectionate "*mrrrow*", leapt from my arms, and pranced away.

Footsteps sounded behind me.

I didn't turn. Just watched the cat disappear behind a tree, then tilted my face toward the sky, trying to thaw the ice forming inside me.

A zipper purred, then leather settled around my shoulders, two warm hands smoothing it into place. I turned to see Cyrus staring down at me, his wordless gesture warming my heart in a way it absolutely shouldn't.

Peeling my eyes off his chiseled face, I said, "You're missing the show."

"I didn't come for their antics."

"What are you doing, Cyrus?"

"I could ask you the same."

"Breathing." I stared at the lake I'd spent so many hours on with my brothers. "The egos in that room are suffocating."

He snorted. A soft *shnick* made me glance back—he held out a cigarette and I plucked one from the case.

Snapping my fingers, I sparked flame from nothing, lit mine, then his. He nodded in thanks.

We stood there in silence, smoke curling around us. Frustration bled off both our shoulders.

"What a shit show," I muttered, watching as he blew out a long stream of smoke.

"Yeah."

"You gather anything else from your encounters?"

"What do you think?"

"I think Reyna's a thorn in your side, and you'd sooner let the world burn than bend to her."

He chuckled darkly, turning to watch me as he took another long drag.

"You came for me," I said, the words feeling heavy with the weight of that new reality. I hadn't said it. Hadn't thanked him. Hadn't acknowledged the significance in him swooping in to scoop me out of harm's way.

"Always," he said, as though it could be that simple.

I gritted my teeth to keep from flinching. "Don't make promises you can't keep, Cyrus."

"That's the gig, isn't it?"

"You're not a Guardian. I don't expect you to drop your own shit to save me when I offer you nothing."

His jaw tensed. "A Mate Bond runs deeper than *physicality*, Freya."

"Our lack of mental connection would beg to differ."

He pulled in deep on his next inhale, holding it as he watched me, then said, "That has everything to do with *you* refusing the karmic tie—and nothing to do with not *wanting* me."

I smirked. "Who said anything about that?"

His eyes tracked the cigarette as I lifted it to my lips.

He smiled, barely. "You saying you like what you see, Jailbait?"

"Don't inflate your ego just because you don't make me claw my eyes out."

"You know what I admire most about you? The poetry."

"Get fucked," I laughed.

He grinned. Dangerous. Effortless. It undid me.

"Weren't you *just* implying that wasn't on the table?" he asked. "I don't do 'tolerable.' I do 'yes—and maybe some begging.'"

"You never lacked for volunteers."

The humor faded from his eyes.

I deflected. "You know what's been bugging me? I've never checked the name in the third tomb."

He blinked at the shift. "The one with the inscription?"

"Yeah. I've only been through there while half-dead or running. Not exactly ideal for sightseeing."

"One of their children, maybe. Probably another royal."

"Maybe."

He paused. "You know what's bugging me?"

I raised a brow.

"Why did Adrastos warn me today? If he and the snake serve the same master, why not let her kill or capture you?"

"He needs me alive. Just like Ally does."

"Because of the prophecy?"

"It would appear so."

He drew deeply, smoke trailing from his lips. "Still doesn't sit right. Doesn't feel very over-lordy. And why unmask himself? Seems like a waste of a perfectly good alias. He had to know I'd be there—know I'd have to defend myself, maybe in front of your brother and Reyna. Why throw that away?"

"To undermine my credibility—or to earn your sympathy. Which he seems to have succeeded at, by the way."

"I'm not *sympathizing*. I'm analyzing."

"They're not mutually exclusive."

"For anyone threatening your safety, they are."

That unquestioning loyalty was maddeningly illogical. We were karmically even—a life for a life—but he kept saying things that made me *feel*, and that just wouldn't do.

"If you say so."

His hand snapped out. I didn't move in time before his fingers gripped my chin, angling my face toward his like he had a right.

"What do I have to do to convince you I mean what I say?" His breath skimmed my skin as he leaned in, voice lower now, urgent. "I choose my words intentionally. My loyalty is not given *lightly*, Freya."

"I've done nothing to earn it." I was proud my retort didn't tremble, though my thumb drifted back to the hilt of my blade. He might've had his father's bone structure and easy charm—but it was Reagan who'd painted his colors. And I wasn't about to forget that when it all went to shit.

"Not yet," he admitted, "but the universe brought you to me. I've read too much to believe that's coincidental. Mates appear when they're most needed—anchors dropped into chaos. Maybe I'm yours. Maybe you're mine."

His touch gentled, sliding from my jaw to the back of my neck, and I hated the part of me that didn't immediately recoil. That let him hold me there. That breathed a little deeper at his nearness.

I didn't want to see the honesty in his eyes. Didn't want to believe in the silent confession threaded through every glance he gave me.

I didn't want to care.

But that's what the Bond did, wasn't it? Twisted something primal until it felt like fate. "What do you need," he asked softly, "to realize we were given a gift?"

"A *gift?*" I scoffed breathlessly, refusing to acknowledge the way my pulse hammered, heat rushing through me at a possessive touch that should've been repulsive. This man had no right to me. No right to touch me or claim me or force me to listen. Yet, I stood there enamored, my lips parting as I stared up at him. *A gift.* My soul was perfectly cut to click into place with my murderer's son like a macabre jigsaw puzzle. What part of that was a fucking gift? "A cruel joke, at best."

"Why did you come back?"

"I was following orders."

He laughed—sharp and humorless. "Bullshit. If you were just here for

Reyna, you'd have locked that alliance in a day. Instead, you stayed. So I'll ask again—why are you finishing the Crucible?"

"To right a wrong," I said quietly, the truth slipping out despite myself.

"Then let me help you."

He stepped in closer, ditching his cigarette as he cupped my face with both hands. His voice was calm. Final. Like he'd already made the choice for us both.

"*You* can't."

"Then tell me what happened so I can find someone who can."

My hands met his wrists—meant to push him away. But I wasn't sure if I was holding him back...or pulling him closer.

"You wouldn't believe me."

"Try me."

I swallowed and tilted my head. "How's that research going, by the way? Find your traitor yet?"

He didn't flinch. "Don't deflect."

"And don't accuse me of murdering two of our souls, and then fail to find answers when I ask for them."

"I cannot provide answers I do not have," he shot back, deliberately using my own words against me. The twitch in his lips told me he knew it. "But the moment I smoke out the rat, you'll know. There is nothing more important than Paladin's honor."

"Of *that,* I'm painfully aware."

"So let me help you reclaim yours."

"You can't—"

"Trust you? You've said that."

"But here you are." My voice dropped, my thumb absently brushing the edge of his sleeve. His scent was all cedar, ash, and leather. The same smell soaked the jacket I hadn't returned. My head tipped just slightly, my chin lifting toward his like my body was making decisions I hadn't cleared.

"You saved me," he said, "when I didn't deserve your mercy."

"I think we're even now."

"Then prove it," he whispered, brushing the tip of his nose along mine. "I can't explain what this is—"

"*A goddamn Bond—*"

"—but I don't want anyone else."

My breath stuttered.

"It wasn't just the Bond transferring your pain into my chest. It was you. You stood your ground against all of us that night."

"A cornered animal does the same."

"I was mesmerized *then*. Something bigger than me stayed my hand at Uptown. Today, when that bastard said you were in trouble...the world stopped existing, Freya. My hierarchy didn't matter, my pride, my honor, all of it meant shit if you needed help. So, *let me.*"

"You don't know what you're saying."

"Then tell me." His fingers curled into my hair, tugging gently. "But don't lie. There's always been something *more.*"

"That's the Bond talking."

"Then tell me I'm wrong. Tell me you feel nothing when I touch you like this." His hands burned paths into my skin, one on my throat, the other in my hair.

I opened my mouth. Tried to lie. But no sound came out. His eyes—smug, hazel, luminous—searched mine.

He *knew.*

"You getting hurt wrecked me," he said. "Call it a tie. Call it fate. But I broke my queen's direct orders because *you* were on the other side of the field. So give me your worst, Freya. I promise—I can take it."

That was the last straw.

Because it wasn't Cyrus's face I saw anymore. It was Reagan's. Regal. Smug. Bleeding out on her throne after I drove a blade through her fucking throat.

I stumbled back, shaking him off as I looked away.

"No. *You can't.* And I didn't come here to break you, Cyrus."

He blinked, pain flashing across his features before he masked it. "Then *don't.*"

"Freya!" August's voice cracked through the clearing. I turned to find him and Ally approaching—blades on their backs, wary eyes flicking between us. "You alright?"

I straightened. "Be right there!" To Cyrus, I murmured, "Word to the wise? Set yourself free before it's too late."

The wind shifted, and he stared at me like he'd already tried. Like I was the one who held the key.

"I don't think that I can."

FIFTY-FIVE
FATE WEAVER
ALVARA

You look perplexed. What secrets is she guarding? August asked, mind-to-mind, a week after we arrived in Santa Bloom—drawing my gaze up from dark hair and mesmerizing aquamarine eyes. I was perched on the leather sofa, luxurious and well-worn, but the ecstatic high of reuniting our coven had long since given way to a morbid, gnawing curiosity: who, precisely, was the woman God carved from the clay of the world to balance my sire?

'Stunning' was inadequate. Magnolia possessed a beauty so arresting it made other women shrink. And when she wasn't locked in battle with her wounds, she radiated a quiet certainty I deeply admired. With another few decades of experience—or another life more carefully guarded—this soul could move mountains. Selfishly, I hoped she would survive the war, if only so Aren's smile might become a permanent fixture.

We'd reconvened with him that afternoon, then jumped the entire coven—sans Freya—back to the Florida Estate, where space and solitude came in abundance.

She's...different, I thought lamely. Lacking a more apt word, I added, *Fragmented.*

It felt cruel. But Magnolia Green's mind was a mosaic: jagged and colorful, soldered together by something stronger. 'Different' didn't begin to cover it.

From one moment to the next, my access to her psyche shifted drastically. When emotion surged, her mind opened wide. I could dissect it—her love, her guilt, her dread—all laid bare, puzzle pieces easy enough to place. But something else restrained her. Something I couldn't name. There were glimpses of surface-level observation and sentiment, but not the depths. And beneath it all, a haunting sense—like she carried the residue of a thousand battles, none of them kind. A shadow I could only ever associate with death. But that couldn't be. She was a new soul, woven into a fresh body. There was nothing in her demeanor to suggest she'd survived war. Had she absorbed it? When her mother died? Or perhaps her sisters' tragic deaths left an imprint deeper than I could see.

The trouble wasn't merely that Magnolia was written in a foreign language. It was that—even now—with her and Blythe in the same room, I could not separate them in any future I glimpsed. Every vision where she existed, Blythe was present. Every triumph, every heartbreak—constant.

They were so painfully entangled, I had never seen anything like it. And our coven was nothing if not interdependent. So, that was saying something.

Blythe—the little blonde healer—radiated warmth in every sense. Like Aren, everything she did was saturated in sincerity: her laughter, her awkwardness, even her discomfort. I envied her presence. Her mind was crystalline—open water, all the way to the bottom. Her reading would be fully saturated in color, should she offer it.

You're staring, my love, August thought, amusement rich in his tone.

Very astute.

Maybe...don't? he offered playfully.

I canted my head, but did not look away from Magnolia. Love for Aren and Blythe, even the Callahans, poured from her in palpable waves. One name kept surfacing—*Bellamy.* Worry. Fear. Guilt. The emotions alternated, dredging him up again and again. My palms itched to touch her and unearth his memory in full. I didn't care for the loyalty she assigned him, though gratitude, perhaps, explained it. He was her protector—and I needed to understand how their threads intertwined.

I did not avert my gaze as I projected my inquiry toward the Old General seated across the room. *Ansel, have you met the Bellpost nomads?*

Two of them.

How many are there?

A small coven. She names three.

Bellamy...

Barry and Smith I've encountered. The third's a detective. Frequently occupied.

Can we arrange a meet?

We need every capable soul we can find, he replied. *I believe, should you ask, Magnolia will be inclined to assist.*

I scowled as no vision came. Confusion tightened my focus on Ansel. *I wouldn't be so certain.*

Visions still unreliable?

They've improved, August interjected. *But it varies, depending on her energy reserves.*

Your encounter with the serpent depleted you?

I shook my head. *No. At least, I didn't think so.*

Blythe rose from where she sat beside her sister and ambled toward me, all sweetness and sunbeams. She was careful not to brush against my exposed skin, her thoughts telegraphing her intention as she summoned a hoodie from the rack. I slid my gloves on, softening my expression as she settled beside me, grinning.

"Aren says you and August are Soul Bound, in addition to being mates. Is that true?"

Confusion prickled as her thoughts drifted toward threads, stripes, and tangled lines. But my heart stilled when I sensed her belief that *our* Bond was incorrectly tied.

No fucking way. I only knew one other person that could see destiny's ropes.

Narrowing my eyes, I asked softly, "Fate weaver?"

Her oceanic eyes widened. She glanced over her shoulder, nervous.

She doesn't know, I thought into her mind, amused by her blinking surprise. *Come now. You knew exactly what I was when you stepped through that door.*

Seven sisters. You really are as good as they say.

Yes, well. I do try.

Her laughter—radiant, unburdened—fit her perfectly. God, she was beautiful, this witch so full of sunlight. Especially as her eyes crinkled from smiling. *I just didn't expect you to see it so quickly. No one ever has.*

Not much experience with psychics?

Apparently not.

May I ask a candid question?

Not like I could say no at this point.

Why do you hide your gift? I hadn't realized Magnolia wasn't the only one running from her fate.

She shrugged, one graceful shoulder rising. A soft smile curved her lips. *My mother told me fate weavers were worth killing for.*

Grief—overwhelming and ancient—poured into the space between us. I leaned back slightly, even as she masked it behind a songbird's smile.

Unfortunately, her death proved her theory.

I don't know many, I admitted. *But I have a friend to the east. Do you know Jason Westerlund?*

I know of the Westerlunds—Nat speaks highly of them.

As do we. You've never met?

Not yet.

Smiling, I offered gently, *I'll take you. Jason is kind—and he owes me a favor or two. I'm certain he could show you the ropes.*

Literally?

A soft laugh slipped out. I glanced at August, watching from the periphery. *Yes. I suppose so, if that's how you see them.*

And how do you see them?

Like film reels in my mind.

Can you change them?

Sometimes. When alternate paths are available.

But you can't see...Bonds?

I shook my head. *Not directly. But it's not difficult to infer, especially if their futures are intertwined—or if I have intimate access to their thoughts.*

My gaze drifted to Aren, then returned. Her smile softened, and she followed my glance before nodding.

Why do you ask?

For a friend, she replied sweetly. *His map is a maze. A tangled mess. I was hoping you might help.*

My eyes widened. *You intend to sever someone's Bonds?*

Is that possible? She rocked slightly, inhaling as she envisioned what had to be hundreds of glimmering threads. A tapestry of golds, blacks, and so many reds.

I don't know, I said honestly. *That's a question for Jason.*

She hummed aloud, tucking strands of pale hair behind her ears. *Very well. Thanks.*

I didn't do much.

No, but it's nice having someone to talk to about these things. Even if this mind-to-mind thing is unnatural as fuck.

You get used to it.

If you say so, Angel of Death.

Ugh, not you too.

She cackled, clapping her hands over her mouth before rising from the sofa and glancing back. *You live up to the legends, you know. They say never meet your heroes, but...*she shrugged airily. *This was pretty cool.*

Aloud she said, "I'm grabbing a drink. Do you want something, Alvara?"

I shook my head at the segue. "Please. Our family calls me Ally."

Her hair tossed over her shoulder as she looked back toward Magnolia—currently squirming in Aren's arms, laughter ringing through the room.

"Okay," Blythe said with a prim nod. "Nickname basis with Aren's second. This just keeps getting weirder."

Laughing, I replied, "And I'm alright. Thanks for asking."

She nodded, dipped her chin reverently toward August, and started for the kitchen.

But August—who had, of course, eavesdropped on the entire mental conversation through our Bond—had other plans.

"Blythe! Wait up. I have a question."

FIFTY-SIX
COMPANY
CYRUS

"Ask stupid questions, get stupid answers, little brother."

"Piss off," I muttered into my beer, draining the last of the pint like it might numb the ache that had been burning in my ribs all damn day. *The Rougarou* was packed. Music thumped through the walls, two nomad biker crews had commandeered the billiards tables, Wings were out in force looking for trouble, and the Guard had claimed a back booth, elbow-deep in fried gator and Boudin balls. Chaos reigned, per usual.

"What'd you want us to say?" Jo teased, dragging one manicured nail along the salted rim of her margarita.

I smeared condensation into a streak on the bar, eyes fixed on the amber inside my glass. "I dunno. Maybe 'forget about her'?"

"I'd love to," Cali laughed, "if I believed you could."

"You've gotta get to the bottom of what happened to her last time, Cy," Jo pressed, licking the salt from her finger. Cali grabbed her wrist and popped it into her own mouth, sucking the tip shamelessly.

"Get a room."

"Jealous?" Cali grinned, leaning in to kiss her.

"No," I groused. I sounded jealous.

I *wasn't*. I was *irritated*.

Irritated that Grayshell's most wanted had stood in my throne room yesterday and I hadn't even known because Mother was scheming with the motherfucker.

Irritated that Freya didn't give a single shit about the Bond we shared. That she'd probably reject it.

It wasn't like I'd ever wanted a love match. I knew I'd end up with some second-string noblewoman positioned just beneath Calypso on the family tree, for the sake of bloodlines. But knowing there was a soul out there wired to be mine—feral, cunning, utterly untamable—and having to stomach some strategic marriage with anyone else?

Bullshit. That's what it was.

"You've been off," my sister noted, pinning me with a look. "Haven't seen you with the usuals."

"The *usuals* took an interest in *Nix.*"

Now that she said it, I realized I hadn't looked at another woman like that since the damn Bond woke and tethered itself to the one person hell-bent on arm's-lengthing me with the Heisman maneuver of the century. Pathetic. I should've punched myself in the face just to knock the stupid out.

"Nothing a cotton swab and blood sample couldn't test for." Jo elbowed me, jerking her chin toward the door. I sighed—and turned.

Red hair.

Green eyes.

Combat boots laced halfway and fishnets under cutoffs. Band tee exposing just enough skin to make my hand twitch.

Freya.

My Freya, standing in my bar like she wasn't about to turn my whole night to ash.

Her gaze landed on me and softened. Mine didn't. My pride wouldn't let it. What the hell was she doing here? If she didn't plan to present herself to Mother, showing up at our bar with a full Guard in tow was a bold way to start a war. Where was Ajax? Had she ditched him again?

Grinding my teeth, I turned back to my beer.

"This'll never work, little brother." Cali slid into the stool beside me, slinging her arm across the backrest like she lived here.

"You assume I'm the one fighting it."

"You, and your earlier tantrum. But I see the way you look at her."

"Like I wanna sink my teeth into that perfect little ass?"

"Ew," she winced. "Like you wanta sink a ring on that dainty little finger."

I recoiled. "Not my style."

Cali snorted, signaling the bartender with two fingers. "Then wipe your chin. You're droolin'. Gonna give people the wrong idea."

With a sigh, I rotated back toward the room, spine braced against the bar. Freya was making her way to the billiards tables, sharp eyes sweeping the setup like she already had her mark.

"She's my mate," I muttered. "Am I not entitled to some entertainment?"

Cali raised a brow, unimpressed. "You hook up with her, you'll be chasing that high until the reaper comes. You know it. That's not a hookup, Cy. That's a Bonnie."

"I'm not Clyde."

She didn't dignify that with a response.

"Ya know me. I'm here for a good time. I make 'em laugh, we have some fun, I send them on their way after a few orgasms and they leave smiling. No strings. No expectations."

And that was true—had always been true. My reputation preceded me. Hell, half the city knew how I operated. But with Freya...I didn't want any of that. I wanted something I couldn't name. Which meant Cali was right, and I hated her for it.

"She broke your nose the first time you fought her."

"And?"

"You're a psychopath and violence gets you off. Which makes this clever little bitch your personal brand of catnip."

I smirked despite myself. She wasn't wrong. I was every shrink's wet dream, wired for chaos. And Freya? She was a one-woman apocalypse.

I should've known I was screwed the second I plucked her out of danger yesterday and my blood wouldn't stop singing her name.

Freya took her shot at the table and the men around her stopped smiling. She was hustling them. And they were dumb enough to fall for it. So much for low profile.

"Like I said," Cali drawled as her glass thunked softly against the counter, "fucking catnip."

I chuckled darkly, emptying my glass. The blond guy stepped closer, and my hackles rose.

"I'm fine, sis. Appreciate the concern." My fingers flexed on the bar. "We don't even know each other."

And yet...Freya's gaze found me.

I straightened, tension hardening in my spine at the blade hidden behind those jade eyes.

The girls were still yammering about something I didn't register—because the blond prick she'd been putting in his place had the audacity to lay a hand on her waist. My grip tightened around my pint. Freya scowled up at him, fingers drifting toward the blade at her hip as she barked something over the music that looked an awful lot like fuck off.

That was enough of that.

On a sigh-turned-growl, I rose from the stool, glass still in hand as I started forward.

"Oh, fuck," Jo muttered behind me.

I heard both of them scramble to follow as I cut a path through the rowdy crowd. Freya had already shaken off the dead man's hand, brows drawn into a warning scowl as she stepped backward, lifting herself with practiced ease onto the table behind her.

Red.

My vision went fucking red.

Deadman's friend reached for him—right as my pale fingers wrapped around his throat.

The bastard didn't even get a full breath before I smashed the glass into his temple, smirking as he crumpled. "*Asshole*," I muttered.

His buddy had better reflexes. Blade already drawn. I was faster.

The shadows clocked every onlooker as Cali moved to cover my back. I caught his wrist, twisted sharply, disarming him and snapping the joint in one fluid motion. "She said—" I jabbed a nerve that dropped him like a sack of bricks. "—*fuck off*."

I twirled the knife once in my grip, flicking my gaze up to Freya. She crouched on the table, wild and gleaming, eyes sparking with mischief. "You okay?"

"I had it handled," she said, voice dry. The annoyance in it warmed my chest.

"No doubt." I quirked a brow and flipped the knife in my hand, letting it fly. It spun once before thunking into the dartboard's bullseye on the far wall. Partially to blow off steam. Partially because if I didn't touch her, I was gonna combust.

I stepped between her knees, hands settling on her thighs—fishnet wrapped, warm, perfect. The ache that lived in my ribs eased at the contact.

"You're a drama king, you know that?"

But her wrists slid easily around my neck, fingers curling in the hair at my nape like they belonged there. She was a damn good actress. Too good. But in Paladin territory, surrounded by eyes that would slit her throat if they knew what she was, pretending to be mine was survival.

Carr materialized at my side, clearly unimpressed. "Was that necessary?"

"She asked nicely," I said flatly, not bothering to hide the smirk tugging at my mouth.

"Hi, *Scooby*," Freya chirped, flashing him a grin as he crouched to inspect the groper.

"Hi, *Maleficent*. Nice to see you not incinerated."

"Aww. I'm touched."

Carr snorted. "Good luck," he muttered, dragging the limp bastard toward the door without another word.

I turned back to Freya, more aggravated than I had any right to be.

"Answer the question," I growled. "Did he hurt you?"

"It takes more than a drunk with a hard-on and grabby hands to hurt me, *Cyrus*." She must've seen the storm gathering behind my eyes because she added, "No. I'm not hurt."

"Good." I let my hands fall, stuffing them into my pockets. "Now—why are you here?"

Her fingers worked into my hair again, and I bit back the groan that threatened to escape. Fuck. How the hell were we supposed to breathe the same air inside Paladin walls without going insane?

I gently caught her wrists, lowering her arms. I couldn't do this. Couldn't *be touched* like that and think straight. She nearly flinched when I pulled away, but I didn't stop, retreating a step like it might help.

It didn't.

"I'm sorry. For...yesterday. I..."

"Yes?" I asked coolly.

"You were kind. Beyond helping me, you were..." She tucked a strand of bright hair behind her ear. "I see your olive branch, Cyrus. I just don't know how to take it without setting you up for disappointment."

"Why's that the only ending you see?"

"We stand on the precipice of a new Great War."

"You rejecting me because we might die?"

"Death is the only inevitable."

"Great. *What* the hell *does that mean?*"

She swallowed hard, wetting her lips—and damn it if my gaze didn't lock on her mouth. Always her mouth. "Paladin will need your leadership in the chaos ahead."

"I'm male. They'll barely notice."

"They will," she said, voice sharp with certainty that pulled me toward her. "How was your day?"

"You ask like you give a shit."

"Because I do. I..." She shifted, visibly uncomfortable. "Detachment is my default. Please don't take it personally."

"How could I?" I said, the sarcasm leaking through. Attachment was weakness. Vulnerability. My mother had made that lesson crystal clear— over and over. And here I was, unraveling because of a single damn Bond, and the woman on the other end of it couldn't give me a real answer.

She was acting like a Paladin. I shouldn't begrudge her that. Shouldn't being the operative word.

"Didn't notice."

Her glare made her feelings on my attitude clear. "*Right.*"

"Why are you here?"

She rolled her lip between her teeth before sighing, like the words pained her. "I needed to see you."

"My condolences."

"*Cyrus.*"

"Don't Cyrus me. I'm man enough to respect your decision, but don't drag this out."

She hopped off the table, stepping into my space, hands landing lightly on my chest.

"You either intend to honor the Bond, or you don't." My voice dropped, rough and bitter. "Stop fucking with me and choose."

"It's not that simple."

"So you've said. But if you won't explain why, I can't simplify it for you."

"The last time I trusted a Paladin, I got my throat slit."

"Gimme a name and I'll return the favor."

"You know how I feel about empty promises."

"Christ, you're maddening," I growled, backing away. Her hands dropped from my chest, the loss of contact landing like a sucker punch to the gut.

A roar of laughter echoed from the billiards table behind us. Games had resumed. Normalcy reasserted itself. It only made me angrier.

Jabbing a finger at her, I ground out, "Don't touch me like that when we both know you don't fuckin' mean it. You tell *me* to stay away—and then show up in my bar."

"We need to talk."

"*You think I don't know that?* What do you think I was trying to do when you ran off with your brother and his mate?"

"We had orders."

"Fuck orders." The words came out sharper than intended. "This impacts more than this lifetime, Freya. You're famous for your little games, but I won't be one of them. I've laid *everything* out—open, raw—and you're standing there like I'm full of shit."

"People are watching," she muttered, her gaze flicking nervously across the bar.

"Fuck them, too."

Her jaw tightened. "My motives mean nothing if we don't get ahead of Adrastos. That's why I'm here. Everything we've both done these last few weeks will burn if we don't cut him off at the knees." She met my eyes. "*I'm here* to ask for your help."

A breath hissed through my nose. Finally. Something tangible.

"Fine." I yanked my hair back, twisting it into a hasty bun.

"Can we go somewhere more private?"

"I'm not sure that's wise."

Arching a brow, she chirped, "I promise to control myself."

From somewhere across the bar, Jo and Cali laughed. *Fucking catnip.* I snorted, shaking my head. Then I met those hazel-ringed jade eyes and exhaled a steadying breath.

"What do you need?"

"To track him down before he sends his men after me—now that you've declared you won't do it yourself. I have a hunch. I'm hoping you'll tell me I'm wrong."

Ten minutes later, we were seated in my usual booth at the back. Neither of us touched the glasses the server left behind.

She'd be the death of me. Infuriating, brilliant, breathtaking, maniacal demon creature.

"All signs point to Bellpost," she said without preamble.

"And yet you played dumb in front of the others."

"I don't offer unvetted leads. I'm not dragging Ally and August into hostile territory unless I'm sure."

Couldn't fault her there. "So, what are you waiting for? Why not accuse them directly?"

"I don't know enough about Moros."

"There's not much to know."

"Expand."

"The hierarchy died," I said, more bitterly than I intended. "The Divide scattered our descendants across the globe. Their dwindled numbers were slaughtered under Koa's reign, and what was left nearly vanished when Moros backed his uncle's war against the Solskari. If Adrastos came out of Bellpost, he doesn't answer to them now. Moros has an ego the size of Helios—he wouldn't sit on a weapon like that without bragging to the rest of us."

I didn't say it aloud, but I was nearly certain she was right.

Her gaze narrowed. "What aren't you telling me?"

I shrugged. "He said as much."

Her brows lifted. "What?!"

She leaned in so fast her cider nearly sloshed over the rim of her cup.

"He claimed he had a right to my mother's throne," I said coolly. "So, I figured Bellpost or the Knights."

"Why wouldn't you lead with *that*?"

"Because I dug back through our history and found nothing. No Adrastos. Not in any Bellpost tome. For a battle hierarchy, the only names more revered than warriors are royals—and he's not on either list."

I watched her lips part slightly, her eyes flicking from one side of the table to the other as she processed. After a moment, she shook her head.

"It's not his name."

"You think both are aliases?"

"Maybe."

"You've got a theory?"

"No. When he struck a deal with Alvara, her brand came back marked A.A."

Alvara of Grayshell. *The* Alvara. The one who didn't barter unless the world was ending.

My mind flared with a thousand questions. "Okay, we're circling back to that later. But for now: there's no one with those initials in any of the historical texts I've read. And I've read everything I could get my hands on."

"In order to command a force that size—"

"What size?"

"At least a thousand Renown."

"Then he's a general at minimum."

Her curt nod matched the unease pulsing in my gut. "Shadows, clairvoyance…Ally says illusions too. He's ancient, Cyrus. No one masters that many gifts unless they've had centuries."

"What does Aren say?"

She wrapped her hands around her mug, drawing it close, eyes going distant. "All gifts present in balance."

"You think your second is his counterweight?"

"We did."

"You said *did*." My voice dropped. "You think you were wrong?"

"I'm starting to wonder if it wasn't the other way around. Something doesn't line up."

No shit. "Like why the fuck he didn't come for you himself?"

She pushed her mug forward, then pulled it back, indecisive. "I've been glamoured against Lonan for at least three lifetimes. Valora has wards too."

I was already shaking my head. "He tipped me off. He saw *something*."

"He might've seen the report come in about the weapons," she offered.

A valid point. "Still doesn't answer the question. Why send others? Why not come himself? How long before he sics his dogs on you?"

Her eyes widened a split second before the front door was kicked open. We both turned.

Two Renown stood silhouetted in the doorway.

Freya

THE ROOM ERUPTED in a torrent of shadow.

Chairs screeched, the music cut out, and screams tangled with shouted orders—but it was the now-familiar hand in mine that had me moving before thought could catch up to instinct. Bodies slammed into mine as we ran. I couldn't see—couldn't hear anything over the rush of blood and chaos—but I kept my footing, kept moving, tethered to Cyrus as he dragged me toward the exit.

Then, suddenly—air. Cool, humid air.

We burst out into the dusk, lungs filling as the bar doors thudded shut behind us. Blinking against the light, I lunged forward, wrapped my arms around his waist—and jumped.

When our boots hit the dirt, we both jolted apart, eyes wide, hands flying over each other, checking for wounds.

Only once we were sure neither of us had been hit did we release our grips and turn, scanning the street. Then, finally, we breathed.

"You were saying?" I muttered.

His gaze flicked toward Luminark Manor behind me, and the scowl returned in full force.

"What the fuck do you think you're doing?"

"We need answers, and we need them now. I've already torn through everything in Reyna's library."

"I've told *you*—I've memorized the history we have. You exposing yourself to my mother was not on my agenda. Unless you're ready to declare your intent to duel in front of the council, this is a shit idea."

"Do you have an alternative?" I snapped. "Who else would have a comprehensive archive on Bellpost?"

He cast another uneasy glance toward the manor. "Reyna's collection is more thorough than ours. If anything survived, it'll be east of the river."

"I've already read everything in it," I said, shaking my head. "She mandated history lessons when I first arrived. I covered every known text on the shadow hierarchies. None of them had answers."

"She let you into the restricted section?" he scoffed.

I scowled. "There is no restricted section. This isn't a fucking academy. She doesn't keep the 'real' books behind a velvet rope."

"Reyna Gwyne absolutely has a restricted section," he said, the smugness in his voice enough to make me want to knock the smirk off his face.

"Where?" I demanded. "I scoured that place."

"In the Middle. Where else?"

Heat prickled beneath my skin. It took every ounce of training not to snap.

"Well, that's bullshit. I asked if I was missing anything."

"Don't take it personally. She's not known for transparency. Hell, even Blaz didn't get access to her personal collection until last year."

"Why on earth would she insist on teaching me the history of the Middle Realm and then withhold..." My breath hitched.

The irritation drained in an instant, replaced by cold calculation. My attention locked on his face—his carved features caught in the dying sun.

Who didn't have access until last year?

"*What* did you just say?"

FIFTY-SEVEN
PRETTY LITTLE LIAR

FREYA

"What?" Cyrus asked, face schooled into that immovable mask of calm.

"How would you *know that?*" I stepped in, jabbing a finger into his chest. "You just said Blaz didn't get access to the restricted library until last year. How. Would. You. Know. That?"

"I must've—"

"So help me God, I will knock your pretty lights out if you lie to me right now, Cyrus Stuart. *You* do not *misspeak.*"

A satisfied smile tugged at his lips, slanting to the left. "You think I'm pretty?"

"This has been well established. Don't change the subject." I gave him a sharp shove. He didn't budge, only let his smirk widen.

"Just nice to hear, given the circumstances."

"The circumstances where you're lying to—" A ribbon of shadow slid up my cheek and wrapped around my mouth. I narrowed my eyes at the smug bastard, yanked on his magic, and conjured shadows of my own. His gaze dipped to where mine surged from the earth, rolling toward his boots like a tide. The beautiful asshole stepped closer, towering above me until I had to crane my neck to hold his gaze as my shadows twined up his legs.

"Not. Here," he said coolly, nodding toward the house.

I lunged for his hand, ready to jump us out of here and rip him a new one, but he twisted away, yanking out of reach. A growl built in my throat as I turned on him again, my shadows stealing the gag off my mouth.

"Oh, stop smiling, you intolerable ass. *I called you pretty*—are you twelve?"

"If we leave, can you be civil long enough to hear me out, or are you determined to remain feral?"

"The last thing you'll ever do is domesticate me."

"So...you're saying there's a chance?"

"Jesus Christ." I hurled my shadows forward, locking him in place long enough to grip his wrist and jump before he could blink. The last thing I heard was his goddamn laugh—then we landed hard on Bellaton's front lawn.

His humor vanished and my smile bloomed. "Not so funny now, is it?"

"Reyna—"

"—is under direct orders from Alvara to summon all souls before the Equinox. She's in the Middle until they return."

His brows twitched, faint surprise leaking through his mask. "What's happening on the Equinox?"

"That's above a liar's pay grade." I offered my sweetest smile. "You and Blaz are in contact? And so help me if you lie again—"

"Yes. We *talk*. Okay?" He caught my arms, dipping his head as though that might lessen the impact of his height.

"Since *when?*"

"Hang tight, for fuck's sake." The world tilted. Sound dulled. He yanked me into the shadows—slipping along the base of the house and through the damn crack in my windowsill. When color and motion returned, I sucked in a breath.

"Does that ever not suck?" I gagged. "I never needed to know what mortar looks like from the inside."

"I think it's cool."

"Stop changing the subject."

"You're the one who asked."

"Cyrus."

He sighed. "He's my cousin."

"And a sworn enemy. Unless..."

"Calypso and I have never treated our mothers' feud as a reason to dishonor blood. Family is family."

Disbelief burned through my ribs. "How long? How? *Where do you meet?*"

"Since we were sixteen. We sent ravens. Met on neutral ground."

"And he just *agreed?* You could've walked into a trap—he could've—"

He clapped a hand over my mouth and cradled the back of my neck, forcing eye contact.

"Calypso and I got wind of a raid that would've endangered him—and Reyna's refugees. We disagreed with innocent lives being collateral in a family war. So, we tipped him off."

I blinked. Tried to breathe. Every inhale reeked of leather and cedar. Hesitantly, he released me.

"Unbelievable."

"Is it though?"

"The raids on Bellaton assets?"

"We told him what we were fighting. He agreed to help."

Fury rose, bright and cutting. "You set him up for treason, and you get away Scott free."

"No," he bit out, anger flaring in his hazel eyes as I shoved him back a step and lifted a hand to stop him from following.

"They've actually been supplying my people with imbued weapons," a familiar voice cut in. I turned, pulse leaping.

Blaz stood in the doorway, arms crossed, the same arrogance dripping off him as Cyrus. "And sending updates on their Reaper's venom research. Until a *certain someone* trashed our labs."

"You *lied* to me," I growled. The betrayal scraped raw and immediate. Blaz was—had been—a friend.

"I *omitted*," he said gently, stepping inside and closing the door. Cyrus flicked his fingers, sealing the space in a soundproof bubble. "To be fair, you never asked if I was on speaking terms with my cousins."

I charged toward him, but shadows snagged my waist, hauling me back into a wall of heat and muscle. An arm locked around me. Cyrus' voice grazed my ear, low and quiet:

"How do you think your friends found you on Valentine's Day?"

"Bullshit," I snapped, stomping on his foot. His arm released. The shadows didn't.

"Think, Freya," he gritted. "He was already in place when you arrived. You think that was an accident?"

I did. I tried to. But memory stirred.

Blaz, unconscious, held carefully in Cyrus' arms—like something irreplaceable. Nix already bloodied. Rage flooding the air, not just at disobedience, but because Blaz had been *hurt*.

And after they'd captured me, Cyrus had vanished.

For hours.

"How long were you out for?" I breathed, snapping my gaze to Blaz—who, to his credit, at least looked apologetic.

"About as long as it took me to get him your location," Cyrus supplied.

The secretive calls. The sideways glances at texts he'd hurried to hide whenever his mother neared. Realization dawned—and landed like a fist. "You were already dressed and *cold* the night we lost Darius." An ache pressed into my ribs, sharp and unforgiving.

It was Cyrus to explain, "We both felt something was wrong. I dropped him at home."

"That's how you knew Reyna had the capacity—and the systems—for those refugees."

Cyrus turned into me, inhaling deeply—relief, maybe. The heat of him scrambled my balance, and I leaned into him for a moment, voice softening as the pieces clicked into place.

"You intend to end the feud?"

"The moment Calypso takes power, we'll push for negotiations. We've already outlined the concessions she's willing to make. Ideally, Blaz will have more ground to stand on—Reyna is an insufferable bigot. No offense," he added, glancing toward his cousin.

"That could be centuries from now," I said, though guilt curled low in my gut. Not because Reyna and I agreed on everything—far from it—but because she fought with honor. And because...perhaps I hadn't given Reagan's heirs the credit they deserved.

"Maybe. But it's better than an eternal war."

"And if Adrastos puts you on opposite sides of this one?" I challenged. As my anger eased, Cyrus' grip softened, too.

He watched me closely as I turned and backed up until my legs hit the bed. I sank onto it, keeping both of them in view. Cyrus' expression had shifted to something open, almost pleading. "Why do you think we were meeting that night?"

"Jesus Christ."

Blaz exhaled, his shoulders sinking. "It has to end, Freya."

I looked between them, shaking my head. So alike. Blaz still held onto that boyish charm, where Cyrus was—God help me—all man. Fully ascended, like me. "The Prince of Paladin wants to broker peace?"

"Hard to believe, I know," he said with a smirk.

"You're not exactly off to a good start with Reyna."

"She belittled you." He said it so simply. As if that slight alone outweighed the centuries of tension and bloodied treaties. "And yes, before you ask, ma moitié, of all her transgressions, condescending to the most infuriatingly brilliant woman I know is the one I will not tolerate."

Blaz dropped his gaze with a grin, like he was intruding on something too private to witness. God, I wished I could speak to him mind-to-mind, if only to spare myself the embarrassment of asking out loud—

"What does that mean?" I snapped.

"It means mates are sacred. Whether they reciprocate or not," Cyrus said, voice clipped. "And I will not let her direct that kind of vitriol at you. Not because of me, or what I want—but because she will show you respect. Or she'll face the consequences."

Not what I meant. But before I could find the words, he turned to Blaz.

"We think Adrastos is using an alias to hide his identity—but we have reason to believe his origins aren't so different from ours. Can you bring us your mother's private collection on Bellpost and the Knights?"

Still reeling, I added, "Anything from the Twelve might help."

"You think the Bellpost survivors are involved?" Blaz asked, glancing between us.

"Signs point that direction, yes."

He tilted his head, that faintly smug little smile lighting up his dimples. "Glad to finally be of some use."

Without another word, he turned and left. I stayed seated, locking eyes with Cyrus in a silent standoff I had every intention of winning.

"Tell me what you remember," I ordered, jerking my chin toward the desk.

For the next hour, he wrote. War generals, commanders, royal bloodlines—more than I'd ever seen in my studies. Dozens of names omitted from Reyna's records, no doubt torn from the pages on purpose.

The Hadriana empire had been formidable. I could see echoes of their tactics in Hazelharbor and Paladin. But it wasn't until he got to the political marriage of Koa Balaskas and Rhiannon Hadrianna that something caught my attention.

They'd had seven children.

The firstborn: Bastien. Eighteen months later, Caius. A year and a half after that, their first daughter, Levana. Then Sirin. Then the twins—Marlana and Moros. And finally, three years later, another son: *Agamemnon.*

"Jesus," I whispered. *"That's him.* Cyrus, that's him. August and I killed Agamemnon in the battle of Grayshell."

He blinked down at his notes, brow furrowing. "I don't understand."

"He was a Renown. He kidnapped me and my brothers. They beat us so badly it triggered my ascension."

"Freya...that's impossible. All the Balaskas children were reported dead—except the twins."

My blood iced over. "Bullshit," I said, eyes wide. "I *bit through his neck.* I remember the taste of his rancid blood."

"Fuck, we need to get you a new strategy."

"It worked, didn't it? August finished him."

"Then...who died in the Ardensian War?"

"A lot of souls, I'd wager."

"Ha-ha," he said flatly. "I mean it. Agamemnon wasn't mentioned after the Pyros fell. According to the records I've seen, only Marlana and Moros made it back alive."

"But that...wait. Adrastos and Agamemnon were brothers. At least, that's what he told Ally."

A line cut into his brow. He blinked, as though that—of all things—was the most confusing part.

"Lonan told my mother that his brother Leo died."

"Leo?"

"She looked surprised to hear it."

"Could it have been a mistranslation?"

He was already shaking his head. "Shouldn't have been. Most of the texts are in Umbrithan—shadow tongue—"

"I know what Umbrithan is," I snapped.

Unbothered, he pressed on. "Others are in Latin or Old English. *Oh!*" His eyes lit. "The third chamber."

"You took a picture of the inscription."

"Yeah. Haven't had time to translate it."

"Send it to me." I tossed my phone onto the table just as Blaz returned. "You don't happen to speak Latin, do you?"

He balked. "Why would I speak Latin?"

"Seems like something Reyna would insist on," I muttered as he hefted an entire cart of books into the room. God help us.

"I'll send it to Dad and Aren," I said. With every tome he stacked on the table, Cyrus and I both slumped a little more—but we joined him in the sitting area, settling into the cushions with shared dread.

"Might as well get started."

"Should I call Carr and Cali?" Cyrus asked.

I glanced at Blaz.

He shrugged. "About time for a family reunion."

FIFTY-EIGHT
FAMILY REUNION
CYRUS

A sharp pain yanked me from sleep—but the flash of blue daggers for eyes had me jolting upright, reaching for a blade that wasn't there. Freya was asleep, curled into my chest, books draped haphazardly across both our laps after studying until the sun threatened the horizon. I lurched up, a protective hand snapping forward, throwing shadows.

The stone-faced female cut them down with a shield.

"Get. Up," she snapped, dagger in hand. Her voice was honed steel, her features even sharper—but something about her struck me as familiar. A relative of the Grayshellian Goddess, Fae, perhaps.

A low rumble of laughter followed.

"Freya, wake up," I barked, tension coiled in my spine.

A mountain of a man stood at the foot of the bed, grinning like this was the highlight of his month. Beside him, a silver-eyed male looked far more likely to slit my throat. But it was the grinning brute who clicked the puzzle into place.

"You're Aren Amadeus."

"And *you're* dead," the female snarled, flipping her knife to throw.

"Oh, come on," Aren said, voice warm. "Like Freya would let her guard down if he were a threat, Lana—honestly."

"Paladin punk," she growled, lip curled. Freya stirred beside me, cleared her throat, and joined me—calmer, though not much clearer-eyed.

"Mom?"

"Get up."

"Let the girl wake," the dark-haired man chided gently—but his eyes never left me, the warning in them unmistakable.

"Oh shit," Carr's voice came from the doorway. He stepped in with Calypso and Blaz, all three balancing trays of food. The blonde still trying to bore a hole through my skull was the only one who didn't pivot to face them.

"Dad? Aren? What are you doing here—is August?!" Freya was up and moving in two seconds flat, abandoning her book beside me as I followed in her wake.

"He's fine, babygirl. But we've got a mission, and we move now."

"Fuckity-fuck-fuck," she muttered, already racing for her armor. I stayed rooted, still caught in the tension between me and the ice-veined woman who'd birthed the girl I—

"Cyrus Stuart," I said, standing tall, extending a hand.

She didn't take it. Just flicked her gaze down like the gesture itself was offensive, then met my eyes again with unconcealed disdain.

Aren cleared his throat and stepped forward, nearly elbowing her aside. "Nice to meet you, *Prince* Cyrus Stuart."

"Likewise," I said, trying—and failing—not to recall the countless legends tied to that name. His companion stepped forward next.

"Ansel Callahan."

The Old General. Holy shit. Which meant—

"And you must be the assassin," I said. Her smile crawled down my spine.

I motioned to my family. "My sister, Calypso. Our cousin, Carr. And I believe you know Blaz."

"What's the assignment?" Freya asked, reemerging in her black Grayshell leathers. I barely restrained a groan. God, she was gonna get me killed.

"It's diadem day," Aren said grimly.

Freya met my eyes and gave a nod. The time had come.

"Adrastos is a Balaskas family Commander," Aren continued. "According to Magnolia's source, their numbers are exponentially higher than any hierarchy had anticipated. We are at *war* with Bellpost *and* their allies."

That brutal confirmation struck like a brand to my chest. My skin went cold. My kingdom...was fractured.

"We move now, or we lose the target, kid."

"Where's Ally?" Freya demanded, dropping into a chair and yanking on her boots.

I didn't wait. I rose, stepped toward the assassin, and met her simmering fury head-on. I walked past her, knowing full well the statement I made by giving her my back.

"We attack in synchronized strikes," Aren said—but his gaze cut to me, thoughtful. Assessing.

"He's good," Freya said, tying her boot.

"He's one of them," her mother hissed.

I sighed, finally meeting Lana's gaze again. "And yet here I am, standing with *you*."

"Cyrus is questioning his allegiances," Freya supplied, rapid-fire. "He helped me prepare."

"This is the *mate*?" Lana bit out, each word a blade.

"Time to be mad later," Freya sing-songed. She moved through the shadows like they were muscle memory, pulling her blades from the dresser and strapping them across her suit with chilling efficiency. "Coordinates?"

Aren provided them. I looked to Carr—he gave me a short nod. We'd been right.

"Are Damien and Tessa ready?"

"Locked and loaded," Aren confirmed. Tessa and Damien. Either shared names, or Westerlund tech support was officially in play.

"Extraction team?"

"The four of us and Jax," Lana said, still glaring.

"Five," I corrected, tugging on my boots. "Five of us and Jax."

If she'd hated me before, it was nothing compared to what lit in her eyes now.

I shrugged. "Where Freya goes, I go."

"Absolutely not," she snapped. Her fists curled at her sides. "Besides, Ally didn't say—"

"I met your second," I cut in, gaze steady. "And I highly doubt she believes I'd abandon my mate as she infiltrates the inner sanctum of a ruthless king."

"These operations require trust, which you have not earned."

I crossed my arms, tone cold but measured. "Nais pas. Have I earned your trust, ma moitié?"

Those harsh blue eyes widened. Lana turned to Ansel, then looked back at me—marginally more amicable this time.

Freya's eyes snapped to her mother's. Her mouth parted before she schooled her expression, blinked, and turned for the door. I'd sell my soul to know what had just passed between them.

"To keep me alive? Yeah. Let's roll."

I smiled, wet my lips, and followed her out. My Paladins fell into step in my wake.

"The boy's got balls," Aren offered behind me.

Ansel gave a noncommittal grunt. The man was a walking myth—and I didn't have time to interrogate him. He'd been an off-limits subject most of my life, yet he probably held answers the archives never could.

As we swept through the estate like a migrating flock, Freya broke down the op. Her voice was sharp, efficient. No hesitation. She rattled off their known security measures—earning sighs, a few curses, and absolute attention.

The Balaskas West Coast estate was buried deep in the Bitterroot Mountains straddling the Idaho-Montana border. Naturally. Where else would genocidal celestial fugitives take cover on this continent?

No one questioned her. Not even once. They trusted her research, trusted the vision. Trusted *her*. If everything went to plan, we'd be in and out before alarms tripped. If not...we were outnumbered and outgunned.

"Mom, I need you on the North Ridge for overwatch and—God forbid —cover fire," Freya said. Right. Alana Callahan. The same assassin who ranked among the most lethal sharpshooters alive. Holy fuck.

"Dad, the entire place is warded. I need you planting gifts in the garage —disable their transports, have a ride ready for exfil." He nodded curtly as we descended toward the foyer.

"Westerlunds are handling power and security disruption."

"I'll run backup," Carr volunteered.

Freya nodded. "If you want overwatch, we'll loop you into Tessa's comms."

He agreed with a grunt, and she continued, turning toward Aren. "I need you and Ajax ready to raise hell on the south wall if plan A fails."

"Fake skirmish?" he asked, voice already smiling.

"Fake skirmish," she confirmed.

"Not bad, kid." He clapped her shoulder. She smiled—genuine and easy. I envied that.

"Contingencies?" he asked.

"Worst case, we brute-force it."

"Excellent. The fun part."

"For *you*, old man," Freya said, elbowing him. "Some of us prefer the quieter route. Which is why Tessa overrides the security grid before lock-down, and Ansel sets off the—"

"Those presents we discussed," he supplied dryly.

"And if the diadem isn't where you believe it is?" Aren pressed.

"We track it. Something with that kind of energetic signature won't be hard to find."

"And if you face resistance?"

"We ask nicely."

He snorted. "If that fails?"

"We ask *less* nicely."

Aren grinned. "Good. If everything goes to shit—walk away. Your life's worth more than a relic. If anyone can find another path, it's Ally."

"It'll work," Freya said without hesitation. "Or Ally wouldn't have sent all of us. How long until they move on the East Coast?"

"Thirty minutes. Expect reaper bullets."

Carr slipped into my mind. *Orders?*

Keep my mother off my trail. Overwatch duty. Cali—keep reading. See if you can identify Adrastos's real lineage. He threatened my mate.

Death warrant issued and signed, she replied coolly. God, I loved my sister.

Calypso grabbed my elbow at the base of the stairs, yanking me down to kiss my cheek.

"Love you, jackass. Don't die."

Grinning, I said, "I'll try."

As Lana passed us, she muttered, "No promises."

Carr snorted. "Like mother, like daughter. I say—watch your back, my Prince."

TWENTY MINUTES LATER, suited in white tactical gear, packs secured, blades and mags tucked tight—we stood atop the northern ridge. Lana was already posted for aerial overwatch, her silhouette sharp against the ice-bitten sky.

Below, the Balaskas estate sprawled like a goddamned fortress in glass—modern brutalist architecture carved into the side of the mountain, sleek parapets and far too many windows for my taste.

We ran through the plan one last time. Then, on Alvara's count, Freya, Ansel, and I jumped to the outer perimeter of the wards.

We advanced from the west—straight up what could only be described as a cliff face from hell.

"I'm from the south," I muttered dryly, my words solidifying in the air in front of my face. Fuck, it was ball-freezing brutal here. "We don't do cold."

"Then go home," Freya said mildly, fingers brushing the bowstring across her chest as she studied the route. Ansel mirrored her movements—calm, calculated. Inside the wards, no jumping. And my shadows? A liability. This place belonged to their creators.

"Just stating facts."

"Noted. Now *climb*."

So we did. Three abreast, scaling jagged stone toward the upper tunnel system. The vault lay at the heart of the stronghold—but to reach it, we had to survive the climb.

"Next time you wanna impress me," I huffed, "a beach vacation would suffice." I worked to test my finger holds before I continued. If we didn't move quickly, our hands would likely go numb from the bitter wind chill long before we scaled high enough to climb into the shelter of the caves.

"You'd burn like a cherry tomato."

"That's what the Middle's for. Bright side—no dead relatives this time."

"That you know of," she countered.

A rock shard cracked under my fingers. I winced, glad I hadn't released the other hand.

"Great," I muttered. "Now I'll have nightmares."

"*Baby.*"

"Feral demon creature."

"Wanna race?"

"To the caves? You're insane."

"This is well-established. Loser deals with Reyna when she finds out Blaz gave us restricted access."

"That's all you. I wouldn't survive it."

"Probably not," she agreed, scampering upward like it was nothing.

"You make this look easy. You sure your dad didn't fuck a mountain goat?"

"Jesus Christ," Ansel muttered behind me.

I didn't dare glance back to gauge humor vs. disapproval—but Freya's laugh echoed off the rugged stone walls.

Insanity. This approach was absolute insanity. But brilliant. It was the least monitored access point, timed perfectly after their last sweep.

The downside? A fall meant death. And my shadows catching us all—in broad daylight—wasn't exactly probable.

Aren waited on the far side, ready to spark a distraction. Lana covered three angles of the building. We were as covered as anyone could hope for.

Then the howls began.

I froze.

Blood wolves.

I broke my number one rule, and looked down.

Three of them stalked the ravine below.

And we weren't even halfway to the tunnels.

FIFTY-NINE

THE VAULT

"Uh, Freya?"

Cyrus's concern quickened my pulse, but I didn't dare look down. My head was already spinning, and I needed to steady it. In every fucking life, a fear of heights had followed me. Moving through it was the only option. So I kept my eyes on the next handhold.

"I hear them."

"Move," Ansel ordered, climbing faster. "Where blood wolves go—"

"Crawlers follow," I finished.

Right on cue, high-pitched chittering pierced the air. When I glanced down, a dozen black, taloned creatures were scaling the cliffs beneath us. I flexed my fingers on the rock and breathed through the panic. So much for the least monitored entrance.

"Shields," Ansel said, though mine was already up. If Cyrus was half the soldier I believed he was, it would be rhetorical for him, too.

We climbed faster. My heart pounded, vision tunneling as adrenaline surged, my arms trembling and fingers screaming. Still, the chittering crept closer, that venom-laced promise of pain tightening around my thoughts.

Only thirty feet to the first tunnel.

But thirty feet on slick rock was a long fucking way for a kid from the flatlands of Louisiana. All of my lives had involved climbing to survive. In this one, I had two older brothers who did it for fun—and who initiated me when I was still in elementary school. I could make it in thirty seconds. Maybe. But that would mean leaving Cyrus behind. The thought made my stomach rebel.

I glanced down. They were climbing side by side, the crawlers gaining fast.

Fuck it.

I shifted into higher gear, redpointing the route we'd studied—each placement like muscle memory, my hands finding holds like I'd done this climb a hundred times.

Had I? The thought struck me upside the head. The stronghold looked too new for my past incarnations, but the last stretch of the climb—the crux —was carved into my bones.

The last thirty feet.

My best hope to gain a vantage point and thin the herd.

"They're gaining," Cyrus warned. I looked again only to wish I hadn't. Talons tore through chunks of stone below.

"Goddammit." With a sharp exhale, I coiled, launching into a desperate dyno, stretching for the next ledge. The world tilted. My fingers caught and slid, and I cried out as my body swung wide over the drop. But I held. My toes scrabbled back onto the edge below, sending dust and loose rocks crumbling, ricocheting off their shields.

Thank fuck.

I lunged for the next hold. My grip locked onto a narrow edge, but my boots slipped.

"*Freya!*" Cyrus shouted, his voice raw and close to breaking.

It did something warm and terrifying to my chest as I breathed through the shake in my forearms. "Focus on your own damn climb!"

Because those clicking screeches were too close. Ghosting over the final ledges, I hauled myself into the tunnel, rolling into a crouch, blade drawn.

Clear.

I darted back to the edge, swung my pack off my shoulder, dropped it to the stone, drew my bow, and snatched an arrow from the quiver. Alvara's voice echoed in my head. *Make room for the bow.*

Thank God for Alvara fucking Porter.

Bow drawn, I peered down, right as a crawler leapt for Cyrus.

No. *Mine.*

"Down!" I shouted. Cyrus pressed against the cliff, just as I released. The creature screamed and fell, the breath returning to my lungs as I assessed our position.

Clear airspace.

Three blood wolves at the base.

Double the crawlers, fifteen feet below my men.

Ten arrows.

With a quick prayer, I aimed and released, this creature's scream more satisfying as it hurdled to the rocky earth below.

"Move your asses!" I yelled as anxiety closed its icy hand around my throat. I picked them off, one by one, guided by air magic until the only remaining threat was gravity.

Ansel reached the ledge first. I helped haul him up, then turned for Cyrus. We dragged him inside just as Ansel took point, disappearing into the darkness.

My hand still clutching his forearm, Cyrus and I locked gazes for an eternal heartbeat, scouring over each other as my mind reached for a connection that wasn't there. *My* doing. My choice.

So why did it taste so bitter as we caught our breath on hell's doorstep?

"Thanks for the cover," he said, eyes full of an ache that set fire to my own.

"Clear!" Ansel barked before I could answer, both of us jerking our heads down the tunnel where The Old General still gave us his back. Cyrus bent to snag my backpack, holding it up in offering. I rotated, allowing him to ease it over my shoulders. A small, steadying gesture. When I met his gaze again, he nodded, and we followed Dad into the mountain.

We're in. How are we looking, overwatch?

Clear, Lana answered. Aren followed.

Clear here too, but this place is…a fortress, *little one. Watch each other's backs. Let us know if there's trouble.*

Ansel and I exchanged a look. Years of unsaid words passed between us.

Ran into wolves and crawlers at the base, Ansel reported as we jogged deeper into the tunnel.

Cyrus's stride made my near-sprint feel like a stroll through a park.

A fortress, Aren rumbled. *They're colluding with demons. And Renown.*

It would seem so.

Nice to have a name for our enemy. Maybe we'll get a face, too.

Not that knowing Adrastos' had helped. That field was painted in blood months ago, and we'd only just now gotten a name.

The tunnel would take five minutes but it felt like a lifetime as we jogged through the darkness.

"Shadows are clear," Cyrus said beside me.

I nodded. "Should I send them further?"

"Too risky," I said, shaking my head. Even my stolen shadows were begging to come out and play—so I imagined what that felt like for him, amplified. To his credit, he didn't argue, and the three of us kept a steady pace until we reached the tunnel's end, where the rugged stone wall jutted up, a steel ladder set in place.

"The door is warded, but a blood rune should work."

"*Should?*" Cyrus asked, eyeing the next climb.

Ansel and I stripped off our white outer layers to lighten the load and improve mobility. My Paladin prince followed suit without complaint.

"I've done this as many times as you have."

"Valid point."

"I'll lead," Ansel volunteered.

Before I could respond, Cyrus said, "I'll cover you."

Fuck me. The idea of his back exposed after what I'd just seen below shouldn't have tied knots in my stomach—but it did.

We filed onto the ladder, following Dad up until he reached the hatch. He didn't hesitate, slicing open his forearm, tracing the rune with a bloody finger. It glowed blue before the latch clicked. In one smooth movement, he pushed the gate open and hauled himself up. The unmistakable sound of a scuffle ensued, followed by the thud of a body hitting stone. I scrambled up, launching through the hatch with a blade drawn.

Two guards were crumpled at his feet.

"*The second one likely got off a distress signal,*" Ansel warned through the bond, signing the same for Cyrus's benefit.

Cyrus responded in kind, and I blinked, surprised.

"*Stick to the plan,*" Cyrus signed. "*If there's a red flag, she can relay it to me.*"

My mouth fell open, part wonder, part wariness.

"*Your shock insults me,*" he added, deadpanning.

"*It's not exactly common.*"

"*Carr's mom was deaf. She mated into Paladin.*"

Meaning she'd never been initiated into the hierarchy. Her only mental link had been with Juno—Reagan's brother.

Ansel pulled me aside and met my eyes, his hands settling on my shoulders.

Just for me, he thought, *Be safe, babygirl. Follow the plan. Signal if you need us.*

I'll see you on the other side.

He kissed my forehead, hugged me tight, then stepped away with a brisk *godspeed.*

Ansel peeled left. We went right, slipping into the maze with nothing but schematics and shadows.

"*You two seem close,*" Cyrus signed.

I nodded. "*Ansel's great. We were closer...before. Last time.*"

"*Your mother's terrifying.*"

Swallowing a laugh, I signed, "*So's yours. Lana barks more than she bites —unless you deserve it.*"

"*That's where you get it?*"

"Maybe. Kinda came out that way this go-around. James called me 'feral Freya' until I was ten."

"Brother?"

"Blood. Like August."

"You just ascended in January?"

I nodded.

"You're incredible. A newborn, and you humiliated us."

The praise caught me off guard. I smiled, then forced my expression neutral. *"Focus, Prince. Keep your eyes up. Last thing we need is them sneaking up on us through the shadows."*

He nodded, and we pressed forward until the tunnel came to an abrupt halt. I knelt, drawing a blade and slicing across my palm. With my blood, I traced a revealing rune over the stone. It hummed, glowing faintly until a shimmering outline appeared in the wall.

I reached into the cut again, this time drawing an unlocking rune.

The stone groaned. A door shifted inward with glacial reluctance—and by some miracle, no guards waited beyond it.

The room was beautiful. Ethereal. A surreal blend of gothic architecture and sleek modern lines. Floor-to-ceiling windows lined the far wall, leading up into spires that curled like fingers toward an unseen ceiling. For one breath, I just stared, until Cyrus elbowed my shoulder. Time to move.

We padded down the corridor in silence until we reached the vault: an enormous glass wall enclosing treasures most rulers would kill for.

Weapons from enemy corpses. Carvings. Tablets. Paintings. Armor polished to gleaming perfection. The king's most prized possessions, and only two guards flanked the exit.

I jerked my head left. Cyrus took the right. We moved like mirrored blades, sprinting forward on silent feet.

I went for the throat. He snapped a neck. Neither body made a sound when it hit the ground.

"Ruthless," I signed, smirking. *"I like it."*

"Looking good yourself."

Flirting over bloodshed. That was new.

We slipped through the arched entry and into the vault.

Fifty yards long, half as wide. Towering shelves. Relics and riches tucked into every crevice.

"Holy shit," Cyrus breathed, eyes wide with reverence.

For a Bellpost descendant and history scholar, this had to feel like finding a vein of gold running beneath his childhood home.

"Focus," I whispered, gesturing for him to split up. We prowled in opposite directions. Each row bled opulence. Ancient portraits. Spellbound treasures. My fingers itched to swipe the more valuable pieces. But we were here to steal *one* thing, not add to my collection.

A bronze music box caught my eye. Ballerina mid-spin, vines coiled around her waist. My fingers hovered, then—

"Freya," Cyrus hissed.

I was at his side in seconds.

There, nestled among velvet and wards, sat a circlet of woven gold vines. A crescent moon flanked by angel wings. A teardrop ruby that gleamed like fresh blood.

Target located, I sent.

Lock it in and get the hell out, Aren replied.

Movement on the perimeter, Lana added. *Should I engage?*

I glanced at Cyrus, who was pulling gloves from his pack.

No. Give us a minute to reach extraction. Don't blow the cover yet.

Roger that. Move your asses.

Ten-four.

I pulled out a metal safe, bracing it under the shelf. Cyrus conjured shadows to shroud the diadem as he levitated it, careful, steady, cautious— like it might bite. Because it might. Rhiannon's curse wasn't some bedtime story. It would kill anyone unworthy who touched it.

The moment it was secured, Lana's voice came down the line like a blade.

Guards inbound. Get out. Now.

My eyes snapped to Cyrus' and I signed the warning.

"It must've triggered a silent alarm."

"Fuck me."

"Maybe if you're good. Let's go."

Freya, do you want us to implement Plan B? Aren's voice was calm. Controlled. Letting me call the shot.

God, I wanted him to take over. Wanted someone to decide for me.

I closed my eyes, sealing the box with a locking rune and shoving it into my pack.

Ansel, how's the exit?

Clear. Busier than I'd like, but nothing I couldn't handle. Can Cyrus ride a snowski?

The swamp gremlin? Probably not.

Before I could ask, a mechanical gear clicked, and we both jerked our gazes back to the front. Without hesitating, I grabbed the bag and bolted toward the archway, horror curdling my stomach as a glass plate descended.

No. No, no, no.

We broke into full sprints, but the gate was dropping like a guillotine. We weren't going to make it. No fucking way.

Emergency respirators gave us ten minutes max.

Mayday, mayday, mayday.

Freya?! Ansel's panic hit me for one stride before I shoved it into a box. Darkness swept out down the shelves, rolling like a storm over the ocean. Cyrus hurled shadows forward, slamming into the glass. It slowed—but not enough.

Five seconds. My lungs burned.

Four. My boots slipped.

Three. I threw the bag forward.

Two. The air vents kicked on.

One.

A body slammed into mine, knocking me forward. I slid under the hatch, tumbling, ribs screaming in pain.

I jerked upright, my heart plummeting as I met sorrowful citrine eyes... where Cyrus stood on the other side of the glass.

Trapped.

Cyrus

I DIDN'T NEED to hear her to know exactly what Freya was screaming on the other side of the impenetrable wall of glass.

No. Again and again, her mouth formed that one word, her fists slamming into the barrier. Wind and shadows surged with every strike, but it didn't make a damn difference.

If Moros was even half as brilliant as his father, this motherfucker was foolproof. If he'd really hidden an entire host while rebuilding the hierarchy under our noses...there wouldn't be weak spots.

I looked up. The vents in the ceiling had activated—so had the ones in the floor.

How long would it take to displace the oxygen in a room this size? Sixty seconds? A hundred and twenty? Less?

"Run," I signed.

Her eyes went wide. Pleading. She shook her head in defiance. *"I'm not leaving you."*

"You have what we needed, Freya. Now, run."

"Get fucked."

I smiled feebly, the barest breath of a laugh sticking in my throat as I grit my teeth. *"Maybe in our next life, my other half."*

Her eyes filled, her mouth falling open in horror. So she understood. That, at least, was something.

"You will not die today, C-y-r-u-s," she signed, jabbing each letter like it

might shake the universe into listening. *"Now open your goddamn pack and get the respirator while I figure out how to get you out."*

Already lightheaded, I nodded and sank to one knee, dragging my pack around and digging into the deepest pocket until I pulled out a small black pouch. Of course, *The Wraith* had a contingency plan. The question was whether her people could implement it fast enough to matter.

Freya was scanning the ceiling now, her hands skimming the edges of the glass as she bolted from one corner to the other—never too far. Never letting me leave her sight.

My head swam harder. I yanked out the escape device and pressed it to my mouth, inhaling deeply. The world steadied in a breath.

Less. Less time than I'd thought. The system had displaced the oxygen in under a minute.

Fuck. Calypso was gonna kill me for this.

She'd be okay. She was raised to reign, whether she wanted to or not. Carr would guard her as ruthlessly as I would. They'd be fine.

Still.

The idea of leaving the three of them behind before the war...

Freya was still searching for seams, for faults, and I did the same. Dropping my pack, I climbed the nearest shelf, trusting the king had reinforced them to secure his precious relics. The vents were flush with the ceiling. Even if I could pry them open, I was way too big to fit through.

No visible mechanism to raise the hatch.

There had to be a failsafe. An emergency override. Moros wouldn't risk condemning himself to death if the alarm were ever triggered while he was inside. So, where the fuck was it?

Too bright to cloak the entire room, but my shadows could still snake beneath each shelf.

In a violent burst, they ripped across the nearest row, scattering treasure like dry leaves in a storm.

Nothing.

I swung to the opposite wall, repeated the motion.

Still nothing.

Under the art?

I tore the mounted portraits from the glass, shredding the velvet and gilded frames, praying for something—anything—that would give. Halfway down the vault, my head was spinning again. I turned to check on Freya— and felt that hit like a punch.

She had blanketed the wall in shadows, her hands moving like a madwoman across every inch of the glass. Searching. Testing. Failing.

Concerned my effort was burning through the respirator faster, I slowed my breath, grounding myself in each inhale like a meditation. Then I made my way back toward the front of the vault.

She was already circling toward me again—pissed off, relentless, more predator than Paladin.

I drew my .45 and stepped back. Then opened fire.

The crack split the air, a sonic blade driving straight through my skull. I staggered, palms to my ears, the ringing cutting through every thought. Blood. There had to be blood. I didn't dare look.

And the glass?

A single spiderweb fracture spread a few inches from where the bullet lodged—nothing more.

Motherfucker.

I turned, and Freya was still there, frozen, devastation written in every line of her face as she stared at the failed attempt like it had broken something in her too.

God, I was tired.

Her little device wasn't built for someone exerting this much effort. I stumbled to the glass, and she sprinted the short distance back, fingers tapping over the spot where the bullet had struck, her eyes racing along the panel like it might yield if she just *believed* hard enough.

But we both knew better.

Her determination was fucking admirable though.

Freya backed up, locked onto her target, and hurled a nearby sculpture into the glass with enough force to make me flinch. I instinctively turned away, shielding my face as the marble collided with a thunderous *crack*— but it was the sculpture that shattered, fragments skidding across the floor in jagged defeat.

Her eyes flew wide, mouth parting in disbelief. I memorized her face in that moment. That compact frame. The blunt edge of her silky red hair. The constellation of freckles scattered over her nose, and the soft curl of pale lashes blinking back tears.

She'd made it. That was what mattered.

And she had the diadem—for the Angel of Death.

Maybe I'd already done my part.

"You're beautiful, ma moitié. You always have been, ever since we were kids," I murmured, knowing full well she couldn't hear me. "Even with a knife to my balls." I smirked faintly, a dark chuckle catching in my throat. "Hell, even when you were covered in blood like a feral avenging angel. Even then...you were beautiful."

"I can't hear you," she signed, frantic now, desperation rising in her eyes as I raised the respirator to my mouth and drew another breath. Would it

last longer if I spaced it out? Or would that fuck with the reaction and deplete it faster?

Shit. I should've asked when she made me memorize the pack contents.

The ground rumbled beneath me, a deep quake that even I could hear, and we both snapped our gazes upward as the lights flickered. Freya spun, arms flared wide as if calling for help from the air itself.

And then the alarm hit.

A screeching howl tore through the corridor, strobes painting the hallway in harsh, erratic bursts.

Freya's wide eyes whipped back to mine.

"*Run,*" I signed again. "*Please.*"

"*I cannot leave you.*"

"*Sure you can.*"

"*Be serious.*"

"*I am. Get to your dad.*" It would be easier if she just ran. Easier if I knew she was on her way to Ansel. On her way to Aren. Easier if I knew someone would get her the hell out of here before my clock ran out.

The Commander would get her out.

But of course, Freya Porter had never done a single fucking thing the easy way.

Fury collided with the terror in her eyes. She slammed her palms into the glass. Then her shoulder. Then her whole damn body. Again. And again. Until I feared she'd shatter her own bones trying to break through.

Her lip trembled as I calmly raised the respirator to my mouth like it was a clunky vape. I shook my head slowly, even as her hands splayed across the barrier like she'd claw her way through it to reach me. Some sick part of me was relieved I wasn't the only one losing my mind.

Movement flicked at the end of the hallway—three men. None familiar.

I pointed that way, heart breaking and grateful all at once when—for once—she listened.

Freya turned on them like a Goddess scorned, hands outstretched, draining their magic before they even realized they'd been stripped.

She reached for her blades, and became a storm.

One after another, she hurled them with calculated, brutal grace, her movements more dance than combat. Shadows lunged for her throat, but she batted them away with a pristine shield, weaving ropes of darkness through their defenses.

She was *incredible*.

Her fury coiled around the last man's throat like a noose, slamming him against the tile and dragging him limp across the floor. She screamed something at him—eyes wild, canines bared—before smashing his skull into the wall.

Once.

Twice.

And again—like she'd shatter his corpse if he didn't give her a way to reach me.

My next breath was thin. The one after weaker. Even with salvation standing on the other side of the glass. Her face split in a scream, shadows snapping his neck in a vicious twist before she tossed him aside.

Savage. *Breathtaking.*

Freya skid to a halt in front of me, her eyes frantic as she searched mine. I swayed. The world tilted. The respirator rasped in my hand.

That couldn't be good.

Another breath. A hiss of resistance. Heat bloomed in my palm.

She was shaking her head. Denying what we both knew. I staggered, shoulder sliding down the glass as my knees gave way. I slumped to the floor, and she mirrored the motion, sinking down on the other side, her eyes never leaving mine.

That rune-etched hilt at her ribs caught my gaze.

She'd taken that blade from me that night on the roof.

A ragged laugh clawed up from somewhere deep. My feral little creature had kept my weapon like a trophy. That was oddly...comforting.

Tears streaked down her cheeks as she pressed her hand to the glass. I shook my head again, wishing I could touch her.

The respirator lit up red.

Fuck.

I tossed it aside and pressed my palm to hers, skin separated by a few inches of Godforsaken glass.

The loathsome emergency lights distorted her radiant face, and I hated them for robbing that from me. For a fleeting heartbeat, our reflections aligned—our faces merging into one fractured image.

Then she moved. Shaking her head. Screaming *something* I couldn't hear. Snarling, canines bared in defiance as she drew back her fist.

No. She'd break.

The thud reverberated through the glass.

Again.

And again.

And again.

And then—the darkness came for me.

SIXTY

MA MOITIÉ

CYRUS

Whoosh…

Whoosh…

Whoosh…

My first thought was that the flow of blood in my ears sounded remarkably like the ocean.

The second was that someone had taken a mallet to my skull.

A breeze ghosted over my skin, the distant roar of waves growing more undeniable with every steady beat of my pulse.

Holy shit, I could feel my heartbeat—thudding in my temples, my fingertips, the tender pinch of skin where my neck was twisted awkwardly to one side.

Eyes flying open, I blinked up at a sunshine-yellow bedroom. French doors stood ajar, letting in salty air and light. Beyond them, a peeling white porch. Beyond that…ocean.

What the fuck?

I sat up too fast. The world spun sideways as I squinted, trying to orient myself.

No shirt.

Someone else's pajama pants.

Something minty smeared across my chest.

A vase of wilted flowers sat on a wicker side table beside a seashell-framed photo of two radiant women—tan, beaming, strangers. One blonde. One with hair darker than Cali's.

Wait. *Not a stranger.*

The teal eyes. The lush lips. The curves that nearly spilled from her swimsuit.

The Hazelharborian Heiress.

What. The. Fuck.

I straightened, reaching for the glass of water beside the photo. Sniffed. Fresh enough. I took a cautious sip, rinsing the cotton from my mouth before rising to my feet and making for the open doors.

I stopped short.

Red hair fluttered in the breeze. Sunlight hit Freya like a prism, turning her into something ethereal. Her forearms were braced on the porch railing, hands clenched around her biceps, her lean frame cloaked in black Grayshellian fighting leathers.

She was armed to the teeth.

The weapons didn't fit the tranquil porch or the quiet garden or the rolling waves beyond.

Oh.

Oh, holy shit.

The memories pummeled my mind like a duel gone wrong. The cliffs. The crawlers. Freya leaping with nothing beneath her. The vault. The glass. The sealed door.

How the hell—

I followed her gaze over grassy dunes and pale sand, all the way to the frothing waves, and pulled in a steadying breath.

We were alive. *Never mind the how.* I'd made peace with death. I remembered that peace—cold and final. I'd handed her through the vault's threshold and braced for the end. And now—

I stepped out into sunlight, the tug of our Bond drawing me forward.

"Freya?"

She spun so fast it was inhuman. Her wide eyes locked onto mine.

"*Oh,*" she exhaled in a stunned rush, crossing the porch in four determined strides before she collided with me, her arms wrapping tight around my waist, her cheek pressing to my chest.

Shock froze me for a moment.

Then I folded into her, one arm circling her shoulders, the other curving around her back. I bowed my head to rest against the crown of her hair.

I didn't know how long we stood like that, breathing in the sunlight and salt and each other, but I committed every detail to memory. The shape of her body against mine. The feel of her heartbeat.

I never thought I'd see her again. My final act—my final breath—had been for her safety. And with the way she'd rejected our Bond, I never thought she'd wanna touch me again.

But here she was.

When the muscles in my neck began to ache, I pressed a kiss to her head and murmured, "Ma moitié."

My other half.

I was grateful I'd memorized the feel of her—because a second later she shoved me away, face drawn in a scowl as she reared back and landed a punishing fist to my gut.

Pain exploded through my ribs as the air whooshed from my lungs.

I staggered, bracing myself on the patio sectional, wheezing, "What the *hell* is wrong with you?"

"What's wrong with *me*?" she shouted, indignant. "What the hell is wrong with *you*?"

"*You*. Right now. At this moment."

She advanced, stomping like some furious, ginger Tinkerbell from hell, and I threw up a hand—either in defense or in plea, I wasn't sure.

"You shoved me through!"

"To save your life," I ground out, trying to breathe past the ache. My throat burned. "You're welcome."

"You loathsome, *reckless*, self-sacrificing, beautiful jackass."

A low laugh rumbled in my chest despite the pain as I took in the fire-bright fury blazing across her face. "Wait—you're *mad* that I *saved you?*"

Her scowl deepened.

Right. That logic clearly made perfect sense.

This time when she aimed for my shoulder, I twisted. Her open palm glanced off bare skin.

"You damned me to *that,*" she growled. "What the fuck is wrong with you!?"

I lifted both hands, palms out, in surrender.

She advanced again, and I stumbled backward over something that looked suspiciously like a bumblebee planter.

"How could you do that to me, Cyrus?" Her voice cracked. "Do you have any idea how horrific it is to feel helpless when—when—*when*—" She broke off, sobbing.

Color flared in her cheeks as tears threatened to spill.

Jesus.

I'd still been under the impression she was more likely to kill me herself than give a shit. But seeing her break nearly shattered me in turn. Her pain splintered me and welded me back together all at once.

Agony I wanted to soothe.

Acceptance I needed down to the marrow.

Her left hook was harder to dodge. My bare heel caught on the patio rug as I twisted, balance still shit. Before I could recover, her palms slammed into my chest, tears streaking down her cheeks.

"I watched you die, asshole." Shove. "You *made me* watch you fight for your fucking life and there was *nothing* I could do—" Shove. "I thought Tessa failed. I thought they wouldn't make it in time and *you*—" Her voice cracked. Another shove, harder now. "You *died*, Cyrus."

I caught her wrists on the next push, locking them in place as she jerked against me, wild with grief.

"I watched the light leave your eyes. I *watched* your body seize, watched you *fall*—"

"Easy, chérie," I murmured, the bridge of my nose stinging as I watched her cheeks grow slick with grief.

Few things had ever brought me to tears. But this woman...

My Freya.

I wasn't alone in this—not anymore. It was written in the pinch of her expression, the tremble of her chin, the shimmer on her skin. Every wall she let collapse made room for me inside her soul. Her grief was a kind of invitation. A vow that we could survive this world together, even when everything else was shattering. Bringing her hands to my chest, I slid her palm over my heart.

"*Real, Freya.* Right here. I'm real."

"Cyrus, I..." Her words drifted off. She wet her lips—lips I suddenly ached to worship. Just to show her we'd made it. Just to prove we were still here.

She'd saved us. Against all odds, she'd dragged us both back.

"I know," I breathed. The waves behind us swallowed the words, but I knew she heard me. She didn't need to say it. Every tear, every tremble in her voice, her hands, her lips—she was already telling me everything she couldn't bear to speak aloud. "I'm sorry."

"You *left* me."

"I'm *sorry*," I repeated, her anguish moving through me like a contagion. But beneath the grief...relief.

This wasn't a soul who'd rejected our Bond.

This was a woman who would've razed the earth to free me, who wouldn't have cared how many souls burned in the fire.

Convinced the fight had gone out of her, I carefully released her wrists, my fingers sweeping up her arms. One hand found her waist and climbed along her ribs, brushing the countless blades she had tucked against her leathers. Her hands ghosted over my chest, down my sides, and back again, finally pausing over the silver scar Nix had left behind.

Each stroke was a forgotten song I never thought I'd hear again.

"*So sorry.*"

The window of vulnerability she'd opened began to narrow again. Her fingers tightened where they clung to my obliques, anger creeping back in to cover the wreckage like a familiar cloak.

I understood. I was trying to do the same thing. Because the thought of half my soul walking around in someone else's body was an inhuman kind of terror.

A vulnerability we could barely afford.

"You think you get to leave me like that and pretend nothing happened?" she snarled, squeezing harder, like she wanted it to hurt but couldn't bring herself to mean it. Her hands trembled. I met her gaze and held it.

"You think you get to go out like that? Looking at me like I'm the last thing you'll ever see? Fuck you, Cyrus Stuart."

She shoved against me—half-hearted, furious—and pulled me closer in the same breath, her nails biting into my skin.

Refusing to let her close herself off again, I slid my hands up her arms, one curving gently beneath her jaw. I lowered my forehead to hers, grounding us both.

She smacked her palms against my chest again, but there was no venom in it this time. "I beat my fists bloody on that glass," she whispered. "And you just...*stared*. Do you have *any* idea what that *felt* like?"

I shook my head slowly, brushing my nose along hers as she pressed her fists tighter against me.

Gently, I slipped one hand around her wrist and brought it to my lips, pressing a kiss to her knuckles—healed now, thank fuck.

"*Don't*," she whimpered. The word splintering in her throat. "Don't you do that to me, Cyrus. *I am* not *built to lose*. I'm the one who leaves. Because I *cannot* breathe air and somehow *let go*." I kissed her knuckles again. And again. The skin too smooth now where she'd broken herself to reach me.

The more she spoke, the more her hands trembled, the adrenaline still running sharp beneath her skin even as her voice turned fierce.

"Pull a stunt like that again and I will shred this realm to get you back. And *mark my words*—if I fail, I *will* follow you. So do us both a favor, and have the decency to take me with you next time. Because I'm *not* doing that again."

A dark laugh broke loose from my chest.

"You were scared for me," I said, unable to stop the smile spreading across my lips.

"Get fucked," she choked, a watery laugh escaping as she shoved her palm against my face, her thumb grazing my jaw, her jade eyes scalding.

"*You* were scared for *me*," I teased, more insistently now.

She let out another laugh-sob and tilted her face away. When I caught her chin, angling her back up to me, her breath hitched.

"What are you doing?"

"Will you just shut up and let me kiss you?"

She inhaled sharply—but didn't retreat. Didn't shove me away. Didn't say no.

When I leaned in, hovering just short of contact, it was Freya who closed the distance, her lips brushing mine in a soft, tentative kiss. And I *knew...*

I'd known on my bed, when I kissed her to cover a lie, that this was different. I'd known when I claimed her mouth to bring her back into her body, to remind her who she was, that I would never recover from touching her.

She wasn't an addiction I couldn't shake—she was oxygen itself. She was life. And I hadn't realized until now that the hunger I carried for this woman didn't burn in my skin. It lived in my soul.

It wasn't just that I wanted to fuck her—which, I did—or that her beauty made my heart stutter. It was that no one had ever felt as natural as breathing until Freya.

Heat flared, not as a firestorm of want, but as something deeper—something vital—rushing through my veins.

One kiss became two. Then three. My hands found her hips, her thighs, the curve of her ass. Hers tangled in my hair until it burned. And *God*, I fucking needed more.

She rose onto her toes with elegance, but it still wasn't enough. I needed her closer. Needed her pressed against me. Needed to bury myself in her and learn what made her cry out—what made her beg, what left her trembling.

Desperate as a dying man dragged to water, I cupped her perfect ass and lifted her into my arms, carrying her to the porch rail. I set her down on the banister and her legs locked around my waist, dragging us flush. Her nails scored my back as the sun beat down on my shoulders and I seized her mouth, forcing it open and tasting her like I'd earned it.

She surrendered sweetly, pulse hammering beneath my fingertips where I cradled her neck.

Mine.

The word echoed through every cell. She was sunlight, blood, and breath. Our kiss found rhythm as we mapped each other's bodies. My fingers ached to strip her leathers—to memorize her without armor, to spread her across a bed and feast.

"We shouldn't," she panted, but she kissed me harder right after, like she already knew it didn't matter. "Doesn't make sense."

"Bullshit," I growled, dragging my teeth along her bottom lip. "You're *the only* fucking thing that makes sense, Freya. The only thing that feels like hope in this shattered world."

"You'll regret me," she whispered. "I'm a mistake." Her eyes searched mine while her hands roamed over my torso, legs still clamped tight around me. I could smell her arousal—feel it pulling me to the edge.

"Your mouth says one thing, but your body disagrees." I pressed my forehead to hers, breathing hard. "You know you're safe with me?"

She nodded, and I exhaled. "I could never hurt you, ma moitié. Not anymore."

She skimmed her nose over mine. "It's not me I'm worried about. I could break you so easily, Cyrus."

I smiled faintly and wrapped a lock of her hair around my finger. "I'm well aware."

"That doesn't scare you?"

"Fuck, chérie, I'm *terrified*," I admitted, grazing her lips. "But trust is earned. And I'm trying."

"There's something I should tell you."

"About your duel declaration?" When she nodded, I gave one in return. "Tomorrow. You can tell me tomorrow."

She watched me in silence for a long beat, then nodded, voice shaking. "You go, I go?"

"As long as I get the same goddamn courtesy."

"I can live with that."

"Good." I cupped her thighs and kissed her again. She matched me with a fire that lit something feral inside me. My hands resumed their exploration—mapping, claiming, savoring.

"I'm gonna shred this armor," I muttered, and she laughed, looping her arms around my neck.

I carried her inside, kissing down her jaw as I moved. When I tossed her onto the bed, my shadows slipped free and pinned her wrists, her laugh lighting me up from the inside.

"Oh, those *are* fun," she teased, smiling like the sun we just abandoned.

Climbing over her, I asked, "Do you trust me?"

"Enough."

I could work with that. For now.

I lowered myself over her, kissing her lips, jaw, and clavicle before plucking a blade from the sheath at her ribs. Her breath hitched. I grinned against her skin, held it up, and let my shadows place it on the dresser. She smirked. I unsheathed another, and another. Before long, I lost count.

"You were prepared to take down the whole compound."

"Just about did," she said, her eyes locking with mine, the truth unspoken.

For me.

"You really are their daughter."

"Damn straight."

I chuckled, trailing my hands down her torso. I emptied her hips, her thigh holsters, then her calves. Finally, I retrieved the last dagger from her ribs, my thumb tracing that familiar rune.

"This is *mine*," I noted, holding it aloft.

"*Was*," she replied with a smug little wrinkle of her nose. "Until I took it off you."

Chuckling, I raised the blade to her throat, feeding on the way she tilted her head, baring her neck. Her pulse fluttered like a hummingbird beneath porcelain skin.

That was trust. And my body roared in satisfaction.

Eyes locked on mine, she wet her lips, that flicker of challenge gleaming in her gaze.

I traced the dagger along her jawline, then slowly dragged the point down her jugular to the collar of her armor.

"Do it and die," she muttered, eyes narrowing.

I tossed the blade aside with a grin and stepped back to admire her tight body stretched over the bed. My shadows released her, and she surged upright, stripping her clothes like they offended her. I helped, wrestling her out of her pants as her hands yanked at mine.

Gazes locked, she slowly lowered to her knees easing the fabric down, my dick jutting free. It wasn't until she tossed my clothes aside that her eyes dropped to my cock, where the needy bastard was at full mast. For a heartbeat, her attention diverted to my thigh tattoo. I could never articulate why, but it had always been my favorite—a skull nestled in Azalea branches, with two accompanying sparrows perched among the leaves. The result of a shroom trip not long after graduation.

Something like fear flashed in her eyes as Freya ran her hand over the ink like a silent benediction before turning her attention back to my shaft. Her eyes gleamed as she took me in hand, her fingers not quite closing around the width. When her thumb brushed the Jacob's ladder piercings, my dick twitched, a groan rumbling from my chest. She licked her lips and slowly ran her tongue up the length of me, teasing each silver bar. When she finally took me into her mouth, I nearly lost it.

She hummed as my hands fisted her hair, satisfaction sparking in her eyes. I was so fucking ravenous for this woman there was a high probability I was about to humiliate myself.

A fear that was amplified when she took me to the back of her throat, her muscles tightening, and then she did it again. Her beautiful eyes watered and those fair lashes fluttered against her creamy skin as she fought to swallow me down.

This fucking woman would be the death of me. The sight of her on her knees—the infamous *Wraith* with my cock in her mouth—peering up at me beneath heavy lids threatened every scrap of control I'd built.

"*Fuuuck*, Freya," I ground between my teeth, tightening my hold on her hair. Goddamn, I was gonna bust like a virgin if she rolled her tongue like that again. When I couldn't take another second, I scooped her up and claimed her mouth, backing her toward the bed.

Stripping the rest of her armor and underthings, I laid her bare and stared at perfection.

"You're soaked."

She smirked. "Kinda the point, don't you think?"

"Smartass."

"Yeah, well, you knew that alrea*dy*." The end of her word trailed into a squeak as my fingers pressed against her clit. Her mouth dropped open, and I grinned. Victory was sweetest when hard fucking earned.

"Cyrus," she breathed, eyes flying wide as I worked her clit. "Oh, fuck."

"I like that. Say it again."

"Oh, *fuck!*" Oh, how I could get used to her being this pliant. When I circled her slick entrance, dipping a finger in, she stiffened beneath me. I froze instantly, even as my whole body trembled with the need to take her.

"What do you need?"

"This body is new." The confusion on my face must've been obvious, because she rolled her eyes. "*This body* is *new*."

"You said that already." Impossible. What she was insinuating couldn't be true. She'd been stunning even in adolescence—the wet dream of half the camp. "Are you a virgin, Freya?"

Her eyes narrowed. "No," she bit out. Then sighed. "Freya *the soul* is not."

"And Freya, the vessel?"

"Has known no men." Flat. Emotionless. Almost irritated. Her annoyance made me smirk.

"I'll leave you with blue balls forever if you make this a thing."

Snorting, I buried my face in her neck, relieved when she tilted her head back to let me in. "You've left me that way for months. Why stop now?"

Her hand slid down to guide mine toward her center. "Just...didn't want to startle you."

"Do you trust me?" I asked again.

This time, I earned a feline smile. "Enough."

That was all I needed. I returned my finger to her center, easing in slowly. Testing. Her heat clenched around me, and a groan cracked out of my chest.

"Good. Then gimme what I want, Freya."

I worked her open, slow and steady, breathless whimpers tumbling from her lips as I relished each reaction. When her slick walls tightened around me, I lost the last threads of restraint.

"I want you to come on my tongue before you come all over my cock, pretty girl."

Burying my face against her sweet cunt, I licked up her center, savoring the taste of her. She whimpered, squirming as I licked, kissed, sucked, held her open. My hands gripped her hips as I devoured her, building her up until she trembled, thighs locking around my face.

"Oh, fuck! *Fuckfuckfuck,*" she cried out, bucking against my mouth. Her body shook as her orgasm hit, and I kept at it, coaxing every aftershock from her until she sagged into the mattress.

Mine.

Her pleasure. Her body. Her soul—if I didn't fuck this up.

By the time I drew out her third orgasm, her eyes were glassy and her body languid.

"Such a pretty pussy, Freya. And so fucking wet."

"My legs are tingling," she sighed.

"Good. I need you ready for me."

"Mm-hmm," she sing-songed, making me chuckle.

I climbed over her, smiling at the hazy contentment in her gaze. Trailing my fingers up her abs, I slid through the sweat-slicked skin until I slipped my knee between her thighs. She opened for me easily, one hand floating to my face.

"Please," she breathed.

Fuck. That word nearly broke me. I set my forehead against hers, grounding myself.

"I need a condom, cher."

She shook her head, our noses brushing. "I'm on a tincture."

Same, but—"Since when?"

"Since you tried to die *without me,* asshole."

I barked a laugh, smiling into her aggressive kiss. Maybe I hadn't ruined her after all.

"Blythe hooked me up."

She'd known. Before I'd even woken up, she knew where this was going. I didn't know whether to beat my chest or smack her ass for putting me through that tantrum first.

"I've never gone bare," I admitted.

"Then you've never put those piercings to good use," she taunted.

Goddamn, I was so fucking sunk. Whether she was sent to complete me or destroy me didn't matter. There was no turning back now.

This time, when I claimed her mouth, there was no hesitation left. Just hunger.

We devoured each other, her hips arching to meet mine as I reached down to guide myself through her slick center and over her swollen clit. She shuddered, thighs tightening around my hips.

"Fuck, yes," I breathed, lining up with her entrance. One hand found her jaw, tipping her face to mine. "Eyes on me, Freya."

She nodded, her gaze unwavering as I eased in. Her mouth parted when the first bar pushed inside.

"Fuuck, you're *so* tight."

"More," she breathed, bucking against me.

My hand flew to her hip, holding her steady. "Easy, beautiful. Unless you're trying to get me to blow like a fucking amateur."

"Might be fun," she smirked.

"Feral demon creature," I muttered, earning that perfect laugh. I nipped her lip, panted, "Fuck," and closed my eyes.

"What happened to eyes on you?"

"Breathing," I grit out, earning her giggle and a scratch down my ribs. I kissed her softly, then met her gaze again. As I eased deeper, that second bar pushed through, and I met resistance.

"Doing okay?"

She nodded, her breath shivering.

"You're gonna feel a pinch," I warned. She dipped her chin in acknowledgment. I pushed through—slow, careful—and swallowed her sharp gasp with a kiss. I didn't move, not yet. Let her adjust. Let her feel the rhythm of us, the trust, the control I wouldn't break.

When I was certain I wouldn't lose myself, I murmured, "You good, ma moitié?"

Another nod. "Fuck me, Cyrus," she whispered, biting my lip hard enough to draw blood. I hissed when I tasted copper, a growl rumbling deep in my chest.

Mine.

Every cell in my body roared that one word as I began a slow, easy rock.

Mine. *Thrust.*

Mine—*thrust.*

"I said *fuck me,* Cyrus," she demanded, her heels digging into my ass. I chuckled against her lips and then followed her order. Who the hell was I to deny her?

She made the most perfect fucking noise as our bodies slid together, my thumb coming to press against her clit. Each thrust was a claiming. A promise. A prayer. My hands eventually roamed her skin, finding every freckle, every scar, every perfect line. My name on her lips wrecked me. Her trust buried the blade deeper.

She'd warned me she could break me.

As her cunt pulsed tight and her scream echoed off the walls, I knew she already had.

One final pump—and I came, a bellow tearing from my throat with her name carved into it.

I was so fucked.

SIXTY-ONE

HOURGLASS

FREYA

Based on the angle of the sun, we'd contentedly reveled in becoming one congealed tangle of limbs for at least an hour before Cyrus pressed a kiss to my shoulder and abruptly left.

"Cyrus?" I breathed, weirded out when he said nothing. Sitting up, I braced myself on my elbows, peering around the corner into the ensuite bathroom he'd vanished into. Was he...rummaging through her shit? *"Cyrus?"*

"Uh—gimme a sec."

"Get your ass back in here," I complained. "What are you doing?"

"One minute, dammit!" Something clattered—bottles, maybe—and a cabinet slammed.

Pinching the bridge of my nose, I muttered, "Jesus Christ, what are you *doing?"*

His voice echoed from what I assumed was the closet. "I thought your kind didn't use that name that way."

My kind. Rolling my eyes, I sat up and pulled the comforter over me, as if modesty could buffer the creeping awkwardness promising my imminent demise. He just...*left.* What the hell was he doing?

"Blythe is a new friend. Please don't raid her cupboards."

"I'll leave her cash." What? What was he even talking about?

"Uh, listen Stuart," I muttered, sliding off the bed. "That was hot and all, but—"

"Sit the hell down—" *Was that a faucet?* "I'll be right there."

Narrowing my eyes, I—naturally—ignored his demand and padded forward on tentative feet. My body was singing, the space between my legs deliciously sore, my soul finally soothed after what had decidedly been the worst night in any incarnation. As it turned out, nobody had ever exaggerated how terrible it was to watch your mate dying. Zero out of ten, do not fucking recommend.

Apparently, my resistance to the *concept* of a Mate Bond shackling the son of my killer to my soul didn't interfere with the thing commandeering my heart.

And as it stood, I was in no way, shape, or form ready for him to stop touching me—every caress a reminder that we'd gotten him out. That Aren and Ansel had stabilized him fast enough for Aren to sling him over a shoulder like a sack of grain and get him to safety.

Fuck, I needed to replace that memory with more of him above me—the weight of him the sweetest sin I'd ever willingly made.

"*Cyrus*," I hissed, popping my head around the corner like a nosy, apprehensive meerkat.

My breath hitched when I stepped into the bathroom. His beautiful, tattooed back faced me, biteable ass on proud display as he poured something into the tub. I rolled my lower lip between my teeth, admiring the view. Lean or not, every inch of him looked sculpted from clay. Cyrus stepped back, nearly grinning as bubbles foamed to life in the water rapidly filling the basin.

Tears shouldn't have stung my eyes, but the maybe-not-an-asshole had lit tea lights around the tub. A towel was laid out on the floor. Lavender oil hung in the air. It smelled like one of those pretentious spas August used to send Layla to.

"Cyrus?" I asked, unable to hide the emotion from my voice.

"Come here," he breathed, extending one long arm toward me.

Swallowing the lump in my throat, I dropped the comforter, lifted my chin, and closed the distance. He pulled me into his beautiful inked arms—heat seeping into my skin—as he traced gentle fingers across my back.

"What are you doing?" I murmured, a cold flicker of fear scraping down my spine. Smart Cyrus, I could handle. Primal, erotic Cyrus? A sight to behold, though I was trying very hard to forget why he was so good at that.

But sweet Cyrus? That was fucking terrifying.

"Thank you," he breathed, not answering the question, but still managing to make my knees buckle in a way I resented. Weak. This man would make me weak if we kept down this path.

Wrinkling my nose, I muttered, "If you thank me for my v-card, my ovaries will shrivel into microscopic raisins."

He snorted, shaking his head. "As much as I'm relishing knowing I'm the only man to fuck that pretty pussy, *no*. That's not what I had in mind."

"Oh. Well. Do carry on then." Blessedly, my tone was light despite the flush heating my cheeks. Look, I'd had lovers in past lives—none of them shabby—but what the actual fuck had that soul-altering, mind-melting insanity been? I was pretty sure I'd glimpsed the pearly gates before spiraling back into my trembling body.

"Thank you for saving my life. *Again*," he added with a rueful smile that turned my pulse traitorous. "Would'a been a shame to miss *that*."

"Agreed."

"And thank you for trusting me with your body. Hottest moment of my life."

I bit the inside of my cheek to keep the smile from breaking through. What the hell was I supposed to say to that? It hadn't been intentional—just the natural result of every boy my age being a fuckwit not worth my time.

Once I ascended, my intolerance for their bullshit had made so much sense.

He pressed a kiss to my forehead, then turned toward the bath, fishing a washcloth from the water.

"Stay." With that single command, he *knelt*, sending a conspiracy of tiny ravens fluttering in my chest as he pressed a kiss to my sternum and lifted the cloth to my skin.

"You don't—"

"For once in your fucking life, Freya, just let it happen."

A snort caught in my throat at the warning in his tone. Swallowing the panic swelling in my chest, I shut up and let him lift one calf, angling my leg to clean the inside of my thigh with agonizing gentleness. Then, with painful precision, he repeated the process.

By the time he finally rose and tossed the cloth aside, I felt more stripped bare than when I'd been splayed out on that bed for him. He guided me into the tub, and I groaned as the heat enveloped my body—sting trailing across sore skin.

I looked up at a man who was more deity than soul. Cyrus's luscious hair fell loose around his shoulders, lids heavy with lust, that satisfied curve ghosting across his mouth. *That mouth*—the one that had mapped every inch of me like a cartographer at war with God.

And that cock. He'd filled me with a pain so sweet I'd thank him for splitting me in two.

Damn, he was tall—languidly stretching above me as he leaned one forearm against the tub's framing wall. Every lean line, every tendon beneath inked skin, had my mouth salivating. He stared until I gave him the faintest nod.

Then, without hesitation, Cyrus climbed over the lip of the tub and slipped in behind me—long legs wrapping snugly around my hips as he hissed at the heat.

"Is it a universal trait that women wanna bathe in Satan's seventh spa?"

Chuckling, I said, "You guessed correctly."

That was it. Without another word, we shimmied down to fit his lanky frame into Blythe's oversized tub, his arms wrapping around my chest as we both leaned back until the water reached my sternum, lapping gently at the emergency drain. Clearly, this place had not been designed with Paladin-sized males in mind.

My eyes slipped closed as his lips found my neck. He nibbled at my earlobe, kissed along my jaw, drawing a hum of satisfaction from deep in my chest. He cupped water in his palms, pouring it over my collarbones, soaking my shoulders and chest before reaching for soap. Lathering his hands, he brought them to my skin—softly cupping my breasts and lavishing my nipples between slick fingers.

"Didn't take you for a sap," I murmured, craning my neck to kiss his jawline in thanks. Every touch felt divine. Unfair.

"I'm not. Don't get used to it," he muttered, squeezing my hips between his thighs. "I'll blame it on the almost dyin'."

"You *did* die, jackass."

"Still mad?"

"Nothing your dick can't remedy."

A laugh rumbled through his chest, rich and pleased. "I'm gonna thoroughly enjoy this arrangement if that's how we solve arguments."

I grinned—not that he could see it—as I leaned back against him. Slowly, I laced our fingers together, palm to palm, and raised his right hand to examine the hooded angel inked across the back of it. Always watching. I turned his arm, scanning through thick wings for the hidden blade. I'd always wanted to ask about the seraphim wings, but after seeing all of Cyrus Stuart, that was no longer the tattoo that squeezed my ribs the hardest.

I would not lift his arm to study that thigh piece. I *would not* lift his arm to study that goddamn thigh piece.

Nope.

I'd add that to my list of shit to ask the big papa in the sky—if I ever made it there.

Thankfully, Cyrus broke the silence before I could spiral further into symbolism that probably wasn't even there.

"You gonna tell me what the hell happened while I was out?"

Where would I start?

The soul-rending desperation of watching him try and fail to claw his way back? The hoarse scream that ripped from my throat when Tessa finally overrode the system and that damned plate opened? The panic of not being able to drag his body into the hall before remembering the shadows could do what this vessel never could?

Giving him CPR as the color leached from his lips. One insane instinct to dive into the depths of my well and haul out the electricity I hadn't realized I'd kept from August.

The stuttered rise of his chest. My guttural sob of relief. The blinding rage that followed.

So many men—Renown and Bellpost alike—slaughtered like animals as my gift eviscerated them, ripping out their power like plugs from sockets.

Aren and Ansel descending like wrathful angels.

Blood. Crimson and black.

Crawlers.

Eleven hours of pure, unrelenting fear that he wouldn't wake. That my pride had robbed me of something sacred.

Throwing myself at Blythe's feet and begging for her help.

Clearing my throat, I whispered, "Maybe tomorrow."

The sound of his teeth grinding was audible. I reached up, stroking his jaw. "Real," I breathed.

"Real," he echoed, hands sliding to my waist as he sat us both up. In the next breath, he turned me to face him, eyes drinking me in. Slowly, he shifted me into his lap, gaze locked on mine as he guided his dick to my entrance, notching the tip in place.

He didn't speak, but he didn't need to.

My choice. Still mine, always mine. And he'd honor it—whether or not I continued.

I wrapped my arms around his neck, held his gaze, and lifted myself before easing down, taking him inch by inch through the sweet, sharp bite of stretched skin. The metal beads of his piercing dragged along my inner walls with sinful precision, and a moan bloomed in my chest as I slid down until he was buried inside me.

I gasped, filled entirely, and that stupidly handsome cheek lifted in a restrained grin as his hands worshipped every inch of slick skin they touched.

But it was those citrine eyes—flashing between mine, suddenly unguarded in their quiet pursuit of something eternal—that undid me completely.

And I willingly spent the day losing myself in the son of my enemy.

FREYA

How ate you?

Ho are you?

How*

Jesus Christ. Ignore me.

CYRUS

Tried that. Didn't end well for me.

FREYA

Laughing emoji Touché.

Just another hour of this cotton candy nightmare, and I'll be back.

Aren's gonna surprise Mags.

CYRUS

Get a feel for her, will you? There was something about that witch I couldn't place my finger on.

Make it thirty minutes, and I won't edge you out until you're begging me for mercy as punishment for leaving me to sift through this shit alone in the first place.

FREYA

That's what vibrators are for.

CYRUS

Hard to reach a vibrator with your hands bound above your head.

FREYA

Filthy.

CYRUS

You can't pretend you're shocked.

FREYA

You can't pretend I won't enjoy *all* of that.

CYRUS

Not sure who will enjoy you coming so hard you pour down your thighs more. Me, or you.

FREYA

Promises, promises.

CYRUS

You did not just question my capabilities.

FREYA

More like this body's.

CYRUS

Chérie, I haven't even gotten started.

Might I point out, you've had lifetimes with these women, and I had to suck death's dick to finally get a chance with you last night.

FREYA

Eyeballs emoji, laughing emojis Oh you must be desperate, playing the almost died card.

Honestly Cyurs.

Cyrus

Jesus, did my thumps have stroke?

*Thubs

THUMBS

Duck.

Never mind.

CYRUS

Crying Laughing emoji, face palm emoji

Can burn down a heavily guarded warehouse, but can't text. Noted.

FREYA

Look, I want your face between my thighs more than you do, but this means a lot to Fae. It's the last chance we have to just…be normal. Do girl things.

CYRUS

Plan on losing?

FREYA

Plan on fighting.

CYRUS

Fine. Enjoy the girls. Then get your fine ass back here.

FREYA

Needy man.

CYRUS

...

WITH HEAT in my cheeks and my teeth clamped onto my lip to keep from grinning, I watched those three little dots load and vanish over and over again. I was on the edge of my hypothetical seat when he finally responded.

CYRUS

In all seriousness, watch your back out there.

Tu me manques.

SCOWLING, I copied his last text and dropped it into a translator. Of all the skill sets that didn't transfer from Valora to me, losing French and being redeployed to Louisiana was an especially cruel joke.

Awe. Fuck me—the menace was a closet romantic.

"You are missing from me," I read aloud in translation, shaking my head as I scrolled through search results. *He missed me.* Jesus. Why was everything more poetic in foreign languages?

FREYA

Ditto.

UGH. I gagged *typing* that. *What* the hell *was wrong with me?* One day of getting properly dicked down and I'd turned into a puddle of goo. I backpedaled, erasing the sappy response.

FREYA

Middle finger emoji Watch your own back.

Your death would be a lukewarm inconvenience.

IRRITATED AT THE soft-hearted monstrosity I was apparently becoming, I slid my phone into my pocket—only to find Ally watching me with a smirk and one perfectly arched brow. She stood sentinel beside the witches' Ferris wheel at the town's Equinox festival, looking for all the world like an omniscient circus freak waiting for her nieces to get off the ride. It was kind of adorable.

"You're...*glowing*," she accused, casting the line.

I bit. "Five orgasms will do that."

"Jesus, Freya," she choked out, blushing as she grinned at her feet.

"Dammit, I *need to get laid*," Blythe groaned, jogging down the creaky metal steps, Magnolia tight on her heels and beaming. I liked the witches—more than I expected to. Fresh, sassy, a little chaotic. They'd cackled when Alvara terrified the mortal psychic fraud. That sealed it. They'd fit into our coven just fine.

"I'm with Freya," Magnolia said. "No better skincare than some toe-curling pleasure."

"Oh shit, Ally is turning red," Lana said dryly, lips twitching.

"Shush, you," Ally snapped, trying to smother a smile. "Like you're thrilled to hear about Freya's sex life."

Lana shrugged one shoulder, but her smile faded as her eyes locked on mine. She didn't need to say it. She'd seen what Ansel had—me unraveling while Cyrus died. "I'm grateful they found each other," she said, voice softer, as if it cost her something. "Even if he is a Paladin."

Fae skipped up beside her with two ice cream cones. I swiped one before Lana could claim it and took a massive bite.

"Brat," Lana squealed, kicking my shin.

I cackled, covering my mouth with one hand.

"Anyone up for the fun house?" Fae chirped.

Unanimous nods. For a moment, it was easy to pretend we were just a group of women laughing at a fair—not the core of a rebellion. It was Ally's eyes on me that gave it away. She saw right through my smile.

She reached out, and I stepped back, sliding Fae between us and untying my sweatshirt from my waist, tugging it on like armor. I hated that I had to keep anything from her—especially *everything*.

Once covered, I rejoined the group, laughing along though I had no idea what they were talking about.

Ally's lips parted. Her jaw tensed. "Hey, Freya. A quick word?"

Nodding, I let the others drift ahead. Fae looped her arms through Lana and Blythe's; Magnolia snagged Blythe's other side. They slithered off in a chain of laughter. I forced my attention back to Ally and lifted my chin with a brittle smile. "You okay?"

"Are *you?*" she countered gently.

Why did she always have to be so kind all the goddamn time. I nodded, hoping she didn't see the lump forming in my throat. "I have something for you, in case things get tricky. We're close."

"How close?"

"A week. Did you finish your business?" Her arched brow made it clear she knew I hadn't.

"Waiting on something," I muttered.

Her gaze sharpened, head tilting like a cat locking onto prey. "Interesting. You intend to take the sister as your second."

My jaw tightened. "Does Aren know?"

"That in eight out of ten threads, you bring us an army? Yes. How you do it? No. Aren is currently burdened with essential information, and nothing more."

I'd take that as her stamp of approval. Thanks very much.

"And the two outliers?"

Her nostrils flared like a predator's before she straightened. "You lose."

So...death. Got it.

A chorus of screams turned our heads toward one of the enormous spinning rides. Metal creaked. Carnival lights spun in dizzying arcs. Somewhere, someone was singing in a makeshift amphitheater. A gaggle of teens fought over turkey legs.

Mortals. Laughing. Celebrating. Blind to the cliff they teetered on.

When I turned back, Ally had drawn something from her bag: a tiny gold hourglass, its sand already trickling between chambers.

"Finish it," she said, holding it out. "I need you back before the last grain falls."

Rolling my lip between my teeth, I took it and inclined my head to study the trinket. That wasn't a week of sand. Not even close. Nerves coiled in my gut. I suddenly wanted nothing to do with the fun house. I wanted Cyrus. I wanted to tell him the truth.

Tomorrow, Calypso would be marked Heiress.

And once she was, I'd be free to strike. She might be young, but she had potential. So did her brother.

Composing myself, I nodded. "Yes, ma'am."

"Time is a delicate thing, Freya. Not all futures are minted. Some choices are broken before they're even made."

Her words echoed for the next hour.

When I returned to Blythe's bungalow, Cyrus was surrounded by a battlefield of papers and sticky notes. His hair was a mess—clearly the result of repeatedly tying it up and yanking it loose.

"There's a gap," he said by way of greeting.

"What?"

"In their children. There's *a gap*, Freya."

"Okay?"

"Bastien, Caius, Levana, Sirin, and the twins were each born eighteen months apart. Then, suddenly, there's a three-year gap before Agamemnon."

I wrinkled my nose. "You pee two watermelons out back-to-back and tell me you're ready for round three."

"First—ouch. Second—not the same thing. But it feels...*ceremonial*. Patterned."

I squinted. "Like...the sex?"

"Eighteen months on the nose, Freya. You can't make this shit up. It can't be coincidence. Maybe twice—but four times? That's deliberate. The marriage contract might've included fertility clauses."

"So...she had trouble getting pregnant. Or miscarried. Or Agamemnon was an oops. Or—"

"Or Adrastos fucking Balaskas was *erased*."

The missing pages. The fragmented records. Goosebumps crawled up my arms.

"Why do you think that?"

He shook his head, running his fingers through his mess of hair. My own itched to do the same. "He claimed Agamemnon was his brother. 'Lonan' lost 'Leo'. I swear I've seen his name before. But it's not in Paladin. I've been looking since before we called our truce."

"There are a lot of books, Cyrus."

"And I've had insomnia for four fucking years."

Since Charles.

Jesus.

He nodded. "It's been itching at my brain for weeks. I can't place it."

Stifling a smile, I murmured, "You're sexy when you go full nerd on me."

"Get fucked," he laughed, arms already opening as I tiptoed through his chaos and curled into his lap.

I plucked the pen from behind his ear with my teeth, twirling it between my fingers. "Add some reading glasses and I'd positively swoon."

"Don't be sweet. It's weird. Unless you want something." His fingers dug into my ass through my jeans.

I leaned in, lips brushing his ear. "*Just you.* For tonight—just you. We go home tomorrow. Then you can nerd out with your cousins and dissect every inch of Reyna's library. But tonight...let me be selfish."

Because tomorrow, once Calypso was marked, I'd owe him the truth.

SIXTY-TWO

THE DIVIDE

FREYA

"Watch your back," Cyrus murmured, pressing his forehead to mine. We stood directly on the divide, unwilling to test our luck now that Reyna had returned to the helm. I nodded, fighting back the anxiety that had bloomed in my belly ever since Ally handed me that inauspicious little hourglass.

A throat cleared in the distance, and we turned to face our respective companions. Jax, Brody, and Alastair stood on the Bellaton side of the river, a grim tableau that deepened the unease already prickling beneath my skin. The last time all three of them had escorted me anywhere, it was out of Cyrus' warehouse with chains clamped around my broken wrists.

Opposite us, on the other side of the bridge, stood Carr and Cali, their expressions equally wary.

We good for a second? I asked silently. Brody responded with a brief jut of his chin—permission granted.

"Why does this feel like a custody exchange after a nasty divorce?" Cyrus muttered, and I half-laughed, the sound catching in my throat as he laced his fingers through mine and guided me toward his family.

"Blaz helping our search now that Reyna's back is going about as well as expected," Calypso announced as we drew near. That, at least, explained the sour expressions. "He's smuggled out what he can, but there's only so many books he can swipe without her noticing."

"The missive confirmed enough, but fuck if I don't want a better grasp of who we're dealing with," Cyrus muttered.

"You're certain he's a Balaskas?" Carr asked as we approached.

"That's what the signature said."

Carr looked like he was two seconds away from throwing a punch. "Where the fuck have they been hiding?"

"Your guess is as good as mine." I squeezed Cyrus' hand as we drew nearer to their side of the river, my eyes scanning the treeline, the water, the shadows—searching for any hint of an ambush, of another Nix crouched in the brush.

"It's not like any of us gave Moros a second thought," Calypso said, her temper tucked neatly behind her calm façade. "He's an entitled prick without the power to back it up."

"Or he *was*," Cyrus corrected softly.

"Right. *That.*"

"I'm heading back to smooth things out with Reyna," I said. "Ally chalked her temper up to grief, but I'd rather ensure our ducks are in a row."

"Line them out quickly, *Maleficent*," Carr said, his stance mirroring my own edginess. He scanned the sky before settling on my face. "The Queen pulled us into her office today."

"What the fuck for?" Cyrus growled.

"She's decided we're allying with Adrastos."

"Fucking bitch," I groaned, jamming my eyes shut before grimacing. "No offense. Mixed company. That was my bad."

Calypso smirked. "None taken. Sometimes I wish being the Heiress gave me an ounce of authority, but I barely have legs to stand on when she's in the room."

"We can push for a vote," Cyrus countered, his thumb brushing over the signet ring on his hand. "This isn't over."

"The Guard will always side with her," Cali said, shaking her head. "We have a few wildcards to play, but not enough to overpower her."

"Portia? Maybe Orion?"

"Maybe," she allowed.

I narrowed my eyes, curiosity getting the better of me. "How many Guards still stand?"

"Six. Not including Dad."

I exhaled sharply. That was going to complicate things. "Twelve hours," I said, glancing up at Cyrus. His hands had moved to his collar, my gaze tracing the edge of his wings where they ghosted beneath his jacket. There was no way Poe had marked him by coincidence. No way we were bound like this by accident.

"Twelve hours," he echoed, resigned. We'd tried to coordinate a full day together, but Reyna's open hostility made that damn near impossible. She'd have an aneurysm if she found out Blaz was aiding him. Until I could thaw that frost, he'd stay behind.

Nodding once, I met Cali's gaze, then Carr's, praying we were right—that we'd find something, anything, to give us an edge.

I turned to leave—but Cyrus' hand clamped around my hip, then into my hair so fast I gasped. He chuckled low, fisting the strands to draw my head back against his shoulder.

"Rude," he whispered against my ear before spinning me to face him.

Heart thundering, I shook my head. "You did *not* just do that."

"*You* did not just walk away without saying goodbye."

"Possessive?"

"Abso-fucking-lutely." He bent down and kissed me like I was air and he'd gone breathless. My hands curled into the leather at his waist, pulling him closer, until stars sparked in the corners of my vision.

"You've got a succubus on your face," Carr called dryly. Cyrus and I raised matching middle fingers, his hand softening on my cheek as he swiped his tongue over my lips.

"Damn, they really did find each other," Calypso murmured.

When he finally released me, we were both flushed and breathless. I smiled, catching sight of my escorts now politely engrossed in their own conversation.

Steeling myself for another parting, I whispered, "Twelve hours?"

"See you then."

I nodded. "You will be missing from me."

A quiet smile curved his mouth, that same reverence from the vault flickering in his eyes like I was the last thing he'd ever see. Swallowing hard, I squeezed his hand and stepped away, waving to Cali and Carr as I crossed the river.

By the time we crossed into Bellaton, my mental to-do list had spiraled out of control—first item: shower off forty-eight hours of sex before presenting myself to Reyna for judgment. I emptied my pockets at the bedside table, taking care with Alvara's hourglass, watching the tiny grains slide through the center—too slowly. And somehow, far too fast.

Time.

We were running out of it.

Bolstering myself, I made quick work of stripping and stepped into the shower, cataloging priorities as the scalding spray hit my shoulders. Today we were briefing the full Flying Squad, syncing strategy with Ally and Aren's allies. My head already hurt.

But the water seemed to knock something loose—a dangling thought that had haunted me for days.

Did I trust Cyrus and Calypso to do the right thing with Paladin?

Yes. I finally did.

And that meant allowing Calypso to bear the Heiress mark before I moved. It promised the return of power to their bloodline—an honor Cyrus had fought his whole life to defend. It was Cyrus Cali relied on for foresight. *Cyrus* who had the loyalty of the Wings. Cyrus who'd already spilled blood to protect the line of succession.

Cyrus, who had defied the treaty to begin building peace with his cousin.

A leader. A friend. A man I trusted.

And he was only twenty-two.

Maybe—if I played my cards right—it didn't have to be me on that throne.

SIXTY-THREE
LIGHTS OFF
CYRUS

The sun had already set by the time we peeled ourselves away from the stack of books Blaz smuggled to Cali. Only Jo's arrival with food from *The Rougarou* had broken our trance—she'd basically spoon-fed Cali to make her stop reading long enough to eat.

"You coming out to celebrate with us?" Jo asked, turning to me with a look that said she already knew my answer.

"Nah. That motherfucker threatened Freya. I'm not in the mood." I jerked my chin toward Cali, who was inhaling fried gator like a woman possessed. "That's a good look for you, sis," I added. She responded with twin middle fingers, which sent Jo into a giggle fit as our oh-so-regal, almost-Heiress returned to Hoovering down calories. Carr snorted, leaned back on the couch, and stretched his neck like he was one nap away from full collapse.

"When do we address the Queen?" he asked without opening his eyes, voice low.

"Fuck. Hopefully never."

"Sooner rather than later," he advised, reaching for the food—only for Cali to slap his hand away with alarming speed.

"She's pissed," Carr muttered. "Asking all kinds of questions."

"I'm sure she is."

"You're coming to the marking ceremony tomorrow," Cali declared, mouth full. When I grimaced, her eyes widened—tearing up slightly as she gulped the food down too fast.

"Christ, Cal. Chew."

She batted Carr away again, and I started wondering how long it would take before he tackled her. "So help me, Cyrus, if you miss this—"

"I'll be there," I said, resigned. "You know I'll be there."

"*I* also *know* you have the most obsessive single-mindedness on the planet."

"She's not wrong," Jo added sagely. "You're like a pit bull once you latch on to something."

"Terrific visual," I muttered, cracking my spine as I leaned back. At this rate, I was gonna look like a hunchback.

"You're not skipping out, right?" Cali said, suddenly serious. "I know that bastard has to pay for what he did to Freya—and, you know, humanity. And yeah, I get that things get harder once Mom announces the alliance, but this is important, Cyrus. I need you there."

"Jesus, Cal. *Breathe.*" I leaned forward and pinched the nerve in her knee that made her squirm. "*Yes.* I'll be there."

She swatted my hand away. "You better be, asshole."

"Wouldn't miss it." I spread my arms wide, giving her a performative grin.

"I mean it."

"Same. Gimme a little credit. When's the last time I let you down?"

"It's a terrible time to start."

"*Exactly.* So, relax." I dropped my hands, elbows braced on my knees. "I said I'll fucking be there, and I will."

"Fine," she huffed, standing with a theatrical sigh and brushing crumbs off her lap.

"Call me if you find anything," she said, already halfway to the door.

"Yeah."

She glanced at Carr. "Watch him."

Carr gave her a lazy two-finger salute. "Always."

"Since when do I need a babysitter?" I barked after her.

She laughed like I was the punchline. Then, as if determined to prove she was still the worst, she bent down and *licked* my cheek.

"Gross," I complained as she cackled her way out the door with Jo right behind her.

"The future leader of our hierarchy, gentlemen," Carr intoned as he stole the last piece of gator.

Shaking my head, I returned to the books. Anything to distract me until Cali's claim to the Heiress title was confirmed. We lost a few hours that way —just ink, anxiety, and that goddamn grandfather clock ticking louder with every passing second. But I couldn't stop thinking about Freya. Hazel-ringed green eyes. Red hair.

Was she safe? Getting anywhere? The total silence from her end could've meant focus...or it could've meant trouble.

I kept checking my phone like some whipped little bitch.

"For fuck's sake, just *call her*," Carr mumbled.

"It's fine," I said, too sharp.

"If you say so." He stretched and yawned, his book sliding off his lap. "Am I the worst cousin in history if I crash?"

"Cousin? No. Right-hand? Probably."

"That's cold, man."

Midnight loomed on my screen. "Go for it. I'm heading out anyway."

"Thank God. Some peace and quiet."

I stood, rubbing my face. "You want a smoke? I'm jonesing."

"Nah, I'm good."

"Be back in five."

"I'll be here," he muttered.

I popped my neck and headed outside. The humidity wrapped around me like wet wool, and for one stupid second I resisted the urge to check my phone again.

She was fine. She had to be fine.

A sharp sting lit up my neck, and I slapped at it—only to feel metal under my fingers. My vision swayed. I yanked a blue dart free and stared at it in horror.

Fuck.

My knees buckled as the ground tipped sideways. I tried to shout for Carr, but my throat was locked up. I flexed my hands, willing my body to fight, but it was like my muscles were underwater.

Two masked figures stepped from the shadows, dressed like Paladins.

I staggered into a defensive stance, but my body wasn't cooperating. The smaller one closed the distance in a blink, grabbing a fistful of my hair and yanking my head up. I couldn't stop him.

He cocked his arm to strike—and the last thought I had before everything went black was that Freya was gonna be so fucking pissed if I was late.

GOD KNOWS how long I was out before I came to in a cold, musty stone room. A sliver of moonlight painted the floor. Chains scraped when I moved, my wrists chafed and burning from the metal restraints. I tried to sit up, only to choke on the pain lancing down my spine. Something scraped—metal against metal—and I turned, blinking against the dark.

A hooded figure stood by the door. Broad-shouldered. Not quite big enough to be Lonan.

Slowly, he turned. A low chuckle spilled out as he stepped into the light. That fucking swagger.

No. *No way.*

He crouched in front of me, blade in hand. My eyes locked on one sapphire and one amber eye—familiar, cruel, and bright as ever.

"I told you this wasn't over," he whispered, grinning with all the victory of a vow made good.

FREYA

WHAT THE FUCK.

I tossed my too-silent phone onto the couch and resumed pacing.

I didn't care for being on this side of the river. Or for the tricks I'd pulled to get inside his building undetected. And I really, *really* didn't care for the fact that Cyrus should've been home three hours ago. With every tick of the clock, breathing got harder—my body aching like I'd run a goddamn marathon.

Texts—unanswered.

Calls—ignored.

Dinner—threatening to reappear.

Crossing the length of the apartment again, I suddenly understood why Ansel kept that dented cigarette tin in his pocket. Something—anything—to keep his hands busy. To keep from stabbing something.

He was fine. It was Cyrus. He was clever. Dangerous in close quarters. Irritatingly resourceful.

We were fine.

Everything was fine.

With a grumble, I collapsed onto his bed, whispering a silent thank-you that he hadn't let housekeeping wash his sheets—because every inch of this ridiculous-thread-count duvet still smelled like him. Leather and heat and that subtle citrus he pretended wasn't cologne.

I suddenly regretted scrubbing his scent from my skin after our...whatever that was. Weekend of orgasms. I hated myself for caring this much. For missing him this much. For aching like he'd been mine forever and not just...briefly.

One weekend of orgasms does *not* a mate make.

I would not fall apart over a feral male.

He was just a guy.

A ridiculously good lay.

A stranger, practically.

Kind of.

Sort of.

Not really. Not when every time I closed my eyes, I saw him. In the theater. On the battlefield. Bent over me in the dark.

The burn of his voice in that crypt. The reverence in his hands. The way he'd said I was his other half—in French, no less. Who the hell says that?

I groaned and rolled off the bed, resisting the urge to steal the pillow and smother myself. Instead, I resumed pacing. Again.

Third lap. Fourth. The buzz of my phone on the coffee table made me lunge so hard I smacked the ever-loving shit out of my shin on the corner. I fumbled the device, heart in my throat.

Not his name.

TESSA

Still nothing. You want me to check the manor, or their cabins?

FREYA

Would you? Please?

TESSA

Give me a sec.

SLIDING the phone into my back pocket, I kept pacing. Tears stung, for two reasons. One—because I had no right to expect Tessa's loyalty, and yet she leapt into action like she'd bled for me in another life. And two—because something was wrong.

"Where are you?" I whispered. For the first time, I reached for that molten thread between us. That heat behind my ribs that pulled me out, out into the world. For the second time—I found nothing. Just a wall. Silence.

He deserved the truth. All of it.

Binding him before he knew why I was here—before he knew what I'd come to do—would be a cruelty even I couldn't stomach. Binding him and then robbing his family of their honor and their tradition?

No. He needed to know. He deserved to choose. That was the point. That was why I was here.

Back and forth, back and forth. My mind spun while my feet wore a trench in the carpet. I checked my phone again. Nothing from Ally, either. They were running security at Hazelharbor tonight. Probably busy.

Probably—

No. The hourglass had been less than half-drained when I'd left for my shower. We had time.

And yet...

Sweat slicked my palms. My throat tightened. My fingers ached, swollen and hot.

Wrong, wrong, wrong.

My phone buzzed, and I about threw my shoulder out of joint reaching for it in the wrong back pocket.

TESSA

The cabin's dark.

FREYA

I'll owe you forever if you get me the coordinates.

TESSA

Already got them. But...you sure you didn't get your wires crossed?

He didn't want to go celebrate with his sister? They seem close.

FREYA

And not tell me?

TESSA

Are you all in?

FREYA

What does that mean?

TESSA

You sure he's not falling back into old habits?

FREYA

No.

I SENT IT. Fast. Certain. But already the pit in my stomach twisted. Because what if—

TESSA

I mean...he is a Paladin.

I just want you to be careful.

You said he had a reputation.

FREYA

He pursued me, not the other way around.

TESSA

I know. But he did look at my tits before
remembering I have eyes.

FREYA

Tessa, darling, with that rack, you confuse straight
women.

TESSA

middle finger emoji

FREYA

Am I wrong?

TESSA

You coming on to me, darling?

FREYA

Little preoccupied atm, but if I find him with one of
his fuckbuddies, I'll let you know.

TESSA

You could take them.

If it means anything, I hope he's fighting Renown or
demons or something.

FREYA

What does it say about me that I hope the same?

TESSA

That you're falling for him. Oh shit—Freya, did you
already fall for him? Did you accept the bond?!

THE DOOR SLAMMED open and I dropped my phone.

Blade drawn. Arm cocked. I nearly launched it before Carr rounded the corner.

"Jesus Christ," he gasped. "You're like a fucking horror film."

"I get that a lot," I said, eyes skimming behind him. "Where is he?"

"Well, hello to you too."

"Hi, *Marley*. Where's Cyrus?"

"I was hoping you could tell me."

"What?" My heart dropped. I sheathed the blade, scooping up my phone as bile rose in my throat. Carr was his ride-or-die. If he didn't know...

"I nodded off. When I woke up, he was gone."

"He's not at the manor?"

"Checked there first. Then *The Rougarou*. Cali hasn't seen him."

I froze. "He just...left you?"

"Lights were off. Everything untouched. He said he'd come here. I figured he'd wake me first."

My chest ached—ribs pulling too tight. "Carr. I've had a bad feeling. Like a *bone deep* sense of panic."

His expression shifted. "What kind of bad?"

"Like...it hurts to breathe."

"Fuck." He turned, pacing as he palmed his face. When he turned back, his eyes were hard, detirmined. "Freya—find him."

"What?"

"You can find him. That *thing* you're suppressing—follow it."

My eyes dropped to where I clutched at my chest. "I can't. Not yet."

"Listen to me." His voice snapped like a whip. "Cyrus is never late. *Never*. Not for anything."

"I kept telling myself he was just *distracted*."

Carr flinched. "You don't fucking deserve him if you believe that. And I know you don't. So stop lying and let him in."

"He has to choose."

"He already did."

"No. There are things he doesn't know. I was supposed to tell him tonight."

The door burst open again.

Calypso.

Shaking. Pale. Eyes glassy. She grabbed Carr like a lifeline.

"They took him," she sobbed. "*They took* Cyrus."

"Who?" he barked, hands on her shoulders.

"Mother and Juno. And I dunno who else. They're saying he committed high treason. That he's trying to steal the throne."

"Bullshit," Carr snapped as my pulse became a roar in my ears, blood chilling.

"I know. But they say they have evidence. They're saying he was colluding with—" she looked at me. "They say he wants you on the throne."

My fault.

This was my fault.

Ciaran.

I'd been so careful. So cautious. No concrete choices. No locked-in vision. Until today. I had been certain today.

"His trial?" I asked, voice barely audible.

"Before my ceremony," Calypso said. "They've had him in interrogation for hours. I tried to see him—they won't let me down. He's in the fucking brig, Freya—they'll kill him."

My blades were already in hand. I was already moving. Already calculating.

This was what I did. I made the impossible possible.

I repeated it like a prayer to keep from puking. From collapsing.

This is what I do.

"Where are the Guards?"

"Orion is with Mother, but the rest are off duty."

"And how many Wings are home?"

"All of them."

Of course.

I turned for the door.

"Freya—" Cali caught my sleeve.

"I'm going to Reyna."

"I'm coming with you."

"No, you're not."

"Don't act like you're the only one here who fucking loves him."

"I'm not risking you."

"That's not your call."

"Yes, it is." I faced her fully. "You'll be a liability."

"Then that's on me."

I opened my mouth to argue—but the look in her eyes stopped me cold.

"They put him in with Nix," she whispered.

Ice flooded my veins.

Nix.

They'd thrown Cyrus to a monster.

And they expected him to come out intact.

SIXTY-FOUR

RATTLE THE CAGE

CYRUS

Fear is a parasite in the soul. It feeds off your life-force, robbing you blind. There is no place for fear in the heart of a Wing.

"This is for being a traitorous little shit!"

Punch.

"Missed you too, you sadistic prick."

Each hit was calculated—enough to snap my head back, to crack skin, but not enough to knock me out. This one, though...this one left me gasping, tears streaking from eyes already swollen shut.

"I prefer my foreplay with fewer bruises, but whatever gets you off."

"Okay, funny man." Nix snarled, fisting a handful of my hair and yanking until my scalp screamed. He wrenched my head back and pressed the blade to my throat.

He wouldn't kill me.

He might make me wish for it, but not yet. Not until they got what they wanted.

And on that front? They could go fuck themselves.

They'd drugged me with reaper's venom, slicing me off from my magic, from the hierarchy. From Poe.

"You think this is funny now?"

"Kinda," I mumbled, careful not to twitch my jugular.

The last thing I registered was his elbow coming straight for my face.

FEAR IS *a parasite in the soul.*

Poison in the well of power.

No place for fear in the heart of a Wing.

Fuck her for teaching me that and leaving me down here with this asshole.

I'd lost track—of time, of the number of times my cousin strolled in like a goddamn *Bond* villain, of how many times he knocked me the fuck out.

Cali once said the venom lasted twelve hours unless re-dosed. Had it been that long? Longer? Were they dosing me while I was out?

This was a special kind of bullshit.

"You know," I coughed, every bone in my body aching. "I think I missed the part of interrogation training where you beat your subject senseless before asking questions."

"Shut the fuck up."

Nix drove his boot into my ribs, and while I might've pissed myself a little, he didn't need to know that.

Eyes squeezed shut, I grunted through the white-hot agony, dragging the pain into a vault and slamming the door. Inside the vault, it couldn't touch me.

Outside the vault—no pain.

No pain, no fear. No poison in the well.

"If you don't start talking—"

"Well, which is it?" I wheezed.

"What?"

"Shut the fuck up or start talking? I can't do both."

"Fuck you." He leaned closer. "Tell me the truth, Cyrus. Give them what they want, or I'll use your own blade to carve my name across your ribs."

He traced the tip of my raven-hilted dagger across what I was pretty sure was a sprawling black-and-yellow bruise.

"How poetic would that be?"

"Just make sure you spell it right," I rasped.

Then spat blood in his face and grinned, or tried to. My lips were too busted to know if I pulled it off.

Crack.

Gun butt to the face.

"COME ON, CYRUS," he growled later, my teeth chattering from cold. "You're being charged with regicidal conspiracy. This isn't a fucking joke."

"No, the joke is you pretending we're fucking family," I muttered. "You don't have a leg to stand on, you piece of shit."

He clicked his tongue, ever the theatrical little bastard.

Every cell in my body throbbed. Except for my neck and head—those were numb. Tingling.

No sleep.

Plenty of ice baths.

A fucking dream vacation.

"I gotta hand it to you, cousin. Didn't think you had it in you."

"You'll have to be more specific. I've had one too many nights with tequila."

Silence.

A beat.

Then his hand cupped the back of my skull. I braced. For the plunge. For the suffocating cold.

He whispered near my ear, "Usurping the crown, huh? Maybe you really do have the balls to rule."

I opened my mouth, but his fingers dug deep, and the basin swallowed my face. No point in thrashing. Not right away. Conserve energy. At least, I told myself that.

Told myself again when my lungs started screaming, when vision dimmed and ribs howled. When instinct took over and I thrashed anyway.

He let me up just before blackout. Threw me back into the chair. Shoulders screaming from the pull of my chained wrists, I gasped a lungful of air that burned on the way in. The cold sank into my bones and didn't leave.

"Refreshing," I rasped.

Didn't need to see him to know I'd pissed him off.

Here's the thing about Nix—he was good at getting under your skin because he was petty and insecure and thought cruelty was clever.

But I could be petty, too.

The fact that he didn't knock me out again? I was impressed.

"How were you gonna do it?" he asked. "Kill your Ma, I assume?"

"You've lost your fucking mind," I croaked.

"Always so stubborn." He paced. "Come on, Cyrus. You know the drill. I can do this all day. You? Not so much. Easy way or hard way?"

"Oh, I always go hard. Just ask your mom—oh wait. You can't. Tragic, really."

Oh, fuck—did I hit a sore spot?

A SLAP to the face yanked me awake a few naps later.

Holy fuck. I was dying. Or close enough to prefer it.

Fear is a parasite in the soul. Poison in the well of power. Fuck the well of power.

That last bit was mine. Added it to the family motto. This shit sucked.

"I've always been a man of my word, Cy," he muttered. Well, that was rich. "And I told you I'd break you, didn't I?"

"Just power napping, Nix." I coughed. "Don't get too excited."

Talking hurt.

Breathing hurt.

Existing hurt.

But I was still here.

Still alive.

And that meant the game wasn't over yet.

They were gonna kill me.

I became sure of it about two knockouts ago, when my head stopped spinning long enough for the nausea to settle in. A nonconsensual ride on the tilt-a-whirl from hell.

But the Queen wouldn't let it happen here—not in some lightless hole where no one could watch. No, her son's death would be a spectacle. A reminder that no one stood above the Accords.

Except, of course, her.

Would she even watch? The trial should've protected me. Should've come before the interrogation. Before the torture. Alas. Rules were for pawns. Not for royals.

She'd make a show of it. Public, symbolic. Tomorrow—today? Maybe during Cali's party. If anyone were gonna act, that would be the window. Unless they bought into the narrative. Then I was cooked.

So fucking be it.

I'd rather die with my honor intact than keep serving this nightmare.

Besides, if this week had proven anything, it was that Freya really was feral—and I kind of hoped she'd show them just how clever she could be. Freya. Fuck, what would this do to her?

"Hmm, thinking about that little thief of yours?"

His words slithered across my nerves, every syllable a blade.

"You know, if you put this much effort into therapy, we wouldn't be here right now."

"Ha. Ha. Ha." He drawled it like a sneer. "*I'm* not the one threatening the monarchy, so maybe worry about yourself."

"I am. I'm thinking about what I'll eat for lunch when they realize you've lost your goddamn mind and I mount your head on a pike at my front gate."

Footsteps thundered above us, dust raining down from the cracked stone ceiling.

God, I hated this place.

"You didn't like that," he drawled, amusement curling around the words. "Me mentioning your pet."

Freya wasn't a pet. Freya was the storm and the silence after. She was the laugh that broke a funeral, the last burst of strength in a losing battle. If revenge had a body, it was five-foot-eight and breathtaking in its savagery.

And whatever she was avenging? It had the Queen shaking.

Would she actually kill me? Or just make it convincing enough to bait Freya? This was for her. It had to be.

Kneeling slowly, like a predator scenting weakness, Nix said, "You know the guard will tear her apart before she even reaches the gates."

"I don't know what you're talking about."

"Freya Porter," he said, and it sounded like venom from his mouth. "They'll enjoy every minute of making her scream—for everything she's done, for corrupting our precious prince. I reckon your mother will savor every sound as payment for your loss."

"They'd have to catch her first."

"You know how the Wings play with their food. What do you think? You think they'll fuck her before they slit her throat?"

I ground my teeth so hard I nearly cracked a molar.

Tried not to react. Really tried.

But my body was already shaking from the cold. My fists ached to clench.

Dammit. I was better than this. Better than letting him see it.

He moved in closer, slow and predatory. "Is that what you're hanging onto, little cousin? That red-haired menace? Oh, you think she'll come for you."

"Not in the way I'd like," I breathed, dragging my eyes up to his. "But yeah. And when she does, she'll slit your throat and burn the body for good measure."

"She could try," he said with an edge of false calm. But the footsteps overhead were growing louder, the guards outside whispering in hurried voices.

A spark lit in my chest.

"She's the protégé of the Angel of Death and the Golden Commander," I said. "It's cute that you think you're not already fucked."

His hand settled on my shoulder.

Revulsion surged. I wanted his hands on me only slightly more than I wanted to masturbate with a meat grinder.

"Do you think"—he walked his fingers down my outstretched arm—"she'll be as mouthy as you are while I break her apart?"

His grip slid to my wrist, the other hand braced on my shoulder. Dread pooled in my gut as I read his intent.

"Or do you think she'll scream the moment I bust that pretty face?"

"Nix. Don't."

"How were you goin' to kill Queen Reagan?" he asked, his fingers tightening.

"I'm not gonna kill my own mother—Nix, *don't*—"

He planted a boot against my good ribs, ignoring the building tremors, the shouting above.

"I'll ask you one more time. How. Were you going. To kill the Queen?"

"Nix, I swear to God, I have no idea what you're talking about. If I did—"

Snap.

My scream tore through the chamber as he dislocated my shoulder.

White-hot agony seared through me, robbing my breath, my vision, everything but the sound of my own heartbeat pounding behind my eyes.

Breathe.

Breathe.

Shove it into the vault. Slam the door.

No pain, no fear.

No poison in the well.

Except this one wouldn't stay locked.

Every inhale was fire. Every twitch, blinding.

Whatever intel Nix had, he clearly didn't want me fit to lift a blade.

A loud clang split the air.

I forced my eyelids open. Fought the vertigo and focused on the creak of Nix's boots as he straightened and stalked toward the gate.

"What?" he barked.

I strained to hear past the ringing in my ears.

"All Wings have orders to respond," someone called.

I wanted to believe she was too smart to fall for it. That she wouldn't fling herself into something so obviously rigged.

But I knew better.

Freya was a living, breathing vendetta. I didn't need to understand her to know exactly what she was capable of.

If I hadn't been in so much pain, I might've laughed.

Rattle the cage, chérie.

FREYA

DISABLE.

Dismantle.

Those were the orders—whenever possible.

Within the hour, assuming I survived, these souls would be mine. And Aren would need every last one of us on the right side of the line.

All except those who'd laid hands on Cyrus.

Them, we would kill.

The sun was rising as we descended on Luminark Manor. Between two hierarchies of shadows, this would become a bloodbath fought between worlds—unless we forced them into the light.

I was waiting for phase two.

More power than I could contain thrummed in my veins, the remnants of four of Reagan's Guardians pulsing beneath my skin after I'd drained them and—let's call it what it was—tucked them away for leverage.

Their fate would depend on Cyrus'.

The fifth one got away.

A bridge I'd burn when I reached it.

But it wasn't the first phase of the siege I was watching now—not the blood, not Reyna and her pyro flyers spiraling through the sky in graceful arcs, hurling fireballs before vanishing again in smoke and soot.

Not even the familiars tearing through them above the spires of the manor I fully intended to raze.

It was Ally's hourglass.

I'd returned to beg Bellaton for backup and suit up. But when I entered my quarters to grab my weapons, the hairs on my neck rose.

I turned toward the bed...and saw it.

That little gold trinket.

Frozen.

The grains of sand unmoving.

Time—ceased.

The path—ended.

I even flicked the glass. Tilted it. Waited. Nothing.

She'd told me she'd need me when the last grain fell. Then she went radio fucking silent when *I* needed *her* most. And now her enchantment was dead. What the fuck did that mean?

Chest tight, I took a breath and focused. Arrow by arrow, firebomb by bomb, the ambush chipped away at Luminark's defenses, quadrant by quadrant. The wards failed, one after another.

I hated waiting.

The second wave was torture.

Not even a blade could kill me faster than standing still.

Somewhere in that gothic tomb, Cyrus was in agony. I couldn't feel him. But I knew. Deep in my chest, I knew.

And my vision was red.

Thumbing the hilts of my blades, I waited—for the signal. For the gifts

I'd stolen, now vibrating inside me, to serve their purpose. For the last piece to fall into place.

Detached.

My heartbeat was steady, trained by a few dozen lifetimes of Aren's battlefield discipline. I would die with honor, or I would rob Reagan of hers. There were no other endings.

My eyes landed on Gio—Cyrus's Wing-Lieutenant. His pick for Captain.

I have eyes on Lieutenant Caruso, I told the line. *What's the ETA on my extra insurance?*

Give us thirty seconds, Brody replied.

But Gio was headed toward Montague. And over my dead fucking body would G fight half-cocked to protect the mission and end up dead. We needed Cyrus's future captain. But we needed G more.

Make it fifteen.

Fucking hell, Porter. Jax's growl came through the bond.

Move, soap boy.

I pounded a gloved fist on the truck roof—twice. Alastair answered with a rev of the engine. I grinned as she roared to life. Me and my two treasonous companions knelt in the truck bed, casting shields as we carved a path through the chaos. The souls scattered as we tore across the property beneath the moss-curtained trees and onto the manicured lawn. My knees braced against the turns as Alastair cranked the wheel hard, drifting until the manor came into full view.

Perfect.

My companions leapt from the truck, casting twin shields around us. I stood tall, bellowing: "Reagan!"

Panting, I fixed my gaze on the front fucking door.

She wasn't on the field. Cowards never fight their own battles. But worse? Monarchs who let others bleed while they stayed hidden behind walls.

The skirmish stilled. Bellaton's soldiers held their shields but ceased advancing. Paladins stared in open horror at my little display, and sadistic satisfaction curled my lips.

Alastair shifted behind me, guarding my back.

I lifted my chin and bellowed again. *"Reagan!"*

My eyes locked on Gio. His furious gaze snapped between me and the truck. I knelt, reached down, and pulled out the first gas can—uncapping it without breaking eye contact. He glanced around for help that wasn't coming.

I pointed the spout at him like a blade.

"You know this is fucked, Gio. Cyrus believes in you. *Defended* you. Tell your people to stand down."

His dark eyes flicked behind me again.

His lip curled.

"This is war," he spat. "What you're doing is declaring war."

"What I'm doing," I said, hopping onto the truck's edge and hoisting the can, "is summoning your Queen for the final stint in my Crucible. Or am I not entitled to finish what *she* started?"

I poured. Gasoline soaked the pyre stacked in the truck bed. I raised the can, letting it flood every inch of my little gift.

"Tell them to stand down."

He did.

"Good boy."

Montague barred his path with a sword when he stepped forward.

The fumes burned in my nostrils as I pulled my mask over my mouth and nose. I breathed deep. Let the reek settle into my lungs. Let it fuel the fire that had been devouring me since I realized how far Reagan had gone.

"Wait!" Gio raised his hand. "Wait! She's coming."

I stepped into a tight circle, splashing more gasoline over the intricately stacked pyre in the back of my goddamn truck. Well, *August's*. He'd have to forgive me later.

The manor doors burst open and Reagan rushed onto the porch, wide-eyed, panting. Her gaze snapped to the pyre. Then to me.

Bingo.

A sick sort of satisfaction flared in my chest and I smiled beneath the mask. Summoning stolen flames into my palm, I lifted them high above my head. Even that was a risk, with the fumes as thick as they were.

"No!" she screamed, lunging forward as shadows rolled off her shoulders and across the grass.

They reached for mine. But froze when I extended my hand over the pyramid. She said nothing. So I tore the mask down and smirked. Tilted my wrist, letting the flames hover—drip.

"Please! *Wait!*"

I steadied my hand but shook my head. "You didn't extend me the same courtesy." She hadn't *waited* before torturing her own son. Just to get me here. "Your move, Reagan."

Chest heaving, she stepped into the sunlight. Her shadows vanished, hands hovering near her blades. She hadn't dulled since last time. If anything, she'd grown stronger. But her eyes—

Her eyes were wide as they landed on what I'd done.

Four of her six Guardians, chained to the pyre.

Unconscious. Stripped of armor. Stripped of shirts. Necks slumped at unnatural angles.Bodies limp from the drugs we'd pumped into them.

Her skin went pale and those sharp blue eyes found mine. "Name your terms."

Rattle the cage, chérie.

His voice sparked hope in my chest and I grinned, widened my stance, and tilted my head.

"Where is my fucking mate?"

SIXTY-FIVE

ILLUMINATION

CYRUS

Where is my fucking mate?

My heavy eyes flew wide. Gray stone walls. Nix's back.

Holy shit, Freya was in my head.

Chérie? That you?

Where are you?

Dungeons. Interrogation chamber. East wing. Nix is here.

Are you okay?

I've been better. I'll survive. You?

A bit preoccupied. Someone will come for you. Carr trusts him. I'm so sorry.

And then she was gone. As quickly as she'd appeared.

If my heart could've flung itself against the walls of my chest, it would have.

"You!" Nix snarled, spinning toward me with more fury than I'd managed to provoke during the endless hours of agony. "You think you're fucking clever?"

"For once in your life, Nix, try making some sense."

The Wing behind him opened the cell gate, dark blue eyes flicking toward mine. "Merikh," I pleaded, "you know me. You know this is bullshit. I live and breathe for our people."

"I'm taking you upstairs, Prince." Flat. Emotionless. The perfect soldier.

"Why?" I barked as he stepped toward the shackles, Nix pacing behind him like a caged tiger.

"Orders," he replied simply.

"Merikh, please. Gimme somethin'." Speaking was an unholy agony.

"Shut up!" Nix snapped, hands flexing at his sides.

"We've been summoned," Merikh muttered as he released my first wrist. My body shrieked in protest with even that minor shift in weight. The vault doors stood open. And now fear laced the very air. "I dunno what you got yourself into, Cy, but—"

"I said shut up!" Nix exploded, storming over and swinging. The Wing barely dodged his fist.

"Traitors get nothing, do you hear me?"

"I'm no traitor," I gritted, clenching my teeth as Merikh unlatched the second shackle. Nix shifted uneasily, his eyes flicking above us as if he could see through the ceiling. My dislocated shoulder lit my right side on fire; my left screamed with each movement, broken ribs grinding.

Merikh locked eyes with me—sympathy, or something close to it, briefly visible in the blue depths. "Can you walk, Prince?"

I swallowed my retort about carrying me and nodded. Because walking, even to the executioner's block, brought me closer to her.

Freya had let me in. She was close enough for us to connect mind-to-mind. But when I reached again, I found only ice—frosted and crystalline. *My own ice.* Guarding her mind.

Despite Nix shoving me forward, I managed the climb. My legs trembled, arms screaming as Merikh wordlessly looped his arm beneath my good one. When I winced, he grimaced—and subtle cooling magic crawled down my side.

You can't run, his voice slid into my mind.

I glanced at Nix. He hadn't heard.

I wasn't planning to. Not in this state.

That complicates things.

What are we walking into?

Your mate unleashed hell on our doorstep.

Sounds about right. Why am I being summoned?

She demands it.

The Queen doesn't take kindly to demands.

Evidently, she takes less kindly to four members of her Guard strapped to a pyre.

My head snapped toward him. Pain lanced down my spine, but I didn't care.

Holy shit.

Did Freya—?

No. A beat. *Not yet.*

Jesus Christ. I wasn't fond of the Guard—but they were mostly decent men. Elite fighters.

Ingenious. Barbaric. Ruthless. All because she thought I'd been hurt.

I was so fucking sunk.

She is addressing the council now, he added.

My pulse quickened. *Is she declaring her duel?*

She...

Focus. She what?

His swallow was audible. *I think she's accusing the Queen of violating the Accord of Blood.*

The world tilted. No. I'd suspected—voiced it to my father—but hearing it aloud made the ground feel unsteady. I'd known, on some gut-deep level, that my mother had a hand in Valora's brutal end. I told my father. And he, coward that he was, insisted I was wrong.

Temper surged like molten ore, filling the cracks of my broken ribs.

At the top of the stairs, the grand foyer opened around us. Raised voices echoed from outside. Nix stormed ahead, hurling open the front doors. I tried reaching the hierarchy. Nothing. My mother had cut me off.

But Merikh's mind still reached mine.

Is she invoking the duel?

She's invoking something more.

Like what?

Accusations of blood magic violations. Council corruption. Treason.

Treason. That word again. Tossed like gravel until someone choked on it.

Sunlight scorched my eyes as we stepped outside. I blinked against it— against the chaos. And there she was. My compass. My anchor. My goddamned salvation.

Lynx and Mars hung from the pyre in the bed of her truck—shirtless, bloodied, and limp. Calypso and Carr flanked her, masks discarded, shielding her back.

One of the Guardians was missing.

Intentional, no doubt.

A message.

Freya spotted me. Her eyes flared—pain, then fury. She dipped her chin, reining it in. Lethal.

"He was your *son*," she said to the Queen.

"He *is* my son," the Queen snapped, "and my *subject* to do with as I please."

"Rules for thee, not for me. It's always been your problem," Freya spat. "You bow to a queen who holds herself above our sacred laws."

"You say '*our*,' but you are no Paladin."

"By your hand," she bit back. "I was your second. I served with my whole soul. Lieutenant Caruso—" Her tone softened. "—your mother saved my life in Appalachia. I returned the favor in New Orleans. She was an honorable fighter. A better friend." Then to Orion: "*Come back with your shield—or on it.*"

Orion shifted. Uneasy. Loyal, yes—but never blindly so.

Where the fuck was my father?

I searched the crowd as Freya called them out, one by one. Named them. Reminded them. She wasn't some upstart challenger. She was *theirs.*

"Cyrus," she whispered, and raised a hand toward me. Carr and Calypso moved instantly. Noctis cut in ahead of them. My knees buckled, vision swimming. I leaned hard into Marikh's arm as his healing magic slowed the fire.

Freya's voice rang out again, this time not for me, but for everyone.

"This prince was imprisoned. Tortured. Silenced. Because the Queen feared him—the cleverness, the resilience, and the truths I returned to share."

"He is being charged with conspiracy!" the Queen snapped.

Freya let a flame slip through her fingers and the Queen *flinched.* She had her. She fucking had her.

"The Accords beg to differ," Freya said coldly. "Or is Paladin blood only sacred if it *kneels?* Was our law written for rulers with egos strong enough to withstand opposition—or the coward who stood unopposed after every stronger rival wound up *dead?*"

My breath caught as the crowd gasped, and the council reeled.

Had she just accused the Queen of *murdering her way to the throne?*

And worst of all—

I didn't doubt her.

I didn't have time to mull it over—Noctis confirmed my suspicion as she yanked off her mask and gently gripped my arm. Pain seared through me. I grunted, unable to stop it as agony devoured every nerve.

"And you," Freya snapped—emotion cracking through her voice for the first time—"you all let your prince be *brutalized* while you stood outside these walls like obedient dogs instead of guardians of the balance. What about *this* is *balanced?*" She threw an indignant hand toward me. "What does your oath even mean if your leaders can be broken beneath the roof you swore to protect, without the honor of a trial?"

A ripple tore through the Wings. As my vision cleared, I caught them shifting, exchanging uneasy glances. A few reached for weapons—but for Freya or the Queen, I couldn't tell. My stomach pitched as if I'd stepped too close to a ravine. Or maybe it was the fresh fire crawling through my bones.

"Move!" a familiar voice snapped, cutting through the chaos. *Jo.* She pushed past immobilized soldiers with practiced fury and reached me just as Carr and Cali arrived at my side. Without a word, Jo replaced

Noctis's hands with her own and gave me a look that made her intentions clear.

Brace.

Merikh stepped back just in time for her to snap my shoulder back into place. I bit down a scream, the world blackening as pain tore through me.

Carr and Cali caught me, positioning themselves on either side to drag me toward safety—but Freya's next words brought us up short.

"Thirty-six years ago, the Oracle declared me the most powerful female in Paladin," she said, her voice slicing through the courtyard. Mother growled. Actually *growled*.

Freya's lips curled into a saccharine smile. "I was silenced, of course— for the good of the realm. Because the Queen couldn't risk anyone knowing I would become Heiress when the magic rotated again. To preserve her bloodline, we came to an agreement. I was to marry her firstborn son. The contract secured the magicline—and placed me as the future Princess of our people."

Cali stiffened beside me, her gaze flicking between Freya and my mother. Her voice dropped to a whisper. "She's talking about you."

Me. Valora—Freya—was the woman I'd been promised to.

"What is she doing?" Cali asked, and I couldn't tell whether it was fear or fury.

"No clue," I rasped, while Jo's magic eased down my arm.

"Orion," Freya said sweetly, turning to the Guardian beside my mother, "what happened the year after that?"

His voice was steady. "You had your first Calling."

"I had my first Calling." Freya nodded, satisfaction lacing her tone. "Many knew I searched. Few knew for whom. Reagan did," she said lightly.

"Her Majesty," Nix barked. "You will address her as such."

Freya didn't even look at him. "*You* will enjoy your head while you have it." She said it like a fact. Then, "*I* will call a spade a spade—and a traitor a traitor."

"You bitch," Mother hissed, her hands twitching toward her blades.

Freya didn't flinch. "As your second, Ciaran and Reagan offered me every tool to find this wandering soul. They assisted me—again and again— never understanding he could not be found because of the power in his blood." *The shield.* The lightning wielder. "Only one person knew when I finally located my Soul Bound target." Her canines descended, that feral grin carving through her lips. "Only, when I arrived, his throat was slit ear to ear. His home was painted red."

"That proves nothing," Mother snapped.

Freya shrugged. "I would agree—except I recognized the wounds. Your blood was in the samples. And beneath the coffee table, I found a very distinctive emerald-encrusted raven blade. You weren't the only one to get in a few good hits."

A stunned silence followed. The weight of her claim—of a Calling slain—was incomprehensible. Even more damning than betrayal. Almost as grievous as destroying a mate bond.

"Did she say they were Soul Bound?" Carr muttered.

Worse. So much worse.

"I didn't want to believe it," Freya said softly. "You were my best *fucking* friend." Her voice cracked, eyes glassy with grief that lanced the Queen like a blade. "I wanted to believe it was a fluke. A setup. But your secrets are always your damnation. Just like hiding your illegal imprisonment of the prince opened the door for me to take your Bonds, so too did your past destroy you."

She turned to the crowd, sweeping over familiar faces—Orion, Gio, Carr, Nix, Cali.

"I am here to challenge Reagan Stuart for her place on the Paladin throne," she declared. "Because treasonous filth is unfit to rule."

"What?" The word ripped out of me.

Chaos erupted. Voices collided. Nix surged forward. Juno and Orion stepped between him and my mother. The Wings reacted—but I couldn't tell who they were protecting anymore.

This was madness.

This was *suicide*.

According to the Accords, any Winged soul could challenge a superior. But a challenge to the Queen herself? It had happened only twice before. Both times it ended in the petitioner's blood.

Where the hell was Dad?

Carr growled, "What is she doing?"

Anger raged beneath my skin, screaming as loud as the pain. This wasn't justice—it was a coup. And I was a fool. I'd believed her. Believed I mattered.

She was the threat to the Crown. The reason they believed I was a traitor.

"All *that* for a power grab?" Cali whispered, our minds reconnecting in shared horror. "She'll die for it."

Freya's eyes burned with conviction as the crowd surged forward. She didn't need to remind us of the stakes—we could feel it in our bones.

"Stop!" Mother barked. "*Hold!*"

"Funny," Cali muttered. "She'll fight for her lovers—but not for us."

"Before you all gallantly throw yourselves on my blades," Freya called, "know this: it was *Reagan* who slit my throat when I told her what I knew. Section Two, Code One of the Accords: No blood shall spill between brothers without trial, for betrayal bleeds the hierarchy dry. As if my blood wasn't enough—she slaughtered an *untrained* Calling. A soul that should have been protected under my Wing."

Gasps. Shifting feet. A chill surged through the gathered Wings.

"She murdered my Calling on orders from a soul you know as Lonan— but who is, in fact, the enemy of the realm. Adrastos Balaskas." Silence. "She didn't know I would reincarnate to remember *everything*. And what I didn't remember?" Her voice dropped. "The Angel of Death did. This isn't the first time she's sold us out. In my first life, she betrayed the realm, too."

Mother stood frozen. No denial. No rebuttal.

Freya cleared her throat. And somehow, it still wasn't over.

"She suppressed Cyrus's power to puppet him. But Adrastos made one mistake—he gave me a gift. Embedded a shred of his power in my soul as payment. I returned it to his ancestors."

To me alone, she thought, *Imagine his rage when I used his own magic to defy him.*

The Crown. He'd paid her with *his* power—and she buried it in the past.

"Reagan didn't just eliminate her rivals," she said, voice ringing out, "she bartered with a slaver to claim the throne. And a queen beholden to a tyrant—is no queen at all."

SIXTY-SIX

THE DUEL

CYRUS

With that final truth, Freya damned my mother and completed her first trial in one fell swoop, leaving the gathering in stunned silence.

The Crucible boxes had been chaotically checked—there was only one left.

And it would be the ultimate dishonor to shirk a challenge with so many witnesses after accusations of treason were hurled like blades. The Queen didn't even deny Freya's claims—didn't flinch at the words *lie, murder,* or *theft.*

She had no choice now.

She didn't spare us a glance before lifting her chin. "I accept. Now, *get away from my Guardians.*"

Freya's smile didn't falter as she extinguished her flames, and the crowd parted like water around stone. "Carrson, and Lieutenant Caruso, would you be so kind as to escort Juno, Nix, and Orion to the Brigg?"

I'll give your mate credit for style. She doesn't fucking play, Carr said into my mind as he stepped forward.

A shaky breath filled my lungs. The venom was wearing off. More and more of them were reaching me mentally.

Orion stepped into line without protest. The bond would force him to defend the Queen if he stayed—and evidently, he had no intention of testing his will against it. The other four Guardians were still mercifully unconscious, strapped to the pyre like corded offerings.

Nix's lip curled in disdain when Carr grabbed his elbow. He snarled but followed bitterly, a leashed wolf pacing toward a cage.

It was Gio who stepped forward to address the crowd. "Form the circle." They did. Everyone shifted to encompass the women at the center. "The rules are simple. One weapon. No magic. The Balance will choose the righteous victor."

"Dagger," they said in unison.

A serpent's smile curved Mother's lips. I couldn't tell if it was admiration, nostalgia, or something colder.

Reyna stood at the edge of the ring. A sharp jerk of her chin called Freya closer. They exchanged a few hushed words before Freya was passed to Jax and his brother. The three embraced quickly—shoulder clasps, whispered advice—and exchanged a Grayshell salute.

No one stepped up for the queen. The men who would were gone or incapacitated.

At the center of the ring, Freya lifted her chin and saluted. "May the light falter on your blade."

Mother sucked her teeth and turned without reciprocating the honor.

This whole thing might be fucked—but *what the fuck?*

Freya wouldn't look at me. Wouldn't lower the wall of ice between us. No words. No farewell.

And maybe I didn't deserve them.

My heart pounded behind an indifferent mask. Calypso's fingers found mine and squeezed. There would be no victor here.

If Mother won, I lost my mate. If Freya won, my family lost its honor.

Honor I'd spent my entire life trying to preserve.

There was no ceremony. No signal. The fight began slow, deliberate. Mother had nearly seven inches on Freya, but Freya was faster, more fluid—ducking, weaving, always just out of reach. She wasn't just fighting. She was baiting. Drawing her closer with each swing of the blade.

I saw it. The pattern. The manipulation. Freya had learned it from her. That was *Mother's* stance, her game. Judging by the sharp hiss from her lips, she saw it too.

Strike for strike, block for block, they moved as if rehearsed. Like a dance learned in secret.

It wasn't Freya in that ring—it was Valora. And still, with every blow, my ribs constricted. Not from the fractures Jo was rushing to heal, but from the sight of *them.*

The first time I watched my mother execute a traitor, I was ten. She hadn't flinched. Not once. It wasn't cruel. Just…clinical. She gave the order. The blade fell, blood hit the marble, and she stepped over it.

"Paladins cannot afford sentimentality," she told me afterward, like we were reviewing footwork. Had he deserved it? Had the man she killed really betrayed us—or had he just crossed *her?*

That same cold detachment now radiated from Calypso and me as we stood rooted, watching the inevitable unfold.

I glanced at her. Her chin was high. Her eyes locked. But it was that memory—the blood on the floor and my mother's unblinking stare—that made it impossible to breathe. Because it begged a question: *If it were me in that ring, would she be just as calculated?*

Would she bleed me dry to protect the throne?

And I already knew the answer.

She had.

She'd let Nix carve his fucking name into my skin. Let me rot in a pit beneath her goddamned floorboards. One word—*one*—and she could've stopped it.

But she threw me to him like a traitor. Like I was expendable. We all were.

Freya drew first blood with a sharp hook that barely missed the Queen's throat. My hands clenched. My chest did too. Calypso squeezed back.

One of my earliest memories was a storm, with thunder so loud it shook the windows, the rain pelting the roof like a drumline from hell.

I was maybe four, and ran, terrified, into her open arms. "Shhh, little prince," she whispered, tucking me into her lap. "It can't touch you. Just a storm, baby."

"Tell me a story?" I'd begged.

She sang instead. A lullaby that was sad and strange—only later did I learn it was about the Battle of Culloden. A massacre, wrapped in melody. Seemed fitting now.

Freya dove for Mother's throat, missed, and was kicked so hard she flew backward. She hit the ground hard, gasping, her eyes flying to mine—panic flashing like lightning in the dark.

I could feel Cali tremble beside me, fighting the same need to move, to do *something*. But what? We dishonored them both to intervene.

Freya challenged.

Mother accepted.

There was only one way this ended.

Carr stuttered to a stop next to me, his breaths coming hard, no doubt from sprinting through the manor to stand beside me for this special kind of hell.

"Pathetic," the Queen sneered, turning to see who Freya had looked to. *Me.* How ironic, considering Freya held her by the balls with her Guardians. Not even sure where *her mate* was.

"After this, you think they'll follow *you*?" Mother spat. "You think you can rule?"

"Me?" Freya scoffed, staggering to her feet. "No." She gestured toward me, her voice shaking with effort. "But *he* sure as fuck can."

"You challenge *me* only to present my son as an alternate?"

"He was chosen," Freya said, breathless. "Marked."

"He's male." She said it like a curse.

And then they were moving again. Every swing, every grunt of pain—it was mine. I would've taken the blade if I could've.

Mother charged. Freya blocked, struck out—but Mother caught her wrist and pulled her in.

And I felt it. Felt it as if I were the one stabbed.

Her steel rammed into Freya's side.

No.

No.

I couldn't move. Couldn't breathe as blood spilled.

For a moment, it was my own, like I'd transported back into the ring with Nix. I catalogued the haunting similarity in their strikes—the eerie pattern between our fights. Before I could wrap my head around it, time rushed in as Freya doubled back, gasping, lips parting around silent pain. My mother pushed her, kept advancing, a victorious gleam in her eyes.

I couldn't do this.

Couldn't watch *this.*

I'd just found her—just started to fight for her.

I couldn't fathom existing without the rumble of thunder or the crack of lightning across a purple summer sky any more than I could fathom breathing if she lost.

Couldn't live without her storm.

All the honor I'd fought for—gone.

The balance I'd protected? Irrelevant. My life's work burned to ash the moment I saw her bleed. I staggered forward but Calypso's hand snapped to my shoulder to anchor me in place. My fists clenched.

Move.

It wasn't a command. It was a prayer. Her eyes locked to mine. Wide. Blinking rapidly. She was still upright, still fighting. Somehow, she *moved.* Somehow, she fought back.

But I saw that dagger leave her side—the black fabric darkening with blood. Saw it stain the grass. And for the first time in my life, I prayed to a God I didn't believe in that she wasn't already gone.

It was impossible to breathe as she struggled to stay upright, struggled to back away or parry.

I fucking need you, Freya Porter. Now, fight.

It wasn't a word so much as a tug—one desperate pull on the line between us. Like she yanked the cord to say she heard me...but couldn't respond.

She blocked two blows and landed a strike to the queen's face, but her next attempt was caught. The queen yanked her arm up. Before she could disarm her, Freya dropped the blade, caught it with her free hand, and twisted—aiming for her throat.

Reagan had to release her to dodge the blow.

When they came face to face, Mother lunged, fisting Freya's hair and jerking her head up. But before she could strike, Freya grabbed her arm and dropped her weight, shoving a boot against her sternum and throwing her over her body.

Both women screamed a beat before colliding with the earth. Freya was quicker to her feet, but Mother wasn't injured—and now she was moving faster.

And Freya was still bleeding.

How long before shock set in?

I'd watched my mother fight my entire fucking life. What was her next strategy? Could Freya still survive?

Your heart, chérie. She's coming for your heart.

I didn't know if she heard me or just sensed the blow, but she lifted a gloved hand and caught the blade an inch from her chest.

Fuck. I couldn't do this. Couldn't watch. Couldn't look away. Couldn't *breathe.*

Whether it was Jo's handiwork or pure adrenaline, my own pain had faded—but it still felt like dying.

Leather creaked. Her glove split. Blood slipped from her grip, but she didn't let go, her whole body shaking as Mother forced the dagger down.

Face inches from my mate, Reagan taunted, "The only place a male has on the Paladin throne is as a *consort.*"

Freya trembled. The blade slid forward. A fractured moan tore through her lips as she growled, voice a snarl of pain and steel, "As *my mate...*Cyrus will be *mine.*"

In one swift movement, she yanked the dagger forward, dropped her shoulder back, and slammed her blade up between the queen's ribs.

FREYA

Well fought, Val.

Reagan's last thought—and I could *hear* it. Tears burned my eyes. No healer could fix that wound—clean through the fifth intercostal space, just to the left of the sternum. *Just like Ally.*

I hadn't realized how many of my favorite combinations came from Reagan until she was the one on the other side of my blade.

But she wasn't the only master who trained me. And I'd watched the best warrior on the planet use that same strike to fell a bigger threat.

Reagan's blade thudded into the grass. Her hands clung to my arms as her knees buckled. We collapsed together. Something shifted in her eyes—just before they closed.

It almost...*almost* looked apologetic.

I bowed my head, chest heaving. Magic crashed into me like a tidal wave.

I killed Reagan Stuart.

Five minutes, and Paladin was—theoretically—mine. *His.*

Each breath came with a pained grunt, but I forced my eyes up. The crowd was silent. Stunned. Brody and Jax nodded their approval as I staggered upright. A blaze of pain lit my arm on fire. My jaw dropped with the breath it stole—only for the pain to vanish as quickly as it came.

The mark had taken.

The Paladin crest would be burned into my skin beneath the leathers.

Still panting, I turned in a slow circle, meeting every gaze but theirs. I couldn't stomach it. Not here. Not yet. Not with all their eyes on me.

"Anyone else?" I asked, breathless. Not sure I could survive another fight. No one moved. Not a single soul. I nodded, turned, and picked up Reagan's blade, wiping it on my leathers.

Calypso. I made a beeline for her, but Carr and Cyrus stepped in front of her.

My jaw tightened. As if they thought I'd hurt her?

I met Carr's hard sapphires—anything to avoid looking at Cyrus—and kneeled, bowing my head as I extended the blade toward Calypso.

Now or never. Respect, yes. But also condemnation. I hadn't *lied* to them outright. Just...omitted things. It got Cyrus out. That was all that mattered. Boots shifted in my periphery as I sucked in another breath, praying I hadn't just executed their mother for nothing.

Calypso gingerly took the blade in both hands. My breath hitched and, tentatively, I lifted my gaze.

Tears glistened in her eyes, her mouth twisting into a grief-stricken grimace. I hated that. Hated that my justice hurt her.

Hated that after all that, the bitch forced my hand when she took my mate.

She nodded slowly. Then turned the blade toward herself, offering me the hilt. "Long live the Queen," she whispered.

The bridge of my nose stung. I blinked the weakness back.

"Long live the Queen," Carr echoed, louder this time, for the crowd.

I rose. Nodded my thanks to Calypso.

And one by one, they all echoed the cry. Kneeling. All except Carr, Cyrus, and Jo.

Carr steadied me as I swayed. Jo appeared on my other side and pressed her hand to my wound.

Her healing worked expeditiously, my breath evening a few heartbeats later.

Keep it, I told Calypso when I found her in the corner of my mind.

You won. It's your right. Cold. Calculated. But honest.

I never intended to take anything more from you, Cali. That's why I waited for the Equinox.

I looked at Cyrus—at those familiar citrine eyes—and swallowed the ache. I wanted to touch him. To fall into him. But I couldn't. Not yet. Instead, I turned to the people.

"Long live the King."

The chorus echoed behind me.

Smiling faintly, I added, "Thank you for honoring my victory. Jax, please see our prisoners delivered to their companions."

He dipped his chin and leapt for the truck.

"This may be unconventional, but then again...that might be my middle name. I am Freya Lynn Porter, the reincarnated soul of your second, Valora Lamb. As Queen by trial, I open a window—for you to leave, if you must. I will not force loyalty. I will rule as my Commander—" I cleared my throat, relief easing the ache as I found Brody and Jax stirred in my mind. Thank fuck. I still had Grayshell. "—my *former* Commander does. Your loyalty will not be bound by command but rather by example. I will fight in the battles we wage, not above them. Paladin was never meant to be a weapon for anything but the balance," I continued. "And to the balance we will return." Some nods. Most were silent.

"The window is open. Go, if you must. May you find another hierarchy to suit you. Because I *am* calling you to war. Cyrus and Calypso are noble souls. I trust them with your lives. But I'm putting out a call to arms—to any who would stand as a shield between humanity and a rising darkness."

They were listening. Holding their breath.

"The Seer of the North says there are three threads where we win. In all three, we fight beside Bellaton and Grayshell. Our enemy thinks they're untouchable. But I'm asking you to do what Paladins do best." My voice hardened. "Rattle the goddamn cage."

A few stood—some angry. Some afraid. I nodded to each as they turned to leave.

The rest stayed.

"*Please* rise," I whispered. I knew Queens weren't meant to beg. But I wasn't a queen. I was a fighter with too much blood on her hands. "Leadership, meet me in the throne room. Wings, return to your stations. Lieutenant Caruso—congratulations on your promotion. You're now Captain. Queen Gwyne, I'll see you in the war room for negotiations."

The crowd stirred—buzzing with new orders.

Three sets of wary eyes found mine. I could only look at one. When I reached for Cyrus's mind, I found exactly what I expected: betrayal, anger, relief. Protection.

"You three, come with me."

"Is that an order or a request, *Your Majesty?*" Carr asked. It hit like a punch.

"*Please,* Carr."

His eyes softened just slightly, and he nodded. We moved for the stairs as I asked Brody to see to Reagan's body.

Only one place felt appropriate: Cyrus's room. The Queen's quarters would be cruel. The meeting rooms were filling. This—this was for them.

No one spoke until Cyrus pushed open the door and found his father shackled to the floor.

"Dad!" he barked. He and Calypso rushed forward.

Carr's eyes snapped to me. Not with accusation—but understanding. "When did you figure it out?"

"I suspected for a while," I whispered. "But the nail in the coffin was turning over his only living son to be brutalized. The Ciaran I knew would *never*. Not even for his mate."

I turned back. Calypso was crying. Cyrus had his face in his hands. Ciaran sobbed on the floor.

"I'll get a healer...*Maleficent,*" Carr muttered, voice wry.

I smiled faintly. Bit back my own emotion. This wasn't the place for it. Not to grieve Reagan. Not to weep in relief. This wasn't for me. It was for them. I told myself that again and again, as Ciaran confessed everything. The Blood Bond. The leash. The love his children had never received. The mistakes that had nearly cost them everything.

And I told myself it would be worth it.

Even if they hated me for it.

SIXTY-SEVEN

THE ROOK

FREYA

"One unified region?"

"That's correct," I confirmed.

Reyna's smile grew as we finished essentially dissolving the treaty between Paladin and Bellaton. We weren't merging the two back into one united hierarchy—or even bridging the mental gap like Westerlund and Grayshell—but there would be no more divide.

No border at the river. Our souls could move freely, clear to the Atlantic. No more feud. No more hoarded resources. No more divided missions. One allied region of shadows. Cyrus and Blaz had set the framework. I'd just pitched it—and with Reagan's body chilling, and Ally's dire warnings still echoing in my ears, Reyna was amicable.

I'd stopped only long enough for Jo to patch me up before she returned her attention to Cyrus in his chambers.

"Congratulations, Freya. You play a good game." The queen stood and reached across the table to shake my hand like we'd just closed a business deal.

Congratulations on your hostile takeover of my estranged sister's king-dom. The day just kept getting more surreal.

I'd stepped out to give the Stuarts a moment—just the three of them. Horrible or not, Reagan had been the pillar of their world for decades—or in her mate's case, centuries. Love didn't have to be healthy to consume you.

"Your Majesty, we need to know what you'd like us to do with Nix and Juno Landry."

I turned to find Gio, standing nearby, hands clasped behind his back.

Nodding, I said, "Gio, if you'd like to avoid me throwing up in my mouth, it's Freya. Just...Freya."

"I don't understand."

"No *my queen*. No *Your Majesty*. I am a warrior, not some gown-wearing, crown-toting tyrant. Call me Freya."

"You just earned every soul's respect. I'd wager you'll have a harder time gettin' them not to honor you than you think."

Reyna sidled up next to me, smirking at my discomfort. "What about Commander? Seems fitting, don'tcha think, Captain?"

Aren's bright smile and wisdom-saturated winter blues flashed in my mind.

I might've had hundreds of cumulative years under my belt, but wearing a title equivalent to his? Ugh. It made my skin itch.

"That could work, if you're more amicable to ranks, Your M—"

"If you must call me something uppity, that would be preferred, yes."

"Yes, Commander. I'll wait for your word on the prisoners, *Commander*."

Gio's lips tipped up at one side, and I couldn't help but think he was quite handsome when he smiled.

We'll talk about that *later.* It was the first thing Cyrus said to me through our connection since the duel. The first acknowledgment of our Bond since I'd taken them upstairs well over an hour ago. My chest loosened incrementally.

The halls were buzzing, and if my ego wasn't getting the best of me...it was predominantly excitement.

The kind that rides a wave of change. The electricity in the air before a battle.

Everywhere I walked, chins dipped—and at least half of them met my gaze. A few were reasonably wary, others, more inquisitive. It was a start.

As Reyna and I reached the front door, her breath hitched and she whirled on me. "Oh my gracious, I nearly forgot." She whipped her bag off her shoulder and around her chest. "Your clothes are in the guest suite you selected, Miss Porter."

Thank God one psycho still talked to me like I was beneath her.

"But this looked...important, and I know it's likely just a trinket, but I felt like I ought to bring it to you in case it's sentimental or..."

Her words drifted out of my consciousness as my eyes fell to the gold hourglass in her palm. My stomach bottomed out.

The top was nearly empty—the last handful of grains in a mad dash for the exit. I snatched it from her, holding it up just in time to watch the final spiral of sand whirl around the funnel and fall to the bottom.

"No," I breathed.

A beat later, a deafening *boom* cleaved the air——and all our windows shattered.

CYRUS

DAD'S VISION didn't strike until it was too goddamn late. We'd barely made it into the hallway when the world exploded. I threw my body over Cali's—only for Carr and Dad to do the same, shielding us both.

Every single stained-glass window shattered, colorful shards raining down as the walls trembled.

The moment the impact shuttered to a stop, I was up and moving, flitting through the shadows to get to Freya.

So much for talking later.

Fuck.

I found her in the foyer, encased in a cocoon of shadow Reyna had conjured. Our eyes locked for one tight beat—then we peeled away to assess the threat. I broke left. Reyna went right.

Fire.

The yard where Freya had won her brutal victory was engulfed in flames.

"What the fuck is it?" I barked, glancing sidelong at a horrified Reyna.

The look on her face said everything she didn't.

"Where's Blaz?"

"At the estate."

"Go!"

With that barked order, she vanished—and I stepped in beside Freya to replace the shield myself.

We were fucked.

The world was going to hell in a handbasket. My mate had just slaughtered my fucking mother for her throne. And I had a sinking suspicion we'd be colliding with the masked man very soon.

I shoved through the shadows—and the chaos roared back to life. Freya's eyes snapped to me, blinking, no doubt trying to figure out how Reyna had just been replaced by her seven-foot, male, extremely pissed-off mate. Gio sprinted toward us, brown eyes flicking from Freya to me like he wasn't sure who to report to.

Luckily, my mate saved him the trouble. "How many falconries are on site?" she demanded.

"Three."

"And the fourth?"

"New Uptown. On their way."

"You're with us," Freya said—like she'd been issuing orders her entire life.

Maybe she had been.

Honestly, I wasn't even sure what her actual role had been in Grayshell. If I'd learned anything in the last hour, it was that I didn't know shit about the woman who'd stolen my fucking heart.

Without hesitation, she rushed into the yard with the rest of the Wings. Gio and I stayed tight on her tail as we bolted down the steps—out into a courtyard ringed in fire. She elbowed me in the waist. I turned to find towers of smoke spiraling from the direction of the city.

And as my ears strained, I could hear them: sirens. Screams. Mortals.

Not now. Not yet. We were supposed to have more time.

But if the three crowned, cloaked motherfuckers emerging through the smoke were any indication, the clock had just run out. The abundance of snarling crawlers behind them only reinforced it.

Freya popped her neck as Gio and I unleashed our ice to smother the blaze.

Wings snapped into formation—three falconries, three perfect defensive walls, merging into a single front.

Like the Spartans: the crime wasn't dropping your shield for yourself. It was dropping it for the person beside you.

But just as we advanced, the energy shifted. The blaze dwindled.

And then—three figures materialized between us and the crowned demons.

Lana. Alvara. Alec.

They looked like they'd seen a ghost.

"Oh, shit—*shields!*" Freya bellowed.

Every single one of us hit our knees, shields up, just as she tossed hers into the air and cast it wide over the manor. Alec appeared beside her, winked, and did the same—his barrier actually visible to the eye.

Incredible.

I turned back toward the now-fleeing horde just as Alvara raised her arms, throwing up a wall of fire.

FREYA

WITH THE WINGS back at their posts, doing their best to repair the wreckage from the demon assault, Alvara stormed straight through the smoldering yard toward Cyrus and me.

"*Now!* Move your asses!" she barked, thrusting a hand toward me.

I pulled my gloves on and crossed the short distance, heart still thudding. "Nice to see you too," I muttered.

She rolled her eyes. "No time. Let's fucking go."

I felt Cyrus's hand land on my shoulder just as Ally's fingers wrapped around mine.

Cali, you're in command.

That was all the time I had before Alvara yanked us through a tear in the world and slammed us down into the middle of pure chaos.

Screams. Sirens. Alarms—buildings, cars, and emergency vehicles all wailing at once. Humans flooding the streets, running from—

"What the fuck in the armageddon black-hole bullshit is that?!" I barked, already lashing ribbons of power out toward the Renown wreaking havoc across the city. Their energy hit me like spoiled milk—rancid, putrid, and foul. But still...it was the fastest way to take them down.

"Good! Yes! I need a jump!" Ally shouted.

"What?" I snapped, glancing to my right—

Cyrus was standing in mute horror, staring at what could only be described as a portal to hell. Fiery red, ringed in a violet-blue halo, with demons pouring from its mouth like floodwater.

"Holy shit," he breathed.

"Go!" Ally shouted again.

The snarl Cyrus turned on her could've curdled blood. "Absolutely fucking not."

"I have her!" Ally insisted. "Now's not the time, Stuart," she snapped. "Hold them off while I get this fucking thing closed."

"I go where she goes."

"Closed?" I echoed, ignoring the argument as I focused on the swirling mouth of the thing. "Ally, how the hell do you intend to close a red hole in the center of the city?"

"Quickly. And just like sewing," she said grimly. "But it takes more power than even August and I have and—"

"That's where I come in," I finished, exhaling hard as I stared down the nightmare. I'd never siphoned a demon before—didn't know if it'd feel more like pulling on Renown, or like what happened in the field with the horseman. "Human jumper cable. Goody."

"Only one way to find out."

"Jesus Christ," I muttered—but I followed her into the chaos, Cyrus flashing through the shadows beside us like a storm on the wind.

It shouldn't have turned me on.

But with a literal gate to hell in front of us, I no longer cared that I was a psychopath because Cyrus kicking demon ass was sinfully sexy.

When we reached what I could only guess was range, Ally stopped, throwing her arms wide. Her power unfurled like ropes of fate, winding through the air and anchoring to the portal's edges. I stared, stunned, as she wrapped her magic around the tear in reality and pulled, like she was lassoing a damn bull.

The portal shrank, inch by inch—

But she had to yell my name before I snapped out of it.

I stepped in close and placed my palm to her spine, casting my own power outward, reaching for the filth and rage and darkness bleeding from the Renown.

I pulled, and she absorbed it.

The more I fed her, the faster the portal shrank. The harder I yanked on the magic polluting the city, the faster the Renown dropped—skin pale, energy leeched from their bones like I'd siphoned blood instead of power.

All the while, Ally screamed her defiance and ripped the portal closed.

"Holy. Shit," Cyrus said—summing up all of our thoughts as the last ember vanished.

But Ally turned to me, death blazing in her eyes. "Bellamy Blackwell is Adrastos. He's infiltrated the coven. He's Blood Bound to Magnolia Green —who just fought off a goddamn dragon. I need you. *Both* of you. You've got ten minutes or less to get your shit together and get to Aren's...or the entire planet is fucked."

"What about Blythe?" I called.

But she was already gone.

Cyrus and I just stood there.

Staring.

And staring.

"...No pressure," I muttered.

Cyrus let out a low, humorless laugh, grabbed my hand, and together, we jumped.

ALVARA

"BABY, *LET GO.*"

My eyes burned as my boots hit the grass—Aren's voice already slicing through the chaos.

Fuck. My. Life.

Everything we'd built—everything August and I had scraped together over months of effort, every stronghold Aren had fortified with centuries of strategy and restraint—was about to be tested.

And God help me, I wasn't sure we'd survive it.

Too many pieces on the board. Too many moving parts I could no longer guarantee were in place. And I'd been too blind, too slow to see what the threads had been trying to show me. Too slow to stop the kindling before it caught. Now, that fire was licking up the path toward a blast I couldn't pull us back from.

They'd never shown me this moment.

Defective magic eight ball.

Motherfucker.

I was juggling threads for Aren, August, Fae, Alec. The Thornquists. The Westerlunds. The Stuarts. Reyna. Nat.

And somehow, in trying to hold them all—I'd failed to see the one that mattered most.

Now the threads were short-firing like manic strobes. Too many, too quickly, with no way to decipher them in time.

But I knew what was about to come out of her mouth, and I winced preemptively.

"Let go," Magnolia growled, trying—and failing—to yank free. "Bell!" she screamed, voice cracked and raw, her bloodshot eyes frantic as she hurled her hands toward him, willing something—anything—to work. "Stay with me, godsdamnit. Bell!"

Aren wrapped his arms under hers and hauled her back—dragging her away from where Adrastos bled out on the pavement. The instant her boots hit the ground, she spun on him.

"I will never forgive you for this," she hissed. "You *coward!*"

Aren's eyes shuttered in agony. His mind reeled—body wracked with pain I could feel even from a distance.

I didn't understand. I hadn't seen this. How the hell hadn't I seen *this?*

Of all things for the threads to withhold...something so crucial, so central? Unheard of.

No matter how tightly I tried to grip the strands, they refused to form sense. Not even when Ansel raised his Glock, training it on the prostrate body at Magnolia's feet. Her cry broke the paralysis in my limbs.

I yanked on the threads, but they gave me nothing. There was no outcome where Adrastos didn't stand. He was meant to bring us a great treasure. But what the fuck was it?

"Ansel, don't!" Magnolia's voice tore apart as she lunged forward. "Please, *gods*, don't—"

Ansel's eyes cut to mine. They were bright with demand—his hands twitching in the air, fingers flicking a silent question.

Do I fire?

A sharp ache bloomed in my chest. Her pain? Mine? It didn't matter.

I gave the smallest shake of my head. It wasn't enough, his eyes steeling in quiet resolution.

When in doubt, eliminate the risk. God, he and Aren had taught me that. But this time was different.

We can't kill him. Not here. Not now. You have to trust me.

Magnolia's wail ripped up her throat, pure grief coating every syllable.

"Don't you *dare!*"

"Magnolia!"

Aren's voice cracked through the chaos, and she froze—her beautiful face folding in confusion as she finally took in Aren's expression. His terror. His grief. His conviction.

"*That's not Bellamy,*" he said, voice trembling with devastated fury. "That's *Adrastos.*"

"*What?*" she breathed. "No...impossible. Aren, I—"

Her mind fractured like glass on stone—each piece reflecting a memory that couldn't quite hold. Her body swayed, shaking, failing to stay upright.

"Ar," I said, crossing the space, my throat tight as I looked between her and Adrastos.

He met my gaze, wide-eyed and pleading.

I jerked my chin toward her, warning him mind-to-mind. *She's lost too much blood. She's going down.*

Magnolia's fogged gaze found him one last time as she whispered, "Save him..."

And then her eyes rolled back, knees buckling.

PART 3
THE ENDGAME

SIXTY-EIGHT

MONSTER

AREN

A blur. The world had reduced to a blur of chaos and color. Someone had sliced apart and peeled away the blood-soaked clothes clinging to Magnolia's skin.

Hers.

His.

A black, viscous liquid that could only be demon ichor.

My eyes burned, hands shaking as I clung to her limp, pale fingers—curling them around mine, clutching them like a lifeline. Unable to breathe. Unable to move. Unable to *think*.

My mate had been sleeping with my enemy.

Loved him—clearly.

Bonded...to *him*.

Her *Guardian*.

Unblinking, I watched four sets of fast-moving hands cleanse her wounds with dishtowels—the same ones she'd used beneath that unholy dinner. Was that last night?

Blood. So much blood.

Mags. *My Mags.* Torn apart. At least, judging by Saraya's wince as she turned her onto her side, more blood spilling—fresh and red and reeking of iron.

The room spun. I leaned back just as Freya came into view, her pained jade eyes flicking to mine as some distant part of my brain recognized she was speaking to me.

I couldn't hear the words over the roar in my ears. All I could do was beg—silently, desperately—that God take me instead.

"Big guy, I need you to move," Freya said gently. "Ally called for Nat and the girls, but they're not answering. We need her. Sar can't do this—certainly not both of them."

"Both?" I echoed distantly. The word sounded foreign in my own mouth, and I blinked at the Wraith. "No."

No? No, I wouldn't move? No, I wouldn't leave her? No, we couldn't save *both*?

But why? Why would we even try? Whatever Mags had said—whatever she'd begged—didn't absolve our enemy of his crimes.

Someone said my name. Or maybe it was the sharp crack of Lana's palm against my cheek that finally snapped my mind from the fog suffocating me.

"Aren!" she barked. I blinked at her, then back down at Magnolia's battered face.

"*Get Nathara,*" she said.

"I don't understand," came Saraya's soft voice. Stray locks of auburn framed her face as she frowned. "There's a *barrier*, Aren. It's not just *her* lifeline—it's like she's tethered…"

My fingers absentmindedly traced the length of her arm, stopping at the brand woven between her tattoos. My thumb stroked over the rune for life, nestled between two others.

"Baby, what did you do?" I whispered.

"She's *Bound* to *him*?" Lana's serpentine hiss cut through the static. I nodded, and Saraya's eyes widened. She glanced over her shoulder, toward the doorway. Toward the bastard now writhing on the sidewalk.

"Bound how?" she demanded. "It's like a shadow. It's sentient. Fighting me."

"I…I don't know. She only told me about it last night. Just before she ran." To keep me from chasing her.

God, I *should've* chased her.

Giving her space had been the wrong choice.

"There wasn't time," I added uselessly.

"It's alive. Like a serpent in her veins," Saraya said.

Ally, I called mentally, *I need a read on Mags. What was entailed in that bond of theirs?*

Her response came back like a shriek: *Aren, she said no. She didn't consent!*

Even now, in crisis, her conscience wouldn't allow her to violate that law she'd created for herself. Even my mental voice turned sharp. *Alvara. I need you to read my mate. Can we save her alone?*

Give me a second. Everything's shattered. I'm trying—God, I'm trying.

That didn't reassure me. I pulled out my phone, dialing Nat. No answer. I tried Blythe. Then Rika.

An argument exploded outside.

"He can get fucked," Alec barked.

Kenna's voice finally answered, hoarse and breathless. "Commander? *What*-in-the-*Jumanji*-is-fucking-happening?"

"Ken, I need every healer you've got at my townhouse. Now."

"We're a little preoccupied—"

"*It's Mags*," I snapped. "My healer doesn't know how—"

But she was already shouting away from the phone, "Mom! Rika! Kari!"

Before I could hang up, boots were pouring over the threshold. My coven spilled into the townhouse, trailed by several bloody, detirmined Hazelharborians, all sprinting. Kenna made straight for Adrastos—Ansel was levitating him in, lip curled in disgust.

"Bell!" she cried.

Nat, Rika, and Kari rushed to Mags, draped over my countertop. My breath caught, and I had to close my eyes against the tide of fury and regret.

"Don't touch him," I growled. "That's *Adrastos*."

Every eye in the room snapped to mine. Every move I'd made in the past few weeks had been wrong.

A vaguely familiar southern drawl cut through the haze, talking about reaper's bullets and making sure the shells were out. Flushing the wound of the venom. Something about it taking five minutes or less to cause irreparable damage.

Nat's eyes flicked to mine and she shook her head—Mags was fine in that regard.

But my focus was still on the bastard as he moaned. The one they were tending to. The one whose blood ran through my mate.

It was brilliant, *really*. Target your enemy's unknowing mate—a healer. Someone not even on a bounty hunting list. Bond to her. Hide behind her power. I had to give him credit. I could be ruthless, but I wasn't a monster. I didn't see this coming and Alvara hadn't, either.

Her jaw was tight as she caught my eye across the room. One grim shake of her head told me everything.

Bound.

Mags had tethered herself to him. Willingly sacrificed her freedom to keep this man alive. And now his death drained her. The web of lies this man must have spun...

There are no threads where he does not live and they both do, she whispered. *We need him to win. Now or months from now, his death solidifies theirs.*

Theirs?

The word hit like a blade in my chest. Visions sparked behind Alvara's eyes, but I turned to Nat, who was already focused on Magnolia.

"Where's Blythe?" I spoke softly. Even still, Nat's eyes were frantic as she shook her head.

"We can't find her," Nat said. "She's not answering. I think she went into the mall chaos and can't reach us. Aren, I can't lose another—"

"She's alive," I reassured when her voice cracked with fear. "Ally sees her. She's in the endgame with us."

Nat gave a shaky nod and returned to work. My gaze drifted to Adrastos' seizing body—to grotesque, black-webbed wounds as they began to glow blue—then back to Mags. I laid my hands on her and pushed my energy into her body.

Come on, baby. Take it. Take everything I have.

Her power stirred—barely. Like a creature waking from a deep, unnatural slumber. It reached for mine, sluggish but alive. I might not be a healer, but I could seal the superficial wounds so Nat could focus on what mattered. Slowly, I shifted from one slice to the next, healing whatever my fingers could find.

But I wasn't a Porter. She couldn't draw directly from my well. And I had never felt more helpless.

"Freya," I rasped.

She appeared beside me in a blink. "Oh! *Yes!* Hang on—this is gonna feel weird."

She placed one hand on my back, the other on Mags.

The moment the connection formed, I felt it. Power pouring through me, through Freya, into Magnolia's innumerable injuries. She'd broken her body. Her gifts—fragmented, scattered—reached greedily for mine.

Christ, she'd *shattered* bones.

I was no healer but even I could sense that much. So much blood loss. "Come on, baby," I whispered, lowering to my knees. I brushed her hair from her swollen face. "I love you so fucking much. Do you hear me? You have to get through this, my Autumn Magnolia. I'm right here. Right here, and I love you. *I love you, goddammit.*"

That sentiment alone should have been enough. Should have somehow magically anchored her here. Given her eyes the strength to open. But mates cleaved apart weren't new to the world. Even I could acknowledge that I wouldn't be enough, should her soul be called elsewhere.

Tears rolled down my cheeks. I couldn't stop them.

August stepped beside me. "Can I help?"

"Please," I croaked.

He laid his hands over her. If anyone could give us a miracle, he was the one made for it.

I brushed bloody tendrils of dark hair away from her bruised cheek, working to heal the wounds I *could*. "I loved you before you ever breathed in this world," I whispered. "Loved the woman you would become before I knew you existed. And all of that pales in comparison to what I feel now. I am yours, Magnolia Green. Unequivocally. Irrevocably. *Stay with me*."

I kissed her bloodied lips, resting my forehead against hers.

She was mine. Always.

A faint *clink, clink, clink* sounded beside Nat. Glass against metal. My teeth ground. Heart pounding. I didn't want to know what they were pulling from her.

"Stay with me," I murmured. Kari cursed softly.

"This Blood Bond is fucking *sentient*," she noted, earning nods around the table. My stomach turned. One healer was bad enough, but for them all to note it...

"Contain it?" Nat offered.

"But *how*?" Rika asked.

Kenna's eyes darted between Magnolia and Adrastos, through a wall of my people fighting to keep him breathing. Sar snapped orders as she dropped a glowing slug onto my damn coffee table.

"Speak," I said, latching onto Kenna like a buoy at sea.

She looked up, hesitant. "I think the bond is mimicking their gifts. Maybe it would respond to that connection."

I snapped my gaze to Ally. "Do we have a Shadowwalker?"

Before she could answer, a rough southern baritone cut in.

"I'm sorry to see you again under these circumstances."

I turned—and froze. The Seer of the South's lookalike, save for blond hair. Cyrus. Freya's mate.

Cyrus' hands were already wreathed in shadow as he knelt beside me, haunted hazel eyes already rimmed in red. He extended his hands, funneled his element through Freya, and Magnolia gasped like a drowning woman breaking the surface.

I exhaled shakily.

"Grateful you're in one piece, Prince," I muttered.

"Likewise."

MAGNOLIA

I WOKE to the coppery tang of blood and antiseptic. Tried to move—whimpered as pain lit every inch of my body. What in the world...

A breath caught sharp in my throat as memory tumbled back through the fog. A concussion. That's what this feeling in my skull was. Like my brain was cotton-wrapped and cracked at once.

Peeling open my eyes, I blinked into the harsh glare of a table lamp, wincing at the sting. The room was all shadow, except for that one blinding spot.

Warm hands held mine.

I looked down to find Aren, slumped over the bed, cradling my hand like it was the only thing keeping him grounded. Aren. The magic had taken me to Aren...

Oh, gods, *Bellamy*.

The bed groaned as I lurched upright—a cry tearing from my throat as pain arched like fire down my spine. Aren straightened at once, blinking groggily.

"*Oh thank God.* Take it slow, baby." His voice—low, rough, warm—settled over me like a weighted blanket. Safe. I was safe.

That word jolted through me, and I remembered that was all I could think of when I was trying to get out of that hell. And the magic had taken me *here*.

My body relaxed instinctively, soothed just by his presence. His voice a balm I didn't deserve. "Take it easy," he said again, softer now. "You're lucky to be alive—even with your sisters."

I turned my head and winced as pain rippled through my bones. I saw that same pain reflected in Aren's eyes.

"I'm sorry," he added. "We'll get you healed up as soon as we can. It took all five of them just to keep...*him* breathing. Reaper's bullets tore him apart. They don't think his magic will return for a while. But...they didn't have much to offer you. And your magic is still tapped out. Apparently, mine can keep you breathing, but Freya doesn't know how to convert it into something it's not."

He wasn't looking at me. Head bowed, hands digging into his temples, elbows braced on his knees. "Magnolia...we kept him alive because Ally says we need him. But we've been hunting that man for *months*. And, uh..." He shifted, one hand squeezing the back of his neck. "He's bound to Alvara's will. Magic Bond from when he lost the battle in January. Die *or serve*—that was the deal. He fled before she could enforce it."

The image of Bellamy bleeding on my doorstep slammed into me. The wound—precise. Between the fourth and fifth ribs, left of the sternum, miraculously angled *away* from his heart instead of toward it. A *millimeter* difference and he'd have been dead.

And *Alvara?* Alvara didn't *miss.*

Not ever.

That timing wasn't a coincidence.

I curled my fingers into the blanket on my lap—Aren's blanket, the one he'd kept so pristine for me. I hated the sight of him curled in on himself. But worse was how quickly he pulled his hand from mine. The way he tugged on his hair. The way his face twisted with words he wasn't saying.

I'd broken him.

And still, here he was—waiting. Sitting vigil beside me even as his heart ached.

"I'm sorry," he murmured. "I know you *thought* you knew him. You obviously loved him. I should've seen it." He dragged both hands over his face, as though trying to scrub the truth away.

"Aren, *no.* It's not like that—"

"You went back to him, Mags. You left me on that sidewalk and ran *to him.*"

Gods, it would've been easier if he'd shouted. If he'd *raged.* But his voice was calm. Disciplined. Like he'd decided he couldn't fault me for it.

"He's a part of you," he said.

"He was in my house with his cousins," I protested. "I didn't seek him out. You have to believe me."

"But you love him."

It wasn't a question, but I answered anyway. "I love Bell, yes. He's saved me more times than I can count, in more ways than I can articulate. But I'm not *in love* with him. Not like I love you."

"Please *don't.*"

The crack in his voice had tears stinging my eyes.

"I just need you to understand. He's alive because the threads show that his life gives *you* and Blythe yours. If that changes...I won't interfere if Ally decides to execute him. That's her call. He's her prisoner."

My head snapped up. Aren lifted his bloodshot winter blues to meet mine. Cold. *Commander*-level detached. *My* Aren was gone. This was the man the battlefield worshipped. Controlled. Calculated.

"He isn't who he told you he was," Aren said. "And I know you don't want to hear that—*especially* not from me—but Alvara will explain. He's not a good man. And if I were you, I'd want this to be about us. I'd *want* it to be personal. But it's not. It's about what the Balaskas have taken from us. The war they're about to wage on the world. And I need you to believe that."

"This isn't right," I whispered. My throat burned. "He can't be—he's not—he *is* a good man. He *saved* me, Aren. In more ways than one. He—"

"Was trying to *acquire* you ." His voice cut through me like ice. "Fuck, I didn't want to be the one to break your heart, baby. But he was using you. This *is war,* Mags. And it was brilliant. Ruthless. But brilliant. I probably should've sent Ansel to say all this—but I couldn't leave you. Couldn't breathe without being near you."

He exhaled, yanking his hands through his hair.

"You are an *asset* to him, Magnolia. A key in the prophecy he gave Alvara about stopping the horsemen. When he couldn't get Ally and August on his side, he came for you. You were his backup plan." Aren shook his head. "But Ally can't tell whether it's you or Blythe who matters more. And he couldn't either. That's why he stayed. To figure out who would win the King's favor."

As much as I wanted to deny it, I saw the sincerity in Aren's eyes. The pain of it.

Was it all a lie? Every moment with Bell—had he planned it? Was it really a coincidence he was waiting in that alley...?

No. He wouldn't have let me be violated. Not like that. *I knew him.* He'd killed men for less.

But...was that all he was, then? A killer?

I thought I knew him...

"I'm so sorry, baby," Aren said softly.

"I didn't know," I whispered, lungs crushed under the horrible weight of it. "*I swear,* I didn't know. I thought—"

"Shh, I know. I know, Mags. If it were up to me, I'd kill him just for hurting you."

He reached toward me—then stopped. Arms folded tightly across his chest, holding himself together.

"Aren," I whispered, pain slicing through me, fracturing my voice. I couldn't stop the memories—every kiss, every laugh, every stupid, joyful moment. I'd broken everything. "*Please.*"

"Can I touch you?" he asked quietly. The fact that he felt he had to ask shattered something inside me. I nodded, tears pouring down my cheeks.

He slid onto the bed beside me like I was made of glass. Gently—always so fucking *gently*—he cupped my face in his broad, careful hands. His thumbs brushed over my cheekbones, and I broke.

I'd broken him.

Monster.

Only a monster could leave a man like Aren so fractured.

He wrapped his arms around me and pulled me to his chest. "I thought

I lost you," he whispered. "I thought I lost you last night. And then you showed up—dying—and I just..."

He smoothed the hair from my face as I wept into his shoulder.

I didn't deserve his kindness.

Didn't deserve *him*.

But gods help me, I didn't know how to let go either.

I'd slept with Aren's enemy. Bound myself to him to save his fucking life—when the whole time he was out there hurting people, *killing* people. Oh gods.

My skin started to crawl, and I wanted to sob for an entirely different reason.

It didn't compute. The man I knew—the nomad with the hard-earned smile, who liked HGTV and argued with Blythe over counter selections and paint samples. The man who saved me from monsters more times than I could count. It didn't make sense.

"I'm so sorry," I whispered, trying and failing to hold back the hysterics. My lips trembled as tears burned. "For everything, Aren. Gods, you deserve so much better."

"Shhh, Mags," he said softly, those beautiful pale blues softening as he shook his head.

There he was. *My* Aren. The man who chased me in the pouring rain. The one who earned my laughter, who wrapped my entire hierarchy around his strong, beautiful fingers. Who loved so deeply he flayed himself open for me—even as I ran.

"Don't," he breathed. "Don't do that to yourself, baby. We make our choices, and then we figure out how to live with them. We do not torture ourselves over decisions already minted."

"I should've done things differently."

"I believe we have that in common."

"What? Aren, you loved me so loudly, and I didn't see—" The mate bond. Gods, I felt so foolish. My gaze fell to his chest, guilt gnawing at my belly. "I didn't see *it*."

"I didn't *say* it," he replied with a shrug, though it couldn't hide the agony in his eyes. "Not directly. And I'll be honest—subtlety's never been my strong suit. I was afraid I'd scare you off. I should've told you."

"You did, though. In all the ways that matter, you did. I just..." I swallowed hard. "That kind of love didn't exist in my world. I never thought it would, not *for me*. I never thought...someone like you..."

"If it means anything...me either. God, baby, I should've chased you."

"I would've kept running," I said with a weak smile, shaking my head. "Bell—*he* tried to send me back. Called me a fool. Told me to go home. Begged me to believe you and stop challenging fate."

With every word, Aren's expression darkened, the pinch in his brow deepening. But he listened. Gods, he listened. That alone was more than I deserved.

"I should've followed."

"*I* should've stayed. Should've come back. That moment has replayed in my head a dozen times, and I hate myself more with every—"

"Please," he cut in, shaking his head. "Please don't say that. You are my *everything*, Mags. It took two of us to make this mess. Learn. Learn what you need. Learn what *you* want. Learn from your mistakes as well as your victories. But don't waste another moment berating yourself."

I nodded, throat tight, and nuzzled into his palm, breathing in his scent. "I'm so sorry I walked away. I panicked, Aren. I *panicked*, and I broke us."

"Broke us?" he repeated, brows raising. "Mags, you cannot break what God meant for you to have. Period. What is intended for you cannot be stolen. Your choices may have delayed the us *I* wanted, but I made mine with a clear mind and a convicted soul—and I stand by it."

He gently tucked chaotic strands of hair behind my ear, those glorious hands trailing down my neck, across my collarbones, and to my shoulders. As if he needed to feel I was still whole. Still here.

"You are *worth waiting for*, Magnolia Green. My love for you isn't so feeble it withers in a storm. *It weathers it.* Always. Whether we find our way home in this life—or I have to wait for my next—I'll still be yours, Mags. The moment *you* want that."

My voice wobbled as much as my lip. "How can you mean that?"

"I've had a long time to think. And I will never cower from the price required to earn you. Not ever."

I raised my hands to his, threading our fingers together as we steadied our breaths.

"What happens now?" I asked softly.

"Now that you're safe? I do what I do best—I go to war. And you help people. As many as you can."

I nodded, heart aching as he gave my fingers a reassuring squeeze.

"No matter how this first wave ends, I need you to do something for me."

"Anything," I whispered.

"Worst case—something happens to me—"

"*Don't,*" I sobbed, my voice cracking.

"I need you to look after my people until I circle back. Get them to your sisters, make them come here. Help them. They'll need a talented healer for a while." He exhaled. "Best case, I still have to forge through the Middle and return Grayshell to full power. Ally says we can't win if I fail. Even then...they'll need you, little dove."

I nodded again, already thinking of the lives I'd tried to protect, even if it meant shattering *us*.

He freed a hand to hook his finger under my chin. "Promise me."

"I promise," I breathed.

"Thank you." He leaned forward and pressed a slow, chaste kiss to my forehead before rising.

"Where are you going?" I blurted, panic rising fast.

"To see what Ally's gleaned from Adrastos."

That dazzling, arrogant smile flashed through my mind, and my ribs clenched.

That's not Bellamy.

I feared that would be my mantra—until the betrayal fully set in.

"Be my good girl," Aren murmured as he walked away, "and get some rest. We're going to need you before you're ready."

SIXTY-NINE

FAMILY QUARREL

ALVARA

I'd seen this interaction play out two hundred ways—each as miserable as the last.

Stabilizing the two of them had been the easy part compared to convincing August and Ansel to let me go in alone. Their seething presence just outside the door had the hair on my neck rising. But he wouldn't talk to them. Not the way he'd talk to me. To *Elizabeth.*

This life or not, the clever bastard we'd nursed back from the brink had once been my twin brother. Best friend. Confidant. The first boy to teach me swordplay, knowing full well he'd be punished if we were caught.

But that was centuries ago—for me, many lifetimes sat between that raven-haired boy and the man my magic showed me waking now.

Dread spooled itself tight in my gut as I pushed through the door, exhaling slowly when I laid eyes on Adrastos, chained to a bed with enchanted metal. He raised his gaze, and a lazy, half-mooned smirk spread across his face.

"Well played, Princess," he rasped. "Well played."

"Still not a game."

"Still not over."

"What are you doing, Adrastos? Or are you *Bellamy* now? Lonan? Paris?" I stepped closer, voice low. "How many aliases can one man have before he forgets where he started?"

His smirk tilted sideways across his face. I could see what Magnolia saw —the clean planes of his jaw, the dark eyes, bronzed skin. He'd benefitted from his time here in California with the witches. Right up until now.

Gone were the fine clothes and tailored suits. Adrastos now wore tattered denim, the shredded remnants of a bloody shirt twisted into a makeshift tourniquet. The rest lay balled in a corner.

"So. If you've run this scene as many times as I have, then you know it only ends one of two ways."

"*Three.*"

Adrastos sucked in a breath. "Ah. So you're passing another Hail Mary."

"They've worked in the past."

"Not against Moros."

"No," I conceded. "Not against Moros. But I've beaten two of his brothers. So I'd say my odds are pretty decent."

"Don't underestimate him, Alvara."

"Him? Not *us*? Not *the cause*?"

"Not this time."

I narrowed my eyes, trying to untangle the threads of his logic. "You're off-script, Balaskas."

"Since we're being honest," he drawled, "I loathe that name."

"It's your name."

"It's *his* name. And I was shown long ago how little it meant. I've no interest in claiming it."

He leaned back, new scars slicing through the ink across his chest and abdomen. I studied him carefully, resisting the pull of my foresight, trying to piece together this puzzle with nothing but the present.

"Except when it came to the book," I said.

A lupine grin stretched across his face. "I was wondering how long you'd resist that particular lure."

"Will it get them home?"

"Not *us*?"

"Not this time. You know that as well as I do."

"Resigned to losing, Princess?"

I smirked, sliding my dagger from its sheath and wiping the blade across my jeans. "Far from it. And you know that, too."

"Arrogant."

"Calculated."

Adrastos cleared his throat, casually crossing an ankle over his knee with a nonchalance that mocked the chains binding him to the bed.

"You don't walk away from this," he said flatly.

It was true. There were still no paths where I walked away, and August remained free. It was one or both of us. And I'd already made up my mind which it would be.

"But Aren might," I clarified. "And August *will*."

"So you sacrifice their queen?"

"So he can take yours."

"Jesus."

"We'll see where His will puts us."

Adrastos smirked again, sighing as he let his head fall back to the wall, eyes on the ceiling. My mind circled back to the one piece of the vision I still hadn't solved.

"Cut the shit. Tell me about the binding."

His glare was sharp. "I can't. Or are you too dense to see that much?"

"I have to guess?"

"It would appear that way."

"You helped Magnolia get the book."

"Interesting theory." He moved as if to run a hand through his hair, the chain clanking as it caught at his wrist. He glanced back at me with an exasperated glare. Like I was an annoyance, and nothing more. "Any other notions bouncing around in that head of yours, *sister?*"

"You're Blood Bound to Moros."

"Until my *dying breath.*"

I smirked, watching his sardonic smile and lazy eyes drift toward the window. "So, I can set you free in death."

"What a mercy."

"Would it be?" I tilted my head, curious whether he was sincere or if it was just another facetious play. "It's easy enough to arrange."

"Should Mor—" He faltered, almost gagging on the name. Tongued a molar. Growled through his breath. "You can only claim your life debt under certain..." He cleared his throat, the words seeming to burn their way out. "...*circumstances.*"

Pleading eyes found mine under a furrowed brow, his jaw snapping shut. The anger wasn't aimed at me. Like static between broken images, Adrastos tried to open his mind to me—and my stomach twisted.

He could only show pieces. And even that was a struggle, his jaw looking liable to snap.

Twins with silver hair we'd encountered briefly in New York.

A much younger Agamemnon on his knees with a blade to his throat.

Adrastos roaring in agony as a silver-tipped whip cleaved through his flesh.

The air slid between my lips with a husky hiss. He was...a slave. Not Commander. At least not entirely. Or maybe that was the trick—shaping how I'd interpreted every interaction up to this point.

"If Moros is here," I said slowly, "his Bond to you outweighs mine. And Magnolia's. She shackled hers with magic. But yours—yours is dependent on proximity and orders. Spoken command."

Adrastos lifted his chin, mouth twitching. "Always knew I liked you."

Fuck.

That smirk was subtle, but it gutted me. This wasn't the swaggering king I'd faced in battle, nor the reckless vigilante Magnolia had romanticized. He wasn't even the defiant bastard I'd nearly executed months ago. My mind flashed to the image of his pleading eyes...and to August plunging the blade into Agamemnon's chest.

"You sold yourself to save Agamemnon."

"His..." Adrastos cleared his throat again, wincing. "Moros became heir to all that power after one of Agamemnon's temper tantrums. But his loyalty was always to his father."

His father. Not *our* father. Not *my* father.

So many questions. And so little time to ask them. Had Agamemnon killed the King? Was that how Moros took the throne? And if so...why? The dreams had never hinted at civil unrest—only the cruelty of a vile ruler who claimed to love his children.

"So you bartered your soul—and your obedience—to spare Agamemnon from the consequences of his actions?" I folded my arms. "Seems to be a pattern between the two of you."

"I did what I had to do," he said, jaw tight. "Wouldn't you? For any of your coven?"

I didn't answer. I wasn't about to follow that road.

"The humans are in full-scale meltdown," I continued. "There's no denying what they saw—hundreds of eyewitnesses. Security footage. Demons. Magic. Bloodshed. The Renown. Magnolia vanishing on camera with you in her arms."

His lips quirked in that knowing, infuriating way. "And so it begins."

"Your plan is flawed. It's been a mess from the gate."

"We can't stop them from coming," he said. "We can't beat them without all the players on the board. So we join them. Lead them until the humans bow. They're broken, Alvara. Stop trying to redeem them."

"They're broken, yes. But they deserve their freedom. You and Moros are monsters—"

"If you think I'm a monster, Princess, then you certainly don't remember Koa."

"I think the healer you fucked out of her future in the room upstairs would argue otherwise."

When I mentioned Magnolia, Adrastos *flinched*—his mouth parted, gaze dropping.

"I knew you were ruthless," I said coolly, "but I didn't know you'd stoop low enough to sleep with a mark."

"Shut. Your mouth."

Defensive.

I inclined my head, stifling a victorious smile. "Well, isn't *this* ironic?" I watched him through narrowed eyes. How could I make him snap? Was she really the key in all of this? I smirked. "You turned your ward into your personal whore, but balk when someone whispers her name."

His jaw flexed and I braced my elbows on my knees, leaning forward conspiratorially.

"Did Magnolia cry out for you the way she cries for him? For *Aren?* They're not exactly quiet. Did she beg for you? Say your name like a prayer? Did she scream when you—"

"*Enough,*" he snarled.

All pretense of humor had been exchanged for rage. His knuckles went white where his fists clenched against the restraints.

A twisted, cruel satisfaction knotted in my gut.

So it had been real. He may have set out to use her—but somewhere along the way, Magnolia had started to mean something to the monster in front of me. And now I needed to know how much...and why.

"She climbs into his lap during our evening nightcaps," I said sweetly. "It's the cutest damn—"

"I said *enough.*"

I smiled. "Stop showing your hand, Adrastos. It's weak. You don't get to bark orders—not after sending the entire plan into chaos at your own request. You burn every alliance before you even give yourself a chance."

His jaw tightened. "I didn't *intend* to hurt her."

"Like you didn't intend to hurt *me?*" I let out a harsh laugh. "Forced allegiance isn't loyalty. You should know that better than anyone."

"My intention—unlike our brothers'—was never to *force* either of you to bend." His voice lowered. "I *told her* not to come. I told her to stay with your lot."

"You kidnapped August's family. Our friends. You made us spill blood to get them back."

"Agamemnon—"

"You outranked him. You could have sent us home whole."

"You speak quite boldly of situations you don't understand."

"Am I wrong?"

"Ag and I were partners. Equals in all but one respect."

"You were placed between him and Moros in the binding."

"That placement alone set me above him."

I watched him carefully. "And still, you failed to use it. You lost. And then you fled here...and *broke* the one thing you've cared about in centuries."

Adrastos surged forward so violently his chains crashed, halting him just as suddenly, the bed's metal feet screeching across the floor. Chest heaving, he loomed over me—his shoulders bowed against the restraints, face inches from mine.

Good.

Either I'd struck a chord...or he was playing me like a fucking fiddle.

I glared up at him, refusing to flinch.

"Face it, Adrastos. You could never have kept her. Magnolia might be broken—in no small part thanks to you—but she's resilient, and courageous, and good at her core. She'll never kneel before a tyrant."

His nostrils flared, eyes blazing. The bed groaned again as he strained against the chains.

Then came the roar. "He's coming to *claim* her!" Adrastos bellowed. "He'll fucking *destroy her*, don't you understand?!"

Finally.

"Moros will never stop. You and your band of bloodthirsty misfits tore the country apart trying to find *the one who held my leash*. Now you know. So do it. Kill me. Spill my life here, stain the floor red. You have the right. But Moros Balaskas will not stop. He will take every piece of the prophecy. Every bond. Every heir. Every drop of blood."

His voice broke. And then...silence. His lips pressed shut, trembling with fury.

"I was going to keep her safe," he whispered. "No matter what. *I...*" He didn't finish. Looked like he couldn't even if he wanted to.

"You care for her."

Adrastos nodded once, jaw locked. His Adam's apple bobbed.

"She's sure become a hell of a problem," I muttered, letting Aren's pain saturate every word.

"You'll protect her," he said, eyes pleading now. "You're too good not to."

"So sure of that?"

Black pupils devoured his irises, swallowing what little humanity remained—then stilled. "You'd never allow harm to come to Aren's mate."

"She just rejected him." My voice cut like a blade. "I don't think you'll like what's left of his heart. Or his sense of mercy."

Come on. Break, motherfucker.

"You would never..." His words trailed off, eyes going glassy a heartbeat before the vision slammed into me.

A neighborhood swallowed in serpent-like flames, the buildings crackling as fire dances through them like living things. Adrastos standing between Magnolia and the white-haired demon king—the one who'd haunted my dreams for months—his hand outstretched protectively in front of Aren. A silver-haired woman siphoning the life from the earth itself, turning everything to ash.

In the next heartbeat, I lunged, fumbling with the key to release the enchantment on his chains. "You so much as split a hair on anyone in my family's head, and we'll put you down. Consequences be damned. Do you understand?"

"We're out of time," he rasped, voice laced with fear. "I tried, El. I did everything I could. I thought...maybe if I could show you the truth, we could change things together."

I jammed the key into the first lock.

"*Keep me* from Moros. You have to protect Magnolia."

"Of course we'll guard her. But it won't fucking be for you."

"You've gotten better with your poker face."

"Product of shit circumstances."

"I'm sorry."

"No, you're not." I flicked my gaze up as the first chain released. "I am who you made me. I'll *be* whatever you sculpt again. Neither of us can pretend we didn't see this coming."

"I don't *want* this." He glared at the next shackle, arching a brow. "Is this really necessary?"

"Is that rhetorical? Because short of killing you now—and dooming us all, for reasons I'm still not entirely clear on—there's not much either of us can do to change this."

I turned back to the second manacle.

"Kill me."

The key slipped from my fingers, landing silently in the carpet. My head snapped up to meet his smoldering stare...just before it turned distant. Pain crossed his face like a storm.

"What?"

"It's the only way to keep them from using me. Do it now. If I could've done it myself, I would have. Believe me. *I've tried.* The witchlings were stronger than I anticipated."

The *Bond.* It must have blocked him. My memory flared with the image of his horrified expression on that rain-soaked field—genuine, unguarded.

"You don't believe that," I said. "I remember. I remember the fear in your eyes."

"I was thinking about *them.*" The word came out as a growl. "Didn't know if you'd get to them in time. I *can't* lie to him—but I can spin truths. Half-truths. Without my orders, my cousins would've been reassigned. Rest assured, it wasn't fear for my own skin."

I stared at him—at the embers of secrets burning in his eyes—and felt dread coil in my stomach.

"I've never seen us win with you dead now," I murmured. "Not since *the field*. Why is that, Adrastos? Don't you believe the tales you've spun?"

"I do."

"Then why?"

"The cause may be just," he said, "but that doesn't guarantee the means are justified."

He looked at me—unblinking. "And with all due respect, we're out of fucking time. Did the little historian bring his sister's serum?"

I nodded and shoved the key into the final lock. Would the Reaper's serum suppress a command from Moros? The Paladins had never tested it against a Blood Bond. I reached into the tether, pressing my thumb into the mark we once shared on my forearm and pushed.

"August will get you to Aren. Show him everything. You harm *no one* who fights for Aren, for August, for me, or our allies. You so much as threaten a member of my family, I will skin you alive. Understand?"

"I love that you're not speaking in euphemisms anymore."

The door groaned open to reveal the hall beyond. August and Ansel stood opposite, arms crossed, death written in the angles of their scowls as they stared past me.

Not yet.

They dipped their heads in silent agreement and I bolted toward the stairwell.

As I rounded the corner, I caught a glimpse of Adrastos behind me— chained wrists extended toward August.

MAGNOLIA

"Wake up!"

It was Alvara's voice that dragged me from the nightmares. "Get up, please—now," she pleaded, frantic, throwing something at my feet. "We have to go."

"Shit," I breathed, blinking into a deluge of sunlight pouring through the windows. She'd tossed a pile of clothes at the foot of the bed and was already tearing through the closet, yanking out a pair of combat boots and dropping them beside the jeans and T-shirt.

"What's going on?"

"Your little side piece in there is going to get us all killed. That's what. We're going to be attacked—now. Shut up and move."

That saccharine, bell-like voice, wrapping around words that were anything but sweet, *should* have pissed me off. It didn't. Not as Alvara snatched a sweatshirt and started shoving clothes into a backpack with blinding speed. She pulled stacks of cash from a shoebox, stuffed them inside socks, then buried them in the bag—making sure I saw where they went. Then she was beside the bed, stripping bloodied bandages off with quick, brutal efficiency, checking my wounds with the practiced swiftness of someone who'd done this a hundred times before.

Only then did I realize the pain was gone.

Had she healed me herself? Had August? Were more of my sisters here?

I didn't have time to ask, because the woman in question was already yanking a shirt over my head like I was a petulant toddler. The shock finally broke, and I started moving as she lunged for the hoodie.

"Fuck."

"Yeah." She zipped the bag, then tore the bloodstained pants off my legs and motioned for me to hurry. "Listen to me very, *very* carefully."

I nodded weakly, shoving my feet into fresh leathers, then the boots.

"There is not a single escape route that doesn't cost me a member of my family today." Her throat bobbed, and for a second, her eyes cracked—just enough for the fear to show before it shuttered again. "Every path is a colossal shit show, and it's *his* fault. Or—mine, for not anticipating him. For not seeing what he was doing to you."

She blew out a breath and yanked my hair back into a knot. "You will do exactly as I say—and *survive this*. I will do everything in my power to make sure it's not you who dies. Do you understand?"

"No," I admitted, breathless, as I scrambled to my feet and she looped the backpack over my shoulders.

Then I heard it. The furniture shifting. The familiar voices of my Grayshell family barking orders.

"Why?" I begged. "Just let it be me. If this is our fault, let it be me."

"Oh, fuck off." Her voice stayed infuriatingly light, though her words gutted me. "You have a part to play—you're essential. Not all of us are. And more than that, I will not lose my best friend of all lifetimes. Goddammit, I will see him happy with you. In this life or the next."

The words hollowed the air, turning my insides icy. Ally seemed to realize she'd said too much. She clapped the backpack and shoved me toward the hall. We moved shoulder to shoulder toward the stairs, her hand wrapped tight around the loop of my bag like she meant to steer me out herself.

"But in order to do that," she said softly, "you and Aren must survive. Okay?"

She looked at me—really looked—and those piercing green eyes pinned me to the spot. I nodded, throat tight, dread choking every thought since I'd walked away from him.

I knew I'd pissed off fate, but retribution had never come this fast.

We started down the stairs, Ally's grip anchored to me like she was afraid I'd vanish.

"If I fight him, I fall prey to his commands. I don't have the strength to break it and survive." That voice—Bellamy's voice—hit like a grenade. English. The motherfucker was *English.* His true voice was a rich, rumbling bass, and it made my skin crawl. Had the accent been an illusion too? Had our entire friendship been one elaborate performance? Seven sisters, the man had softened his godsdamned *voice.*

Had he lied while buried inside me?

My stomach turned. He'd saved me. Or made me think he had.

Tears welled up, but I blinked them away. "What's happening? Who's attacking?"

"Moros Balaskas is coming to claim his ward."

"Moros?" My shock-riddled brain barely kept up. "His *what?"*

"Moros of Bellpost. Adrastos is Blood Bound to him—a slave, of sorts."

"So he's...*not* the enemy?" My heart thudded. "What does that mean for my Bond?"

"Oh, he's still a villain. He believes in the cause. He just would've been more *diplomatic* about it than his siblings."

The pieces clicked. Ally saw it too—her jaw tensed as I asked:

"The war?"

She nodded once, eyes solemn. "The Horsemen are already here. And they serve him."

Every inch of skin prickled. It had begun. The apocalypse. The war. Bellamy—*Adrastos*—was serving the ones bringing hell to earth.

At the base of the stairs, we joined Aren, August, and *him*—the betrayer. All three looked at me with variations of sympathy I didn't want.

"Witchling, I—"

"Save it." I couldn't bring myself to look at him.

Freya and her Paladin prince burst through the front entrance.

"Aren!" she barked, rage sharpening the edges of his name. *"Tessa.* She found Blythe. They have her. The Renown took her from the mall—T saw it on the security footage."

The world tilted and swayed, my heart stuttering.

"Blythe?" I gasped. *"My* Blythe?"

"We'll get her back," Adrastos and Ally said together. It made my stomach twist.

The monsters who slaughtered Sorin, Zehra, Jaycee and Aideen...had *Blythe.* My sister.

No.

August caught Ally's eye, scowling.

"He needs a prize," Adrastos said, voice grave. Alvara was already nodding.

"Fuck off," August growled.

I couldn't make sense of it. How could they argue like this while my world was collapsing? How could they *know* she'd come back?

I'd seen what the monsters did to witches.

I gagged, and Ally pressed a hand to my back.

Then Aren dropped in front of me, cupping my face. "Breathe, Mags. We will not leave her. We'll set up an op."

"How?"

"Give us today. We'll assemble a team. I swear to you, she will not be forgotten."

My shadows coiled around me like panicked whispers. A warning I didn't understand.

"*Fuck*," Adrastos and Alvara said in unison, the word more growl than breath.

Adrastos lunged, slamming into *Aren* hard enough to knock him flat. At the same time, Alvara tackled me, shielding my smaller frame beneath hers.

Both seers shouted—

"Shields!"

And then we hit the ground.

BOOM.

SEVENTY

MAYHEM

MAGNOLIA

The world exploded. The townhouse burst into fragments, fire slamming against the bubble Alvara had cast around us.

Trapped.

I was trapped in a body I couldn't move, pinned to the floor.

Sirens. Flashing lights. The reek of charred wood and melting plastic. I stood in our front yard, the chill of the earth creeping into my bare feet. My pajama dress clung to my legs, my arms hanging limp at my sides as I stared at the inferno devouring our home.

Nathara running past the firemen, tears already glistening on her cheeks when she hit her knees in front of me.

Alvara's growl yanked me back into my body. Back into a different fire. A different home.

The seer braced herself on her forearms, shielding me with her body. Her eyes—wide and glossy—were fixed not on the flames but on something beyond them. *Sight.*

Shadows curled protectively around us, my element responding not to me, but to her. Guarding my protector, even as fire consumed the world.

Everything beyond Alvara's face and whipping hair vanished behind the wall of orange and falling debris. No sound reached me but the screaming silence in my ears and the echo of my pulse. A temporary threshold shift, I knew, but that knowledge didn't make it less surreal.

Her face twisted—effort or a snarl, I couldn't tell—as she pushed herself upright and hurled her arms wide, magic erupting from her like a crashing wave. I tried to move, to rise and help, but her hand dropped to my chest, pinning me with painful force to the floor.

Stay down.

Her eyes slammed shut. Fists clenched. Flames bent toward her, pouring into her body like a second skin. She devoured the fire as if it belonged to her. When her eyes snapped open, embers glowed beneath her emerald irises.

I dared a glance sideways—toward what used to be the kitchen—and caught a flash of winter-blue eyes. Aren. His shield surrounded those who'd been huddled near the counters, and I huffed a relieved breath. Alec and August stood at his sides, casting nets of power wide across the block, as though they alone could protect the entire street.

Beside them, the alleged enemy knelt, hands outstretched in the opposite direction. Still alive. All of them. For now.

Aren met my gaze across the wreckage, and something in my chest loosened. His calm steadied me. But the moment didn't last.

He, Freya, and Ansel raised their hands—drawing from the well of their magic—and suddenly it was hard to breathe. Not from the hit to my ribs, but from the sudden vacuum of oxygen in the room. Alvara swallowed the fire; they swallowed the air.

The silence thickened, iron-weighted and absolute. And then, the inferno extinguished, only seconds passing in an eternity of holding my breath.

Alvara launched to her feet, whirling toward the front door—or what remained of it. She barked a command I couldn't hear through the ringing in my skull.

Heal your ears, witchling. His voice crashed through my mind. I snapped my gaze to Bellamy—no, *Adrastos*—watching me with a haunted expression. *Now.*

The shock nearly knocked the breath from me. He could mind-speak. He'd been able to all along. Which meant he'd been lying—just like Alvara said. He could *see.* Like her.

Betrayal surged.

Followed by shame.

He'd been inside me. I had trusted him. With my body. My sisters. My life.

And all the while, he'd known.

I blinked, barely hearing him as he tried to speak again. Red flared at the edges of my vision. I wanted a knife. Glass. Anything sharp enough to draw blood.

Strong hands seized my arms, pulling me upright. *Aren.*

His piercing gaze swept over me, and then his hands came to my face, cupping my cheeks. His lips moved, forming words I couldn't make out. I raised one trembling hand to my ear, fingers coming away slick and red.

Aren's palms pressed over my ears like muffs, and cool, tingling healing magic bled into my skull.

And the world came *roaring* back.

"Fuuuuck," I cried, throwing my hands over my ears to stifle the noise.

Screaming. Dogs howling. Alarms blaring. The thunderous collapse of broken homes.

Fire still crackled, chewing through the remains.

Aren pulled me into his chest, arms wrapping around me in an embrace that said: you're safe.

And for a breath, I believed it. I let myself feel it—his warmth, the weight of him, the drum of my own heartbeat syncing to his.

But then he shifted, placing his body in front of mine, bringing reality crashing back.

Nathara.

Horror surged in my gut. The block was leveled—nothing left but scattered protection bubbles. I looked for her, but—

She's not here. Alvara's voice rang clear in my mind, sharp as a bell. I flinched at the intrusion—but then relief struck. Nat was safe.

I blinked hard, trying to push down the panic.

This was my fault. All of this.

No time for that, sweetheart. We have to go.

"Don't call me that," I snapped, glaring at Adrastos. "And get the fuck out of my head."

His mouth tightened, eyes going glossy and distant.

How hadn't I seen it? The way he'd spaced out while watching TV. Staring at the ocean. All of it. He'd never been who he claimed to be.

The Grayshellians moved as one, drawing their pistols with practiced ease. Alec stepped in front of Fae, just as Aren stood guard over me. The Porters formed a line—each slightly angled, guarding the group with silent coordination. Their shields had held. None bore even a scratch.

Bellamy's gaze flicked to their hands. Then to Alvara.

Some silent exchange passed between them had her sneering. With a huff, she pulled a second handgun from a back holster and tossed it to him. He caught it, checked the chamber, cocked it, and aimed it forward. As if he belonged. As if he hadn't been the enemy all along.

Aren bristled, spine stiffening—clearly displeased that she had armed his enemy. His rival. I echoed the sentiment, betrayal still eating at my nerves.

What the fuck was going on? What weren't they telling me? Nothing made sense.

Aren's hand reached back, and I grabbed it like a lifeline, breathing steadier as his calloused fingers curled around mine. Then we were moving —shifting into some kind of formation I hadn't been taught. I stayed tucked against his back as Grayshell led us through the wreckage of the house, toward the yard where a handful of startled survivors were staggering from their homes.

The wards. That's why we hadn't jumped yet. Even with the house obliterated, the old magic still bound us within the perimeter.

A lot of fucking good they'd done.

We jumped off the foundation one at a time. Aren went first, then turned and caught me at the waist, lifting me easily, setting me gently on what was left of the lawn.

I felt like a ghost haunting the skeleton of the place I'd fallen in love— with Aren. With my shadows. With his family. Gone.

Numbness settled into my bones as I took in the smoldering ruin through drifting walls of smoke.

Gunshots cracked across the block. Bellamy had moved several paces ahead, quickly picking off demons with cursed ammunition. He shot with precision—eliminating targets sprinting toward fleeing humans, and the Grayshellians did the same, covering escape routes.

Aren halted just feet from the ward's edge, and I nearly stumbled into him. Freya and Cyrus vanished into mist, and I had to resist the familiar pull of the shadows. Not with creatures like Balorath lurking there.

Bellamy swore and closed the distance. He reached for my hand— snatching it from Aren's grip—and pressed his firearm into my palm, his expression haunted and pleading. I nodded, bringing my other hand up to brace my grip.

"Run, Green," he murmured. "I beg of you."

Then he turned to Aren, his hand landing on Aren's shoulder, earning a growl of disapproval.

"*Amadeus*," Bellamy said, low and cold. The name locked my feet in place. Roots. Like magic winding through the soles of my boots, anchoring me to the scorched grass. Aren's head snapped toward him, his eyes wild with rage.

"There's no going back."

Aren's hand flexed on the pistol. He didn't lift it, but I saw the tremor. His gaze flicked to mine, a war of pain and conflict shadowing his face.

"No. She won't forgive you. But she will understand, eventually. *Now, Commander.*"

What were they talking about? Why did Aren look ready to break, and Bellamy look like he'd already shattered?

The ground trembled. In the distance, I heard music—a music box, eerily out of place.

Bellamy swore and barked Aren's name again, this time with a note of desperation. Alvara seized him by the shoulder, yanking him into place like a human shield. He didn't resist. His shackled hands dropped limply in front of him as she pressed a gun to his head, marching him forward.

I knew who he was. I knew what monster he was bound to. And still the sight of him like that turned my lungs to stone.

Two figures materialized from the shadows. I went still, staring at the monochrome pallor of the twins—hair like snow, skin like marble. They didn't look human. They looked like illusions brought to life.

These were the monsters leading the charge against my people.

Fury ignited under my skin, white-hot and demanding justice—for my sisters, for Aren's kin…for Bell.

I couldn't believe he was one of them. Not fully. The man who had ripped evil off of me couldn't live the same kind of sickness.

But the twins—oh, I believed it of them.

They moved like mirror images, reflections in a warped glass. Their black coats glimmered with silver thread. The only things they shared with their half-brother were their otherworldly beauty—and those onyx eyes gleaming beneath the moonlight.

They sneered at us with twin expressions of disgust.

If it came down to it—if they slipped into the shadows—only Cyrus, Bellamy, and I could follow. And if the Blood Bond still overpowered Alvara's influence…not good. Not even close to good.

The music box's song grew louder, and I spotted it in Moros's hand—bronze, winding slowly, the melody dragging like a death march. His smirk widened as recognition seemed to flicker through the Grayshellians.

And then I felt it.

The chill yanked through my bones—pulling, siphoning my magic away like a rip tide.

No.

I shoved a shield up, but it flickered and died like a zapped fly.

"Reaper," Aren breathed as the line *erupted.*

Everyone except Alvara, August, and Bellamy opened fire on the twins. Civilians screamed, scrambling for shelter. The seers didn't waste bullets—either unwilling or unable to fire as the shots bounced harmlessly off the twins' shields.

The twins didn't flinch. Not once. What the fuck *were* they?

Ally's voice was tight, her lips an inch from Adrastos' ear. "I *can't.*"

Can't what?!

"Well, if this isn't a happy surprise." Moros's voice slithered through the chaos—low, sickly, and laced with command. "So pleased to find you in one piece, little brother."

Bellamy went rigid. His jaw locked, his eyes dead. But he still managed to grit out one solitary word:

"*Run.*"

FREYA

From within the shadows, Cyrus and I watched hell prepare to descend.

Moros and that death bitch—allegedly *Marlana*—had brought friends. Lots of them. Standing proudly beneath banners of black, red, and silver.

This could go belly-up faster than a frog in a pot. Just beyond the curtain of flame, there had to be a thousand troops—some fully infested Renown, others horribly clear-eyed. I hated the latter more. Hated them for choosing this, for following without a demon whispering promises in their ears.

Cyrus had barely said a word since we left Paladin.

Not that I blamed him. He'd had maybe an hour to process what I'd done to his family before being thrust into a war that might be humanity's *last*. And still, he was here. Still bound and determined to fight beside me.

The storm inside his head was rivaled only by the size of the enemy host.

Fuck, I hoped Ally knew what she was doing. She'd evacuated ten blocks this morning—an order issued while Magnolia was still trapped in the shadow realm.

Now, our job was to draw the fight back inside the boundary line.

Anything? Cyrus clipped through the tether. Alec and Ally had patched him up quickly, his injuries superficial compared to the wreckage of Magnolia and Adrastos, who'd been hauled back from the brink.

The bulk of Hazelharbor was already deployed—scattered to other allied hierarchies or manning hospital wards.

Yeah. Ally was right. But you're not going to like it.

I think we're past the point of liking things, don't you?

Fuck. I huffed. *Go.*

I go where you go, Your Majesty.

There was no fondness in it. Just the cold, dutiful cadence of a soldier fulfilling his orders. I'd been demoted from *ma moitié* to a strategic liability. A memory of what we could've been.

But now wasn't the time to mull that over.

I still trusted him to fight. To defend the balance. To protect our people. That would have to be enough.

Right now, I need you to defer to my experience—and to Aren and Alvara's. Follow orders, Stuart.

Same old, same old.

With a huff, he misted to Aren and Magnolia, tapping her shoulder to drag her into the molasses-thick hush of the realm between. She blinked, startled, shadows already curling around her like smoke.

"No dragons," I purred, earning a wary nod. "That's cool as shit. I'm kind of fucking jealous."

"You say that now, but that thing was horrific."

"The first monster always is. You get used to it."

"I don't know how long my magic will hold," she said, voice tight.

"Then we better make it fucking count."

Before I could add more, Cyrus laid a hand on Aren's shoulder and dragged him under. Magnolia reached back a beat later, pulling Fae into the monochrome veil.

"Ally was certain?" Fae's voice wobbled. Her eyes locked onto Alec's profile, all terror and longing. She trembled with the urge to run to him but didn't. Didn't let go of Magnolia's hand.

Two threads.

That's all we had left. Somewhere between Magnolia breaking Aren's heart and Reagan having Cyrus tortured, the optimal future vanished.

Just two fucking threads remained.

I couldn't tell her that—not my pregnant aunt. So, I just nodded.

"I'm betting on Ally," Aren said, voice steady.

"Y'all realize this plan is insane, right?" Cyrus drawled, gaze fixed on Moros like he was weighing the odds of dragging the bastard into the dirt now. The temptation had certainly crossed my mind. "Your seer made us bait."

"You get used to that, too," Aren and I said in unison. Cyrus's citrine gaze flicked to us, unconvinced.

"She's rarely wrong," Aren added, and there was something heavy beneath the words. Something final.

It *was* brilliant—Ally's plan. Broken into phases. Scalable. Strategic. All we had to do was stick to it, even if it sucked like a bag of donkey dicks to walk away from our family while they faced down a fucking legion.

"We follow the plan."

The shadows stirred—serpents winding through our feet—and Magnolia and Cyrus both turned sharply, scanning.

"We've got company," Cyrus muttered.

"Move," Aren ordered.

And just like that, we hauled ass—dragging Fae and Aren through the heart of the city.

AUGUST

"*Run.*"

One gritted word—and everything changed.

Magnolia, Fae, and Aren vanished the instant Adrastos spun, disarming Ally like it was a goddamn drill. In the same breath, he looped his chained wrists around her neck and yanked her against his chest.

With a roar, Alec's shield surged forward—blocking the Reaper's strike and the spears of dark magic the twins hurled our way. But not even Alec could stop a horseman alone. I threw my own shield forward to reinforce his.

Ally had gone full Angel of Death, battling her ancient brother with the kind of fury that made even seasoned soldiers hesitate. Every part of me screamed to protect her.

But I followed the goddamn plan. Trusted her to signal if she needed me.

I dropped to one knee as the whites of the silver-haired witch's eyes turned black.

Marlana. That was the name Ally had pulled from Adrastos's mind.

And now the slippery bitch was pressing her hand into the dirt, that oily smile spreading as the ground beneath us turned to ash.

Oh, we were so, so fucked.

That's the spirit, Alec muttered through the tether as we both drew our bows.

"After them!" Moros barked, pointing into the city—no doubt toward Freya, who'd just whisked away half the damn prophecy like a fucking legend. Thank God at least one part of this plan had worked. I prayed her reinforcements would show up before this turned into a massacre.

With her shadowwalker, she'd gotten them out of the Reaper's radius. That was all I could ask.

Because our shields were cracking, smoke sputtering through the fissures as the serpent shifter grinned.

My chest seared with effort as I patched the damage, but we were still in the wrong goddamned place. If this was going to work, we had to lure them east—at least two blocks. That was where Freya had set the trap.

The army marching up behind the Horsemen would flank our position before we even had a chance to hold ground.

Fire erupted beside me—bright orange and blessed white—but I kept my focus on Marlana. On the base of our barrier, where the ground was rotting to nothing.

"August," Alec warned, voice tight.

"I see it," I muttered, eyes locked on the spreading black.

And Ansel, clearly feeling the tension spike, snapped down the line: *Hold.*

We would not buckle before Freya was ready. Had to make it mean something.

Marlana hissed, Ally cursed—and Adrastos fucking *laughed.*

"It's rather endearing," he said, his voice syruped with mockery, "that you all think resistance matters."

I anchored deeper into the earth, tapping into the shared well Ally and I had built, drawing on her full reserves. Alec's grunt of pain mirrored the strain lancing through my spine, but before I could stabilize it—

Moros's eyes turned onyx.

Just like the serpent's.

My skull screamed. Pain spindled behind my eyes, pressure needling into my temples like nails made of fire. He stepped forward, smiling like a butcher, and set his hand on the edge of our shield.

I cried out, knees hitting the dirt as the agony ripped through me, like he'd driven a jackhammer into my mind.

Mentalist! Alec roared down the line. *Shields up—move your asses!*

Remember. This quarter's lost, Ansel snapped.

I shoved back against the pressure, breath hitching. The ink-black magic clawed at every line of my concentration. Nobody else dropped. Moros had zeroed in on me.

Good. Let the bastard focus on the anchor. Let someone else flank him while he tried to crack me open. He'd identified the source. Now he was trying to hollow it out.

Good luck, asshole.

Wait for it, I gritted through the bond, thoughts fraying under the weight of his assault. *Wait for Freya. Wait for the signal. Hold the fucking line.*

It would've been easier to believe in the plan if my brain wasn't being pulverized like a walnut under a boot. If the silver-haired witch wasn't *molting* at our feet.

Marlana hissed and tipped her head to the moonlight, her skin sloughing off like silk as she *shed it*—revealing something massive and terrible underneath.

The snake rose.

Towering.

"Motherfucker," Ansel muttered as we watched her ascend, mouths agape. A grunt sounded to my left—Ally hitting the dirt, scrambling up again as Adrastos followed. She'd gotten free. Both of them squared off, ready for round two.

Fire erupted. A wall of it roared between us and them—blazing high as the moon, a barrier of heat and fury.

The ground quaked. The soldiers—every last one—snapped their heads toward the city.

Now, Ansel barked.

And though every instinct in me rebelled at leaving the humans behind —we jumped.

SEVENTY-ONE

TAPPED OUT

AREN

Fires bloomed in the streets below, the world a cacophony of explosions and the screams of humans who hadn't evacuated in time. I didn't have space to pity them. Every ounce of focus was reserved for ticking off the steps. Magnolia watched in mute horror, her eyes glassy, as I moved between the truck Ally had parked for us and our rooftop vantage point.

Perk: full three-sixty view of the siege of Santa Bloom.

Downside: we were sitting ducks if Reyna and Cyrus's people stayed pinned in the south.

I hefted the last duffle out of the silver pickup, dropped it at the roof's edge, and began assembling a sniper rifle with mechanical precision, clearing my head. No reaper bullets—so this setup was either meant for human targets, or to take advantage of the Reaper's null field while it was active.

Past Mags, where she'd lowered into a crouch, the city burned. Demons clawed through already-leveled buildings.

Phase One had worked. The moment Freya lit up the city with that blast of power, every Renown and crawler within radius had veered toward the center. Our coven was in position. From what I could see, Moros's army had taken the bait.

Nine out of ten prophecy pieces had been placed within ten city blocks —only Mags and I shared a quadrant. The others had been intentionally scattered to make capture harder. Effective. But it also meant we couldn't fight like the unit we were.

Fae was long gone. Thank God she was the best tracker I'd ever met —she'd find a place to vanish where they wouldn't even smell her shadow.

Nat's once-beautiful Santa Bloom had become an ocean of destruction. The air was thick with sulfur and burning asphalt. Crawlers and Second Hierarchy assholes moved in formations too clean for demons—which meant there was a Commander nearby.

Vulnerable or not, Ally had been right—this rooftop gave us everything. Every skirmish, every perimeter team. Every bloody death.

I blew out a slow breath and turned, fishing out the stashed armor. I held it up for Mags, who nodded numbly. As I helped her into it, I dropped to one knee to fasten the garter holsters.

"Remember what you've been taught." She barely nodded. I tightened the strap until her eyes met mine. "*Focus*. Fight only if you *have to*. Stay where we placed you. We'll bring the wounded to you."

Another small nod.

"And remember—it's okay to fight like a healer. Shut down their organs. I'd fucking prefer it."

"Heart and lungs," she recited softly. Her voice wavered, but her hands stilled.

"Good girl." I slid the last blade into its sheath. Some for fighting. Some for the delicate work. I had a feeling she'd be digging bullets out of more than one of us before the night was over.

Movement caught my eye. Down on the street, Cyrus and Freya misted into place. The chittering rose instantly—blood-hungry demons swarming toward them. I gritted my teeth. I hated using Freya as bait, but she hadn't even blinked when Ally pitched the idea. Judging by her smirk, she was thoroughly enjoying herself.

And Cyrus?

Jesus. I thought *my* love life was complicated. Didn't seem to be slowing him down, though—he stayed tight to her flank, cutting through ichor-soaked bodies like he was born to it.

"What are they doing?" Mags whispered, narrowing her eyes on the perimeter teams.

"Driving the demons inward."

"Like a corral?"

"Exactly."

"Why?"

"For Ally." Two words. All I needed to say.

Guilt pierced my concentration. I'd been so twisted up in my own head, I'd questioned *Ally*. My little shadow. The soul who always came home. I'd never unraveled like that. Never lost control like I did.

Stop moping—it's not your color, Ally snapped down the bond. *We're fine.*

Snorting, I thought back, *I owe you.*

Duh. Now stay alive so you can bribe me with a house in Italy or another McLaren.

I'm sorry.

I know.

But I need you to hear it.

You needed to unload that bullshit on someone who could take it. So I could have you up there now, acting as overwatch.

You didn't deserve it.

And you deserve to be happy. If you're not—

The story's not over.

Amen. Now are we doing this sappy sire-calling nonsense, or are you calling plays, Commander?

I chuckled aloud.

Mags raised an eyebrow. "Sorry," I said. "Making up with Ally."

Guilt flickered across her face—but then we both flinched as Ansel and Lana appeared on the roof, striding toward us.

"Second Hierarchy grouping at the west barricade," Ansel greeted, all business. "August's shield is holding, but we need to break that formation before they push through."

"Send Ally's pyros to flank from high ground."

On it, Ally chirped in my mind, like this was a training op.

"Where's our aerial?"

"Cyrus still hasn't heard from his people."

"Okay—then send the earth elementals in behind. Pin them between the walls and our blades."

"And Moros?"

"We give him a reason to come front and center."

"Alec's working on it."

"Adrastos?"

"At his side."

Dread curdled in my gut. *Should've killed him.* The moment he demanded it of me, I should've slid my blade over his throat. I knew it. But Ally insisted we needed him. The problem was, I didn't know how many of us would survive having them both in play. Adrastos was too good at this game—and I still didn't understand how his death tied to Magnolia and Blythe's.

"Godspeed," I murmured. Ansel and Lana echoed the word before vanishing as quickly as they'd come.

Fuck me, Ally whined through the link. *Marcus is about to need us.*

Not sure if you noticed, but we're a little preoccupied, Freya fired back.

Still, that dread twisted deeper. Grayshell never failed Westerlund. We couldn't start now.

Why? I asked.

They're hitting us on all fronts, Ally answered. *But if we go now, we can do it. We left enough strength here to contain the chaos. That gate's smaller than this monstrosity.*

Can we focus the demons where we want them? I asked.

That's the idea.

Then go.

"Um..." Magnolia's voice shook. "Did Freya and Cyrus just vanish?"

I sighed, "Yep."

"They're going after the gates?"

"Yep."

"It's like a giant chess game," she whispered. "Moving pieces across the board, even when it costs you."

"Yes," I said quietly—but when I looked down, her skin had gone pale. "Mags?"

She blinked up at me. "Which soul would you say is your most observational?"

CYRUS

Three portals and several hours later, we returned to Santa Bloom.

Freya stumbled on impact, chest heaving, swiping a shaking arm across sweat-slick skin as her eyes locked on mine—searching for reassurance I couldn't give.

Impossible.

This was impossible.

The war Grayshell had chosen to stand against would consume us all. Santa Bloom was under siege—but so were Chicago, New York, New Orleans, and God knew how many others. We'd made a detour through Ivy Springs—a hellscape of blood and fire, once cradled by now-burning mountains.

But August and Freya still had mortal family. So, we punched through the lines, dropped their loved ones in a safe house, and closed the gate behind us without explanation.

It wasn't sustainable. They were just two souls. And both had to be standing on the razor's edge of burnout. No one else had a clue how to close the goddamn portals, so the lightning wielder and I ran defense while the girls stitched shut one rift after another.

Impossible. Continuing like this was impossible.

Which brought us back here. Alvara staggered into her mate, gasping, coughing on the thick smoke clinging to the air like poison. This city was already lost. The war unwinnable. But still they moved. Still they fought. The walls reinforced themselves, Grayshell's blades cut through enemy lines with relentless precision. For every one of ours that fell, ten Renown followed—and twice that in demons. But it wouldn't last. Fatigue and burnout would claim us before the enemy did.

The allies they'd promised us? Nowhere to be seen.

Successfully divided. Inevitably conquered.

Alvara dropped us into a parking lot beside what used to be a mall. The walls had been blown apart, windows shattered and blackened with the soot of an inferno. The stench of excrement, carrion, and charred flesh made my stomach turn. Even my shadows flinched away from the dark magic soaked into these walls.

Hell no, they whispered, curling back beneath my skin despite the pitch-black cocoon surrounding us.

"This feels like suicide," I muttered, my element pulling me back toward the carnage, toward the red-and-gold flashes of light painting the sky in apocalyptic bursts. The witches' once-beautiful city was now smoldering.

Even here, the air was thick with ash. It fell like cursed snow. Lightning arced overhead, no doubt August's doing, as his frustration surged.

"My love, he's right," he said, shaking his head. "We can't keep this up. Not like this."

"No choice," Ally panted, her voice fraying at the edges. Screeching demons tore past us—unbothered by our presence. We were too inconsequential to kill, apparently.

"Just...give us a second," Freya wheezed, hunched over, gripping her ribs with a blood-soaked hand. "Need to catch my breath."

I looked at her, *really* looked.

Her bravado was paper-thin. Sweat clung to her pale skin. Her mask was back in place, but it wasn't fooling anyone. Determined? Yes. But she was scared. Drained. And I didn't need to touch the Bond to know it.

She was done. But she wouldn't admit it.

And I—I couldn't stop staring at her.

She lied to me. Used me. Manipulated Cali and Carr too. Used my fury to get what she needed—to get her throne.

It wasn't about Reagan. That monster deserved to die after chaining me up and letting Nix beat me half to death.

It was that I was the fool she used to do it.

And yet...

Even now, as she trembled from exhaustion, something primal inside me wanted to gut every creature that had put that fear on her face. With every surge of protective rage, I forgave my father a little more.

She was barely upright. Blood soaked her glove as she dragged her thumb across it, testing her strength like she could will herself to keep going.

"Your Majesty," I murmured, arching a brow. "I believe this is where the witch faced the dragon."

She shot me a venomous glare. "Cut the shit, Cyrus."

"Just assessing the odds."

"That's *my* job," Ally growled, planting her hands on her hips. "And Aren is sending reinforcements."

I deadpanned. "Can he actually spare them?"

"That's his call, Prince, not mine."

"Did somebody say dragon hunting?" Alec's voice broke through the haze as he emerged from the ash-drenched lot like it was just another goddamn Tuesday. He was streaked in blood, his quiver empty—explaining the casual way he bent down to yank arrows from corpses at our feet.

"I do believe we fight as a coven, or not at all," he said. "That was the impression you gave Westerlund. This splitting up bullshit isn't working."

Ally gave a ragged laugh and collapsed into his arms for a moment, her posture relaxing against him.

The assassins came next, silent and sure-footed, appearing behind Alec with the same practiced ease.

I'd seen shit running ops for the Wings—but none of it compared to this. No nightmare had prepared me for *this*.

"Freya," Alec hedged, "can you haul us through the shadows?"

I already knew the answer. The way her eyes dropped told me as much.

"No," she murmured. "Not all of us. Not anymore." She hesitated. "And Balorath's still kicking."

I nodded. "My shadows won't go near this place. They know something's wrong."

"Our willingness won't matter," Ansel said as he approached, his tone grave. "There's no border left to contain it. If that beast comes out to play, we need to be ready." He pulled Freya close, and she leaned into him. "You alright, babygirl?"

"Better now," she whispered, lifting her eyes to Alvara. "Let's end this. Shut it off at the source. Or die trying."

Ally's jaw clenched. Her magic stirred.

"Move," she ordered. And we did.

I fell into formation with the others, flanked by Grayshell's elite. We moved like one creature.

The blown-out mall swallowed us whole. The blackness deepened.

My shadows hissed in my ear. *Evil,* they whispered. *Unspeakable evil within.*

Fantastic. Just fucking fantastic.

The Grayshellians flowed like a single tide, curling and snapping around me with lethal grace. Their mental line must've been crystal clear—because without a word, they shifted to place me at the center. Their formation folded around me like it was second nature. Like they'd done this a hundred times before. Like it was nothing new to carry an outsider through the carnage.

The chitter and screech of demons had Alvara lifting a fist—hold—and we froze. Silent, tense. She scanned the shadows. Freya's elbow nudged my waist, and I looked down as she fired off instructions down the bond.

A dozen guard the portal. It's quiet—for now. Bad news? They're probably flooding out somewhere else.

One problem at a time, I answered. She nodded, and we fanned out.

Seven of us. Twelve of them. Best odds we'd had all night.

To my surprise, August slotted in as an archer too. Alec, The Great Commander, and his mate fanned out in sync—shields up, bows drawn. Three arrows loosed. Three crawlers dropped. A clean, coordinated strike that sent the rest screaming in our direction.

Demonic shrieks echoed off the busted concrete like birds cawing through hell. The rest scrambled toward us. I lost track of them in the black, but another volley of arrows shot past—and three more fell.

No need for blades.

Ansel and Lana tore through the remaining demons like water through silk. Gutting them before they reached the rest of us.

Smooth. Efficient. Practiced.

No wonder the third coven was legendary. How many wars did you have to survive before this shit looked like a sparring match?

"They'll send backup," Ally predicted grimly, striding toward the portal beneath the mezzanine. The glass above was shattered, jagged edges framing the ceiling like a monster's mouth.

The hair on my neck prickled in response. I turned toward the darkness, watching our backs—same as August and I had done three times already tonight.

But this time...

I grabbed Freya's arm before she could follow.

"You're tapped," I noted flatly.

"She doesn't have enough left," she shot back, flicking a glance toward Alvara, whose face was tight with strain as she examined the portal's edge.

"There's nothing here to siphon from," I growled. "What are you gonna do—pull it from the floor?"

"Maybe," she snapped.

"I'm not letting my queen burn out with enemies surrounding her."

Her jaw clenched. Eyes flashed—not anger, but hurt.

Queen. Not mate. I hadn't meant it to cut like that. Maybe I had. I didn't know anymore. I only knew one thing—she wasn't passing out on my watch. Not in enemy territory. Not happening.

"I'm fine," Alvara lied. August didn't look convinced either.

"West wall is flagging," Ansel called. "Brody says ravens inbound. Jax dropped the snake into the sewer and is heading west. Aren's gonna need us back ASAP, Al."

Alvara nodded shakily, and raised trembling hands. My attention split—Alvara straining to close the tear. Freya standing ready, fury in her eyes. And the darkness pressing in from all sides.

Water dripped somewhere behind us. Steady. Measured. A countdown. The walls creaked around us like bones shifting in a corpse.

Anguish. That's what filled the air. Not just the scent of rot—but grief. And something else. Something feeding on it. I didn't like it. Not one fucking bit.

Alvara whimpered, her power flickering. Her mate didn't cast a shield—*couldn't,* judging by the drained look in his eyes.

The shadows whispered: *Run, Prince.*

And I braced, letting them pour forward, scouring the black for a threat I couldn't see.

"We've got company," I warned. August and Ansel nodded wordlessly. Moonlight—red as blood—filtered through the atrium.

Alvara grunted, voice thick with strain. Her mate flinched. August's gaze swept the black.

An unnatural silence settled. Dense. Electric. The kind that came before the scream.

Lana must've felt it too—she turned, tight and deliberate, gun sweeping the upper floor in a steady arc.

Then—ice down my spine. Every hair on my arms lifted.

"Hurry, baby," August whispered.

Shnick. Blades were drawn all around us. My hand closed around the weapon up my sleeve—but my shadows were the better bet now.

"Fucking trying," Alvara snapped. Then screamed in unseen agony, like a soul cleaved from its flesh.

"She's burning out," August muttered. "We're almost tapped."

"Just find me a target," Freya snarled. A breeze swept past our faces. Rubble clattered in the distance.

Wind inside? Not a good omen.

"You're no better off," I muttered. She glared but didn't argue.

The shadows slammed into me, urgent, and terrified. I cast ribbons of smoke into the dark—heart pounding, lungs straining.

Empty. Nothing there.

For now.

The fight, I could handle. The waiting? That was the real torture.

A metallic rattle rang out in the distance, stiffening my spine.

"Pretty sure those are talons," Alec muttered. Ally cried out again—raw and cracked—and he turned to Freya, eyes frantic. "Take mine," he begged, arms out, practically offering his throat. "Freya, take mine. She's gonna drop."

"I know," Freya whispered, anguished. "But it's not enough. Alec—I could kill you."

"This is Ally," he snapped. "If she and August go down, we're all fucked anyway."

"Alec, I—"

"*Now*, Freya," he barked, eyes flicking from her to the portal behind.

Alvara sobbed—the tear was shrinking. But not fast enough.

A swirl of ash passed over us. I turned, but no one was there.

But then—the shadows deepened. Thickened.

Something massive fell from the mezzanine, and Freya screamed as I yanked her back. The shadows shielded her and Alec *roared* as the thing collided with him.

Shouts and clatters of steel cleaved the air. The shield swung his blade into the darkness as it swallowed him whole, and blood sprayed across my face.

SEVENTY-TWO
THE BELL TOLLS
ALVARA

Fucking shifting shadow birds.

Alec was lucky to make it out—barely. Talons slashed across his arm before the bird shifted midair, spearing forward. Thank God he'd always been the fastest of us, parrying and striking with desperate precision.

But Adrastos moved like me. Just as lethal. Just as relentless. He must've lost his blades along the way because he came in swinging with bare fists—*goddamned fists*—like a monster unbothered by steel.

Aren! The cry echoed through my mind like a scream. *Kingsley!*

A desperate plea. A Hail Mary hurled into the ether.

None of it—none of the planning, the sacrifice, the strategy—would matter if I didn't get this damn portal closed.

My body burned. Sweat poured from my skin as a scream curdled in my throat, fighting its way up as I funneled every scrap of power I had into sealing the rupture.

And then she was there. *Freya.* Her hand slammed to my spine as she bellowed her fury to the heavens. Darkness surged around us—raw and radiant. Fire bloomed back to life in my chest. I gasped as my clairvoyance flared open, vision bending and snapping as familiar magic surged into me.

Oh.

Oh.

I knew this magic. It poured through my veins like it had always belonged there. Like I was built for it.

Him.

Adrastos hit his knees. Arms wide. Palms open. Shadows ripping away from his skin as Freya—now screaming—tore them from him strand by strand.

But his eyes locked on mine. Dark. Determined. Pleading.

My mouth opened, but no words came. I didn't understand—none of it made sense.

Still, I turned back. Threw up my hands. Another wall of flame exploded from my core, this one jagged with shadow, streaked in shades of orange and ash. It devoured the Renown. Sent crawlers skittering from the light.

Grabbing the border of the portal again, I yanked.

Seal. Please seal.

Still, I pulled. Still, I begged. My limbs shook with the effort as the Callahans, Alec, and Cyrus surrounded Adrastos where he knelt.

Wait! I tried to cast it down the bond, but I couldn't hear anything beyond my own thundering heartbeat. My hands trembled, vision blurring.

Did they hear me?

We need him.

A vision slammed into me—vivid and brutal. Him. Stealing Magnolia away.

I gasped. Eyes flying wide as I cried out and shoved the last of my power into the portal's closing edge.

With a deafening *snap*, the magic sealed. The flow stopped. And Adrastos *vanished*.

"*Mags*," I whispered.

***A*REN**

In a rapid burst of motion, my coven appeared on the rooftop, all of us heaving for breath.

Eyes wide, I scanned each face, but it was Ansel who answered the unspoken question with a nod. Portal closed.

Then why the hell were they all looking between me and Mags like the world had just snapped in two?

"They're coming," Ally finally wheezed.

She didn't need to explain. For Magnolia. They were coming for my mate.

I drew my blades just as Ally raised hers. Screams echoed from below, followed by a massive *crunch* that twisted our heads in grim recognition.

"They're *here*," Alec muttered, just as the serpent curled around the street corner.

Ally's eyes met mine. She nodded once.

"Godspeed," Ansel whispered, right before she, Alec, and August vanished. Thunder cracked overhead. A split second later, a hiss curled up from the street—chilling and furious. They'd found their mark.

Lightning split the sky as fire licked up the edge of the building. Magnolia's hand found mine, warm and trembling. I turned to her, wanting—*aching*—to kiss her. To tell her I loved her.

Instead, I pressed my lips to the crown of her head and whispered, "Stay down. Stay behind us."

"Why?" she breathed. But I was already moving toward the vortex of shadow forming across the rooftop.

Freya and Lana flung their knives. Moros flicked them away with a casual whip of power as he stepped through the spiral. His brother followed, that oily smile nearly distracting enough to overlook the two Renown at their backs.

Nearly.

We knew our roles and wore them like skin. Ansel and Lana would handle the Renown. Freya and I had the Balaskas brothers.

That was the last coherent thought before Adrastos lunged—and Freya and Cyrus vanished into the melee. Moros smirked once before he disappeared too.

Steel screamed as it met steel. Shadow tangled with shadow. My blood sang with war cries of vengeance. Adrastos struck downward with brutal force, nearly cleaving through my guard. I barely sidestepped, the displaced air skimming over my skin. I countered, but he slipped aside, unnaturally fast. Every blow pushed me back across the parking garage. I parried, blades shaking beneath the weight of each hit.

He was relentless. As relentless as Ally.

A kick slammed into my ribs mid-block, knocking me off balance. I grunted and shoved forward to stop his next strike, pushing into him instead of yielding ground.

You don't get near her. Not while I breathe.

He was fast. Good—too good. But so was I. A headbutt landed, sending him reeling.

Freya spilled out of the shadows, her small body skidding across the rooftop—but I couldn't break focus as this fucker advanced. Block for block, I realized with growing rage: he was my match. Nearly my size. Just as strong. Just as precise. He *knew* my moves a beat before they landed—like Ally did. Brute strength wouldn't cut it. I had to outthink him. When he lunged, I dodged his blade and let his hand clamp around my throat. Magnolia screamed—but I kept my eyes on him.

Fire flared, embers swirling around us.

Time slowed.

I gripped his sword hand. Twisted. Hard. The blade clattered to the ground. With a roar, I spun him by the shoulder and slammed a dagger into his arm.

Shadows surged, and he vanished—only to reappear a foot away.

He stared at the blade protruding from his arm, then looked up at me with an expression that said, *Really?*

He retrieved his sword without breaking eye contact. I jerked my chin. *Come on, then.*

He charged. Our blades met again—but then we both *froze.*

A vision slammed down the bond.

Marlana. Appearing on the rooftop's edge and severing Cyrus's head in one clean, brutal swing.

A second vision hit like a punch to the chest.

I can't! Ally's voice—ragged and panicked—shattered down the line.

A blast of heat swept across the roof engulfing the building in white flame.

Pressure exploded in my side.

I looked down—blood pooled in my armor, and I hadn't even felt the wound. A ripple of energy burst from me, slamming Adrastos back. It was enough. I turned. Toward the shadows. Toward the swirl of magic where Freya staggered upright, planting herself between the darkness and Mags.

Ansel's quicksilver eyes met mine, shining with something I couldn't bear to read. *It has been an honor to fight with you.*

"No!"

My roar cracked the air as the shadows imploded—like a bomb had gone off inside the dark realm. Three warriors tumbled from the void, bleeding, snarling. Marlana stepped forward, naked and soaked in blood. Her poisoned sword gleamed as she lunged at Freya.

Cyrus appeared—*just in time*—his arms flung wide, shadows colliding with hers, wings exploding from his back in a burst of light.

Freya shrieked. I bellowed as I hit the ground running. But I was too late.

Ansel appeared between the blade and the prince, his sword raised to block.

Everything stopped.

The world tilted.

The thud of my pulse drowned out sound.

Only the ragged, soul-wracking scream that ripped from my chest proved I was still alive.

Because the witch's blade fell...

And Ansel lost his head.

MAGNOLIA

The world stilled—and suddenly I was floating, unmoored in a body that didn't feel like mine, watching in horror.

Like a rag doll, Aren's oldest friend crumpled to the concrete, blood pooling at Cyrus's boots as he staggered back, arms outstretched protectively over Freya's slight form.

Freya lunged, canines bared. Even the moonlight seemed steeped in red, tainted by the death clinging to the air. Cyrus caught her by the waist, his face contorted in an agonized bellow as he hauled her back.

Marlana smiled. A thin, blood-red curve of cruelty.

I blinked.

Ansel.

Ansel was—

Gods, no.

My shaking hands scrambled across his armor, muscles seizing as I clung to him. A high-pitched ringing filled my ears. There was no fixing this. Not even with all my sisters. Not even with time itself rewound.

The world moved like molasses as I pulled myself closer, as if proximity might shift reality, as if I'd see something different. Something reversible.

But it was his blood. Hot, wet. Soaking my hands, my knees. And I couldn't fix it.

Couldn't do anything but stare as the rest were forced to keep fighting.

Lana's face twisted into something unrecognizable—rage incarnate. Her eyes went wild, veins bulging at her throat as her mouth split open in a scream so full of anguish it split the world. She vaulted over her mate's brutalized body.

And the serpent woman *laughed.*

My horror sharpened into rage when I found her oily smile mirrored in her twin's face.

The Grayshell assassin wiped both smirks away in a blur of motion.

It was impossible, the way Lana moved. She struck at both twins with a fury that bent light, that blurred edges. I turned back to Ansel, my hands still glowing, still trembling over the deluge of blood, as if I could stitch the pieces together.

"No," I sobbed, the sound tearing up my throat as time snapped back into motion and I rocked over The Old General—my friend. My teacher. "No, no, no. Gods, *please.*"

I scrambled back, staring at my hands. At his blood. I wiped it across my leathers in frantic denial.

Freya was *screaming.* Cyrus cursing, trying to pull her away—but his free hand remained raised, fingers curled tight as shadows flowed *into* him and the sun crested the horizon.

I turned toward Lana again. She had them bleeding now, parrying with such precision she was driving the twins into each other.

Alec appeared in the center of the lot, rage radiating from him like a heat wave. Flames crawled down his arms, the ground shaking beneath his feet. With Alec inbound, I twisted around, hunting for Aren.

I found him as his dagger plunged into Bellamy's side, his face contorted in brutal, frozen rage, mouth open in a war cry that rattled the bones in my chest.

My heart cracked.

Bellamy looked down at the blade in his gut. Shock. Anger. Disbelief flickered in his eyes before Aren wrenched the dagger free.

Violence reigned around me. Every beautiful thing I had ever loved was breaking—Blythe, Ansel...Bellamy. My city. My soul.

Tremors shook my limbs. My vision burned. One horror bled into the next.

The rooftop's edge still burned with fire, the street below echoing with Ally's pain—so tangible it felt like it lived in my bones. The sky cracked open in answer. Thunder boomed. Rain fell in torrential sheets as forks of lightning stabbed the ground again and again, turning the street into a battlefield.

Boom. Boom. Boom. Each strike shook the earth, lighting new fires.

Alec bellowed as he lunged for Moros, nearly skewering him—until Marlana dove, dragging her brother off the roof. My breath hitched.

Hope flared. But two ravens took their place, trailing blood in their wake.

"Motherfucker!" Alec roared, hurling a blade after them. It missed. Of course it missed.

And I—

I could do nothing.

Just wait for the next body to fall at my feet. Just pray.

"I'm sorry," I whispered. Then louder: "I'm so, so sorry." I staggered to the edge of the roof. Felt the bruises from where my knees had slammed into the concrete as I'd crawled for Ansel, desperate to save him. To make it right. I welcomed the pain. I *deserved* the pain.

My heart was splintering—no, *shattering*—into something unrecognizable.

Tears streaked my cheeks as I turned to see Freya break free of Cyrus's hold and fling herself over Ansel's body. Cyrus dropped to his knees beside her, haunted eyes meeting mine. His mouth parted, hopeless. Despair clung to him like ash.

Then strong arms wrapped around me. I was hoisted off the ground. The energy shift hit me like a blade.

Across the rooftop, I locked eyes with winter-blue ones, wide and terrified. Aren lunged. His sword clattered to the concrete.

I screamed, fighting against the grip, trying to plant my feet—

Too late.

"*Please*, Green!" Adrastos shouted.

Then he jumped.

SEVENTY-THREE

VALLEY OF DEATH

MAGNOLIA

The instant my feet hit the dirt, I threw my head back, cracking into Adrastos' nose. The sound of splintering bone rewarded me as I found my balance, his arms flying off me. An enormous conspiracy of shifter-sized ravens tore across the sky overhead, and I prayed they were Freya's.

"You pathetic little cockroach!" I shouted, whirling to face him as shadows rippled down my arms and fury surged. His hand was clamped over his bleeding nose as he set and healed the bone. When he opened his mouth to speak, I cut him off, screeching, "Traitorous filth!" I slammed my shield into him—one hand outstretched, the other pulling a dagger from my hip, rage curling in my grip. "I *trusted* you. I fucking *loved* you. You made me *love* you."

"Green, please—" My enemy raised a hand in surrender. I slammed my shield into his again, forcing him back another satisfying step.

"Don't you call me that." Every moment of our friendship, every laugh, every touch, every lie crashed into me like a freight train, and I channeled it into my attack. "Don't you speak to me." Every kiss, every compliment—crafted to *manipulate*. "I fucking trusted you, you piece of shit. I *believed* in you."

"It was real!"

"Don't you fucking dare." I slammed against his shield again, a seam cracking down the center. Adrastos' eyes flicked to it, a cocky smile tugging at his mouth.

"Nice work, witchling. You've gotten better."

"Shut the fuck up. You're dead to me." I relished his flinch, marching forward and hammering our shields together with deafening cracks. "You died when the lie you spun as *Bellamy* did." I threw my shadows out, raging, shoving him toward the treeline. Only then did I realize we were in some kind of park. We couldn't be far from the city—the air still lined with smoke, the glimmer of sunrise a mercy I hadn't expected to see. "You let me believe you were my *friend*. You knew what would happen if I broke Aren's—"

"I warned you," he snapped. "I warned you what it would do to *your mate*, what he could do to me—and still you refused. Determined to free yourself of him. Well," he gestured vaguely between us, "congratulations. You won."

"You knew!" I cracked another glittering fracture in his shield. His eyes darted to it. "You knew you were going to use me, betray me—and you still fucked me. You're no better than that monster."

His eyes flared. Jaw clenched. Good. He deserved to hurt. Deserved to feel every lie that had dripped from his tongue.

"Oh, own up to *something*, darling. This pathetic redirect is beneath you."

"Don't call me that."

"Back to that game, are we?"

"You think this is a fucking game?!" *Crack.* "Ansel is *dead.*" *Crack.* "A good man lost his head. A *noble* man. It should've been *you.*" Crack. "My city is under siege. What part of this looks like a game to you?" *Crack.* This time, he flinched, grabbing the wound Aren had inflicted as the force of holding his shield tweaked his muscles. I adjusted my angle, pressing into the weakness. "Lives are on the line, you spineless coward."

Crack—only this time, it was my shield that glimmered. His lip curled.

"I may be many wicked things, Magnolia Green—both despicable and divine—but I promise you, a coward *I am not.*"

"Prove it," I snarled, throwing my power against his again. Another fracture shimmered like light through crystal, sparks skittering off the edges. The earth rumbled beneath our feet. "Stand for what's right. Stand up for those who can't. Don't you realize what you are?"

"What am I?" His eyes bored into mine. "Tell me, Magnolia—what am I?"

"You could change things. Help people. Instead, you're a fucking *monster.*"

"Yes," he said flatly. "And yet, you're shocked I'm doing what monsters *do?*" He slammed his fists into the shield wall, and the entire barrier rippled around him. My eyes widened.

"It doesn't have to be that way. I've seen the good in you, Bell. I..." My voice cracked. "I've seen you save people. Save *me.*"

"You think it's a coincidence they knew where you were? That Aren's house exploded after you took *me* inside the wards? Read between the lines, Green. I am exactly what you say I am."

I was gaping. The shock of his words struck like physical blows. My jaw slackened. I couldn't even summon the sense to shut it.

He chuckled, and the sound was entirely foreign—not the sweet rumbles or the barks of laughter I'd once known. His smirk was sly, lopsided. Not subtle. Not timid.

"But those other women..."

"Wrong place, wrong time. And I take pleasure in killing psychos."

"Rich sentiment, coming from *you*." My voice was mercifully steady, though my heart thundered. The betrayal burrowed into my marrow.

"Isn't it?" he bit back. "I was *supposed* to bring you in. Bring you into the bloody fold. Win you over. I was never supposed to love you. Never supposed to give a shit about you. Or your fucking life, or your *cat*, or your fucking pain-in-my-ass best friend."

"Good to know."

"But I *did*, Magnolia. I *do*. Don't you see that?" His voice cracked with desperation. "This is fucking *killing me*."

One could only hope.

When my silence stretched, he forged on. "You and Blythe are the most resilient, most brazen women I've encountered. And I fucking love you both. More than you know."

I was going to evaporate—dissolve into the wind and gladly welcome it. Because he *couldn't* mean it. Couldn't be telling the truth. Or maybe he was so starved for love that this web of convoluted tales was as close as he'd gotten. The lie was his reality.

"I'm not," Adrastos snapped. "*Lying*. I'm not lying. I broke the rules, Magnolia, and I fell in love with *my mark*. How's that for picking your poison?" He barked a laugh. "You have my word—I'll do everything in my power to protect her. But Moros will expect me to bring back a prize."

"You're lying." My voice finally betrayed me, the tremor creeping in as the world tilted around me.

"I'm not. Gods, I wish I were. But I'm not. You can come willingly—or they'll come for you. And ask Alvara—my siblings do not extend the same civility that you know of me. Moros will take your power. Just like he'll take Alvara's, August's, and your precious Aren's. He will. He'll see it through."

"Grayshell beat him back."

"For now." The certainty in his voice—the glint in his eye—sent spiders walking along my spine.

"What did you do?"

Adrastos snorted. "Sweetheart, this has been in play longer than you've been alive. You can't even fathom it. Moros has every piece exactly where he wants them. You'll stand with us...or he'll pocket you like the pawn you are."

"Bellamy...What did you do?" Panic tore through me as the distant shriek of screams pierced the air.

"What was asked of me," he said, so calmly a chill radiated down my spine.

Not good.

I threw up every mental guard Ally had jammed into my mind, praying they'd hold.

I began pacing, fear and confusion crashing inside my skull. I didn't look away from those dark brown eyes as he watched me circle.

"It was real?" It came out half-statement, half-question. He nodded, features twisted with something close to pain.

"Why? Why help *us?*"

His lips quirked—and for a heartbeat, he looked like my Bell. Like my friend. "Some things, darling, are best left a mystery, are they not?" Those eyes I'd memorized turned pleading. "I'm not a man prone to begging, but I'm begging you now: forgive me, witchling, for what comes next."

My lower lip trembled. The dimple in my chin deepened as I fought back tears.

"Why?" I asked again. "Why do all of this, if...if..."

"If I love you?"

I nodded.

"I have to think about the greater good."

"But you did?"

"Love you?" His brow furrowed as I nodded. "Yes, sweetheart. That part was real."

The dam broke. Tears slid down my face as I lowered my hands, my shield dissipating with a flicker. His shoulders sagged in relief.

Slowly, tentatively, Adrastos crossed the distance. I forced myself not to recoil as his hands cupped my face and neck. His scent curled through my senses, familiar beneath the iron tang of blood. He leaned into my hair and whispered, "I never thought I'd see you again."

A breathless laugh escaped me as I rested my face against his chest, heart thundering like a war drum. "I love you too." I sniffled, trembling like a leaf as his arms tightened, pulling me flush to him. "And I'm sorry."

Adrastos stiffened. "Sweetheart...what part of this are *you* possibly sorry for?"

I sobbed into his chest, breathing him in one last time as grief carved through me—

—and drove the Erebos blade into his back.

AUGUST

It was a battle we couldn't win. We all knew it. But that didn't stop us from charging headlong into the chaos below.

The wolves were everywhere, shredding through humans like warm butter. Their screams reverberated between the walls and buildings—right up until their abrupt ends—filling the city with a chorus of agony. Ally was doing her damndest to rein in the fires, trying to pull the element back inside her body, but her strength was fading. She'd expended too much trying to hold the city. Just the two of us. I could sense her flagging, energy waning.

My lightning crackled through two more wolves, their roasted carcasses flying before crashing to the pavement beside the would-be victims. Aren was a whirlwind of righteous fury at my back, the bodies in his wake stacking up like a deck of cards. Ally did the same at my other side.

Where is she? Aren demanded.

Coming back, Ally promised. *You equipped her well.*

Then rain down hell, he ordered.

For Ansel. Ally leapt airborne, slicing her blade clean through the neck of a beast lunging for a family's balcony. Their horrified faces were wide-eyed behind the glass. Its enormous skeletal form cracked to the earth seconds before the head did, rolling away in a trail of black blood.

Her agony was palpable as Lana hissed, *For Ansel,* running her blades through two Renown, telekinetically impaling them as fire licked up in a wall, incinerating the demons on her heels. I'd never seen Lana use flame before—not even flimsy sparks.

With bloody howls, the wolves began circling, herding us toward the square at the center of town. Aren let loose a roar more beast than man, and Alec swung his blades wide, then motioned for the wolves to come and get it.

Dozens. Dozens of them barreled forward, fear licking up my spine as my lightning thundered into the earth, smashing through enemies. But rarely could one strike take two. It was too slow—not like Ally's fire, which tore across the ground, devouring them as they shrieked and ran.

Just as the wall of demons leapt within feet of us, the energy in the square shifted—like the earth had been shoved off its axis. I blinked, clearing my vision. Checking myself.

But there—between the demons—stood at least a hundred souls.

Elements flickered in their hands. Blades screeched from their sheaths as they poured into the melee. It took all my focus to kill the wolf lunging for me as I scanned the chaos—Kingsley, Rosaleigh, surrounded by wolves the size of Clydesdales with coats of every color.

My eyes found Ambroise, Ajax, Alastair, and a handful of beautiful, heavily armed souls I didn't recognize—but they had to be Bellatons, judging by the familiar, long-haired blonde in silver armor at their center, her ponytail whipping on the wind.

Thank fuck! Alec cried down our bond.

I sent a bolt through the wolf and whirled to see souls scattered throughout the carnage, already helping the screaming humans flee their homes, engaging the demons and a few scattered Renown.

Hundreds—dressed in low hoods and modern black tac suits—had shadows coiling around their arms.

Holy shit, it must be a cold day in hell, Aren thought, gratitude pointing clearly toward my sister—and my mate.

Don't thank me yet.

Those are mine, Freya announced flatly. No pride laced her words.

You bold bitch, Lana hissed, a breathy, relieved sound climbing up the bond.

Hey guys, love you all. We gotta focus. For once, it was Alec reigning us back in. Ally jumped to his side as the wolves surrounded him. He cracked his neck as she pressed her back to his, and they began to swirl in a slow circle, matching the demons' movements.

The shadows flitted in and out of the world between us all—popping into reality long enough to drive in a blade, then vanishing before the beasts could retaliate.

Wicked. The thought went wayside as I climbed toward the park, a soft tug pulling me toward the treeline. The line of bodies in my wake did little to lift my wounded ego, but the look on Magnolia's face as she burst through the bushes did plenty.

Shock skittered across her expression as she looked from me to the corpses scattered behind me.

"Hey," I said softly, opening my arms just as she hurled herself into them.

"August. Oh gods, August," the little healer sobbed, burying her face against my chest, the warmth of her tears mixing with the chilled blood on my clothes.

I pushed her back to look her over, noting how much more blood coated her hands. I blew out a breath. "Is he...?"

"I don't think so. I ran when I could." Because of course that would've been too easy.

"Good. Get to Aren."

Magnolia nodded, stepping over a body toward the brawl—then staggered.

"Aren's allies came through."

I nodded, stepping up beside her, taking in the reinforcements just as the light seemed to shift. Nathara, Rika, and Kenna appeared on the border of the trees, with a massive huddle of witches in their wake. All of their eyes flicked to Mags just as a sob tore from her chest.

"Girls," Magnolia called, her voice morphing into a doctor's calm, collected tone. "I'm going to need those of you who jump to bring Nat the injured."

She swallowed her grief, assessing the chaos. Her bright eyes found mine, jaw set as she gave me a final nod.

"Stay safe, little witch," I said, offering a soft smile.

She nodded, then buried herself against Nathara. And then the healers turned to the carnage—heads held high, hands already glowing with blinding white.

ALVARA

Never in all my lives had I seen Aren fight like this. He had always been formidable—a force few would dare challenge—but this...this was different. There was no restraint. Only raw, righteous fury, rippling off him with every strike, every lunge, every howl of anguish he didn't voice aloud.

It took only moments of watching him tear through demons to realize: he wasn't himself.

The weight of betrayal. The agony of losing Ansel. It had undone him.

Again and again, he threw himself into the onslaught, and still his fury grew—compounding, mutating. Each snapped neck, each severed spine, only deepened the fire behind his eyes. And with every decapitation, he roared louder. Angrier.

He'd paused only once—when the allies arrived. A flicker of recognition. A flash of pride. But it passed like breath on glass, and then he was whirling on a tormentor and rending it apart with his bare, glowing hands.

Ansel had been his oldest and most loyal friend. The only one of us who had never disappointed him. His brother. His anchor. His heart.

But even that grief didn't encompass the storm inside him. No—the storm was wider. Darker. His gaze had already drifted to the beautiful healer throwing herself into the devastation as though she'd been born to it.

Over and over, she plunged into the chaos, pulling limp bodies from the wreckage and jumping them to safety, always away from the epicenter. Her magic flared white, bright and ruthless. She didn't hesitate. Didn't flinch. Even among countless casualties, her mind worked with trauma-trained precision—identifying wounds that could be saved and triaging the rest.

She gave preference to the humans. Just like Aren would've told her to. My heart both sank and soared. And I sent up a silent prayer—for them. For their bond. For it to hold fast through this hell.

But as Aren crashed into a wall of walkers, oblivious to the claws raking through his shirt and skin, blades flashing in rhythm with his rage, I feared we might not get the chance. I had seen glimpses of it in the threads—that tether between them—but I hadn't let myself believe.

Aren was Aren. Infallible. The hinge upon which all fate turned.

If we lost him now, we would fail. Long before August could rise.

And yet...even the visions had begun to blur in the wake of his fury, as though the fates themselves hesitated to look him in the eye.

The skeletal, horned bodies began to collapse at our feet, and slowly—just barely—the sound began to change. The screams of humans grew muffled by distance. The demons had abandoned their hunt of the mortals the moment the hierarchies arrived, drawn to us instead.

And I relished it. *Come get me, motherfuckers.*

As if summoned, a dozen wolves prowled toward me, but it was the two figures behind them that made my stomach twist.

My flames nearly gone, I laced what little remained into my blade and offered a grin that would've made Aren proud. Even as he beheaded two more demons, I felt his approval down the bond a heartbeat before he appeared at my side.

Marlana stood poised on a rooftop, her gaze locked sharp as flint. Beside her, Moros looked every bit the predator he was—eager, unblinking, smiling for blood. If they were looking for trouble, they'd found it.

Her blight didn't scare me. August's magic burned in my blood. Not even Moros' reaper gifts could cut through the wall of protection my mate had left in me.

But then—

A ripple of dread coiled in my gut.

Because neither of them was looking at me.

AREN

Ally was a blur of flame and steel, and pride burned in my chest as she poured herself again and again between me and the threat. Between her and the Paladins, the twins were fully occupied, her hold on August's shield keeping a barrier between us and Marlana's venomous assaults.

I spared a glance sideways, surveying the field as exhaustion dragged at my muscles. My limbs trembled. August stood guard over the healers. Panic bloomed sharp and fast as I scanned their line—once, twice, three times—without spotting her. No flash of slick black hair. No spark of aquamarine eyes.

Fuck.

But then Magnolia emerged from the wreckage, hauling a limp body—one of Reyna's men—his arms slung over hers. She laid him in front of Nathara, then vanished into the chaos again.

Dear God. She was diving *into the fight* to pull out the wounded.

I made to move toward her when pain lanced through my torso, the force of the attack driving me forward. Agony tore down my side, and I doubled over, clutching my now-bleeding abdomen. Hot liquid gushed between my fingers.

With a roar of defiance, I forced myself upright, blade raised in a shaking hand as the wolf settled in front of me, its maw slick with blood.

"You just *bit me*, motherfucker."

It growled in response, circling. Then it lunged—and I twisted, bringing my blade up and through. The wolf hit the ground in two twitching pieces.

"*Aren!*" Ally's voice snapped my attention sideways—just in time to block a descending Renown blade. Steel shrieked as I came face to face with Moros.

"One by one, we will pluck them all from your grasp," he sneered.

Even as my magic faltered beneath his, I struck. He met every blow with cruel efficiency, but I could feel it—his exhaustion. The reaper gifts were waning.

"You'll watch your pets kneel before me from hell itself," he promised.

"As long as the seats are decent," I growled. God, what was it with villains and their monologues?

We traded strike for strike. I didn't need magic to make this bastard bleed. My next blow grazed his shoulder, splitting black ichor down his arm. He hissed, stumbling back.

Then I felt it—oily, invasive. The demon blade's poison crawling beneath my skin.

Marlana moved in, launching her plague. I flung out a shield with my free hand, forming a barrier just as the disease scorched the sidewalk beside us, rotting stone to ash. The distraction cost me—Moros nearly took my head off.

My periphery caught Alvara, surrounded and outnumbered.

Time was running out.

I surged forward, shoving past the rot creeping up the city walls, the buildings around us crumbling into dark ash. Marlana's blight thickened, coiling around my shield. Black veins etched across the dome as my duel with Moros raged on.

Screams split the air, the ground trembling.

Somewhere, someone was screaming my name.

But my focus was on the snarling bastard in front of me.

Using the maneuver that had saved Ally and me countless times, I closed the gap. One hand seized the back of Moros' neck, the other driving my blade deep into his chest. Panting, I held him there, dragging the sword upward toward his sternum.

"For Ansel," I rasped.

Blood sprayed across my face as he coughed something between a laugh and a curse.

"Fruere inferos, motherfucker." *Enjoy hell.*

"Ibi te videre" he snarled. *See you there.*

Agony exploded through me. He'd shoved a dagger into the side of my neck.

We staggered apart. The blight collapsed. So did my shield.

Marlana misted in between us, her hiss like venom in the air. She loomed above me as I dropped to my knees, clutching at the knife in my throat. My blades slipped from numb fingers when she kicked me.

I hit the ground, bone cracking against pavement. I swung at her—slow, sloppy—but she blocked it, stepped on my hand, and wrenched the blade across my neck.

Blood gushed. I rolled, choking, gasping, my mouth filling with copper. Panic. Blind, suffocating panic. My hands pressed against the wound, but it was too deep. Too fast.

The crunch of boots over asphalt.

Marlana lifted Moros into her arms, pressing a hand to his wound before they vanished into shadow.

I was drowning.

Every breath a torment.

My chest seized. My throat blazed.

I clawed at my neck, slick fingers trying to stem the bleeding. My vision blurred.

And then—flames. Orange and wild.

Alvara's face appeared above me, twisted in horror. Her scream tore through the morning.

Her hands trembled over my throat, blazing with light.

A wall of fire burst outward from her body, a last desperate defense.

I tried to speak—to tell her I loved her. That I forgave her. That none of this was her fault. That I was sorry for the things I'd said. That I was grateful.

I wanted to thank her.

I wanted—

My hand lifted to hers, feeble, blood-soaked.

And then something fractured. Time bent. And everything happened at once.

Tears welled in Alvara's eyes.

I remembered a girl dancing on a bar top. A promise I'd made to a friend—one I hadn't yet kept.

I remembered oceanside rides. Her thighs clamping around me. The way her laughter sounded like music. The motion of her hips beneath my hands.

When the sun again rises, little dove, I just want to take you dancing.

If I died now, she'd never know.

Never know my final wish was to hold her again. That I'd already forgiven her. That I'd always find her. In every life. Every realm. Every breath.

I tried to tell her.

But my throat filled with blood, and the world went dark.

Magnolia

Agony shredded through my chest and throat, stealing the air in a violent, crushing assault. My eyes burned as tears carved hot paths down my cheeks. I looked down, half-expecting to see a blade, an exit wound—something to explain the pain. But my leathers were intact. The blood staining my clothes was the same as moments before.

The shadows swelled and stretched in great black tendrils as I collapsed to my knees. The world rocked and halted all at once. The screams of the city muffled, distant—like I'd been hurled to the bottom of a pool. Dread and terror merged into a single, molten weight in my gut.

I knew the truth before the shadows hissed in my ear.

Aren.

Run, little witch. Run for the Commander.

"Aren!" I wasn't sure if I screamed or mouthed the word. His name.

But I knew. I knew in my core that Aren had fallen—before the whispers, before the shadows even spoke. It was the rippling agony at my center. The silent rift of something essential, irrepably broken.

I screamed. The sound tore from me, flaying my throat as if my soul itself were unraveling. My arms wrapped tight around my ribs, instinctively trying to hold myself together. But the pain was everywhere. The worst of it burned within—the torment of being ripped in half. Drawn and quartered by fate itself.

Aren. Aren. *Aren.*

Each heartbeat howled his name. The tears came fast and hot, blinding me as I surged to my feet.

I saw it. The wall of fire erupting across the square. The Angel of Death, bloodied and broken, collapsing to her knees just as I had. Alvara Porter's arms were outstretched, flames erupting in a roaring inferno that engulfed the Renown and demons around her.

And then—I was there.

Kneeling in a lake of blood, black and crimson twining in a slick pool that soaked my shredded pants and coated my skin. My hands shook as I lifted them, and the trembling worsened when I saw the source of all that red.

Alvara's face was twisted in panic and grief as she threw herself over the massive form of her sire. Her scream was raw, scraping, barely human.

Aren's body lay limp across her lap. All strength gone from that towering, sculpted frame. And for the barest breath of a moment, he looked... small.

Agony eviscerated what remained of my composure. My breath hitched. My vision blurred.

The tearing in my soul—it was *him. My Aren.* My mate.

My heart thundered so violently I thought it might rupture.

Because my *mate* was dying.

And he didn't know. Didn't know that I *knew.* That I had accepted him, on a level deeper than thought or will. That the bond had taken root—had sealed into place. That I had *chosen* him, even after ruining everything. Chosen him on that rooftop. Chosen him again when I drove my dagger into his enemy's back.

My pulse roared in my ears. My lungs fought to keep up, the world tilting on its axis as I reached him.

The part of me that bled out in front of me.

Aren. Perfect, even now, his face streaked with soot and blood.

Sound returned slowly, like thick honey poured too long untouched.

"*Save him!*" Alvara's scream ripped through the haze. It struck me like a blade.

I lunged forward, her words anchoring me. Snapping me back into the world.

You were born for this, the shadows whispered.

Alvara's hands stayed pressed hard over the gaping wound in Aren's throat. Tears cut paths through the grime caked on her face. I threw my arms over his chest and sent my magic crashing down into him.

Too much blood loss. Not good.

But—his mind was intact.

His heart was still beating. Fast. Much too fast.

Help me. Please—anyone.

He could survive. If I moved quickly—*very* quickly. But I'd never attempted something like this on my own. Not without my sisters. And my magic was nearly drained.

If I could anchor to another energy source...

If his lungs were intact.

If the brain hadn't been without oxygen too long.

If the *blade* hadn't been demon-forged or cursed.

If hypovolemic shock wasn't too advanced.

Alvara's eyes widened as the calculations raced through my head. All the *ifs* holding Aren's life by a thread.

Ally raised her trembling hands, desperation etched into every line of her face.

I pressed both palms to the gash in his throat just as she pulled her fingers back. Light burst from my hands—clean, bright white—and I drove the magic down into the torn tissue. Purging infection. Closing vessels. Reweaving what had been undone.

Alvara looked down at me, her eyes glazed with a Seer's knowing.

Soft as a breath, she said, "In walls of white, we fight faux blight."

When her gaze cleared, she met mine. Shadows lived behind that gaze —deep shadows. Pain. Regret. Fear.

She exhaled. "Just the one."

My left hand skimmed above Aren, my magic probing, scanning, while the right stayed firm on his neck.

"Heal him, witchling," Alvara said—this time a command. The tremor in her voice slight, but unmistakable. Her emerald eyes brimmed, the tears pouring fast now. "Tell Aren...he has to get to Grayshell. Taking Grayshell is the key. Tell him to hold the line."

"Ally?" I gasped. "*What are you—?*"

"Calling an audible. Can you do this for me?"

I nodded, barely able to breathe.

She did the same. "Tell him to bring rope. *Don't trust the water.* Save the arrows and blades for a beast with many teeth." Her voice cracked. "Tell him I love him. And thank him...for making me into a weapon." I stared at her. I didn't want to hear more. I couldn't bear it. "He needs to wait at the gate for the signal. Tell August..." A sob shook her. "...Tell him *I'm sorry.* There's only one thread left. And I love him."

Another pause.

"Tell him to fuck the odds. To fight the lightning *with* lightning." Her gaze blurred again. Fuzzy. Distant. And through the tremors wracking her, she whispered: "The shadow frees the unkempt flame."

Alvara lifted her chin, eyes snapping back into focus as she narrowed them on me.

"What are you going to do?" My voice was quiet, but not weak. Somewhere within it, I could hear the demand of a Priestess.

"What I have to."

Alvara pressed a kiss to Aren's forehead and rose in one smooth motion. She honored her Commander with the Grayshell salute, then turned to face whatever monsters still lurked behind us.

I hated her for the finality in that gesture—for the way it felt like goodbye. But I didn't look. I couldn't. Not at what the Angel of Death was about to face.

My breath came in short, heated pants, but I barely noticed. My concern wasn't *my* body.

It was his.

It was the way Aren's ribs rose and fell—too fast. The way those shallow, panicked breaths turned terrifyingly thin. His pulse, already weak, began to falter beneath my hands. My magic was still working, still pouring through his veins, but the damage...

The bluish tinge on his lips. The wan pallor of his skin.

My hands went clammy as death turned toward us. As that cold, hollow shadow—my lifelong warning, my constant companion—neared.

"No." It was barely a whisper, ragged and raw. I shoved more energy into him, desperate. But my magic recoiled. *Too late.* The shield rippled around us, trembling as if it too knew what approached. Not even his angel could hold Death at bay.

He didn't care for the bodies Alvara had thrown to the earth. Didn't notice the thousands of mortals laid out like offerings.

No. Death had come for the one soul who'd evaded him for over a millennium. And he would not be denied.

The hair at the nape of my neck rose, reaching skyward. Gooseflesh raced down the blood-slick skin of my arms. I couldn't tell if it was my heartbeat or Aren's pounding in my ears.

"You can't have him," I hissed through my teeth. "You can't have him. He's *mine*."

But Death didn't turn away. He lingered behind me, his chill brushing against my back like a hand made of frost and ash. There was an eagerness to him this time—an anticipation.

He had waited too long for the man who'd sent him so many.

All debts must be paid. That voice was a blade across my spine. The last time I heard it, it had nearly broken me.

"Haven't you had *enough?!*" I screamed. Shadows spun around my hands and surged outward, wrapping Aren in coils of mist like they could hide him. Like I could protect him by sheer will.

But his heart—

Gods, his heart was still slowing. His blood pressure was crashing.

Too late, my magic screamed. *Too late.*

Tears streamed down my cheeks and splashed onto Aren's chest. My palms still glowed, still worked, still healed. But it wasn't enough.

"Please."

I didn't know who I was begging anymore. The world shook beneath us. The battle still raged beyond Alvara's shield, but it all sounded so far away now. Distant. Irrelevant.

All that mattered was this:

I loved him.

"Aren!" My voice broke, wild and cracking. "Please, baby, please. I love you! Don't you do this. Don't you leave me. Not like *this!*"

An icy hand closed around my shoulder, and I sobbed.

"Aren! Come back here, gods damn it. *Please!*"

I'm sorry, little witch, Death said. His voice was one and many. Ancient. Haunted.

Light and shadow, grief and hunger all woven together.

"Then don't take him!" I screamed, voice raw with every hatred I'd ever buried—my mother, my sisters, all the people I'd failed. "Please!"

The hand on my shoulder patted me. Almost...gently. A mockery of comfort.

Beneath my palms, Aren's breath came shallower. I'd seen it before. Too many times to pretend. The dying breath. The slowing heart. The end.

My hands shook. Sobs ripped through my body as my magic finished its work. His wounds were long-since closed. A slender violet scar now shimmered faintly across his throat.

Perfect.

He looked perfect. His lips, slightly parted, were stained with blood. His lashes dark against his cheeks. If I closed my eyes, I could almost pretend—

Pretend he would shift closer if I lay beside him. That his hand would reach for me, the way it always had in the dark.

"Please," I whispered. "I love him."

And I knew it was true. Gods help me, I *knew.* Despite everything, despite all the walls I'd built, all the ways I'd tried to resist—I had fallen. Hopelessly, irrevocably. I loved Commander Aren Amadeus of Grayshell.

And he had loved me for months. I felt it in every piece of the Bond anchoring us together. Felt it in the splintering agony that now ripped through me.

If Death took him, I would never forgive myself. Because the last thing he knew of me was pain. Fear. Abandonment.

Still, that bony hand rested on my shoulder.

"Jesus Christ, *please*," I whispered. If anyone had ever deserved that name's mercy—it was Aren.

Death squeezed my arm once, an apology carved in bone and silence.

And then...he let go.

"*No!*"

The word shattered from my throat as the world turned cold.

And Aren's chest lifted one final time.

One last, shuddering breath—

And then his heart stopped.

SEVENTY-FOUR

DEATH, GIVEN FORM

ALVARA

Magnolia's hands glowed with perfect, mesmerizing white as they trembled over Aren. But within the wound, venom and filth rose like a tide—and slowly, his muscle and flesh began to stitch back together.

I had no time.

The visions had shown me as much. If I didn't leave now, this battle would take every person I loved—and then it would take me. August.

"Archangel Michael, protect Aren. Protect Magnolia," I whispered under my breath as I raised my swords above my head. The shield rippled, almost in response. As if the saints were watching. Helping. Lending me power I didn't have.

Look at me. Pay attention to me. I am your threat. I am your undoing. I am your damnation.

With each thought, I clapped my blades together in a deafening crash. Power screamed from them. Each crack of steel echoed like thunder.

Perhaps I had become lightning—through August. August, who unleashed his gift now, a storm unhinged, leveling demon after demon with bolts hurled from furious hands.

Clash. Clash. Clash. My blades rang again and again. And finally, they began to turn toward me. The covens knew better than to look directly, but some couldn't resist flicking their eyes this way.

But it was Adrastos' gaze that met mine—full of hate, of pain, of a fear I didn't understand. This was *his* doing. This chaos, this carnage. There would be no redemption.

For Aren—Adrastos' blood would paint the earth. His *master's* blood would paint the earth. He seemed to recognize the promise in my eyes, slinking back into shadow like the coward he was.

Lana's gaze met mine for less than a heartbeat before she returned to her furious hunt, a hurricane of vengeance. I wished—for once—that she could wield my fire, just to exact the retribution she deserved. Freya fought at her back. A lethal duet of rage and justice.

I kept clapping the blades as I stepped beyond the barrier of the shield. Carrion reek and the sound of a dying world hit me all at once.

I am your damnation. Look at me. Come to me.

My gaze snapped to the tormentors—their true forms towering over the last fleeing humans. My furious war cry bought them a moment.

Run, I commanded into their minds. *Don't look back.*

Horse legs. Humanoid torsos. Antlers like crowns. Meant to strike fear in our hearts. And they did, for the mortals. But for me—they were just more demons. Just more monsters to hunt and destroy.

They would pay for what they'd taken.

For Ansel.

For the witches.

I would rain hell upon them before I met my own.

Clash. Clash. Clash.

And now, they ran.

Barreling toward me in a tide of snarls and claws. The distraction cost them—August's lightning forked through half a dozen at once. But I didn't feel fear. Not even facing my end.

I watched August fight, Alec at his back. I knew, then—there would be no escaping the vision.

The end was certain.

I would just make it worth it.

For Aren, I let my cruelest smile curl over my fangs. For Aren, I snarled a primal warning.

For Ansel, I held the line.

Hold. The Old General's voice rang in my mind—hundreds of years of battle, shoulder to shoulder. When the tormentors and Renown were close, I bellowed my war cry—

—and unleashed hell.

After our months with Kingsley, I no longer wielded fire.

I *was* fire.

There should've been nothing left in me—but I vanished into it now, consumed by the white heat. Even the crowned demons screeched to a halt as my body shifted, blue flame overtaking my form. I hurled whips of orange and livid red into their ranks.

They cracked as they struck—ripping flesh, beheading monsters.

I am the blade on which justice is found. I am the executioner the devil fears. I am death, given form. I will not be denied.

That icy calm rolled over me.

The calm that had won us battles.

The calm Aren had carved into me.

The calm that let me kill without blinking.

Now, it was forged in fire.

They began to turn—to run.

But they couldn't run from *me*.

A wall of rippling flame rose behind them, forcing them forward again. Fear lit their eyes—fear and knowing. That they were already dead.

I *smiled*.

Not a beautiful thing, but a victorious one. A promise of the end.

"Burn," I whispered. And the wall obeyed, crashing down like a tidal wave. Those closest made for a fight—but my blades found every mark. Too easily.

When the first wave fell, I turned toward August and Alec, still locked in battle. Lana and Freya fought like fury itself. But the demons were after their marks. I swore under my breath.

I am with you, always. Aren's voice cracked through my mind—too clear. His goodbye.

Eyes burning, I leapt toward August and Alec. I would not let the only vision I couldn't survive come true.

Until we meet again.

My hands trembled as I returned the salute I'd prayed I'd never give. Fear rippled across the square. But the coven echoed in my head:

Until we meet again.

It's been an honor—

His voice turned translucent. My stomach twisted and I drove my blade through the demon lunging for Alec's throat.

Stay with me, I begged.

The creature dropped at our feet.

But Aren was gone. Silence where his mind should've been. Empty.

I didn't fight the tears streaking my face. Didn't fight the raw, inhuman sound that tore from my throat.

I flipped over another demon's back, tore out its spine, drove my blade through the blood wolf leaping for Alec's back.

I grabbed his bloody hand. My voice cracked. "Live to be a *father*, Alec!"

His eyes flared with disbelief—betrayal. And I hurled him through time and shadow, back to the safe house. Back to his mate. Back to their unborn child.

August withdrew his blades from two more demons, spinning to strike down two others. I decapitated a limping tormentor, then grabbed August by the back of the head and dragged him to me for one final kiss.

My voice broke against his lips. "I love you. I'm sorry."

His eyes flew wide—noticing Alec was gone. "Ally, *don't*—"

But I already had.

I hurled him after Alec. My heart slammed against my ribs as I turned toward Lana and Freya. Too slow. I had been too slow.

So I did what I could. "Bomb!" I screamed.

Lana flung herself over her daughter. Both fell to the asphalt, arms over heads.

And then—

The scream I had dreaded tore the world in half.

Magnolia.

It wasn't a cry—it was the sound of someone being ripped apart. Her voice split the battlefield, louder than death, louder than God. A supersonic screech that nearly cleaved me in two.

Something warm trickled from my nose.

I touched it. Red. A *nosebleed.* I wiped it away with shaking fingers.

Shadows licked across the grass and pavement—fleeing, like smoke dragged by wind.

I dropped to the ground, curled into a ball, arms clutched over my ringing ears.

And the world was swallowed by blinding light.

By shadow.

By glory.

By the inky ribbons of death itself.

Magnolia

Someone was screaming so loud it felt like my skull would split open. Like an axe had cleaved through the center of my mind. I clutched my head in both hands, as if I could hold the fragments of myself together. Even my shadows abandoned me—a green mist curling from my fingertips, fleeing across the pavement like they could outrun the pain.

But as my soul shattered, so too did the world.

A blast of light flung my arms wide. My throat tore with the scream still erupting from me as death claimed his prize. And the light—gods, the light—came from everywhere.

Went everywhere.

It wasn't until the earth reeled that I understood: the light came *from* me. From deep in my chest.

I was light and shadow. Life and death. All wrapped in flesh, disguised as a healer bearing forbidden magic.

Too much.

The power was too much. It would destroy me from the inside out as my magic detonated—burning, expanding, unfurling like a sunburst. An eruption.

I had spent so many years suppressing it. Tamping it down. Pretending I was smaller than I was. But grief had shattered the seal I'd so carefully forged. Broken open the cage that held a goddess' fury at bay.

Now there was no stopping it. I was a volcano of pain and light. Of death and shadow. Of love and grief so sharp it could split the heavens.

And I would burn the world for taking him from me.

So, I let go. Let the power sear through me—burning, burning, *burning*—

Until the darkness took me.

FREYA

I pushed myself up from the pavement, ash raining around me like snow from a dying sky. Every window on the street had shattered, now charred and blackened—like the hollow eyes of a skull, rimmed with shadow. A chill climbed down my spine as I staggered to my knees, hands pressing to my temples while I grunted through the pain still throbbing behind my eyes. I popped my jaw, blinking into the smoke-thick dusk. The sun itself was muted, choked by the ash still falling over the city.

I crawled the few paces to Lana, who lay unconscious on the ground. I flung myself over the corpse of a slain tormentor and lunged for her limp form. My hands trembled as I grabbed her shoulder and turned her over—only to recoil.

Where there had been cuts, bruises, a split lip and brow, Lana's face was...perfect. Even the old scars were gone. *Healed.* Her silvery hair, still matted with gore, was the only sign the battle had ever happened at all.

I blinked, then looked down at my own hands. Clean. No blood. No scrapes or bruises. No signs of the fight we had just survived.

My heart pounded as I scanned the square, listening. I could hear heartbeats—the covens who had come to aid us. Cyrus lay nearby, his chest rising and falling in slow rhythm, sandwiched between Calypso and Carr. At their feet, the demons were dead.

But the Renown...

The Men of Renown were *gone.*

Shit. *Adrastos—*

I scrambled to my feet and sprinted toward Alvara's collapsed form. My fingers found her throat, sliding to a halt just below her jaw.

There. A pulse—barely—but present.

"Ally," I hissed, shaking her. "Ally, wake up. Come on."

She stirred with a pained grunt, blinking up at me as her trembling fingers lifted to her temples. She nodded, just barely.

Good enough.

I bolted across the square, heart in my throat, until I reached Magnolia—collapsed over Aren's still body. I dropped to my knees, skidding to a stop beside her. The pavement tore at me, but I barely registered the pain. I reached for her, my focus narrowed to the rise and fall of her breath.

She was alive. The witch who had exploded—*with both light and shadow*—was still breathing.

Thoughts for another time.

I leaned toward Aren's parted lips, preparing to check for breath—when I saw something worse than death.

Adrastos stood behind Alvara, cloaked in flickering shadows. One dagger pressed to her throat. Another to her back. Her head lolled against his shoulder, her arms limp at her sides. She looked like a doll left in the rain. Exhausted. Defenseless. With one flick of his wrist, the pendant at her neck slid free, falling silently to the mud.

His black eyes locked with mine.

There was no rage in them. No triumph. Only the cold weight of numbness.

He pressed the blade harder. Alvara arched in response, her breath catching in pain.

"Wake her," he ordered, nodding toward Magnolia beside me.

I hesitated.

"Wake her, little Wraith," he said again, his voice unnervingly calm.

My hand shook as I reached for Magnolia's fever-hot skin. *Please,* I begged inwardly. *Don't burn the world again.* She stirred, licking cracked lips, then winced as she pushed herself upright—just enough to see. And froze.

Her gaze landed on Alvara, helpless in Adrastos' grip.

"Bell..." Her voice cracked, thick with anguish. His name fell like lead. "Please don't do this."

For a moment, I thought I saw something ripple through his expression—pain. Regret. Something human.

But then it was gone. His face hardened, mouth drawing into a tight, bloodless line. His eyes shimmered, throat bobbing.

And then—just one word. Dry. Flat. Final.

Before I could register it, before Magnolia could scream—

Adrastos drove the blade into Ally.

Our screams tore through the square—raw, brutal things. They echoed off the smoking ruins like a funeral bell no one rang.

The shadows swallowed them both.

No trace.

No sound.

No mercy.

Only darkness.

And one word.

A death knell.

A parting shot.

A promise.

"Checkmate."

EPILOGUE
THE KING

King Moros Balaskas was greeted by the stomp of boots and chants of victory as his feet struck the black marble floor of the palace. His sister's magic had already staunched the bleeding from the stab wound in his abdomen—enough to hold him together until a proper healer could finish the work.

A cruel smile stretched across his lips, and he threw up a victorious fist, the gesture met with raucous applause. Pride simmered in his chest, threatening to boil over as the final pieces slid into place. For all his work—for all the decades of planning—he had not dared hope the first wave would end in so complete a victory.

A healer dressed in sheer scraps of crimson rushed to his side, the jewels adorning her curves clinking with every step. She wordlessly dropped to her knees and reached beneath his tunic, fingers finding the wound left by Amadeus' blade. Her magic surged, stitching flesh from within. The king traced a slow line down her cheek, her red lips parting, lashes fluttering as she leaned into the touch. She looked up at him, cheeks flushed with color—but his attention was already moving elsewhere.

"Sire. On your order, we retreated prior to the wave of light. Casualties were minimal," came the silken voice of his sister.

Marlana's penchant for death without bloodshed had proven more useful than he'd expected. It would prove so again, soon.

With an affectionate smile, Moros patted the healer's cheek, and she rose wordlessly to her feet, leaving his flesh perfectly restored.

"Well executed," he said, rubbing at the blood still drying on his palms. "And what of our brother?"

"Last I saw, he was still engaged."

Anticipation sparked through the king's veins. If Adrastos had fallen, the people's thirst for vengeance would be unquenchable. Holy. Hellfire would rain from the sky, hotter than any prophet had dared envision.

But satisfaction evaporated as a collective gasp swept through the hall. His smile faltered. Every face around him shifted—bewilderment morphing into reverence—as his people dropped to their knees.

With a grim twist of resignation, he turned.

Adrastos stood beneath the high arch of the entry, wreathed in lashing shadows. A limp female body hung from his chest, a blade protruding cleanly through her abdomen. She wore the black and gold armor of Grayshell. Her face was obscured beneath gore-slicked hair.

A cruel smile played across his half-brother's lips as their eyes met. Of course. For all his flaws, Adrastos had always known exactly how to make the people eat from the palm of his hand.

"Brother," came the curt greeting—arrogance sharpening the slant of his mouth.

Only Adrastos would dare omit his title. Only this insolent creature could survive such disrespect, and it ate at Moros like rot beneath the skin.

"*Commander*," the king returned, the title bitter as ash, twisted into something macabre—like the corpse of a sacrifice strung up between them.

Adrastos let the woman drop. With a wet squelch and a hoarse cry, she slid off his blade, crumpling at his feet. "Is it wise to strut so smugly as the bearer of such a spectacular failure?"

"*Failure?*" Adrastos scoffed, nudging her away with his boot as if sweeping filth from an alley. A low groan left her lips as her face tilted to the side. Another gasp rippled through the chamber. Even bloodied and broken, Alvara of Grayshell was unmistakable.

But she hardly looked like a legend now—her eyes fluttered, unfocused, her limbs slack as blood soaked the floor beneath her. And Adrastos, the arrogant shit, was still smiling. "I fear you're just as short-sighted as Agamemnon," he said, voice thick with promise. "Your lack of vision will be your undoing."

Gasps followed. Nervous eyes bounced between the brothers, watching —waiting—for another blow.

He would deserve it, Moros thought. Adrastos' defiance, his endless provocations, had earned a blade to the gut a hundred times over. But would it hold up with the people? Unlikely.

Adrastos stepped forward, unbuckling his sheaths and tossing the weapons aside. A nearby soldier rushed to catch them before they hit the floor, reverent hands lifting the bands over his shoulder like sacred relics.

It had always been this way. Even when they were children, the people had scrambled to honor the twins.

Still, their loyalty bewildered him. Moros thought of Adrastos, strung up by Grayshellian Commanders only hours ago. Of the feral female they'd dragged in, thrashing against her captors.

His gaze narrowed as his brother offered a hand to a kneeling soldier and clapped him once on the back. Then another. And another.

"You don't expect me to believe this was your *intended* outcome," the king drawled, gesturing to the still-bleeding gash along Adrastos' side.

"You don't expect me to believe she wouldn't go down swinging," Adrastos returned smoothly, brow raised. He bowed low—just enough to maintain formalities, and no more. "Your Majesty, I bided my time, studied the prophecy, weighed every risk. I returned with my life and a victory."

He paced slowly, voice gaining volume as he turned to the room. "We have drawn every last piece onto the board. All but one. But given the babe in her womb, I don't foresee the fertility Goddess surfacing on any battlefield soon. She'll be buried under Grayshellian wards, I imagine."

He paused to pluck a mug from a soldier's hand. "Once the child comes screaming from her cunt, we'll have the leverage we need to bring her to heel without protest." He raised the cup. "To a kingdom on its knees." A crooked smile tugged the corner of his mouth as he turned back to Moros. "Congratulations, my king, on a victory hard-earned."

Then, louder—commanding, reveling, relentless: "Rise, brothers and sisters. Celebrate! Grayshell will fall by sunrise, and her allies within the year."

Chaos ignited.

Cheers broke like waves as the crowd surged toward their bastard prince. Hands outstretched, voices raised—some shouting praise, others begging for answers, still more clamoring to touch his bloodied hands. Healers rushed forward, guiding him to his seat on the dais as though escorting a holy man. Scrapes and bruises vanished beneath their magic, unable to bear the sight of him wounded.

It made Moros vaguely ill.

And yet, Adrastos absorbed their hysteria with all the usual grace—stroking the cheek of a fawning girl, clasping hands with men who wept at his feet. He'd always humored their worship. Always knew exactly how far to lean into myth.

Behind the king, a song broke out.

The people cried thanks for the return of their lost prince. All the while, Adrastos' gaze kept flicking back to his own, defiant and sharp.

Yet again, the bastard had outmaneuvered him. This was what he did. His insolence was forgiven again and again—because somehow, his unorthodox strategies *worked*. And the half-dead seer of the North was, begrudgingly, living proof of that.

"I must admit, when Bartholomew brought us word of your capture, I feared the worst," the king said, accepting a towel and scrubbing the blood from his hands. "How did you convince them not to gut you?"

"The demagoguery of an opportunist never fails to pacify fools." Adrastos' roguish grin widened, scraping across Moros' fraying nerves. "And as we both know, arrogance *always* breeds fools."

With a creak, the massive hall doors groaned open, and an abrasive chill swept through the chamber. Candle flames danced violently in their sconces. Adrastos didn't turn, but Moros caught the slight tick in his jaw as a feral scream rang off the cathedral ceiling.

The witch was still fighting.

For a healer, she had a curious willingness to break her own body.

Moros turned to watch the petite blonde being dragged—literally kicking and screaming—through the parting crowd. Her face was swollen and bloodied, her arms slick with crimson from wounds likely self-inflicted during her resistance.

Then her eyes—electric blue—found Adrastos. They flew wide with recognition.

"Bell!" she cried, voice hoarse and ragged. His gaze flicked to her slowly, a sneer curling his lips. Her chin trembled. Eyes darted from Adrastos to Moros, then to the gathered host.

"Bell?" she whispered again, more desperate now. Even with Adrastos seated in his throne, she crawled forward when thrown at his feet, one hand reaching out. "Bell!"

Adrastos flinched, disgust twisting his face as he jerked back like her touch might stain him.

"The world in chaos? Check," Adrastos said, his eyes now fixed on the woman sprawled at his boots.

Alvara stirred nearby. The nearest soldiers recoiled, as though the mere shift of her weight might kill them all. But Adrastos' focus didn't stray.

A cruel smile played across his lips as he leaned forward, bracing his elbows on his knees, blood-streaked hands clasped. The king watched with something like grim satisfaction. In the end, they weren't so different—both of them took a certain joy in torment before triumph.

"The satisfaction of the Commander of Grayshell's heart ceasing to beat?" Adrastos cocked his head. "*Check.*"

"*No!*" the witch screamed, launching toward him.

Adrastos didn't so much as blink. He flicked his hand, and shadows leapt from the marble, spearing forward to seize her throat. Darkness dragged her upright just as the Commander forced himself to his feet.

"*Oh yes*," Adrastos said, smug. Then, as an afterthought: "Admittedly, that part was...personal."

Alvara groaned behind them, trying to rise. A soldier stepped in, landing a brutal kick to her ribs. She collapsed with a choked gasp, blood pouring from reopened wounds. If they didn't tend her soon, she and the great Commander might both be lost.

Adrastos barely spared her a glance. His dark eyes slid toward the soldiers now swarming the Angel of Death. "Torment her all you want," he said, voice cool. "By all means—you've earned some enjoyment after so many years. But I need her alive for the next part."

He leaned back, satisfaction gleaming in his eyes. "Thanks to my foresight, we now possess three pieces. And as Aren has no heirs, that gives us half the puzzle, *brother*. I'd say I've done more than my part in your grand design."

"Glad to see math still isn't your strong suit." Moros ground his molars as Adrastos sighed dramatically, canting his head with wolfish delight.

His shadows lifted the witch again, suspending her by the wrists, arms stretched overhead. Her head lolled back, neck bared as the darkness wrapped a gag around her mouth. Tears streaked her bruised cheeks, but her eyes refused to leave the prince's.

Still staring at her, Adrastos gestured lazily to Alvara. "I believe you're all well acquainted with Amadeus' pet—the *Angel of Death*," he said. "*The Raven* has always stood in these halls." He tapped his own chest, devilish smile cutting sharp across his face as he stepped closer to the witch.

At last, their cousins flanked the blonde. It was Bartholomew who grinned first, looking her over with open curiosity.

"Good to see you, witchling. Bit of a predicament you've gotten yourself into."

Her eyes flew wide before contorting into a snarl. She thrashed against the binds, shadows muffling her screams. Her face snapped toward Adrastos—now only inches from her own.

He inhaled slowly, deeply, and the king narrowed his eyes.

"Your fear is a *delicacy*," Adrastos purred. Then, louder, lifting his voice for all to hear:

"Brothers. Sisters. I am pleased to introduce you to Blythe Briar...the prophesied witch of the *East*."

To be continued...

. . .

If you love the found family vibes, and strong, sassy FMCs in the Grayshell world, and you're a sucker for contemporary romance (or maybe need a hug after that ending), be sure to check out my contemporary romance series, *The Nomadic Rhodes*, and *The Hearts of Emerald Bay*.

The books are all interconnected stand alone romances following the journey of twelve siblings. Book one, *South of The Skyway*, is my ode to the bookish community. Readers say it has '*Hallmark* vibes under the Florida sun', but make it *spicy*. Consider it my penance for what I just put you through.

AFTERWORD

Well. *Clears throat*. You okay there, little soul?

No? Well, me either, frankly. Alas, misery loves company, so welcome to the aftermath. We have a recovery group on discord, as well as the Grayshell Babes group on Facebook. Come commiserate together.

What did Ally tell Aren? *"...you deserve to be happy. If you're not—"*

"The story's not over."

After all...we're only at our mid-point. This book was an absolute roller-coaster to write, taking me to the highest highs (Freya was hands down my favorite FMC to write. She's so chaotic and I'm here for it) and lowest of lows (don't need to explain that one, do I?).

When I say that I am a conduit for this story, and the characters inside it, that's not an exaggeration. They have wills of their own, and go rogue (way off my fucking outline, btw) and somehow once they do, the dominoes all fall and I can't seem to fix it. Because, believe me, I have never had to type blind for as long as I did in this book. Tears just pouring down my face in a full, snotty, ugly cry.

Book four is being written, but per my vow to myself and my team, I can't give y'all a ballpark on a release date yet. Just know that nobody wants these books out more than I do. I'm letting them flow through me as fast as my health allows, and I'll get these last two installments published as quickly as budget allows.

Promise.

Until we meet again.

Xoxo-SJB

ACKNOWLEDGMENTS

My readers. The fact that y'all have stuck with me through the lows in the last two years means more than you will ever begin to comprehend. Thank you for being here. Thank you for taking a chance on a baby author and then having my back as I figure out this whole author thing. You are forever my why.

Jessica Hoffa. The best friend and critique partner combo a woman could ever ask for. Girl, you were my rock through this one. It's not an exaggeration when I say I could not have done this without you, babes. Thanks for pushing me to grow. To be better. To lean into the character development, even for the leg lamp. (Dear gentle reader, if you like cozy fantasy romance, I got to beta read her upcoming release, *Charmed, I'm Sure*, which is releasing October, 2025, and it is to die for. Think *Gilmore Girls* meets *Practical Magic* in small-town Louisiana. I'm obsessed. Read it. Thank me later.)

Heather, thank you for straightening my noodles on a daily basis. I don't even know how to summarize how much you mean to me. Just know I'm forever grateful for everything you do.

In Sam we trust. Seriously. Could I ask for a better editor? Hell no. You saw my vision, you hear my heart in these stories, and for that I am eternally grateful. The fact that you carved more than 40,000 mother forking words out of this monstrosity while maintaining the plot points?!? Un-fucking-real.

My badass beta team. Jess, Heather, Mercedes, Amanda, Vendy, Kate, Amber, Christana, & Heather H. Y'all looked at that behemoth of a word count, and said hell yeah! Thank you for all of your hard work, for the feedback, for the love and encouragement. For helping us really make this puppy shine. For loving Freya in all of her chaotic glory and Cyrus in his broody rant-filled storm cloud.

MERCEDES. Yes you get to be listed twice, because you went through all that heartache and said, 'sure, I'll do it again' when I needed new eyes on the revision. Girl. Like you didn't already have my undying, eternal loyalty.

STEF, for creating the coolest freaking covers on the planet for my babies. You are our hero.

LAST, BUT NEVER LEAST, MY FAMILY. Thank you for loving me through countless missed events and gatherings—through events where my body was present but my mind was in another world, scaling cliffs, escaping vaults, and hunting down the pieces of a prophecy that's haunted me since 2009. Thank you for sliding food onto my desk with caution befitting approaching a rabid she-beast. Thank you for lifting the heavy things and taking out the trash when my wrists gave out on me after hitting my personal word count record. You guys are my world.

ABOUT THE AUTHOR

Sydne Barnett is a lover of spunky, badass heroines, and heroes that embrace their wild. She's an avid reader, never turns down a good cup of coffee, loves hiking with her hubby, and lives for finding their next adventure.

If she's not writing, you can probably find her behind her camera, swimming, or curled up with a homemade pastry, watching Friends, HIMYM, or Gilmore Girls.

ALSO BY S.J. BARNETT

Romantic High Fantasy as S.J. Barnett

Commanding Flame And Shield (Grayshell Rising, book one)

Commanding Earth And Shadow (Grayshell Rising, book two)

Commanding Blood and Bonds (Grayshell Rising, book three) <—you are here.

CSAS (Grayshell Rising, book four, coming soon)

Contemporary Romance as Sydne Barnett

Nomadic Rhodes

South of The Skyway (book 1)

Brewing Temptation (book 2)

Finding A Way Back Home (book 3)

The Hearts of Emerald Bay

Salvaged Hearts (book 1)

Mended Hearts (book 2)

Winning Hearts, release date TBD

Catching Hearts, release date TBD